THE LAST

"Why after a ... ize a biography of ... was lucrative." W... over. There was no anger in her eyes. "Mrs. Rockwell, when I insult you I'm prepared to be kicked back."

She smiled for the first time. It touched her eyes and gave her face a calm, rather sweet vulnerability. He felt a twinge of guilt and a tug of attraction, both unexpected.

DANCE TO THE PIPER

When he drew away again Maddy could only look into his eyes, and what she saw wasn't desire. It was anger.

"I get the feeling that you're annoyed at what happened." Tears came to her easily, as easily as laughter, but she wouldn't shed them now. "I'll see myself home."

Reed stood there until he saw her get safely inside a cab. He'd done them both a favour—that was what he told himself. He continued to tell himself that over and over as he remembered how soft and fragile she'd looked in the bright glow of the streetlight.

SKIN DEEP

Quinn could drum up little sympathy for a woman who deliberately projected an image designed to arouse men, then complained about a few phone calls.

"Oh, I see. I parade myself on the screen, therefore I asked for what I got. And I deserve it."

Chantel's cool beauty was compelling, but her passionate outburst was like seeing fire in ice.

International bestseller **Nora Roberts** was the first author inducted into the Romance Writers of America's Hall of Fame. She has received a lifetime achievement award from the *Romantic Times* magazine and her books often appear in the *New York Times* bestselling lists.

Also available in Worldwide

SWEET REVENGE
HOT ICE

NORA ROBERTS

A COLLECTION

THE LAST HONEST WOMAN
DANCE TO THE PIPER
SKIN DEEP

WORLDWIDE BOOKS
LONDON • SYDNEY • TORONTO

The Last Honest Woman   *First published in Great Britain in 1988 as a Sihouette Special Edition © Nora Roberts 1988*

Dance to the Piper   *First published in Great Britain in 1988 as a Silhouette Special Edition © Nora Roberts 1988*

Skin Deep   *First published in Great Britain in 1989 as a Silhouette Special Edition © Nora Roberts 1988*

This publication published 1993 by Worldwide Books, Eton House, 18-24 Paradise Road, Richmond, Surrey TW9 1SR

ISBN 0 373 59029 6

99 / 9310

Made and printed in Great Britain

CONTENTS

THE LAST HONEST WOMAN   Page   9

DANCE TO THE PIPER   Page 261

SKIN DEEP   Page 507

This special collection of three stories from bestselling author **Nora Roberts** features three beautiful, talented and impetuous sisters. This is what Nora has to say about the collection:

"Writing interlocking stories is always a pleasure. I get such a kick out of discovering what happens to the characters once their particular story closes! With the O'Hurleys I discovered a family I could admire, a family I could laugh with and hurt for. I'm glad I had the chance to know them, and I hope that you'll feel the same way."

THE LAST
HONEST WOMAN

Prologue

"**Y**ou can yell all you want, Mrs. O'Hurley."

Her breath came in gasps. Sweat rolled down her temples as she dug her fingers into the side of the gurney and braced herself. "Molly O'Hurley doesn't yell her babies into the world."

She wasn't a big woman, but her voice, even at a normal tone, reached all corners of the room. It had a lilting, musical sound, though she had to dig for the strength to use it. She'd been rushed into the hospital by her husband only minutes before in the last stages of labor.

There'd been no time to prep her, no time for comforting words or hand-holding. The obstetrician on call had taken one look and had her rolled into the delivery room fully dressed.

Most women would have been afraid, surrounded by strangers in a strange town, depending on them for her life and for the life of the baby that was fighting its way into the world. She was. But she'd be damned if she'd admit it.

"A tough one, are you?" The doctor signaled for a nurse to wipe his brow. The heating in the delivery room was working overtime.

"All the O'Hurleys are tough." She managed to say, but she wanted to yell. God, she wanted to as the pain screamed through her. The baby was coming early. She could only pray it wasn't too early. The contractions piled one on top of another, giving her no time to recharge for the next.

"We can be grateful your train wasn't five minutes later, or you'd be having this baby in the club car." She was fully dilated, and the baby was crowning. "Don't bear down yet, pant."

She cursed him with all the expertise she'd developed in seven years of living with her Francis and seven more of playing the clubs in every grimy town from L.A. to the Catskills. He only clucked his tongue at her as she breathed like a steam engine and glared.

"That's fine, that's fine now. And here we go. Push, Mrs. O'Hurley. Let's bring this baby out with a bang."

"I'll give you a bang," she promised, and pushed through the last dizzying pain. The baby came out with a wail that echoed off the walls of the delivery room. Molly watched, tears streaming as the doctor turned the small head, the shoulders, then the torso. "It's a girl." Laughing, she fell back. A girl. She'd done it. And wouldn't Francis be proud? Exhausted, Molly listened to her daughter's first cries of life.

"Didn't have to give this one a slap on the bottom," the doctor commented. Small, he thought, maybe five pounds tops. "She's no heavyweight, Mrs. O'Hurley, but she looks good as gold."

"Of course she is. Listen to those lungs. She'll knock them out of the back row. A few weeks ahead of schedule, but . . . Oh, sweet God."

As the new contraction hit, Molly pushed herself up.

"Hold her." The doctor passed the baby to a nurse and nodded to another to brace Molly's shoulders. "Looks like your daughter had company."

"Another?" Between pain and delirium, Molly started to laugh. There was nothing hysterical about it, but something robust and daring. "Damn you, Frank. You always manage to surprise me."

The man in the waiting room paced, but there was a spring to his step, even as he checked his watch for the fifth time in three minutes. He was a man who spent as much time dancing as walking. He was slim and spry, with a perpetual optimism gleaming in his eyes. Now and again he'd pass by the little boy half dozing in a chair and rub his hand over the top of his nodding head.

"A baby brother or sister for you, Trace. They'll be coming out any minute to tell us."

"I'm tired, Pop."

"Tired?" With a great, carrying laugh, the man whisked the boy out his chair and into his arms. "This is no time for sleeping, boy. It's a great moment. Another O'Hurley's about to be born. It's opening night."

Trace settled his head on his father's shoulder. "We didn't make it to the theater."

"There's other nights for that." He suffered only a moment's pang over the canceled show. But there were clubs even in Duluth. He'd find a booking or two before they caught the next train.

He'd been born to entertain, to sing, to dance his way through life, and he thanked his lucky stars that his Molly was the same. God knew they didn't make much of a living following the circuit and playing in second-class clubs and smoky lounges, but there was time yet. The big break was always just one show away. "Before you know it, we'll bill ourselves as the Four O'Hurleys. There'll be no stopping us."

"No stopping us," the boy murmured, having heard it all before.

"Mr. O'Hurley?"

Frank stopped. His hands tightened on his son as he turned to the doctor. He was only a man, and terrifyingly ignorant of what went on in childbirth. "I'm O'Hurley." His throat was dry. There wasn't even any spit to swallow. "Molly. Is Molly all right?"

Grinning, the doctor lifted a hand to rub his chin. "Your wife's quite a woman."

Relief came in a wave. Overcome by it, Frank kissed his son hard. "Hear that, boy? Your mom's quite a woman. And the baby. I know it was early, but the baby's all right?"

"Strong and beautiful," the doctor began. "Every one of them."

"Strong and beautiful." Beside himself with joy, Frank went into a quick two-step. "My Molly knows how to have babies. She might get her cues mixed up, but she always comes through like a trouper. Isn't that..." His words trailed off and he stared at the doctor who was continuing to smile at him. "Every one of them?'

"This is your son?"

"Yes, this is Trace. What do you mean every one of them?"

"Mr. O'Hurley, your son has three sisters."

"Three." With Trace still in his arms, Frank sank into the chair. His wiry dancer's legs had turned to water. "*Three* of them. All at once?"

"A couple minutes apart, but three at last count."

He sat a minute, stunned. Three. He hadn't yet figured out how they were going to feed one more. Three. All girls. As the shock wore off, he started to laugh. He'd been blessed with three daughters. Francis O'Hurley wasn't a man who cursed fate. He embraced it.

"You hear that, boy? Your mom's gone and had herself triplets. Three for the price of one. And I'm a man who loves a bargain." Springing up, he grabbed the doctor's hand and pumped it. "Bless you. If there's a man luckier than Francis Xavier O'Hurley tonight, I'm damned if I know him."

"Congratulations."

"You've got a wife?"

"Yes, I do."

"What's her name?"

"It's Abigail."

"Then Abigail it is for one of them. When can I see my family?"

"In just a few minutes. I'll have one of the nurses come down and look after your son."

"Oh, no." Frank caught Trace's hand in his. "He goes with me. It isn't every day a boy gets three sisters."

The doctor started to explain the rules, then caught himself. "Are you as stubborn as your wife, Mr. O'Hurley?"

He poked his slight chest out. "She took lessons from me."

"Come this way."

He saw them first through the glass walls of the nursery, three tiny forms lying in incubators. Two slept, while the other wailed in annoyance. "She's letting the world know she's here. Those are your sisters, Trace."

Awake now, and critical, Trace studied them. "Pretty scrawny."

"So were you, little baboon." The tears came. He was too Irish to be ashamed of them. "I'll do my best for you. For each and every one of you." He placed a hand on the glass and hoped it would be enough somehow.

Chapter One

It wasn't going to be an ordinary day. Now that the decision had been made, it would be a long time before things settled down to the merely ordinary again. She could only hope she was doing the right thing.

In the quiet, animal scented air of the barn, Abby saddled her horse. Maybe it was wrong to steal this time in the middle of the day when there was still so much to be done, but she needed it. An hour alone, away from the house, away from obligations, seemed like an enormous luxury.

Abby hesitated, then shook her head and fastened the cinch. If you were going to steal, you might as well go for the luxurious. Because it was something her father might have said, she laughed to herself. Besides, if Mr. Jorgensen really wanted to buy the foal, he'd call back. The books needed balancing and the feed bill was overdue. She could deal with it later. Right now she wanted a fast ride to nowhere.

Two of the barn cats circled, then settled back into the hay as she led the roan gelding outside. His breath puffed out in a cloud of mist as she double-checked his cinch. "Let's go, Judd." With the ease of long experience, she swung herself into the saddle and headed south.

There would be no fast ride here, where the snow and mud had mixed itself into a slushy mire. The air was cold and heavy with damp, but she felt a sense of anticipation. Things were changing, and wasn't that all anyone could ask? They kept to a fast walk, with both of them straining for what always seemed just out of reach. Freedom.

Perhaps agreeing to be interviewed for this book would bring some portion of it. She could only hope. But the doubts she'd lived with ever since the arrangements had been made still hovered. What was right, what was wrong, what were the consequences? She'd have to assume the responsibility, no matter what occurred.

She rode over the land she loved yet never quite considered her own.

The snow was melting in the pasture. In another month, she thought, the foals could play on the new grass. She'd plant hay and oats, and this year—maybe this year—her books would inch over into the black.

Chuck would never have worried. He'd never thought about tomorrow, only about the next moment. The next car race. She knew why he'd bought the land in rural Virginia. Perhaps she'd always known. But at the time she'd been able to take his gesture of guilt as a gesture of hope. Her ability to find and hold on to thin threads of hope had gotten her through the last eight years.

Chuck had bought the land, then had spent only a few scattered weeks on it. He'd been too restless to sit and watch the grass grow. Restless, careless and selfish, that was Chuck. She'd known that before she'd married him. Perhaps that was why she'd married him. She couldn't claim he'd ever pretended to be anything else. It was simply that she'd looked and seen what she'd wanted to see. He'd swept into her life like the comet he was and, blinded with fascination, she'd followed.

The eighteen-year-old Abigail O'Hurley had been stunned and thrilled at being romanced by the dramatic Chuck Rockwell. His name had been front-page news as he'd raced his way through the Grand Prix circuit. His name had been in bold type on the scandal sheets as he'd raced his way through the hearts of women. The young Abigail hadn't read the tabloids.

He'd spun her into his life in Miami, charmed and dazzled her. He'd offered excitement. Excitement and a freedom from responsibilities. She'd been married before she'd been able to catch her breath.

Though a light drizzle was falling now, Abby stopped her horse. She didn't mind the rain that dampened her face and jacket. It added another quality she'd needed that morning. Isolation. A coward's way, she knew, but she'd never thought herself brave. What she had done—what she would continue to do—was survive.

The land curved gently, patched with snow, misted with a fog that hovered over it. When Judd pawed the ground impatiently, she patted his neck until he was quiet again. It was so beautiful. She'd been to Monte

Carlo, to London and Paris and Bonn, but after nearly five years of day-to-day living and dawn-to-dusk working, she still thought this was the most beautiful sight in the world.

The rain splattered down, promising to make the dirt roads that crisscrossed her land all but unmanageable. If the temperatures dropped that night, the rain would freeze and leave a slick and dangerous sheen of ice over the snow. But it was beautiful. She owed Chuck for this. And for so much more.

He'd been her husband. Now she was his widow. Before he'd burned himself out he'd singed her badly, but he'd left her two of the most important things in her life: her sons.

It was for them she'd finally agreed to let the writer come. She'd dodged offers from publishers for more than four years. That hadn't stopped an unauthorized biography of Chuck Rockwell or the stories that still appeared from time to time in the papers. After months of soul-searching, Abby had finally come to the conclusion that if she worked with a writer, a good writer, she would have some control over the final product. When it was done, her sons would have something of their father.

Dylan Crosby was a very good writer. Abby knew that was as much a disadvantage as an advantage. He'd poke into areas she was determined to keep off-limits. She wanted him to. When he did, she'd answer in her way, and she'd finally close that chapter of her life.

She would have to be clever. With a shake of her head she clucked to her horse and sent him moving again. The trouble was, she'd never been the clever one. Chantel had been that. Her older sister—older by two and a half minutes—had always been able to plan and manipulate and make things happen.

Then there was Maddy, her other sister, younger by two minutes and ten seconds. Maddy was the outgoing one, the one who could usually make her own way through sheer drive and will.

But she was Abby, the middle triplet. The quiet one. The responsible one. The dependable one. Those titles still made her wince.

Her problem now wasn't a label that had been pinned on her before she could walk. Her problem now was Dylan Crosby, former investigative reporter turned biographer. In his twenties he'd unearthed a Mafia connection that had eventually crumbled one of the largest mob families on the East Coast. Before he'd turned thirty he'd unhinged the career of a senator with an unreported Swiss bank account and aspirations to higher office. Now she had to handle him.

And she would. After all, he would be on her turf, under her roof. She would feed him information. The secrets she wanted kept secret were locked in her own head and her own heart. She alone had the key.

If she'd learned nothing else as the middle daughter of a pair of road-roving entertainers, she'd learned how to act. To get what she wanted, all she had to do was give Dylan Crosby one hell of a show.

Never tell the whole truth, girl. Nobody wants to hear it. That's what her father would have said. And that, Abby told herself with a smile, was what she'd keep reminding herself of over the next few months.

A bit reluctant to leave the open road and the rain, Abby turned her horse and headed back. It was almost time to begin.

Dylan cursed the rain and reached out the window again to wipe at the windshield with an already-drenched rag. The wiper on his side was working only in spurts. The one on the other side had quit altogether. Icy rain soaked through his coat sleeve as he held the wheel with one hand and cleared his vision with the other. He'd been mad to buy a twenty-five-year-old car, classic or not. The '62 Vette looked like a dream and ran like a nightmare.

It probably hadn't been too smart to drive down from New York in February either, but he'd wanted the freedom of having his own car—such as it was. At least the snow he'd run into in Delaware had turned to rain as he'd driven south. But he cursed the rain again as it pelted through the open window and down his collar.

It could be worse, he told himself. He couldn't think of precisely how; but it probably could. After all, he was finally going to sink his teeth into a project he'd been trying to make gel for three years. Apparently Abigail O'Hurley Rockwell had decided she'd squeezed the publisher for all she could get.

A pretty sharp lady, he figured. She'd snagged one of the hottest and wealthiest race car drivers on the circuit. And she'd hardly been more than a kid. Before she'd reached nineteen she'd been wearing mink and diamonds and rolling dice in places like Monte Carlo. It was never much strain to spend someone else's money. His ex-wife had shown him that in a mercifully brief eighteen-month union.

Women were, after all, born with guile. They were fashioned to masquerade as helpless, vulnerable creatures. Until they had their hooks in you. To shake free, you had to bleed a little. Then if you were smart, you took a hard look at the scars from time to time to remind yourself how life really worked.

Dylan struggled with the map beside him, held it in front while steering with his elbows, then swore again. Yes, that had been his turn. He'd just missed it. With a quick glance up and down the stretch of rain-fogged road, he spun into a U-turn. The wipers might be pitiful, but the Vette knew how to move.

He couldn't imagine the Chuck Rockwell he'd followed and admired choosing to settle in the backwoods of Virginia. Maybe the little woman had talked him into buying it as some sort of hideaway. She'd certainly been hibernating there for the past few years.

Just what kind of woman was she? In order to write a thorough biography of the man, he had to understand the woman. She'd stuck with Rockwell like glue for nearly the first full year on the circuit, then she'd all but disappeared. Maybe the smell of gas and smoking tires had annoyed her. She hadn't been in the stands for her husband's victories or his defeats. Most importantly, she hadn't been there when he'd run his last race. The one that had killed him. From the information Dylan had, she'd finally shown up at the funeral three days later but had hardly spoken a word. She hadn't shed a tear.

She'd married a gold mine and turned a blind eye to his infidelities. Money was the only answer. Now, as his widow, she was in the position of never having to lift a finger. Not bad for a former singer who'd never made it past hotel lounges and second-rate clubs.

He had to slow the Vette to a crawl to make it down the slushy, rut-filled lane marked by a battered mailbox with Rockwell painted on the side.

Obviously she didn't believe in spending much money on maintenance. Dylan wiped his window again and set his teeth against each jarring bump. When he heard his muffler scrape, he stopped cursing the rain and started cursing Abigail. The way he saw it, she had a closetful of silk and fur but wouldn't shell out for minimal road repair.

When he saw the house, he perked up a bit. It wasn't the imposing, oppressive plantation house he'd been expecting. It was charming and homey, right down to the rocker on the front porch. The shutters on the windows were painted Colonial blue, providing a nice contrast to the white frame. A deck with a double railing skirted the second floor. Though he could see the house needed a new paint job, it didn't look run-down, just lived-in. There was smoke trailing up from the chimney and a bike with training wheels leaning on its kick-stand under the overhang of the roof. The sound of a dog's deep-throated barking completed the scene.

He'd often thought of finding a place just like this for himself. A place away from crowds and noise where he could concentrate on writing. It reminded him of the home he'd had as a child, where security had gone hand in hand with hard work.

When his muffler scraped the road again, he was no longer charmed. Dylan pulled up behind a pickup truck and a compact station wagon and shut off his engine. Dropping his rag on the floor mat, he rolled up his window and had started to open the door when a mass of wet fur leaped on it.

The dog was enormous. Maybe it had meant to give a friendly greeting, but in its current bedraggled state, the animal didn't look too pleasant. As Dylan gauged its size against that of a small hippo the dog scraped two muddy paws down his window and barked.

"Sigmund!"

Both Dylan and the dog looked toward the house, where a woman stood near the porch steps. So this was Abigail, he mused. He'd seen enough pictures of her over the years to recognize her instantly. The fresh-faced ingenue in the pits at Rockwell's races. The stunning socialite in London and Chicago. The cool, composed widow by her husband's grave. Yet she wasn't precisely what he'd expected.

Her hair, a honey blond, fell across her forehead in wispy bangs and skimmed her shoulders. She looked very slender, and very comfortable in jeans and boots and a bulky sweater that bagged at her hips. Her face was pale and delicate through the rain. He couldn't see the color of her eyes, but he could see her mouth, full and unpainted as she called to the dog again.

"Sigmund, get down now."

The dog let out a last halfhearted bark and obeyed. Cautious, Dylan opened the door and stepped out. "Mrs. Rockwell?"

"Yes. Sorry about the dog. He doesn't bite. Very often."

"There's good news," Dylan muttered, and popped his trunk.

As he pulled out his bags, Abby stood where she was while her nerves tightened. He was a stranger, and she was letting him into her home, into her life. Maybe she should stop it now, right now before he'd taken another step.

Then he turned, bags in hand, and looked at her. Rain streamed from his hair. It was dark, darker now wet and plastered around his face. Not a kind face, she thought immediately as she rubbed her palms on her thighs. There was too much living in it, too much knowledge, for kindness. A woman had to be crazy to let a man like that into her life. Then she saw that his clothes were drenched and his shoes already coated with mud.

"Looks like you could use some coffee."

"Yeah." He gave the dog a last look as it sniffed around his ankles. "Your lane's a mess."

"I know." She gave him a small, apologetic smile as she noted that his car had fared no better than he. "It's been a hard winter."

He didn't step forward. With the rain pelting between them, he stood watching her. Summing her up, Abby decided, and she thrust her nervous hands in her pockets. She'd committed herself, and she wouldn't get what she wanted if she allowed herself to be a coward now.

"Come inside." She went to the door to wait for him.

Her eyes looked dark, a soft green, and if he hadn't known better he'd have said they were frightened. The delicacy he'd seen at a distance became more apparent at close range. She had elegant cheekbones and a slightly pointed chin that gave her face a triangular piquant look. Her skin was pale, her lashes dark. Dylan decided she was either a magician with cosmetics or wasn't wearing any. She smelled of rain and woodsmoke.

Pausing at the door, Dylan pried off his shoes. "I don't think you want me tramping around the place in those."

"I appreciate it." He stepped easily into her house in his stockinged feet while she stood with her hand on the knob feeling desperate and awkward. "Why don't you just leave your things there for now and come into the kitchen? It's warm; you can dry out."

"Fine." He found the inside of the house as unexpected as he'd found the exterior. The floors were worn, their shine a bit dull. He saw on a table by the staircase a crude papier-mâché flower that appeared to have been made by a child. As they walked, Abby bent down to pick two little plastic men in space regalia and continued without breaking rhythm.

"You drove down from New York?"

"Yeah."

"Not a very pleasant ride in this weather."

"No."

He wasn't purposely being rude, though he could be when it suited him. At the moment, the house interested him more than small talk. There were no dishes in the sink, and the floor was scrubbed clean. Nevertheless, the kitchen was hardly tidy. On every available space on the refrigerator door were pictures, drawings, memos. On the breakfast bar was a half-completed jigsaw puzzle. Three and a half pairs of pint-size tennis shoes were jumbled at the back door.

But there was a fire in a brick fireplace, and the scent of coffee.

If he wasn't going to bother to speak to her, they wouldn't get far, Abby mused. She turned for another look. No, his face wasn't kind, but it was intriguing, with its untidy night's growth of beard. His brows were as dark as his hair, and thick over eyes that were a pale green. Intense eyes. She recognized that. Hadn't she been fatally attracted to intensity before? Chuck's eyes had been brown, but the message had been the same. I get what I want because I don't give a damn what I have to do to win.

He hadn't. Abby was very much afraid she'd just opened her life to the same kind of man. But she was older now, she reminded herself. Infinitely wiser. And this time she wasn't in love.

"I'll take your coat." She held out her hands and waited until he shrugged out of it. For the first time in years she found herself noticing and reacting to a male body. His was tall and rangy, and a response trickled into her slowly. Abby felt it, recognized it, then put a stop to it. Turning, she hung his coat on a peg by the door. "What do you take in your coffee?"

"Nothing. Just black."

It had always been true for Abby that to keep occupied was to keep calm. She chose an oversize mug for him and a smaller one for herself. "How long have you been on the road?"

"I drove through the night."

"Through the night?" She glanced over her shoulder as he settled at the bar. "You must be exhausted." But he didn't look it. Though he was unkempt, he seemed to be completely alert.

"I got my second wind." He accepted the mug and noticed that her long, narrow hands were ringless. Not even a gold band. When he lifted his eyes, they were cynical. "I'd guess you know how that is."

Lifting a brow, she sat across from him. As a mother, she knew what it was to lose a night's sleep and will herself through the next day. "I guess I do." Since he didn't seem interested in polite conversation, she'd get right down to business. "I've read your work, Mr. Crosby. Your book on Millicent Driscoll was tough, but accurate."

"Accurate's the key word."

She sipped coffee as she watched him. "I can respect that. And I suppose there was enough pity for her from other sources. Did you know her personally?"

"Not until after her suicide." He warmed his hands on the mug as the fire crackled beside him. "I had to get to know her afterward in order to write the book."

"She was a sensational actress, a sensational woman. But her life wasn't an easy one. I knew her slightly through my sister."

"Chantel O'Hurley, another sensational actress."

Abby smiled and softened. "Yes, she is. You met her, didn't you, when you were researching Millicent?"

"Briefly." And there'd been no love lost there. "All three of the O'Hurley triplets seemed to have made their mark . . . one way or the other."

Her eyes met his, calm, accepting. "One way or the other."

"How does it feel having sisters causing ripples on both coasts?"

"I'm very proud of them." The answer came immediately, without any extra shades of meaning.

"No plans to break back into show business yourself?"

She would have laughed if she hadn't detected the cynicism in his voice. "No. I have other priorities. Have you ever seen Maddy on Broadway?"

"Couple of times." He sipped. The coffee was making up for those last few filthy miles of road. "You don't look like her. You don't look like either one of them."

She was used to that, the inevitable comparisons. "No. My father always thought we'd have been a sensation if we'd been identical. More coffee, Mr. Crosby?"

"No, I'm fine. The story goes that Chuck Rockwell walked into that little club where you and your family were playing on a whim, and that he never looked twice at either of your sisters. Only you."

"Is that how the story goes?" Abby pushed her coffee aside and rose.

"Yeah. People generally lean toward the romantic."

"But you don't." She began to busy herself at the stove.

"What are you doing?"

"I'm starting dinner. I hope you like chili."

So she cooked. Or at least she was cooking tonight, perhaps to build some sort of impression. Dylan leaned back in his stool and watched her brown meat. "I'm not writing a romance, Mrs. Rockwell. If the publisher didn't make the ground rules clear to you, I'll do it now."

She concentrated on the task at hand. "Why waste time?"

"I haven't any to waste. First rule is, *I'm* writing this book. That's what I'm paid for. You're paid to cooperate."

Abby added spices with a deft hand. "I appreciate you pointing that out. Are there other rules?"

She was as cool as her reputation indicated. Cool and, a good many had said, unfeeling. "Just this. The book is about Chuck Rockwell; you're a part of it. Whatever I find out about you, however personal, is mine. You gave up your privacy when you signed the agreement.''

"I gave up my privacy, Mr. Crosby, when I married Chuck." She stirred the sauce, then added a touch of cooking wine. "Am I wrong, or do you have reservations about writing this book?"

"Not about the book. About you."

She turned to him, and the momentary puzzlement in her eyes vanished as she studied his face. He wouldn't be the first to have come to the conclusion that she'd married Chuck for money. "I see. That's frank enough. Well, it isn't necessary for you to like me."

"No, it isn't. That goes both ways. The one thing I will be with you, Mrs. Rockwell, is honest. I'm going to write the most thorough and comprehensive biography of your husband I can. To do that I'm bound to rub you the wrong way—plenty—before we're done."

She set the lid on the pot, then brought the coffee to the bar with her. "I'm not easily annoyed. I've often been told I'm too...complacent."

"You'll be annoyed before this is over."

After adding more coffee to her mug, she set the pot on a hot pad. "It sounds as though you're looking forward to it."

"I'm not much on smooth water."

This time she did laugh, but it was a quick, almost regretful sound. She lifted her cup. "Did you ever happen to meet Chuck?"

"No."

"You'd have understood each other very well. He was a man with one goal in mind. To win. He'd run the race his way, or not at all. There was very little flexibility."

"And you?"

Though the question was offhand, she took it seriously. "One of my biggest problems growing up was that I'd tend to bend whenever I was asked. I've learned." She finished her coffee. "I'll show you to your room. You can unpack and get your bearings before dinner."

She led him down the hall and took one of his suitcases in hand before he could tell her not to bother. He knew it was heavy, but while he gathered the rest of his things, he watched her carry it easily up the stairs. Stronger than she looked, Dylan mused. It was just one more reason not to take her—or anything about her—at face value.

"There's a bath at the end of the hall. The hot water's fairly reliable." After pushing open a door, she set his case down next to the bed. "I brought a desk up here. I do have a study of sorts downstairs, but I thought this would be more convenient."

"This is fine."

It was more than fine. The room smelled faintly of lemon oil and spice, fresh and inviting. He liked antiques and recognized the Chippendale headboard and the museum-quality shaving stand. There were sprigs of dried weeds mixed with silver-maple twigs in a brass pot on a chest of drawers. The curtains were drawn back to give him a view of rolling, snow-covered hills and a barn whose wood had mellowed to gray.

"It's a nice place."

"Thanks." She looked out the window herself and remembered. "You should have seen it when we bought it. There were probably five spots where the roof didn't leak, and the plumbing was more wish than reality. But I knew it was for me as soon as I saw it."

"You picked it out?" He carried his typewriter to the desk. It was his first order of business.

"Yes."

"Why?"

She was still looking out the window, so her back was toward him. He thought he heard her sigh. "A person needs to sink down roots. At least some people do."

He unearthed his tape recorder and set it next to his typewriter. "A long way from the fast lane."

"I never raced." She looked over her shoulder, then turned, seeing his tools already set out. "Do you have everything you need?"

"For now. One question before we get started, Mrs. Rockwell. Why now? Why after all this time did you agree to authorize a biography of your husband?"

There were two reasons, two very important, very precious reasons, but she didn't think he'd understand. "Let's just say I wasn't ready before. Chuck's been gone for nearly five years now."

And after five years the money might be running out. "I'm sure the deal was lucrative." When she didn't answer, he glanced over. There was no anger in her eyes. He would have preferred it to the cool, unreadable expression that was there.

"Dinner should be ready at six. We keep early hours here."

"Mrs. Rockwell, when I insult you I'm prepared to be kicked back."

She smiled for the first time. It touched her eyes and gave her face a calm, rather sweet vulnerability. He felt a twinge of guilt and a tug of attraction, both unexpected. "I don't fight well. That's why I generally avoid it."

There was a crash outside, but she didn't even jolt. It was followed by a wailing yell worthy of an Indian circling a wagon train. The dog sent up a riot of barking just before something along the lines of an elephant stampede landed on the porch.

"There are fresh towels in the bathroom."

"Thanks. Mind if I ask what that is?"

"What?"

And for the first time he saw real humor in her eyes. The vulnerability was gone. Here was a woman who knew who she was and where she was going. "It sounds like an invasion."

"That's just what it is." She crossed the room, then paused when the front door slammed open, then shut, shaking the pictures on the walls.

"Mom! We're home!"

The greeting echoed, followed by another riot of crashing feet and the beginnings of a heated argument. "My children always feel as though they have to announce themselves. God knows why. If you'll excuse me, I have to try to save the living room carpet."

With that, she left him alone with his thoughts.

Chapter Two

By the time she got to the kitchen, her sons were shedding their outdoor clothes. She'd followed the thin stream of water from the front door.

"Hi, Mom." Both boys grinned at her. School was out and the world was beautiful.

"Hi, yourself." A few damp books sat on the bar. A small puddle was forming in front of the refrigerator where the two boys stood. The door was wide open and the cool air vied with the heat from the fire. Abby surveyed the damage and found it minimal. "Chris, that looks like your coat on the floor."

Her youngest glanced around in apparent surprise. "Tommy Harding got in trouble on the bus again." He gathered up his coat and hung it on one of the lower hooks by the rear door. "He has to sit up in the front for two whole weeks."

"He spit at Angela," Ben announced with relish as he got a sturdy grip on a jug of juice. "Right in her hair."

"Lovely." Abby picked up Chris's dripping gloves and handed them to him. "I don't suppose you had anything to do with it."

"Uh-uh." Juice sloshed, but Ben made it to the counter. "I just said she was ugly."

"She's only a little ugly." Chris, always ready to root for the underdog, busied himself with his boots.

"Toad face," Ben stated as he poured juice in a glass. "Chris and I raced from the bus. I gave him a head start, but I still won."

"Congratulations."

"I almost won." Chris struggled with his second boot. "And I got awful hungry."

"One cookie."

"I mean *awful* hungry."

He had the face of a cherub, round, pale and pretty. His blond hair curled a bit around his ears, and his hazel eyes were luminous as he looked up at her. Abby relented with a sigh. "Two." He was going to be a heartbreaker.

"I'm starving." Ben gulped down his juice, then swiped the back of his hand across his mouth. Her little heathen. His hair was already darkening from blond to a sandy brown and fell every which way around his face. His eyes were dark and wicked.

"Two," Abby told him, accepting the fact that they knew each other's measure. She was boss. For now.

Ben dipped his hand in a cookie jar shaped like a duck. "Whose car's out front? It's neat."

"The writer, remember?" Going to the closet, Abby took out a mop and began to scrub quickly at the water on the floor. "Mr. Crosby."

"The guy who's going to write the book about our dad?"

"That's right."

"Don't see why anybody'd want to read about somebody who's dead."

There it was again, Abby thought. Ben's frank and careless dismissal of his father. Was Chuck to blame for it, or was she at fault for refusing to carry her child papoose-style around the circuit? Blame didn't matter, she decided. Only the result.

"Your father was very well-known, Ben. People still admire him."

"Like George Washington?" Chris asked, stuffing the last of his cookie in his mouth.

"Not exactly. You two should go up and change before dinner. And don't disturb Mr. Crosby," she added. "He's in the spare room nearest the stairs. He had a long drive, and he's probably resting."

"'Kay." Ben sent Chris a significant look behind their mother's back. "We'll be real quiet."

"I appreciate it." Abby waited until they were gone, then leaned on the mop handle. She was doing the right thing, she told herself again. She had to be.

"Don't make the stairs creak," Ben warned and started up in a pattern he'd discovered a few months before. "He'll know we're coming."

"We're not supposed to bother him." But Chris meticulously followed his brother's path.

"We're not gonna. We're just going to look at him."

"But Mom said—"

"Listen." Ben paused dramatically three steps from the top, keeping his voice to a whisper. "Suppose he isn't a writer really. Suppose he's a robber."

Chris's eyes widened. "A robber?"

"Yeah." Warming to the theme, Ben bent close to his brother's ear. "He's a robber and he's going to wait until we're all sleeping tonight. Then he's going to clean us out."

"Is he going to take my trucks?"

"Probably." Then Ben played his ace. "I bet he has a gun, too. So we've gotta be real quiet and just watch him."

Sold, Chris nodded. The two boys, hearts thumping, crept up the last steps.

With his hands tucked in his back pockets, Dylan stood looking out the window. The hills weren't so different from the hills he'd seen out of his bedroom window as a boy. The rain pelted down, the fog rolled. There wasn't another house in sight.

Unexpected. But then, he preferred the unexpected. He'd thought Abigail O'Hurley Rockwell's home would have been a showplace of the ornate and the elegant. He'd been certain he'd find a houseful of servants. Unless they were out on errands, she didn't appear to have any at all, and her house was simply comfortable.

He'd known, of course, that she had children, but he'd expected nannies or boarding school. The woman whose picture he had in his file, dressed in white mink and glittering with diamonds, wouldn't have the time or inclination to actually raise children.

If she wasn't that woman, who the hell was she? It was his job to research the life of Chuck Rockwell, but Dylan found himself more interested in the widow.

Hardly looked like a widow, he mused as he moved to drop one of his suitcases on the bed. Looked more like a graduate student on winter break. But then she had been an actress of sorts. Perhaps she still was.

He flipped back the top of his suitcase. A small sound, hardly more than a murmur, caught his attention. As an investigative reporter, Dylan had found himself in enough back alleys and seedy bars to develop eyes in the back of his head. Casually he pulled out a stack of shirts and sweaters while he shifted his gaze to the mirror at the foot of the bed.

The bedroom door opened slowly, just a crack, then a tiny bit wider. He tensed and waited, though it appeared as though he simply continued to unpack. He saw two eyes in the mirror one above the other. Moving to the dresser, he heard the sound of nervous breathing. When the door opened a bit wider, he saw small fingers wrap around the edge.

"He looks like a robber." Ben said in a piercing whisper, hardly able to contain the excitement. "He's got shifty eyes."

"Do you think he's got a gun?"

"Probably a whole arsenal." Wildly pleased, Ben followed Dylan's movements around the room. "He's going to the closet," he whispered frantically. "Be quiet."

The words were hardly out of his mouth when the door was yanked open. The two boys tumbled into the room.

Sprawled on the carpet, Chris looked up at the man's face, which seemed miles above his. His bottom lip poked out, but his eyes were dry. "You can't have my trucks." He was ready to yell frantically for his mother at a moment's notice.

"Okay." Amused, Dylan crouched down until they were almost eye-to-eye. "Maybe I could see them sometime."

Chris's eyes darted back to his brother. "Maybe. Are you a robber?"

"Chris!" Mortified, Ben struggled to untangle himself from his brother and stand. "He's just a kid."

"Am not. I'm six."

"Six." Dylan struggled to look suitably impressed. "And you?"

"I'm eight." Ben's conscience tugged at him. "Well, I will be pretty soon. Mom thinks you're a writer."

"Sometimes I think so, too." A good-looking boy, Dylan decided, and with such an eager gleam of curiosity in his eyes he was hard to resist. "I'm Dylan." He held out his hand and waited while Ben pondered.

"I'm Ben." He took Dylan's hand, appreciating the man-to-man offer. "This is Chris."

"Nice to meet you." Dylan offered his hand to Chris. With a sheepishly pleased smile, he took it.

"We thought your car was neat."

"It has its moments."

"Ben said it probably goes two hundred miles an hour."

"It might." Unable to resist, he ruffled the boy's hair. "I don't."

Chris grinned. He liked the way the man smelled, so different from his mom. "My mom said we weren't supposed to disturb you."

"Did she?" Dylan set the boy on his feet, then rose himself. "I'll let you know when you do."

Accepting the words at face value, Chris climbed onto the bed and chattered while Dylan unpacked. Ben held back, saying little and watching everything.

Doesn't trust easily, Dylan thought. Though he agreed with the sentiment, he thought it was a pity to find it in such a small boy. The little one was a crackerjack, and one who'd believe whatever tumbled out of your mouth. It would pay to watch what you said.

Chris watched as Dylan pulled out a carton of cigarettes. "Mom says those are a dirty habit."

Dylan tossed them into a dresser drawer. "Moms are pretty smart."

"Do you like dirty habits?"

"I . . ." Dylan decided to let that one ride. "Why don't you hand me that camera?"

Willing to please, Chris drew the compact 35-millimeter out of the case. He held it for just a moment, eyeing the knobs. "It's pretty neat."

"Thanks."

"You going to take our picture?"

"I just might." As he set in on the dresser, Dylan glanced in the mirror and saw Ben poking gingerly at his tape recorder. "Interested?"

Caught, Ben snatched his hands back. "Spies use these."

"So I've heard. Got any around here?"

Ben sent him a quietly measuring look he wouldn't have expected from a boy twice his age. "Maybe."

"We thought Mr. Petrie who helps with the horses was a spy for awhile." Chris looked in the suitcase to see if there was anything else interesting. "But he wasn't."

"You have horses?"

"We got a bunch of them."

"What kind?"

Chris shrugged. "Mostly big ones."

"You're such a dope," Ben said. "They're Morgans. One day I'm going to ride Thunder, that's the stallion." As he spoke, the caution in his eyes vanished, to be replaced by enthusiasm. "He's the best there is."

So this was the key to the boy, Dylan mused, that someone could turn if he cared to. "I had a Tennessee walker when I was a kid. Sixteen hands."

"Sixteen?" Ben's eyes widened before he remembered he shouldn't be too enthusiastic. "He probably wasn't as fast as Thunder." When Dylan made no comment, Ben struggled, then gave up. "What'd you call him?"

"Sly. He had a way of knowing which pocket you had the carrot in."

"Ben. Chris."

Ben flushed with guilt as he spotted his mother in the doorway. She had that look in her eye. Oblivious, Chris bounced happily on the bed. "Hi, Mom. I don't think Dylan's a robber after all."

"I'm sure we're all relieved to hear that. Benjamin, didn't I tell you not to disturb Mr. Crosby?"

"Yes, ma'am." You had to use "ma'am" when she used "Benjamin."

"They weren't." Dylan took a pair of slacks and hung them in the closet. "We were getting acquainted."

"That's kind of you." She sent him an even look, then ignored him. "Maybe you boys have forgotten about your chores?"

"But, Mom—"

She cut Ben off with a look. "I don't think we have to discuss responsibilities again."

Dylan stuck a shirt in his drawer and tried not to chuckle. He'd heard the same line in the same tone from his own mother countless times.

"You have animals depending on you for their dinner," Abby reminded her sons. "And—" she rustled a paper "—this seems to have fallen on the floor. I'm sure you were going to show it to me."

Ben shuffled his feet as she held up his C in spelling. "I sort of studied."

"Mmm." Walking over, she cupped his chin in her hand. "Delinquent."

He smiled, knowing the crisis had passed. "I'm going to study tonight."

"You bet you are. Now scram. You too." She held out a hand for Chris as Ben scrambled from the room.

"Ben said he might steal my trucks."

Abby lifted him up by the elbows to kiss him soundly. "You're very gullible."

"Is that okay?"

"For now. Change your clothes."

At six, Chris couldn't have defined charm—but he knew he had it. "I'm still *awful* hungry."

"I guess we could eat a little early. If you get your chores done."

Since it seemed cookies were out, he wiggled down and walked to the door. He stopped and aimed a smile at Dylan. "Bye."

"See you."

Abby waited a moment, then turned back. "I'm sorry. I'm afraid they're used to having the run of the house and don't think about other people's privacy.

"They didn't bother me."

She laughed and tossed her hair back from her shoulder. "That won't last, I promise you. If you don't mind, we'll eat when they've finished their chores and cleaned up."

"Anytime."

"Mr. Crosby." The laughter was gone, and her eyes were calm and sober again. But it was her mouth, he realized, that drew his attention. It was full, sensual, serious. "I'm going to try to give you my cooperation with this project. That doesn't include my children."

He drew his shaving kit out of the case. "Which means?"

"I don't want them involved. You aren't to interview or question them about their father."

After setting the kit on his dresser, he turned back to her. Soft. She was a woman who looked soft as butter and she had a voice to match, but he had a feeling she'd grow talons if her children were threatened. That was fair enough. "I hadn't really given that any thought. I'd think both of them a little young to remember much."

You'd be surprised, she thought, but nodded. "Then we understand each other."

"Not yet. Not by a long shot . . . Mrs. Rockwell."

She didn't care for the look in his eyes. It was too . . . intrusive. How much of herself would she have left when he finished his assignment? It was a gamble, and she'd already decided to take it. "I'll have one of the boys let you know when dinner's ready."

After she'd closed the door and started down the hall, she found herself chilled, so chilled that she rubbed her hands up and down her arms. She wanted to call her family, to hear her parents' comforting voices. Or Chantel's caustic one. She dragged a hand through her hair as she walked down the steps. Maybe she could call Maddy and absorb some of her carelessly upbeat views on life in general. She couldn't call Trace. Big brother was roaming his way through Europe or Africa or God knew where.

She couldn't call any of them, Abby reminded herself as she stepped into the kitchen again. She was on her own and had been for years, by her own choice. They'd come, any and all of them would come if she so much as hinted at need. So she couldn't call. She wasn't simply the middle triplet now. She was Abby Rockwell, mother of two sons. She had to see to them, provide for them, raise them. And by God, she was going to make certain they had some kind of legacy from their father.

She pulled vegetables out of the crisper and began to prepare a salad both her sons would mutter over.

When the stock was fed and hands and faces reluctantly washed, Abby turned off the flame under the pot of chili. "Chris, go up and tell Mr. Crosby dinner's ready."

"I'll do it." Ben's offer was quick and out of character. When Abby sent him a questioning look, he shrugged. "I want to get something upstairs anyway."

"All right, thanks. But no fooling around. Everything's ready."

"I don't have to eat mushrooms, do I?" Chris was already pulling himself onto his stool.

"No, you don't have to eat any mushrooms."

"You gonna pick them out?"

"Yes."

"All of them. If I eat one, I'll throw up."

"Understood," she said, and glanced up to see Dylan and Ben come in. "Go ahead and sit, I'm just setting things up." Moving automatically, she began to dish salad into bowls.

"I don't want any," Ben told her as he slid onto his stool.

"Your body does." She added dressing. "Here, Chris, not one mushroom."

"If there is I'm gonna—"

"Yes, I know." She dished up a third bowl and set it in front of Dylan. "Now if you'll—" She caught herself when she glanced over and saw him grinning at her. "Oh, I'm sorry." She looked down at the salad she'd fixed him just as tidily as she had fixed her sons'. "I guess I'm just used to dishing it up."

"It's all right." He picked up a bottle of dressing and shook it lazily. "I think we can handle it from here."

She sat down and began to eat as Chris chattered between and during mouthfuls. Ben was picking at his salad and watching Dylan out of the corner of his eye. Odd, she thought, he looked...what? Wary? Resentful? She couldn't be sure. He wasn't the most open child, but...

Then it occurred to her all at once that Dylan was sitting in what had been Chuck's seat. True, he'd only sat there a handful of times, and those times had been few and far between, but it had been his. Did Ben remember? He'd been barely three the last time his father had stayed at the house. Barely three, she thought, and yet so stiffly adult in too many ways. She felt the elbow nudge her ribs and blinked herself back.

"What?"

Ben pushed his salad bowl aside. "I said I ate most of it."

"Oh." She started to reach for the ladle to spoon out chili.

"I can get it myself."

She started to serve him then caught Dylan's eyes over Ben's head. Something in them made her pass Ben the pot and sit back, annoyed with herself. "The rain seems to be letting up," she commented as she offered the chili to Dylan.

"Seems to." Dylan helped himself. "I guess things'll be a mess for the next few days."

"Mud up to your ankles." Abby set Chris's chili next to him to cool. "If you like being outdoors, I hope you brought something more substantial than your tennis shoes."

"I'll get by." He tasted the chili. Either it was delicious or he was starving. Whatever the reason he dug in. "The boys tell me you have some horses."

"Yes, we breed Morgans. Use your napkin, Chris."

"Breed?" Dylan deftly avoided being splattered with sauce as Chris jiggled his bowl. "I didn't know you were in business."

"Unfortunately, a lot of people don't." Then she smiled and tugged at Ben's ear. "But they will. Do you know anything about horses?"

"He had a rocker," Chris piped up.

"A walker." Ben rolled his eyes and would have wiped his mouth on his sleeve if he hadn't caught the warning look from his mother. "He said it was sixteen hands."

"Did he?"

"I was raised on a farm in Jersey."

"Seems stupid to be a writer, then," Ben commented as he scraped the bottom of his bowl. "Must be boring, like being in school all the time."

"Some people actually enjoy using their minds. More, Mr. Crosby?"

"A little." He took another scoop. Though he wasn't a talkative man, preferring to listen, he found himself compelled to justify his profession to the boy. "You know, when I write I get to travel a lot and meet a lot of people."

"That's pretty good." Ben made patterns on the bottom of his bowl with his fork. "I'm going to travel, too. When I grow up I'm going to be a space marauder."

"Interesting choice," Dylan murmured.

"Then I can fly from galaxy to galaxy and loot and pil...pil..."

"Pillage," Abby finished for him. "Ben's fond of crime. I've already started saving up bail money."

"It's better than Chris. He wants to be a garbage man."

"Not anymore." The fire was in Chris's eyes as he talked through his last mouthful of chili.

"Don't talk with your mouth full, love." She scooted Ben's milk in front of him as a reminder. "We visited Maddy in New York last year. Chris was fascinated with the garbage trucks."

"Dumb." Ben's voice dripped with scorn as he looked at his brother. "Real dumb."

"Ben, isn't it your turn to wash up?"

"Aw, Mom."

"We made an agreement. I cook, you guys take turns with the dishes."

He sulked a moment, but then a wicked gleam appeared in his eyes. "He's living here now." With a jerk of his head, Ben indicated Dylan. "He should have a turn, too."

Why was it, Abby wondered, that Ben was only logical when it was to his advantage? "Ben, Mr. Crosby is a guest. Now—"

"The kid has a point." Dylan spoke casually, but he was rewarded by a grin of approval from Ben. "Since I'm going to be around a while, the least I can do is follow the rules."

"Mr. Crosby, you don't have to humor the monsters around here. Ben will be glad to do the dishes."

"No, I won't," he muttered.

"You know, when someone cooks you a good meal, the least you can do is pitch in and clean up the mess." As he pushed away from the counter, Dylan saw Ben hang his head. "I'll take the shift tonight."

Ben's head came up immediately. "No fooling?"

"Seems fair to me."

"Great. Come on, Chris, let's go—"

"Do your homework," Abby finished. She watched Ben's mouth open and close. He knew better than to press his luck. "Then you can watch television." With a clatter of feet, they were down the hall and racing up the stairs. "Such unpretentious children," she murmured. "I suppose I should apologize for their lack of manners again."

"Don't bother. I was a kid once myself."

"I suppose you were." With her elbows on the counter, Abby dropped her chin onto her hands and looked at him. "It's difficult to imagine certain people being small and vulnerable. Would you like anything else, Mr. Crosby?"

"Your kids don't have any problem with my first name. We've had a meal together now, and we're going to be together for a number of weeks. Why don't we try something a little less formal? Abigail?"

"Abby," she corrected automatically.

"Abby." He liked the pretty, old-fashioned sound of it. "It suits you better."

"Dylan's an unusual name."

"My father wanted something solid, like John. My mother was more romantic, and more stubborn."

He was staring at her again in that cool unblinking way she'd already determined meant questions were forming. She wasn't ready to start answering them yet. "My parents always preferred the unusual," she began as she slid off the stool to stack dishes.

"That's my job."

Abby continued to clear the bar. "I'm sure you've earned Ben's undying gratitude for getting him off the hook. But you don't have to feel obligated." She turned with a stack of bowls in her hands and all but ran into him.

"A deal's a deal," he said very quietly, and reached out to take the bowls from her. Their fingers brushed, as lightly as fingers brush every day in ordinary situations. Abby jerked back and nearly sent the dishes crashing to the floor.

"A little jumpy?" He watched her. He had discovered that you learned more from faces than from words.

"I'm not used to having anyone else in the kitchen." A feeble excuse, and one that didn't ring true even to herself. "I'd better give you a hand, at least tonight, until you learn where things go. There's a dishwasher." She grabbed more dishes from the counter, filling her hands and her mind with ordinary chores. "It seems ridiculous that the boys make such a fuss over the dishes when they don't have to do much more than load and unload."

"We could spread out the pain a little more if I cooked once a week and you cleared up."

She was bent over the dishwasher, and she had to straighten to stare at him. "You cook?"

He nudged her aside. "Surprised?"

It was silly to be, she knew. But none of the men in her life had ever known one end of the stove from another. She remembered her father quite clearly hard-boiling eggs on a hot plate in a motel room, but that was as far as it had gone. "I suppose when you live alone, it helps."

He thought of his marriage. She heard him laugh, but he didn't sound amused. "Even when you don't, it helps." The dishwasher rattled a bit as he added dishes. "This thing's a little shaky."

She frowned at the back of his head. "It works." She wasn't about to admit that she'd bought it secondhand and, with a lot of sweat and skinned knuckles, installed it herself.

"You'd know best." With the last of the dishes in, he closed it. "But it sounds to me like a couple of the bolts have shaken loose. You might want to have it looked at."

There were a lot of things that needed to be looked at. And they would be, once the manuscript was submitted and the rest of the advance was in her bank account. "I imagine you want to work out some sort of schedule."

"Eager to start?"

Abby went to the coffeepot and poured two cups without asking. "You're here to get background, I'm here to give it to you. The best times for me are midmorning or early afternoon, but I'll try to be flexible."

"I appreciate it." He took the coffee, then leaned on the stove, close to her, as a kind of test for both of them. He thought he could just smell the rain on her hair. She stood very still for a moment, still enough that he could see his own reflection in her eyes. When he saw it, he forgot to look for anything else. Incredibly, he found he wanted to reach out, to touch the hair that brushed her shoulders. She stepped back. The reflection vanished, and so did the need.

"Breakfast is early." Concentrate on routine, Abby warned herself. As long as she did, there wouldn't be room for these sudden, sharp desires to sneak up on her. "The kids have to catch the school bus at 7:30, so if you're a late sleeper you're on your own."

"I'll manage."

"If I'm not in the house, I'm probably in the barn or one of the other outbuildings, but I should be ready for you by ten."

And what in hell did a woman with hands like a harpist do in a barn for an hour and a half in the morning? He decided to find out for himself rather than ask. "We'll figure on ten. The time element might vary from day to day."

"Yes, I understand that." The tension was draining as they focused in on business. Abby relaxed against the counter and savored what would be her last cup of coffee for the night. There were hours yet to fill between this and the cup of herbal tea she'd pamper herself with at bedtime. "I'll do the best I can. The evenings, of course, are taken up with the children. They go to bed at 8:30, so if there's something important we can go over it after that. But generally I do my paperwork at night."

"So do I." She had a lovely face, soft, warm, open, with just a touch of reserve around the mouth. It was the kind of face that could make a man forget about feminine guile if he wasn't careful. Dylan was a careful man. "Abby, one question."

"Off-the-record?"

"This time. Why'd you give up show business?"

This time she really laughed. It was low and smooth, a distinctly sensuous sound. "Did you ever happen to catch our act? The O'Hurley Triplets, I mean."

"No."

"I didn't think so. If you had, you wouldn't ask."

It was difficult to resist people who could laugh at themselves. "That bad?"

"Oh, worse. Much worse." Taking her cup to the sink, she rinsed it out. "I have to go up and check on the boys. When they're this quiet for this long, I get antsy. Help yourself to more coffee. The TV's in the living room."

"Abby." He wasn't satisfied with her, with the house, with the situation. Nothing was precisely what it seemed, that much he was sure of. Still, when she turned toward him, her eyes were calm. "I intend to get to the bottom of you," he murmured.

She felt a little jolt inside, but quickly smoothed it over. "I'm not as complex as you seem to want to believe. In any case, you're here to write about Chuck."

"I'm going to do that, too."

That was what she was counting on. That was what she was afraid of. With a nod, she walked out to go to her children.

Chapter Three

For the second time, Dylan heard his door creak open. In bed, abruptly awake, it took him only a moment to remember he wasn't in some hotel room on assignment. Those days were over, and the gun he'd kept under his pillow for three years running wasn't there. Out of habit, he kept his eyes closed and his breathing even.

"Still sleeping." The quiet, slightly disdainful whisper was Ben's.

Chris jockeyed for position and a better view. "How come he gets to sleep late?"

"'Cause he's grown-up, stupid. They get to do whatever they want."

"Mom's up. She's a grown-up."

"That's different. She's a mom."

"Ben, Chris." Dylan judged the low call to be coming from the bottom of the stairs. "Let's move it. The bus'll be here in ten minutes."

"Come on." Ben narrowed his eyes for one last look. "We can spy on him later."

When the door closed, Dylan opened his eyes. He couldn't claim to be an expert on kids, but he was beginning to think that the Rockwell boys were a different kettle of fish altogether. So was their mother. Pushing himself up, he glanced at his watch. 7:20. It seemed things ran on time around here. And it was time he began.

Twenty minutes later, Dylan walked downstairs. The house was quiet. And empty, he decided before he came to the bottom landing. The scent of coffee drew him to the kitchen. It looked as though a hurricane had struck and moved on.

There were two cereal boxes on the breakfast bar, both open, with a trail of puffed wheat and little oat circles leading to the edge. A half-open bag of bread lay on the counter between the sink and stove. Next to it was a good-sized dollop of what Dylan assumed to be grape jelly. There was a jar of peanut butter with the top sitting crookedly and an assortment of knives, spoons and bowls. Muddy paw prints ran just inside the back door, then stopped abruptly.

Didn't get far, did you? Dylan thought as he searched out a cup for coffee. With the first swallow of caffeine rushing through his system, he walked to the window. However confused things looked inside, outside seemed peaceful enough. The rain had frozen and covered what was left of the snow with a shiny, brittle layer. It glistened as the sun shone brightly. By the end of the day, he decided, it would be a mess.

Without the fog, he could see past the barn to the rolling hills beyond. If she had neighbors, he thought, they were few and far between. What made a woman bury herself like this? he wondered. Especially a woman who was used to lights and action.

There was something else that bothered him, something that had been bothering him all along. Where were the men in her life? He took another sip, letting his gaze sweep over paddock and outbuildings. Surely a woman who looked like Abby had them. She'd been a widow for four years. A young, wealthy widow. Though he was willing to concede that she took motherhood seriously, that hardly answered the question. Two boys under ten didn't make up for male companionship.

For some reason, she seemed to want him to take her little farm and her domesticity at face value. His mouth twisted in a grimace and he downed the rest of the coffee. He took nothing at face value. Particularly not women.

Then he saw her. She came out of a little shed and closed the door carefully behind her. Her hair caught the sunlight as she combed her fingers through it and just stood there. Her coat was bundled up to her chin and stopped just short of her hips, where slim jeans ran down and tucked into scarred boots.

Was she posing? he thought as a rush of arousal pushed, unwanted, into his system. Did she know he was there, watching as she stood with her face lifted to the sun and a quiet smile on her face? But she never glanced toward the house. She never turned. Swinging the bucket she carried, she walked across the frozen ground to the barn.

Abby had always liked the feel and scents of a barn, especially in the morning, when the animals were just stirring from sleep. The lights was dim, the air a bit musty. She heard the purring of the barn cats as they woke for breakfast. After setting the bucket beside the door, she switched on the lights and began her morning routine.

"Hello, baby." Opening the first stall, she stepped inside to check the chestnut mare, which was nearly ready to foal. "I know, you feel fat and ugly." She chuckled as the mare blew into her hand. "I've felt that way a couple times myself." Gently, expertly, she ran her hands along the mare's belly. The mare's muscles quivered, then relaxed as Abby murmured to her. "In a week or two it'll all be over, then you'll have such a pretty baby. You know Mr. Jorgensen's interested in buying your foal." With a sigh, she rested her cheek against the mare's neck. "Why does that make me feel like a slave trader?"

"First sale?"

She hadn't heard Dylan come in. She turned slowly, one arm still slung around the mare's neck. He'd shaved, and though his face was smooth now, and still attractive, it seemed no kinder to her than before. "Yeah. Up until now I've just been buying and setting up."

He stepped inside to get a closer look. The mare was beautiful, strong and full-bodied in the way of Morgans, with alert eyes and a glossy coat. "You pick this mare out?"

"Eve. I call her Eve because she's the first of my breeders. She was just weaned when I got her at auction. Mr. Petrie said to bid on her, so I bid."

"Looks like your Petrie knows his horseflesh. I'd say this little lady's going to give you plenty of foals. Plan to breed her back?"

"That's the idea." Eve nuzzled into her shoulder. "It doesn't seem fair."

"That's what she's built for." It had been a long time since he'd been around horses. He'd forgotten how good a barn could smell, how soothing it could be to work around and with animals. Maybe people had consumed him for too long. The mare shifted. Abby shifted with her and brushed against him. The contact was anything but soothing. "How many do you have?"

Her mind, usually so orderly, was blank. "How many?"

"Horses."

"Oh." She was being ridiculous, reacting as though she'd never touched a man before. "Eight—the stallion, two mares already bred and two we'll breed in the spring, three geldings for riding." The last was a luxury she'd never regretted. "Not exactly the big leagues," Abby went on, relaxing again.

"Four mares and a decent stallion, properly managed, sounds like a pretty good start to me."

"That's what I've got." She scratched the mare between the ears. "A start."

He watched her reach for a halter. "What are you doing?"

"They need to go out in the paddock while I clean the stalls."

"You? Alone?"

She went to the next stall to repeat the process on a second mare. "Mr. Petrie comes by three times a week to help out, but he's down with the flu like half the county. Come on, girls.'' Taking the two lead ropes she led the horses out.

For a moment Dylan just stood there with his hands in his pockets. The woman looked to him as though she'd keel over after one shovelful of manure. What was she trying to prove? The martyr act might work on certain men, but he'd always believed that if you asked for it, you probably deserved it.

Then he looked down the line of stalls. He swore as he pulled a halter down. Whether she was doing all this for his benefit or not, he couldn't just stand around and let her work alone.

Outside, Abby closed the paddock gate behind the first two mares, then turned to see Dylan leading out another pair. ''Thanks.'' She met him halfway and automatically reached for the rope. When he just looked at her, she stepped back, feeling foolish. ''Look, that wasn't a hint. I don't want you to feel obligated.''

''I don't.'' He walked past her and released the horses in the paddock.

''Mr. Crosby—'' she corrected herself ''—Dylan. I can handle things. I'm sure you have other things you'd rather do with your morning.''

He closed the gate. ''Off the top of my head I can only think of about two dozen. Let's get the others.''

She lifted her brow, then fell into step beside him. ''Well, since you're being so gracious about it.''

''I'm known for being gracious.''

''I don't doubt it. The geldings go out, the first three stalls on this side. I leave the stallion in until the rest is dealt with. He's apt to bite one of the geldings or mount any mare than isn't fast enough to get away.''

''Sounds like a sweetheart.''

"He's as mean as they come, but his line's just as pure." As she slipped a halter around a roan, the horse lowered his head, then shoved her hard. Instinctively Dylan made a grab to right her, but she was shoving the horse back and laughing. "Bully," she said accusingly, burying her face in his mane. "He'd rather be taken for a ride than go into the paddock. Maybe later, fella, I've got my hands full today."

When the horses were settled, Abby pulled on a pair of work gloves. "Sure?" she asked as she offered a second pair to Dylan.

"You take the left side." He grabbed a pitchfork and went to work, figuring he'd have the four stalls cleaned out and spread with fresh hay before she'd finished the first.

It had been a while since he'd indulged in pure manual labor. Workouts kept his body in tune but didn't, he discovered, give the same kind of gratification. His muscles coiled and tensed. As the wheelbarrow filled, he rolled it to the rear of the barn and added to the pile. Abby had switched on a portable radio and was singing along as she worked. He ignored her. Or tried to.

She'd never worked alongside a man before. Oh, there was Mr. Petrie, she thought as she wiped a light film of sweat from her brow. But he was different. Chuck had never so much as lifted a hoof pick in the barn. And her father... Abby grinned as she spread fresh hay. Whenever Francis Xavier O'Hurley visited the farm, he always found something vital to do when there was work. One mustn't forget the man was an artist, Abby reminded herself, trying not to think of just how much she missed him and the rest of her family.

The little farm in Virginia didn't suit their life-styles. It hadn't suited Chuck's. It suited her, and it suited her children. That was something she'd never forget. Whatever compromises she had made, whatever compromises she had yet to make, she wouldn't bend there.

Dylan sent his pitchfork into the soiled hay, then glanced up when Abby moved to the stall beside him. "Why don't you finish over there?"

"I already did." She started shoveling.

Dylan glanced over his shoulder, then turned completely around. The three stalls were clean and fresh. Frowning, he turned back. He'd barely started on his third. "You work fast," he muttered.

"It's routine." Because she'd never really understood the male ego, she didn't give it a thought as she filled the wheelbarrow behind them.

"I said I'd do this side."

"Yeah, I appreciate the help." Abby tossed in a last forkful, then walked over to grasp the handles of the wheelbarrow.

"Put that down."

"It's pretty full. I'd just as soon make an extra trip as—"

"Put the damn thing down." He sliced his pitchfork down in the hay and walked toward her. Anger— male anger. Though she hadn't been around it in a good many years, she still recognized it. Cautiously Abby lowered the cart and released the handles.

"All right, it's down."

"I'm not having you haul that thing while I'm around."

"But I—"

"You're not hauling twenty pounds of horse manure while I'm around." He grasped the handles himself. "Understand?"

"Possibly." Calm, patient, Abby picked up her pitchfork again and leaned on it. "I can haul it all I want when you're not around?"

"That's fine." He began to roll it down the sloping concrete.

"That's silly," she said. He muttered something she couldn't quite catch. Shaking her head, she walked outside to begin leading the horses back.

After the one outburst, they worked in silence. As Dylan finished up, Abby returned all the horses to their stalls and fed them. Then only the stallion remained.

"I'll take him out." Abby held a halter behind her back and opened only the top half of the stall door first. "He's moody and unpredictable. Don't care much for being closed up, do you, Thunder?" she murmured, cautiously opening the bottom half and stepping inside. He danced back, eyeing her, but she continued to talk. "In the spring you can just graze and graze. And have your way with those two pretty mares." She slipped the halter around his neck, taking a firm hold as he swung his head in annoyance.

"High-strung," Dylan commented.

"To say the least. Better stand back. He likes to kick, and he isn't particular who."

Taking her at her word, Dylan moved aside. Thunder started to rear, then subsided when Abby scolded him. Scolded him in much the same way, Dylan thought as she continued out of the barn, as he'd heard her scold her sons. He picked up his pitchfork and put his back into it. When Abby came back in, he was nearly done.

"You don't seem to be a stranger to this sort of work." Because he'd shed his coat, she could see the muscles rippling along his forearms. He grunted an answer, but she didn't hear. She wondered what it would feel like to touch those arms when they were flexed with strength. It had been so long, so incredibly long since... She caught herself and stepped away to stroke one of the mares which was busily gobbling grain.

"Did you raise horses?"

"Cows." Dylan spread hay over the floor of the stall. "We had a dairy farm, but there were always a couple of horses around. I haven't mucked out a stall since I was sixteen."

"Doesn't look like you've forgotten how."

No, he hadn't forgotten how. And it wouldn't be wise to forget what he'd come for. Still, at the moment, he wanted to finish what he'd started. "Got a broom?"

"It's Ben's job to sweep the barn." She took the pitchfork from him and set it on its hook. "I usually leave Thunder out in the paddock through the morning unless it's filthy out, so we're done for now. The least I can do after you saved me all this time is to fix you some fresh coffee."

"All right." Then he'd get his tape recorder and his notebook and start doing what he'd come to do.

"The kitchen was a mess," she recalled. "Did you have any trouble finding breakfast?"

"Just coffee."

She bent over to pick up her bucket. Her back ached, just a bit. "I guess I can give you some bacon and eggs. I can guarantee the eggs're fresh."

He glanced into the bucket and saw a mound of light brown eggs. "You have chickens?"

"Over there." She indicated the shed he'd seen her come out of earlier. "They're the boys' responsibility in the summer. I haven't the heart to make them trudge around before school, so—"

He slipped. The ice was rapidly turning to slush. Next to him, Abby reached out, then slid herself. Instinctively they grabbed for each other, teetered, then righted themselves. Her face was buried in his shoulder, and she began to giggle.

"You wouldn't laugh if you'd landed on your back and broken your... eggs." His hand was deep in her hair. It shouldn't be, he knew, but it was so soft, and the neck beneath was so slender.

"I always laugh when I escape catastrophe." Still smiling, she looked up. Her face was flushed, her eyes glowing. Without thinking, without being able to think, he tightened the arm around her waist. The smile faded, but the glow in her eyes deepened. He was so close, his body so hard, and he was looking at her as though they'd known each other all their lives rather than one day.

She wished they had. She wished desperately that they had and that he was someone she could talk to, share with, lean on, just a little. His fingers brushed the nape of her neck and she shivered, though they were warm.

"I should have warned you—" she began. Suddenly she found her heart was beating too fast to allow her to think, much less speak.

"Warned me about what?" It was crazy. It was wrong. He had no business forgetting his purpose here in this sudden wild desire to taste her. But crazy or not, wrong or not, he wanted to feel her mouth meet his and give.

He lowered his head, watching her. The sun shone on her face, warm and bright, but her eyes were shadowed, and as wary as the mare's had been when he'd slipped the halter over her head.

"The path." Abby inched her head back in a gesture of confusion that was easily mistaken for teasing. Her eyes never left his. Her lips parted. "It gets slippery."

"So I found out." The fingers at the nape of her neck pressed lightly, drawing her closer, still closer, until their lips were only a whisper apart.

Longings, needs she'd thought she'd finished with, sprang out fresh and terribly strong. She wanted, oh, she wanted to give way to them and feel. Just feel. But she'd always been the sensible one. Only once had she forgotten that, and... She couldn't forget again. "Don't."

His mouth brushed over hers, and he felt the tremulous movement he knew women used as seduction. "I already have."

"No." She was weakening. The hand that she brought to his chest simply lay there. "Please don't."

Her breath was unsteady, her eyes half-closed. Dylan had little respect for a woman who pretended reluctance so that a man was left with the responsibility. And the blame. Need crawled through him, but he released her. His eyes were flat and cool as he nodded. "Your choice."

She was chilled and churning. There was something biting, something hurting, in his tone, but she couldn't think about that now. Careful of the melting ice, she picked her way back to the house.

After using the boot pull on the back porch, she took the eggs to the sink and began washing up. Dylan came in behind her. "If you'll give me a few minutes, I'll have something hot."

"Take your time." He walked past her and out of the kitchen.

She washed each egg meticulously, waiting for her mind to empty and her system to calm. Serenity was what she relied on, what she'd worked for. She couldn't allow an accidental embrace with a man she barely knew to change that. Hadn't he released her without a second's hesitation? Abby began to put the eggs in one of the empty cartons she kept under the sink. He was safe. She only sighed over that once.

She'd never been terribly sexual in any case, she reminded herself as she pulled a slab of bacon from the refrigerator. Hadn't Chuck pointed that out with complete clarity? She simply wasn't enough to fulfill a man's needs. Abby heated the cast-iron skillet and watched the bacon bubble and shrink. She was a good wife, dependable, responsible, sympathetic, but she wasn't someone a man burned for in the middle of the night.

She didn't need to be. She put on more water for coffee. She was happy being what she was. She intended to go on being what she was. Taking a deep breath, she unclenched her hands. Dylan was coming back.

"I didn't ask you how you wanted your eggs," she began then turned to see him set his tape recorder on the counter. Nerves threatened and were conquered. "You want to work in here?"

"Here's fine. And I'd like the eggs over easy." He found an uncluttered spot at the counter and sat. "Listen, Abby, I don't expect you to cook three meals a day for me."

"The check you sent for expenses was more than adequate." She broke an egg in the pan.

"I thought you'd have a staff."

"A staff of what?" She broke the second egg, then glanced over. Abruptly, nerves gone, she laughed. "A staff? As in maid and cook and so on?" Delighted, she shook her hair back, then gave the eggs her full attention. "Where in the world did you get an idea like that?"

Automatically he turned on the tape recorder. "Rockwell was wealthy, you were his heir. Most women in your position would have a servant or two."

She remained facing the stove so that her face was curtained by her hair. "I don't really care to have people around. I'm here most of the time; it'd be silly to have someone dusting around me."

"Didn't you have a staff before your husband died?"

"Not here. In Chicago." She scooped up his eggs. "That was before and right after Ben was born. We lived in a suite in his mother's house. She had a full staff. Chuck traveled a great deal, and we didn't really have a family yet, so we hadn't decided where to settle."

"His mother. She didn't approve of you."

Abby set the plate in front of him without a tremor. "Where did you hear that?"

"I heard all sorts of bits and pieces. It's part of the job. It couldn't have been easy living in Janice Rockwell's home when she didn't approve of the marriage."

"I don't think it's fair to say she didn't approve." Abby went back for coffee, choosing her words carefully. "She was devoted to Chuck. You probably knew she raised him alone when her husband died. Chuck was only seven then. It isn't easy raising children without a partner."

"You'd know about that."

She sent him an even look. "Yes, I would. In any case, Janice was very protective of Chuck. He was a dynamic, attractive man, the kind who attracted women. On the circuit, there are all manner of groupies hovering around."

"You weren't a fan."

"I never followed racing. We were always traveling around, playing in clubs and so forth. I didn't even know who Chuck was when we first met."

"Hard to believe."

She poured coffee into two cups on the counter. "Janice thought so, too."

"And resented you."

Abby took a calming sip of coffee. "Your job isn't to put words in my mouth, is it?"

She wasn't going to be easy to shake. It seemed to him that she had her answers down pat. Too pat. "No. Go on."

"Janice didn't resent me personally. She would have resented any woman who took Chuck away from her. It's only natural. In any case, I think we got along well enough."

Though he intended to dig a bit deeper there, he let it pass for now. "Why don't you tell me how you met Rockwell?"

That was easy. She could talk about that without hedging. "We were playing—my family and I—in a club in Miami. My parents did this little comedy routine and a couple of songs. Then my sisters and I ran through our bit—show tunes with a sprinkling of popular music. God, the costumes—" She broke off, laughing, then began to set the kitchen to rights as she talked. "Anyway, we did bring some business in. I always thought Chantel was responsible for that. She was stunning, and though she never had Maddy's range, she could sell a song. The race brought the drivers into town, the mechanics, backers, groupies. We always had a pretty good crowd."

He watched her move around the kitchen with a smile on her face as though she were amused by the memory. "Every night Pop had to ward men off who wanted to ah . . . see Chantel home. Then one night Chuck walked in with Brad Billinger."

"Billinger's retired now."

"He quit racing after Chuck was killed. They were close. Very close. I haven't seen him in a couple of years now, but he always sends the boys something on their birthdays and for Christmas. As soon as they sat down at a table, there was a lot of noise and confusion, right during the middle of a set. You get used to that kind of thing in clubs and have to know how to handle it. Noise, hecklers, drunks."

"I can imagine."

"Pop had delegated me to deal with that kind of problem when the three of us were on because Chantel tended to lose her temper and Maddy had a habit of walking right offstage until things calmed down again. So I leaned into the mike and made some joke, something about our next number being so dangerous that we needed absolute quiet. They didn't pay a lot of attention, but we kept on. Then we went into 'Somewhere,' from *West Side Story*. Do you know it?''

"I've heard it." Dylan leaned back and lit a cigarette. Eighteen, and handling drunks and hecklers. She couldn't be as soft as she looked.

"I looked over to where most of the noise was still coming from, and Chuck was looking right at me. It was an odd feeling. When you perform, people watch, but they rarely really look at you. At the break Chantel made a comment about Superdriver staring at me. That was the first inkling I had of what Chuck did for a living. Chantel was always reading gossip columns.''

"Now she's in them."

"She loves every minute of it."

After searching through the kitchen drawers, Abby came up with the lid of a mason jar for Dylan to use as an ashtray. "Sorry, I don't have anything else."

"Chris has already given me your views on smoking. So it was love at first sight?"

"It was..." How did she explain? She'd been eighteen, and naive in ways the man sitting in her kitchen would never understand. "You could call it that. Chuck stayed until the last set was over, then came back and introduced himself. Maybe part of the attraction for him was that I really didn't know he was someone I should be impressed with. He was very polite and asked me to dinner. It was after midnight and he asked me to dinner."

She smiled again. She'd been so young and, like Chris, so gullible. "Of course, Pop wouldn't hear of it. The next afternoon there were two dozen roses delivered to the motel where we were staying. Pink roses. Nothing that romantic had ever happened to me. And that night he was back again. He kept coming back until he'd charmed my mother, persuaded my father and infatuated me. When he left Miami for the next race, I left with him. And I had his ring on my finger."

She glanced down. Now it was bare. "Life's a funny thing, isn't it?" she murmured. "You never know what trick it's going to pull next."

"How did your family feel about you marrying Chuck?"

She pulled herself back to the business at hand. Give him enough, Abby reminded herself. Just don't give him everything. "You'd have to understand that my family rarely all think the same thing about anything. My mother cried, then altered her wedding dress to fit me even though we were married by a justice of the peace. Pop cried, too. After all, he was marrying me off to a stranger, and his act had just been shot to hell." Picking up an apple, she polished it absently on her sleeve. "Maddy said I was crazy, but that everyone deserved to do something crazy now and then. And Chantel . . ." She hesitated.

"Chantel what?"

It was time, she felt, for caution again. "Chantel's the oldest of the three of us—two and a half minutes older than me, but that still makes her big sister. She didn't think Chuck, or anyone, was good enough. She had plans to have a great many love affairs, and decided I was blowing my chance to have them, too."

With a laugh, she bit into the apple. "If you believe everything you read, Chantel's had so many love affairs she's lucky to be alive. Trace didn't hear about the wedding until, oh, three or four months later. He sent me a crystal bird from Austria."

"Trace...that's your brother. Older brother. I don't have much information on him."

"Who does? I doubt it matters in this case, really. Trace never even met Chuck."

Dylan made a note anyway. "From there, you hit the circuit. Some might call it an odd sort of honeymoon."

In some ways, that entire first year had been a honeymoon. In other ways, there'd been no honeymoon at all, no solitary time for settling in and learning. "I'd traveled before." She shrugged. "I was born traveling, literally. Pop got my mother off a train in Duluth and to a hospital twenty minutes before she gave birth. Ten days later we hit the road again. Until this place, I'd never lived in one spot for more than six months at a time. You follow one circuit or you follow another."

"But the Grand Prix's more exciting."

"In some ways. But like performing, there's a lot of sweat and preparation for a few minutes in the spotlight."

"Why did you marry him?"

She looked back at him. Her eyes were calm enough, but he thought her smile was just a little sad. "He was a knight on a white charger. I'd always believed in fairy tales."

Chapter Four

She wasn't being honest with him. Dylan didn't need a lie detector to know that Abby veered away from the truth every time they talked. When she veered, she did so calmly, looking him straight in the eye. Only the slightest change in her tone, the briefest hesitation, tipped him off to the lie.

Dylan didn't mind lies. In fact, in his work he expected them. Reasons for them varied—self-preservation, embarrassment, a need to gloss over the image. People wanted to paint themselves in the best light, and it was up to him to find the shadows. A lie, or more precisely the reason for the lie, often told him more than a flat truth. His background as a reporter had taught him to base a story on fact, corroborated fact, then leave judgment to the reader. His opinion might leak through, but his feelings rarely did.

His main problem with Abby was that he'd yet to satisfy himself as to her motivation. Why lie, when the truth would undoubtedly sell more books? Sensationalism was more marketable than domestic bliss. She hadn't reached the point where she portrayed her marriage as idyllic, but she certainly had managed to skim over problem areas.

And there'd been plenty of them.

Alone in his room with only the desk lamp to shed light, Dylan took out a stack of tapes. A glance at this watch showed that it was just past midnight. The rest of the house was long since in bed, but then, regular hours had never been a part of his life. Schedules and time frames boxed a man in. Dylan didn't like walls unless he built them himself. He could work through the day if he chose, or he could work through the night, because hours didn't matter. Only the results.

The house was quiet around him, with only a faint wind scraping at the windows. He might have been alone—but he was aware, maybe too aware, that he wasn't. There were three people in the house, and he found them fascinating.

Chris and Ben, Dylan recalled sympathetically, had gone to their rooms after a firm scolding and a few tears. Using their mother's best china to feed the dog hadn't been the smartest move they could have made. She hadn't lifted a hand to them or even so much as shouted, but her lecture and disapproval had had both boys' chins dragging on the ground. A nice trick. Though it amused him, Dylan pushed the whole business aside. He had work to do, and a woman to figure out.

He'd already interviewed several people about Chuck Rockwell. Opinions and feelings about the man were varied, but none of them were middle-of-the-road. The one firm fact Dylan had picked up was that people had either adored Rockwell or detested him. Dylan picked up the tape marked Stanholz and turned it over in his hand.

Grover P. Stanholz had been Chuck's original backer, a wealthy Chicago lawyer with a love of racing and personal ties to the Rockwells. For ten years he'd played father, mentor and banker to Rockwell. He'd seen the young driver go from an eager rookie to one of the top competitors on the circuit. Just over a year before his death, Stanholz had pulled the financial rug out from under his famous protégé.

Thoughtful, Dylan slipped the tape into the recorder and ran it nearly to the end. It only took him a moment to find the spot he was looking for.

"Rockwell was a winner, a money-maker and a friend." Dylan's own voice came through the speaker, low and distinct. Automatically he turned the volume down so that the sound reached no farther then the end of his desk. "Why, when he was favored to win the French Grand Prix, did you pull out as his backer?"

There was a long silence, then a rustling sound. Dylan remembered that Stanholz had drawn out a cigar and taken his time unwrapping it. "As I explained, my interest in Chuck wasn't simply financial. I had been a close friend of his father's, was a friend of his mother's." There was another silence as Stanholz lit his cigar. "When Chuck started out, he was already a winner. You could see it in his eyes. The beauty was, he had a tremendous love and respect for the sport. He was . . . special."

"How?"

"He was going straight to the top. Whether I had backed him or he'd had to scramble to find the money to race, he was going to the top."

"Couldn't he have used the Rockwell money?"

"To race?" Stanholz's laugh came as a wheeze over the tape. "Chuck's money was tied up tight in trust. Janice adored that boy. She'd have never released the money so he could drive at 150 miles an hour. Believe me, she fried me for doing it, but the boy was hard to resist." It came on a sigh, wistful, regretful. "Men like Chuck don't come along every day. Racing takes a certain arrogance and a certain humility. It takes common sense and a disregard for life and limb. It's a balance. He was devoted to his profession and eager to make a name for himself. I've always wondered if the trouble was that he won too much too soon. Chuck began to see himself as indestructible. And unaccountable."

"Unaccountable?"

There was another pause here, a hesitation, then a quiet sigh. "Whatever he did, however he did it, was all right, because of who he was. He forgot, if you can understand what I mean, that he was human. Chuck Rockwell was on a collision course with himself. If he hadn't crashed in Detroit, he'd have done so elsewhere. I felt pulling out as his backer might give him something to think about."

"What do you mean, he was on a collision course with himself?"

"Chuck was racing his own engine. Sooner or later he was going to burn out."

"Drugs?"

"I can't comment on that." It was a lawyer's voice, dry and flat.

"Mr. Stanholz, it's been rumored that Rockwell had been using drugs, most specifically cocaine, for some time before his fatal crash in Detroit."

"If you want that substantiated, you'll have to go elsewhere. Chuck didn't die an admirable man, but he'd had his moments. I remember them."

Unsatisfied, Dylan stopped the recorder. It was a non-denial at best. He had substantiated through others who'd refused to go on record that Chuck Rockwell had developed a dangerous dependence on drugs. But he'd been clean during the last race. The autopsy had determined that. In any case, that was only one area. There were others.

The next tape was marked Brewer. Lori Brewer was the sister of the man who had been Rockwell's backer during his last year. The divorced former model was by her own admission a woman who liked men who took risks. Rockwell's wife hadn't been in the stands during his final race. But his mistress had.

Dylan put in the tape and pushed the play button.

"... the most exciting, dynamic man I've ever known."

Lori's voice had the low-key sensuality of the South. "Chuck Rockwell was a star, fast and hot. He knew his own worth. I admire that in a man."

"Ms. Brewer, for nearly a year you'd been Rockwell's constant companion."

"Lover," she corrected. "I'm not ashamed of it. Chuck was as devastating a lover as he was a driver. He did nothing by half measures." She gave a low, warm-sugar laugh. "Neither do I."

"Did it bother you that he was married?"

"No. I was there, she wasn't. Look, what kind of a marriage is it when people only see each other three or four times a year?"

"Legal."

He remembered she'd taken that good-naturedly enough, her only response a shrug. "Chuck was planning to divorce her anyway. The problem was that she had a stranglehold on his bank account. The lawyers were negotiating a settlement."

Dylan turned off the tape with a muttered oath. Not once during any of his conversations with Abby had she mentioned divorce. There was always the possibility that Rockwell had lied to Lori Brewer. But then, Dylan didn't believe the very sharp Ms. Brewer would have been duped for long. If divorce proceedings had been underway, Abby was doing her best to cover it.

Dylan hadn't pushed the point yet, nor had he brought up Lori Brewer. He was aware that once he did she would probably look at him as the enemy. Whatever he got out of her after that point would have to be pried out. So he'd wait. What he wanted from Abby had to be won through patience.

He pushed aside tapes of other drivers, mechanics, other women, and chose the one marked Abby. It didn't occur to him that out of all the tapes he had, hers was the only one not marked with just a last name. He'd stopped thinking of her as Mrs. Rockwell. The tape was from this morning, when he'd cornered her in the living room. She'd been folding laundry, and it had occurred to him that he hadn't seen anyone do that quiet, time-consuming little chore in more years than he could count. There'd been an old fifties record on the stereo, and the doo-wops and the sha-la-las had poured out as she'd sorted socks.

He remembered how she'd looked. Her hair had been pulled back in a ponytail so that her cheekbones stood out with subtle elegance. The collar of a flannel shirt had poked out of the neck of an oversize sweatshirt, leaving the curve and line of her body a mystery. She'd worn thick socks and no shoes. The fire had been crackling behind her, flames curling greedily around fresh logs. She'd looked so content and at peace with herself that for a moment he hadn't wanted to disturb her. But he'd had a job to do. Just as he had one to do now. Dylan pushed the play button again.

"Did racing put a strain on your marriage?"

"You should remember, Chuck was a driver when I married him." Her voice on the tape sounded calm and solid after Lori Brewer's honey-laced one. "Racing was part of my marriage."

"Then you enjoyed watching him race?"

There had been a lengthy pause as she'd given herself time to find the right words. "In some ways I think Chuck was at his best behind the wheel, on the track. He was exciting, almost eerily competent. Confident," she added, looking beyond Dylan into her own past. "So confident in himself, in his abilities, that it never occurred to me he would lose the race, much less lose control."

"But after the first eight or nine months you stopped traveling with your husband."

"I was pregnant with Ben." She'd smiled a little as she'd pulled a small, worn sweater out of the basket. "It became difficult for me to jump from city to city, race to race. Chuck was—" And there it was, Dylan noted, that slight variance in tone. "He was very understanding. It wasn't too long after that that we

bought this place. A home base. Chuck and I agreed
that Ben, then Chris, needed this kind of stability.''

"It's hard to picture a man with Chuck Rockwell's
image settling down in a place like this. But then, he
didn't settle, did he?''

She had very carefully folded a bright red sweatshirt. "Chuck needed a home port, like anyone else.
But he also needed to race. We combined the two.''

Evasions, Dylan thought as he stopped the tape.
Half-truths and outright lies. What game was she
playing? And why? He knew her well enough now to
be certain she wasn't stupid. She would have known of
her husband's infidelities, and most particularly of his
relationship with Lori Brewer. Protecting him? It
hardly seemed feasible that she would protect a man
who'd cheated on her, and one who'd cheated bla-
tantly, in public, without a semblance of discretion.

Was she, had she been, the kind of woman content
to stay in the background and keep the home fires
burning? Or was she, had she been, a woman with her
eye on the main chance?

And what kind of man had Rockwell been? Had he
been the egotistical driver, the generous lover or the
understanding husband and father? Dylan found it
hard to believe any man could be all three. Abby was
the only one who could give him the answers he
needed.

Dragging a hand through his hair, he pushed away
from the desk. He wanted to get something down on
paper. Once he did, he might begin to put it all in some
sort of perspective. Dylan looked at his typewriter and
the tapes. Coffee, he decided. It was going to be a long
night.

There was a low light burning in the hall. Automatically he glanced across the corridor to where Abby slept. Her door was partially open, and the room was dark. He had an urge to cross over and push the door open a little wider so he could see her in the light from the hall.

What did he care for her privacy? He poked and scraped at her privacy whenever he questioned her. She'd cashed a check that gave him permission to.

No, he didn't give a damn for her privacy. But his own self-preservation was a different matter. If he looked, he'd want to touch. If he touched, he might not be able to pull back. So he turned from her room and started down the stairs, alone.

The fire in the living room was burning low and well. He'd watched Abby bank it one night and had been forced to admit that she did a better job of it than he would have. He left it alone and walked down the hall to the kitchen.

She was sitting at the bar in the dark. The only light came from the kitchen fire and the half-moon outside. She had her elbows on either side of a cup, her chin propped by both hands. He thought she looked unbearably lonely.

"Abby?"

She jumped. It might have been funny if he hadn't seen just how white her face was before she focused on him.

"Sorry, I didn't mean to scare you."

"I didn't hear you come down. Is anything wrong?"

"I wanted coffee." But instead of going to the stove, he went to her. "I thought you were in bed."

"Couldn't sleep." She smiled a little and didn't, as he'd expected, fuss with her hair or the lapels of her robe. "The water's probably still hot. I just made tea."

He slid onto the stool beside her. "Problem?"

"Guilt."

His reporter's instincts hummed, at war with an unexpected desire to put his arm around her and offer comfort. "About what?"

"I keep seeing the tears welling up in Chris's eyes when I sent him to bed without letting him watch his favorite show."

He didn't know whether to laugh at himself or her. "Odds are he'll recover."

"The plate wasn't that important." She lifted her tea, then set it down without drinking. "I never use them. They're ugly."

"Uh-huh. Maybe they should take a place setting or two out to the barn for the horses."

She opened her mouth, then laughed. This time, when she picked up her tea, she drank. It soothed a throat that was dry and a little achy. "I wouldn't go quite that far. Janice gave them to Chuck. To Chuck and me," she corrected, a little too quickly. "They're Wedgwood."

"And should be treated with due respect," he said. He hadn't missed her slip. "So what's the problem?"

"I hate to lose my temper."

"Did you? You never raised your voice."

"You don't have to yell to lose your temper." She looked out the window again and wished fleetingly that it wasn't so cold. If it were spring she could go out, sit on the porch and watch the sky. "It was only a plate, after all."

"And it was only a television show."

With a sigh, she settled against the back of the stool. "You think I'm being foolish."

"I suppose you're being a mother. I don't have much experience there."

"It's just so hard when you're the only one to make the rules and the decisions . . . and the mistakes." She combed a hand through her hair in an unconscious gesture that had it settling beautifully around her face. "Sometimes, late at night like this, I worry that I'm too hard on them. That I expect too much from them. They're just little boys. Now I've sent them off to bed, Chris sniffling and Ben sulking, and—"

Dylan interrupted her. "Maybe you're too hard on their mother." She stopped, stared at him, then looked at her tea again.

"I'm responsible."

And that was that, he could hear it in her tone. He started to drop it, to leave her to her own unhappiness. But whatever he thought of her, whatever he didn't think of her, he knew she was devoted to her children. "Look, I don't know a lot about kids, but I'd say those two are pretty normal and well adjusted. Maybe you should congratulate yourself instead of dragging out the sackcloth."

"I'm not doing that."

"Sure you are. You'll have the ashes out any minute."

She waited for the annoyance to come, but it didn't. Instead, she felt the guilt fade. "Thanks." At ease now, Abby warmed her hands on her cup. "I guess it helps to have a little moral support from time to time."

"No problem. I hate to see a woman sulking in her tea."

She laughed, but he couldn't be sure if it was at herself or at him. "I never sulk, but I'm a real champ at guilt. There were times when Ben was going through his terrible twos when I'd call my mother just to hear her tell me he probably wasn't going to be a homicidal maniac."

"I'd have thought you'd talk to your husband about it."

"That wouldn't have done any—" She cut herself off. It was late, and she was tired and much too vulnerable. "I'll make you that coffee," she began, and started to stand.

"I don't want you to wait on me." He had his hand on her arm, and though the touch was still light, it was enough to keep her from moving away.

She felt, incredibly, impossibly, an urge to just turn into his arms. She wanted to be held in them, to have him fold her to him and ask no questions. But of course he would. He would always ask, and she couldn't always answer. Abby held her ground and kept her distance.

"And I don't want you to interview me now."

"You've never mentioned Chuck in the area of fatherhood, Abby. Why is that?"

"Maybe because you've never asked me."

"So I'm asking now."

"I told you, I'm not in the mood for an interview. It's late. I'm tired."

"And you lie." His grip tightened just enough to make her heartbeat unsteady.

"I don't know what you're talking about."

He was sick of evasions, sick of looking at her face and knowing the truth wouldn't be there. "Every time I touch on certain areas you give me these tidy answers. Very pretty and well rehearsed. I have to ask myself why. Why do you want to whitewash Chuck Rockwell?''

He was hurting her. Not her arm—she could barely feel his fingers on her—he was hurting her deep in places she'd deluded herself into believing were safe. "He was my husband. Isn't that answer enough for you?''

"No." He could hear the emotion trembling in her voice. So he'd push, and he'd push now. "The theory I've come up with is, the better he looked, the better you looked. And if your marriage seemed to be going well, Janice Rockwell was happy. Chuck was her only son, and somebody was bound to inherit all that money.''

For the second time he watched her face pale, but this time he recognized rage, not fear. It ripped through her; he could feel it just by the touch of his hand on her arm. He wanted it. He wanted to tear holes in her composure and get to the truth. And to her.

"Let go of me." Her voice vibrated in the quiet kitchen. Behind them, a log broke and tossed sparks against the screen. Neither of them noticed.

"I want an answer first."

"You seem to have them already."

"If you want me to believe otherwise, tell me."

"I don't give a damn what you think." And that, Abby realized was the biggest lie of all. She cared, and because she cared, his accusation had crushed her. She'd been crushed before and understood that whining about it brought nothing but humiliation. "I'll give you what you want to hear and be done with it. I chose to exploit my marriage, to cash in on my dead husband's fame and reputation. Since I'm all but certain Janice Rockwell will read the book, I want to be sure she's satisfied with the results. Obviously I want her to see that my marriage to Chuck was solid. Whatever dirt you manage to dig up won't come from me. Satisfied?"

He let her arm go. In the space of seconds, she'd confirmed everything he'd thought of her, and contradicted everything he'd begun to feel. "Yeah, I'm satisfied."

"Fine. If you have more questions, ask them tomorrow, when the tape's running."

He watched her walk away and wondered how long it would take him to separate the lies from the truth.

Abby invariably woke quickly, and after her first half cup of coffee was completely alert and ready to take charge. Today, she found herself reluctant to leave her bed. Her muscles ached, her temples throbbed. Blaming it on a restless night, she went into her morning routine in low gear.

The boys were cheerful enough as they gobbled down their breakfast. The altercation of the evening before was already forgotten, in the way children had of putting things behind them. After she'd seen them off to school she indulged in another cup of coffee, waiting for her system to catch up with her schedule.

Still dragging, she bundled herself in her coat and went outside. The sun was bright, the air already warming with the first promise of spring, but she shivered and wished she'd put on an extra sweater. Catching a cold, she decided as she rubbed at the ache in the back of her neck. Well, she just didn't have time for it. Moving on automatic pilot, she gathered the eggs, then walked to the barn.

The stalls needed cleaning, the horses needed to be fed and groomed. For the first time in as long as she could remember, she resented the hours she spent working. All she ever did was clean up after others, take care of problems and deal with the jobs that had to be done. When was she going to have time for herself? Time to curl up with a book and while away an afternoon.

A book. Nearly laughing at herself, she gathered halters. Now wasn't the time to think of books—especially not one book in particular. She'd forgotten she could be hurt. It had been so long since she'd been involved with anyone who could—

Pressing her fingers against her eyes, Abby cut herself off. She couldn't call her relationship with Dylan an involvement. Business and business only, the kind that was meant to benefit both of them—that was all there was. It didn't matter, couldn't matter to her that he thought she was an opportunist. Abby supposed that was the kindest word for what he thought of her. If she followed her wounded feelings and tossed him out, she'd have accomplished nothing. In any case, she'd signed the papers and was committed to keeping him around.

And when did her obligations end? Abby let the first two horses loose in the paddock, then made the return trip to the barn. She'd been obligated to Chuck, then to her children. Now, because of them she was again duty-bound, however obliquely, to Chuck. So let Dylan Crosby think what he wanted of her as long as he wrote the book.

Tired, she rested her head against the gelding's flank. His flesh felt cool and friendly. God, she needed a friend. How could she think straight when her head was pounding? Yet she had to. The flare of temper last night might have cost her. If Dylan thought the worst of her, wouldn't it color his writing? Damn, what did he care about her reasons for authorizing the book? Whatever they were, he was being paid to write it. Her motivations had nothing to do with the story of Chuck's life. Yet they had everything to do with it.

She made a second trip outside and returned for the rest of the horses. After she'd finished in the barn, maybe her head would be clear. Then she'd know the right way to handle Dylan.

She remembered the morning when the sun had been bright and hard on her face and he'd held her. Wanted her. She could still remember the way his eyes had looked, the way his mouth had felt when it had brushed against hers. For a moment, for one indulgent moment, she'd wished he could be someone she could depend on, someone she could confide in. That was foolish. She'd known before they'd met that he had a job to do. So did she.

By the time she'd finished with the first stall, her skin was filmed with sweat. The pitchfork seemed heavier than usual as she lifted it to start on the next.

"Seems to me you ought to hire yourself a couple of hands."

Dylan stood just inside the door, the sun at his back, his face in shadow. Abby stopped long enough to squint at him. "Does it? I'll take it under advisement."

He picked up a pitchfork but just leaned on it. "Abby, why don't you drop this masquerade—you know, the struggling little homemaker who works from dawn to dusk to keep her family going."

She leaned into her work. "I'm trying to impress you."

"Don't bother. The book's about Chuck Rockwell, not you."

"Fine. I'll drop the act as soon as I get rid of this manure."

So she had claws. His fingers tightened on the worn wood handle until he deliberately relaxed them. He wanted to get to her, but he had to keep control to do it. "Listen, as long as things don't jibe, the book goes nowhere. Since we both want it to move, let's stop playing games."

"Okay." Because she needed to rest a moment, she stopped and leaned on her pitchfork. "What do you want, Dylan?"

"The truth, or as close as you can get to it. You were married to Rockwell for four years. That means there are parts of his life you know better than anyone. Those are the parts I want from you. Those are the parts you were paid to give me."

"I said I'd talk to you when the tape was running, and I will." She turned back to the stall. "Right now I've got work to do."

"Just drop it." Dylan grabbed her by the lapels and spun her around. Her pitchfork went clattering to the concrete. "Call back whoever usually takes care of this business and let's get to work. I'm tired of wasting time."

"My staff?" She'd have pulled away, but she didn't think she had the strength. "Sorry, I gave them the month off. If you want to work, bring your little pad and tapes out here. My horses need tending."

"Just who the hell are you?" he demanded, giving her a quick shake. He was no less surprised than she when her knees buckled. Keeping his grip firm, he braced her against the stall. "What's the matter with you?"

"Nothing." She tried to brush his hands away but failed. "I'm not used to being knocked around."

"You get jostled more on the subway," he muttered. She made him feel like a rough-handed clod, and he hated it. He let her go.

"You'd know more about that than I." Infuriated with herself, she bent down to scoop up the pitchfork. When her head spun, she grabbed the side of the stall for support.

Swearing, Dylan took her by the shoulders. "Look, if you're sick—"

"I'm not. I'm never sick, I'm just a little tired."

And pale, he realized as he let himself really look at her. He yanked off his glove and held a hand to her face. "You're burning up."

"I'm just overheated." Her voice rose a bit with her panic at being touched, even though being touched was exactly what she needed. "Leave me alone until I'm finished in here."

"Can't stand a martyr," he mumbled, taking her by the arm.

It was rare, very rare, for Abby's Irish heritage to break through in sheer blind rage. She'd always left that to the rest of her family and calmly worked her way through difficulties. This wasn't one of those times. She yanked her arm away and shoved him hard against the side of the stall. The strength she'd dredged up surprised them both.

"I don't care what you can stand. I don't give a damn what you think. Those papers I signed don't give you the right to interfere in my life. I'll let you know when I have time for your questions and for your accusations. Whether you believe it's a game or a facade, I have work to do. You can go to hell."

She was panting as she turned and grasped the handles of the wheelbarrow. She jerked it up, took two steps, then dropped it again as her strength drained away.

"You're doing great." He was fed up with her, and with himself, but he'd have to deal with that later. Now, unless he was very much mistaken, the lady needed a bed. This time, when he took her by the arm, she could do no more than try to shake him off.

"Don't put your hands on me."

"Babe, I've been doing my damnedest to keep them off you all week." When she stumbled, he swore, then scooped her up in his arms. "This time we're both going to have to put up with it."

"I don't have to be carried." Then she started to shiver. Too weak to help herself, she let her head fall on his shoulder. "I haven't finished."

"Yeah, you have."

"The eggs."

"I'll get them later—after I dump you in bed."

"Bed?" She roused herself again, noticing dimly they were stepping onto the porch. "I can't go to bed. The horses haven't been dealt with, and the vet's coming at one to look over the mares. Mr. Jorgensen's coming with him. I have to sell that foal."

"I'm sure Jorgensen's going to be thrilled to buy the foal after you've given him the flu."

"Flu? I don't have the flu, just a little cold."

"Flu." Dylan laid her on the bed, then began to pry off her boots. "I'd say you'll be hobbling around again in a couple of days."

"Don't be absurd." She managed with a great deal of effort to prop herself up on her elbows. "I just need a couple of aspirin."

"Can you get undressed by yourself, or do you want help?"

"I'm not getting undressed," she said evenly, though if she could have had one wish at the moment, it would have been to sleep.

"Help then." Sitting down, he began to unbutton her coat.

"I don't need or want your help." She clung to what dignity she had left and struggled to sit up. "Look, I might have a touch of the flu, but I also have two children who'll walk in the door at 3:25. In the meantime I have to groom the horses, Eve in particular. I have a lot riding on the deal with Jorgensen."

Dylan studied her face. Her skin was pale, her eyes glazed with fever. The quickest way to bring her around was to agree with her. "Okay, that's at one. Do yourself a favor and rest for an hour." When she started to object, he shook his head. "Abby, you'll really impress Jorgensen by fainting at his feet."

She was wobbly. There was no use denying it. To be honest, she didn't think she could have lifted a curry comb at the moment. She was a practical woman, and the practical thing to do was to rest until she built up a little strength. If it galled a bit to agree with him, she'd just have to swallow the gall. "I'll rest an hour."

"Fine, get into bed. I'll bring you a couple aspirin."

"Thanks." She peeled off her coat as he rose. Then, as it had a habit of doing, her conscience poked at her. "Really. I appreciate it."

"No problem."

When he left, Abby took a grip on the bedpost and pulled herself out of bed. Her body punished her by throbbing all over. Moving slowly, she went to her dresser and pulled out a cotton gown. She tugged off her sweater, then her jeans. Exhausted from the effort, she stood rocking on her feet and shivering. Just an hour, she told herself, and I'll be fine.

Later, she couldn't even remember dragging on the gown and crawling into bed.

Dylan found her there when he came back. Sprawled on her stomach, she was sleeping, so deeply that she never stirred when he tucked the blankets around her. Nor did she stir when he bent closer and brushed the hair away from her face.

She never stirred for the hour he sat in the chair beside the bed, watching her. And wondering.

Chapter Five

Sweaty, aching and disoriented, Abby woke. How long had she been asleep? Pressing the heels of her hands against her eyes, she tried to gather her reserves of strength. Her skin felt clammy, and she thought for a moment that the lining of her throat had been coated with something hot and bitter. She was forced to admit that whatever had hit her had hit her with both fists. Because she was alone, she moaned a little as she sat up. Then, studying the clock beside her, she moaned again.

2:15. She'd slept nearly four hours. Mr. Jorgensen. Desperate, Abby swung out of bed. The pounding in her head began immediately, along with a throbbing that seemed to reach every inch of her body. She realized she was damp with sweat. Abby snatched up her jeans, then leaned against the bedpost, waiting for the weakness to pass.

They might still be here, she told herself. They could have come late and right now be standing in the barn, looking over the mare. Eve hadn't been groomed, but Jorgensen had already seen her at her best. And the vet—the vet was bound to vouch for the fact that the mare was strong and healthy. All she had to do was get dressed and go outside and apologize.

Dylan strolled in, carrying a tray. "Going somewhere?"

"It's after two." Though weak, it was definitely an accusation.

"You got that right." He set the tray down on the dresser and studied her. The nightgown scooped low at her neck and drooped carelessly over one shoulder—one very slender, very smooth shoulder. The rest of her was just as slender, from the long dancer's legs to the high, subtly rounded breasts.

A man was entitled, Dylan told himself, to feel a little tightening, a little heat, a little longing, when he looked at a half-naked woman and a rumpled bed. He just couldn't let it get personal. "Interesting," he murmured. "This is the first time I've seen you in something that isn't three inches thick."

"I'm sure I look ravishing."

"Actually, you look like hell. Why don't you get back in bed before you keel over?"

"Mr. Jorgensen—"

"An interesting little man," Dylan finished. Walking to her, Dylan took the jeans out of her hand and tossed them on a chair. "He talked about his horses with more passion than he did his wife." He eased her down on the bed as he spoke.

"He's still here? I've got to go out and talk to him."

"He's gone." With little fuss, Dylan arranged the pillows at her back.

"Gone?"

"Yeah. Open up. I managed to find this among the bottles of antiseptic spray and colored Band-Aids."

She waved the thermometer away as she tried to concentrate on her next move. "I can call him and reschedule. Did you explain why I wasn't available? I can't believe I missed him. The vet...did the vet...?"

Dylan stuck the thermometer in her mouth, then captured both her hands before she could pull it out again. "Shut up." When she started to mumble around it, he caught her chin in his other hand. "Listen, if you want to hear about Jorgensen you'll leave that thing in and keep your mouth shut. Got it?"

She slumped back, nearly ready to sulk. He was speaking to her as she might to one of the boys. Seeing no alternative, Abby nodded.

"Good." Releasing her hands, he went back for the tray.

Abby immediately pulled the thermometer out. "Did the vet give Eve an exam? I need to—"

"Put that thing back in or I'll leave you up here alone and wondering." After setting the tray on her lap, he stood waiting. He felt a nice sense of satisfaction when she obeyed. "The vet said Eve was in perfect shape, that he didn't foresee any complications, and you can expect her to deliver the foal within a week."

She reached for the thermometer. He only had to lift a brow to stop her. "About the other mare, Gladys?" When she nodded, he shook his head. "Hell of a name for a horse. Anyway, she's just as fit. Jorgensen said to tell you if all goes well he'll call you to discuss terms after the foal's born. He also said," Dylan continued, grabbing her wrist again as she reached up, "that he has a couple of names for you. People who might be interested in the other foal. I have a feeling he might be interested himself if his wife doesn't skin him. You can call him when you're on your feet. Satisfied?"

She closed her eyes and nodded. It was happening, at last it was really happening. The money from the foals would go a long way toward paying off the rest of the loan she'd been forced to take after Chuck's death. To be nearly out of debt, to know that in a year or two she'd be essentially stable again. Foolishly she wanted to cry. She wanted to burrow under the covers and weep until tears of relief washed everything else away. Keeping her eyes closed, she waited until she could compose herself.

An odd woman, Dylan thought as he watched her. Why should she get so emotional over the sale of a couple of horses? He was certain the price was right, but it could hardly be more than a drop in the bucket compared to the estate she must have inherited from Rockwell. Money must be important, he decided, though he'd be damned if he could see where she spent it.

The furniture perhaps. Her bed was eighteenth-century and not something you'd pick up at a yard sale. And the horses, of course. She hadn't bought that stallion for a song and a smile. He glanced over at her closet. He'd wager that a good chunk of the rest was hanging in there.

When she opened her eyes again, he plucked the thermometer out. "Dylan I don't know what to say."

"Um-hmm. A hundred and three. Looks like you win the prize."

"A hundred and three?" Her gratitude disappeared. "That's ridiculous, let me see it."

He held it out of reach. "Are you always such a lousy patient?"

"I'm never sick. You must have read that wrong."

He handed it over, then watched as her brows drew together. "Well, that should make you feel a whole lot worse." He took the thermometer again, shook it, then slipped it into its plastic case. "Now, can you feed yourself or do you want help?"

"I can manage." She stared without appetite at the soup steaming on the tray. "I don't usually eat lunch."

"Today you do. We're pushing fluids. Try the juice first."

She took the glass he handed her, then sighed. No wonder he was treating her like one of the boys, she thought. She was acting like one. "Thanks. I'm sorry for complaining. I don't mean to be cranky, but there are so many things I have to do. Lying here isn't getting them done."

"Indispensable, are you?"

She looked at him again. Something moved in her eyes—emotion, hope, questions, he couldn't tell which. "I am needed."

She said it with such quiet desperation that he reached out to stroke her cheek before he thought about it. "Then you'd better take care of yourself."

"Yeah." She lifted the spoon and tried to work up some enthusiasm for the soup. "I *am* a lousy patient. Sorry."

"It's all right. So am I."

To please him, she began to eat. "You don't look like you're ever sick."

"If it makes you feel better, I had the flu a couple of years ago."

She smiled, a self-deprecating humor in her eyes. "It does. Anyway, I'm more used to doing the doctoring. Both boys were down with the chicken pox in September. The house was like a ward. Dylan..." She'd been working up to this for some time. Now, idly stirring her soup, she thought she had the courage. "I'm sorry about last night, and this morning."

"Sorry for what?"

She looked up. He seemed so relaxed, so untouched. Apparently harsh words and arguments didn't leave him churning with guilt. But he hadn't lied, and they both knew it. She figured they both knew she'd go on lying. "I said things I didn't mean. I always do when I'm angry."

"Maybe you're more honest when you're angry than you think." He was tense. However it looked on the outside, he was baffled by her, moved by her. "Listen, Abby, I still intend to push you and push you hard. But I've got some scruples. I don't intend to start wrestling with you until you can hold your own."

She had to smile. "As long as I'm sick, I'm safe."

"Something like that. You're not eating."

"I'm sorry." She set down the spoon. "I just can't."

He picked up the tray to set it beside the bed. "Anyone ever tell you that you apologize too much?"

"Yes." She smiled again. "Sorry."

"You're an interesting woman, Abby."

"Oh?" It felt so good just to snuggle back. Chilled, she drew the blankets higher. Incredibly, she was tired again, so tired it would have taken no effort at all to simply ease back and drift off. "I always thought I was rather humdrum."

"Humdrum." He glanced down at her elegant hands and remembered how competently they had worked. He remembered the woman in mink, diamonds glittering at her ears, and thought of how she had folded laundry. It didn't add up to humdrum. It simply didn't add up at all. "I've got a picture of you in my file that was taken in Monte Carlo. You were wrapped to the eyebrows in white mink."

"The white mink." She smiled drowsily as the energy drained from her degree by degree. "Made me feel like a princess. It was fabulous, wasn't it?"

"Was?"

"Mmm. Just like a princess."

"Where is it?"

"The roof," she said, and slept.

The roof? She had to be delirious if she was picturing fur coats on the roof. She murmured a bit when he settled her more comfortably.

A very interesting woman, Abby, he thought again as he stood back to look at her. All he had to do was fill in all the blank spaces.

When Dylan heard the first crash, he was in the middle of transcribing his notes on Rockwell's first year of professional racing. He swore, though without heat, as he turned off the typewriter. Leaving the half-typed sheet in the machine, he went downstairs to greet the boys at the front door.

"It wasn't my fault." Ben glared at his brother, his arm around the dog.

"It was, too, you—" Chris reached into his vocabulary and brought out his top insult "—idiot."

"You're the idiot. Just because—"

"Problem?" Dylan asked as he opened the door. Both boys had fire in their eyes, and Chris was covered with mud from head to foot, as well. His bottom lip trembled as he pointed a dirty, self-righteous finger at his brother.

"He pushed me down."

"I did not."

"I'm telling Mom."

"Hold it, hold it." Dylan blocked the door and got a smear of fresh mud on his jeans. "Ben, don't you think you're a little too big to be pushing Chris down?"

"I didn't." His chin poked out. "He's always saying I did things when I didn't. *I'm* telling Mom."

Big tears welled up in Chris's eyes as he stood, a major mess, on the porch. Dylan had a strong and unexpected urge to hunker down and hug him. "Look, it'll clean off," he said, contenting himself with flicking at the boy's nose with a finger. "Why don't you tell me what happened?"

"He pushed me down." The first tears spilled over. He was still too young to be ashamed of them. "Just 'cause he's bigger."

"I did not." Not far from tears himself, Ben stared at the ground. "I didn't mean to, anyway. We were just fooling around."

"An accident?"

"Yeah." He sniffled, embarrassing himself.

"It never hurts to apologize for an accident." He put a hand on Ben's shoulder. "Especially when you're bigger."

"I'm sorry," he mumbled, shooting a look at his brother. "Mom's going to be mad 'cause he's got mud all over. I'm going to get in trouble. And it's Friday."

"Uh-huh." Dylan considered. Chris was over his tears now and running his fingers curiously through the mud on his coat. "Well, maybe we won't have to tell her this time."

"Yeah?" Hope sprang into Ben's eyes, then was quickly displaced by mistrust. "She's gonna see anyhow."

"No, she's not. Come on." Seeing no other way, Dylan hoisted Chris up. "We'll dump you in the washing machine."

He giggled and swung a friendly, filthy arm around Dylan's neck. "You can't put people in there. It's too small. Where's Mom?"

"Upstairs. She's got the flu."

"Like Mr. Petrie?"

"That's right."

Ben stopped as they entered the kitchen. "Mom's never sick."

"She is this time. Right now she's sleeping, so let's try to keep it down, okay?"

"I want to see her myself."

Dylan stopped in the act of pushing the door to the laundry room open. He glanced back and saw Ben just inside the kitchen, his mouth set, his eyes defiant. Though it disconcerted him, Dylan found himself admiring Ben's determination to defend his mother.

"Don't wake her up." He swung through to the laundry room. "Okay, tiger, strip."

Ready to oblige, Chris struggled out of his coat. "My teacher had the flu last week, so we had a substitute. She had red hair and couldn't remember our names. Is Mom going to be sick tomorrow?"

"She won't be as sick tomorrow." Dylan found the soap and began figuring out the mechanics of the washing machine.

"She can use my crayons." Chris plopped down on the floor and began yanking at his boots. "And we can read her stories. She reads me stories when I'm sick."

"I'm sure she'll appreciate it."

"If she feels real bad, I can let her have Mary."

"Who's Mary?"

"Mary's my dog, the one Aunt Maddy gave me when I was little. I still sleep with her, but don't tell Ben. He teases me."

Dylan smiled and sent water gushing into the machine. It was nice to be trusted. "I won't say anything."

"If she's better tomorrow, do you think we can go to the movies? She said she'd take us to the movies on Saturday."

"I don't know." Turning back, Dylan saw that the boy had taken him at his word. He'd stripped down to the skin. His sturdy little body was covered with goose bumps and dirt. "I don't think we have to go that far." After taking a folded towel off the dryer, Dylan bent down and wrapped the boy in it. "You're going to need a bath."

"I hate baths." Chris tilted his head and gave Dylan a solemn look. "I really hate them."

"Trouble is, you were right." Dylan dumped the rest of the clothes in the machine and closed the lid. "You won't fit in the washing machine."

Laughing, Chris raised his arms in an open, uncomplicated gesture that left Dylan speechless. Helpless to do anything but respond, Dylan lifted him up. Good God, he thought as he nuzzled him, I've managed to keep things in perspective for over thirty years and now I'm falling for a six-year-old kid with mud on his face.

"About that bath."

"Hate them."

"Come on, you're bound to have a boat or something to fool around with in there."

Resigned, Chris let himself be carried toward the inevitable. "I like trucks better."

"So take a truck."

"Can I take three?"

"As long as there's room for you." He set Chris down again by the bathroom door. "Now you've got to be quiet, right?"

"Right," Chris returned in a whisper. "Are you going to help me wash my hair? I can almost do it myself."

"Ah..." He thought about the work waiting on his desk. "Sure. Get yourself started."

Baby-sitting, Dylan thought as he hesitated in the hall, hadn't been part of the deal. Still, he knew Abby wasn't enjoying it any more than he was. He glanced at Ben's room. The door was closed. His first thought was to leave the boy to himself and deal with the less complicated task of washing Chris's hair. Swearing at himself, Dylan walked over and knocked.

"You can come in."

Dylan opened the door to see the boy sitting on his bed, an army of miniature men spread out in front of him. "Did you see your mother?"

"Yeah. I didn't wake her up." He sent two of the men crashing together. "I guess she's pretty sick."

THE LAST HONEST WOMAN

"She just needs to rest for a couple of days." Dylan sat on the edge of the bed and picked up one of the men. "She'll probably want some company later."

"Once I came home from school and she was on the couch because she said she had this headache. But I knew she'd been crying."

At a loss, Dylan lined up men in tandem with Ben's. "Moms need to cry sometimes. Everybody does, really."

"Not guys."

"Yeah. Sometimes."

Ben digested that, but he wasn't ready to believe it. "Was Mom crying again?"

"This time she's just sick. I guess she'll feel better if we don't give her any trouble."

"I don't mean to cause trouble." Ben's voice was very young and very small.

"I'm sure you don't." Dylan thought of himself, of how he'd pushed and tugged and pressured. His job. But it didn't go very far toward the guilt.

"I didn't really mean to push Chris down in the mud," he mumbled.

"I didn't think you did." But Dylan *had* meant to push Abby up against a wall.

"Mom would've punished me."

"I see." Dylan found himself admiring Ben's candor, but now he'd have to do something, and what the hell did he know about handling kids? He dragged a hand through his hair and tried to be logical. "I guess we'll have to think of something. Want me to go push you down in the mud?"

Ben glanced up warily. After meeting Dylan's eyes, he laughed. "Then Mom would be mad at you."

"Right. Why don't you do Chris's chores tonight?"

"Okay." That was no big deal. He liked spending time with the horses, and Chris usually got in the way.

It both pleased and surprised Dylan that he could read the boy's mind. "That includes the dishes—it's Chris's turn."

"But—"

"It's a tough old world, kid." Dylan tugged his earlobe and went to see to his other charge.

Abby awoke to the sounds of an argument. An argument in whispers was still an argument. Opening her eyes, she focused on her sons, who were standing at the foot of the bed.

"We should wake her up now," Ben insisted.

"We should wait until Dylan comes up."

"Now."

"What if she still has a temperature?"

"We'll take it and find out."

"Do you know how?" Chris demanded, ready to be impressed.

"You use that little skinny thing. We just put it in her mouth, then wait."

"While she's asleep?"

"No, dummy. We have to wake her up."

"I'm awake." Abby pushed herself up against the pillows while both boys eyed her.

"Hi." Not at all sure how to deal with a sick mother, Ben fooled with the bedspread.

"Hi yourself."

"Are you still sick?"

Her throat was so dry that she was surprised she could talk at all. Every muscle in her body rebelled as she pushed herself up a bit higher. "Maybe a little."

"Do you want my crayons?" Not one to stand on ceremony, Chris crawled onto the bed to get a closer look.

"Maybe later," she told him, running a hand through his hair. "Did you just get home from school?"

"Heck, no. We've been home forever. Right, Ben?"

"We had dinner," Ben confirmed. "And did the chores."

"Dinner?" After she'd cleared her mind of sleep, she saw that the light was dim with evening. A glance at the clock had her moaning. She'd lost another three hours. "What did you have?"

"Tacos. Dylan makes them real good. Do you have a temperature?" Interested, Chris put his hand on her head. "You feel hot. Do you have to take medicine like Ben and me did? I can read you a story after."

"You can't read," Ben said in disgust.

"I can too. Miss Schaeffer said I read real good."

"Kid stuff, not Mom's kind of stories."

"Fighting again?" Dylan walked in with another tray. "It's nice to see everything's normal. Scoot over, Chris. Your mom has to eat."

"We all made it," Chris told her as she shifted aside. "Dylan made the eggs and Ben heated the soup. I made the toast."

"Looks great." She wished she could toss it, tray and all, out the window. When Dylan arranged the pillows behind her, she glanced up and saw the grin. Apparently writers read minds. Since he did, he'd also be aware that she had no choice but to eat.

"Dylan said you need your strength," Ben put in.

"Did he?"

"And Dylan said we had to be quiet so you could rest. We were real quiet." Chris waited for his mother to sample the toast he'd smeared overgenerously with butter.

"You were very quiet," Abby told him, washing down the soggy toast with juice.

"Dylan said he'd play a game with us later if we didn't mess up." Chris sent him a sunny smile. "We didn't, did we?"

"You did just fine."

Unwilling to let Chris get all the attention, Ben moved closer. "Dylan said you'd probably be too sick to go to the movies tomorrow."

"It seems Dylan says a lot," she murmured, then reached out to touch Ben's cheek. "We'll have to see. How was school?"

"It was pretty good. A bird got into the classroom during math and Mrs. Lieter chased it around. It kept crashing into the windows."

"Pretty exciting."

"Yeah, but then she opened one of the windows and got a broom."

"Tricia fell on the playground and got a big bump on her head." Chris leaned over to fuss with the thin gold chain his mother wore, which had fascinated him since childhood. "She cried for a long time. I fell down and didn't cry at all. Well, not very much," he corrected meticulously. "Dylan was going to put me in the washing machine."

Abby stopped running a hand over Chris's hair. "I beg your pardon?"

"Well, there was all this mud and stuff and—"

Dylan interrupted before Chris's storytelling got his brother in deep water. "A little accident, it's still pretty slippery outside."

As Abby looked on, Ben tilted his head and sent Dylan a quick sidelong look. A mixture of guilt and gratitude. "I see." At least she thought she did. She was also wise enough not to pursue it. "This is a great dinner, you guys, but I don't think I can eat any more right now."

Dylan took the remaining juice off the tray and set it on the nightstand. "Why don't you two take the tray down? I'll be along in a minute."

As soon as they'd gone, Dylan picked up the thermometer.

"Dylan, I really appreciate all this. I don't know what to say."

"Good." He stuck the thermometer in her mouth. "Then you can be quiet."

Unwilling to start another battle she'd lose, Abby sat back and waited until he drew the thermometer out again. "It's down, right?"

"Up two-tenths," he corrected, entirely too cheerfully for her taste, and handed her the aspirin.

"The boys were counting on that movie tomorrow."

"They'll survive." After replacing the thermometer, he started to leave her. Abby grabbed his hand impulsively.

"Dylan, I'm not trying to be a bad patient, but I swear I'll go crazy if I spend another minute alone in this bed."

He cocked his head. "Is that an invitation?"

"What? Oh, no." She snatched her hand back. "I didn't mean that. I only meant—"

"I get the picture." Bending over, he wrapped the spread around her and lifted her into his arms.

"What are you doing?"

"Getting you out of bed. I'll take you down, plop you in front of the TV. Odds are you'll be dead to the world inside of an hour."

"I've already slept all day." This time she could allow herself to enjoy, to appreciate, the sensation of being held in strong arms, of being carried as though she were fragile. For tonight, just for tonight, she could pretend there was someone to stand by her, to stand with her. Fairy tales, Abby warned herself, and stopped before she could lay her head on his shoulder.

"I appreciate you watching the children like this. I don't want to impose, though. I can call a neighbor."

"Forget it." He said it lightly, not wanting to admit he'd enjoyed the afternoon. "I can handle them. I worked my way through college as a bouncer."

"That kind of experience certainly helps," she murmured. "Dylan, did Chris get hurt when Ben pushed him down?"

"I don't know what you're talking about."

"You certainly do."

"Did Chris look hurt to you?"

"No, but—"

"Then you wouldn't want me to be a stool pigeon, would you?"

She sent him a mild look as he settled her down on the living room couch. "Men always stick together, don't they?"

Without answering, he switched on the set. He'd needed to set her down quickly, to break contact. She'd seemed so sweet, so small, so frail in his arms.

A man made his biggest mistakes when he was sucked in by fragility.

"If you need anything, we'll be in the kitchen. Men stuff, you know?"

"Dylan—"

"Look, if you thank me again I'm going to belt you." Instead he bent down, took her face in his hands and kissed her, hard. "Don't thank me and don't apologize."

"I wouldn't dream of it." Before she could think, before she could reason, Abby reached out and brought his mouth back to hers again.

It wasn't sweet. It wasn't magic. It was solid and strong. She tasted, for the first time in too many years, the flavor of man. She wanted, for the first time in too many years. And wasn't it wonderful just to want again—not to think, not to reason, just to let go and want.

The touch, the taste, brought back no memories of her marriage, of the only other man she'd known. It was fresh and new, as beginnings should be.

Her skin was hot. He felt the yielding he knew came as much from weakness as from passion. Yet he thought, or rather wanted to think, that there was something more, something unique in the way her mouth fit his. So he wanted more. From the kiss alone, desire sprinted out until he wanted everything—to feel her skin, feverishly hot under the thin nightgown, to feel her body melt against his.

There was no artifice in her kiss, no expertise. The gesture seemed to be as pure and as generous as Chris lifting his arms to him. He drew away, reluctant and more than a little puzzled. He was finding that the more he knew her, the less he knew.

She lay back, her eyes half-closed, knowing he was studying her and helpless to slip on any mask. Whatever he wanted to see was there. She had no way of knowing that his own doubts were blinding him.

"That's something else we're going to deal with when you're on your feet, Abby."

"Yes, I know."

"You'd better rest." He put his hands in his pockets because it would be too easy to touch her again and forget.

"I will." She closed her eyes because it would be too easy to reach out again and forget. There were children in the next room. Her children, her responsibility. Her life.

When she opened her eyes again, he was gone.

Chapter Six

She didn't remember going back upstairs, but in the morning she woke in her own bed. And she woke late. There was something warm and fuzzy against her cheek. Her initial alarm turned to puzzlement, then to love, as she cuddled the ragged stuffed dog Chris prized. He must have brought it to her as she'd slept. Shifting, she saw the big pink sheet of contact paper taped sloppily to the bedpost that read Get Well Mom.

She recognized Ben's slanted, uneven printing, and tears blurred her vision. Maybe they were monsters, but they were her monsters, and they came through when it counted.

Did she? She rubbed Mary absently against her cheek. It was nearly ten in the morning, and she hadn't even fixed her children breakfast.

Disgusted, Abby pulled herself out of bed. Pretending her legs didn't wobble, she yanked her robe out of the closet and headed for the shower. There were things to be done, and she couldn't accomplish them in bed.

After she'd cleared the tub of a convoy of trucks, she just stood under the spray. It beat against aching muscles and feverish skin. She braced her hands against the tile and lifted her face so that the water sluiced over her. Gradually the chill passed and her mind cleared.

Dylan. Was it wrong that when her mind cleared he was the first thing to form in it? Perhaps it wasn't wrong, but it certainly wasn't safe. She'd started more there than she'd bargained for. Alone, she could admit that she hadn't the vaguest idea what to do next. The attraction she felt for him hadn't been in the plans. The wisest move would be to ignore it. But could she? Would he?

Once before, she'd felt this kind of quick excitement. And once before, she'd acted without giving herself a chance to reason. It wasn't a mistake she could afford to make twice. She couldn't say how long it had taken her to get over the hurt Chuck had caused, but she knew she couldn't deal with that sort of pain again. No, she didn't think she would survive to rebuild a second time, so the choice was clear. No involvement was worth the risk of losing. No man was worth the price. Now she had children to think of, a home, and the life she'd made for them.

Overlaying the doubts she had about herself were doubts about the project that had brought Dylan to her. It was going to be more difficult to evade, to lie, to hide, if she let herself feel something for him. So she couldn't.

Abby wearily turned off the shower. She couldn't risk feeling or giving or even taking when it came to Dylan. She'd stick by her plan because the plan was survival; he was only the biographer of her children's father.

Dry, she walked back into the hall. A quick peek showed her the boys were already up. She'd go down, fix coffee, make them breakfast and get them away from their cartoons long enough to feed the stock.

She found them where she'd expected, huddled in front of the TV with the latest action-adventure cartoon whizzing by on the screen. What she hadn't expected was to find Dylan huddled with them.

"You call this a cartoon?" Chris was snuggled beside him on the sofa and Ben lay sprawled at his feet as though the three of them spent every Saturday morning together.

"It's a great cartoon," Ben told him. "Asteroid John tracks down the bad guys, but he never gets them all. Especially Dr. Disaster."

Dylan thought he knew who Ben was rooting for. "Listen, Bugs Bunny's a cartoon. It has style and wit, not just laser beams. Wile E. Coyote trying to catch the Roadrunner. Bugs outmaneuvering Elmer Fudd. That's a cartoon."

Ben just snorted and gave Asteroid John his attention.

Chris tugged on Dylan's shirt. "I like Bugs Bunny." Amused by the boy's earnest face, Dylan swung an arm over his shoulders.

"Chris looks like Bugs Bunny," Ben stated. He grinned, waiting for retaliation. Before Chris could scramble down, Dylan shifted the boy onto his lap.

"Nope," he said after a careful study of Chris's face. "Ears are too short. But Ben..." Reaching down, he tugged on an unguarded ear. "These might just make it."

Giggling, Ben put both hands over his ears and rolled over. "I'm Dr. Disaster and I'm going to blow up the planet Kratox."

"Yeah? You and who else?" He scooped the boy up and held him in a loose headlock. "You space marauders are all the same."

"Evil?"

"No, ticklish." He dug a finger into the boy's ribs and sent him squealing. It only took a moment for the three of them to roll off the sofa. Delighted, Chris climbed onto Dylan's shoulders. It was then he saw his mother standing in the doorway.

"Hi, Mom."

"Good morning." She watched her sons, who were flushed from the tussle, then looked at Dylan. He hadn't shaved, and might have been any man on a lazy Saturday morning.

"We're not supposed to roughhouse on the furniture," Ben whispered in Dylan's ear.

"Right." Dylan untangled himself, then gave Abby a long, measuring look. "You should be in bed."

"I'm fine, thanks." Why did he become only more arousing when he was a little rough around the edges? Would she always be attracted to men who had so little tenderness in them? "I'm just going to fix some coffee."

"It's on the stove."

"Oh." She hesitated, hating to drag the kids away. "Ben, Chris, as soon as that show's over I need you to come eat and help me feed the stock."

"We already did it," Ben told her, relieved that there would be no lecture on showing the proper respect for the furniture.

"You fed the stock already this morning?"

"And we had breakfast. Pancakes," Chris told her. "Dylan makes them real good."

"Oh." She stuck her hands in her pockets, feeling foolish and, worse, useless. "Then I'll heat up the coffee."

"Let me know how the planet makes out," Dylan said, then rose and followed Abby into the kitchen. "Problem?" he asked her.

"No." Just dozens of them, she thought as she turned the flame on under the pot. How was she supposed to keep promises to herself when she saw him playing with her children? How was she supposed to keep her mind busy when all the chores were done before she could even begin? No tenderness in him, no kindness—she needed to go on believing that if she wanted to stay whole.

She stiffened when he took her by the shoulders, but he ignored it and turned her to face him. With his eyes on hers, he put a hand to her forehead. "You still have a fever."

"I feel much better."

"You feel like hell," he said. Taking her by the arm, he led her to a stool. "Sit."

"Dylan, I'm used to running my own life."

"Fine. You should be able to get back to it by Monday."

"And what am I supposed to do until then?" The words came out in a heated rush as she gave in to her weakness and dropped down onto the stool. "I'm tired of lying in bed and eating soup. I'm tired of having a thermometer stuck in my mouth and aspirin poured down my throat.''

"One of the first signs of getting well is crankiness.'' He set a glass of juice in front of her. ''Drink.''

''You're good at giving orders.''

''You're lousy at taking them.''

She scowled at him, then picked up the juice and drained it. ''There. Satisfied?''

Not certain whether he should be amused or annoyed, Dylan skirted the counter. ''What's eating you?''

''I've just told you. I…'' Her voice trailed off as he took her face in his hand.

''You haven't told me half of it. But you will.'' Unable to resist, he stroked his thumb along her cheekbone.

''Don't.'' She lifted a hand to his wrist but couldn't make herself push him aside.

''People are my speciality,'' he murmured. ''So far, I'm having a hard time getting through to what makes you tick. Do you like challenges, Abby?''

''No.'' She said it almost desperately. ''No, I don't.''

''I do.'' He combed his other hand through her hair, which was still damp from the shower. ''I find them intriguing, and in some cases very arousing.'' He'd thought about her during the night. Thought about her and what he wanted. The more he thought, the more he believed the two might be the same thing. He touched his mouth to hers, just enough to awaken her. ''You arouse me, Abby. What the hell are we going to do about that?''

''Stop.'' She fought to keep a tight hold on her emotions but her grip kept slipping. ''The children.''

"If they haven't seen their mother kissing a man before, they should have." The hand in her hair grew firmer. This time his mouth didn't merely touch hers, it absorbed it.

His lips were softer than they should have been, warmer, more...patient. None of it was expected. Was this how a man kissed a woman he desired, a woman he cared for? Was this what she'd been missing in her life, what she'd been craving without understanding? If it was, she wouldn't be able to fight it for long. Gentleness shattered her defenses in a way demands never could. Slowly, reluctantly, she opened to him. If her head was spinning it was the fever. She needed the excuse.

He couldn't explain the sense of innocence he felt from her, but it excited him. He couldn't explain his own sudden need, but it churned through him. He wanted her, alone. He wanted to see that look of panic and passion in her eyes when he touched her. He wanted to feel that slow, gradual melting of her body against his—half reluctant, half eager. He wanted to hear that quickening of breath that meant she'd forgotten everything but him. Whatever game she was playing, whatever lies she told, didn't matter when her mouth yielded to his.

He'd have his answers. He'd have hers. At the moment, he didn't care which came first.

"I want to take you to bed." He murmured it against her mouth, then against her skin as his lips skimmed over her face. "Soon, Abby, very soon."

"Dylan, I—"

"Are you taking Mom's temperature?"

Abby jerked back and stared, speechless, at Chris. He looked at her and at Dylan with the open, friendly curiosity that was an innate part of him.

"Mom kisses my forehead sometimes when I have a fever. Can I have a drink?"

"Yes." Abby fumbled for words while Chris found a glass. "Dylan was just—"

"Telling your mother she should get back in bed," Dylan finished for her. "And you and Ben need your coats. We have to run into town."

"Into town?" When she looked at him, she saw only cool amusement. She knew she should have expected that.

"We're out of a few things," he said easily enough. And he needed to get out, away from her, until he had himself back in order.

"Can I have some gum? Sugarless," Chris added, remembering his mother.

"Probably."

Leaving half a glass of juice on the counter, Chris went running for his brother.

"You don't have to take them," Abby began.

"I like the company."

Amusement helped fade the tension. "Oh, you'll have plenty of that. Have you ever taken two boys to the store?"

"I told you." He wasn't smiling now. "I like challenges."

"Yes, you did." Struggling to be calm, Abby rose. "They'll try to talk you into buying twice as much as you need."

"I'm a rock."

"Don't say I didn't warn you."

Then Ben and Chris came barreling in again, ready for the next adventure.

Abby compromised with herself. She did indeed have work to do and barely enough energy to stand. In order to accomplish some of the first and give in to the second, she took her paperwork to bed with her. The least she could do was pay the bills and bring her account and checkbooks up-to-date.

Because the house was quiet, she turned on the radio beside the bed before she began. Though she'd long ago accepted it as an unending cycle, it continued to give Abby a sense of satisfaction to pay bills and diminish the amount of her debts.

The house came first, and always would. It was security for her family and, undeniably, for herself. Fourteen years and two months to go, she mused as she sealed the envelope.

Fourteen years, she thought again. Her boys would be men. She wanted the home where they'd grown up to matter, to be full of good memories, love, laughter and a balancing sense of responsibility. That wasn't something she could give them merely by writing a check. That was something else she wanted them to grow to understand. What you had wasn't nearly as important as what you were. There were those, she knew, who never found the serenity to understand that.

She wrote her monthly check to Grover Stanholz with a mixture of gratitude and resentment—gratitude to the man for the loan, resentment that the loan itself had been necessary. Resentment didn't help, she reminded herself. Fulfilling the obligation would. Her answer there was the foals. If their price was right, she'd have come a long way toward being free of at least one of her obligations. Settling back, Abby wrote the note she always attached to the check.

Dear Grover,

I hope this finds you well and happy. The children are great and looking forward, as I am, to the end of winter. The weather's finally beginning to clear up, though there are a few patches of snow and ice here and there. I want to thank you again for the invitation to join you in Florida. I know the boys would have enjoyed a few days, but it just wasn't possible to leave the farm or take them out of school.

Two of our mares are nearly ready to foal. Spring promises to be exciting. If you consider a trip north, please come. I'd like you to see what you helped me accomplish.

As always,
Abby

It never seemed enough. Abby folded the letter and sighed. There was so little she could say. She could have mentioned Dylan. They had discussed their joint contribution to the book and she knew that Dylan had already interviewed him. Somehow, she thought, it would help both of them to avoid the subject until it was all finished. Stanholz had loved Chuck like a father and had grieved like one. It seemed she could do no more than send him pictures of the children a couple times a year and a tidy note attached to a check once a month.

Shaking off the mood, she continued to sort through bills. Some she could pay, some she knew she had to put off just a little while longer. When she was finished, she had a grand total of $27.40 in her checking account.

So she'd dip into the emergency fund, she told herself. That was what emergency funds were for. The boys were going to need new shoes within the month, and twenty-seven dollars wasn't going to do it. It only proved she'd made the right decision in agreeing to the book. With that money to fall back on, she could keep everything afloat. When the foals were born...

She had to stop. Abby closed the books firmly and tidied the papers. She wasn't going to fall into the trap of thinking about money every waking moment. There would be enough. That was all she needed to know.

Laying back, she frowned at the ceiling. Want to or not, she didn't think she had the strength to tackle the kitchen floor or any of the other heavy household chores on her list for the day. But she wasn't going to vegetate, either. When was the last time she'd had a Saturday free? Thinking of it made her laugh at herself. And how many times had she wished for one so she could do nothing at all? Well, she'd gotten her wish, and she hated it.

Turning her head, she spotted the thermometer. She refused to touch it. But beside it was the phone. Abby hesitated, then reached for it. She'd just paid most of the bills, hadn't she? What better time for a little extravagance?

Abby dialed the phone, then waited impatiently until the third ring.

"Hi."

Just hearing the syllable made her smile. "Maddy."

"Abby!" The rest of the words tumbled out quickly, as though Maddy wanted to hurry them aside so she could say something else. "Terrific. I was just thinking about you. Must be another triplet flash. What's going on?"

"I've got the flu and I'm feeling sorry for myself."

"Now you don't have to. I'll feel sorry for you. Are you getting plenty of rest and liquids? I bet you've never taken one of those megavitamins I sent."

"Yes, I did." She'd taken a total of five before they'd ended up in the back of a cupboard. "Anyway, I'm feeling a bit better today."

Maddy stepped over a boot and sat on a pile of magazines. "How are the monsters?"

"Wonderful. They hate school, very often hate each other, never pick up anything and make me laugh at least six times a day."

"You're lucky."

"I know. Tell me about New York, Maddy. I want to get away for a while."

"We had some snow last week. It was beautiful." Maddy rarely noticed how quickly it turned to gray sludge. "On my day off I walked through Central Park. It was just like fairyland. Even the muggers were charmed."

There was no use telling Maddy it might not be wise to walk through fairyland alone. "How's the play going?"

"Looks like it could run forever. Did you know Mom and Pop made a swing through here last month? They had a couple of gigs in the Catskills and I talked them into a detour through Manhattan. Pop had this terrific argument with the choreographer."

"I bet he did. How are they?"

"The older we get, the younger they get. I don't know how it works." The pause was so slight that no one but her sister would have detected it. "Abby, did you go ahead with the book?"

"Yes." She concentrated on keeping her tone easy. "As a matter of fact, the writer's already here."

"Everything okay?"

"Everything's fine."

"I wished you'd waited until one of us could have been there with you."

"That's silly. But I do miss you—you and Chantel and Mom and Pop. And Trace."

"I got a telegram."

"From Trace? Where is he?"

"Morocco. He wanted me to know he'd shown my picture to some sheikh and got an offer of twelve camels for me. Pretty exciting."

"Did he take it?"

"I wouldn't be surprised. Abby, I'm thinking about leaving the show."

"Leaving? But you just said it could run forever."

"Yeah, that's why. It's getting too easy. I've been with it for a year now." Poking at the table beside her, Maddy found an earring she'd been certain had been lost forever. Without giving it a thought, she clipped it on. "I think it might be time to move on to something else. If I do, would you mind company for a few days?"

"Oh, Maddy, I'd love it."

"Well, keep the light burning, kid. I've got to go. Saturday matinee. Give my love to the boys."

"I will. Bye."

Abby sat back and pictured her sister grabbing her bag, searching for her keys, then dashing out of her apartment, already ten minutes late for makeup. That was Maddy's style. She had a critically acclaimed

Broadway musical under her belt and was thinking of leaving it to see what was around the corner. That, too, was Maddy's style.

And hers was to do the laundry. With a little sigh, Abby got out of bed.

An hour later, she was satisfied she had some portion of her life under control. Dressed in baggy sweats, she carried the first load of clean, folded laundry toward the stairs. The front door burst open and two boys and a dog bounded in.

"Sigmund!" She made a quick evasive maneuver before the dog could knock her and the fresh linen to the floor.

"Mom, Mom! I got a new truck." Thrilled with himself, Chris brandished a shiny new pickup as he shouted over a mouthful of gum.

"Hey, very fancy." She set her basket down to examine it from hood to taillights as she knew was expected of her.

"I got a plane." Ben was bouncing up and down to get her attention. "A jet."

"Let's see." Abby took it and duly gave it the once-over. "Looks pretty fast. Where's—"

Dylan walked through the door, a bag of groceries under each arm. "More bags in the car, fellas."

"Okay!" They tore out again, the dog at their heels.

"A rock, huh?" Abby smiled at him as he walked past her.

"Aren't you supposed to be in bed?"

"I was. Now I'm not." She followed him into the kitchen. "Dylan, it was very nice of you to buy things for the boys, but you shouldn't let them pressure you."

"Easy for you to say," he muttered. He wasn't quite ready to admit the pleasure it had given him to buy a couple of plastic toys. "I did pretty well, all in all. I think Ben wanted an atomic bomb."

"It was on his Christmas list." She poked in the first bag and pulled out a box of little vanilla cakes with cream filling. "Twinkies?"

"I happen to like Twinkies."

"Mmm. And chocolate ice-cream bars."

"And chocolate ice-cream bars," he agreed, snatching them out of her hand.

"Got any teeth left?"

"Keep it up and I'll show you."

"And guess what else?" Chris staggered into the room under the weight of a grocery bag. Abby saved the bag, set it on the counter, then scooped him up.

"What else?"

"We have a surprise." He hooked his feet behind her waist and laughed.

"You're not supposed to tell." Ben walked in, trying not to show the strain as he carried the last bag.

"I see. Well, it seems to me that anyone who worked so hard must be ready for lunch."

"We ate already." Ben set his bag down and eyed the box of Twinkies. "Hamburgers."

"And French fries," Chris added.

"Sounds like quite a day."

"It was neat. I want to put the stickers on my plane now. Come on, Chris."

At the imperial order, Chris was scrambling down and racing after his brother.

"Don't walk much, do they?" Dylan commented as he stashed the groceries away.

"I guess you found that out in the store." She started to empty bags but she was more interested in

Dylan. "I'm a little surprised," she began. "You don't look ready for a bottle of aspirin and a nap."

"Should I be?"

"I don't know. Actually, you look as if you enjoyed yourself."

"I did." He closed a cupboard door and turned. "Surprised?"

"Yes." Chuck had never enjoyed them. He'd been frustrated, baffled and annoyed by them and he'd never enjoyed them. "Most men—bachelors—don't consider an afternoon shopping with kids a barrel of laughs."

"You generalize."

She moved her shoulders dismissively. "I suppose I've never asked if you have children of your own."

"No. My ex-wife was a model. She wasn't ready to take time out for children."

"I'm sorry."

He turned, giving her a mild, half-amused look. "For what?"

The question left her stumbling. "Divorce—it's usually a difficult experience."

"In this case, marriage was the difficult experience. It only lasted a year and a half."

Such a short time, she thought. Yet he did seem like a man who would admit a mistake quickly and deal with it. "But still, divorce is never pleasant."

"And marriage rarely is."

She opened her mouth to disagree but discovered she had very little ammunition. "But divorce is like admitting you're a failure, isn't it?"

She wasn't talking about him. He took a gallon of milk and put it in the refrigerator, wondering if she knew how transparent she was. "The marriage was a failure. I wasn't."

She shrugged off the feeling. In the way he'd seen his own mother do, she neatly folded the empty bags. "I suppose it's easier when children aren't involved."

"I wouldn't know about that. I'd say when a marriage is bad, it's bad. It doesn't do anyone any good to pretend otherwise."

She glanced up to see him staring at her. Too close to the bone, Abby thought, keeping her hands busy. "Well, we seem to have things under control here."

"Not yet. But nearly." He crossed over and put his hand to her brow. "Fever's down."

"I told you I was feeling better."

"Good. Because I want you to have all your strength back before we start again. I like to play fair whenever possible."

"And when it's not?"

"Then it's not. Do you believe in rules, Abby?"

"Of course."

"There's no 'of course.' People make rules, then they use them or they ignore them. Smart people don't box themselves in with them. I've got to get something else out of the car."

Dissatisfied with him and with the situation, Abby went back and picked up the laundry. She heard the boys shuffling around in Ben's room and went into her own.

How much did Dylan suspect about her marriage? She hadn't intended to make it sound as though it had been made in heaven. Or had she? She'd wanted to give the illusion of normalcy, of contentment. The agreement with herself had been made. There would be no mention of the tears and broken promises, of the lies and disillusionment. She would never have been able to hide the infidelities already gleefully recorded in the scandal sheets, but she'd thought she could play them down. And never, never had it occurred to her that he might discover that divorce papers had been filed weeks before Chuck's last race.

He probably didn't know, she told herself as she walked to the window and looked out over her land. He would have no reason to question her lawyer. And if he did, wasn't that privileged information? Four years earlier she'd agonized over how to tell her children she was divorcing their father. Instead, she'd had to tell them their father was dead.

Chris hadn't understood. He'd barely known who his father was and hadn't comprehended death at all. But Ben had. They'd wept together, and that first night they'd lain together in the bed where she'd spent so many other nights alone.

Now she was trying to give them what she felt they needed to understand their father and themselves. And she had to protect them. The problem was, she was no longer so sure she could do both.

"Mom." Ben pushed open her door without knocking. "You've got to come down. The surprise is ready."

She looked at him as he stood in the doorway, eager, flushed with excitement and miserably untidy. "Ben." She walked over and caught him up in a fierce hug. "I love you."

Pleased, embarrassed, he laughed a little. And since there was no one to see, he hugged her back as hard as he could. "I love you, Mom."

Then, because she knew him, she nuzzled into his neck until he squealed. "What's the surprise?" she demanded.

"I'm not telling."

"I can make you talk. I can make you beg to tell me everything you know."

"Mom!" Chris yelled impatiently from the bottom of the stairs. "Come down, we can't start till you're here, Dylan says."

Dylan says, she thought with a sigh. Taking advantage of her momentary distraction, Ben squirmed away and danced to the stairs. "Hurry," he ordered, then bolted downstairs.

Amused, Abby started after him. "Okay, where is everybody?" She found them in the living room, huddled over a VCR. "What's this?"

"Dylan rented it." Chris, nearly delirious with pleasure, climbed onto the couch and bounced. "You play tapes of movies on it."

"I know." She glanced at Dylan as he handily attached the necessary plugs.

"He said since we couldn't go to the movies we could have them at home. We got *Warriors in Space.*"

She caught Chris on an upswing. *"Warriors in Space?"*

"I was outvoted," Dylan told her. "They had some very interesting movies in the back room."

"I bet they did."

"I did pick up this as well." He tossed her a second tape.

"Lawless," she murmured. "Chantel's big break. She was really wonderful in this movie."

"I've always been partial to it."

"I still remember sitting in the theater and watching her come on the screen. It was an incredible feeling." Just holding the tape brought her sister closer and reminded her that she was never really alone. "It's funny, I just talked to Maddy a couple of hours ago, and now—"

"Can we watch Chantel, too?" Ben was nearly beside himself with the idea of such extravagance. "I like to see when she shoots the guy in the hat."

She hesitated, struggling with a feeling of obligation she didn't know what to do with. Both boys looked at her with eager impatience. Dylan simply lifted a brow and waited. She gave in, as much for herself, she realized, as for anyone else.

"Seems to me we should have popcorn."

He grinned, understanding very well the process that had gone on inside her head. "You up to making it?"

"Oh, I think I can manage."

Twenty minutes later they were spread out on the sofa, watching the first in a series of flashy laser battles. Ben, as usual, was rooting ferociously for the bad guys. Chris's little fingers tensed on Abby's arm, and she leaned down and whispered something that made him laugh.

It was so normal. That was what kept running through her head as the movie rolled noisily on. Watching movies and eating homemade popcorn on a chilly Saturday afternoon—it seemed so easy, almost nonsensically easy, but she'd really never wanted much else. Relaxed, Abby draped her arm on the back of the sofa. Her hand brushed Dylan's. She started to draw away, then glanced over at him.

He watched her over the heads of her sons. The questions that always seemed to be in his eyes were still there, but she was growing accustomed to them. And to him. He had done this for her, for her children. Maybe, just maybe, he'd done it for himself, as well. Maybe that was all that really mattered. With a smile, she linked her fingers with his.

He wasn't used to such simplicity from a woman. She'd just smiled and taken his hand. There had been no flirtation in the gesture, no subtle promises. If he'd been willing to take the gesture at face value, he'd have said it was a simple thank-you.

He thought this must be what it was like to have a family. Not-so-quiet weekends with sticky faces and mundane chores and a living room littered with toys. Warm smiles from a woman who seemed happy to have you there. Dozens of questions that leaped out of young minds and demanded answers. And contentment, the kind that didn't require hot lights and fast music.

He'd always wanted a family. Once he'd told himself he wanted Shannon more—Shannon with the slim, amazing body and the dark, sultry looks. She'd touched off things inside him—exploded was more accurate, Dylan admitted. He found it much easier to remember now than it once had been. They'd met, made love and married, all in a whirling sexual haze. It had seemed right. They'd both lived on the edge and enjoyed it. Somehow it had been incredibly wrong. She'd wanted more, more money, more excitement, more glamour. He'd wanted . . . He was damned if he knew what he'd wanted.

But if he could believe the woman sitting two children away from him was real, it might be her.

Chapter Seven

A backlog of work had helped Abby avoid Dylan throughout the morning. His typewriter had been clicking when she'd woken the boys for school. It had clattered steadily, almost routinely, rather than in the quick on-again, off-again spurts of creation she'd expected. Perhaps it was routine for him, digging into and recording the lives of other people.

The sound had reminded her forcibly that the weekend had only been a reprieve. It was Monday, she was recovered, and the questions were about to begin again. She wished she could recapture the confidence of a week ago and believe she could answer only the ones she chose to, and answer them in her own way.

Still, her own routine soothed her—the breakfast clatter, the scent of coffee, the typically frantic search for a lost glove before she sent her sons racing off to catch the bus. She watched them go down the lane as she did every morning. It struck her, unexpectedly and sharply, as it did now and then, that they were hers. *Hers.* Those two apprentice men in wool caps heading off to face the day at a fast trot had come from her. It was fascinating, wonderful and just a little frightening.

When they disappeared, she continued to watch a little longer. Whatever happened, whatever strange twist life tossed at her, no one could take away the wonder of her children. The day no longer seemed so hard to face.

As she headed toward the barn a few minutes later, she heard the sound of a car. Changing direction, she walked around the side and saw Mr. Petrie hopping out of the cab of his truck. She could have kissed his grizzled face.

"Ma'am." He grinned at her, then spit out a plug of tobacco.

"Mr. Petrie, I'm so glad to see you." She shifted the bucket of eggs as she studied him. "Are you sure you're well enough to work?"

"Right as rain."

He did look fit. His small, stubby body appeared well fed. Beneath several days' growth of beard, his color was good, ruddy, windburned and reliable. He was hardly taller than she and built somewhat like a thumb—sturdy and unexpectedly agile. The boots he wore were black and worn and tied up over his ankles. "If your wife let you out of the house, I guess you're ready to pitch some hay."

"Old nag," he said affectionately. "She kept a mustard plaster on me for a week." His small, slightly myopic eyes narrowed. "You look a might peaked."

"No, I'm fine. I was just about to get started in the barn."

"How are the ladies?"

"Wonderful." They began to walk together over the slowly drying ground. "The vet was here on Friday and gave them both a checkup. It looks like Eve and Gladys are going to be mothers before the week's out."

Petrie spit again as they crossed to the barn. "Jorgensen came by?"

"Yes, he's very interested."

"Don't let that old horse thief buffalo you. Top dollar." Petrie swung the door open with a hand that was missing the first knuckle of the ring finger.

"No one's going to buffalo me," she assured him.

He'd known her five years and worked for her for nearly two, and he believed her. She might look like something out of one of the magazines his wife kept on the coffee table, but she was tough. A woman alone had to be. "Tell you what now, you take the horses out and groom them. I'll clean out the stalls."

"But—"

"No, now you've been swinging a pitchfork on your own all last week. Looks like you need some sun to me. 'Sides, I gotta work off some of this food my wife pushed on me when I was too weak to stop her. There now, sweetheart." He stroked Eve's head when she leaned it over the stall. His ugly, callused hands were as gentle as a lute player's. "Old Petrie's back." He pulled out a carrot and let her take it from his hand.

Abby appreciated his easy touch with the horses, just as she had always relied on his judgment. "She's missed you."

"Sure she has." He moved down to the next stall and gave the second mare equal attention. "I tell you something, Miz Rockwell, if I had the means I'd have myself a mare like this."

She knew the position he was in, knew the limitations of living off social security and little else. The regret that she couldn't pay him more came quickly, as it always did. "I wouldn't have either of them if you hadn't helped me."

"Oh, you'd've got by all right—but maybe you'd've paid too much." With a cackle, he went down to the next horse. "You were a novice back then, Miz Rockwell, but I think you've lost your green."

From him, it was an incredible compliment. With more pleasure than she'd been able to drum up in days, Abby began to lead the horses out. She groomed them in the sunshine.

Dylan watched her from his window. She was singing. He couldn't hear her, but he could tell by the way she moved. He watched as she meticulously cleaned out hooves, brushed manes and curried. There was a lightness about her that he hadn't seen before. But then, she thought she was alone.

Her gloves were on a post, and she ran her bare hands over the flank of one of the geldings. Tea-serving hands, he thought. Yet somehow they looked just as right brushing hard over the gelding's coat. How would they look brushing over his skin? How would it feel to have those hands running with abandon over his body, arousing, exciting, exploring? Would she have that dreamy look in her eyes? He thought she had it now, but he was too far away to be certain.

And if he was smart, he'd stay away.

Her face wouldn't be pale now. The early-morning air would bring the color up as the strong sunlight and exercise warmed her muscles. Her face wouldn't be pale when he made love with her. Excitement would flush it. Passion would make her agile. He could imagine what it would be like to have her skin slide over his. He could almost taste the flavor of her flesh in those dark, secret places made only more mysterious by the layers of thick winter clothing. He wanted to peel them off her while she stood watching him, wanting him, waiting for him. Just thinking of it made his pulse thud.

He'd wanted other women. Sometimes his wants had been eased, sometimes they hadn't. Passion came and passion went. It erupted and it vanished. He understood that well. Just because he churned for her now, just because he stood at the window and watched her with needs bouncing crazily inside him that didn't mean he'd want her tomorrow. Desire couldn't rule your life—not desire for money, not for power and certainly not for a woman.

But he continued to watch her while his typewriter hummed impatiently behind him.

He watched as she led the horses, two and three at a time, into the barn. He waited until she came out again not even calculating the time that passed. Then, abruptly and obviously on impulse, she swung herself onto the big gelding she'd called Judd. With a halter and nothing else, she sent the horse racing out of the paddock and up the rough, narrow track that led in to the hills.

He wanted to throw the window open and yell at her not to be an idiot. He wanted to watch her ride. He could see her knees pressed tight to the gelding's side and her hand holding the halter rope. But more, as the sun fell like glory over her face, he saw the look of absolute delight.

She let the gelding run up and down the track—ten minutes, fifteen, Dylan was too mesmerized to notice. Her hair rose and fell in the wind they created, but she never bothered to push it from her face. And when she swung to the ground he knew she was laughing. She nuzzled the horse, stroking again. Stroking, soothing, murmuring. Dylan wondered what soft, pretty words she spoke.

A man was losing his grip when he became jealous of a horse. He knew it but continued to stand by the window, straining for control, or perhaps for the inevitable. She disappeared inside the barn again, and he told himself to turn away, to get back to his work, but he waited.

She returned with the stallion, holding the rope close under his chin as he danced impatiently, bad-temperedly. Abby tied him securely to the rail and began to groom him.

The animal was beautiful, his head thrown high and an arrogant look in his eyes that Dylan could see even from the window. And he was skittish. When Abby took his hind leg to clean his hoof, he jerked it twice, nearly pulling out of her grip before he settled down and let her do her business. When she set it down again, Dylan caught his breath as the horse took a hard, nasty kick at her. Abby avoided it and calmly picked up the next leg. He could almost hear her gently scolding as she might have if one of the boys had had a fit of temper.

Damn it, who are you? He pressed a hand to the glass as if demanding she look up, hear him and an-

swer. Who the hell are you? If she was genuine, why
the lies? If she had the kind of morals, the kind of
values she seemed to have, how could she lie?

Yet she was lying, Dylan reminded himself. And she
would continue to lie until he tripped her up. Today,
he promised himself as he watched her brush out the
smooth, dark skin of the stallion. Today, Abby.

Turning, he went back to his typewriter and told
himself to forget her.

It was after eleven when he heard her come back
into the house. He had Rockwell's early professional
years, his earlier family background, drafted out.
He'd written of Rockwell's meeting with Abby from
her perspective, using quotes from her and bits of her
family history. People would be interested in the sister of one of Hollywood's rising stars, and in the sister of a successful Broadway actress. He hadn't
overlooked the triplet angle or the theater background. Three sisters, three actresses. But he was
about to rewrite Abby's script.

She heard him come down but continued to wash
the eggs. "Good morning." She didn't look back at
him, and continued to keep her hands busy. "Coffee's on."

"Thanks."

When he walked to the stove, she glanced over. He
hadn't shaved. It always made her stomach quiver—
perhaps at the thought of having that rough, slightly
uncivilized face scrape against hers.

"Mr. Petrie's back. I think he could have used another day or two, but he missed the horses."

"You finished out there?"

"For now. I'm going to be checking on the mares off and on."

"Fine." He took his coffee to the bar, lit a cigarette, then turned on his tape recorder. "When did you and Rockwell decide to divorce?"

An egg hit the floor with a splat. Abby stared down at it in dull surprise. Without a word, she began to clean it up.

"Do you want me to repeat the question?"

"No." Her voice was muffled, then came stronger. "No, but I would be interested to know where you got the idea."

"Lori Brewer."

"I see." Abby cleaned up the last of the mess, then turned to wash her hands.

"She was sleeping with your husband."

"I'm aware of that." Abby dried her hands meticulously. They were steady. She hung on to that.

"She wasn't the first."

"I'm also aware of that." She went to the stove and poured coffee.

"You got ice for blood, lady?" When she turned to look at him calmly, it goaded him all the more. "Your husband slept with any woman who could crawl between the sheets. He made a career out of cheating on you. Lori Brewer was only the last in a long line."

Did he think she was hurting her? she wondered. Did he think she should feel a stab of pain, a wave of betrayal? She'd felt it all before, but that was long since over. She felt nothing now but a sort of vague curiosity about the anger she saw in Dylan's eyes.

"If we both know that, why talk about it?"

"Was he going to dump you for her?"

She took a sip of coffee. It steadied the nerves. She would give him the truth as long as it was possible to give him the truth. "Chuck never asked me for a divorce." She drank again, and the liquid slipped, hot and potent, into her system. "Though he may very well have told Lori Brewer that he did."

That was the truth. His gut told him that this time she spoke with pure honesty. It only made it more of a morass. "She's not a stupid woman. She had it in her head that she and Rockwell would be married before the year was out."

"I can't really comment on what she thought."

"What can you comment on?" His anger surged, and because he trusted it, he moved with it. Perhaps with anger he could finally break through her shield. "Tell me this—how did it feel knowing your husband wasn't faithful to you?"

She'd known the question would come up. She'd prepared herself for it. But now, somehow, the answer didn't come as easily. "Chuck and I... understood each other." How flat that sounded, how foolishly sophisticated. "I...well I knew he was under a great deal of pressure, and being on the road like that month after month..."

"... is a license to relieve the pressure anyway you chose?"

She wasn't as calm as she wanted to be, but she was still in control. "I'm not talking about a license, or even an excuse, Dylan. But it is a reason."

"You consider being separated from you, being on the road and pressured by a need to win, is a reason for the women, the booze, the drugs?"

"Drugs?" Her face went a dead white. If the shock in her eyes wasn't real, Dylan decided, she should be the sister in Hollywood. "I don't know what you're talking about."

"I'm talking about cocaine. Freebasing." His voice was clipped and hard, a reporter's voice. He tried not to hate himself for it.

"No." There was a sudden sheen of desperation in her voice. He watched her knuckles blanch as she gripped the counter. "No, I don't believe that."

"Abby, I have it from four different sources." His tone had softened. She was hurting inside. She might have lied to him before, but the pain was real. "You didn't know."

"You can't write that. You can't. The children." She put her hands over her eyes. "Oh, God, what I have done?"

He had her arm. She hadn't heard him get up. "Sit down." When she started to shake her head, he pulled her over to a stool. "Sit down, Abby."

"You can't write that," she repeated, and her voice was a roller coaster of ups and downs. "You can't be sure it's true. If you try to put that in the book, I'll withdraw my authorization. I'll sue."

"What you'd better do right now is calm down."

"Calm down?" She clutched her hands together until her fingers ached. Only determination kept her facing him, and her eyes were drenched with despair. "You've just told me that Chuck was—" She swallowed and got a grip on herself. "Turn that off," she said quietly, then waited until the recorder stopped. "We're off the record now, do you understand me?"

Her eyes were dry again and her voice steady. He had a sudden flash of her carrying his suitcase up the stairs. Stronger than she looked. "All right, Abby. Off the record."

"If Chuck—if he used drugs, I never knew."

"Do you think you would have?"

She closed her eyes. A sense of failure reached up and grabbed her by the throat. "No."

"I'm sorry." He touched her hand, swearing at himself when she drew back. "I am sorry. His mother knew. I have it that she tried to get him into rehab."

A sudden hysterical thought drummed through her. "The last race. The crash."

"He was clean." He thought he heard the relief sweep through her, though she didn't make a sound. "He just took the turn too fast."

She nodded and straightened her shoulders. If Abby had learned anything over the past eight years, it was to take one step at a time, deal with it, then go on. "Dylan I'm not asking for favors, but I'd like you to remember there are two innocent people involved. The children deserve some legacy from their father. If you try to print anything about this I'll find a way to stop you, even if I have to go to Janice."

"How much will you try to cover up, Abby?"

She gave him a clear, direct look. "You'd do better to ask me how much I'd do to protect my children."

He felt a twinge and fought to grind it down. "Once a ball's rolling, it rolls. You'd have been smarter to stop the book in the beginning."

"Isn't the sex enough for you?" she lashed out, desperate to find solid ground again. How could she take the first step when each time she did she was knee-deep in quicksand? "Do you have to put this ugly business in, too? Can't you leave the boys something?"

"Do you want me to write a fairy tale?" He grabbed her wrists before she could push away from the counter. He should have resented her for making him feel responsible, yet he couldn't. She looked lost and helpless. "Abby, it's too late to stop the book now. The publishers would sue you, not the other way around. Talk to me, tell me the truth. Trust me to tell it."

"Trust you?" She stared at him, wishing she could see inside him, find some soft, giving spot. "I trusted myself and I've made a mess of it." Faced with the inevitable, she stopped resisting his hold on her hands. "I've got no choice, do I?"

"No."

She waited a moment until she was certain she was strong enough. "Turn your recorder back on." She withdrew from him, not by inches but by miles. As soon as the machine was running, Abby began speaking again. But she never looked at him. "Chuck never used drugs in my presence. We were married for four years, and I never saw him with drugs of any kind. As far as I'm concerned, he never used them at all. Chuck was an athlete, and he was very disciplined about his body."

"For most of your marriage, you only lived together for short periods."

"That's true. We each had certain responsibilities that kept things that way."

"It would seem to me that you had certain responsibilities that should have kept you together."

She would ignore that. She wouldn't wallow in guilt or in self-pity ever again. If the time had come to compromise herself, so be it. She'd take the lesser demon. "To go back to your earlier question, Chuck was often lonely. He was attractive and women were a part of the circuit."

"You accepted that?"

"I accepted that Chuck was not capable of being faithful. I realized that a marriage is the responsibility of two people. In certain areas, I wasn't able to give him what he needed."

"What are you talking about?"

Pride was brushed aside. Abby had found it was rarely useful in any case. "I was only eighteen when we were married. Despite the fact that we were entertainers and on the road continually, I was very sheltered. I was a virgin when I married Chuck, and he often said I remained one. I failed him in bed and so he looked elsewhere. Maybe that was wrong, but it was also natural."

"Stop humiliating yourself this way."

She heard the barely restrained fury and turned to look at him. "You wanted answers, I'm giving them to you. Chuck slept with other women because his wife didn't satisfy him."

"The hell with this." He spun her on the stool until she faced him. "You're a fool if you believe that."

"Dylan, I know what went on in my own bedroom. You don't."

"I know what goes on inside you."

"You asked me if I had ice for blood. I'm answering you."

"No, you're not." He pulled her off the stool to stand beside him. "Now you will."

He had her close. His mouth came down on hers, hot, furious, before she could even think about protesting. Excitement bubbled up inside her to war with a strong desire for self-preservation. She tried to resist. There was something wild and frightening about the way he could take her over, make her hurt with need. The hands in her hair weren't gentle, but held her to him in a kind of angry possession. Slowly, inevitably, she let herself go.

He'd burned for her through the night, through the morning, but he hadn't expected it to be like this. There were waves of fire and smoke blinding him. Her body was tight as a bowstring against his, holding back against the passion he could feel building. Her fingers didn't push at his shoulders, but dug into them. He could almost hear her heart thudding in her throat—fear, excitement, desire, he didn't care. As long as it was for him.

Then, with incredible ease, she relaxed. Her lips softened, her body yielded, and she was his.

Her heartbeat didn't slow. Somehow it increased even as her arms wound slowly around him. She sighed. He felt the soft trickle of air whisper against his mouth. He combed his hands through her hair, gently, soothingly, because she seemed to need it. The flame had gone out of him, but the heat was still there, simmering, sizzling. He could have burned alive with tenderness.

"Come upstairs, Abby." He murmured it against her ear, then against her mouth. "Come upstairs with me."

She wanted to. The fact that she did jolted her. She'd already accepted that she was attracted to him, but it was a different matter to slip into bed with a man. "Dylan, I—"

"I want you." His mouth loitered along her chin, where he bit gently. "You know that."

"I think I do. Please . . ." Her voice was trembling. Her muscles felt like putty. She couldn't allow herself to tumble over the edge a second time without keeping her eyes open. "Please, Dylan, I just can't. I'm not ready."

"You want me." He skimmed his hands up, molding her hips, tracing her ribs, teasing her breasts. "I can feel it every time you take a breath."

"Yes." She was through denying. "But I need more than that." She took his hand and brought it to her cheek. "I need some time."

Dylan brought his hand up under her chin and held it there. Her cheeks were flushed, as he'd once imagined they would be. Her eyes were dark and unsure. If it hadn't been for them, watching him, almost trusting him, he'd have ignored her protests and taken her.

"How badly did he mess up your head, I wonder."

"No." She shook her head. "This has nothing to do with what happened between Chuck and me."

"You don't believe that and neither do I. He's your yardstick. Sooner or later you're going to find out you can't measure me by it."

"I don't think of Chuck when I'm kissing you. I don't think at all."

His fingers tightened on her skin. "Abby, if you want time, you'd better watch yourself."

She felt the energy that had poured into her so quickly drain out again. "I don't know how to play the games, Dylan. That's the reason I messed up so badly once before."

"I'm not interested in games. And I'm not interested in hearing you shoulder blame. Let's make a deal."

She moistened her lips and wished she could be sure of herself again. "What sort?"

"You tell me the truth. The truth," he repeated, laying his hands on her shoulders. "I'll write it objectively. Then we'll let the blame fall wherever it belongs.''

He made it sound so simple, but then he had nothing to lose. ''I don't know if I can do that, Dylan. I have the children to think of. Sometimes the truth hurts.''

''Sometimes it cleanses,'' he countered. ''Abby, I'll find out everything I need to know one way or the other.'' It was a threat. He understood that, and he saw by the look that came and went in her eyes that she did, as well. ''You should think about that. Don't you think it would be better if it came from you? I don't want to hurt those kids.''

Trapped, she studied him, carefully, critically. ''No, I don't think you do, but you and I might not agree on what's best for them.''

He rubbed a hand over his face, then paced around the kitchen. It wasn't like him to make compromises. He didn't care for it. Yet he was compelled to find one. The book? He was beginning to think the book didn't mean much of anything. He wanted the truth from her, about her. And he wanted it for himself. He thought perhaps he wanted it for her.

''Okay, you give me the real story, the true story, without all the little evasions. I'll write it, and then before I submit anything for publication I'll give it to you to read. If there's a problem, we'll work it out. Both of us have to be satisfied with the manuscript before it flies.''

She hesitated. ''Do you mean that?''

He turned back. She wasn't ready to trust him. The woman had been lied to before, he thought, and lied to in a big way. ''You've got it on record.'' He gestured to the recorder which was still running.

She took the step, though her legs were a little wobbly. "All right."

When he came forward and offered his hand, Abby held her breath and accepted it. Another bargain, she thought, hoping she could keep it better than the one she'd made with herself.

"He hurt you."

Dylan said it quietly, so quietly she answered without hesitation. "Yes."

It made him angry. No, it made him furious. He couldn't explain it, but he knew that fury wouldn't help him get to the truth. And for years, maybe too many years, that had been his driving ambition. "Why don't you sit down again?"

She nodded, then sat with her hands neatly folded and her face placid.

"Abby, you and Rockwell were having serious marital problems."

"That's right." It seemed so easy to say it now. Just as he'd said, cleansing.

"Was it the other women?"

"That was part of it. Chuck needed more than I could give him in so many areas. I guess I needed more than he could give me. He wasn't a bad man." The words were quick and earnest. "I want you to understand that. Maybe he wasn't a good husband, but he wasn't a bad man."

Dylan planned to use his own judgment there. "Why did you stop traveling with him?"

"I was pregnant with Ben." She let out a little breath. "I can't honestly say whether that was a convenient excuse or a legitimate reason, but I was pretty far along, and traveling had become difficult. We were living with his mother in Chicago. At first . . . at first he managed to fly back fairly often. I think he was happy, maybe a little awed at the idea of being a father. In any case, he was attentive when he was home, and he encouraged me to stay in Chicago and take care of myself. He tried, really tried to ease the uncomfortable relationship I had with his mother. There were long separations."

She looked back, remembering those weeks, months in the luxurious house in Chicago, long idle mornings, quiet afternoons. It seemed like a dream, one in soft focus but with surprisingly sharp edges.

"I was content and rather pleased with myself. I decorated the nursery and took up knitting... badly." She laughed at herself as she remembered her fumbling attempts. "I figured I had just about everything under control. Then one day I found one of those gossip papers on my bed. I've always wondered if Janice left it there." Abby shook that away, it hardly mattered. "There was a picture of Chuck and this really beautiful woman, and a short, nasty article."

She looked out the window and watched the trees bend a little. "I sat there, big and clumsy and nearly eight months pregnant. I was crushed and betrayed and absolutely certain the world was over. Chuck came home at the end of the week and I tossed the paper at him demanding an explanation."

"He gave you one."

"He was angry that I'd believe a story like that. He called it trash and threw it in the fire. He didn't defend himself, so I was abruptly in the position of apologizing. Do you understand?"

He thought he could picture her, fragile and alone. His anger only burned brighter. "Yeah, I understand."

"I was one month away from having a baby, and scared to death. I decided to believe him, but of course I knew, because I'd seen it in his face, that he was lying. I accepted the lie. Do you understand?" Why did she keep asking that? Why was it so important? She pressed her fingers against her eyes a moment and swore not to ask again. "I think by accepting it I only hurt him."

"You believe if you'd had a showdown then it would have stopped."

Her eyes were solemn. "I'll never be sure."

"And there were other women."

"There were others. Remember that Chuck and I weren't living together under normal circumstances and that our physical relationship had deteriorated. He was a man who needed victories, but as soon as he'd achieved them, he needed more. If you could try to understand that even as a child he was under tremendous pressure to succeed, to be the best—to be number one."

Weary of it all, she let out a little sigh. "Because of that, he required constant reassurance that he was the greatest. After a while, I don't think I gave him that. In any case, I'd thought—hoped—that after Ben was born we'd settle down. But I knew, or should have known, when I married Chuck, that he was far from ready to settle. There was an ugly little scandal with one of the groupies. She wrote me letters, threatened to kill herself if Chuck didn't marry her. That's when we bought this place. Chuck was upset because things had gotten out of hand. It was an attempt to make it up to me, to Ben, maybe to himself. But then there was another race."

"You didn't go with him."

"No. For a while I concentrated on making a home. I felt he needed one. The fact was, I needed one." She watched the smoke from Dylan's cigarette curl slowly toward the ceiling. "During that time, after Ben was born and before I became pregnant with Chris, I began to realize that our marriage wasn't working, that Chuck and I were only pretending it had ever worked. He came home. He'd won in Italy. He wanted to sell the farm. We had a terrible fight about it. While we were fighting, Ben toddled in. Chuck just went wild. He yelled at Ben, who was crying."

She dragged a hand through her hair as the misery of that memory came back to her. "Ben was barely a year old. I lost my temper and told Chuck to get out. He got in his car and went tearing up the road. I calmed Ben down and finally got him to sleep.

"It was late and I went to bed. I didn't expect Chuck to came back, I didn't care. But he came back." Her voice had dropped almost to a whisper. As he watched her, Dylan realized she wasn't talking to him any longer. She was exorcizing her own ghosts. "He'd been drinking. He never drank very much because he couldn't handle it well, but this time he'd been drinking heavily. He came upstairs and we argued again. I was trying to get him to go sleep in one of the guest rooms so he wouldn't disturb Ben. He was too furious and too drunk to listen to reason. He said I'd never been any kind of wife, and less of a lover. He said I only cared about Ben and the farm. God, it was true. It hadn't always been but he was right and I wouldn't admit it. He said it was about time I learned what it was a man wanted from his wife. What it was a man expected and was entitled to. So he shoved me back on the bed . . . and he raped me," she said flatly as Dylan stared at her. "Then he cried like a baby. He left before dawn. A few weeks later I found out I was pregnant."

Her hand trembled as she ran it through her hair. "That's honest, Dylan. That's the truth." She focused on him again. "Should I tell Chris that he was conceived the night his father forced himself on me? Is that the truth I owe my son?"

She didn't wait for him to answer, but stood slowly and walked out of the room.

Chapter Eight

He couldn't work. Dylan stared almost resentfully at his typewriter, but he couldn't bring himself to put words on paper. The words were there, jammed tight in his head. The emotion was there, still churning through him. He could remember, point by point, precisely what had happened throughout the afternoon and evening.

When Abby had walked out of the kitchen, he'd just sat there staring at the tape, which had continued to run. Shocked? How could he say he was shocked? He'd taken off his rose-colored glasses years before. He knew how ugly life could be, how violent, how petty. He'd chipped his way into lives before and found the sores, the scars and the secrets. They didn't shock him, and they had stopped affecting him a long time ago.

But he'd sat in the kitchen a long time, where the scent of coffee had still lingered. And he'd hurt. He'd hurt because he could remember how pale her face had been, how calm her voice had sounded when she'd told him. Then he'd left her alone, knowing privacy was what she'd wanted.

He'd driven into town. Distance, he'd told himself, would help. A journalist needed distance, just as he needed intimacy. It was the combination of the two that brought truth and power to a story. And wasn't it always the story that came first?

The air had warmed, though the wind was starting to kick up to welcome March. Snow was just a memory on the still-soggy ground. Spring was beginning to push its way through. And when spring faded the book should be finished. He no longer knew precisely `how.

When he'd come back, the boys had been home from school. They'd been playing in the yard, racing with the dog and each other. Dylan had sat in the car for a few moments, watching them, until Chris had rushed over to invite him to play catch.

Even now, hours later, Dylan could remember just how bright Chris's face had been, how open and innocent his eyes had looked. The little hand had gripped his with absolute trust as he'd begun to ramble on about his day in school. Someone named Sean Parker had thrown up at recess. Big news. Ben had said something childishly obscene about Sean Parker's dilemma, and Chris had giggled until he'd been ready to burst.

They'd raced around the back and had barreled into the kitchen. Standing behind them, Dylan had seen Abby at the stove. When she'd turned, their eyes had held for one long moment. Then she'd fallen into the predinner routine with the easy efficiency he'd come to expect from her.

He'd waited for the tension, but it hadn't come, not then, not during dinner, not later when she'd played a board game with the children and he'd been drafted to join them. Normal was the order of the day, and if it was forced, even he couldn't tell. She'd seen the children off to bed, then had retreated to her room. She'd been there ever since.

In his own room, he found it impossible to get settled. What was he going to do? He had the makings of a tough, honest story in the palm of his hand. Romance, betrayal, sex, violence. And it wasn't fiction, it was real. It was his job to write it and to write it honestly, thoroughly.

He remembered how trustingly that small hand had fit into his.

Swearing, Dylan pushed away from his desk. He couldn't do it. It wasn't possible to put down in black and white what Abby had told him that afternoon. No matter how he wrote, no matter how carefully he phrased it, it would be ugly, hollow, unforgivable. And the child was so beautifully untouched and open.

It shouldn't matter. All the instincts that had driven him through his years of reporting, all the skill that had made his biographies hard-edged and genuine, pushed him to the truth. But he could remember the way a small boy had grinned and lifted his arms for a hug. He remembered Ben sitting alone and sulky on a bed surrounded by tiny men. And he remembered how Abby had linked her fingers with his and made him feel whole.

They'd gotten to him. Dylan dragged a hand through his hair. There was no use pretending otherwise. Inside him was a tug-of-war that they'd created and he was still fighting. He'd forgotten the cardinal rule, the one he'd learned in his first week as a pool reporter: don't get involved. Well, he was involved, and he had no idea how to draw back.

The hell with drawing back.

Without giving himself a chance to think it through, Dylan walked out of his room, crossed the hall and knocked on Abby's door.

"Yes, come in."

She was sitting at a small writing desk, finishing a letter. She glanced up, then set it aside as if she'd been expecting him.

"We need to talk."

"All right. Close the door."

He closed it, but he didn't speak at once. There was no barrier between them now, no recorder that made everything profession and ethical. What was said now would be between the two of them. Or more accurately, he realized, *for* the two of them. He wasn't certain how it had come down to this. Like a man walking down a dimly lit road, he walked over and sat on the bed.

The room was quiet, soft, feminine—as she was. If there had been violence here, it had long since been eradicated. She'd locked it away, he realized, because she wouldn't let her life or the lives of her children be destroyed by it. By putting the knowledge in his hands, she'd made him responsible. Something within her had reached in and discovered the compassion that made him accept the responsibility.

"Abby, you know I can't write what you told me this afternoon."

A wave of relief rolled over her. She'd hoped, she'd dared to trust, but she hadn't been sure. "Thank you."

"Don't be grateful." In some ways he felt he could deal with her resentment more successfully. "I'm going to write plenty that you won't like."

"I'm beginning to think it doesn't matter as much as I once believed it did." She looked beyond him to the tiny pattern of flowers that was repeated over and over again in the wallpaper. Life was like that, patterns that repeated. She'd tried to change them without looking at the overall picture. "You know, I thought the children needed an image to look up to, to be able to say, 'This is my father.' The more I think about it, really think about it, it's more important that they be proud of themselves."

"Why did you tell me?"

She looked at him—at the man who had finally changed the pattern. How could she explain? She'd found kindness in him where none had been expected. He'd worked beside her though he hadn't been required to. He'd been warm and generous with her children. He had cared for her when she'd been ill. She'd found the kindness beneath the tough exterior, and she had fallen in love with it. With a half sigh, Abby picked up her pen, unconsciously shifting it from hand to hand.

"I can't tell you all the reasons. Once I started talking, it just came, all of it. Maybe I needed to say it out loud now, after all these years. I've never been able to before."

There was a paperweight by her hand, pale pink flowers encased in glass. Fragile to look at, difficult to shatter. "You didn't tell your family?" Dylan asked.

"No. Maybe I should have. You go through all these stages—shame, self-reproach, fury. I needed to work them through."

"Why in God's name did you stay with him?" He thought of the money again, of the woman in mink and diamonds. He no longer wanted to believe that was the reason.

She looked down at her hands. The wedding ring had been gone for a long time, and the bitterness had faded even before that. "After—after it happened, Chuck was devastated. He was miserably sorry. I thought we might salvage something out of that awful night. For a while we nearly did. Then Chris was born. Chuck couldn't look at him without remembering. He'd look at the baby and he'd resent him because of the way he'd come into the world, because Chris reminded him of his own weakness, maybe his own mortality."

"And you? How did you feel when you looked at Chris?"

The smile came slowly. "He was so beautiful. He's still beautiful."

"You're a remarkable woman, Abby."

She looked at him, surprised. "No, I don't think so. I'm a good mother, but there's nothing remarkable about that. I wasn't a good wife. Chuck needed someone who'd pick up and go on a moment's notice. He needed someone who'd race with him. I was too slow."

"What did you need?"

Now she looked at him, her expression blank. No one but her family had ever asked her that. And the pat answers wouldn't come. "I'm not sure what I needed, but I'm happy now with what I have."

"It's enough? The children, this place?" He rose and crossed to her. "I thought you were going to tell me the truth."

"Dylan." He wasn't supposed to be so close. She couldn't think when he stood so close. "I don't know what you expect me to say."

"Don't you?" Taking her hand, he drew her to her feet. He felt her fingers tremble and tightened his grip. "I don't want you to be afraid of me."

"I'm not."

"I don't want you to be afraid of what's between us."

"I can't help it. Dylan, don't do this." She put her free hand on his arm. "I really couldn't stand making a mess of it. I think—I hope we're at the point of being friends."

"We're past that point." He brought her hand to his lips and watched the surprise come into her eyes. "Has anyone ever made love with you?"

Panic sprinted up her spine. "I—I have two children."

"That's not an answer." Curious, he turned her hand over and pressed his lips to the palm. Her fingers curled and tensed. "Was there anyone besides Chuck?"

"No, I—"

His look sharpened, and his fingers tightened. "No one?"

The shame came quickly, the price of failure. "No. I'm really not a physical person."

In how many ways had Rockwell managed to humiliate her? Dylan wondered. Rage came swiftly, and he banked it. Noninvolvement? He was far beyond that now. He wanted to prove to her it could be different. Maybe, for the first time, he wanted to believe it himself.

"Why don't you let me find out for myself?"

"Dylan—" The words clogged in her throat as he brushed his lips over her temple.

"Don't you want me, Abby?" Seduction. He'd never consciously seduced a woman before. Women had always come to him, knowing, experienced, expectant. None of them had ever trembled. He had a moment of panic himself. Did he have it in him to be careful enough, gentle enough, thorough enough?

"Yes." She tilted her head to look at him. "But I don't know what I can give you."

"Let me worry about it." With more confidence than he felt, he took her face in his hands. "For now, just take."

He kissed her slowly, dreamily. Her hands lifted to his wrists and held on. It was that, that hesitant, vulnerable movement, that touched him in a way he'd never expected to be touched. The lamplight fell across her face as he tilted his head and nibbled lightly at her lips. She felt the pulse in his wrists speed up and tightened her hold. He wanted her, really wanted her. And God, she was terrified she'd disappoint both of them. He urged her closer. She stiffened.

"Easy," he murmured, finding patience he hadn't been aware of possessing. "Relax, Abby." He stroked soothingly until he felt her muscles give. Her hands went around his waist, hesitant, tentative. He felt the sweetness of the gesture shoot through him. He'd never looked for sweetness before, never expected it. Now, finding it, he didn't want to lose it.

Slowly, easily, carefully, he made love to her with his mouth alone. Tasting, seducing, then relaxing, he drew her ever so gradually to him. He felt her hands clutch, then loosen at his back. When her mouth warmed and softened against his, he took her deeper. He felt her breath shudder, heard the low, quiet moan that came from wonder. For the first time in years, he felt the wonder himself.

He slipped his hands under her sweater. When she jumped, he stroked and whispered promises he hoped he could keep. Her skin was smooth, her back long and slender. Need whipped through him quickly, painfully. He fought back.

Inch by inch, he brought the sweater up until he could slip it off. It dropped at their feet.

The panic returned. She was vulnerable now. Her breath was coming quickly, somehow clouding her brain. Didn't she have to think? How could she protect herself, how could she give him what he expected if she couldn't think? But his hands felt so wonderful gliding over her skin. Strong, patient, touching her when she needed so badly to be touched. Perhaps when they became demanding she would freeze up, but for now she could only feel the heat building.

Then he led her toward the bed. Fear snapped back into place. "Dylan—"

"Lie down with me, Abby. Just lie down with me."

She held on to him as they lowered to the bed. She saw everything with perfect clarity, the pattern of roses repeated over and over on the walls, the dark spiral of the bedpost, the white square of ceiling. And his face. Nerves tangled and twisted until she was afraid she couldn't move. She struggled with them, trying to remind herself she wasn't a young, inexperienced girl, but a woman.

"The light."

"I want to see you." He kissed her again, eyes open and on hers. "I want you to see me. I'm going to make love to you, Abby. That's nothing that has to be done in the dark."

"Don't—don't expect too much."

He cupped the back of her neck and lifted her face toward his. "Don't expect too little." Then he silenced her.

The kiss sent her spinning. It was hard and pungent. Her body, already tingling with panicked excitement, went hot with passion. The moan ripped out of her and into him. She felt, as she'd once imagined, the scrape of his face against her cheek. Dozens of pulses began to beat in a rhythm that drummed over and over in her head.

She was driving him crazy. Couldn't she feel it? The way her body tensed and shuddered and relaxed, the way her hands reached and hesitated and caressed. He hadn't known he'd wanted her this badly. Not this badly. Now that she was here, warm and solid beneath him, he knew he had to think of her first and his own needs second.

So he showed her. Restlessly, ruthlessly, he stroked his hands over her, feeling her arch, hearing her tangled breaths. He inhaled the passion rising to her skin, that musky, heady, womanly scent a man could drown in. The light slanted over her face so that he could see surprise, pleasure and desire mix and mingle. Impatient, he pulled off his shirt so he could feel his skin against hers.

He was smooth. His torso was hard as iron, but the skin over it was soft. She could glide her fingers over it and feel his muscles tense. Strong. She'd always needed strength, but she'd found it only in herself. Patience. Once she'd nearly wept for patience, but then she'd stopped looking. Now she'd found it. Passion. She'd wanted it, craved it, then dismissed it as something she'd have to live without. Here it was, wrapped around her, burgeoning inside her. He moaned her name, and she was dizzy from the sound of it.

His lips were on her breast. The muscles in her stomach contracted as he encircled the tip with his mouth. Unconsciously she pressed a hand to the back of his head and arched under him. With teeth and tongue and lips he brought her an exquisite torture. Mindlessly she let herself go with it.

He opened the snap of her jeans, but she didn't even notice. She felt the slow movement of his hands, the soft scrape of denim down her legs. She wanted to call out to him, but his name evaporated with a moan as his tongue skimmed over her thigh.

She was beautiful. Her body was slim and subtly muscled, the legs long, the hips narrow. He wondered as he looked at her how she'd ever carried children. Somehow he could only imagine her as untouched. Then he began to see just how high he could take her. And how fast.

The first peak rocked her with uncontrollable speed. Helpless, dazed, Abby gave a muffled cry. It seemed as though her body filled, then burned, then emptied. Struggling to right herself, she reached for him, only to have him send her miles higher.

She was gasping for breath, pulsing with sensations she'd never experienced before. Were there names for them? she wondered frantically. Had anyone ever found the right words to describe those feelings? Her skin was so sensitized that even the brush of his fingertip sent her spiraling. He'd wanted to see her like this, floundering in her own pleasure. When he slipped into her, her eyes flew open. He saw the astonished pleasure in them before she reached out to bring him closer.

Her hips moved like lightning, tearing down the control he'd laboriously built. Her fingers dug into his back, the short, rounded nails scraping his skin. She wasn't aware. And soon neither was he.

It had never been like that before. No one had ever made her feel so complete, so important, so alive. Doors had been opened, windows raised, and the air that blew in was wonderful.

She wanted to tell him but was afraid he'd think she was foolish. Instead, she contented herself with placing a hand over his heart. It was beating more steadily than hers, but it was beating very fast.

It had never been like that before. No one had ever made him feel so real, so strong, so open. She'd turned on a light inside his head, and it shone clear and bright. He wanted to tell her but was afraid she'd think he was feeding her a line. Instead, he contented himself with drawing her against him.

"Not very physical, huh?"

"What?"

"You told me you weren't very physical. I guess you didn't want to brag."

She turned her face into his shoulder. Her scent was there, she realized. It was an odd and wonderful sensation to find her own scent clinging to his skin. "I never have been very good at the... at the technical parts."

"Technical parts?" He didn't know whether to laugh or shout at her. "What does that mean?"

"Well, the..." Embarrassed, she let her words trail off. "Sex," she said firmly, reminding herself she was a grown woman.

"We didn't have sex," he said simply, rolling on top of her. "We made love."

"It's just a matter of semantics."

"Like hell it is. No, don't close up on me." He grasped her shoulders hard before she could. "I'm not Chuck. Look at me, really look."

She calmed herself and did what he asked. "I am. I know."

"What do you want, Abby, an evaluation?"

"No." Color flooded cheeks already flushed with passion. "No, of course not. I just—"

"Wonder how it was for me. If you did the right things at the right times." He sat up, pulling her with him, and kept his hands firmly on her shoulders even when she fumbled for the sheet. "Did it ever occur to you that Chuck Rockwell wasn't the devastating macho lover the gossip sheets touted him to be? Did you ever consider that what happened or didn't happen between the two of you in this bed was his fault?"

It hadn't. Of course it hadn't. "All those other women..." she began, then fell silent.

"Let me tell you something. It's easy to wrestle under the sheets with a different woman every night." He felt a little twinge, remembering all those times. "You don't have to think, you don't have to feel. You don't have to worry about making the other person see stars. All you do is satisfy yourself. It's very different when you've got a partner, someone you've made promises to, someone you're supposed to want to make happy. It takes care and time and waiting until it's right."

She stared at him, lips parted, eyes wide. With an oath he lifted a hand and ran it through her hair. "Listen, right now I don't much want to hear about Chuck Rockwell. I don't want you to think about him or anyone else. Just concentrate on me."

"I am." A little uncertain, she touched a hand to his cheek. "You're the best thing that's happened to me in a long time." She saw his expression change, felt his hand tighten in her hair, and went on quickly. "You've made me face a lot of things I thought I should keep under lock and key. I'm grateful."

"I'm getting tired of telling you not to thank me." But his hand gentled in her hair and slipped down to the curve of her shoulder.

"This is absolutely the last time." Lifting her arms, she twined them around him and held tight. She felt safe there, as she'd known she would once before, when the sun had shone down on them. "Don't laugh."

He skimmed his lips over her collarbone. "I don't feel much like laughing."

"I feel as though I've just mastered a very complex and important skill."

He chuckled earning himself a whack on the back. "Like the backstroke?"

"I said not to laugh."

"Sorry." Then he tumbled her over until she lay beneath him. "You don't master anything unless you practice. A lot."

"I guess you're right." This playfulness was something she'd never tasted before. Abby clung to it. Her lips met his, already warm, open and accepting. "Dylan?"

"Hmm?"

"I did see stars."

He smiled. She felt it. When he drew back to look at her, she saw it. "Me, too."

He started to lower his head again, but then he heard the sobbing. "What the—"

"Chris." Abby was out of bed in an instant. She whipped a robe out of her closet, pulled it out and was out of the room before he'd picked up his jeans.

"Oh, baby." Abby hurried into Chris's room, where he was bundled under the covers, sobbing his heart out. "What's the matter?"

"They were green and ugly." He burrowed into the safety of his mother's breasts, smelling her familiar smell. "They looked like snakes and went *Ssss*, and they were chasing me. I fell down in a hole."

"What a nasty dream." She held and rocked and soothed him. "It's all over now, okay? I'm right here."

He sniffled but relaxed. "They were going to cut me up in little pieces."

"Bad dream?" Dylan hesitated in the doorway, not certain whether it was his place to come in.

"Ugly green snakes," Abby told him as she rocked Chris in her lap.

"Wow. Pretty scary, huh, tiger?"

Chris sniffled again, nodded and rubbed his eyes. Whether it was his place or not, Dylan couldn't resist. He came in and hunkered down in front of the boy. "Next time you should dream yourself a mongoose. Snakes don't have a chance against a mongoose."

"Mongoose." Chris tried out the word, giggling over it. "Did you make it up?"

"Nope. We'll find a picture of one tomorrow. They have them in India."

"Trace went to India," Chris remembered. "We got a postcard." Then he yawned and settled back against Abby. "Don't go yet."

"No, I won't. I'll stay until you're asleep again."

"Dylan, too?"

Dylan rubbed his knuckles over the boy's cheek. "Sure."

They sat there, Abby snuggling the boy and singing something that sounded to Dylan like an Irish lullaby. Dylan felt an amazing satisfaction, not like the one he'd found with Abby in the old bed, but one just as strong. It was a firm sense of belonging, as if he had finally reached a place he'd been moving toward all his life. It was foolish, and he told himself it would pass. But it stayed. The hall light slanted into the room and fell on a jumble of trucks next to an old, half-deflated ball.

She settled the boy smoothly, tucking Mary under the sheets with him. Abby kissed his cheek, then straightened, but Dylan stayed for a moment, idly brushing at the curls over Chris's forehead.

"Pretty irresistible, isn't he?" she murmured.

"Yeah." He brought his hand back and stuck it in his pocket. "He's going to be hard to live with when he figures it out."

"He's a lot like Trace—all charm. According to Pop, Trace figured out how to exploit it before he could crawl." In a natural gesture, she took Dylan's hand and drew him out of the room. "I just want to look in on Ben."

She pushed the door open and saw the morass that was her son's room. Clothes, books, toys were one tangled heap that stretched from wall to wall. Abby sighed and promised herself she'd make him see to it over the weekend. At the moment, though, her first-born was sprawled in bed, half in and half out of the covers.

Going in, she rolled him over, pulled a tennis shoe from under the pillow, tossed aside a squadron of small plastic men and covered him up.

"He sleeps like a rock," she commented.

"So I see."

She took a last look around the room. "He's also a slob."

"Yeah, no argument there."

With a quiet laugh, she bent over and kissed her son. "I love you, you little jerk." She made her way expertly over the heaps in the semidarkness. When she came to the doorway again, Dylan ran his hands down her arms.

"I like your kids, Abby."

Touched, she smiled, then kissed his cheek. "You're a nice man, Dylan."

"There aren't a lot of people who'd agree with you."

She understood that. "Maybe they haven't seen you the way I have."

That much was true, but he couldn't tell her why. He didn't know. "Come back to bed."

She nodded and slipped an arm around his waist.

Chapter Nine

So much could happen in twenty-four hours. Abby faced the morning with a kind of dazed wonder. She'd discovered passion. She'd found affection. And maybe, just maybe, she was taking the first step toward finally severing her ties and obligations to the past. She had Dylan to thank for that, but she didn't think he'd tolerate hearing the phrase again. She couldn't express her gratitude without annoying him. She couldn't tell him that she loved him without risking losing what had just begun. So she would say nothing and hope that simply being with him was enough.

Abby sent the boys off to school, zipped through her morning chores and left a note for Dylan on the breakfast bar, then hopped in her car. She had the energy of ten.

She'd planned to spend the morning mopping, waxing and scrubbing Mrs. Cutterman's house—and earning a good portion of the grocery money. She thought it was a lucky thing she was over the flu and could get back to the part-time job that helped keep the ledgers balanced until she could sell the foals. Tomorrow was also her day to do the twice-monthly cleaning at the Smiths. Mentally she went over her schedule and calculated that she had just enough time to fit everything in, including a shopping expedition for new shoes at the end of the week.

Abby told herself to concentrate on that and not to think too deeply about what had happened the night before. What it had meant to Dylan and what it had meant to her were two different things. She had to be wise enough to understand that. But he'd given her something she'd never had from a man before: respect, affection, passion. She was still relishing it. Switching the radio on, she turned onto the main road.

When Dylan came downstairs, he went straight for the coffee. He didn't usually wake up groggy, even after a sleepless night, but working through the night and lying awake in bed seemed to have different effects. He wasn't sure yet why he'd been so restless. Abby had slept beside him as peacefully as her children had slept in the other rooms.

His body had been relaxed, even serene. He could tell himself that was pure physical relief. But his mind had been tense and active. What had happened between them hadn't been ordinary. Part of him wished it had been, while another—a part he hadn't explored in years—rejoiced that it hadn't. He wasn't a man who enjoyed contrasts within himself. Over and above those contradictions, there was the mystery of the woman who had slept beside him.

He'd begun to dissect the opinion he'd had of her before they'd met and compare it to the feelings he had about her now. Nothing lined up. What did the woman in mink, laughing at the spin of the wheel, have to do with the woman who'd trembled in his arms? Were they both real—or were they both an act?

His blood still curdled when he thought of what she'd told him. For the first time in his life, the urge to protect was stronger than any other. He knew better than to let his feelings color the facts, and he tried to be objective. If she had been physically and emotionally abused, why had she stayed? Chuck Rockwell had publicly thumbed his nose at his wedding vows, so a divorce would have been simple. But she'd stayed. He couldn't resolve the contradiction any more than he could resolve what was happening inside him.

He wanted her, just as much as he had before—no, even more. There was a sweetness about her love-making that he'd never tasted before, and he craved it again. But there was more. He could close his eyes and hear the way she laughed at herself, easily and without guile. He could see the way she worked, steadily and without bitterness. There was the way she handled her children, with a firm hand and tremendous love.

A special woman. He knew only a fool believed there was anything as fanciful as a special woman. Maybe he was becoming a fool.

He glanced out the window and wondered if she was in the barn feeding the stock. He could wait for her to come in again, have his recorder ready, and they'd get down to work. Dylan pictured her hefting a bag of grain or hefting another bale of hay. With a shake of his head, he turned and reached for his coat. Then he saw the note.

> Dylan
> I'm at Mrs. Cutterman's through the morning. The number is in the book if there's a problem. I need to swing into town and pick up a few things before I come home. See you around one.
> > Abby

He felt ridiculously depressed. She wasn't there, wouldn't be there for hours. He wanted to see her, to look at her in the morning, see her face after their night together. He wanted to talk to her, calmly, logically, until what he knew and what he felt drew closer together. He wanted to make love with her in the daylight in the big, empty house.

He wanted to be with her.

Shrugging off the feeling, Dylan poured a second cup of coffee and took it upstairs. There was work to be done.

When Abby pulled up in front of the house, the sky had darkened again. She muttered halfheartedly at the clouds as she carried the bread and milk to the house. Rain, she thought, disgusted because the radio had promised clear skies. Neither of the boys had their boots with them. Well, they needed new shoes anyway, she reminded herself, and pushed open the door. On her way to the kitchen, she picked up two trucks, two plastic men and a sock.

After shedding her coat, she switched on the portable radio and began to deal with the ground beef she'd taken out to defrost that morning.

"Hi."

She jumped a little, a frying pan in one hand. Dylan was only two feet away. "Lord, you're quiet. I didn't hear you come in."

"You always play the radio too loud."

"Oh." Automatically she lowered the volume. She felt awkward, but she'd expected to. "I had to pick up some milk. The way the boys go through it, I'm tempted to buy a cow." She busied herself at the stove and felt a little easier. "You've been working?"

"Yeah." He felt awkward. He hadn't expected it. Soft and straight, her hair was tied back with a bandanna. He wanted to loosen it, to feel it flow through his hands the way it had during the night. "Did you have a good time?"

"What?"

"A good time." The meat began to sizzle. "With your friend."

"My—oh, Mrs. Cutterman. She's very nice." Abby thought briefly of the acres of furniture she'd polished. Dismissing the thought, she began to rummage for tomato paste. "It's going to rain," she said. "I don't think the boys are going to make it home before it does."

"You had a call."

"Oh?"

"Betty something from the PTA."

"Bake sale." With a sigh, Abby opened the can of tomato paste. The whirl of the electric can opener sounded like an earthquake. How long, she wondered, could she hide behind routine? "Cupcakes?"

"Three dozen. She said she knew she could count on you."

"Good old reliable Abby." She said it without sarcasm, but with a self-mocking tone. "When does she need them?"

"Next Wednesday."

"Okay." The silence went on as she diluted the paste and added spices. Spaghetti was Ben's favorite, she thought. He packed it away like a lumberjack. At the moment, she didn't know if she would ever eat again. "I guess you'd like to ask me more questions."

"A few."

"I'll be finished here in a minute. If we can do it while I'm seeing to the laundry, then..." Her voice trailed off when he touched her shoulder. No longer knowing what to expect, she turned slowly. He was looking at her again, looking deep, looking hard. She wished she understood what he was searching for.

Then he kissed her, softly, gently, and her heart melted like butter.

"Oh, Dylan." The breath she hadn't been aware of holding escaped unevenly as she put her arms around him. "I was afraid you had regrets."

"About what?" God, it felt good to hold her. He'd told himself it made no difference, but it did. It made all the difference.

"About last night."

"No, I have no regrets." She smelled of soap—just as fresh as that. "I'm dazed."

"Really?" Only half believing him, she drew back.

"Yeah, really." He smiled, incredibly relieved, and kissed her again. "I missed you."

"Oh, that's nice." She ran her hands up his back as she drew him closer. "That's very nice."

"Want to play hooky?"

With a laugh, she tossed back her head. "Hooky?"

"That's right. You look like someone who never played enough hooky."

"I was never in one school long enough to work up to it. Besides, it's going to rain. What kind of fun is it to play hooky in the rain?"

"Come upstairs, I'll show you."

She laughed again, but her eyes widened when she saw he was serious. "Dylan, the kids'll be home in a couple of hours."

"You can pack a whole day into a couple of hours." On impulse, he scooped her up. It felt good, he realized, to hear that quick, breathless laugh, to see those wide, wondering eyes.

Her heart pounded as he carried her from the room. It was thrilling, illicit. Abby buried her face against his throat and murmured. "No one's going to have any clean socks."

"And only you and I will know why."

They made love quickly, desperately, with a wild kind of abandon she'd never experienced before. Clothes were tossed helter-skelter around the room. The curtains were thrown wide so that the soft, gloomy light crept into the room. He took her places she'd never been, places she knew she'd be afraid to go with anyone else. Like a child treated to her first roller coaster, she lost her breath on the ride, then fretted to go again.

He felt free, so incredibly free, as they rolled over on the old bed. Her body was furnace-hot and open to him, open to anything he could teach her. She was pliant, she was strong. And she was his. Amazingly agile, she arched back, lost in mindless pleasure.

Unable to get enough, he rose with her. Their bodies met, torso to torso, hip to hip, as they knelt on the bed. Tight as bowstrings, then limp, they tumbled together.

It began to rain, slow and steady against the windows.

Their loving slowed and steadied as passion turned to yearning. Quiet sighs, gentle movements took the place of frenzy. There was no need to rush. The bed was wide and soft, the rain quiet and soothing. They drew from each other all the sweet, simple things lovers bring to one another and no one else.

He tasted her skin, warm with pleasure, damp with excitement. He'd never known a flavor more intoxicating. Her fingers trailed over his back, finding the muscles that contracted and gave. She'd never known strength in itself could be so arousing.

They went deep into each other where the rain could no longer be heard. She found what she'd needed to find—the kindness, the compassion.

There were so many layers to her—serenity, wisdom, passion. He wondered if he would ever discover them all. He could look at her one way and see the headstrong woman who'd thrown caution to the winds and left family and familiar things to grab at something as elusive as love. He could look at her another way and see the vulnerability and the control. He felt compelled to know her, to fit the pieces together. Abby was becoming his obsession. But when they were like this, desire peaking, senses swimming, it only mattered that she was there with him.

The hands that had once been hesitant moved over him as though they'd always known him. The mouth that had once been unsure fused to his as though there were no other tastes in the world she would ever need. Her long, limber body came to his without inhibitions. Her arms and legs wrapped around him like warm silk. Passion poured through them, swirled around them, until there was nothing else.

Abby was walking downstairs, delighted with herself, when the front door burst open. "Wipe your feet," she said automatically, then laughed and hurried down the rest of the stairs to hug her two dripping children.

"It's raining," Chris informed her.

"Really?"

"My papers got wet." Ben took off his soaking hat and let it fall on the floor.

"They wouldn't if you used your book bag."

"They're for girls." He picked up his hat because his mother was looking at it, then handed her a wet, wrinkled paper.

"An *A*!" Abby put a hand to her heart as if the shock were too much for her. "Why, Benjamin, someone put your name on their paper."

He chuckled, a bit embarrassed. "No, they didn't. It's mine."

"This spelling test—unit 31—with none, absolutely none, marked wrong, belongs to Benjamin Francis Rockwell? *My* Benjamin Francis Rockwell?"

He wrinkled his nose as he always did when reminded of his middle name. "Yeah."

She put a hand on his shoulder. "You know what this means?" she asked solemnly.

"What?"

"Hot chocolate all around."

A grin split his face. "Can I have marshmallows?"

"Absolutely."

"Hot chocolate?" Dylan asked as he came down the steps.

Abby hooked an arm around Ben's shoulder. "We're celebrating the one hundred percent, grade *A*, unit 31. Twenty death-defying words spelled correctly." She held up the paper where the little gold star glittered damply.

"Pretty impressive." Dylan scrubbed a hand over Chris's head, then held it out to Ben. "Congratulations."

"It's no big deal," he murmured, but looked secretly pleased with the handshake. "Can I have three marshmallows?"

"The boy knows how to take advantage of a situation," Abby stated. "Let's go. Hang up your coats," she said automatically when they stepped into the kitchen.

For the next twenty minutes, the air was filled with stories of the adventures young boys go through in a day. Then bloated with chocolate, Ben and Chris tugged on their boots and coats and went out to tend the stock.

"I bet I haven't had any of this for twenty years," Dylan mused as he studied his empty cup.

"Bring back memories?"

"My mother used to make it." When Abby leaned on the counter opposite him and smiled, he found himself continuing. "She's a great cook. I still think she bakes the best custard pies in New Jersey."

"Do you get to see them often? Your parents?"

"Couple of times a year." He shrugged, feeling the familiar tug of guilt and resignation. "There never seems to be enough time."

"I know." Abby glanced over her shoulder at the window. There would come a time when her boys would go, when she'd have to let them go. That was the price of being a parent. "I don't see mine very often, either. They're never in one place long enough."

"Still playing the clubs?"

"They'll always be playing the clubs." Affection came into her voice, deep and natural. "Put two people into a room and they're ready to entertain. It's in the blood, if you believe my father's theory. He's desperately proud of Chantel and Maddy for carrying on the tradition in grand style. He stays annoyed with Trace because he didn't."

"What does your brother do?"

"Travels." She moved her shoulders. "None of us really have any idea just what it is that Trace does." She took another cookie off the plate and offered Dylan one. "Pop claims Trace doesn't know, either."

"What about you? Any problems because you don't sing for your supper?"

"Oh, no." She grinned. "I gave them Ben and Chris—better than a command performance. Your parents must be proud of you."

"My father would have preferred it if I'd stayed on the farm and milked cows." He drew out a cigarette. "But my mother tells me he's read every word I've written."

"Isn't if funny how—"

"Mom!" Chris came barreling through the door, dripping wet and tracking mud. Abby caught him halfway into the room, checking for injuries.

"What is it? What's wrong?"

"It's Eve. She's sick. She's lying down and all sweaty."

Abby already had her coat off the hook. Not bothering to change into her boots, she dashed out the door in her sneakers. When she got to the barn, Ben was sitting next to the mare, struggling not to cry as he stroked her.

"Is she going to die?"

Abby crouched beside him and put a hand on the mound of the mare's stomach. "No, no, of course not." She circled her arm around Ben and squeezed hard. "She's just going to have a baby. Remember, we talked about it."

"She looks awful sick."

"When babies come, it hurts some. But she's going to be fine." With her heart in her throat, Abby prayed she wasn't making promises she couldn't keep. "She's having contractions," she murmured, soothing the mare. "Her body's helping the baby come out."

All Ben could see was the mare's shudders. Sweat rolled, dampening her coat and overwhelming the scent of fresh hay. "Why does it have to hurt?"

"Because life hurts a little, Ben. But it's worth it." One of the barn cats mewed in sympathy as Eve moaned. "Now, Ben, I want you to go in and call the vet. Tell him who you are first, okay?"

He sniffed. "'Kay."

"Then tell him that Eve's in labor."

"In labor?"

"Having a baby's work," she told him, and kissed his cheek. "Go ahead. Then come back. This is something you'll want to see."

He dashed off, recovered enough to be pleased with the responsibility. As the mare suffered her pangs, Abby shifted Eve's head onto her lap.

"Anything we can do?"

She looked up to see Dylan standing at the entrance to the stall, Chris's hand firmly caught in his. Her son was wide-eyed and fascinated. She smiled.

"I've helped the vet with deliveries before, and I found that you end up doing little more than cheering her on. Eve has the starring role here." Eve moaned with the next contraction, and Abby leaned over and crooned to her. "Oh, I know it hurts, baby." The mare's sweat transferred to her own skin. Abby wished she could take some of the pain as easily.

Chris swallowed with a little click. He'd never seen anything like it. One of the cats had had kittens once, he remembered. But he'd come out to the barn to find them snuggled, clean and naked, against their mother. "Did it hurt when I was born?"

"You were a slowpoke." The mare's eyes half shut, and she breathed heavily. With her hand on Eve's stomach, Abby felt the power of the contraction. "For a while I thought you'd decided not to come out after all. The doctor had music on. They were playing 'Let It Be' when you were born."

"Would Eve like the music?"

"I bet she would."

Anxious to help, Chris dashed over and turned on the radio. A familiar ballad filled the air.

"The vet said he'd come as soon as he could but not to worry 'cause Eve's real strong." Ben dashed back in and took his place beside his brother.

"Of course she is."

But as the minutes dragged on and the contractions built, Abby worried. She knew she could handle a simple foaling, with or without the vet. When a woman lived on her own, raised children on her own, she had no choice but to develop self-confidence. But if there were complications... She shook her head and cleared her mind. Whatever happened, she was going to give Eve the best she could. The horse meant more, much more, than a means to an end to her. Eve was flesh and blood, something she'd cared for day after day for over a year. When pain went through the mare, it rippled through her. Then Dylan crouched beside her.

"She's doing fine," he assured her. "Look, I never delivered any horses, but I helped with my share of cows."

She leaned her head on his shoulder briefly in a gesture that caught Ben's attention. "Thanks."

But when it began, Abby rushed to help the foal into the world before Dylan could. Her own sweat mixed with the mare's, and her voice was raised in encouragement. The blood that came with new life streaked her hands. The hope that came with new life shone in her eyes. She looked, Dylan realized as he watched her, magnificent. He glanced at the boys and saw them watching the foal's birth with their mouths hanging open.

"Incredible, isn't it?"

Ben looked at him and made a face. "It's pretty gross." Then he saw spindly legs emerge, a small head and a compact body. "It's a horse. It's a real horse." Both he and Chris scrambled for a closer look.

"But he's big." Intrigued, Chris measured the foal. "How'd he fit in there?"

"She," Abby corrected, weeping shamelessly. "Isn't she beautiful?"

"She's kind of sloppy," Ben commented. Then Eve immediately went about her business and cleaned up her baby.

"Good job." Dylan stroked a hand down Abby's hair, then kissed her. "Real good job."

Chris reached out a tentative hand to touch the foal. "Can we play with her?"

"Not yet . . . but you can touch. Isn't she soft?"

Then Chris jerked back as the foal shook and shivered and tried out her legs for the first time. "She stood up!" Amazed, he stared at his mother. "She stood right up. Cathy Jackson's little sister didn't stand up for months and months." It pleased him enormously to find his horse superior. "What can we name her?"

"We can't name her, love. If Mr. Jorgensen's going to buy her, then he'll want to name her."

"We can't keep her?"

"Chris . . ." She looked at him and at Ben. "You know we can't. We talked about this."

"You didn't sell Ben and me."

"Horses grow up faster," Dylan put in. "One day you'll have a house of your own. The foal's going to be ready for her own place in a few months."

"We can visit her." Ben set his chin and waited for someone to shoot him down.

"I'm sure we can." Abby smiled at him. Her baby was so grown-up already. "Mr. Jorgensen's a very nice man."

"Can we watch when Gladys has her baby?" Ben reached out for the first time to touch the foal's ears.

"If you're not in school." She heard the sound of an engine and looked down at her hands. For the first time, she noticed they were streaked with blood. "That must be the vet. I'd better wash."

The excitement didn't die down until long after bedtime. Because she understood, Abby let her boys go out and say good-night to the foal after they should both have been in bed themselves. Tired, but pleasantly so, she settled down in front of the living room fire.

"Quite a day," Dylan murmured as he sat beside her.

"And then some. I'm so glad the boys were there. It's something they'll never forget. It's something I'll never forget." She felt a stirring inside her, one she hadn't experienced for a long, long time. She knew what it was like to have life grow inside her, what it was like to bring it into a not-so-perfect world. Would she ever carry another child? She sighed, reminding herself she had two beautiful healthy sons.

"Tired?"

"A little."

"Your mind's wandering."

She curled her legs under her and watched the flames dance. "I think you see too much in there too easily."

"Funny, I would have said I haven't seen nearly enough."

She blocked off wishes and longings and faced reality. "Tomorrow you're going to have more questions, and you're going to expect me to answer them."

"That's what I'm here for, Abby." But he wasn't sure that was the complete truth, not now.

"I know." She accepted it as truth. She had to. "I've made myself a few promises, Dylan. I'm going to try to keep them."

He touched her hair, wishing there were other ways to get what he needed to get from her. "There aren't any questions right now."

She closed her eyes a moment. Maybe there was a little room for longings after all. "For tonight, just for tonight, I'd like to pretend there isn't any book, that there aren't any questions."

He knew he could have pressed. He understood that at that moment she was open enough to tell him everything. If he pushed the right buttons, the answers would simply pour out. He had an obligation to do it. He slipped an arm around her shoulder and watched the fire with her.

"We had a big stone fireplace at home. My mother used to say you could roast an ox in it."

She relaxed against him as if it were the most natural thing in the world. "Were you happy?"

"Yeah. I never much cared for milking cows before the sun came up, but I was happy. We had a creek and a big oak tree. I'd sit under it, listen to the water and read books. I could go anywhere."

She smiled, picturing him as a child. "And you decided to be a writer."

"I decided to single-handedly spread the truth. I guess that's why reporting came first. I went into that with the First Amendment playing in my head." He laughed at himself, something he didn't yet realized he'd learned from her. "I found out you've got to crawl through a lot of dirt to make it work."

"The truth." She closed her eyes and wished the word didn't have such a sharp edge. "It's very important to you."

"Without it the rest is just dressing, just excuses."

She'd made plenty of those, Abby thought. "Why biographies, then?"

"Because it's fascinating to explore one person's life, one person at a time, and find out how many other lives were affected, what marks were left, what mistakes were made.''

"Sometimes mistakes are private."

"That's why I've never done a bio that wasn't authorized."

"And if one day someone wrote yours?"

He seemed to find that amusing. She heard his chuckle as his cheek brushed over her hair. He couldn't know how deadly serious she was. "Maybe I'd do it myself—warts and all."

"Have you ever done anything you were really ashamed of?"

He didn't have to think for long. A man didn't live beyond thirty without shame. "I've had my share of wrong turns."

"And you'd write about them, no matter what anyone thought of you after it was done?"

"You can't bargain with the truth, Abby." He remembered what she had told him about Chris's conception and continued, "Sometimes, when it's important enough, you can pretend you didn't hear it."

She watched the fire and thought about that. She thought about it a long time.

Because he wanted to get an early start, Dylan was downstairs before the boys had finished breakfast. The main topic, as expected, was the foal. The boys were arguing, though without heat, about whether Gladys would mess things up and deliver while they were in school. Veterans now, they were prepared to step in as midwives. To prove their valor, each one had a Polaroid snapshot of the new addition to take to class.

"They're having hamburgers for lunch today," Ben remembered, looking expectantly at his mother.

Abby put the jar of peanut butter back in the cupboard. "Get my purse."

"Me, too?" Chris asked dribbling milk down his chin.

"Okay." She opened her bag when Ben brought it in, and dumped out the contents. Along with her wallet, she pulled a pair of rubber gloves in a plastic bag out of the pile and dropped them on the counter. "Here you go. Don't lose it."

"We won't." Chris scrambled for his coat while he stuffed the money in the pocket of his jeans. "Mom, I know where babies come from."

"Um-hmm." She was pouring her second cup of coffee.

"But how do they get there?"

"Oh." She spilled the coffee on the counter, and caught Dylan's grin as she turned to look at Chris. His round young face was lifted to hers. But he's only six, she thought, wondering just what she was supposed to tell him. She knelt down in front of him and asked herself how to tell a six-year-old about making babies in the two minutes he had left before he had to catch the bus for school.

"Love puts them there," she told him, and kissed both his cheeks. "A very special kind of love."

"Oh." Satisfied, he gave her one of his quick, energetic hugs and dashed for the door. "Come on, Ben." Then, seeing that his brother was still pulling on his coat, Chris grinned. "I'll beat you." He flew off with the challenge and left Ben struggling to zip up and run at the same time.

"Bye, Ben," Abby murmured. Then, with a shake of her head, she went back to mop up the coffee.

Dylan sat at the counter and watched her tidy up the spill with a secret smile of amusement on her face. "I like your style, lady."

"Oh?" Laughing, she tugged at the hem of an over-laundered sweatshirt. "It is rather *today* isn't it?"

"I was talking about your answer to a very important and very ticklish question from a six-year-old boy. Some people would've given him a biology lesson, and others would have brushed him off. You gave him exactly the answer he needed. Still..." He toyed with the last of his coffee. "I wish I'd had that Polaroid when the question popped out of his mouth. Your face was worth the price of a ticket."

"I'm sure it was." She walked over to pull on her boots.

"I like the way you look in the morning."

She stopped, still bent over, and looked at him. "Frazzled?"

"Fresh." The smile on her face faded. "Soft." His voice lowered. "I'd like to be able to lie in bed with you during the morning, watch you wake up, fall back to sleep and know when you wake up again I could make love with you."

Her pulse thudded, and she wondered he didn't hear it. "I'd like that, too. But the children—"

"I didn't say I didn't understand. But the idea warms me up a little."

It warmed her more than a little, she thought as she finally managed to get into her boots. "As it is, there isn't a lot of time around here for lazing around in bed in the morning. I always figure I'll know the kids are growing up when they sleep past seven." Not quite steady, she walked over to clear the counter.

"I'll do that," he said, and caught her hand.

"It's all right."

"Abby..." He flicked a finger over her wrist. "Haven't you ever heard of women's liberation?"

She lifted a brow. In her way, she'd been liberated since she'd taken her first breath. Her parents had seen to that. "Sure. That's why the boys take turns doing the dishes, put away their own clothes—on a good day—and know how to use the vacuum. Their wives will thank me. In the meantime, someone has to man the oars."

"There are usually two oars."

She tilted her head, smiled, then nodded. "Fine. You clean up the kitchen, I'll feed the stock. It'll save some time."

"Okay. We'll get started when you come back in."

"Can't." She started to clear the contents of her purse from the counter. "I have to run over to the Smiths' this morning. I'll be back around noon."

He started to object, then made himself stop. She had her own life. He watched her fill her purse again. "Do you always carry rubber gloves in there?"

"What? Oh." With a laugh, she dropped them in. "I do when I'm going to the Smiths'. She's a fanatic about ammonia."

"Come again?"

"Ammonia." Abby zipped up her purse and wondered if there was enough spaghetti in the fridge for leftovers. "The straight stuff. The woman has a fetish about having all the floors cleaned with ammonia."

His brow creased as he tried to follow her. "You clean them?"

"Twice a month." Her mind on dozens of other matters, Abby went for her coat.

"What is it, like volunteer work?"

She have a quick, appreciative roll of laughter as she turned back. "Not on your life. I make six dollars an hour. Look, don't run the dishwasher. I think—"

"You work as a maid?"

"Housekeeper." She grinned and pulled a bandanna off a peg to tie her hair back with. "I suppose that's really a glorified term, but I always see a maid in a little black skirt, and..." She let the words die when he rose out of his seat and walked to her. Something in his eyes had her throat clogging up. She'd never dealt well with anger.

"Why in the hell are you getting down on your hands and knees and scrubbing someone else's floor?"

Her chin came up. "It's honest work."

"Why?"

"Because the only other thing I'm good at is singing in three-part harmony. There isn't a lot of call for that, and the pay's lousy."

Ignoring her evasions, he went straight to the point. "Why does Chuck Rockwell's widow have to wash floors for six dollars an hour?"

She went very pale. It was in his voice, the doubt, the derision. "I don't have time or the inclination to discuss my financial business with you, Dylan." She yanked the door open, but he slammed it again.

"I asked you a question."

"And I've given you the only answer I intend to." The fire came into her eyes, briefly but powerfully. "I don't have to tolerate this from you, from anyone,

Dylan. I don't have to stand here while you look at me as though I'm less of a person because I mop other people's floors and dust their furniture for pay. If I did it for charity I'd be a hero, but I do it for money."

"I want to know why you do it at all."

"I do exactly what I have to do. Nobody knows it better."

With that she yanked the door open again and strode out. He could have followed her, and he started to. Then, just as determined as she, Dylan shut the door. It was time to get back to business, he told himself. And back to the truth.

Chapter Ten

Moving with a dull, grinding fury, Dylan drafted out twenty pages. Chuck Rockwell had become more than a name, less than an image to him now. Over the course of time, Dylan had come to know him as a man, a badly flawed one, insecure, self-absorbed, intemperate. The skill and the training couldn't be overlooked, nor could the daring that some would have called heroics. He'd been born not just with a silver spoon in his mouth, but with the whole place setting at his disposal. Yet he hadn't chosen to simply sit back and enjoy his wealth, he'd refused a meaningless title in the family conglomerate. He had, instead, chosen to make his own mark in his own way. There was something to be said for that.

Chuck Rockwell had become a success and had earned respect, even adulation. His associates had considered him one of their best, even if they hadn't liked him personally. The press had gloried in him, on the track and off. His fans had made him a celebrity within a year of his first professional race. He'd attained all that, plus a devoted wife and two sons.

Then he'd set out—systematically, it seemed to Dylan—to destroy it all.

He'd lost his backer and first supporter, he'd alienated most of his associates and had torn irreparable holes in his marriage. Yet Abby had once described him as a knight on a white charger. And she'd stuck by him for four years.

Why?

Chuck had abused their marriage, abused her and left her to raise his children while he ran the next race and pursued the next woman. But she'd made a home for him.

Why?

Until she told him, until he cornered her again and pulled the answers out of her, what he wrote would just be words.

Until she told him, until she trusted him with the truth, what he felt for her couldn't be acknowledged.

How long could he deny it? Dylan crushed his cigarette out with quick and deliberate violence. How long could he live in the same house with her, watch her, want her, deny he'd lost his head over her? Lost his head. With self-mocking laugh, he ran his hands over his face. It was easier to plead insanity than to admit he'd lost his heart. What he'd done was fall in love.

But he'd always thought that falling in love meant you'd stumbled, slipped, that you hadn't looked for the rocks in the road or noticed the edge of the cliff. And he'd been right. He felt as if he'd slipped, stumbled and caught himself on one of those rocks, then taken a nosedive off the cliff. In all likelihood, it was going to screw up his book, his objectivity and his life.

He wished to God she would come home.

That was another problem, he admitted. He'd been on the farm less than three weeks and he already thought of it as home. He'd been with Abby less than three weeks and he already thought of her as his. And the boys... Dylan pushed away from his desk and strode around the room. All right, so he was crazy about them. He wasn't made of stone, was he?

It didn't have to make any difference. He'd worked too hard to get his life exactly the way he wanted it. The only person he was responsible to was himself, the only person he had to satisfy was himself. The only person who had to approve of him was Dylan Crosby.

Maybe he wasn't rolling in money, but he certainly made enough. If he wanted to take off tomorrow for three weeks in the South Seas, there was no one he'd have to clear it with first. Selfish? Dylan turned that over in his mind with a shrug. What if he were? He was entitled. He'd milked cows until the time he'd gone to college. He'd studied hard, worked hard, and had established himself professionally and personally. His years as an investigative reporter had been fiendish in their way, but he'd gotten through them. His marriage hadn't exactly been made in heaven, but he'd done the best he could with it while it had lasted. Now he was free, with no ties, no strings. He set his own schedules, made his own demands. Just because he liked the farm and was fond of a couple of kids didn't mean he was going to turn his world upside down. He'd been through one marriage, and so had Abby. They'd be smart not to step back into the ring.

When was she coming home?

The minute he heard the engine, he was at the window. But it wasn't Abby's sturdy station wagon that pulled up. It was a huge gunmetal-gray limo.

"Ah, fresh air. Country air." Frank O'Hurley bounced out of the limo as though it were act one, scene one. "Clears the mind. Cleanses the soul. Everybody should breathe it in." He did, then screwed up his face. "God save us. What is that smell?"

"Horse manure'd be my guess." Maddy stepped out beside him, then looked around with quick, avid curiosity. Fifty-second Street or Dogpatch, it made no difference to her. "Mom, did I leave my purse in there?"

"Right here." Molly, slim and pretty, accepted the driver's hand before stepping out. She stood on sturdy legs and shaded her eyes against the sun. Sunlight made wrinkles. She wasn't particularly vain, but her face was part of her act. "Ah." With a look that was half pleased, half baffled, she stared at the house. "Such a place. I can never quite imagine our Abby here."

"Where'd we go wrong?" Frank asked her, and got a quick swipe on the shoulder from his youngest daughter.

"Cut it out, Pop. Abby loves this place."

Dylan came to the door just in time to see Chantel O'Hurley step from the limo onto the sparsely graveled drive. It struck him first that Abby had the same million-dollar legs as Chantel. He watched as her skirt flared beautifully around her and she took the driver's hand, then flashed a smile designed to turn a man to putty.

"Thank you, Donald." Her voice was like smoke and seemed to encircle her listeners sensuously. "If you'd just put our bags on the porch, that will be all for today."

"Very good, Miss O'Hurley."

"You do that so well," Maddy murmured as the driver popped the hood.

"Darling, I was born to do it." Then, as she laughed and linked her arm through her sister's, she spotted Dylan. "Well, well." It might have been a purr, but kittens didn't purr when they showed their teeth. "What have we here?"

"Must be the writer." Maddy gave him a brief and thorough summing-up. "Be nice."

"Maddy, remember my image." Chantel slid her oversize sunglasses down her nose and continued to stare. "Nice had nothing to do with it."

As the two women paused, Dylan did some summing-up of his own. One sister was dressed in baggy slacks and an oversize jacket whose contrasting shades of green and blue should have hurt the eyes. Instead, the pattern was as bright and cheerful as her short mop of strawberry-blond hair. Beside her was the image of cool, understated glamour, from the long silvery-blond mane to the toes of her alligator pumps. Standing next to them were a small, pretty woman of about fifty and a wiry little man making theatrical gestures toward the barn.

Maddy was the first to step forward. "Hello, we're Abby's family."

She walked up the steps with the quick, swinging gait of a born optimist. Her sister followed with the slow, alluring moves of a born siren. "Dylan Crosby." Chantel extended the tips of her fingers. "We've met."

"Miss O'Hurley." If he'd ever seen a woman who'd have liked to ram a knife into him—and one who would have known precisely the right spot to aim for—it was this one. Dylan turned to Maddy.

"You're the writer." She sent her sister an amused, knowing glance. "Abby told us you'd be here. These are our parents."

"Frank and Molly O'Hurley." Frank stuck his hand out and shook with fast, friendly exuberance.

"Molly and Frank," his wife said with a smile. Dylan could see where Abby had inherited her looks.

"Always worried about billing." Frank pecked his wife's cheek before turning back to Dylan. "Where's my girl?"

"Abby had to run some errands." Dylan was a man who believed in first impressions, and he was immediately drawn to the small, spry man with the big grin and the well-timbred voice.

"Errands." Frank slipped an arm around his wife and gave her a squeeze. "Just like our Abby."

"And totally unlike the rest of us. Hello." Molly didn't offer her hand, but smiled at Dylan. "You must be the writer. Abby told us she'd decided to authorize the book."

"That's right." She didn't have to say any more to convey her disapproval. Yet Dylan felt it was directed at the project rather than himself. It wasn't everyone who could make such a fine distinction felt so easily. "I don't know exactly when she'll be back, but—"

"No problem." Frank gave him a companionable pat on the arm, then strode past him into the house. The move was so smooth, so natural, that it took Dylan a minute to realize Frank had ignored the pile of luggage. Maddy hauled up two bags and sent Dylan a wink.

"Pretty sharp, isn't he? Come on, Chantel, just like old times."

Chantel cast a long, considering look at the pile, paused, then chose one small leather tote.

"Takes after her father," Molly commented as she leaned over to grasp the handle of a suitcase.

"I'll take care of it," Dylan began, but Molly laughed and hefted the bag herself.

"I've been lugging trunks since I could stand. Don't worry about me, you'll have your hands full with the rest, because I can promise you they won't be back for them. Put on some coffee, Frank," she called out, then walked up the staircase without a backward glance.

With a shrug, Dylan stacked and lifted the remaining bags and followed. It looked as if it might be an interesting afternoon.

Abby decided there was little purpose in nursing her temper. Perhaps it was justified, perhaps in its way it was satisfying. But it just didn't accomplish anything. Dylan didn't trust her. If she was honest, she had to admit he had no real reason to. While she could rationalize that she hadn't lied to him, neither had she been completely honest. Dylan Crosby was a man who required the unvarnished truth.

He'd hurt her. His doubts and derision had hurt her. She had wanted to believe they'd reached some point of understanding. She'd hoped they'd come far enough in their relationship for him to accept her for who and what she was.

She had wanted too much. The trouble was, Abby longed for more. She wanted his trust, though she hadn't been able to give her own. She wanted his support, though she was afraid to offer hers. She wanted his love most of all, yet she wouldn't admit her own feelings for him.

Temper had given her a smug sense of self-satisfaction, but only temporarily. It had also left her unsettled and unhappy. Maybe the time had come for her to put her feelings on the line and give Dylan what seemed most important to him. Complete honesty. If she opened up and he still walked away from her, she could have no regrets.

When Abby pulled up in the drive, she had decided to tell Dylan everything—the mistakes, the regrets, the compromises. Without faith, love was just another word. She would put her life in his hands and believe in him.

The minute she opened the front door, her nerve started to weaken. She had to talk to him and talk to him quickly, before she pulled back. Then she saw him coming from the direction of the kitchen. Abby stood where she was and waited for her resolve to harden. "Dylan." She shifted her bag from hand to hand. "We need to talk."

"Yeah." He'd made his own decisions that morning. "It might have to wait a little while."

"It can't. I—" Abby caught a movement out of the corner of her eye and turned toward the stairs. Maddy stood there, barefoot, her hands deep in the pockets of baggy slacks. She grinned as though she knew every secret in the world and was ready to tell them.

"Maddy!" Before the name was fully formed, Abby rushed toward the staircase and threw herself into her sister's arms. First came laughter; then they both began to talk at once. Somehow, in the torrent of words, they both managed to ask and answer a half a dozen questions.

"You two always stepped on each other's lines." From the top of the staircase, Chantel looked down. Dylan noted that she looked just as cool, just as elegant, as she had when she'd stepped from the limo. Then, with a whoop, she was clattering down the stairs at a dangerous speed to launch herself at her sisters.

"Both of you." Abby had an arm around each sister, holding them close. One smelled free, easy, fresh, the other dark and tempting. "How did you manage it?"

"I backed out of the play." Maddy said with a laugh. She hadn't realized until it was done, how badly `she'd needed to move on. "My understudy is building a shrine to me."

"We shot the final scenes of the movie last week." Chantel gave a lazy shrug. "I left my leading man desolate." Then she stepped back, taking Abby's face in her hand. She turned it one way, then the other, her eyes narrowed. "Incredible," she muttered. "Not a bit of makeup. That's why I hate you."

Abby hugged them both again. "Oh, God, I'm so glad to see you."

There was a hint, only a hint, of desperation in her voice. It was enough. Over Abby's head, Chantel aimed a long, hard look at Dylan. Her eyes were blue, a very dark, very intense blue. She knew how to use them.

Sensitive to changes in mood, Maddy felt the tension. The best way to deal with it, in her opinion, was to slide over it. "I hate to use old lines," she said easily, "but you ain't seen nothin' yet. Come into the kitchen. How about some coffee, Dylan?"

Her look was so friendly that he wondered if he imagined the message beneath. Her eyes weren't the vivid blue of Chantel's or the deep green of Abby's. They were a warm shade of brandy uniquely her own. But the challenge was there. Acknowledging it, he walked in to the kitchen with them.

"Mom. Pop." Stunned, Abby stared at her parents, who were sitting cozily at the breakfast bar.

"It's about time you got home, girl." Frank swiveled in his chair and grinned at her. His arms opened in the wide, inviting gesture that had always warmed her. "Let's have a kiss."

"What are you doing here?" She had an arm around each parent, drawing in the old, familiar scents—peppermint and Chanel. Her father couldn't get through a day without peppermints, and her mother would go without shoes before she denied herself her perfume. "There isn't a theater within twenty miles."

"Vacation." Her father have her another smacking kiss. "It was either here or Paris."

Molly gave a quick, none-too-subtle snort, then picked up her coffee. "Where are the boys?"

"In school. They'll be home a bit after three."

"All day stuck with books." Frank shook his head. "It's a tragedy."

"Just keep that to yourself," Abby warned. "They'll be too glad to agree with you."

"What's this?" Frank reached up and brushed a tear from her lashes.

"Abby's entitled to get emotional." Maddy went to the stove to pour more coffee. "She's wondering how she's going to feed four extra people for three days. Abby, is there a trick to this stove? I can't get the burner going.''

"Push the knob in before you turn it. Can you really stay?'' She looked at her mother first because she knew who really called the shots.

"We're between engagements,'' Molly told her dryly then patted her arm. "If you can put up with us, we'll stay until the end of the week.''

"Of course I can put up with you.'' She hugged Molly again, hardly able to believe her family was in one place at one time. "I only wish Trace were here.''

Frank made a hissing sound. "That boy. No sense of responsibility, no ambition. Can't think how I could raise a son to be so feckless.''

"It's a mystery.'' Chantel's dry voice was lost on him.

"He's got talent.'' Frank slammed his fist on the counter. "Taught him everything I knew. He hasn't walked through a stage door in ten years.''

"Did I mention that Chris was in his school Christmas play?'' Abby knew how to soothe and distract. "He played a sheep.''

Frank positively preened. "A man's got to start somewhere.''

"Nice touch, Abby,'' Maddy murmured.

"Years of practice.'' She saw Dylan standing slightly off to the side, observing and absorbing— something he did well. She wished she could tell if the smile on his face was one of amusement or disdain. "Coffee?'' she asked. He only nodded.

"Dylan, my boy.'' Frank perked up as he remembered his audience. "Come, sit down here. Let me tell you about the time we played Radio City.''

Chantel didn't bother to disguise a moan, and Frank glared at her. "Have some respect."

"Frank, Dylan may not be interested in show business."

Frank looked at his wife as if she'd grown horns. "There's not a person alive who isn't interested in show business." He added two heaping spoonfuls of sugar to his coffee, hesitated briefly, then added a third. "Besides, the man's a writer. That means he likes a story."

"Story's right." Chantel gave her father a loud kiss on the cheek. "Tall story."

Frank raised his chin. "Sit down, Dylan. Ignore the family. I could teach them a time step, but I never could teach them manners."

Frank told his story, interrupted by asides from all three of his daughters and the occasional chuckle from his wife. Dylan would never be sure whether it was fact or fiction, but he was certain that Frank O'Hurley believed every word.

Abby relaxed. Dylan could all but feel the tension that had held her stiff when she'd first come in drain out of her. She seemed to meld with the odd mix of people who were her family. Though she was totally unlike any of them, she fit in like a piece of a jumbled jigsaw puzzle.

He enjoyed them. They were loud, talking over and against each other, laughing at one another. Each one had a habit of grabbing the spotlight and clinging a moment before passing it on. Their stories were exaggerated and dramatic. Yet some of them, though ridiculous, had the ring of truth. Instinctively he found himself making mental notes. The O'Hurleys, singly and as a group, might make a hell of a book.

Not his style, Dylan reminded himself. It wasn't his style at all, of course. But he continued to observe.

When the boys came home, it was chaos. To a casual observer it might have seemed as though the O'Hurleys were competing for the attention of a new audience. Dylan saw something deeper: their innate love of confusion and each other. Ben and Chris were part of Abby and therefore part of themselves. There were hugs, exclamations, quizzes and presents. Some children might have been overwhelmed by all the sudden attention. Dylan watched as Ben and Chris simply lapped it up as if it were their due. From what he'd gathered, Dylan was certain the boys didn't see their grandparents or their aunts often, but he sensed none of the awkward shyness that might have been expected. At one point, Chris climbed up onto Dylan's lap as though it were his natural place and began bombarding his grandfather with stories of his day at school. Without thinking, Dylan hooked an arm around the boy's waist to secure him. They sat that way for nearly an hour, with the fire crackling in the hearth, the scent of coffee lingering and the echo of voices bouncing off the kitchen walls.

The minute Abby started dinner preparations, Frank was up. Taking both of his grandsons by the hand, he demanded that they take him upstairs and show him some of their more fascinating toys.

Maddy watched them go with a shake of her head. "As quick on his feet as ever."

"The nice thing about your father is that he doesn't consider cooking women's work any more than he considers changing a tire men's work." Molly leaned back in her stool with a smile. "He considers them both work and avoids them at all costs. What can I do, dear?''

"Nothing. This is going to be pretty simple tonight, I'm afraid. Meat loaf."

Chantel walked over and slipped onto a stool in such a way that her skirt flared and settled around her legs. "I guess you want me to peel potatoes or something."

Abby glanced down at her sister's beautifully manicured hands. There was a sunburst of diamonds and sapphires on one finger, and a slim gold watch with an amber face on her wrist. Abby smiled, hefted a bag of potatoes out of the pantry and dropped it on the counter.

"A dozen ought to do it."

With a sigh, Chantel took the paring knife. "I suppose I should learn to keep my mouth shut. You've always been so literal-minded."

Though it would have amused him to watch one of Hollywood's reigning princesses skin potatoes, Dylan rose. "I'll feed the stock."

"But the boys—" Abby began.

"Special circumstances." Dylan grabbed his jacket off the hook.

"I'll give you a hand." Maddy was up and bouncing toward the door. "I'd rather play with the horses than peel potatoes." When the first blast of cool air hit her face, she tossed her head back. "I hope you know your way around the barn. I don't."

"I can manage."

Sigmund bounded around the side of the house and leaped toward her, tongue lolling. Maddy evaded him with the ease of a woman used to dodging foot traffic on crowded sidewalks. She bent down and rubbed his fur vigorously with both hands until he settled down.

"I don't know what to make of you, Dylan." Still leaning over the dog, she turned her head to look up at him. "I'd almost decided not to like you until I saw you with the boys. Generally I think kids are the best judge of people, and they like you." When he said nothing, she straightened and looked directly at him. "The main reason I came down to see Abby was because of you."

Dylan decided the stock could wait, and drew out a cigarette. "I don't think I follow you."

"When I talked to Abby a week or so ago, she sounded unnerved. It takes a lot to unnerve Abby." Maddy dipped her hands into her pockets, but her candid, friendly gaze remained on his. "She's been through a lot. I wasn't always around, Chantel wasn't always around, it wasn't possible to give her support when it turned out she needed it most. That's why we're here now."

He let out a long stream of smoke. "It seems to me that Abby can take care of herself."

"Absolutely." She dragged a hand through her hair, but the wind tossed it back again. "Look at this place. She loves it, and whether she's told you or not, she's done it all on her own. All. I don't know what she's told you, or might tell you, about Chuck Rockwell, but everything here is Abby's."

"You didn't like him."

"For an actress, I'm often transparent. No, I didn't like him, and there are really very few people I can say that about. But my feelings are my own, and Abby's are hers. I won't see her slapped down again, though." She smiled a little, but her smile took nothing away from her firm tone. "Thing is, I'd expected to stand between you and Abby with my fists raised. I don't think that's going to be necessary."

"You don't know me."

"I think Abby does," she said simply. "If she cares for you, there's a reason. I guess that's enough." She linked her arm through his as though she'd been doing so for years. "Let's feed the horses."

Dinner was a babble of conversation. The food might have been simple, but it was consumed enthusiastically, down to the last crumb. When it came time to deal with the dishes, Frank made his escape with his banjo. Because he was entertaining the children, Abby said nothing and went about the task herself. It was reward enough to hear her father's voice over the sound of clattering china and silverware.

"Let me do that."

"Mom, you're on vacation."

"Do you know the last time I washed dishes?" Molly stacked plates in the quick, expert style that demonstrated her on-again, off-again career as a waitress. "God, I don't. I used to think it was relaxing."

Maddy wrinkled her nose and grabbed a few glasses. "I wish you'd come to my apartment and relax. Come on, Chantel, grab that platter."

"I peeled the potatoes," She looked critically at her hands. "Unless you have surgical gloves, I'm not putting these in dishwater."

"Vain," Maddy grumbled as she stacked more dishes. "Always vain."

"It's only vanity if you haven't a right to it." Chantel smiled and slid off the stool. "I think I'll give Pop a hand."

Dylan began to stack plates in the dishwasher. "I imagine you've done enough housework for one day," he said to Abby. "Why don't you go sit with your father?"

One look was enough to remind her of the harsh words he'd spoken that morning. Wanting to avoid a scene in front of her family, Abby backed off. "It looks as though you have things under control."

There was the sound of three-part harmony from the living room. "Frank'll be in heaven," Molly commented. "He's got his girls singing with him again. Go ahead, Maddy, we're nearly done here."

Maddy needed no urging to slip out of the kitchen and into the spotlight. Within seconds the voices were joined by another. Frank picked up the beat with the banjo and went into the next number. Molly began to hum as she wiped off a counter.

"Guess I'm sentimental," she said, "but it does my soul good to hear them."

"You've quite a family, Mrs. O'Hurley."

"Oh, Lord, don't call me that. Call me that and you remind me I'm too damn old to be running around the country and smearing on greasepaint. Molly, just plain Molly."

Dylan closed the door of the dishwasher and looked at her, really looked. She was lovely, with soft, small features and a full, youthful mouth. The lines made no difference that he could see, no difference at all. "I wouldn't say just plain Molly."

She laughed, a full, robust sound that contrasted with her height and build. "Oh, you're a smart one, you are, and you've a way with words. I read your last book, the one about that actress, on the train." She laid the dishcloth over the spigot.

"And?" There was an *and* in there, though he wasn't certain it would be complimentary.

"You're a hard man, the kind who sees things that would probably be better left alone. But you're fair." When she turned and looked at him again, really looked, he saw that her eyes were like Abby's, deep and vulnerable. "Be fair with my girl, Dylan. That's all I want. She's strong. Sometimes it scares me just how strong. When she's hurt, she doesn't ask for help, but binds her wounds herself. I don't want her to have to bind anymore."

"I didn't come here to hurt her."

"But you may unintentionally hurt her in the end." She sighed a little. Her children were grown. They'd started taking steps without her help years before. "Can you sing?" she asked him abruptly.

Off balance, he looked at her a moment, then laughed. "No."

"Then it's time you learned." She took him by the arm and led him out to join the others.

It was after midnight before the house settled down. Abby thought Maddy and Chantel might still be talking and laughing in the room they were sharing. Her parents would be asleep, as comfortable in the strange bed as they had been in hundreds of other strange beds. She was restless, too restless to sleep, too restless to join her sisters. Instead, she slipped a coat over her robe and went out to the barn. The foal that had pleased Maddy so much was asleep, curled contentedly in the hay with her mother guarding him. Gladys

was awake, perhaps too close to her own time to rest.
Abby stroked her, hoping to soothe both herself and
the mare.

"You need some sleep."

Her fingers tightened in the mare's mane, then
slowly relaxed before she turned to Dylan. "I didn't
hear you come in. I thought everyone was in bed."

"You should be. You look tired." He came closer,
almost afraid to get close enough to touch her. "I saw
you leave. I was standing at the window."

"Just checking on Gladys," Abby rested her cheek
against the mare's. The morning's argument seemed
so far away. It seemed like years since she'd lain beside him and felt excitement build. "With my family
here, it's going to be a little difficult for us to work
together for the next couple of days."

"I've got enough to work on my own for a while.
Abby..." He wanted her, wanted to gather her close
and pretend things were every bit as simple as sitting
around the living room and singing. He wanted to offer her the kind of unconditional support her family
did, yet there seemed to be a wall between them. "I'd
like to talk to you about this morning."

She'd known he would. For a moment, she continued to stroke Gladys. "All right. Would you like to go
inside?"

"No." He caught her as she turned, caught her before he could give himself the chance to remember he
should keep a certain distance. "I want you alone.
Damn it, Abby, I want some answers. You're driving
me crazy."

"I wish I could give you the ones you want." She
took a deep breath and put her hands on his arms,

both to comfort, and to emphasize her point. "Dylan, I decided as I was driving back here today to tell you everything, to be completely open with you. I may not give you the answers you want, but I'm going to trust you with the truth."

That was all he wanted from her, or so he told himself. He watched her in the dim, slanting light. "Why?"

She could have evaded him, and perhaps she should have, but honesty had to begin somewhere. "Because I'm in love with you."

He didn't step back, but his hands slid slowly away from her until he was no longer touching her. Abby felt a little tingle of pain. "I told you it might not be the answer you wanted."

"Wait a minute. Wait a minute," he repeated as she turned away. Even through his own shock he'd seen the flicker of hurt in her eyes. "You can't expect to say something like that and not leave me a little stunned." When she turned toward him, he didn't reach out to her, because she terrified him. "I don't know what to say to you."

"You don't have to say anything." Her words were calm and low, and there was a touch of amusement in her eyes now. "I'm responsible for my own feelings, Dylan. That's something I learned a long time ago. I answered your question honestly because I decided that avoiding this and the rest of your questions will only put me into a hole I may never get out of. About this morning—"

"The hell with this morning." He caught her face in his hands and stared at her as though he were seeing her for the first time. "I don't know what to do about you. I sure as hell don't know what to do for you."

It would have been so easy just to step forward into his arms. To ask to be held. She knew he wouldn't refuse. Abby shook her head and kept her arms at her sides. "That's a problem I can't help you with."

She was closer now, but he didn't even realize that he'd closed the distance between them. "I don't want to get tangled up in a relationship. I had one marriage hit the skids. I have a career that requires me to be selfish to begin with."

"I'm not asking you for a relationship, Dylan. I'm not asking you for anything at all."

"That's the trouble, damn it. If you asked, I could tell you to forget it." Or so he hoped. "If you asked I could give you two dozen reasons why it would never work." She looked at him, her eyes warm and calm. He swore at her, then at himself, before he drew her into his arms. "I want you. There doesn't seem to be anything I can do about it."

"There's nothing you have to do."

"Shut up," he muttered. Then he closed his mouth over hers.

It was as if the day had never happened. The heat, the passion, the glow, were just as strong as they'd been before. She softened against him as if she knew he needed her to be soft. Her lips were avid and hungry on his, meeting every demand. In the dim light of the barn he could see her eyes flutter closed, then open to watch him as their mouths met again and again. The scent of animals and hay and leather was strong, but as she entwined her arms around him he could only smell the fresh, light hint of soap on her skin.

"I don't want to talk." He skimmed his lips over her cheek before he drew her back. "I don't really want to think."

"No." She linked her fingers with his. "Not tonight. I'll give you all the answers, Dylan. I promise."

He nodded but wondered if she already had.

Chapter Eleven

Things got a little crazy when Gladys went into labor. Abby was walking through her morning routine, her father strolling along beside her. The ground was hard again and just beginning to show signs of new life. Her father's shoes hit the path in their own cheerful rhythm. She never tired of listening to him spin his stories of life on the road. Even though she'd been there herself for more than half her life, Abby was able to suspend reality and believe it was all glamour and excitement and opening nights.

"I tell you, Abby, it's a great life. City after city, town after town. What a way to see the world."

He never mentioned the back-alley entrances, the smoke- and liquor-filled rooms, or the disinterested crowds. There were no such things in Frank O'Hurley's world. Abby was grateful for it.

"Vegas, what a place. The neon flashing, the slot machines clinking. People waltzing around in evening clothes at 8:00 a.m. Ah, I'd give a lot to play Vegas again."

"You will, Pop." Maybe not on the Strip, maybe not with his name several feet high on a marquee, but he'd play Vegas again. Just as he'd play in dozens of other towns. A man like Frank O'Hurley couldn't stop performing any more than he could stop breathing and survive. In the blood, he'd often said to her, and in the blood it was. And it was because the O'Hurley blood was thick that he was up before eight o'clock and walking in a farmyard with his daughter when he usually considered noon a barely civilized hour. Knowing that only made Abby love him more.

"This place." He stopped but was careful not to breathe too deeply. "It suits you, I guess. Must take after your grandma. Never would leave that farm in Ireland." He had a moment's pang for early memories that were more dreams than memories. "You happy, Abby?"

She thought about the question because she sensed the answer was important. The farm brought her contentment and personal satisfaction. The children... Abby smiled as she remembered their complaints at being sent off to school when the excitement was at home. The children gave her roots and pride and the kind of love she could never describe. And Dylan. He brought her passion and fire and serenity all at once. He made life complete. Even though she knew it was only temporary, it seemed to be enough.

"I'm happier now that I've been in a long, long time." That was true enough. "I like what I've done here. It's important to me."

It was beyond Frank how anyone could be happy staying rooted to one spot. But he'd always wanted his children to have what they wanted most. It didn't matter what it was, as long as they had it. "This writer..." He felt his way along here. It was untested ground. "Well, Abby, a body would have to be blind not to see the way you look at him."

"I'm in love with him." Strange how easily the words came out now without a pang of regret, without a twinge of fear.

"I see." He let out the whistling sound through his teeth. "Should I talk with him?" For a moment she went blank. Then the laughter came. "Oh, no, Pop, no. You don't have to talk to him." She stopped and kissed her father's smoothly shaven cheek. "I love you."

"And so you should." He pinched her chin. "Now I can admit that your mother and I are concerned about you, living alone out here and trying to run things all on your own." He grinned and tugged on her hair. "Fact is, your mother claims there's not a reason in the world to worry about you, but I worry just the same."

"You don't have to. The boys and I have a good life. The life we want."

"That's easy to say, but a father considers worrying over his daughters a serious matter. Chantel, well, she gave me enough anxiety as a teenager, so I figure we're past that stage now. And Maddy can talk her way in and out of anything under the sun."

"Like her pop."

He grinned. "Like her pop. But you've been a different matter. Never a minute's trouble with you as a child, and then..." He let his words trail off. It wasn't fair or right to tell her now about the hours he'd spend agonizing over what had happened in her life, the heartbreaks, the struggles. Though he was a caring man, he hadn't grieved for his son-in-law. He had only prayed for his daughter's peace of mind. "But now that I know you're going to be settling down with a man, a good, solid man, if I don't miss my mark, I can rest easy.

The early-morning breeze whispered through her hair. It was warm, almost balmy. What a difference a few weeks could make. "I'm not settling down with Dylan, Pop. It's not like that."

"But you just said—"

"I know what I said." She kicked a small stone out of her path and wished other obstacles could be dealt with as easily. "He won't stay, Pop. This isn't the life for him. And I can't go, because this is the life for me."

"I've never heard such a barrel of nonsense." She opened the barn door, and though it hadn't been his intention to actually go in, he was compelled to follow. He'd led his family over the country, crisscrossing, overlapping, circling. Shouldn't he be able to lead his Abby where she already wanted to go? "People in love make certain adjustments. Not sacrifices." Abby knew her father didn't believe in sacrifices. "Compromises and such, Abby. You didn't have that with the other..." He wouldn't say Chuck's name. His throat simply closed over it. "That's because it takes two people to compromise. If one's doing all the adjusting, it's like a rubber band. It's either going to fly away or break."

She studied him. He wasn't a handsome man, but he was an engaging one, with his small, agile build and animated face. Often he played the clown, because bringing laughter was what he felt he'd been fashioned for. But he was no fool.

"You're very wise, Pop." Abby kissed him again and remembered all the times he'd been right there when she'd stumbled. "Dylan's nothing like Chuck. And I'm beginning to realize that I'm nothing like the woman who married that excitingly irresponsible man."

"Just how does this man feel about you?"

"I don't know." She hit the lights. "I guess I really don't want to because it would make the situation harder one way or the other. Now don't worry." She put both hands on his spindly shoulders. "I told you I was happy here just as I am. I'm not looking for a man to take care of me, Pop. I did that once before."

"And a poor job he did of it, too."

She had to laugh and kiss him again. When Frank O'Hurley lost his temper, it was quite a scene. "He wasn't made to take care of me, Pop, and I just couldn't take care of him. You know very well that's not what marriage is about. It's a team, like you and Mom."

"Those two young boys need a man around."

"I know that." That was where the guilt ultimately came from. "I can't give them everything."

He cut himself off because he heard it in her voice, the faint regret, the obvious guilt. He took her hands and squeezed. "You've done a damn fine job with them. Anyone says different, they have to take on Frank O'Hurley."

She laughed, remembering a few brawls. He might be small, but her father enjoyed a tussle. "Why don't you help me feed the horses instead?"

He drew back a little, naturally cautious. "Well, I don't know about that, Abby girl, I'm a man of the city."

"Come on now, you'll want to see the foal."

She started to walk to the first stall when instinct had her looking into Gladys's. With quick moves, Abby was swinging open the stall door and going to the laboring horse.

"What's the matter? What's the matter?" Her father was practically skipping behind her. "Is it sick? Contagious?"

Abby had to laugh even as she checked the mare. "Having babies isn't a communicable disease, Pop. Go into the kitchen, look in my book and call the vet."

He let loose a string of Irish and American curses. "You need water? Hot water?"

"Just call the vet, Pop, and don't worry. I'm an old hand at this."

He scurried off, and didn't come back. Abby hadn't expected him to. He did send Dylan, though to Abby's surprise, Chantel poked her head in the stall behind him.

"Should we get ready to pass out cigars?"

"Soon enough. Did Pop call the vet?"

"I did." Dylan took his place beside her. "Frank ran into the kitchen demanding boiling water. I think your mother's calming him down. How's Gladys doing?"

"Pretty good." She glanced up at her sister. Chantel was as cool and polished as ever in buff-colored slacks and a silk blouse. "You're up early."

Chantel just shrugged, not bothering to mention that when your life revolved around 6:00 a.m. calls you got in the habit of rising early. "I couldn't miss all the excitement.'' Then, because her heart went out to the mare, female to female, she crouched down. ''Anything I can do?''

''It's nearly done,'' Abby announced.

And so she and Dylan delivered their second foal, working together in a kind of unstated partnership that had Chantel's eyes narrowing. Perhaps she'd misjudged him, she thought. But she wasn't accustomed to misjudging a man. Not any longer.

''What's going on?''

Rumpled from a night's sleep and dressed in overalls that swamped her, Maddy staggered in. ''I'm supposed to bring a message to the front. It seems the vet's on call. His service is tracking him down, but it might be a while.'' She yawned hugely. ''Pop's got water boiling on every burner. If the vet doesn't show up soon he's threatening to call the paramedics. You can't even get a cup of coffee in there.''

''We're getting ready to knit four little pink bootees,'' Chantel told her. She brushed off the knees of her slacks as she rose.

''Would you look at that.'' Maddy focused her sleep-bleared eyes on the foal. ''Hey, wait, don't anybody move. I've got to go get my camera. The guys in dance class won't believe it.'' She was off and running.

''Well, now that the excitement's over I think I'll just toddle inside and see if I can get Pop to give up some of his boiling water. I'm dying for coffee.'' Chantel sauntered off, trailing a tantalizing scent behind her.

''Your family's something,'' Dylan murmured.

''Yeah.'' Abby wiped sweat from her face with her shirtsleeve. ''I know.''

* * *

When Maddy suggested riding, Abby rearranged her schedule and saddled Judd. Dylan was working and her parents weren't interested, so it would be the three of them, as it so often had been in the past. She watched Maddy adjust a stirrup with breezy confidence before she turned to Chantel.

"Need some help?"

"Oh, I think I can manage." Chantel fastened the cinch on the little mare.

"I didn't think you rode at all." Cautious, Abby rechecked the saddle. "But Matilda here is gentle."

Chantel adjusted the collar of her blouse. "We'll just poke along."

Once outside, Maddy swung into the saddle with athletic ease. Chantel hesitated, fumbled and finally managed to mount the mare. Abby decided to keep Judd to a walk beside her sister. "We can go up this road. It runs along the east side of the property where we'll be planting hay in a couple of weeks."

"Planting hay." Chantel's mare stood soberly while she looked lazily around. "How rural of you."

Maddy chuckled. "Okay, Miss Hollywood, let's ride."

Chantel shifted down in the saddle. "Better, Miss New York, let's race." As Abby's mouth dropped open, Chantel pressed her heels to the mare's sides and lunged forward. Maddy started to shout a warning, then realized it wasn't necessary. Chantel was laughing and riding beautifully.

"Always full of surprises," Maddy said to Abby.

Abby skimmed her own heels over Judd. "What are we waiting for?"

For more than half a mile she rode free, easily matching Maddy's pace. It brought memories of childhood. Chantel had always been the leader then, as well. Even with the grueling schedules of trains and buses and one-night stands, they'd managed to fight and play like most children. Even prior to birth, they'd had each other. Nothing had changed that.

They pulled up, breathless and laughing, where Chantel waited at the top of the crest.

"Where'd you learn to ride like that?" Maddy demanded.

Chantel simply fluffed her hair. "Darling, just because you gulp vitamins and jog ten miles a day doesn't mean you're the only O'Hurley with any athletic ability." When Maddy snorted, she grinned. The Hollywood actress was gone, and Chantel was just a woman enjoying a joke. "I've just come off a Western, Wyoming circa 1870." She arched her back and rolled her eyes. "I swear I spent more time in the saddle than any cattle rustler. Lost a half inch off my hips."

Abby controlled Judd as he danced sideways. "It's not all flashy premieres and lunches at Ma Maison, is it?"

"No." Then she tossed her hair back and shrugged. "But you do what you do best, it you're smart. Isn't that what you're doing?"

Abby glanced around the land she'd fought so hard to keep. "Raising children and planting hay. Yes, I suppose it's what I do best."

"I can't say I envy you, but I do admire you." They began to walk the horses, Chantel in the middle, Abby to the left and Maddy to the right, in the same position they'd used before more audiences than they could have counted.

Maddy adjusted the stride of her horse to match her sisters'. "Do you remember that time in that little place just outside Memphis?"

"The place where all the customers drank straight bourbon and looked as though they could chew raw meat?" Abby shook her hair back and looked at the sky. "God, it's hard to believe we lived through that one."

"Lived through it," Chantel repeated, buffing her nails on her suede jacket. "Darling, we were a smash."

"Yeah, there were about six bottles smashed that night, as I recall."

Remembering made Maddy chuckle. "On opening night I pretend I'm about to play in Mitzie's Place outside Memphis. I tell myself whatever happens can't be as bad."

"What are you going to do when you get back?" Abby asked her. "Are you really leaving *Suzanna's Park*? It looks like it'll have a long run on Broadway."

"Over a year of dancing the same routines, saying the same words." Maddy clicked to her horse as he took an interest in the shrubbery on the side of the road. "I wanted something new, and as it turned out, there's a play in the works now. If they find an angel, we could be in rehearsals in a couple months. I'm a stripper."

"A what?" Chantel and Abby said in unison.

"A stripper. You know, bump, grind, take it off. The character's wonderful, a lady of free spirit and morals who meets the guy of her dreams and pretends she's a librarian. And no, I won't actually bare my full talent on stage. We want to bring in the family crowd, as well.''

''What about you, Chantel? Taking a break?'' Abby asked.

''Who could stand it? I'm going to start shooting a miniseries in about ten days. Did you read *Strangers*?''

''God, yes, it was wonderful. I thought...'' Maddy's words trailed off, and her eyes widened. ''You're going to play Hailey. Oh, Chantel, what a wonderful part. Abby, did you read it?''

''No, I don't get a lot of time to read anymore.'' It was said simply, without malice.''

''It's all about this—''

''Maddy.'' Chantel cut her off as they rode beside a big spreading elm. ''Let's not give her the whole story line. You can watch it in the comfort of your own home in a few months, Abby.''

It no longer surprised her that she could indeed snuggle on the living room sofa and watch her sister on television. ''Somehow I never thought you'd do TV again,'' Abby commented.

''Neither did I, but the script was too good. Anyway, it might be interesting to go back.'' She rarely admitted she liked challenges. The image of glamour and ease had been too hard-won. ''I haven't worked the small screen since my sensuous-shampoo and brighter-than-white-toothpaste ads.'' They were far enough away from the house now, and Abby seemed relaxed. Chantel and Maddy exchanged a glance. Agreement needed no words.

''What about you, Abby?'' Chantel tugged on the reins and skirted around easily to put Abby in the middle. ''What's the story with you and Crosby?''

"The story," she said simply, "*is* what Dylan came here to write. I have to tell it, at least parts of it."

"Does feeling the way you do about him make it easier?"

Abby absorbed Maddy's question. She didn't have to tell either of her sisters that she was in love. They could feel it almost as strongly as she did. "In some ways. I'd planned to, well ... I guess I'd planned to restructure the facts. That doesn't work with Dylan, because he knows just by looking at me whether or not I'm being up-front with him. So I have to tell him the truth."

Chantel felt her temper start to rise. "Have you told him what a bitch Janice Rockwell is? How she treated you and the boys after Chuck died?"

"That's not really relevant, is it?"

"Well, I for one would like to read it in black and white," Maddy muttered. "What she did was criminal."

"What she did was perfectly within the law," Abby corrected. "Just because it wasn't right doesn't mean it wasn't legal. Anyway, I think I'm better off the way things turned out. Made me shape up."

"I think he should know it all," Chantel insisted. "All the details, all the angles. Race driver's wealthy mother leaves widow and children impoverished."

"Oh, Chantel, it wasn't as bad as that. We were hardly begging for pennies."

"It was as bad as that," she corrected. "Abby, if you're going to trust him with some, you should trust him with everything."

"She's right." Maddy was silent a moment. The sun was warm and bright, the scent of new grass pungent, but she could sense the turmoil within her sister. "I thought the whole idea was a mistake, but now that it's being done, it should be done properly. Look, I know there were plenty of things you didn't tell us. You didn't have to. Don't you think you'd feel better, feel freer, if you finally got it all out?''

"I'm not thinking of me. I've learned to deal with it. I'm thinking of the boys."

"Do you think they don't know?" Chantel said quietly.

"No." She looked down at her hands, voicing what she'd been avoiding for the longest time. "They know; not the details, but they've sensed the mood. What they don't know now they'll find out sooner or later. I just want Dylan to write it with enough compassion so when they're old enough they can accept it all."

"Does he have any?" Chantel asked her.

"Any what?"

"Compassion."

"Yes." Abby smiled then, relaxing again. "A surprisingly large amount."

That was something Chantel intended to test for herself. "How does he feel about you?"

"He cares." In unspoken agreement, they turned the horses back. "I think he cares more than he ever bargained for, not only about me but the kids. It won't make any difference when he's finished. He'll leave."

"Then you have to make him stay."

Abby smiled at Maddy. "You got all the optimism. Chantel got all the guile."

"Thank you very much." Only half-amused, Chantel picked up the pace.

"Maddy can just believe strongly enough and things happen. You make them happen. I just shuffle around the cards I've been dealt until I have the best hand I can manage. I can't make Dylan stay, because if he asked, I couldn't go. I'm not eighteen and impulsive anymore. I have two children.''

Chantel held her head high and let the wind take her hair. It was a sensation of absolute freedom she couldn't often allow herself. ''I don't see why you should make him stay in the first place. Some women put too much emphasis on having a man complete their lives. They should be fulfilled in the first place— then a man might be a nice addition.''

''Spoken like a true heartbreaker,'' Maddy put in.

''I don't break hearts.'' Chantel smiled slowly. ''I only bruise them a little.''

''I'll gag any minute,'' Maddy said to her horse. ''In any case, just because you and I aren't ready to settle down doesn't mean that Abby isn't entitled to dirty dishes in the sink and someone to take out the garbage.''

''An interesting description of a meaningful relationship,'' Abby murmured. ''As the only one of the three of us who's ever been married, I feel qualified to say that there's a bit more to it than that.''

''Hold on, Abby.'' Concerned, Chantel slowed her horse. ''Who's talking marriage? I'm not saying you shouldn't have a good time with him, enjoy him, certainly, but you can't seriously be thinking about locking yourself in again.''

''Another interesting description,'' Maddy commented, making Abby laugh.

''If I thought we had a shot at it and if I could find a foothold for compromise, I'd ask him myself.''

''Then go for it.'' The sun shot a halo around Maddy's bright, rumpled hair. ''If you love him, if he's right for you, why anticipate problems?''

Chantel gave a quick, amused laugh. "The bulk of this woman's experience with men has been limited to socializing with dancers who stand in front of mirrors all day and admire themselves."

"Dylan's not a dancer," Maddy pointed out, unbruised. "And the actors you spend time with can't figure out who they really are after a day on the set."

"Jaded." Abby shook her head and struggled not to laugh. "I think all of us better stay single."

"Amen to that," Chantel breathed.

"Who has time for romance, anyway?" Maddy commented. "Between dance classes, rehearsals and matinees, I'm too tired for candlelight and roses. Who needs men?"

"Darling, that depends on whether you're talking about a permanent addition or an occasional escort."

"You're starting to believe your own press," Abby said as the house came into view.

"Why shouldn't I?" Chantel lifted a brow. "Everyone else does." With a laugh and a kick of her heels, she plunged ahead.

"Damned if she's going to beat me again!" Maddy was off like a shot.

Abby took a moment to smile after them before she signaled to Judd, knowing his long, powerful stride would bring her in ahead of her sisters.

Chapter Twelve

The moonlight was soothing, thin white, and quiet as it fell over the bed. The house, though silent, almost seemed to ring with the echo of voices and laughter, music—the music her family created wherever they went. Her mother playing the banjo while her father danced. Her father playing while all of them sang. Tomorrow they would be gone, but Abby thought it would be a long time before those echoes faded completely.

Content but far from sleepy, she cradled her head on Dylan's shoulder and just listened.

It was silly, she supposed, to feel as though she was stealing this time with him. With her family in the house, being with him was like walking on eggshells. He must have felt something of it as well. Now he came to her late at night, after the others were asleep, and left early, at first light.

They hadn't discussed it. He'd seemed to have understood that she would feel awkward. She was a grown woman, a widow, the mother of two, but she felt entirely too much like a daughter when her parents were under the same roof.

They might laugh about it later, but for now the echoing silence was too lovely.

He was listening to his own echoes. The phone calls he'd made while Abby had been occupied with her family had added more pieces to the puzzle. He didn't like all of them. When her family was gone the questions would start again, but he already had a number of answers.

It was more important to him now that she tell him things he was already aware of, that she trusted him with secrets he already knew. When she did, if she did, maybe they could put yesterdays behind them and deal with tomorrows.

"Are you asleep?"

"No." He brushed his lips over her hair. Tonight was the last night for pretenses, and he wanted badly to give her whatever she needed. "I was thinking of your parents. I've never met anyone like them."

"I'm not sure there is anyone like them." It pleased her. Abby let her eyes half close as memories fluttered through her head.

"The only thing that scared me was that your father was really insisting he could teach me to tap-dance."

"The thing is, Pop could teach anyone to dance. I'm living proof." She yawned and settled more comfortably against him.

"They'll take the limo to the bus station and travel to Chicago."

"For a three-day gig." She smiled a little, picturing them going over their routine in a cramped motel room. "Chantel wanted to put them on a plane, first class. They wouldn't hear of it. Mom said she'd managed to get where she was going for fifty years without leaving the ground and saw no reason to start now."

"Your mother's a sensible woman."

"I know. Sort of a contradiction in terms, isn't it? I think if she ever found herself in suburbia, with a lawn and a chain-link fence, she'd go crazy. She found the perfect partner when she hooked up with Pop."

"How long have they been together?"

"Hmmm. About thirty-five years now."

He was silent for a moment. "Kind of lifts your confidence in the institution."

"I think one of the reasons I married so quickly was that Mom and Pop made it seem so easy. For them, it really is. I'm going to miss them."

He heard the wistfulness in her voice and drew her closer. "Never a dull moment. I thought you were going to lose a couple of lamps when Frank decided to teach the boys how to juggle."

Abby turned her face into his shoulder as she laughed. "There won't be an apple worth eating until Ben gets it out of his system."

"Better than having him throw them at Chris."

"Every time." She lifted her head, and though she was still smiling, her eyes were serious as she looked down at him. "I'm glad you were here to meet them. Someday you might be traveling through some small, half-forgotten town and see their names on a marquee. You'll remember me."

In a habit he knew would be hard to break, he combed his fingers through her hair. "Do you think I'll need a marquee?"

"It wouldn't hurt." Lowering her mouth, she let it linger on his, warm and sweet. "I'd like to think you'd remember this." She brushed her hand through his hair, then skimmed her lips over his temple. "And that."

"I've a good memory, Abby." He took her wrists. The pulses in them were just beginning to quicken. "A very good memory."

Still holding her, he rolled over, pinning her body with his. There it was, instantly, that splinter of excitement, that calming feeling of rightness. With his lips, he found hers. He didn't release her hands. Not yet. Somehow he knew if she touched him then, he'd explode, go mad, take frantically what he wanted to savor. They had all night, they had years. If he believed hard enough, they had forever. So he held himself a prisoner as much as he held her, letting his lips soothe, arouse and entice.

He sucked at her tongue, drawing it deep into his mouth, teasing it with his own. Feeling her breath shudder against his mouth, he groaned at the sensation. At each move, her body sank into the mattress, strong enough to take, pliant enough to give. Still holding her wrists, he skimmed down the long line of her throat. There was pulse hammering, a flavor tempting. He could have spent hours exploring each tiny spot where her blood pulsed close to the surface. He felt at home. Her body offered him both peace and rest, passion and excitement. He had only to take what he needed most.

She loved him. It was a wild, terrifying thought. Yet when he released her wrists her arms wrapped around his so naturally, hands soothing and tormenting all at once. She asked for nothing, and by doing so asked for more than he'd thought he could ever give again.

He was so gentle. Abby wondered if she'd ever get used to the quiet tenderness beneath the fire. His hands molded, caressed. At times his fingers dug unheedingly into her flesh, but there was always such underlying care, such overlying sweetness.

Whenever she heard his breath grow uneven, she was amazed. She reveled in feeling his muscles quiver and tense beneath her exploring hands. It was for her, from her, with her. Never before, not even in her dreams, had there been a man with such a compelling need for her.

Yet she wondered if he knew. Even as they took each other deep and fast, feeling the blood heat the surface of their skin, she wondered if he knew what that beyond wanting her, beyond desiring her, he needed her in his life.

Unless he did, their relationship would end when he had his answers. And she'd already promised to give them to him.

"Dylan." The sudden stark realization ran through her that he was slipping through her fingers just when she'd learned to grab hold. She had no tricks, no wiles, knew no secret ways to keep a man and bind him to her. She could only give him what was in her heart and hope it was enough for both of them.

He heard his name come softly from her. He felt the sigh run deep inside her. Because he felt she needed it, he brought his lips back to hers and let her take what she wanted.

"Slowly." He slipped inside her, cushioning her gasp with his mouth. "I want to watch you climb, Abby."

The flickers of passion, of pleasure, of wonder on her face aroused him more than he'd ever imagined possible. He'd thought he wasn't the sort of man to give, but with her he was driven to. For years he'd taken, sometimes carelessly, often selfishly. It was never like that with Abby. It left him shaken. It left him wondering.

Between packing, last-minute details and Saturday-morning cartoons, everyone in the house was occupied. Chantel bided her time. When Dylan went to help the boys tend the stock, she waited a few moments, then slipped out to join them. It was warm for March by East Coast standards, but she shivered inside her jacket and decided she'd be glad to get back to Southern California. Before she went, she had something to do.

Most of the horses were in the paddock. Chantel wandered over to lean on the fence. He'd come out sooner or later. She could wait.

Dylan let out the two geldings and saw her. He'd known for days that she had something to say to him. It appeared the time was now. He released the horses and carefully closed the gate behind them. In silence he moved over and joined her at the fence. She took the cigarette he offered. She rarely smoked; it all had to do with mood. She inhaled deeply then let out a long stream of smoke, watching the horses as she spoke.

"I haven't decided if I like you. It's not really important. Abby's feelings are."

Dylan decided she couldn't know how closely her words echoed Maddy's. It was just part of the bond. Together they watched as Eve's foal began to nurse. The mare steadied herself against the pull and tug, then stood patiently.

"I can tell you I didn't like you when you interviewed me about Millicent Driscoll for your last book. Some of it had to do with that period of my life, and the rest was your attitude. I found you abrasive and unsympathetic, so I wasn't as open with you as I might have been. If I had been, maybe you'd have found a little more room for compassion in your story. But Abby's my sister."

For the first time, she turned to look at him. Even in the strong, unrelenting sunlight, her face was stunning. The classic oval shape, the sweep of cheekbone, the flawless skin. A man could look at that face and forget there was anything else to the woman. But it was her eyes that held his interest. He imagined they'd ruthlessly flayed a great many men.

"I think you care about Abby, but I'm not sure if you're too tough to let that matter. I want to tell you about Chuck Rockwell in a way I don't think Abby can." She drew in more smoke, appreciating its rough taste. "This is off-the-record, Dylan. If Abby consents to this you can use anything I say. If she doesn't, you're out of luck. Agreed?"

"Agreed. Tell me."

"When Chuck came into the club that first night, he was utterly infatuated with Abby. Maybe, for a little while, he was even in love with her. I don't know the kind of women he'd been running with before, but I can imagine. Abby, was, even with the tacky costume and greasepaint, untouched. Gullible's a hard word unless you understand the person, and Abby was and still is gullible.'' She smiled, not the clever, ice-edged smile she used so often but a simple, easy curving of the lips that was as beautiful as it was revealing. ''She believed in love, devotion, till death us do part. She went into marriage with stars in her eyes.''

He could imagine Abby then, open, innocent, trusting. ''And Rockwell?''

''He loved her, I think, as far as he was capable and for as long as he was capable. Some people say weakness doesn't make a person bad.'' Something flickered in her eyes but was quickly masked. ''I disagree with that. Chuck was weak emotionally. I could make excuses for him, knowing that he was raised by an impossibly domineering mother and a workaholic father. Personally, I don't care much for excuses.''

She glanced over, waiting for him to comment. ''Go on.'' Dylan had already researched Rockwell's upbringing.

''They had trouble almost from the start. She'd cover it up, but it's difficult to hide anything from another triplet. She went with him to Paris, London, wore beautiful clothes and was offered the sort of lifestyle a lot of women dream of. Not Abby.'' Chantel shook her head, and her fingers began to drum lightly on the fence rail. ''I'm not saying she didn't enjoy it at first, but Abby had always looked for roots. The O'Hurleys have a difficult time sinking them.''

''That's why she wanted this place.''

Chantel dropped her cigarette on the ground and left it to smolder. ''Chuck bought it after a particularly messy affair with a girl too young to know any better. Then, almost as soon as he did, he grew bored with it. He made it clear to Abby that if she wanted to keep the place and maintain it she had to do it herself.''

"She told you that?"

"No. Chuck did.'' She sent him an odd, self-mocking look. "He breezed into L.A. and decided it might be interesting to put the moves on his wife's sister. Charming. Give me another cigarette.''

While he lit if for her, Chantel composed herself. "As it happened, he wasn't my type, and though my morals are often in doubt, I do have standards. He did manage to get drunk and tell me all the problems he was having with the little woman at home. She was boring.'' Chantel blew out a vicious stream of smoke. "She was too ordinary, too middle-class. She'd dug into this farm and was holding on, and he had better things to do with his money. If she wanted the damn roof fixed, she could deal with it herself. If she wanted the plumbing brought up to twentieth-century standards, she'd just have to figure out how to manage it on her own. He wasn't interested. He went on about how she had this wild idea to raise horses. He laughed at her." Chantel's jaw stiffened. When she realized she was speaking too quickly, she deliberately slowed. "I didn't throw him out, because I wanted to hear it all. While she'd been going through this, I'd been busy carving out my own career. Too busy, you see, to pay much attention, even though I knew instinctively that things weren't right with Abby.''

And how much attention had *he* really paid over the past weeks? That thought stung him. He'd expected her trust and honesty—had demanded it—but all he'd given her were questions.

He'd seen her, listened to her, watched her, and he'd known in his gut that all the preconceptions he'd come

with were wrong. Yet why had she stayed with
Rockwell? And why did he hate himself for still needing to know?

He drew back, "Why do you think he told you all
this?" he asked his voice unemotional.

Her look was hard. It was amazing how quickly her
expression could change from cool to frigid without
her moving a muscle. "Obviously he thought I'd be
just as amused as he." She smiled again and drew
more calmly on her cigarette. "Anyway, I got rid of
him, then I called Maddy and we came here. Abby was
living in a place that was nearly ready to fall down
around her ears. Chuck wasn't giving her a dime, so
she was working part-time at places she could take Ben
along. She was glad to see us, but she wasn't ready to
listen to any advice that led to divorce."

"Why?" Dylan touched her for the first time, just
a hand on her arm, but she could feel the intensity of
his response. "Why did she stay with him?"

So, that was the crux of it, Chantel realized. He
cared, and that made it difficult to hold her grudge
against him. "I think you'll need to get that answer
from her, but I can tell you this. Abby has a large capacity for hope, and she kept believing that Chuck
would come around. Meantime, there was the imme-
diate problem of making the house livable. We went
to Richmond and sold her jewelry. Chuck had been
very generous in the first six or eight months of their
marriage and it brought in enough to get her going. I
bought her mink." What she didn't mention was that
she hadn't been able to afford it at the time. "She
joked later that she saw a picture of me wearing her
roof."

"She sold the mink to fix the roof," he murmured.

"There were a lot of repairs. It amazed me then how stubborn she was about this place. But when I see her here now, it's obvious how right it is for her and the kids. After that, things settled down a bit. She was pregnant with Chris. I have my own theory on that, but it's best left alone."

He looked at her and saw that she understood more than Abby would ever have guessed. "It's being left alone."

"Maybe I do like you." She relaxed a little and tossed the cigarette aside. "After Chris was born, things went from bad to worse. Chuck was blatant about his affairs. I don't consider it a point in his credit, but I believe he wanted to push Abby into a divorce for her own good. When she did, when she finally did, I think he realized just how much he was losing."

"Are you saying that Abby had filed for divorce?"

"That's right. She could have raked him over the coals—I certainly would have—but she didn't charge him with adultery and she didn't ask for alimony. All she wanted was the farm and some reasonable support for the kids. He was involved with Lori Brewer at the time, and they went on quite a binge. Somewhere along the line, it must have hit him. He'd compensated for the loss of the thrill of racing with other things. He'd had a wife who'd stuck by him and two wonderful children he'd traded for a life-style that only led to more misery. I know how he felt because he called me a few days before that last race. God knows why. I was hardly sympathetic. He said he'd called Abby and had asked her to reconsider and she'd refused. He wanted me to go to bat for him. I told him to grow up. A couple days later, he crashed."

"And she was left feeling guilty because she'd planned to divorce him."

"You catch on." She tapped a beautifully manicured nail against the rail. "There's never been any use telling her not to feel that way, or not to let herself be punished."

Dylan was having problems enough with his own sense of guilt, but he focused on Chantel's last words. "What do you mean, punished?"

"Did you ever consider how difficult it is to maintain a place like this, to raise two children—I'm not speaking of emotionally or physically now, but financially."

"Rockwell had plenty of money."

"Rockwell did—Janice Rockwell did, and she still does. Abby didn't get a penny." She shook her head before he could interrupt her. Every time she thought of it she tasted venom. "She saw to it that Abby didn't get a penny of Chuck's trust fund, not for herself, not for the farm, not for the children."

While Chantel tasted venom, something like acid rose in Dylan's throat. Everything he'd said to Abby from the first day in the rain dreary kitchen to the morning he'd watched her drop rubber gloves in her purse came back to him. And he realized, as his stomach twisted, that he'd have to live with that.

"How has she managed to hold on to the farm?"

"She took out a loan."

There was a bitter taste in his mouth that had nothing to do with tobacco. He hadn't believed in her, hadn't trusted his own feelings enough. She'd been too proud to tell him the things Chantel was saying now.

The hell with her pride, he thought suddenly, viciously. Didn't he have a right to know? Didn't he have a right to... Checking his thoughts, he stared over the paddock and to the hills beyond. No, it was *his* pride that was bruised, he realized, both the man's and the reporter's. She'd known what he'd thought of her, and she'd accepted it—and him.

"Why are you telling me this?"

"Because someone has to convince Abby that it wasn't her fault, that she couldn't have prevented anything that happened. I think you're the one to do it. I think you're the man, if you've got the spine for it, to make her happy."

Her chin was up, her eyes dark as she tossed the challenge at him. Dylan found himself smiling. "You're a hell of a woman. I missed that the first time around."

She smiled back. "Yeah. I missed a few things about you, too."

Maddy stuck her head out of the back door. "Chantel, the limo's here."

"I'm coming." She took a step back, then gave him one last piercing look. "One more thing, Dylan. If you hurt Abby, you're going to have to deal with me."

"Fair enough."

He offered his hand. As though she were amused by both of them, Chantel accepted it. "I guess I'll wish you luck."

"I appreciate it."

The goodbyes were long, tearful and noisy. Maddy came to Dylan and gave him a surprisingly hard and affectionate hug. "Lucky for you I think you're good for her," she whispered in his ear. Then she backed off with a smile. "Welcome to the family, Dylan."

Each member made the rounds twice before climbing into the limo. Chris and Ben had to be coaxed out once they discovered all the knobs and automatic buttons inside the car. After they'd raised and lowered the windows half a dozen times, blasting the stereo and the sleek compact TV, Abby pulled them out so that the rest of her family could climb in. Serene as an ocean liner, the limo cruised up the rut-filled lane.

"I'm going to drive a limo," Chris decided on the spot. "I can wear a neat hat like the one Mr. Donald had and ride in the front seat."

"I'd rather ride in the back with the TV."

Laughing, Abby ruffled Ben's hair. "There's a lot of O'Hurley in this boy. I don't know about you, but I want something long and cold before I tackle the mess in the kitchen."

"Can we go play with the foals?" Ben was already off the porch as he asked.

"Not too rough," Abby called after them. With a sigh, she turned into the house. "I miss them already."

"Quite a family."

"To say the least. Do you want a soda?"

"No." Restless, he wandered around the kitchen. Chantel's words were still eating at him. That, and everything else he'd learned over the last couple of days. The fact that he'd misjudged Abby so completely and so unfairly left him unsure of himself. "Abby, this place, the farm, it's very important to you."

"Aside from the boys, it's the most important." She filled a glass with ice.

"You're not a pushover." He said it so strongly that she turned back to stare at him.

"I don't like to think so."

"Why did you let Rockwell push you around?" he demanded. "Why did you let his mother push you out of everything you were entitled to?"

"Wait a minute." She'd expected a day, even a few hours, before she had to plunge into it all again. "Janice had virtually nothing to do with the rest of it, certainly nothing to do with Chuck's biography."

"The hell with the biography." He took her by the arms. It wasn't until that moment that he realized the book meant nothing, had meant nothing for some time. Abby meant everything. He could only see what she'd been through, what she had done, what had been done to her. If she wouldn't hate, he would hate for her. "She made certain you didn't get a penny of Rockwell's trust fund. With that money the farm would have been free and clear. You were entitled, your children were entitled. Why did you tolerate that?"

"I don't know where you got your information." She struggled to keep her voice calm. There had been bitterness long ago, and she'd swallowed it. She had no desire to taste it again. "Janice had control of the trust. Chuck would have inherited at thirty-five, but he didn't live that long. The money was hers."

"Do you really think that would have stood up in court?"

"I wasn't interested in going to court. Chuck left us some money."

"What was left after he'd blown most of it away."

Abby nodded, keeping her voice even. This was an old argument, one she'd had with herself years before. "Enough so I can be sure that the kids can go to college."

"In the meantime you had to take out a loan just to keep a roof over their heads."

It humiliated her. He couldn't know how it had humiliated her to ask for money, how it embarrassed her that Dylan was now aware of it. "Dylan, that isn't your concern."

"I'm making it my concern. You're my concern. Do you know how it made me feel to know that you're scrubbing some woman's floors?"

She let out an impatient huff of air. "What difference does it make whose floors I scrub?"

"It makes a big difference to me because I don't want you—I can't stand thinking of you..." He swore and tried again. "You could have been honest with me, maybe not at first, but later, after we'd come to mean something to each other."

To mean *what*? she wanted to ask. At least she'd been honest about her feelings. She took the coffeepot from the stove and calmly moved to the sink to fill it with soapy water. "I was as honest as I could be. If it had only been me, I might have told you everything, but I had to think of the boys."

"I wouldn't do anything to hurt them. I couldn't."

"Dylan, why should any of this be important?" She wasn't calm, she thought. Damn it, she wasn't calm at all. She could feel anger building up and throbbing in her head. "It's only money. Can't you just let it go?"

"It's not just about money, and no, I can't let it go. You haven't let it go either or you'd have been able to tell me about it." The frustration hit him, the guilt, the anger. And suddenly he flashed back to the picture of her, wrapped like a princess in white fur. "You sold that damn white mink to fix the roof."

Baffled, she shook her head. "What difference does that make? I hardly need a mink to feed the stock."

"You knew what I thought of you." Dylan's anger with himself only made him more unreasonable with her. "You let me go on thinking that. Even when I was busy falling in love with you, you never really trusted me with all of it. Double-talk and evasions, Abby. You never told me you were going to divorce him, you never told me you had to struggle just to keep food on the table. Do you know how it makes me feel to find out all of these things in bits and pieces?"

"Do you know how it makes me feel?" Her voice rose to match his. "Do you know how it feels to rake it all up, to remember what a miserable failure I was?"

"That's ridiculous. You have to know how foolish that statement is."

"I know how foolish I was."

"Abby." His tone roughened, but his hands grew gentle on her arms. "*He* failed you, he failed his children, and he failed himself." He gave her a quick shake, desperate to make her see what she'd done and how much he respected her for it. "You were the one who made things work. You're the one who built a home and a life."

"Stop yelling at my mom."

Rigid and pale, Ben stood just inside the kitchen doorway. Already upset, Abby could do little more than stare at him. "Ben—"

"Let go of my mom." His bottom lip quivered, but the look he sent Dylan was devastatingly man-to-man. "Let go of her and go away. We don't want you here."

Disgusted with himself, Dylan released Abby and turned to the boy. "I wouldn't hurt your mother, Ben."

"You were, I saw you."

"Ben." Abby stepped between them quickly. "You don't understand. We were angry with each other. People sometimes yell at each other when they're angry."

His jaw was set in a way that reminded Abby almost painfully of her father in full temper. "I don't want him to yell at you. I'm not going to let him hurt you."

"Honey, I was yelling back." She said it softly, dropping her hand to stroke his head. "And he wasn't hurting me."

His eyes shone with a mixture of humiliation and anger. "Maybe you like him better than me."

"No, baby—"

"I'm not a baby!" His pale face filled with color as he pushed away. "I'll show you!" Abby was still crouched on the floor as the back door slammed behind him.

"Oh, God." Slowly Abby rose to her feet. "I didn't handle that very well."

"It was my fault." Dylan dragged both hands through his hair. He'd wanted to give, to offer whatever he could to all of them. Instead, he'd managed to hurt Abby and alienate Ben in one instant. "Let me go talk to him."

"I don't know. Maybe I should—oh, my God! Ben, Ben, stop!" She was through the back door before Dylan could call out. He was behind her in an instant, then past her. Ben was mounted on top of

Thunder, and the high-strung stallion was bucking nastily.

Abby's heart lodged in her throat as the boy clung to the horse's back and she couldn't even call his name again. For a moment she thought he'd be able to control the horse and slip off safely, but then the stallion reared so violently that for an instant horse and boy were one form, raised high against the blue sky behind them. Then Ben was tossed off as carelessly as a fly.

She heard his cry mingle with the shrill whinnies of the animal. Slowly, as if suspended in time, she watched, devastated, as hooves danced around Ben's body, miraculously missing him. She tasted her own fear, which rose like rust in her mouth as she raced over the last few feet of ground.

"Ben. Oh, Ben." She wasn't weeping, but along with Dylan began to check his limp body for signs of life.

"He's okay, but he's unconscious. I think his arm's broken." His own hands were shaking. If he'd only been quicker, just a few seconds... "Abby, can you pull the car around?"

Ben lay quietly, his face pale as milk. She wanted to cover his body with hers and weep. "Yes." Glancing up, she saw Chris standing beside her, shaking like a leaf. "Come on, Chris." She took his hand in hers. "We've got to take Ben to the hospital."

"Is he okay? Is he going to be okay?"

"He's going to be fine," she murmured as she hurried for the car.

"Can you drive?" Dylan asked her when she came back. "I don't know the way."

With a nod, she helped him settle her firstborn on his lap in the front seat. Teeth set, she went slowly down the lane, terrified of jolting him with bumps. The moment she got onto the highway, she pressed the accelerator and stopped thinking.

When Ben stirred, she felt tears well up and forced them back. The first whimpering sounds he made became full-fledged sobbing as he regained consciousness fully. She began to talk to him, nonsense, anything that came into her head. From the back seat, Chris leaned up and tentatively stroked Ben's leg. Not knowing what else to do, Dylan held the boy tight in his arms and brushed gently at his hair.

"Almost there, Ben," he murmured. "Just hang on."

"It hurts."

"Yeah, I know." When the boy turned his face into his shirt, Dylan held on. For the first time in his life, he fully understood what it meant to feel someone else's pain.

Abby left the car by the curb outside the emergency room and leaped out to help Dylan with Ben.

It seemed to take hours. Her teeth began to chatter as she gave the admissions clerk insurance information and Ben's medical history. She took deep, gulping breaths and tried to compose herself when they wheeled Ben away for X rays. Her little boy had tried, in his angry way, to prove he was a man. Now he was hurt, and she could only wait. Beside her, Dylan stood holding Chris in his arms.

"Sit down, Abby. It's bound to take some time."

"He's just a little boy." She couldn't fall apart now. Ben was going to need her. But the tears poured out and ran silently down her cheeks. "He was so angry.

He'd never have gotten on the stallion if he hadn't been angry."

"Abby, boys are always breaking bones." But his own stomach was knotted and rolling.

"What's going to happen to Ben?" When he saw his mother's tears, Chris's breath began to hitch.

"He's going to be all right." Abby pushed both hands over her cheeks to dry them. "The doctors are taking care of him."

"I think he's going to have a cast." Dylan ran his hands down Chris's short, sturdy arm. "When it's dry you can sign your name on it."

Chris sniffed and thought about it. "I can only print."

"That'll be fine. Let's sit down."

Abby forced herself not to pace. When Chris climbed into her lap, she had to stop herself from clinging too tightly. With each minute that passed, the empty feeling inside her increased until she knew she was hollow.

She was up and dizzy with fear when the doctor came out.

"A nice clean break," he said to her. Recognizing her anxiety, he gave her shoulder a quick squeeze. "He's going to be a sensation at school with that cast."

"He's... Is there anything else?" Everything from concussion to internal injuries had passed through her mind.

"He's a strong, sturdy boy." His hand still resting lightly on her shoulder, the doctor felt the relief run through her. "He's a little queasy, and he's got some bruises that'll be colorful. I'd like him to rest here for a couple of hours, keep an eye on him, but I don't think you've got anything to worry about. We'll give you a prescription and a list of dos and don'ts. I've already told him he has to stay off wild horses for a while."

"Thank you." She pushed her hands against her eyes for a moment. A broken bone. Bones healed, she thought with relief. "Can I see him now?"

"Right this way."

He looked so small on the white table. She fought back a fresh bout of tears as she went over to hold him. "Oh, Ben, you scared me to death."

"I broke my arm." He was getting used to the idea as he showed off his cast.

"Very impressive." She was already forgiven. Abby could see it in his eyes, feel it in the way his fingers curled into hers. "I guess it hurts, huh?"

"It feels a little better."

Chris walked over to inspect the clean white plaster. "Dylan said I could put my name on it."

"I guess so." Ben looked up for the first time at Dylan. "Maybe you all could. Did Thunder run away?"

"Don't worry about Thunder," Abby told him. "He knows where the grain barrel is."

He stared down at his own fingers, wriggling them tentatively. "I'm sorry."

"No." She cupped a hand under his chin. "I'm sorry. You were standing up for me. Thanks."

He breathed in her familiar scent when she kissed him. He didn't feel so brave now, just tired. "'S okay."

"They want you to stay a little while. I'm going to get your medicine."

"Why don't you and Chris do that, Abby?" Dylan moved closer to the table. "I'd like to talk to Ben awhile."

Because she saw embarrassment rather than anger in Ben's face, she nodded. "All right. We won't be long."

"Can I have a drink?" Ben asked.

"I'll ask the doctor." Bending over, Abby kissed both of his cheeks. "I'm crazy about you, you jerk."

He grinned a little and stared down at his cast. When she glanced over her shoulder from the doorway, he was looking at Dylan.

"I guess you were pretty mad at me," Dylan began.

"I guess."

"Yelling at someone you care about's pretty stupid. Adults can be stupid sometimes."

Ben thought so, too, but he was cautious. "Maybe."

How could he approach the boy? With the truth. He spouted off about honesty, demanded it, expected it. Maybe it was time he gave it. Still cautious, Dylan rested a hip against the table. "I've got a problem, Ben. I was hoping you could help me out with it."

The boy shrugged and began to toy with the edge of the sheet. But he listened.

It was almost dusk when they were home again, settling Ben down and stacking up piles of books and toys for his pleasure. The day had worn him out, and he was asleep before he'd finished his supper. Even while Abby was tucking him in, Dylan carried a dozing Chris up to his room.

"Fell asleep in his pizza," he told Abby with a half grin.

"I'll be right there."

"I can do it. Why don't you do down and fix us both a drink?"

There were a few bottles of wine left over, gifts from Chantel. Abby poured two glasses, then dove into the pizza, realizing she hadn't eaten since early that morning. She was halfway through a piece when the tears started again. She closed the cardboard box carefully, put her head on the counter and wept it all out.

Dylan found her that way and didn't hesitate. He gathered her into his arms, held her close and let her cry against him. "Silly now," she managed. "He's all right. I just keep seeing him in the air, hanging there for that one horrible second."

"I know. But he is all right." He drew her away from him and began wiping away the tears. "In fact, besides one broken bone, he's great."

Abby touched his cheek, then kissed it. "You were great. I don't know what I'd have done without you."

"You'd have done fine." He drew out a cigarette because he was more than a little shaken himself. "That's one of the most intimidating things about you."

"Intimidating?" She hadn't been sure she would ever laugh again, but it was easy. "Me?"

"It isn't easy for a man to get involved with a woman who's totally capable of handling anything that comes along. Running a house, raising children, building a farm. It isn't easy for a man to believe that there are women who can not only do those things but enjoy them."

"I'm not following you, Dylan."

"I don't guess you would." He crushed out the cigarette, discovering he really didn't want it. "It's all natural for you, isn't it? It's incredible."

She picked up his glass and handed it to him. "If I didn't know better, I'd think you'd already been dipping in the wine."

"I'm just beginning to think clearly."

"I am, too." She picked up her glass and sipped. The wine was unfamiliar and wonderfully cool. "I know you were angry with me this morning."

"Abby—"

"No, wait a minute. The last thing you said to me before Ben came in turned on all sorts of lights. I'd like to get it out now—all of it—and end it."

He could have told her that it didn't matter anymore, not to him. But he could see it mattered to her. "Okay."

"You've asked me why I stayed with Chuck. Very simply, I'd stayed because I'd made a promise. Eventually, when I knew I had to break it and end my marriage, I needed to take all the blame. Somehow it was easier for me to go on believing that I'd made a mistake, I'd failed in some way."

Her voice was strained. Abby took another sip of wine, then continued. "But I hadn't made a mistake, Dylan, and I have two beautiful children to prove it. You said Chuck failed himself and you were right. He was capable of so much more, but he made the wrong choices. It's time I admit that I made the right ones. I've got to thank you for that."

"I'll take your gratitude, but it's not what I'm after."

As it had in the hospital waiting room, her stomach worked itself into knots. "I'll never forget what you did, what you've done just by being here."

"I have a hard time hearing you put all that in the past. Don't you want to know what Ben and I talked about while you were gone?"

She looked down at her wine. "I thought you'd tell me if you wanted me to know." Then she smiled up at him. "Besides, I could always get it out of Ben if you didn't."

"That's one of the things I love about you."

She looked at him with eyes that were clouded and no longer calm. "Dylan, this morning when you were shouting, you said—"

"That I'd fallen in love with you. You have a problem with that?"

She was holding her glass with both hands now, but she didn't look away. "I wish I knew."

"Let me explain it to you the way I explained it to Ben." He set his glass down, then took hers and set it on the counter. "I told him I was in love with his mother. And that I was new at being in love and didn't know quite how to handle it. I told him I knew I'd make some mistakes and that I hoped he'd give me a hand."

He combed a hand through her hair, let it rest on her cheek, then removed it. "I told him I knew a little about running a farm, but I didn't have much experience at being a husband and none at being a father, though I wanted to give it a shot."

Her eyes had grown wide, so wide and vulnerable that he wanted to pull her against him and promise to protect her from everything. But there'd be no rash promises with Abby. She'd had rash promises before, and had them broken. He thought second chances should be based on faith. "Are you going to give me a chance?"

She couldn't swallow. She wasn't even sure how she could still manage to breathe. "What did Ben say?"

Smiling, he reached out and touched her cheek. "He thought it sounded like a pretty good idea."

"So do I." She flung herself into his arms. "Oh, Dylan, so do I."

Perhaps it was gratitude he felt, perhaps it was relief. Mixed with it was a sense of coming home at last. "Just don't start thinking about buying cows."

"No. No cows, I promise." When she laughed, he pressed his mouth to hers. There was everything— love, trust, hope. There were second chances in life, and they'd found theirs.

"Abby..." He could spend hours just holding her.

"Mmm-hmm?"

"Do you think we could talk your father into dancing at our wedding?"

Her eyes laughed at him. "I'd hate to see you try to stop him."

*　*　*　*　*

DANCE TO
THE PIPER

Prologue

During the break between lunch and cocktails, the club was empty. The floors were scarred but clean enough, and the paint on the walls was only a little dull from fighting with cigarette smoke. There was the scent intrinsic to such places—old liquor and stale perfume mixed with coffee that was no longer fresh. To a certain type of person it was as much home as a cozy fire and plump cushions. The O'Hurleys made their home wherever audiences gathered.

When the after-dinner crowd strolled in, the lights would be dimmed, and it wouldn't look so grimy. Now, strong sunlight shone through the two small windows and lighted the dust and dents mercilessly. The mirror in back of a bar lined with bottles spread some of the light around but reflected mostly on the small stage in the center of the room.

"That's my girl, Abby, put a nice smile on."

Frank O'Hurley took his five-year-old triplets through the short dance routine he wanted to add to the show that night, demonstrating the prissy moves with his wiry body. They were playing a family hotel at a nice, reasonably priced resort in the Poconos. He figured the audience would have a soft spot for three little girls.

"I wish you'd time your brainstorms better, Frank." His wife, Molly, sat at a corner table, hurriedly sewing bows on the white dresses her daughters would wear in a few hours. "I'm not a bloody seamstress, you know."

"You're a trouper, Molly my love, and the best thing that ever happened to Frank O'Hurley."

"There's nothing truer than that," she muttered, but smiled to herself.

"All right, my darlings, let's try it again." He smiled at the three little angels God had blessed him with in one fell swoop. If the Lord saw fit to present him with three babies for the price of one, Frank figured the Lord was entitled to a sense of humor.

Chantel was already a beauty, with a round cherub's face and dark blue eyes. He winked at her, knowing she was more interested in the bows on the dress she'd wear than in the routine. Abby was all amiability. She'd dance because her pop wanted her to and because it would be fun to be onstage with her sisters. Frank urged her to smile again and demonstrated the curtsy he wanted.

Maddy, with an elfin face and hair already hinting toward red, mimicked his move perfectly, her eyes never leaving his. Frank felt his heart swell with love for the three of them. He laid his hand on his son's shoulder.

"Give us a two-bar intro, Trace, my boy. A snappy one."

Trace obligingly ran his fingers over the keys. It was Frank's regret he couldn't afford lessons for the boy. What Trace knew of playing he'd learned from watching and listening. Music rang out, jumpy and bright.

"How's that, Pop?"

"You're a pistol." Frank rubbed a hand over Trace's head. "Okay, girls, let's take it from the top."

He worked them another fifteen minutes, patiently, making them giggle at their mistakes. The five-minute routine would be far from perfect, but he was shrewd enough to recognize the charm of it. They'd expand the act bit by bit as they went on. It was the off-season at the resort now, but if they made a bit of a mark they'd secure a return engagement. Life for Frank was made up of gigs and return engagements. He saw no reason his family shouldn't be of the same mind.

Still, the minute he saw Chantel losing interest he broke off, knowing her sisters wouldn't be far behind.

"Wonderful." He bent to give each of them a smacking kiss, as generous with affection as he'd have liked to be with money. "We're going to knock them dead."

"Is our name going on the poster?" Chantel demanded, and Frank roared with delighted laughter.

"Want billing, do you, my little pigeon? Hear that, Molly?"

"Doesn't surprise me." She set down her sewing to rest her fingers.

"Tell you what, Chantel, you get billing when you can do this." He started a slow, deceptively simple tap routine, holding a hand out to his wife. Smiling, Molly rose to join him. A dozen years of dancing together had them moving in unison from the first step.

Abby slid onto the piano bench beside Trace and watched. He began to improvise a silly little tune that made Abby smile.

"Chantel's going to practice till she can do it," he murmured.

Abby smiled up at him. "Then we'll all get our names on the poster."

"I can show you how," he whispered, listening to his parents' feet strike the wooden stage.

"Will you show us all how?"

As an old man of ten, Trace was amused by the way his little sisters stuck together. He'd have gotten the same response from any of them. "I just might."

Content, she settled back against his shoulder. Her parents were laughing, enjoying the exertion, the rhythm. It seemed to Abby that her parents were always laughing. Even when her mother got that cross look on her face, Pop would make her laugh. Chantel was watching, her eyes narrowed, experimenting a bit but not quite catching the movements. She'd get mad, Abby knew. But when she got mad, she made sure she got what she wanted.

"I want to do it," Maddy said from the corner of the stage.

Frank laughed. With his arms around Molly's waist, the two of them circled the stage, feet tapping, sliding, shuffling. "Do you now, little turnip?"

"I *can* do it," she told him, and with a stubborn look on her face she began to tap her feet—heel, toe, toe, heel—until she was moving center stage.

Caught off balance, Frank stopped on a dime, and Molly bumped heavily into him. "Look at that, will you, Molly."

Pushing her hair out of her eyes, Molly watched her youngest daughter struggling to capture the basics of their tap routine. And she was doing it. She felt a mixture of pride and regret only a mother would understand. "Looks like we'll be buying another set of taps, Frank."

"That it does." Frank felt twice the pride and none of the regret. He released his wife to concentrate on his daughter. "No, try this now." He took the moves slowly. Hop, shuffle, stamp. Brush, step, brush, step, and step to the side. He took Maddy's hand and, careful to keep his steps small to match hers, moved again. She moved right with him.

"Now this." His excitement growing, he looked at his son. "Give me a downbeat. Listen to the count, Maddy. One and two and three and four. Tap. No body weight here. Toe stab front, then back. Now a riff." Again he demonstrated, and again she imitated the steps.

"We'll put it all together now and end with a step slide, arms like this, see?" He brought his arms out to the side in a sharp, glitzy move, then winked at her. "You're going to sell it."

"Sell it," she repeated, frowning in concentration.

"Give us the count, Trace." Frank took her hand again, feeling the pleasure build as she moved in unison with him. "We've got ourselves a dancer here, Molly!" Frank hefted Maddy into his arms and let her fly. She squealed, not because she feared he wouldn't catch her but because she knew he would.

The sensation of dropping through the air was every bit as thrilling as the dance itself had been. She wanted more.

Chapter One

Five, six, seven, eight!

Twenty-four feet hit the wooden floor in unison. The echo was wonderful. Twelve bodies twisted, swooped and plunged as one. Mirrors threw their images right back at them. Arms flowed out on signal, legs lifted, heads tilted, turned, then fell back.

Sweat rolled. And the scent was the theater.

The piano banged out notes, and the melody swelled in the old rehearsal hall. Music had echoed there before, feet had responded, heartbeats had raced and muscles had ached. It would happen again and again, year after year, for as long as the building stood.

Many stars had rehearsed in that room. Showbusiness legends had polished routines on the same boards. Countless unknown and unremembered line dancers had worked there until their muscles had gone stringy with fatigue. It was a Broadway that the paying public rarely saw.

The assistant choreographer, his glasses fogging a bit in the steamy heat, clapped out the beat constantly as he shouted the moves. Beside him the choreographer, the man who had sculpted the dance, stood watching with eyes as dark and alert as a bird's.

"Hold it!"

The piano music stopped. Movement stopped. The dancers drooped with a combination of exhaustion and relief.

"It drags there."

Drags?

The dancers, still a unit, rolled their eyes and tried to ignore their aching muscles. The choreographer studied them, then gave the signal to take five. Twelve bodies dropped against the wall, shifting together so that heads fell on convenient shoulders or abdomens. Calves were massaged. Feet flexed, relaxed, and flexed again. They talked little. Breath was an important commodity, to be hoarded whenever possible. Beneath them, the floor was battle-scarred, covered with masking tape that had set the marks for dozens of other shows. But there was only one show that mattered now: this one.

"Want a bite?"

Maddy O'Hurley roused herself to look down at the chocolate bar. She considered it, coveted it, then shook her head. One bite would never be enough. "No, thanks. Sugar makes me light-headed when I'm dancing."

"I need a lift." The woman, her skin as dark and rich as the candy, took a huge bite. "Like now. All that guy needs is a whip and a chain."

Maddy glanced over at the choreographer as he bent over the accompanist. "He's tough. We'll be glad we've got him before this is over."

"Yeah, but right now I'd like to—"

"Strangle him with some piano wire?" Maddy suggested, and was rewarded with a quick, husky laugh.

"Something like that."

Her energy was coming back, and she could feel herself drying off. The room smelled of sweat and the fruity splash-on many of the dancers used to combat it. "I've seen you at auditions," Maddy commented. "You're real good."

"Thanks." The woman carefully wrapped the rest of the candy and slipped it into her dance bag. "Wanda Starre—two *r*s and an *e*."

"Maddy O'Hurley."

"Yeah, I know." Maddy's name was already well-known in the theater district. The gypsies—the dancers who wandered from show to show, job to job—knew her as one of their own who'd made it. Woman to woman, dancer to dancer, Wanda recognized Maddy as someone who hadn't forgotten her roots. "It's my first white contract," she said in an undertone.

"No kidding?" White contracts were for principals, pink for chorus. There was much, much more to it than color coding. Surprised, Maddy straightened to get a better look. The woman beside her had a large-featured, exotic face and the long, slender neck and strong shoulders of a dancer. Her body was longer than Maddy's. Even sprawled on the floor, Maddy gauged a five-inch difference from shoulder to toe.

"Your first time out of chorus?"

"That's right." Wanda glanced at the other dancers relaxing and recharging. "I'm scared to death."

Maddy toweled off her face. "Me, too."

"Come on. You've already starred in a hit."

"I haven't starred in this one yet. And I haven't worked with Macke." She watched the choreographer, still wiry at sixty, move away from the piano. "Show time," she murmured. The dancers rose and listened to the next set of instructions.

For another two hours they moved, absorbed, strove and polished. When the other dancers were dismissed, Maddy was given a ten-minute break, then came back to go through her solo. As lead she would dance with the chorus, perform solo and dance with the male lead and the other principals. She would prepare for the play in much the same way an athlete prepared for a marathon. Practice, discipline and more practice. In a show that was slated to run two hours and ten minutes, she would be on stage about two-thirds of the time. Dance routines would be absorbed into the memory banks of her mind, muscles and limbs. Everything would have to respond in sync at the call of the downbeat.

"Try it with your arms out, shoulder-level," Macke instructed. "Ball change before the kicks and keep the energy up."

The assistant choreographer gave the count, and Maddy threw herself into a two-minute routine that would have left a linebacker panting.

"Better." From Macke, Maddy knew that was praise indeed. "This time, keep your shoulders loose." He walked over and laid his blunt, ugly hands on Maddy's damp shoulders. "After the turn, angle stage left. I want the moves sharp; don't follow through, cut them off. You're a stripper, not a ballerina.''

She smiled at him because while he was criticizing her he was massaging the exhausted muscles of her shoulders. Macke had a reputation for being a grueling instructor, but he had the soul of a dancer. "I'll try to remember that.''

She took the count again and let her body do the thinking. Sharp, sassy, acerbic. That was what the part called for, so that was what she'd be. When she couldn't use her voice to get into the part, she had to use her body. Her legs lifted, jackknifing from the knee in a series of hitch kicks. Her arms ranged out to the side, contracted to cuddle her body and flew up, while her feet moved by memory to the beat.

Her short, smooth crop of reddish-blond hair flopped around a sweatband that was already soaked. She'd have the added weight of a wildly curled shoulder-length wig for this number, but she refused to think about that. Her face glowed like wet porcelain, but none of the effort showed. Her features were small, almost delicate, but she knew how to use her whole face to convey an expression, an emotion. It was often necessary to overconvey in the theater. Moisture beaded on her soft upper lip, but she smiled, grinned, laughed and grimaced as the mood of the dance demanded.

Without makeup her face was attractive—or cute, as Maddy had wearily come to accept—with its triangular shape, elfin features and wide, brandy-colored eyes. For the part of Mary Howard, alias the Merry Widow, Maddy would rely on the expertise of the makeup artist to turn her into something slick and sultry. For now she depended on her own gift for ex-

pression and movement to convey the character of the
overexperienced stripper looking for an easy way out.

In some ways, she thought, she'd been preparing all
her life for this part—the train and bus rides with her
family, traveling from town to town and club to club
to entertain for union scale and a meal. By the age of
five she'd been able to gauge an audience. Were they
hostile, were they laid-back, were they receptive?
Knowing the audience's mood could mean the difference between success and failure. Maddy had discovered early how to make subtle changes in a routine to
draw the best response. Her life, from the time she
could walk, had been played out onstage. In twenty-
six years she'd never regretted a moment of it.

There had been classes, endless classes. Though the
names and faces of her teachers had blurred, every
movement, every position, every step was firmly
lodged in her mind. When there hadn't been the time
or money for a formal class, her father had been there,
setting up a makeshift *barre* in a motel room to put his
children through practice routines and exercises.

She'd been born a gypsy, coming into the world with
her two sisters when her parents had been on the way
to a performance. Becoming a Broadway gypsy had
been inevitable. She'd auditioned, failed, and dealt
with the misery of disappointment. She'd auditioned,
succeeded, and dealt with the fear of opening night.
Because of her nature and her background, she'd
never had to deal with a lack of confidence.

For six years she'd struggled on her own, without
the cushion of her parents, her brother and her sisters. She'd danced in chorus lines and taken classes.
Between rehearsals she'd waited tables to help pay for
the instructions that never ended and the dance shoes

that wore out too soon. She'd broken through to principal, but had continued to study. She'd made second lead, but never gave up her classes. She finally stopped waiting tables.

Her biggest part had been the lead in *Suzanna's Park*, a plum she'd relished until she'd felt she'd sucked it dry. Leaving it had been a risk, but there was enough gypsy in her to have made the move an adventure.

Now she was playing the role of Mary, and the part was harder, more complex and more demanding than anything that had come before. She was going to work for Mary just as hard as she would make Mary work for her.

When the music ended, Maddy stood in the center of the hall, hands on hips, labored breathing echoing off the walls. Her body begged to be allowed to collapse, but if Macke had signaled, she would have revved up and gone on.

"Not bad, kid." He tossed her a towel.

With a little laugh, Maddy buried her face in it. The cloth was no longer fresh, but it still absorbed moisture. "Not bad? You know damn well it was terrific."

"It was good." Macke's lips twitched; Maddy knew that was as good as a laugh, for him. "Can't stand cocky dancers." But he watched her towel off, pleased and grateful that there was such a furnace of energy in her compact body. She was his tool, his canvas. His success would depend on her ability as much as hers did on his.

Maddy slung the towel around her neck as she walked over to the piano where the accompanist was already stacking up the score. "Can I ask you something, Macke?"

"Shoot." He drew out a cigarette; it was a habit Maddy looked on with mild pity.

"How many musicals have you done now? Altogether, I mean, dancing and choreographing?"

"Lost count. We'll call it plenty."

"Okay." She accepted his answer easily, though she would have bet her best tap shoes that he knew the exact number. "How do you gauge our chances with this one?"

"Nervous?"

"No. Paranoid."

He took two short drags. "It's good for you."

"I don't sleep well when I'm paranoid. I need my rest."

His lips twitched again. "You've got the best—me. You've got a good score, a catchy libretto and a solid book. What do you want?"

"Standing room only." She accepted a glass of water from the assistant choreographer and sipped carefully.

He answered because he respected her. It wasn't based on what she'd done in *Suzanna's Park*; rather, he admired what she and others like her did every day. She was twenty-six and had been dancing for more than twenty years. "You know who's backing us?"

With a nod, she sipped again, letting the water play in her mouth, not cold but wonderfully wet. "Valentine Records."

"Got any idea why a record company would negotiate to be the only backer of a musical?"

"Exclusive rights to the cast album."

"You catch on." He crushed out the cigarette, wishing immediately for another. He only thought of them when the music wasn't playing—on the piano, or in his head. Luckily for his lungs, that wasn't often. "Reed Valentine's our angel, a second-generation corporate bigwig, and from what I'm told he's tougher than his old man ever thought of being. He's not interested in us, sweetheart. He's interested in making a profit."

"That's fair enough," Maddy decided after a moment. "I'd like to see him make one." She grinned. "A big one."

"Good thinking. Hit the shower."

The pipes were noisy and the water sprayed in staccato bursts, but it was cool and wet. Maddy propped both forearms against the wall and let the stream pour over her head. She'd taken a ballet class early that morning. From there she'd come directly to the rehearsal hall, first to go over two of the songs with the composer. The singing didn't worry her—she had a clean voice, excellent pitch and a good range. Most of all, she was loud. The theater didn't tolerate stingy voices.

She'd spent her formative years as one of the O'Hurley Triplets. When you sang in bars and clubs with faulty acoustics and undependable audio equipment, you learned to be generous with your lungs.

She had a pretty good handle on her lines. Tomorrow she'd be rehearsing with the other actors—after jazz class and before dance rehearsal. The acting itself gave her a few flutters. Chantel was the true actor in the family, just as Abby had the most fluid voice. Maddy would rely on the character of Mary to pull her through.

Her heart was in the dancing. It had to be. There was nothing more strenuous, more demanding, more exhausting. It had caught her—mind, body and soul—from the moment her father had taught her her first simple tap routine in a dingy little lounge in Pennsylvania.

Look at me now, Pop, she thought as she shut off the inconsistent spray. I'm on Broadway.

Maddy toweled off quickly to avoid a chill and dressed in the street clothes she'd stuffed in her dance bag.

The big hall echoed. The composer and lyricist were performing minor surgery on one of their own tunes. There would be changes tomorrow, changes she and the other vocalists would have to learn. That was nothing new. Macke would have a dozen subtle alterations to the number they'd just gone over. That was nothing new, either.

Maddy heard the sound of dance shoes hitting the floor. The rhythm repeated over and over. Someone from the chorus was vocalizing. The vowel sounds rose and fell melodically.

Maddy swung her bag over her shoulders and descended the stairs to the street door with one thing on her mind—food. The energy and calories that she'd drained after a full day of exercise had to be replenished—but replenished wisely. She'd trained herself long ago to look at a dish of yogurt and a banana split with the same enthusiasm. Tonight it would be yogurt, garnished with fresh fruit and joined by a big bowl of barley soup and spinach salad.

At the door she paused a moment and listened again. The vocalist was still doing scales; piano music drifted, tinny and slight with distance. Feet slapped the floor in rhythm. The sounds were as much a part of her as her own heartbeat.

God bless Reed Valentine, she decided, and stepped out into the balmy dusk.

She'd taken about two steps when a sharp jerk on her dance bag sent her spinning around. He was hardly more than a boy, really—sixteen, seventeen—but she couldn't miss the hard, desperate look in his eye. She'd been desperate a few times herself.

"You should be in school," she told him as they began a tug-of-war over her bag.

She'd looked like a pushover. A hundred pounds of fluff to be tossed aside while he took the bag and fled. Her strength surprised him but made him all the more determined to have whatever cash and plastic she carried. In the dim light beside the stairs of the old building, no one noticed the struggle. She thought of screaming, then thought of how young he was and tried reason instead. It had been pointed out to her once or twice that not everyone wanted to be reformed. That never stopped her from trying.

"You know what's in here?" she asked him as they pulled and tugged on the canvas. He was running out of breath more quickly than she was. "Sweaty tights and a towel that's already molding. And my ballet shoes."

Remembering them, she held on tighter. A pro, she knew, would have given up and looked for an easier mark. The boy was beginning to call her all sorts of names, but she ignored them, believing that he was entitled. "They're almost new, but they won't do you any good," she continued in the same rational tone. "I need them a lot more than you do." As they scuffled, she banged her heel against the iron railing and swore. She could afford to lose a few dollars, but she

couldn't afford an injury. So he didn't want to be re-
formed, but maybe he'd compromise.

"Look, if you'll let go a minute I'll give you half of
the cash I have. I don't want to have to bother changing my credit cards—which I'll do by calling that 800
number the minute you take off. I don't have time to
replace the shoes, and I need them tomorrow. All the
cash," she decided as she heard the seam in her bag
begin to give. "I think I have about thirty dollars."

He gave a fierce tug that sent Maddy stumbling
forward. Then, at the sound of a shout, he released his
hold. The bag dropped like a stone, its contents tumbling out. The boy, not wasting time on a curse, ran
like a rocket down the street and around the first corner. Muttering to herself, Maddy crouched down to
gather up her belongings.

"Are you all right?"

She reached for her tattered leg warmer and saw a
pair of highly polished Italian shoes. As a dancer, she
took a special notice of what people wore on their feet.
Shoes often reflected one's personality and self-
esteem. Polished Italian shoes meant wealth and appreciation for what wealth could provide to Maddy.
Above the exquisite leather were pale gray trousers
that fell precisely to the middle of the foot, their
creases perfectly aligned. An organized, sensible man,
she decided as she gathered the loose change that had
spilled from the bottom of her bag.

Looking higher, she saw that the trousers fit well
over narrow hips and were buckled by a thin belt with
a small, intricately worked gold buckle. Stylish, but
not trendy.

The jacket was open, revealing a trim waist, a long
torso smoothed by a light blue shirt and a darker tie.

All silk. Maddy approved highly of silk worn against the body. Luxuries were only luxuries if they were enjoyed.

She looked at the hand that reached down to help her up. It was tanned, with long, attractive fingers. On his wrist was a gold watch that looked both expensive and practical. She put her hand in his and felt heat and strength and, she thought, impatience.

"Thank you." She said it before she looked at his face. From her long visual journey up his body, she knew he was tall and lean. Rangy, not in the way of a dancer but in the way of a man who knew discipline without the extremes of sacrifice. In the same interested way she'd studied him from shoes to shoulders, she studied his face.

He was clean-shaven, and every line and plane showed clearly. His cheeks were slightly hollow, giving his otherwise hard and stern look a poetic hint. She'd always had a soft spot for poets. His mouth was in a firm line now, signalling disapproval or annoyance, while below it was a trace, just a touch, of a cleft in his chin. His nose was straight, aristocratic, and though he looked down it at her, she took no offense. The eyes were a dark, flinty gray, and they conveyed as clearly as words the message that he didn't care to waste time rescuing damsels in distress.

The fact that he didn't, and yet had, made Maddy warm toward him.

He brushed his fingers through his burnished blond hair and stared back at her and wondered if she was going into shock. "Sit down," he told her in the quick, clipped voice of a man accustomed to giving orders and having them obeyed. Immediately.

"I'm okay," she said, sending him an easy smile. He noticed for the first time that her face wasn't flushed or pale, that her eyes weren't mirroring fear. She didn't fit his picture of a woman who'd nearly been mugged. "I'm glad you came along when you did. That kid wasn't listening to reason."

She bent down again to gather her things. He told himself he should go and leave her to pick up her own scattered belongings, but instead he took a deep breath, checked his watch, then crouched down to help her. "Do you always try to reason with muggers?"

"Apprentice mugger would be my guess." She found her key ring where it had bounced into a deep crack in the sidewalk. "And I was trying to negotiate."

He held up Maddy's oldest practice tights, gingerly, by the backs of the knees. "Do you really think this was worth negotiating over?"

"Absolutely." She took them from him, rolled them up and stuffed them in her bag.

"He could have hurt you."

"He could have gotten my shoes." Maddy picked up her ballet slippers and stroked the supple leather. "A fat lot of good they'd have done him, and I only bought them three weeks ago. Hand me that sweatband, would you?"

He retrieved it, then grimaced. Dangling it by his fingertips, he handed it over. "Shower with this, do you?"

Laughing, she took it and dropped it in with the rest of her practice clothes. "No, it's just sweat. Sorry." But there was no apology in her eyes, only humor. "Dressed like that, you don't look as though you'd recognize the substance."

"I don't generally carry it around in a bag with me." He wondered why he didn't simply move by her and start on his way. He was already five minutes late, but something about the way she continued to look up at him with such frank good humor kept him there. "You don't react like a woman who very nearly lost a pair of tights, a faded leotard, a ratty towel, two pairs of shoes and five pounds of keys."

"The towel's not that ratty." Satisfied she'd found everything, Maddy closed her bag again. "And anyway, I didn't lose them."

"Most of the women I know wouldn't negotiate with a mugger."

Interested, she studied him again. He looked like a man who would know dozens of women, all elegant and intelligent. "What would they do?"

"Scream, I imagine."

"If I'd done that, he'd have my bag and I'd be out of breath." She dismissed the idea with a graceful shrug of strong shoulders. "Anyway, thanks." She offered her hand again, a delicate one, narrow and naked of jewelry. "I think white knights are lovely."

She was small and completely alone, and it was getting darker by the minute. His natural instinct for noninvolvement warred with his conscience. The resolution took the form of annoyance. "You shouldn't be walking around in this neighborhood after dark."

She laughed again, the sound bright, rich and amused. "This is my neighborhood. I only live about four blocks away. I told you the kid was green. No self-respecting mugger's going to look twice at a dancer. They know dancers are usually broke. But you—" She stepped back and took another long look. He was definitely worth taking the time to look twice.

"You're another matter. Dressed like that, you 'd be better off carrying your watch and your wallet in your shorts."

"I'll keep that in mind."

Deciding one good turn deserved another, Maddy merely nodded. "Can I give you directions? You don't look as though you know your way around the lower forties."

Why had he been the one feeling responsible for her? In another minute that kid might have planted a fist in her face, but she didn't appear to have considered that. "No, thanks. I'm just going inside here."

"Here?" Maddy glanced over her shoulder at the ramshackle building that housed the rehearsal hall, then looked at him speculatively. "You're not a dancer." She said that positively. It wasn't that he didn't move well—from the little she had seen, he'd looked good. He simply wasn't a dancer. "And not an actor," she decided after only a brief mental debate. "And I'd swear...you aren't a musician, even though you've got good hands."

Every time he tried to walk away from her she drew him back. "Why not?"

"Too conservative," Maddy told him immediately, but not with scorn. "Absolutely too straight. I mean you're dressed like a lawyer or a banker or—" It struck her, clear as a bell. She positively beamed at him. "An angel."

He lifted a brow. "You see a halo?"

"No, I don't think you'd be willing to carry that kind of weight around. An angel," she repeated. "A backer. Valentine Records?"

Yet again, Maddy offered her hand. He took it and found himself simply holding it. "That's right. Reed Valentine."

"I'm Merry Widow."

He frowned. "I beg your pardon?"

"The stripper," she said, and watched his eyes narrow. She might have left it at that, just for the possible shock value, but then he *had* helped her out. "From *Take It Off*. The play you're backing." Delighted with him, she covered his hand with her free one. "Maddy O'Hurley."

This was Maddy O'Hurley? This compact little urchin with the crop of disheveled red-blond hair and the scrubbed face was the same powerhouse he'd watched in *Suzanna's Park*? She'd worn a long blond wig for that, an *Alice in Wonderland* look, and period costumes of the 1890s, but still... Her voice had boomed out, filling every crack in the theater. She'd danced with a frenzied, feverish energy that had awed a man who was very difficult to impress.

One of the reasons he'd been willing to back the play was Maddy O'Hurley. Now he was face-to-face with her and swamped with doubts.

"Madeline O'Hurley?"

"That's what it says on the contract."

"I've seen you perform, Miss O'Hurley. I didn't recognize you."

"Lights, costume, makeup." She shrugged it off. When there weren't footlights, she prized her anonymity and acknowledged her own unremarkable looks. She'd been born one of three—Chantel had gotten the heart-stopping beauty, Abby the warm loveliness, and she'd gotten cute. Maddy figured there were reasons for it, but she couldn't help being amused by Reed's cautious look. "Now you're disappointed," she concluded with a secret smile.

"I never said—"

"Of course, you wouldn't. You're much too polite. Don't worry, Mr. Valentine Records, I'll deliver. Any O'Hurley's a wise investment." She laughed at her own private joke. The streetlight behind them flickered on, signaling that night was coming, like it or not. "I guess you've got meetings inside."

"Ten minutes ago."

"Time's only important when you're on cue. You've got the checkbook, captain, you're in charge." Before she stepped out of his way, she gave him a friendly pat on the arm. "Listen, if you're around in a couple of days, come by rehearsals." She took a few steps, turned and walked backward, grinning at him. "You can watch me bump and grind. I'm good, Valentine. Real good." With a *pirouette*, she turned away, eating up the sidewalk with an easy jog.

In spite of a penchant for promptness, Reed continued to watch her until she disappeared around the corner. He shook his head and started up the stairs. Then he noticed a small round hairbrush. The temptation to leave it where it lay was strong. Curiosity was stronger. When Reed scooped it up he noticed that it carried the faintest scent of shampoo—something lemon-scented and fresh. He resisted the urge to sniff at it, and stuck it in his jacket pocket. Would a woman like that miss a hair brush? he wondered, then shrugged the thought away. He'd see that she got it back in any case.

He was bound to see Maddy O'Hurley again anyway, he told himself. It wouldn't hurt to do one more good deed.

Chapter Two

Nearly a week passed before Reed managed to schedule another visit to the rehearsal hall. He was able to justify the trip to himself as good business sense, but just barely. It had never been his intention to become directly involved with the play itself. Meetings with the producer and sessions with the accountants would have been enough to keep him informed. Reed understood balance sheets, ledgers and neatly formed columns better than he did the noises and the scents inside the decaying old building. But it never hurt to keep a tight rein on an investment—even if the investment involved an odd woman with a vivid smile.

He felt out of place. He was a twenty-minute cab ride from his offices, yet just as out of place in the rehearsal hall in his three-piece suit as he would have been on some remote island in the South Seas where the natives wore bones in their ears.

He would never have considered his life sheltered. In the course of his career he'd visited some seamy areas, dealt with people from varied backgrounds. But he lived uptown, where the restaurants were sedate and the view of the park out his apartment window was restful.

As he started up the stairs, Reed told himself it was natural curiosity that had brought him back. That, coupled with the simple matter of protecting his interests. Valentine Records had sunk a good chunk of capital into *Take It Off*, and he was responsible for Valentine Records. Still, he reached into his pocket and toyed with Maddy's hair brush. Going against his natural inclinations, he headed toward the sounds of music and talk.

In a room wrapped with mirrors, he found the dancers. They weren't the glittery, spangly chorus one paid to see on a Broadway stage, but a ragtag, dripping group of men and women in frayed tights. To him they were a helter-skelter mix of faded, damp leotards without any hint of the precision or uniformity expected of professionals. He felt uneasy for a moment as they stood, most of them with their hands on their hips, and stared at the small, thin man he knew was the choreographer.

"Let's have a little more steam, boys and girls," Macke instructed. "This is a strip joint, not a cotillion. We've got to sell sex and keep it good-natured. Wanda, I want a hesitation on the hip roll, then make it broader. Maddy, raise some blood pressure when you step up in the shimmy. Bend it from the waist."

He demonstrated, and Maddy watched, considered the move, then grinned at him. "I saw the design for my costume, Macke. If I bend over like that, the boys in the front row are going to get an anatomy lesson."

Macke looked her over. "A small one, in your case."

The dancers around her snorted and cackled. Maddy took the ribbing with a good-humored laugh as they moved back into position to take the count. They moved, with gusto, on eight.

Reed watched with steadily growing astonishment. Over a floor shiny with sweat, the dancers sprang to life. Legs flashed, hips rolled. Men and women found their partners in what seemed to be a riot of churning bodies. There were lifts, jumps, spins and the soft stamp of feet. From his vantage point he could see the exertion, the drip of perspiration, the deep, controlled breathing. Then Maddy stepped out, and he forgot the rest.

The leotard clung to every curve and line of her body, with the dark patches only accentuating her shape. Her legs, even in battered tights, seemed to go all the way to her waist. Slowly at first, with her hands at the tops of her hips, she moved forward, then right, then left, always following the rotation of her hips. He didn't hear the count being called now, but she did.

Her arm snaked across her body, then flew out. It didn't take much imagination to understand that she had tossed aside some article of clothing. She kicked up, so that for a moment her foot was over her head. Slowly, erotically, she ran her fingertips down her thigh as she lowered her leg.

The pace picked up, and so did her rhythm. She moved like a leopard, twisting, turning, sinuous and smooth. Then, as the dancers behind her went into an orgy of movement, she bent from the waist and used her shoulders to fascinate. A man broke from the group and grabbed her arm. With nothing more than the angle of her body, the placement of her head, she conveyed teasing, taunting acceptance. When the music ended, she was caught against him, arched backward. And his hand was clamped firmly on her bottom.

"Better," Macke decided. The dancers sagged, unwilling to waste energy by standing upright. Maddy and her partner seemed to collapse onto each other.

"Watch your hand, Jack."

"I am." He leaned over her shoulder just a little. "I've got my eye right on it."

She managed a breathless laugh before she pushed him away. For the first time, she saw Reed standing in the doorway. He looked every inch the proper, successful businessman. Because she'd wanted to see him again, had known she eventually would, Maddy sent him an uncomplicated, friendly smile.

"Take lunch," Macke announced as he lit a cigarette. "I want Maddy, Wanda and Terry back in an hour. Someone give Carter the word I want him, too. Chorus is due in room B at 1:30 for vocals."

The room was already emptying. Maddy took her towel and buried her face in it before she walked over to Reed. Several of the female dancers passed him with none-too-subtle invitations in their eyes.

"Hello again." Maddy slung her towel around her neck, then gently eased him out of the way of the hungry dancers. "Did you see the whole thing?"

"Whole thing?"

"The dance."

"Yes." He was having a hard time remembering anything but the way she had moved, the sensuality that had poured out of her.

With a laugh, she hung on to the ends of the towel and leaned against the wall. "And?"

"Impressive." Now she looked simply like a woman who'd been hard at work—attractive enough, but hardly primitively arousing. "You've, ah . . . a lot of energy, Miss O'Hurley."

"Oh, I'm packed with it. Are you here for another meeting?"

"No." Feeling a little foolish, he pulled out her hairbrush. "I think this is yours."

"Well, yeah." Pleased, Maddy took it from him. "I gave it up for lost. That was nice of you." She dabbed at her face with the towel again. "Hang on a minute." She walked away to stuff the brush and towel in her bag. Reed allowed himself the not-so-mild pleasure of watching her leotard stretch over her bottom as she bent over. She came back, slinging the bag over her shoulder.

"How about some lunch?" she asked him.

It was so casual, and so ridiculously appealing, that he nearly agreed. "I've got an appointment."

"Dinner?"

His brow lifted. She was looking up at him, a half smile on her lips and laughter in her eyes. The women he knew would have coolly left it to him to make the approach and the maneuvers. "Are you asking me for a date?"

The question rang with cautious politeness, and she had to laugh again. "You catch on fast, Valentine Records. Are you a carnivore?"

"I beg your pardon?"

"Do you eat meat?" she explained. "I know a lot of people who won't touch it."

"Ah...yes." He wondered why he should feel apologetic.

"Fine. I'll fix you a steak. Got a pen?"

Not certain whether he was amused or just dazed, Reed drew one out of his breast pocket.

"I knew you would." Maddy rattled off her address. "See you at seven." She called for someone down the hall to wait for her and dashed off before he could agree or refuse.

Reed walked out of the building without writing down her address. But he didn't forget it.

Maddy always did things on impulse. That was how she justified asking Reed to dinner when she barely knew him and didn't have anything in the house more interesting than banana yogurt. *He* was interesting, she told herself. So she stopped on the way home, after a full ten hours on her feet, and did some frenzied marketing.

It wasn't often she cooked. Not that she couldn't when push came to shove, it was simply that it was easier to eat out of a carton or can. If it didn't have to do with the theater, Maddy always looked for the easiest way.

When she reached her apartment building, the Gianellis were arguing in their first-floor apartment. Italian expletives streamed up the stairwell. Maddy remembered her mail, jogged back down half a flight and searched her key ring for the tiny, tarnished key that opened the scarred slot. With a postcard from her parents, an offer for life insurance and two bills in hand, she jogged back up again.

On the second landing the newlywed from 242 sat reading a textbook.

"How's the English Lit?" Maddy asked her.

"Pretty good. I think I'll have my certificate by August."

"Terrific." But she looked lonely, Maddy thought, and she paused a moment. "How's Tony?"

"He made the finals for that play off-Broadway." When she smiled, her young, hopeful face glowed. "If he makes chorus he can quit waiting tables at night. He says prosperity's just around the corner."

"That's great, Angie." She didn't add that prosperity was always around the corner for gypsies. The roads just kept getting longer. "I've got to run. Somebody's coming for dinner."

On the third floor she heard the wailing echo of rock music and the thumping of feet. The disco queen was rehearsing, Maddy decided as she chugged up the next flight of steps. After a quick search for her keys, she let herself in. She had an hour.

She switched on the stereo on her way to the kitchen, then dropped her bag on the twelve-inch square of Formica she called counter space. She scrubbed two potatoes, stuck them in the oven, remembered to turn it on, then dumped the fresh vegetables into the sink.

It occurred to her vaguely that she might tidy the place up a bit. It hadn't been dusted in . . . well, there was enough clutter on the tables to hide the dust, anyway. Some might call her rooms a shade messy, but no one would call them dull.

Most of her furnishings and decorations were Broadway surplus. When a show closed—especially if it had flopped—the markdown on props and materials was wonderful. They were memories to her, so even after the money had started to come in regularly she hadn't replaced them. The curtains were red and dizzily ornate—a steal from *Best Little Whorehouse in Texas*. The sofa, with its curvy back and dangerously hard cushions, had been part of the refuse of a flop she couldn't even remember, but it was reputed to have once sat on the parlor set of *My Fair Lady*. Maddy had decided to believe it.

None of the tables matched; nor did any of the chairs. It was a hodgepodge of periods and colors, a tangle of junk and splendor that suited her very well.

Posters lined the walls, posters from plays she'd been in, posters from plays where she hadn't gotten past the first call. There was one plant, a philodendron that hovered between life and death in its vivid pot by the window. It was the last in a long line of dead soldiers.

But her most prized possession was a hot-pink neon sign whose curvy letters spelled out her name. Trace had sent it to her when she'd gotten her first job in a Broadway chorus. Her name in lights. Maddy switched it on as she usually did and thought that while her brother might not often be around, he always made himself known.

Deciding not to spend too much time picking up when it would only be cluttered again in a couple of days, Maddy cleaned off a couple of chairs, stacked the magazines and the unopened mail and left it at that. More pressing was the task of washing out her dance clothes.

She filled the tub with warm water and soap, then added the tights and leotard she'd worn to class that morning. With them she added her rehearsal clothes.

For good measure she dropped in sweatbands and leg warmers. With the sleeves of her knee-length sweatshirt rolled up, she began the monotonous job of washing out, rinsing and wringing. Using the makeshift clothesline she'd fashioned in the tub, Maddy hung every piece up to dry.

The bathroom was no larger than a closet. When she stood up and turned, she faced herself in the mirror over the sink. Mirrors were an intimate part of her life. There were days when she danced in front of them for eight hours, watching, recording, assessing every muscle and move of her body.

Now she looked at her face—fairly good bones, satisfactory features. It was the combination of pointed chin, wide eyes and glowing skin that won those awful accolades like 'cute' and 'wholesome.' Nothing earth-shattering, she thought, but she could give them a hand.

On a whim she swung the mirrored door open and grabbed two handfuls of makeup at random. She bought it, stored it, even hoarded it. It was almost an obsession. The fact that she rarely used it unless she was performing didn't make her hobby seem odd to her. Whenever she wanted to play with her face, she had all the tools handy.

For ten minutes she experimented, putting on, creaming off, then putting on again, until the result was simply a bit of exotic color on her eyes and the faintest hint of warmth on her cheekbones. Maddy put the pots and tubes and pencils back into the cabinet, then shut the door before anything could fall out.

Was she supposed to chill that wine? she thought abruptly. Or maybe she should serve it at room temperature—which was now hovering around eighty degrees.

She must have given him the wrong address. Reed didn't doubt his memory. He'd been taught early the importance of remembering names, faces, facts, figures. When your teacher was your father and you adored your father, you learned. From years of practice rather than from natural inclination, Reed could hold three columns of figures in his head and tally each of them. Edwin Valentine had taught his son that a smart businessman hired the best accountants, then made certain he knew as much as they did.

He hadn't forgotten the address or mixed up the numbers, but he was beginning to believe she had.

The neighborhood was tough and seedy and rapidly getting seedier as he drove. A broken chair, with its stuffing pouring out the side, sat on the sidewalk. A group of people was arguing over ownership. An old man in an undershirt and shorts sat on a grimy stoop and chugged a can of beer. He eyed Reed's car owlishly as it passed.

How could she live here? Or more to the point, he thought, why would she live here? Maddy O'Hurley had just come off a year's engagement in a solid show that had brought her a Tony nomination. Before that, she'd had another year as the second lead and understudy to the star in a successful revival of *Kiss Me, Kate*.

Reed knew, because he'd made it his business to know. His business, he assured himself as he pulled to the curb in front of the building that corresponded with the numbers Maddy had given him. A woman who was about to embark on her third major

Broadway show could afford to live in a neighborhood where they didn't mine the sidewalks at night.

As Reed stepped out of his car he spotted a young hood leaning against a lamppost, eyeing his hubcaps. With a quiet oath, Reed approached him. He'd dressed casually, but even without tie and jacket he looked as if he belonged at the country club.

"How much to watch it?" Reed began bluntly. "Instead of strip it?"

The boy shifted his position and smiled with practiced arrogance. "Pretty elegant wheels you got there, Lancelot. Don't see many BMWs cruise through here. I'm thinking of getting my camera."

"Take all the pictures you want. Just don't take anything else." Reed slipped a twenty out of his wallet. "Let's say you're gainfully employed. There's another ten if the car's intact when I come out. You won't get more by hocking the hubcaps, and this way all you have to do is take in the evening air."

The boy studied the car, then its driver. He knew how to size up an opponent and figure the odds. The flinty eyes were direct and calm. If he'd seen fear in them, the boy would have pushed. Instead, he took the twenty.

"You're the boss. I got a couple hours to kill." He grinned and showed a painfully crooked front tooth. The twenty had already disappeared before Reed started toward the front door.

Her name was on a mail-slot in what might loosely have been called a foyer. Apartment 405. And there was no elevator. Reed started up the steps to the accompaniment of squalling kids, ear-splitting jazz and the swearing Gianellis. By the time he reached the third floor, he was doing some swearing himself.

When the knock came, Maddy was up to her wrists in salad. She'd known that he'd be on time just as surely as she'd known she wouldn't be. "Hang on a minute," she shouted, then looked around fruitlessly for a cloth to dry her hands with. Giving up, she shook what moisture she could from them as she walked to the door. She gave the knob a hard yank, then grinned at him.

"Hi. I hope you're not hungry. I'm not finished yet."

"No. I—" He glanced back over his shoulder. "The hall . . ." he began, and let his words trail off. Maddy stuck her head out and sniffed.

"Smells like a cow pasture," she said. "Guido must be cooking again. Come on in."

He should have been prepared for her apartment, but he wasn't. Reed glanced around at the vivid red curtains, the shock of blue rug, the chair that looked as though it had come straight out of a medieval castle. It had, in fact, come from the set of *Camelot*. Her name in pink neon glowed brilliantly against a white wall.

"Quite a place," he murmured.

"I like it when I'm here." Overhead came three simultaneous thuds. "Ballet student on the fifth," Maddy said easily. "*Tours jeté*. Would you like some wine?"

"Yes." Reed glanced uneasily at the ceiling again. "I think I would."

"Good. So would I." She walked back to the kitchen, which was separated from the living room by a teetering breakfront and imagination. "There's a corkscrew in one of these drawers," she told him. "Why don't you open the bottle while I finish this?"

After a moment's hesitation, Reed found himself searching through Maddy's kitchen drawers. In the first one he found a tennis ball, several loose keys and some snapshots, but no corkscrew. He rifled through another, wondering what he was doing there. On the fifth floor, the ballet student continued his leaps.

"How do you like your steak?"

Reed rescued the corkscrew from a tangle of black wire. "Ahh...medium rare."

"Okay." When she bent down to pull the broiling pan out of a cupboard, her cheek nearly brushed his knee. Reed drew the cork from the bottle, then set the wine aside to let it breathe.

"Why did you ask me to dinner?"

Still bent over and rummaging, Maddy turned her face upward. "No concrete reason. I rarely have one, but if you'd like, why don't we say because of the hairbrush?" She rose then, holding a dented broiling pan. "Besides, you're terrific to look at."

She saw the humor come and go in his eyes and was delighted.

"Thank you."

"Oh, you're welcome." She brushed away the hair that fell into her eyes and thought vaguely that it was about time for a trim. "Why did you come?"

"I don't have any idea."

"That should definitely make things more interesting. You've never backed a play before, have you?"

"No."

"I've never cooked dinner for a backer. So we're even." Setting the salad aside, she began to prepare the steak.

"Glasses?"

"Glasses?" she repeated, then glanced at the wine. "Oh, they're up in one of the cupboards."

Resigned, Reed began another search. He found cups with broken handles, a mismatched set of fabulous bone china and several plastic dishes. Eventually he found a hoard of eight wineglasses, no two alike. "You don't believe in uniformity?"

"Not really." Maddy set the steak under the broiler, then slammed the oven door. "It needs a boost to get going," she told him as she accepted the glass he offered. "To SRO."

"To what?"

"Standing room only." She clicked her glass to his and drank.

Reed studied her over the rim of his glass. She still wore the oversize sweatshirt. Her feet were bare. The scent that hung around her was light, airy and guileless. "You aren't what I expected."

"That's nice. What did you expect?"

"Someone with a sharper edge, I suppose. A little jaded, a little hungry."

"Dancers are always hungry," she said with a half smile, turning to grate cheese onto potatoes.

"I decided you'd asked me here for one of two reasons. The first was to pump me for information about the finances of the play."

Maddy chuckled, putting a sliver of cheese on her tongue. "Reed, I have to worry about eight dance routines—maybe ten, if Macke has his way—six songs, and lines I haven't even counted yet. I'll leave the money matters to you and the producers. What was the second reason?"

"To come on to me."

Her brows lifted, more in curiosity than shock. Reed watched her steadily, his eyes dark and calm, his smile cool and faintly amused. A cynic, Maddy realized, thinking it was a shame. Perhaps he had a reason to be. That was more of a shame. "Do women usually come on to you?"

He'd expected her to be embarrassed, to be annoyed, at the very least to laugh. Instead, she looked at him with mild curiosity. "Let's just pass over that one, shall we?"

"I suppose they do." She began to hunt for a kitchen fork to turn the steak with. "And I suppose you'd resent it after a while. I never had to deal with that sort of thing myself. Men always came on to my sister." She found the fork, squeaked open the oven door and flipped the steak over.

"There's only one," Reed pointed out.

"No, I've got two sisters."

"Steak. You're only cooking one steak."

"Yes, I know. It's yours."

"Aren't you eating?"

"Oh, sure, but I never eat a lot of red meat." She slammed the oven door again. "It clogs up the system. I figured you'd give me a couple bites of yours. Here." She handed him the salad bowl. "Take this over to the little table by the window. We're nearly ready."

It was good. In fact, it was excellent. As he'd watched her haphazard way of cooking, Reed had had his doubts. The salad was a symphony of mixed greens in a spicy vinaigrette. Cheese and bacon were heaped on steaming potatoes, and the steak was done precisely as he preferred. The wine had a subtle bite.

Maddy was still nursing her first glass. She ate a fraction of what seemed normal to Reed, and seemed to relish every bite.

"Take some more steak," he offered, but she shook her head. She did, however, take a second small bowl of salad. "It seems to me that anyone who has as physical a job as you do should eat more to compensate."

"Dancers are better off a little underweight. Mostly it's a matter of eating the right things. I really hate that." She grinned, taking a forkful of lettuce and alfalfa sprouts. "Not that I hate the right kind of food, I just love food, period. Once in a while I splurge on thousands of calories. But I always make sure it's a kind of celebration."

"What kind?"

"Well, say it's rained for three days, then the sun comes out. That's good enough for chocolate-chip cookies." She poured herself another half glass of wine and filled his glass before she noticed his blank expression. "Don't you like chocolate-chip cookies?"

"I've never considered them celebrational."

"You've never lived an abnormal life."

"Do you consider your life abnormal?"

"I don't. Thousands would." She propped her elbows on the table and rested her chin in her hands. Food, so often dreamed over, could always be forgotten when the conversation was interesting. "What's your life like?"

The light from the window beside them was dying quickly. What was left of it gleamed darkly in her hair. Her eyes, which had seemed so open, so easy, now glowed like a cat's, tawny, lazy, watchful. The neon was a foolish pink shimmer that curled into her name. "I don't know how to answer that."

"Well, I can probably guess some of it. You have an apartment, probably overlooking the park." She poked into the salad again, still watching him. "Ming vases, Dresden figures, something of the sort. You spend more time at your office than in your home. Conscientious about your work, dedicated to the business. Any responsible second-generation tycoon would be. You date very casually, because you don't have the time or inclination for a relationship. You'd spend more time at the museum if you could manage it, take in a foreign film now and then, and prefer quiet French restaurants."

She wasn't laughing at him, he decided. But she was more amused than impressed. Annoyance crept into his eyes, not because of her description but because she'd read him so easily. "That's very clever."

"I'm sorry," she said with such quick sincerity that his annoyance vanished. "It's a bad habit of mine, sizing people up, categorizing them. I'd be furious with anyone who did it to me." Then she stopped and caught her bottom lip between her teeth. "How close was I?"

It was difficult to resist her frank good humor. "Close enough."

With a laugh, she shook her head back so that her hair flared out then settled. She brought her legs up into the lotus position. "Is it all right to ask why you're backing a play about a stripper?"

"Is it all right to ask why you're starring in a play about a stripper?"

She beamed at him like a teacher, Reed thought, whose student had answered a question with particu-

lar insight. "It's a terrific play. The trick to being sure
of that is to look at the script without the songs and
the dance numbers. The music punctuates, empha-
sizes, exhilarates, but even without it, it's a good story.
I like the way Mary develops without having to change
intrinsically. She's had to be tough to survive, but she's
made the best of it. She wants more, and she goes after it because she deserves more. The only glitch is that
she really falls for this guy. He's everything she's ever
wanted in a material way, but she really just plain loses
her head over him. After she does, the money doesn't
matter, the position doesn't matter, but she ends up
with it all anyway. I like that."

"Happy ever after?"

"Don't you believe in happy endings?"

A shutter clicked down over his expression, quickly,
completely. Curiously. "In a play."

"I should tell you about my sister."

"The one the men came on to?"

"No, my other sister. Would you like an éclair? I
bought you one, and if you have it you could offer me
a bite. It would be rude for me to refuse."

Damn it, she was getting more appealing by the
minute. Not his type, not his speed, not his style. But
he smiled at her. "I'd love an éclair."

Maddy went into the kitchen, rummaged noisily,
then came back with a fat chocolate-iced pastry. "My
sister Abby," she began, "married Chuck Rockwell,
the race driver. Do you know about him?"

"Yes." Reed had never been an avid fan of auto
racing, but the name rang a bell. "He was killed a few
years back."

"Their marriage hadn't been working. Abby really
had been having a dreadful time. She was raising her

two children alone on this farm in Virginia. Financially she was strapped, emotionally she was drained. A few months ago she authorized a biography of Rockwell. The writer came to the farm, ready, I think, to gun Abby down," Maddy continued, placing the éclair on the table. "Are you going to offer me a bite?"

Reed obligingly cut a piece of the pastry with his fork and offered it to her. Maddy let the crust and cream and icing lie on her tongue for a long, decadent moment. "So what happened to your sister?"

"She married the writer six weeks ago." When she smiled again, her face simply lighted up, just as emphatically as the pink neon. "Happy-ever-after doesn't just happen in plays."

"What makes you think your sister's second marriage will work?"

"Because this is the right one." She leaned forward again, her eyes on his. "My sisters and I are triplets, we know each other inside out. When Abby married Chuck, I was sorry. In my heart, you see, I knew it wasn't right, that it could never be right, because I know Abby just as well as I know myself. I could only hope it would work somehow. When she married Dylan, it was such a different feeling—like letting out a long breath and relaxing."

"Dylan Crosby?"

"Yes, do you know him?"

"He did a book on Richard Bailey. Richard's been signed with Valentine Records for twenty years. I got to know Dylan fairly well when he was doing his research."

"Small world."

"Yes." It was full dusk now, and the sky was deepening to purple, but she didn't bother with lights. The ballet student had long since stopped his practicing. Somewhere down the hall, a baby could be heard wailing fitfully. "Why do you live here?"

"Here?" She gave him a blank look. "Why not?"

"You've got Attila the Hun on the street corner, screaming neighbors . . ."

"And?" she added, prompting him.

"You could move uptown."

"What for? I know this neighborhood. I've been here for seven years. It's close to Broadway, handy to rehearsal halls and classes. Probably half the tenants in this building are gypsies."

"I wouldn't be surprised."

"No, chorus-line gypsies." She laughed and began to toy with the leaf of the philodendron. It was a nervous gesture she wouldn't have begun to recognize herself. "Dancers who move from show to show, hoping for that one big break. I got it. That doesn't mean I'm not still a gypsy." She glanced back at him, wondering why it should matter so much that he understand her. "You can't change what you are, Reed. Or at least you shouldn't."

He believed that, and always had. He was the son of Edwin Valentine, one of the early movers and shakers in the record industry. He was a product of success, wealth and survival. He was, as Maddy had said, devoted to the business, because it had been part of his life always. He was impatient, often ruthless, a man who looked at the bottom line and the fine print before changing it to suit himself. He had no business sitting in a darkening apartment with a woman with cat's eyes and a wicked smile. He had less business entertaining fantasies about what it would be like to remain until the moon began to rise.

"You're killing that plant," he murmured.

"I know. I always do." She had to swallow, and that surprised her. Something in the way he'd been looking at her just now. Something in the tone of his voice, the set of his body. She could always be mistaken about a face, but not about a body. His was tensed, and so was hers. "I keep buying them, and keep killing them."

"Too much sun." He hadn't meant to, but brushed the back of her hand with his fingers. "And too much water. It's as easy to overlove as underlove."

"I hadn't thought of that." She was thinking about the tremors that were shooting up her arm, down her spine. "Your plants probably thrive with the perfect balance of attention." She caught herself wondering if it was the same with his women. Then she rose, because her system wasn't reacting as she'd expected it to. "I can offer you tea, but not coffee. I don't have any."

"No. I have to go." He didn't—there were no schedules to be met, no appointments to keep. But he was a survivor, and he knew when to back away. "I enjoyed the dinner, Maddy. And the company."

She let out a long breath, as if she'd just come down from a very high leap. "I'm glad. We'll do it again."

It was impulse. It was usually impulse with Maddy. She didn't think about it twice. With friendly warmth, she put her hands on his shoulders and touched her lips to his. The kiss lasted less than a second. And vibrated like a hurricane.

He felt her lips, smooth, curved a bit in a smile. He tasted the sweetness, fleeting, with a touch of spice.

Her scent was there, hovering, light enough to tease. When she moved back, he heard her quick, surprised intake of air and saw the same surprise reflected in her eyes.

What was that? she thought. What in God's name was that? She was a woman who made a habit of light, friendly kisses, quick hugs, casual touches. None of them had ever rocked her like this. She felt hints of everything she'd ever imagined in that one brief contact. And she wanted more. Because she'd practiced self-denial all her life, it was easier to control the desire to touch the fire a second time.

"I'm glad you came." The tremor in her voice amazed her.

"So am I." It wasn't often he had to use restraint. It wasn't often he had to deny himself anything. In this case, he knew he had to. "Good night, Maddy."

"Good night." She stood where she was while he let himself out. Then, listening to her body, she sat down. Better to think this one through, she warned herself. Better to think long and hard. Then her gaze drifted over to the plant that was wilting and yellowing in the dark window. Strange, she hadn't realized she'd been in the dark herself for so long.

Chapter Three

Her muscles warmed, her eyes dreamy, Maddy stretched at the *barre* with the line of dancers. The instructor called out every position, *plié*, *tendu*, *attitude*. Legs, torsos, arms responded in endless repetition.

Morning class was repetition, a continual reminder to the body that it could indeed do the unnatural and do it well time and time again. Without it, that same body would simply revolt and refuse to strain itself, refuse to turn the leg out from the hip as though it were on a ball hinge, refuse to bend beyond what was ordinary, refuse to stretch itself past natural goals. It would, in essence, become normal.

It wasn't necessary to concentrate fully. Maddy's body had built-in discipline, built-in instinct that carried her through the warm-up. Her mind floated away, far enough to dream, close enough to hear the calls.

Grand plié. Her knees bent, her body descended slowly until her crotch hovered over her heels. Muscles trembled, then acquiesced. She wondered if Reed was already in his office, though it was still shy of nine. She thought he would be. She imagined he would arrive as a matter of habit before his secretary, before his assistant. Would he think of her at all?

Attitude en avant. Her leg raised, holding at a ninety-degree angle. She continued to hold as the count dragged on. He probably wouldn't, Maddy concluded. His mind was so crowded with schedules and appointments that he wouldn't have time for a single wayward thought.

Battement fondu. She brought her foot under her supporting knee, which bent in synchronization. Gradually, slowly, she straightened, feeling the resistance, using it. He didn't have to think of her now. Later, perhaps, on his way home, over a quiet drink, his mind might drift to her. She wanted to think so.

Maddy's serviceable gray leotard was damp when she moved onto the floor for center practice. The exercises they had just practiced at the *barre* would be repeated again. On signal, she went into the fifth position and began.

One, two, three, four. Two, two, three, four.

It was raining outside. Maddy could watch the water stream down the small frosted windows as she bent, stretched, reached and held on command. A warm rain, she thought. The air had been steamy and heavy when she'd rushed to class that morning. She hoped it wouldn't stop before she got out again.

There hadn't been much time for walking in the rain when she'd been a child. Not that she regretted anything. Still, she and her family had spent more time at rehearsals and in train stations than in parks and playgrounds. Her parents had brought the fun with them—games, riddles and stories. Such high-flown, ridiculous stories, stories that were worlds in themselves. When you were blessed with two Irish parents who possessed fantastic imaginations, the sky was the limit.

She'd learned so much from them—more than timing, more than projection. Little formal education had seeped through, but geography had been taught on the road. Seeing the Mississippi had been more illuminating than reading about it. English, grammar, literature had come through the books that her parents had loved and passed on. Practical math had been a matter of survival. Her education had been as unconventional as her recreation, but she considered herself more well-rounded than most.

Maddy hadn't missed the parks or playgrounds. Her childhood had been its own carousel. But now, as a woman, she rarely missed a chance to walk in a warm summer rain.

Walking in the rain wouldn't appeal to Reed. In fact, Maddy doubted it would even occur to him. They were worlds apart—by birth, by choice, by inclination. Her right foot slid into a *chassé*, back, forward, to the side. Repeat. Repeat. He would be logical, sensible, perhaps a bit ruthless. You couldn't succeed in business otherwise. No one would consider it logical to stretch your body into unnatural positions day after day. No one would consider it sensible to throw yourself body and soul into the theater and subject yourself to the whims of the public. If she was ruthless, she was only ruthless in the demands she made on herself physically.

So why couldn't she stop thinking about him? She couldn't stop wondering. She couldn't stop remembering the way the dying sunlight had lingered on his hair, darkening it, deepening it—or the way his eyes had stayed on hers, direct, intrigued and cynical. Was it foolish for an optimist to be attracted to a cynic? Of course it was. But she'd done more foolish things.

They'd shared one kiss, and barely a kiss at that. His arms hadn't come around her. His lips hadn't pressed hungrily to hers. Yet she'd relived that instant of contact again and again. Somehow she thought— somehow she was sure—he hadn't been unmoved. However foolish it was, she dredged up that quick flood of sensation and reexperienced it. It added a fine sheen of heat to already-warmed skin. Her heartbeat, already thudding rhythmically with the demands of the exercise, increased in speed.

Amazing, she thought, that the memory of a sensation could do so much. Launching into a series of *pirouettes*, Maddy brought the feeling back again and spun with it.

With her hair still dripping from the shower, Maddy pulled on a pair of patched bright yellow bib overalls. The rehearsal hall showers themselves were ripe with the scents of splash-on cologne and powdered talc. A tall woman, naked to the waist, sat in the corner and worked a cramp out of her calf.

"I really appreciate you telling me about this class." Wanda, resplendent in jeans and a sweater as snug as skin, tugged her own hair back into a semiorganized bun. "It's tougher than the one I was taking. And five dollars cheaper."

"Madame has a soft spot for gypsies." Maddy straddled a long bench, bent over and began to aim a hand drier at the underside of her hair.

"Not everyone in your position is willing to share."

"Come on, Wanda."

"It isn't all a big sisterhood, sweetheart." Wanda jammed in a last pin and watched Maddy's reflection in the mirror. Even with the reddish hair curtaining her face, Wanda saw the faint frown of disagreement. "You're the lead, and you can't tell me you don't feel newcomers breathing down your neck."

"Makes you work harder." Maddy shook back her hair, too impatient to dry it. "Where'd you get those earrings?"

Wanda finished fastening on the fiercely red prisms, which fell nearly to her shoulders. A movement of her head sent them spinning. Both she and Maddy silently approved the result. "A boutique in the Village. Five-seventy-one."

Maddy got up from the bench and stood with her head close to Wanda's. She narrowed her eyes and imagined. "Did they have them in blue?"

"Probably. You like gaudy?"

"I love gaudy."

"Trade you these for that sweatshirt you've got with the eyes all over it."

"Deal," Maddy said immediately. "I'll bring it to rehearsal."

"You look happy."

Maddy smiled and rose on her toes to bring her ear closer to Wanda's. "I am happy."

"I mean, you look *man* happy."

With a lift of her brow, Maddy studied her own face in the mirror. Free of makeup, her skin glowed with health. Her mouth was full and shaped well enough to do without paint. It was a pity, she'd always thought, that her lashes were rather light and stubby. Chantel had gotten darker, longer ones.

"Man happy," Maddy repeated, enjoying the phrase. "I did meet a man."

"Shows. Good-looking?"

"Wonderful-looking. He's got incredible gray eyes. Really gray, no green at all. And a kind of cleft." She touched her own chin.

"Let's talk body."

Maddy let out a peal of laughter and hooked her arm around Wanda's shoulders. Friendships, the best of them, are often made quickly, she thought. "Good shoulders, very trim. He holds himself well. I'd guess good muscle tone."

"Guess?"

"I haven't seen him naked."

"Well, honey, what's your problem?"

"We only had dinner." Maddy was used to frank sexual talk. A lot more used to the talk than to acting on it. "I think he was interested—in sort of a detached way."

"So you've got to make him interested in an attached way. He's not a dancer, is he?"

"No."

"Good." Wanda sent her earrings for a last spin, then began to unfasten them. "Dancers make lousy husbands. I know."

"Well, I'm not thinking of marrying him . . ." she began, then widened her eyes. "Were you married to a dancer?"

"Five years ago. We were in the chorus of *Pippin*. Ended up getting married on opening night." She handed the earrings over. "Trouble was, before the play closed he'd forgotten that the ring on my finger applied to him."

"I'm sorry Wanda."

"It was a lesson," she said with a shrug. "Don't jump into something legal with a smooth-talking, good-looking man. Unless he's loaded," she added. "Is yours?"

"Is my— Oh." Maddy pouted into the mirror. "I suppose."

"Then grab ahold. If it doesn't work out, you can dry your eyes with a nice fat settlement."

"I don't think you're as cynical as you'd like to appear." Maddy gave Wanda's shoulder a quick squeeze. "Hurt bad?"

"It stung." Wanda found it odd that she'd never admitted that to anyone but herself before. "Let's just say I learned that marriage doesn't work unless two people play by the rules. How about some breakfast?"

"No, I can't." She glanced down to where her drooping philodendron sat under the bench. "I've got to deliver something."

"That." Wanda broke into a grin. "Looks like it needs a decent burial."

"It needs," Maddy corrected as she fastened on her new earrings, "the proper balance of attention."

He hadn't stopped thinking about her. Reed wasn't used to anything interfering with his schedule—especially not a flighty, eccentric woman with neon on her walls. They didn't have a thing in common. He'd told himself that repeatedly the night before, when he hadn't been able to sleep. She had nothing to attract him. Unless you counted whiskey-colored eyes. Or a laugh that came out of nowhere, and that could echo in your mind for hours.

He preferred women with classic tastes, elegant manners. The companions he chose wouldn't drive through Maddy's neighborhood with an armed guard, much less live there. They certainly wouldn't nibble at the meat on his plate. The women he dated went to the theater. They didn't act in it. They certainly wouldn't allow a man to see them sweat.

Why, after a few very brief encounters with Maddy O'Hurley, was Reed beginning to think the women he'd dated were raging bores? Of course they weren't. Reed began to study the sales figures in front of him again. He'd never dated a woman merely for her looks. He wanted and sought intelligent conversation, mutual interests, humor, style. He might want to discuss the impressionist show at the Metropolitan over dinner or the weather conditions in St. Moritz over brandy.

What he avoided—studiously avoided—was any woman connected with the entertainment field. He respected entertainers, admired them, but kept them at arm's length on a social level. As head of Valentine Records he dealt constantly with singers, musicians, agents, representatives. Valentine Records wasn't just a business. Not as his father had seen it. It was an organization that provided the best in music, from Bach to rock, and prized the talent it had signed and developed.

Reed had entertained musicians from childhood. He considered himself understanding of their needs, their ambitions, their vulnerabilities. In his free time he preferred the company of the less complicated. The less driven. His own ambitions were intense enough. Valentine Records was at the top of the heap and would remain there. He would see to that. Not only for his father, but for himself. If, as it often happened, he had to work ten hours a day for and with entertainers, he needed a breather from them when the day was over.

But he couldn't stop thinking of Maddy.

What made her tick? Reed pushed aside the sales figures and turned to look at his view of midtown. The rain turned it all into a misty gray fantasy. She didn't appear to have developed the protective shield that her profession seemed to require. She was rising to the top, like cream, but didn't seem awed by it. Could she really be as basic and uncomplicated as she seemed?

Why did he care?

He'd eaten dinner with her—one short, simple dinner. They'd had an interesting, somewhat intimate conversation. They'd shared a brief, friendly kiss. That had rocked him back on his heels.

So he was attracted. He wasn't immune to bright, vital looks or a firm, compact body. It was natural to be curious about the woman, with her odd philosophies and dangling thought patterns. If he wanted to see her again, there was no harm in it. And it was simple enough. He'd just pick up the phone and call her. They could have dinner again ... on his terms. Before the evening was over, he'd discover what it was about her that nagged at him.

When his door opened, Reed's glance of annoyance turned into a warm smile few were ever treated to. "A little wet for golf?"

"Club's a tomb when it rains." Edwin Valentine walked into the room with the long, slow steps of a big man, then dropped heavily into a chair. "Besides, I start to feel old if I don't make it in here every couple of weeks."

"Yeah, you look feeble." Reed leaned back in his chair and studied his father's ruddy, strong-featured face. "What's your handicap these days?"

"Four." Edwin grinned, pleased as a boy. "All in the wrist. Got wind you've all but signed Libby Barlow away from Galloway Records."

Cautious, always cautious, Reed merely inclined his head. "It looks that way."

Edwin nodded. The office had been his for nearly twenty years. The decisions had been his then. Still, he didn't feel any twinge of regret, any twist of envy at seeing his son behind the desk. That was what he'd worked for. "Great set of pipes on that little lady. I'd like to see Dorsey produce her first album with us."

Reed's lips curved slightly. His father's instincts were, as always, bull's-eye. "It's been discussed. I still think you should have an office here." He held up a hand before his father could speak. "I don't mean you should tie yourself down to regular hours again."

"Never had regular hours in my life," Edwin put in.

"Well, irregular hours, then. I do think Valentine Records should have Edwin Valentine."

"It has you." Edwin folded his hands, and the look he gave his son was direct and calm. More, much more passed between them than the words. "Not that I don't think you could use some advice from the old man now and again. However, you're at the helm now. The ship's holding steady."

"I wouldn't let you down."

Edwin recognized the intensity in his son's voice, and understood a portion of the passion behind it.

"I'm aware of that, Reed. I don't have to tell you that of all the things that have touched my life, nothing's made me prouder than you."

Emotion rippled through him. Gratitude, love. "Dad—"

Before he could finish, or even properly begin, his secretary wheeled in a tray of coffee and sweet rolls.

"By damn, Hannah, you're as sharp as ever."

"So are you, Mr. Valentine. Looks like you've dropped a pound or two." She fixed his coffee the way he preferred it. The flash of a wink she sent Reed was too quick to measure. She'd been with the company twelve years and was the only person on staff who would have dared the cheeky look.

"You witch, Hannah. I've gained five." Edwin heaped two rolls on his plate anyway.

"You wear it well, Mr. Valentine. You have a meeting at eleven-thirty with Mackenzie in Sales." She set another cup on Reed's desk. "Would you like for me to reschedule?"

"Not on my account," Edwin put in quickly.

Reed glanced at his watch and calculated the next thirty-five minutes. "I'll see him at eleven-thirty, Hannah. Thank you."

"Hell of a woman," Edwin said with a full mouth as the door shut behind Hannah. "Smart move, taking her on as your secretary when I retired."

"I don't think Valentine Records could run without Hannah." Reed glanced at the rain-drenched window again, thinking of another woman.

"What's on your mind, Reed?"

"Hmm?" Bringing himself back to the conversation, Reed picked up his coffee. "The sales figures look good. I think you'll be pleased with the results at the end of the fiscal year.''

Edwin didn't doubt that. Reed was a product of his mind, of his heart. Only rarely did it concern him that he'd molded his son a little too closely after himself. "Doesn't look to me like you've got sales figures on the brain.''

Reed nodded, deciding to answer the question while evading it. "I've been giving a lot of thought to the play we're backing.''

Edwin smiled a little. "Still nervous about my hunch there?''

"No.'' He could answer that honestly enough now. "I've had several meetings with the producer and the director. I've even looked in on a couple of rehearsals. My guess is that the play itself will hit big. The score—more our concern, really—is wonderful. What we're working on now is promotion and marketing for the cast album.''

"If you wouldn't mind, I might like to squirrel my way in on that end a bit.''

"You know you don't have to ask.''

"I do,'' Edwin corrected. "You're in charge, Reed. I didn't step down figuratively, but literally. As it happens, though, this is a pet project of mine. I've got a bit of personal interest.''

"You've never explained why you do.''

Edwin smiled a bit and broke off a corner of his second roll. "Goes back awhile. A long while. Have you met Maddy O'Hurley yet?''

Reed's brows drew together. Did his father read him that well? "As a matter of fact—'' When the buzzer sounded on his desk, he accepted the interruption without heat. "Yes, Hannah.''

"I'm sorry to disturb you, Mr. Valentine, but there's a young woman out here." Hannah could be tough as nails, but she found herself smiling at the drenched figure in front of her. "She says she has something to deliver to you."

"Take it, will you, Hannah?"

"She prefers to give it to you personally. Her name is, ah . . . Maddy."

Reed paused on the brink of refusal. "Maddy? Send her in, Hannah."

Dripping rain and carrying her dance bag and her dying plant, Maddy rushed into the office. "I'm sorry to bother you, Reed. It's just that I've been thinking and I decided you should have this before I murder it. I always get these spasms of guilt when I kill another plant and I figured you could spare me."

Edwin rose as she passed his chair, and she broke off her tumbling explanation. "Hello." She sent him an easy smile and tried to ignore the sweet rolls on the tray. "I'm interrupting, but it's really a matter of life and death." She set the wet, wilting plant on his spotless oak desk. "Don't tell me if it dies, okay? But if it survives, you let me know. Thanks." With a last flashing grin, she started to leave.

"Maddy." Now that she'd given him a moment to speak, Reed rose, as well. "I'd like you to meet my father. Edwin Valentine, Maddy O'Hurley."

"Oh." Maddy started to offer her hand, then dropped it again. "I'm soaked," she explained, smiling instead. "It's nice to meet you."

"Delighted." Edwin beamed at her. "Have a seat."

"Oh, I can't, really. I'm wet."

"A little water never hurt good leather." Before she could protest, Edwin took her arm and led her to one of the wide, biscuit-colored chairs beside the desk. "I've admired you onstage."

"Thank you." It didn't occur to her to be awed, though she was sitting almost toe-to-toe with one of the richest and most influential men in the country. She found his wide, ruddy face appealing, and though she looked, she couldn't find a single resemblance to his son.

Reed brought her gaze back to his. "Would you like some coffee, Maddy?"

No, he didn't resemble his father. Reed was sharp-featured and lean. Hungry. Maddy found her blood moving just a bit faster. "I don't drink coffee anymore. If you had any tea with honey, I'd love a cup."

"Have a roll," Edwin said when he saw her give them a quick, wistful look.

"I'm going to miss lunch," she told him easily. "I guess I could use a little sugar in the bloodstream." She smiled at him as she chose one that dripped with frosting. If she was going to sin, she preferred to sin well. "We've all been wondering if you'd come by rehearsals, Mr. Valentine."

"I've given it some thought. Reed and I were just talking about the play. He's of the opinion it's going to be a hit. What do you think?"

"I think it's bad luck for me to say so until we try it out in Philadelphia." She took a bite of the roll and could almost feel her energy level rise. "I can say that the dance numbers should knock them back in the aisles." She looked gratefully at Hannah as the secretary brought in her tea. "We're working on one this afternoon that should bring down the house. If it doesn't, I'll have to go back to waiting tables."

"I trust your judgment." Edwin reached over to pat her hand. "To my way of thinking, if an O'Hurley doesn't know when a dance number works, no one does." At her puzzled smile, he leaned back. "I knew your parents."

"You did?" Her face lighted with pleasure, the roll forgotten. "I don't remember either of them talking about it."

"A long time ago." He sent Reed a quick glance as if in explanation, and continued. "I was just getting started, hustling talent, hustling money. I met your parents right here in New York. I was on the down end right then, scrambling for pennies and backers. They let me sleep on a cot in their hotel room. I've never forgotten."

Maddy sent a meaningful glance around the office. "Well, you scrambled enough pennies, Mr. Valentine."

He laughed, urging more rolls on her. "I always wanted to pay them back, you know. Told them I would. That was a good twenty-five years ago. You and your sisters were still in booties. I do believe I helped your mother change your diaper."

She grinned at him. "It was very difficult to tell Chantel, Abby and me apart, even from that angle."

"You had a brother," he remembered. "A pistol."

"He still is."

"Sang like an angel. I told your father I'd sign him up once I got myself going. By the time I did and managed to find your family again, your brother was gone."

"To Pop's continued lamentations, Trace decided against a life on the road. Or at least he opted to follow a different road."

"You and your sisters had a group."

Maddy was never sure whether to wince or laugh at the memory. "The O'Hurley Triplets."

"I was going to offer you a contract," he said, and watched her eyes widen. "Absolutely. About that time, your sister Abby got married."

A record contract? More, a contract with Valentine Records! Maddy thought back to those times and imagined the awe that would have accompanied such an announcement. "Did Pop know?"

"We'd talked."

"Lord." She shook her head. "It must have killed him to see that slip through his fingers, but he never said a word. Chantel and I finished out the bookings after Abby married, then she went west and I went east. Poor Pop."

"I'd say you've given him plenty to be proud of."

"You're a nice man, Mr. Valentine. Is backing the play a kind of repayment for a night on a cot?"

"A repayment that's going to make my company a lot of money. I'd like to see your parents again, Maddy."

"I'll see what I can do." She rose then, knowing she was pushing her luck if she wanted to get back across town on time to rehearsals. "I didn't mean to take up your visit with your father, Reed."

"Don't apologize." As he stood he continued to watch her, as he had been for the entire visit. "It was enlightening."

She studied him then. He looked so right there, behind the desk, in front of the window, in an office with oil paintings and leather chairs. "We mentioned small worlds once before."

Her hair was dripping down her back. Ridiculous red glass triangles dangled from her ears, looking somehow valiant. The yellow bib overalls and the bright blue T-shirt seemed the only spots of color on a gloomy day. "Yes, we did."

"You'll take the plant, won't you?"

He glanced at it. It was pitiful. "I'll do what I can, but I can't promise a thing."

"Promises make me nervous, anyway. If you take them, you have to make them." She took a deep breath, knowing she should go but not quite able to break away. "Your office is just how I pictured. Organized elegance. It suits you. Thanks for the tea."

He wanted to touch her. It amazed him that he had to fight an urge to walk around the desk and put his hands on her. "Anytime."

"How about Friday?" she blurted out.

"Friday?"

"I'm free on Friday." Now that she'd done it, Maddy decided not to regret it. "I'm free on Friday," she repeated. "After rehearsal. I could meet you."

He nearly shook his head. He had no idea what was on his calendar. He had no idea what to say to a woman who took a casual statement as gospel. He had no idea why he was glad she had. "Where?"

She smiled at him so that every part of her face moved with it. "Rockefeller Center. Seven o'clock. I'm going to be late." She turned and held out her hands to Edwin. "I'm so glad you were here." In her easy way, she leaned down to kiss his cheek. "Goodbye."

"Goodbye, Maddy." Edwin waited until she'd dashed out before turning back to his son. It wasn't often Edwin saw that dazed look on Reed's face. "A man runs into a hurricane like that, he better strap himself down or enjoy the ride.'' Edwin grinned and took the last roll. "Damned if I wouldn't enjoy the ride.''

Chapter Four

Reed wondered if she was playing tricks with his mind. Maddy O'Hurley didn't look like most people's idea of a witch, but that was certainly the most reasonable explanation for the fact that he was loitering around Rockefeller Center at seven on a humid Friday evening. He should have been home by now, enjoying a quiet dinner before diving into the mass of paperwork he carried in his briefcase.

Traffic streamed along Fifth, bad-tempered from heat and noise. Those lucky enough to have a place to go and the time to spare were heading out of town, hoping the heat wave would ease by Monday. Pedestrians hurried by, ties loose, shirts wilting, looking like desert nomads in search of an oasis—an air-conditioned lounge and a long, cold drink.

He watched without interest as a few children, their eyes shrewd enough to mark out-of-towners, tried to push stiff red carnations for a dollar each. They did a fair trade, but not one of them bothered to approach Reed. He looked neither generous nor naive.

Though he caught snippets of conversation as people shuffled past, he didn't bother to wonder about them. He was too busy wondering about himself.

Why had he agreed to meet her? The answer to that was obvious enough. He'd wanted to see her. There was no use picking at that bone again. She aroused his . . . curiosity, Reed decided, unable to find a better term. A woman like her was bound to arouse anyone's curiosity. She was successful, yet she shrugged off the trappings of success. She was attractive, though she rarely played on her looks. Her eyes were honest—if you were the type who trusted such things. Yes, Maddy was a curiosity.

But why in hell hadn't he been able to pull his thoughts together and suggest some place more . . . suitable, at least?

A group of teenage girls streamed past, giggling. Reed sidestepped in lieu of being mowed down. One of them glanced back at him, attracted by the aloof expression and lean body. She put her hand over her mouth and whispered urgently to her companion. There was another round of laughter, and then they were lost in the crowd.

A sidewalk vendor hawked ice-cream bars and did a thriving business with a pack of office workers who hadn't escaped the heat of the city for the weekend. A panhandler milled through the crowd and was far less successful. Reed brushed off a scalper who promised the last two tickets for the evening show down the street at Radio City, then watched him pounce on an elderly pair of tourists. A block away, a siren began to scream. No one even bothered to look.

Reed felt perspiration trickle down his collar and ease down his back. His watch showed 7:20.

His temper was on its last notch when he saw her. Why did she look different, he wondered, from the dozens of people churning around her? Her hair and clothes were bright, but there were others dressed more vividly. She walked with a relaxed sort of grace, but not slowly. It seemed she did nothing slowly. Yet there was an air of ease about her. Reed knew that if he bothered to look he could find five women in that many minutes who had more beauty. But his eyes were fixed on her, and so was his mind.

Sidetracked by the panhandler, Maddy stood near the curb and dug into her purse. She pulled out some change, exchanged what appeared to be a few friendly words, then slid through the crowd. She spotted Reed a moment later and quickened her pace.

"I'm sorry. I'm always apologizing for being late. I missed my bus, but I thought I'd be better off going home and changing after rehearsal because you'd probably be wearing a suit." She looked him over with a bright, satisfied smile. "And I was right."

She'd traded the overalls for a full-skirted dress in a rainbow of colors that made her appear to be the gypsy she claimed she was. Everyone on the sidewalk seemed to fade to gray beside her.

"You might have taken a cab," he murmured, keeping that short but vital distance between them.

"I've never gotten in the habit. I'll spring for dinner and make up for it." She hooked her arm through his with such quick, easy camaraderie that his normal hesitancy toward personal contact never had a chance.

"I bet you're starving after standing around waiting for me. I'm starving, and I didn't." She shifted her body to avoid a collision with a woman in a hurry. "There's a great pizza place just down—"

He cut her off as he drew her through the crowd. "I'll buy. And we can do better than pizza."

Maddy was impressed when he caught a cab on the first try, and she didn't argue when he gave the driver an upscale address off Park Avenue. "I suppose I can switch gears from pizza," she said, always willing to be surprised. "By the way, I like your father."

"I can tell you the feeling was mutual."

Maddy didn't blink when the cab was cut off at a light and the driver began to mutter what might have been curses in what might have been Arabic. "Isn't it odd about him knowing my parents? My pop loves to drop names until they bounce off the walls—especially if he's never met the person. But he never mentioned your father."

Reed wondered if her scent would linger in the stale, steamy air of the cab after they left. He thought somehow it would. "Perhaps he forgot."

Maddy gave a quick, chuckling snort. "Not likely. Once Pop met the niece of the wife of a man whose brother had worked as an extra on *Singin' in the Rain*. He never forgot that. It does seem odd that your father would remember, though, or that it would matter, one night on a cot in a hotel room."

It had seemed unlikely to Reed, as well. Edwin met hundreds and hundreds of people. Why should he remember so clearly a pair of traveling entertainers who had given him a bed one night? "I can only guess that your parents made an impression on him," Reed answered, thinking aloud.

"They are pretty great. So's this," she added as the cab pulled up in front of an elegantly understated French restaurant. "I don't get up this way very often."

"Why?"

"Everything I need's basically concentrated in one area." She would have slid from the cab on the street side if Reed hadn't taken her hand and pulled her out with him onto the curb. "I don't have time to date often, and when I do it's usually with men whose French is limited to ballet positions."

She stopped herself when Reed opened the door for her. "That was a remarkably unchic thing to say, wasn't it?"

They stepped inside, where it was cool, softly scented and quietly pastel. "Yes. But somehow I don't think you worry about being chic."

"I'll figure out whether that was a compliment or an insult later," Maddy decided. "Insults make me cranky, and I don't want to spoil my dinner."

"Ah, Monsieur Valentine."

"Jean-Paul." Reed nodded to the maître d'. "I didn't make a reservation. I hope you have room for us."

"For you, of course." He cast a quick, professional look at Maddy. Not the *monsieur*'s usual type, Jean-Paul decided, but appealing all the same. "Please, follow me."

Maddy followed, wondering what kind of juggling act the maître d' would have to perform. She didn't doubt that Reed would make it worth his while.

It was precisely the sort of restaurant Maddy had thought he would patronize. A bit staid but very elegant, quietly chic without being trendy. Floral pastels on the walls and subdued lighting lent an air of relaxation. The scent of spice was subtle. Maddy took her seat at the corner table and glanced with frank curiosity at the other patrons. So much polish in one small place, she mused. But that was part of the charm of New York. Trash or glitz, you only had to turn a corner.

"Champagne, Mr. Valentine?"

"Maddy?" Reed inclined his head, holding the wine list but leaving the decision to her.

She gave the maître d' a smile that made his opinion of her rise several notches. "It's always difficult to say no to champagne."

"Thank you, Jean-Paul," Reed said, handing back the list after making his selection.

"This is nice." Maddy turned from her study of the other diners to smile at Reed. "I really hadn't expected anything like this."

"What did you expect?"

"That's why I like seeing you. I never know what to expect. I wondered if you'd come by rehearsals again."

He didn't want to admit that he'd wanted to, had had to discipline himself to stay away from something that wasn't his field. "It's not necessary. I have nothing creative to contribute to the play itself. Our concern is the score."

She gave him a solemn look. "I see." Slowly she traced a pattern on the linen cloth. "Valentine Records need the play to be a hit in order to get a return on its investment. And a hit play sells more albums."

"Naturally, but we feel the play's in good hands."

"Well, that should be a comfort to me." But she had to drum up enthusiasm when the champagne arrived. Because rituals amused her, Maddy watched the procedure—the display of the label, the quick, precise opening resulting in a muffled pop, the tasting and approval. The wine was poured in fluted glasses, and she watched the bubbles rise frantically from bottom to top.

"I suppose we should drink to Philadelphia." She was smiling again when she lifted her glass to his.

"Philadelphia?"

"Opening there often tells the tale." She touched her glass to his, then sipped slowly. She would limit her intake of wine just as religiously as she limited her intake of everything else. But she'd enjoy every bit of it. "Wonderful. The last time I had champagne was at a party they threw for me when I left *Suzanna's Park*, but it wasn't nearly this good."

"Why did you?"

"Did I what?"

"Leave the play."

Before she answered, she sipped again. Wine was so pretty in candlelight, she mused. It was a pity people stopped noticing things like that when they could have wine whenever they liked. "I'd given the part everything I could and gotten everything I could out of it." She shrugged. "It was time to move on. I have restless feet, Reed. They dance to the piper."

"You don't look for security?"

"With my background, security doesn't come high on the list. You find it first in yourself, anyway."

He knew about restlessness, about women who moved from one place to the next, never quite finding satisfaction. "Some might say you bored easily."

Something in his tone put her on guard, but she had no way of answering except with honesty. "I'm never bored. How could I be? There's too much to enjoy."

"So you don't consider it a matter of losing interest?"

Without knowing why, she felt he was testing her somehow. Or was he testing himself? "I can't think of anything I've ever lost interest in. No, that's not true. There was this calico-cat pillow, an enormous, expensive one. I thought I was crazy about it, then I bought it and got it home and decided it was awful. But that's not what you mean, is it?"

"No." Reed studied her as he drank. "It's not."

"It's more a matter of different outlooks." She ran a finger around the rim of her glass. "A man like you structures his own routine, then has to live up to it every day because dozens of people are depending on you. A great deal of my life is structured for me, simply to keep me on level ground. The rest has to change, fluctuate constantly, or I lose the edge. You should understand that, you work with entertainers."

His lips curved as he lifted his glass. "I certainly do."

"They amuse you?"

"In some ways," he admitted easily enough. "In others they frustrate me, but that doesn't mean I don't admire them."

"While knowing they're all a little mad."

It took only an instant for the humor to spread from his mouth to his eyes. "Absolutely."

"I like you, Reed." She put her hand over his, friend to friend. "It's a pity you don't have more illusions."

He didn't ask her what she meant. He wasn't certain he wanted to know. Conversation stopped when the waiter arrived with menus and a list of specials delivered in a rolling French accent Maddy decided was genuine.

"This is a problem," Maddy muttered when they were alone again.

Reed glanced up from his menu. "You don't like French food?"

"Are you kidding?" She grinned at him. "I love it. I love Italian food, Armenian food, East Indian food. That's the problem."

"You suggested pizza," he reminded her. "It's hard to believe you're worried about calories."

"I was only going to have one piece and inhale the rest." She caught her bottom lip between her teeth and knew she could have eaten anything on the menu. "I have two choices. I can order just a salad and deny myself. Or I can say this is a celebration and shoot the works."

"I can recommend the *côtelettes de saumon*."

She lifted her gaze from the menu again to study him very seriously. "You can?"

"Highly."

"Reed, I'm a grown woman and independent by nature. When it comes to food, however, I often have the appetite of a twelve-year-old in a bakery. I'm going to put myself in your hands." She closed the menu and set it aside. "With the stipulation that you understand I can only eat this way once or twice a year unless I want to bounce around stage like a meatball."

"Understood." He decided, for reasons he didn't delve into, to give her the meal of her life.

He wasn't disappointed. Her unabashed appreciation for everything put in front of her was novel and
somehow compelling. She ate slowly, with a dark,
sensual enjoyment Reed had forgotten could be found
in food. She tasted everything and finished nothing,
and it was clear that the underlying discipline was always there, despite her sumptuous appreciation.

She teased herself with flavors as other women
might tease themselves with men. She closed her eyes
over a bite of fish and gave herself to the pleasure of
it as others gave themselves to the pleasures of love-
making.

Champagne bubbles exploded in their glasses, and
the scents rising up were rich.

"Oh, this is wonderful. Taste."

Wanting to share her pleasure, she held her fork out
to him. His body tightened, surprising him. He had
been aroused just by watching her, but he discovered
in that instant that what he really wanted was to sample her, slowly, as she sampled the tastes and textures
on her plate.

He opened his mouth and allowed himself to be fed.
As he savored the bite, he watched her eyes and saw
they were aware. Mixed with that awareness was a curiosity that became intensely erotic.

"It's very good."

She knew she was getting in over her head, and she
wondered why the feeling was so alluring. "Dancers
think about food too much. I suppose it's because we
watch so much of it pass us by."

"You said once that dancers are always hungry."

He wasn't speaking of food now. To give herself a
moment, Maddy picked up her glass and sipped. "We
make a choice, usually in childhood. We give up foot-

ball games, TV, parties, and go to class instead. It carries over into adulthood.''

''How much do you sacrifice?''

''Whatever it takes.''

''And it's worth it?''

''Yes.'' She smiled, more comfortable now that she could feel her body pull away from that trembling edge of tension. ''Even at its worst, it's worth it.''

He leaned back just enough to distance himself from her. She sensed it and wondered whether he had felt the same intensity between them. ''What does success mean to you?''

''When I was sixteen, it meant Broadway.'' She looked around the quiet restaurant and nearly sighed. ''In some ways, it still does.''

''Then you have it.''

He didn't understand, nor did she expect him to. ''I feel successful because I tell myself the show's going to be a smash. I don't let myself think it might flop.''

''You wear blinders, then.''

''Oh, no. Rose-colored glasses, but never blinders. You're a realist. I suppose I like that in you because it's so different from what I am. I like to pretend.''

''You can't run a business on illusions.''

''And your personal life?''

''That either.''

Interested, she leaned forward. ''Why not?''

''Because you can only make things work your way if you know what's real and what's not.''

''I like to think you can make things real.''

''Valentine!''

Reed's considering frown lingered as he glanced up at a tall, lanky man in a peach jacket and a melon tie. ''Selby. How are you?''

"Fine. Just fine." The man sent Maddy a long look. "It looks like I'm interrupting, and I hate to use a tired line, but have we met before?"

"No." Maddy extended her hand with the easy friendship she showed everyone.

"Maddy O'Hurley. Allen Selby."

"Maddy O'Hurley?" Selby cut into Reed's introduction and squeezed Maddy's hand. "This is a pleasure. I saw *Suzanna's Park* twice."

She didn't like the feel of his hand, but she always hated herself when she made snap judgments. "Then it's my pleasure."

"I'd heard Valentine was dipping into Broadway, Reed."

"Word gets around." Reed poured the last of the wine into Maddy's glass. "Allen is the head of Galloway Records."

"Friendly competitors," Selby assured her, and Maddy got the distinct impression that he'd cut Reed's professional throat at the first opportunity. "Have you ever considered a solo album, Maddy?"

She toyed with the stem of her glass. "It's a difficult thing to admit to a record producer, but singing's not my strong point."

"If Reed doesn't convince you differently, come see me." He laid a hand on Reed's shoulder as he spoke. No, she didn't like those hands, she thought again. It couldn't be helped. Maddy noticed that Reed's eyes frosted over, but he merely picked up his glass. "Wish I could join you for some coffee," Selby went on, ignoring the fact he hadn't been asked, "but I'm meeting a client for dinner. Give my best to your old man, Reed. Think about that album now." He winked at Maddy, then sauntered off to his own table.

Maddy waited a beat, then finished off the rest of her wine. "Do most record producers dress like they're part of a fruit salad?"

Reed stared at her a moment, seeing the bland, curious smile. The tension dissolved into laughter. "Selby's one of a kind."

She took his hand again, delighted to have made him laugh. "So are you."

"Do I need time to decide if that was a compliment or an insult?"

"A definite compliment." She glanced over to where Selby was signaling a waiter. "You don't like him."

He didn't pretend not to understand who she was referring to. "We're business rivals."

"No," Maddy said with a shake of her head. "You don't like *him*. Personally."

That interested him, because he had a well-earned reputation for concealing his emotions. "Why do you say that?"

"Because your eyes iced over." Involuntarily she shivered. "I'd hate to be looked at that way. Anyway, you won't gossip, and you're annoyed that he's here, so why don't we go?"

When they walked outside again, the heat of the day had eased. Traffic had thinned. Hooking her arm through his, Maddy breathed in the rough night air that was New York. "Can we walk awhile? It's too nice to jump right into a cab."

They strolled down the sidewalk, past dark store windows and closed shops. "Selby had a point, you know. With the right material, you could make a very solid album."

She shrugged. That had never been part of her dream, though she wouldn't completely dismiss it. "Maybe someday, but I think Streisand can sleep easy. You never see enough stars," she murmured, looking up as they walked. "On nights like this I envy Abby and her farm in the country."

"Difficult to sit on the porch swing and make the eight-o'clock curtain."

"Exactly. Still, I keep planning to take this wonderful vacation some day. A cruise on the South Seas where the steward brings you iced tea while you watch the moon hovering over the water. Or a cabin in the woods—Oregon, maybe—where you can lie in bed in the morning and listen to the birds wake up. Trouble is, how would I make it to dance class?" She laughed at herself and moved closer. "What do you do when you have time off, Reed?"

It had been two years since he'd taken anything more than a long weekend off, and even those were few and far between. It had been two years since he'd taken over Valentine Records. "We have a house in St. Thomas. You can sit on the balcony and forget there is a Manhattan."

"It must be wonderful. One of those big, rambling places, pink-and-white stucco with a garden full of flowers most people only see in pictures. But you'd have phones. A man like you would never really cut himself off."

"Everyone pays a price."

She knew that very well every time she placed her hand on the *barre*. "Oh, look." She stopped by a window and looked in at an icy-blue negligee that swept the mannequin's feet and left the shoulders bare but for ivory lace. "That's Chantel."

Reed studied the faceless mannequin. "Is it?"

"The negligee. It's Chantel. Cool and sexy. She was born to wear things like that—and she's the first one to say so." Maddy laughed and stepped back to make a note of the name of the shop. "I'll have to send it to her. Our birthday's in a couple of months."

"Chantel O'Hurley." Reed shook his head. "Strange, I never put it together. She's your sister."

"Not so strange. We're not a great deal alike on the surface."

Cool and sexy, Reed thought again. That was precisely Chantel's image as a symbol of Hollywood glamour. The woman beside him would never be termed cool, and her sexuality wasn't glamorous but tangible. Dangerously so. "Being a triplet must be a very unique sensation."

"It's hard for me to say, since I've always been one." They began to walk again. "But it's special. You're never really alone, you know. I think that was part of the reason I had enough courage to come to New York and risk it all. I always had Chantel and Abby, even when they were hundreds of miles away."

"You miss them."

"Oh, yes. I miss them dreadfully sometimes, and Mom and Pop and Trace. We were so close growing up, living in each other's pockets, working together. Yelling at each other."

She chuckled when he glanced down at her. "It's not so odd, you know. Everyone needs someone they can yell at now and then. When Trace left, it was like losing an arm at first. Pop never really got over it. Then Abby left, and Chantel and I. I never thought how hard it was on my parents, because they had each other. You must be close to your parents."

He closed up then, instantly; she thought she could feel the frost settle over the heat. "There's only my father."

"I'm sorry." She never deliberately opened old wounds, but innate curiosity often led her to them. "I've never lost anyone close to me, but I can imagine how hard it would be."

"My mother's not dead." He didn't accept sympathy. He detested it.

Questions sprang into her head, but she didn't ask them. "Your father's a wonderful man. I could tell right away. He has such kind eyes. I always loved that about my own father—the way his eyes would say 'Trust me,' and you knew you could. My mother ran away with him, you know. It always seemed so romantic. She was seventeen and had already been working clubs for years. My father came through town and promised her the moon on a silver platter. I don't think she ever believed him, but she went with him. When we were little, my sisters and I used to talk about the day a man would come and offer us the moon."

"Is that what you want?"

"The moon?" She laughed again, and the sound of it trailed down the sidewalk. "Of course. And the stars. I might even take the man."

He stopped then, just outside the beam of a streetlight, to look down at her. "Any man who'd give it to you?"

"No." Her heart began to thud, slowly at first, then faster, until she felt it in her throat. "A man who'd offer it."

"A dreamer." He combed his hand through her hair the way he'd wanted to, though he'd told himself he wouldn't. It spread like silk through his fingers. "Like you."

"If you stop dreaming, you stop living."

He shook his head, moving it closer to hers. "I stopped a long time ago." His lips touched hers, briefly, as they had once before. "I'm still alive."

She put a hand on his chest, not to keep him away but to keep him close. "Why did you stop?"

"I prefer reality."

This time, when his mouth came to hers, it wasn't hesitant. He gathered and took what he'd wanted for days. Her lips were warm against his, exotic in flavor, tempting in their very willingness to merge with his. Her hand pressed against the back of his neck, drawing him nearer, eagerly accepting the next stage of pleasure as their tongues met and tangled.

The streetlight washed the sidewalk beside them, and the buildings blocked out most of the sky. They were alone, though traffic shuttled by on the street. His fingers spread against her back, bringing enough pressure to align her body with his, hard and firm. The scent she wore made the musky smell of the city disappear, so there was only her.

Trapped in his arms, she was already soaring up so that in a moment she could touch the chilled white surface of the moon and learn its secrets. She hadn't expected to be breathless, but she swayed against him with a helplessness neither of them could comprehend.

He tasted of power and ruthlessness. Her instinct for survival should have had her turning away from it, even scorning it. Yet she remained as she was, wound around him in the warm evening air. The hand at the back of his neck stroked to soothe a tension she sensed intuitively.

He knew better. From the first moment he'd seen her, Reed had known better. But he'd continued to take steps toward her rather than away. He was no good for her, and she could only mean catastrophe for him. There would be no casually complementary relationship here, but something that would draw you farther and farther into a slowly burning fire.

He could taste it. The frank surrender that was seduction. He could hear it in her quiet sigh of acceptance. With her body hugged tightly against his, he could feel the need expand beyond what should, what must, be controlled. He didn't want it. Yet he wanted her more than he'd wanted anything that had come into his life before.

He drew away. Then, before he could stop himself, he framed her face in his hands to kiss her again. He wanted to be sated by her, done with her. But the more he took, the more he wanted.

A woman like this could destroy a man. Since childhood his life had been based on the premise that he would never allow a woman to be important enough to hurt him. Maddy was no different, he told himself as he all but drowned in her. She couldn't be.

When he drew away again, Maddy's legs were rubber. She had no flip remark, no easy smile. She could only look into his eyes, and what she saw wasn't passion now, wasn't desire. It was anger. She had no answer for it.

"I'll take you home," he told her.

"Just a minute." She needed to catch her breath, needed to feel firm ground under her feet again. He released her, and she stepped to the street lamp and rested a hand on the solid metal surface. Light washed white over her and left him in shadow. "I get the feeling that you're annoyed at what happened."

He didn't respond. When she studied him, she saw that his eyes could be colder than stone. It made her hurt, as much for him as for herself. "Since I'm not, I'm left feeling like a fool." Tears came to her easily, as easily as laughter, but she wouldn't shed them now. She'd inherited a good deal of pride as well as quick emotions from her parents. "I'd just as soon see myself home, thanks."

"I said I'd take you."

Inner strength came back. It might have been the underlying fury in his voice that did it. "I'm a big girl, Reed. I've been responsible for myself a long time. See you around."

Maddy walked to the corner and lifted a hand. Fate took pity on her and sent a cab steering toward the curb. She got in without looking back.

He stood there until he saw her get safely inside. Then he stood there longer. He'd done them both a favor—that was what he told himself. He continued to tell himself that over and over as he remembered how soft and fragile she'd looked in the bright glow of the streetlight.

Turning away, he began to walk. It was late before he headed for home.

Chapter Five

Maddy stood stage left and took her cue from Wanda. There was no audience, but the theater was far from empty. The rest of the dancers were positioned across the stage, and Macke stood at the front, ready to dissect every move. In addition, there were the stage manager, the lighting director, their assistants, the accompanist—with the composer standing nervously close by, along with several technicians and the one who would make it all work—the director.

"Listen, honey," Wanda began, in character as Maureen Core, a fellow stripper, "this guy's a pipe dream. You're asking for trouble."

"He's an answer," Maddy shot back, and crossed to an imaginary bar on the empty stage. She poured herself an invisible drink, tossed it back and grinned. "He's the ticket I've been standing in line for all of my life."

"Get it in diamonds, babe." Wanda walked toward her, running her fingers up her arm as if she were enjoying the sensuous feel of a diamond bracelet. "And put them in a nice dark safe deposit box, 'cause when he finds out what you are he's going to be gone before you can shake your—"

"He's not going to find out," Maddy told her. "He's never going to find out. You think a class act like him is ever going to find his way to a dump like this?" She cast a disdainful look around the empty stage. "I tell you, Maureen, I've got a chance. For the first time in my life, I've got a chance."

The accompanist gave her her intro, and Maddy's mind went blank.

"Maddy." The director, known more for his skill than his patience, snapped her back. She swore with the ripe expertise she reserved solely for foul ups on stage.

"Sorry, Don."

"You're only giving me about fifty percent, Maddy. I need a hundred and ten."

"You'll get it." She rubbed at the tension in her neck. "Give me a minute first, will you?"

"Five," he said, clipping off the word so that the dancers shifted uneasily before they dispersed. Maddy walked off stage left and dropped down on a box in the wings.

"Problem?" Wanda sat down beside her, casting a look around designed to keep anyone else at a safe distance.

"I hate to mess up."

"I make it a policy to keep my nose out of other people's business. But ..."

"There's always a but."

"You've been walking around on three cylinders for about a week. I'd say you're due for a tune-up."

She couldn't deny it; she didn't try to. Instead, she set her jaw on her hand. "Why are men such jerks?"

Wanda considered a moment. "Same reason the sky's blue, honey. They were made that way."

Another time, she might have laughed. Now she only nodded grimly. "I guess it's smarter just to leave them alone."

"A hell of a lot smarter," Wanda agreed. "Not much fun, but smarter. Your guy giving you trouble?"

"He's not my guy." Maddy sighed and frowned down at her shoe. "But he's giving me trouble. What do you do when a man kisses you as though he'd like to nibble away at you for the next twenty years, then brushes you aside as though you were never really there in the first place?"

Wanda cupped a hand around her instep, then brought her leg up to keep the muscles limber. "Well, you can forget him. Or you can give him another chance to nibble until he's hooked."

"I don't want to hook anybody," Maddy mumbled.

"But you are," Wanda put in, stretching the other leg. "Hooked and dangling."

"I know." Misery was something completely foreign to her. She tried to shake it off, but it clung. "The problem is, I think he knows, too, and he doesn't want any part of it."

"Maybe you should think about what you want first."

"Yeah, but first you have to know what that is."

"Is it him?"

Maddy gave a sulky shrug and hated herself for being petulant. "It might be."

"Take a lesson from Mary on this one." Wanda gave her advice as she rose into a *plié*. "Go after what's good for you."

It sounded so easy. Maddy knew better than most how it was to get to what was good for you. "You know the problem with being a dancer, Wanda?"

Two members of the chorus, currently in the midst of a blistering affair, began to argue with low, steady malice. Wanda eavesdropped without a qualm. "I can name a couple hundred, but go ahead."

"You never have time to learn how to be just a person. When other girls were out snuggling at the drive-in with their boyfriends, we were sleeping so we could get up and go to class the next morning. I don't know what to do about him."

"Get in his way."

"Get in his way?"

"That's right. Get in his way enough and he'll end up doing it to himself."

Laughing, Maddy took her own chin in her hand. "Does this look irresistible?"

"Never know unless you try."

Maddy's fingers stroked down her chin. Then she dropped her hand. "You're right." She stood then, nodding. "You're absolutely right. Let's go. I think I'm ready to give Don a hundred and ten percent."

They ran through the dialogue again, but this time Maddy used her own nerves to give an edge to her character. When the accompanist cued her for the song, she poured herself into it. Part of the staging called for her to go toe-to-toe with Wanda. When she did, the other's dancer's eyes glittered with a combination of appreciation and approval that had Maddy's adrenaline soaring higher.

She was all over the stage during the chorus, interacting with the other dancers, moving so quickly that the intense control she kept on her breathing went unnoticed. She whirled to stage center, threw out her arms—selling it, as her father had shown her years before—and let the last note ring out.

Someone threw her a towel.

They went over the scene again and again, sharpening, making a few changes in the blocking. The lighting director and the stage manager went into a huddle, and then they went through it again. Satisfied—for the moment—they walked through the next scene. Maddy took a break, downed a pint of orange juice and a carton of yogurt, then went back for more.

It was twilight when she left the theater. A group of dancers were going to a local restaurant to unwind and recharge. Normally Maddy would have tagged along, content to remain in their company. Tonight, she felt she had two choices. She could go home and collapse in a hot tub, or she could get in Reed's way.

Going home was smarter. The last run-through had drained her store of energy. In any case, a woman who pursued an uninterested man—or a man who pursued an unwilling woman—showed a remarkable lack of good sense.

There were plenty of other people, people who had her own interests and ambitions, who would make less complicated companions. It wasn't as though men looked at her and ran in the other direction. She was well liked by most, she was usually appreciated for what she was, and if she really wanted to she could find an easy dinner partner and while away an enjoyable evening.

She went to five phone booths before she found one with its phone book still attached. Just checking, she told herself as she looked up Reed's name. It never hurt to check.

More than likely he lived way uptown. She'd just have to forgo her impulsive visit until she wasn't so tired. Her heart sank just a little when she found his address. He lived uptown, all right. Central Park West. There were nearly fifty blocks between them, fifty blocks that meant a great deal more than linear distance.

When she closed the phone book, it didn't occur to her that she could have lived there as well. She couldn't live there because she didn't understand Central Park West. She understood the Village, she understood SoHo, she understood the lower forties and the theater district.

She and Reed had nothing in common, and it was foolish to think otherwise. She began to walk, telling herself that she was going home, getting into the tub, climbing into bed with a book. She reminded herself that she'd never wanted a man in her life anyway. They expected things. They complicated things. She had dozens of dance routines filed in her head. There wasn't enough room left to let her think about a relationship.

Maddy went down into the subway, merging with the crowd. After a search, she unearthed a token from the bottom of her bag. Still lecturing herself, she went through the turnstile that would take her to the uptown train.

It would have been smarter to call first, Maddy decided as she stood on the sidewalk in front of the tall, intimidating building where Reed made his home. He might not be there. She paced down the sidewalk and back again. Worse, he might be there, but not alone. A woman in raw silk slacks strolled by with a pair of poodles and never gave Maddy a glance.

That was what this neighborhood was, she thought. Silk slacks and poodles. She was a mongrel in denim. She glanced down at her own roomy jeans and worn sneakers. At least she should have had the foresight to go home and change first.

Listen to yourself, Maddy ordered. You're standing here complaining about clothes. That's Chantel's line, it's never been yours. Besides, they're good enough for you. They're good enough for the people you know. If they're not good enough for Reed Valentine, what are you doing here?

I don't know, she mused. I'm an idiot.

No argument there.

Taking a deep breath, she walked forward through the wide glass doors into the quiet, marble-floored lobby.

She'd been an actress for years. Maddy put on an easy smile, tossed back her hair, then strolled over to the uniformed man behind the oak counter. "Hello. Is Reed in? Reed Valentine?"

"I'm sorry, miss. He hasn't come in yet this evening."

"Oh." She struggled not to let the depth of her disappointment show. "Well, I just dropped by."

"I'd be happy to take a message. Miss—" When he looked at her, really looked, his eyes widened. "You're Maddy O'Hurley."

She blinked. It was a very rare thing for her to be recognized outside the theater. Maddy knew better than anyone how different she appeared onstage. "Yes." She offered her hand automatically. "How do you do?"

"Oh, what a pleasure this is." The man, not much taller than she and twice as wide, took her hand in both of his. "When my wife wanted a treat for our anniversary, the kids got us two tickets for *Suzanna's Park*. Orchestra seats, too. What an evening we had."

"That's lovely." Maddy glanced at his name tag. "You must have wonderful children, Johnny."

"They're good sports. All six of them." He grinned at Maddy, showing one gold tooth. "Miss O'Hurley, I can't tell you how much we enjoyed watching you. My wife said it was like watching a sunrise."

"Thank you." Compliments like that one made the years of classes, the days and weeks of rehearsals, the cramped muscles, worthwhile. "Thank you very much."

"You know that part—Lord, my wife cried buckets—when you think Peter's gotten on the train, you think he's gone, and all the lights come down, with just that pale, pale blue one on you. And you sing, ah..." He cleared his throat. "How can he go," he began in a shaky baritone, "with my love wrapped around him?"

"How can he go," Maddy continued in a strong, vibrant contralto, "with my heart in his hand? I only know that I gave him a choice. And he didn't choose me."

"That's the one." Johnny shook his head and sighed. "I have to admit it brought a tear to my eye, too."

"I'm in a new musical that's scheduled to open in about six weeks."

"Are you now?" He beamed at her like a proud father. "We won't miss it, I promise you."

Maddy took a pencil from the counter and scrawled the name of the theater and the assistant stage manager on a pad. "You call this number, ask for Fred here and give my name. I'll see to it that you have two tickets for opening night."

"Opening night." His look of astonished pleasure was enough to warm Maddy all over. "My wife's not going to believe me. I don't know how to thank you, Miss O'Hurley."

She grinned at him. "Applaud."

"You can count on that. We'll— Oh, good evening, Mr. Valentine."

Maddy straightened from the counter like a shot, feeling guilty for no reason she could fathom. She turned and managed a smile. "Hello, Reed."

"Maddy." He'd come in during the brief duet, but neither of them had noticed.

When he only stared at her, she cleared her throat and decided to wing it. "I was up this way and decided to drop in and say hello. Hello."

He'd just come out of a long meeting where thoughts of her had distracted him. He wasn't pleased to see her. But he wanted to touch her. "Are you on your way somewhere?"

She could try being casually chic and lie about a party around the corner. She could just as easily grow a second head. "No. Just here."

Taking her by the arm, Reed nodded at Johnny, then led her to the elevators. "Are you always so generous with strangers?'' he asked as they stepped inside.

"Oh.'' After a moment's thought, she shrugged. "I suppose. You look a little tired.'' And wonderful, she added silently. Just wonderful.

"Long day.''

"Me too. We had our first full rehearsal today. It was a zoo.'' Then she laughed, nervously dipping her hands in her pockets. "I guess I shouldn't say that to the man with the checkbook.''

With an unintelligible mutter, he led her out into the hallway. Maddy decided silence was the best tack. Then he unlocked his door and brought her inside.

She'd expected something grand, something elegant, something tasteful. It was all that and more. When the lights were switched on, there was a feeling of space. The walls were pale, set off by vibrant impressionist paintings and three tall, wide windows that let in a lofty view of the park and the city. The pewter-toned rug was the perfect contrast to the long, spreading coral sofa. Two lush ficus trees stood in the corner, and set in two wall niches were the Ming vases she'd once imagined. A curved, open staircase led to a loft.

There wasn't a thing out of place, but she hadn't expected there to be. Still, it wasn't cold, and she hadn't been sure about that.

"It's lovely, Reed.'' She crossed to the windows to look down. If there was a problem, she felt it was here. He kept himself so aloof, so distant from the city he lived in, away from the sounds, the smells, the humanity of it. "Do you ever stand here and wonder what's going on?''

"What's going on where?''

"Down there, of course." She turned back to him with a silent invitation to join her. When he did, she looked down again. "Who's arguing, who's laughing, who's making love. Where's the police car going, and will he get there in time. How many street people will sleep in the park tonight. How many tricks turned, how many bottles opened, how many babies born. It's an incredible place, isn't it?"

She wore the same scent, light, teasing only because it was so guileless. "Not everyone looks at it the way you do."

"I always wanted to live in New York." She stepped back so that there were only lights, just the dazzle of them. "Ever since I can remember. It's strange how the three of us—my sisters, I mean—seemed to have this gut instinct where we belonged. As close as we are, we all chose completely different places. Abby's in rural Virginia, Chantel's in fantasyland, and I'm here."

He had to stop himself from stroking her hair. There was always that trace of wistfulness when she spoke of her sisters. He didn't understand family. He had only his father. "Would you like a drink?"

It was in his tone, the distance, the formality. She tried not to let it hurt. "I wouldn't mind some Perrier."

When he went to the compact ebony bar, she moved away from the window. She couldn't stand there, thinking about people milling around together, when she felt so divorced from the man she had come to see.

Then she saw the plant. He'd set it on a little stand where it would get indirect sunlight from the windows. The soil, when she tested it with her thumb, was moist but not soaking. She smiled as she touched a leaf. He could care, if only he allowed himself to.

"It looks better," Maddy said as she took the glass he offered.

"It's pitiful," Reed corrected, swirling the brandy in his snifter.

"No, really, it does. It doesn't look so, well…pale, I guess. Thank you."

"You were drowning it." He drank, and wished her eyes weren't so wide, so candid. "Why don't you sit down, Maddy? You can tell me why you came."

"I just wanted to see you." For the first time, she wished she had some of Chantel's flair with men. "Look, I'm lousy at this sort of thing." Unable to keep still, she began to wander around the apartment. "I never had time to develop a lot of style, and I only say clever lines when they're fed to me. I wanted to see you." Defiantly she sat on the edge of the sofa. "So I came."

"No style." It amazed him that he could be amused when this unwanted need for her was knotting his gut. "I see." He sat, as well, keeping a cushion between them. "Did you come to proposition me?"

Temper flared in her eyes and came out unexpectedly as hauter. "I see dancers don't have a patent on ego. I suppose the women you're used to are ready to tumble into bed when you crook your finger."

The smile threatened again as he lifted his brandy. "The women I'm used to don't sing duets in the lobby with the security guard."

She slammed down her glass, and the fizzing water plopped dangerously close to the rim. "Probably because they have tin ears."

"That's a possibility. The point is, Maddy, I don't know what to do about you."

"Do about me?" She rose, completely graceful, totally livid. "You don't have to do *anything* about me. I don't want you to do anything about me. I'm not an Eliza Doolittle."

"You even think in plays."

"What if I do? You think in columns." Disgusted, she began to pace again. "I don't know what I'm doing here. It was stupid. Damn it, I've been miserable for a week. I'm not used to being miserable." She whirled back, accusing. "I missed my cue because I was thinking about you."

"Were you?" He rose, though he'd promised himself he wouldn't. He knew he should see to it that she was angry enough to leave before he did something he'd regret. But he was doing it now, moving closer to brush his thumb over her cheek.

"Yes." Desire rose and anger drained. She didn't know how to make room for both. She took his wrist before he could drop his hand. "I wanted you to think of me."

"Maybe I was." He wanted to gather her close, to feel her hard against him and pretend for just a little while. "Maybe I caught myself looking out the window of my office and wondering about you."

She rose on her toes to meet his lips. There was a storm brewing in him, she could feel it. She had storms of her own, but she knew his would be for different reasons and have different results. Was it necessary to understand him, when being with him felt so right? It was enough for her. But even as she thought it, she knew it would never be enough for him.

"Reed—"

"No." His hands were hard and tense on her back, in her hair, as he pulled her closer. "Don't talk now."

He needed what she could give him, with her mouth, with her arms, with the movement of her body against his. His home had never seemed empty until she had come into his life. Now that she was here, with him, he didn't want to think about being alone again.

Her mouth was like velvet, warm and smooth, as comforting as it was arousing. When she touched him, it felt as though she wanted to give, rather than take. For a moment he could almost believe it.

How easily he could lure her under. A kiss had always been a simple thing to her. Something to show affection to a loved one with, something to be given casually to a friend, even something to be played up onstage for a theater full of people. But with Reed, the simplicity ended. This was complex, overwhelming, a contact that shot sparks through every nerve ending. Passion wasn't new to her. She experienced it every day in her work. She'd known that it was different when it involved a man and woman, but she hadn't realized it could turn her muscles to water and cloud her brain.

He ran his hands through her hair. She wished he would move them over her, over every inch of the body that throbbed and ached for him. He wanted her. She could taste the frenzied desire every time his mouth met hers. Yet he did nothing more than hold her close against him.

Make love with me, her mind requested, but her lips were captured by his and couldn't form the words. She could picture candlelight, soft music and a big, wide bed with the two of them tangled together. The image made her skin heat and her mouth more aggressive.

"Reed, do you want me?"

Even as her mouth skimmed over his face, she felt him stiffen. Just slightly, but she felt it. "Yes."

It was the way he said it that cooled her blood. Reluctance, even annoyance, glazed over the answer. Maddy drew away slowly. "You have a problem with that?"

Why couldn't it be as simple with her as it was with other women? Mutual enjoyment, rules up front, and nobody's hurt. He'd known from the first time he'd touched her that it wouldn't be simple with her. "Yes." He went back for his brandy, hoping it would steady him. "I have a problem with that."

She was going too fast, Maddy decided. It was a bad habit of hers to move at top speed without looking for the bumps in the road. "Would you like to share it with me?"

"I want you." The statement wiped away what she'd hoped was a casual smile. "I've wanted to take you to bed since I watched you gathering up loose change and sweaty clothes off the sidewalk."

She took a step closer. Did he know that was what she'd wanted to hear, even though it frightened her a little? Did he know how much she wanted him to feel some portion of what she felt? "Why did you send me away the other night?"

"I'm no good for you, Maddy."

She stared at him. "Wait a minute. I want to be sure I understand this. You sent me away for my own good."

He splashed more brandy into the glass. It wasn't helping. "That's right."

"Reed, you make a child wear scratchy clothes in the winter for her own good. Once she gets past a certain age, she's on her own."

He wondered how in the hell he was supposed to argue with an analogy like that. "You don't strike me as the kind of woman interested in one-night stands."

Her smile chilled. "No, I'm not."

"Then I did you a favor." He drank again because he was beginning to despise himself.

"I guess I should say thank you." She picked up her dance bag, then dropped it again. It just wasn't an O'Hurley trait to give up easily. "I want to know why you're so sure it would have been a one-night stand."

"I'm not interested in the long term."

She nodded, telling herself that was reasonable. "There's a big difference between one night and the long term. I get the feeling that you think I'm trying to put a cage around you."

She didn't know that the cage was half formed already, and that he'd built it himself. "Maddy, why don't we just leave it that you and I have nothing in common."

"I've thought about that." Now that she had something solid to dig her teeth into, she relaxed again. "It's true to a point, you know, but when you really think about it, we have plenty in common. We both live in New York."

Lifting a brow, he leaned back against the bar. "Of course. That wipes everything else out."

"It's a start." She caught it, that faint glimpse of amusement. It was enough for her. "We both, at the

moment, have a vested interest in a certain musical."
She smiled at him, instinctively and irresistibly
charming. "I put my socks on before my shoes. How
about you?"

"Maddy—"

"Do you stand up in the shower?"

"I don't see—"

"Come on, no evasions. Just the truth. Do you?"

It was useless. He had to smile. "Yes."

"Amazing. So do I. Ever read *Gone with the
Wind*?"

"Yes."

"Ah. Common ground in literature. I could probably go on for hours."

"I'm sure you could." He set his brandy down and
went to her again. "What's the point, Maddy?"

"The point is, I like you, Reed." She put her hands
on his forearms, wishing she could ease the tension
and keep that smile in his eyes just a bit longer. "I
think if you'd loosen up, just a little, we could be
friends. I'm attracted to you. I think if we take our
time we could be lovers, too."

It was a mistake, of course. He knew it, but she
looked so appealing just then, so honest and carefree.
"You are," he murmured as he toyed with a strand of
her hair, "unique."

"I hope so." With a smile, she rose up on her toes
and kissed him, without heat, without passion. "Is it
a deal?"

"You might regret it."

"Then that's my problem, isn't it? Friends?" She
offered her hand solemnly, but her eyes laughed at
him, challenging.

"Friends," he agreed, and hoped he wouldn't be the one to regret it.

"Great. Listen, I'm starving. Have you got a can of soup or something?"

Chapter Six

On the surface, it appeared to be every bit as simple as Maddy had said it could be. For a great many people it would have been simple beneath the surface, as well. But not everyone wanted as deeply as Reed or pretended as well as Maddy.

They went to the movies. Whenever their schedules meshed and the weather cooperated, they had lunch in the Park. They spent one quiet Sunday afternoon wandering through a museum, more interested in each other than in the exhibits. If Reed hadn't known himself better, he would have said he was on the brink of having a romance. But he didn't believe in romance.

Love had brought his father betrayal, a betrayal Reed himself lived with every day. If Edwin had put it behind him, Reed had not, could not. Fidelity, to the majority of the people he worked with, was nothing if not flexible. People had affairs, not romances, and they had them before, during and after marriage, so that marriage itself was a moot point. Nothing lasted forever, particularly not relationships.

But he thought of Maddy when he wasn't with her, and he thought of little else when they were together.

Friends. Somehow they'd managed to become friends, despite their differing outlooks and opposite backgrounds. If the friendship was cautious on his part and careless on hers, they'd still found enough between them to form a base. Where did they go from here?

Lovers. It seemed inevitable that they would become lovers. The passion that simmered under the surface every moment they were together wouldn't be held back for long. They both knew it and, in their different ways, accepted it. What worried Reed was that once he'd taken her to bed, as he wanted to, he would lose the easy companionship he was coming to depend on.

Sex would change things. It was bound to. Intimacy on a physical level would jar the emotional intimacy they had just begun to develop. As much as he needed Maddy in his bed, he wondered if he could afford to risk losing the Maddy he knew out of bed. It was a tug-of-war he knew he could never really win.

Yet he didn't believe in losing. Given enough logical thought, enough planning, he should be able to find a way to have both. Did it matter if he was being calculating, even cold-blooded, when the end result would please both of them?

The answer wouldn't come. Instead, an image ran through his head of Maddy as she'd been a few afternoons before, laughing, tossing bread crumbs to pigeons in the Park.

When the buzzer sounded on his desk, he discovered he'd lost another ten minutes daydreaming. "Yes, Hannah."

"Your father's on line one, Mr. Valentine."

"Thank you." Reed pushed a button and made the connection. "Dad?"

"Reed, heard a rumor that Selby's taken on a fresh batch of indies. Know anything about it?"

Reed already had a preliminary report on the influx of independent record promoters taken on by Galloway. "Keeping your ear to the ground on the 'nineteenth' hole?"

"Something like that."

"There's talk of some pressure on some of the Top 40 stations to add a few records to their playlist. Nothing new. A few whispers of payola, but nothing that gels."

"Selby's a slippery sonofabitch. You hear anything concrete, I wouldn't mind being informed."

"You'll be the first."

"Never liked the idea of paying to have a record air," Edwin muttered. "Well, it's an old gambit, and I'm thinking more of new ones. I wanted to see a rehearsal of our play. Would you like to join me?"

Reed glanced at his desk calendar. "When?"

"In an hour. I know it's the form to let them know; they'd like to be on their toes when the bank roll's expected, but I like surprises."

Reed noted two appointments that morning and started to refuse. Giving in to impulse, he decided to reschedule. "I'll meet you at the theater at eleven."

"Stretch it into lunch? Your old man's buying."

He was lonely, Reed realized. Edwin Valentine had his club, his friends and enough money to cruise around the world, but he was lonely. "I'll bring an appetite," Reed told him, then hung up to juggle his schedule.

Edwin entered the theater stealthily, like a boy without a ticket. "We'll just slip into a seat on the aisle and see what we're paying for."

Reed walked behind his father, but his gaze was on the stage, where Maddy was wrapped in the arms of another man. He felt the lunge of jealousy, so surprisingly fierce that he stopped in the center of the aisle and stared.

She was looking up at another man, her arms linked behind his neck, her face glowing. "I really had a wonderful time, Jonathan. I could have danced forever."

"You're talking like it's over. We have hours yet." Reed watched as the man pressed a kiss to her forehead. "Come home with me."

"Come home with you?" Even with the distance, Reed could sense the alarm in the set of Maddy's body. "Oh, Jonathan, I'd like to, really." She drew away, just a little, but he caught her hands. "I just can't. I have to... I have to be at work early. Yes, that's it. And there's my mother." She turned away again, rolling her eyes so that the audience could see the lie while the man beside her couldn't. "She's not really well, you know, and I should be there in case she needs anything."

"You're such a good person, Mary."

"Oh, no." Guilt and distress were hinted at in her voice. "No, Jonathan, I'm not."

"Don't say that." He drew her into his arms again. "Because I think I'm falling in love with you."

She was caught up in another kiss. Even knowing it was only a play, Reed felt something twist in his stomach.

"I have to go," she said quickly. "I really have to." Pulling away, she darted across stage right.

"When will I see you again?"

She stopped and seemed at war within herself. "Tomorrow. Come to the library at six. I'll meet you."

"Mary—" He started toward her, but she held up both hands.

"Tomorrow," she said again, and ran offstage.

"All right." The director's voice boomed out. "We'll have fifteen seconds here for the drops and set change. Wanda, Rose, take your marks. Lights go on. Cue, Maddy."

She came rushing onstage again to where Wanda was lounging in a chair and the woman named Rose was primping in a mirror.

"You're late," Wanda said lazily.

"What are you, a time clock?" Maddy's voice had an edge of toughness now; her movements were sharper.

"Jackie was looking for you."

Maddy stopped in the act of pulling on a wild red wig. "What'd you tell him?"

"That he wasn't looking in the right places. Don't stretch your G-string, Mary. I covered for you."

"Yeah, she covered for you," Rose agreed, snapping a wad of gum and fussing with her outrageous pink-and-orange costume.

"Thanks." Maddy whipped off her skirt. Nudging Rose aside, she began to paint her face.

"Don't thank me. We gotta stick together." She watched negligently as Rose practiced a routine. "Think you're nuts, though," Wanda added.

"I know what I'm doing." Maddy slipped behind a screen. The blouse she'd worn flapped across it. "I can handle it."

"You better make sure you can handle Jackie. Any idea what he'd do to you and your pretty boy if he found out what's going on?"

"He's not going to find out." She came out from the screen in a long, slinky gown covered with red spangles. "Look, I'm on."

"Crowd's pretty hot tonight."

"Good." She sent Wanda a grin. "That's the way I like them." She walked off stage right again.

"Lights stage left," the stage manager called. "Cue Terry."

A dancer Reed recognized from the only other rehearsal he'd seen paced out on stage left. His hair was slicked back, and he'd added a pencil-thin moustache. He wore a brilliant white tie against a black shirt. When Maddy came out behind him, he grabbed her arm.

"Where the hell you been?"

"Around." Maddy pushed back the mane of red hair, then settled a hand saucily on her hip. "What's your problem?"

Edwin leaned over and whispered to Reed. "Doesn't look like the little lady who came into your office with a dead plant."

"No," Reed murmured as the two on stage argued. "It doesn't."

"She's going to be big, Reed. Very, very big."

He felt twin surges of pride and alarm and could explain neither of them. "Yes, I think she is."

"Look, sugar." Maddy gave her partner a pat on the cheek. "You want me to go strip or stay here and read you my diary?"

"Strip," Jackie ordered her.

"Yeah." Maddy tossed her head back. "That's what I do best."

"Lights," the stage manager called out. "Music."

Maddy grabbed a red boa and walked—no, sauntered—to center stage, then stood there like a flame. When she began to sing, her voice came slowly and built, as arousing and teasing as the movements she began to make. The boa was tossed into the audience. It would be replaced dozens of times before the play closed.

"I never took you to a strip joint, did I, Reed?"

He had to smile, even as Maddy began to peel off elbow-length gloves. "No, you didn't."

"Hole in your education."

Onstage, Maddy let her body take over. It was just one routine among nearly a dozen others, but she knew it had the potential to be a showstopper if she played it right. She intended to.

When she whipped off the skirt of the dress, some of the technicians began to whistle. She grinned and went into a series of thunderous bumps and grinds. When the two-minute dance had run its course, she sat on the stage, arched back, wearing little more than spangles and beads. To her surprise and pleasure, there was a smattering of applause from the center of the audience. Exhausted, she propped herself on her elbow and smiled out into the darkened theater.

Word traveled quickly, from assistant to assistant to stage manager to director. Money was in the house.

Don went down the aisle, swearing because the grapevine hadn't gotten to him sooner. "Mr. Valentine. And Mr. Valentine." He offered hearty handshakes. "We weren't expecting you."

"We thought we'd catch something a little impromptu." Reed spoke to him, but his gaze wandered back to the stage, where Maddy still sat, dabbing at her throat now with a towel. "Very impressive."

"We could be a little sharper yet, but we'll be ready for Philadelphia."

"No doubt about that." Edwin gave him a friendly slap on the shoulder. "We don't want to hold things up."

"I'd love you to stay longer, if you could. We're about to rehearse the first scene from the second act. Please, come down front."

"Up to you, Reed."

He was going to have to put in an extra two hours with paperwork to make up for this. But he wasn't going to miss it. "Let's go."

The next scene was played strictly for laughs. Reed didn't know enough to dissect the comedic timing, the pacing, the stage business that made the simplest things funny. He could see, however, that Maddy knew how to play it to the hilt. She was going to have the audience eating out of her hand.

There was something vivid about her, something convincing and sympathetic even in her role as the brazen, somewhat edgy stripper. Reed watched her play two roles, adding the innocence necessary to convince the eager and honest Jonathan that his Mary was a dedicated librarian with a sick mother. He'd have believed her himself. And it was that quality that began to worry him.

"She's quite a performer," Edwin commented when the director and stage manager went into a huddle.

"Yes, she is."

"I suppose it's none of my business, but what's going on between you?"

Reed turned, his face expressionless. "What makes you think anything is?"

Edwin tapped the side of his nose. "I'd never have gotten this far in the business if I couldn't sniff things out."

"We're . . . friends," Reed said after a moment.

With a sigh, Edwin shifted his large bulk in the seat. "You know, Reed, one of the things I've always wanted for you is a woman like Maddy O'Hurley. A bright, beautiful woman who could make you happy."

"I am happy."

"You're still bitter."

"Not with you," Reed said immediately. "Never with you."

"Your mother—"

"Leave it." Though the words were quiet, the ice was there. "This has nothing to do with her."

It had everything to do with her, Edwin thought as Maddy took the stage again. But he knew his son well, and kept his silence.

Edwin couldn't turn back the clock and stop the betrayal. Even if it were possible, he wouldn't. If he could, and did, Reed wouldn't be sitting beside him now. How could he teach his son that it was a matter not of forgiveness but of acceptance? How could he teach him to trust when he'd been born of a lie?

Edwin studied Maddy as her bright, expressive face lighted the stage. Could she be the one to do the teaching?

Maybe she was the woman Reed had always needed, the answer he'd always searched for without acknowledging that he was looking. Maybe, through Maddy, Edwin could lay all his own past hurts to rest.

Even though it was simply a walk-through, Maddy kept the energy at a high level. She didn't believe in pacing herself through a performance, or through life, but in going full out and seeing where it landed her.

While she ran through her lines, practiced her moves, part of her concentration focused on Reed. He was watching her so intently. It was if he were trying to see through her role to who and what she really was. Didn't he understand that it was her job to submerge herself until there was no Maddy, only Mary?

She thought she sensed disapproval, even annoyance—a completely different mood from the one he'd sat down with. She wanted badly to jump down from the stage and somehow reassure him, though of what she wasn't sure. But he didn't want that from her. At least not yet. For now he wanted everything casual, very, very light. No strings, no promises, no future.

She stumbled over a line, swore at herself. They backtracked and began again.

She couldn't tell him how she felt. For a woman with an honest nature, even silence was deception. But she couldn't tell him. He didn't want to hear her say she loved him, had begun to love him from the moment she'd stood on the sidewalk with him at dusk. He would be angry, because he didn't want to be trapped by emotion. He wouldn't understand that she simply lived on emotion.

Perhaps he'd think she simply gave her love easily. It was true enough that she did, but not this kind of love. Love of family was natural and always there. Love of friends evolved slowly or quickly, but with no qualms. She could love a child in the park for nothing more than his innocence, or an old man on the street for nothing more than his endurance.

But loving Reed involved everything. This love was complex, and she'd always thought loving was simple. It hurt, and she'd always believed love brought joy. The passion was there, always simmering underneath. It made her restless with anticipation, when she'd always been so easygoing.

She'd invited him into her life. That was something she couldn't forget. More, she'd argued him into her life when he'd been ready to back away. So she loved him. But she couldn't tell him.

"Lunch, ladies and gentlemen. Be back at two, prepared to run through the two final scenes."

"So it's the angel," Wanda murmured in Maddy's ear. "The one in the front row who looks like a cover for *Gentleman's Quarterly*."

"What about him?" Maddy bent from the waist and let her muscles relax.

"That's him, isn't it?"

"What him?"

"*The* him." Wanda gave her a quick slap on the rump. "The him that's had you standing around dreamy eyed."

"I don't stand around dreamy eyed." At least she hoped she didn't.

"That's him," Wanda said with a self-satisfied smile before she strolled offstage.

Grumbling to herself, Maddy walked down the steps beside the stage. She put on a fresh smile. "Reed, I'm glad you came." She didn't touch him or offer the quick, friendly kiss she usually greeted him with. "Mr. Valentine. It's so nice to see you again."

"I enjoyed every minute of it." He sandwiched her hand between his big ones. "It's a pleasure to watch you work. Did I hear the man mention lunch?"

She put a hand on her stomach. "That you did."

"Then you'll join us, won't you?"

"Well, I..." When Reed said nothing, she searched for an excuse.

"Now, you wouldn't disappoint me." Edwin ignored his son's silence and barreled ahead. "This is your neck of the woods. You must know a good spot."

"There's a deli just across the street," she began.

"Perfect. I could eat a good pastrami." And it would only take a quick call to cancel his reservation at the Four Seasons. "What do you say, Reed?"

"I'd say Maddy needs a minute to change." He finally smiled at her.

She glanced down at her costume of hot-pink shorts and tank top. "Five minutes to get into my street clothes," she promised, and dashed away.

She was better than her word. Within five minutes she had thrown a yellow sweat suit over her costume and was walking into the deli in front of Reed and his father.

The smells were wonderful. There were times she stopped in for them alone. Spiced meat, hot mustard, strong coffee. An overhead fan stirred it all up. Most of the dancers had headed there from the theater like hungry ants to a picnic. Because the proprietor was shrewd, there was a jukebox in the rear corner. It was already blasting away.

The big Greek behind the counter spotted Maddy and gave her a wide white grin. "Ahhh, an O'Hurley special?"

"Absolutely." Leaning on the glass front of the counter, she watched him dish up a big, leafy salad. He used a generous hand with chunks of cheese, then topped it off with a dollop of yogurt.

"You eat that?" Edwin asked behind her.

She laughed and accepted the bowl. "I absorb it."

"Body needs meat." Edwin ordered a pastrami on a huge kaiser roll.

"I'll get us a table," Maddy offered, grabbing a cup of tea to go with the salad. Wisely she commandeered one on the opposite end of the room from the music.

"Lunch with the big boys, huh, Maddy?" Terry, with his hair still slicked back *á la* Jackie, stooped over her. "Going to put in a good word for me?"

"What word would you like?" She turned in her chair to grin up at him.

"How about 'star'?"

"I'll see if I can work it in."

He started to say something else but glanced over at his own table. "Damn it, Leroy, that's my pickle."

Maddy was still laughing when Reed and his father joined her.

"Quite a place," Edwin commented, already looking forward to his sandwich and the heap of potato salad beside it.

"They're on their best behavior because you're here."

Someone started to sing over the blare of the jukebox. Maddy simply pitched her voice higher. "Will you come to the Philadelphia opening, Mr. Valentine?"

"Thinking about it. Don't travel as much as I used to. There was a time when the head of a record company had to be out of town as much as he was in his office."

"Must have been exciting." She dipped into her salad and pretended she didn't envy Reed his pile of rare roast beef.

"Hotel rooms, meetings." He shrugged. "And I missed my boy." The look he gave Reed was both rueful and affectionate. "Missed too many ball games."

"You made plenty of them." Reed sliced off a corner of his sandwich and handed it to Maddy. It was a small, completely natural gesture that caught Edwin's eye. And his hope.

"Reed was top pitcher on his high school team."

Reed was shaking his head with a smile of his own when Maddy turned to him. "You played ball? You never told me." As soon as the words were out, she reminded herself he had no reason to tell her. There were dozens of other details about his life that he hadn't told her. "I never really understood baseball until I moved to New York," she went on quickly. "Then I caught a few Yankee games to see what the fuss was about. What was your ERA?"

He lifted a brow. "2.38."

It pleased her that he remembered. She rolled her eyes at his father. "Big-league material."

"So I always told him. But he wanted to work in the business."

"That's the big leagues, too, isn't it?" She nibbled on the portion of sandwich Reed had given her. "Most of us only look at the finished product, you know, the album we put on the turntable, the cassette we stick in the car stereo. I guess it's a long trip from sheet music to vinyl."

"When you've got three or four days free," Edwin said with a laugh, "I'll fill you in."

"I'd like that." She drank her honeyed tea, knowing it would seep into her bloodstream and get her through the next four hours. "When we recorded the cast album for *Suzanna's Park*, I got a taste of it. I think the studio's so different from the stage. So, well . . . restricted." She swallowed lettuce. "Sorry."

"No need."

"A studio has certain restrictions," Reed put in. He took a sip of his coffee and discovered it was strong enough to melt leather. "On the other hand, there can be untold advantages. We can take that man behind the counter, put him in a studio and turn him into Caruso by pushing the right buttons."

Maddy digested that, then shook her head. "That's cheating."

"That's marketing," Reed corrected. "And plenty of labels do it."

"Does Valentine?"

He looked at her, and the gray eyes she'd admired from the beginning were direct. "No. Valentine was started with an eye toward quality, not quantity."

She slanted Edwin a wicked look. "But you were going to offer a recording contract to the O'Hurley Triplets."

Edwin added an extra dash of pepper to his sandwich. "You weren't quality?"

"We were . . . a slice above mediocre."

"A great deal above, if what I saw onstage this afternoon is any indication."

"I appreciate that."

"Do you get time for much socializing, Maddy?"

She plopped her chin on her hands. "Asking me for a date?"

He seemed taken aback, though only for an instant. Then he roared with laughter that caught the attention of everyone in the deli. "Damned if I wouldn't if I could drop twenty years. Quite a prize right here." He patted her hand, but looked at his son.

"Yes, she is," Reed said blandly.

"I'm thinking of giving a party," Edwin said on impulse. "Sending the play off to Philadelphia in style. What do you think, Maddy?"

"I think it's a great idea. Am I invited?"

"On the condition that you save a dance for me."

It was as easy for her to love the father as it was for her to love the son. "You can have as many as you like."

"I don't think I can keep up with you for more than one."

She laughed with him. When she picked up her tea, she saw that Reed was watching her again, coolly. The sense of disapproval she felt from him cut her to the bone.

"I, ah, I have to get back. There are some things I have to do before afternoon rehearsal."

"Walk the lady across the street, Reed. Your legs are younger than mine."

"Oh, that's all right." Maddy was already up. "I don't need—"

"I'll walk you over." Reed had her by the elbow.

She wouldn't make a scene. For the life of her she couldn't pinpoint why she wanted to so badly. Instead, she bent down and kissed Edwin's cheek. "Thanks for lunch."

She waited until they were outside before she spoke again. "Reed, I'm perfectly capable of crossing the street alone. Go back to your father."

"Do you have a problem?"

"Do *I* have a problem?" She pulled her arm away and glared at him. "Oh, I can't stand to hear you say that to me in that proper, politely curious voice." She started across the street at a jog.

"You have twenty minutes to get back." He caught her arm again.

"I said I had things to do."

"You lied."

In the center of the street, with the light turning yellow, she turned toward him again. "Then let's say I have better things to do. Better things than to sit there and be put under your intellectual microscope. What's wrong, don't you like the fact that I enjoy your father's company? Are you afraid I have designs on him?"

"Stop it." He gave her a jerk to get her moving as cars began to honk.

"You just don't like women in general, do you? You put us all in this big box that's labeled 'Not To Be Trusted.' I wish I knew why."

"Maddy, you're becoming very close to hysterical."

"Oh, I can get a lot closer," she promised with deadly sincerity. "You froze up. I saw you when I was onstage and you were watching me with that cold, measuring look in your eyes. It was as if you thought you were looking at me instead of the part I was playing—and you didn't want either of us to win.''

Because he recognized the glimmer of truth, he shifted away from it. "You're being ridiculous."

"I'm not." She shoved away from him again as they stood by the stage door. "I know when I'm being ridiculous, and in this instance I'm not. I don't know what ate away at you, Reed, but whatever it was, I'm sorry for it. I've tried not to let it bother me, I've tried not to let a lot of things bother me. But this is too much."

He took her by the shoulders and held her against the wall. "What is too much?"

"I saw your face when your father was talking about having a party, about me being there. Well, you don't have to worry, I won't come. I'll make an excuse."

"What are you talking about?" he demanded, spacing each word carefully.

"I didn't realize you'd be embarrassed being seen with me."

"Maddy—"

"No, it's understandable, isn't it?" she rushed on. "I'm just plain Maddy O'Hurley, no degrees behind the name, no pedigree in front of it. I got my high school diploma in the mail, and both my parents can trace their roots back to peasant stock in the south of Ireland."

He caught her chin in his hand. "The next time you take a side trip, leave me a map so I can keep up. I don't know what you're talking about."

"I'm talking about us!" she shouted. "I don't know why I'm talking about us, because there *is* no us. You don't want an us. You don't even want a you and me, really, so I don't—"

He cut her off, out of total frustration, by pressing his mouth over hers. "Shut up," he warned when she struggled to protest. "Just shut up a minute."

He filled himself on her. God, if she knew how frustrated he'd been watching her seduce an empty theater, how empty he'd felt sitting beside her, unable to touch her. The anger poured through. He'd hurt her. And would probably hurt her again. He no longer knew how to avoid it.

"Calm?" he asked when he let her speak again.

"No."

"All right, then, just be quiet. I don't know exactly what I was thinking while I was watching you onstage. It's becoming a problem to think at all when I look at you."

She started to snap, then thought better of it. "Why?"

"I don't know. As for the other business, you are being ridiculous. I don't care if you got your education in a correspondence school or at Vassar. I don't care if your father was knighted or tried for grand larceny."

"Disturbing the peace," Maddy mumbled. "But that was only once—twice, I guess. I'm sorry." As the tears rolled out, she apologized again. "I'm really sorry. I hate this. I always get so churned up when I'm angry, and I can't stop."

"Don't." He brushed at her tears himself. "I haven't been completely fair with you. We really need to clear up what the situation between us is."

"Okay. When?"

"When don't you have a class at the crack of dawn?"

She sniffed and searched in her dance bag for a tissue. "Sunday."

"Saturday, then. Will you come to my place?" He brushed a thumb along her cheekbone. She was being reasonable, too reasonable, when he knew he couldn't promise to be. "Please?"

"Yes, I'll come. Reed, I didn't mean to make a scene."

"Neither did I. Maddy—" He hesitated a moment, then decided to start clearing the air now. "The business with my father. It had nothing to do with the party he's planning. It had nothing to do with you coming or being with me."

She wanted to believe him, but an insecurity she hadn't been aware of held her back. "What was it, then?"

"I haven't seen him so . . . charmed by anyone in a very long time. He wanted a house full of children, and he never had them. If he'd had a daughter, I imagine he'd have enjoyed one like you."

"Reed, I'm sorry. I don't know what you want me to do."

"Just don't hurt him. I won't see him hurt again." He touched her cheek briefly, then left her at the stage door.

Chapter Seven

When Maddy let herself into her apartment she was thinking about Reed. That didn't surprise her. Thoughts of Reed had dominated her day to the point where she had had to make a conscious effort to concentrate on her role as Mary Howard. The Philadelphia opening was only three weeks away. She couldn't afford to be distracted by speculation on what-if and how-to when they concerned Reed Valentine.

But what was going to happen on Saturday? What would she say? How should she behave?

Maddy jammed the key into her lock and called herself a fool. But she kept thinking.

The lights were on. As the door closed behind her, Maddy stood in the center of the room frowning. True, she was often absentminded or in too much of a rush to remember little details, but she wouldn't have

left the lights on. She'd retained the habit of conserv-
ing energy—and electrical bills—from her leaner days.
Besides, she didn't think she'd even turned them on
that morning before she'd left for class.

Odder still, she could have sworn she smelled coffee. Fresh coffee.

Maddy was setting down her dance bag and turning toward the kitchen when she heard a noise from
the bedroom. Heart thudding, she pulled a tap shoe
from the bag and held it up like a weapon. She didn't
consider herself the aggressive type, but it didn't even
occur to her to run and call for help. It was her home,
and she had always defended what was hers.

Slowly, careful to make no sound, she moved across
the room.

She heard a jangle of hangers from the closet and
gripped the shoe tighter. If the thief thought he'd find
anything of value in there, he was too stupid for
words. She should be able to send a dim-witted thief
on his way with the threat of a rap over the head with
a reinforced heel. Still, the closer she came, the more
often she had to swallow past the little flutter of panic
in her throat.

Holding her breath, Maddy closed her free hand
around the knob, then pulled. There were simultaneous shrieks of alarm.

"Well." Chantel put a hand to her heart. "It's nice
to see you, too."

"Chantel!" With a whoop of delight, Maddy tossed
her shoe aside and grabbed her sister. "I almost put a
dent in your head."

"Then I'd have one to match yours."

"What are you doing here?"

"Hanging up a few things." Chantel kissed Maddy's cheek, then tossed back her silvery-blond mane. "I hope you don't mind. Silk wrinkles so dreadfully."

"Of course I don't mind. I meant, what are you doing in New York? You should have let me know you were coming."

"Darling, I wrote you last week."

"No, you—" Then Maddy remembered the stack of mail she'd yet to open. "I haven't gotten to some of my mail yet."

"Typical."

"Yeah, I know." She drew her sister back just to look. It was a face she knew as well as her own, but one she never ceased to admire. The subtle French fragrance that wafted through the room suited Chantel as perfectly as the deep blue eyes and the cupid's-bow mouth. "Oh, Chantel, you look wonderful. I'm so glad to see you."

"You look pretty wonderful yourself." Chantel studied her sister's glowing complexion. "Either those vitamins you guzzle are working or you're in love."

"I think it's both."

One thin, shapely brow rose. "Is that so? Why don't we get out of the closet and talk about it?"

"Let's sit down and have a drink." Maddy linked her arm through Chantel's. "Oh, I wish Abby were here, too. Then it would be perfect. How long are you in town?"

"Just a couple of days," Chantel explained as they walked back to the living room. "I'm presenting one of those America's Choice Awards Friday night. My publicists thought it would be 'just nifty'."

Maddy began to search the cupboards for a bottle of wine. "And you don't."

Chantel tossed a glance at the darkening window. "You know New York's not my town, darling. It's too..."

"Real?" Maddy suggested.

"Let's just say noisy." Outside, two sirens were competing in volume. "I hope you have some wine, Maddy. You were out of coffee, you know."

"I gave it up," Maddy told her with her head stuck in a cupboard.

"Gave it up? You?"

"I was drinking too much of it. Just pouring that caffeine into my system. I'm drinking mostly herb tea these days." Maddy sniffed again and caught the rich, dark scent of coffee. "Where did you get it?"

"Oh, I borrowed a few scoops from your next-door neighbor."

Wine bottle in hand, Maddy drew out of the cupboard. "Not Guido."

"Yes, Guido. The one with the biceps and large teeth."

Maddy unearthed two glasses. "Chantel, I've lived next door to him for years and I wouldn't exchange a good-morning with him without an armed guard."

"He was charming." Leaning against the counter, Chantel pushed her hair away from her face. Although I did have to discourage him from coming over to fix the coffee for me."

Maddy glanced at her sister, at the classic face, the stunning body, the Wedgwood-blue eyes that easily hypnotized men. "I bet." Maddy poured two glasses, then tapped hers against her sister's. "Here's to the O'Hurleys."

"God bless them every one," Chantel murmured, and sipped. After a grimace, she swallowed. "Maddy, you're still buying your wine at the flea market."

"It's not that bad. Let's sit down. Have you heard from Abby?"

"I called her before I left so she'd know I'd be on the same coast. She was refereeing a fight between the boys and sounded blissfully happy."

"Dylan?"

Chantel sank into the sofa, grateful for its stationary comfort after a long, tedious flight. "She said he was nearly finished with the book."

"How does she feel about it?"

"Content. She trusts him completely." Chantel sipped again. There was a trace of cynicism in her voice that she couldn't completely disguise. She had trusted once, too. "Abby seems to have put her life with Rockwell behind her. She tells me Dylan's going to adopt the boys."

"That's great." Maddy felt her eyes fill, and swallowed more wine. "That's really great."

"It's what she's needed. He's what she's needed. Oh, and Abby said she'd gotten a lace tablecloth from Trace as a wedding gift."

"I guess we were all hoping he'd manage to get back for the wedding. Where is he?"

"Brittany, I think. He sent his apologies, as usual."

"Do you ever wonder what he does?"

"I decided to stop wondering in case it was illegal. Are Mom and Pop going to make it to your opening?"

"I hope so. They've got three weeks to work their way to Philly. I guess you won't be able to make it back east."

"I'm sorry." Chantel closed her hand over her sister's. "Filming on *Strangers* was postponed—couple of problems with the location site. I should be starting week after next. You know I'd be here if I could."

"I know. You must be so excited. It's such a wonderful part."

"Yes." A frown moved into her eyes and out again.

"What's wrong?"

Chantel hesitated, on the verge of telling Maddy about the anonymous letters she'd been getting. And the phone calls. She shrugged it off. "I don't know. Nerves, I guess. I've never done a miniseries. It's not really television, it's not a feature film."

"Come on, Chantel. This is Maddy."

"It's nothing." She made up her mind not to discuss what was probably nothing more than a minor annoyance. When she returned to California, the whole thing would probably have blown over. "Just a few loose ends I have to tie up. What I want to talk about is the man you're thinking about." She smiled when Maddy blinked back to full attention. "Come on, Maddy. Tell your big sister everything."

"I'm not sure how much there is to tell." Maddy brought her legs up into a comfortable lotus position. "Do you ever remember Pop talking about knowing Edwin Valentine?"

"Edwin Valentine?" Narrowing her eyes, Chantel searched her memory. One of the reasons for her quick rise as an actress in Hollywood was the fact that she never forgot anything—not lines, not names, not faces. "No, I don't remember the name at all."

"He's Valentine Records." Chantel merely lifted a brow again and waited for Maddy to go on. "It's one of the top labels in the business, maybe *the* top.

Anyway, he met Mom and Pop when we were babies. He was just getting started, and they let him sleep on a cot in their hotel room.''

"Sounds like them," Chantel said easily. She slipped out of her shoes and slouched, something she would never have done with anyone but family. "What's next?"

"Valentine Records is the backer for the play."

"Interesting." She started to sip, then latched on to her sister's hand. "Maddy, you're not involved with him? He must be Pop's age. Look, I'm not saying that age should be a big factor in a relationship, but when it's my little sister—"

"Hang on." Maddy giggled into her wine. "Didn't I read that you were seeing Count DeVargo of DeVargo Jewelers? He must be hitting sixty."

"That was different." Chantel muttered. "European men are ageless."

"Very good," Maddy decided after a moment. "That was really very good."

"Thanks. In any case, we were nothing more than friends. If you're getting dreamy eyed over a man old enough to be your father—"

"I'm not dreamy eyed," Maddy said. "And it's his son."

"Whose son? Oh." Calmer, Chantel settled back again. "So this Edwin Valentine has a son. Not a dancer?"

"No." She had to smile. "He's taken over the record company. I guess he's a magnate."

"Well." Chantel rolled out the word. "Coming up in the world, aren't we?"

"I don't know what I'm doing." Maddy unlaced her legs and rose. "Most of the time I think I must be

crazy. He's gorgeous and successful and conservative. He likes French restaurants.''

"The beast."

Maddy dissolved into laughter. "Oh, Chantel,
help."

"Have you slept with him?"

It was like Chantel to get right down to brass tacks.
Maddy let out a deep breath and sat again. "No."

"But you've thought about it."

"I can't seem to think of much of anything but
him."

Chantel reached for the bottle to fill her glass again.
Once you got past the first swallow, the wine was almost palatable. "And how does he feel about you?"

"That's where I hit the brick wall. Chantel, he's
kind and considerate and has the capacity for such—
well, goodness, I guess. But he has this safety net when
it comes to women. One minute he's holding me and
I feel as though this is what I've been waiting for all of
my life. The next minute he's putting me aside as
though we hardly know each other."

"Does he know how you feel?"

"I'm half-afraid he does. I wouldn't dare tell him.
He's made it clear he's not interested in what he calls
'the long haul'."

Chantel felt a little twist of alarm. "And you're
thinking in terms of the long haul?"

"I could spend my life with him." With eyes
abruptly serious, abruptly vulnerable, she stared at her
sister. "Chantel, I could make him happy."

"Maddy, these things work two ways." God, how
well she knew it. "Can he make you happy?"

"If he'd let me in. If he'd let me in just a little so I
could understand why he's so afraid to feel. Chantel,

something happened, something devastating, I know it, to make him so untrusting. If I knew what it was I could do something about it. But I'm flying blind."

Chantel set down her glass and took both of Maddy's hands. "You really love him?"

"I really love him."

"He's a very lucky man."

"You're prejudiced."

"Damn right. And no matter how aloof he is, I don't think he stands a chance. I mean, look at that face." She took Maddy's chin in her hand. "It says trustworthy, loyal, devoted."

"You make me sound like a cocker spaniel."

"Maddy..." It was so easy to give advice, Chantel thought, so easy to give what she would never take herself. "Very simply, if you love this guy, the best way to get him to love you back is to be what you are."

Discouraged, Maddy picked up her wine. She'd throw caution to the winds, she decided, and have another half glass. "I figured you'd give me some tried-and-true tips in the art of seduction."

"I just did. For you," Chantel added. "Honey, if I told you some of my secrets, your hair would curl. Besides, you're looking for marriage, right?"

"I guess I am."

"Then while I don't recommend honesty in most relationships, this is different. If you want this man in your life for better or for worse, then you should be up-front. When are you seeing him again?"

"Not until Saturday."

Chantel frowned a moment. She'd wanted to get a look at this Valentine character herself, but she'd be on a plane heading west on Saturday. "Well, it wouldn't hurt for you to have a new outfit." She cast a look at

Maddy's sweats. "Something alluring, of course, but something that will suit you."

"Do they make things like that?"

"Leave it to me." Chantel took another quick glance and gauged that she and Maddy still wore the same size. "The only thing I really like about New York is the shopping. Speaking of shopping, did you know you only have three carrots and a jug of juice in your fridge?"

"I was going to get something at the health food shop around the corner."

"Spare me from that. I don't like eating twigs."

"There's a restaurant a block away that serves great spaghetti."

"Terrific. Do I have to change or do you?"

Maddy studied her sister's elegant nubby silk suit while fingering her own sweats. "You do. Did you bring anything with you that doesn't look so Rodeo Drive?"

"I can't bring what I don't have. Keeping up an image that looks glamorous and a little decadent is hard work."

With a quick snort, Maddy rose. "I've got something you can toss on that shouldn't tarnish that image of yours too badly. Besides, no one's going to recognize you down at Franco's."

Chantel smiled slowly as she rose. "What odds do you give me?"

Maddy opened her arms to grab her sister. "Chantel, you're one in a million."

Chantel rested her cheek against her sister's. Things should be as simple, she thought, things should be as easy as they were at this moment. "No, we're three in a million. And I'm so glad to have you."

* * *

When Maddy came home from rehearsal on Saturday, the apartment was empty. She'd had almost three days with Chantel. During the brief visit her sister had charmed the surly Guido, awed the production staff of the play with a brief visit during rehearsal and bought out half the stores on Fifth Avenue.

Maddy missed her already.

If Chantel had been able to stay just one more day...

Sighing, Maddy headed for the shower. It was silly to think she needed moral support just to go talk to Reed. She didn't need a pep talk or a vote of confidence. She was simply going to talk to the man about the meaning of their relationship and where it was going.

Maddy turned on the shower and stood, face into the spray, as the water poured over her. She was going to wash, change, then catch the subway uptown. It wasn't as though it were the first time she would have spent an evening in Reed's apartment. Besides, they needed to talk. There was no use being nervous about something that had to be done.

The play was going well. She could tell him that. She could start things off by telling him how right it was beginning to feel. Everything was coming together. When they left the following week for the last days of intense rehearsal in Philadelphia, it was only going to get better. Would he miss her at all? Would he tell her?

Lecturing herself, Maddy stepped out of the shower and immediately searched through the rubble of her linen closet for her hair drier. Within minutes she'd fluffed her hair dry, teased a bit of height on the top and ruffled the sides to give more volume. She pulled out a pile of makeup and began to experiment with an expert hand.

More than once she'd done her own hair and makeup for the stage. She'd learned early that if she didn't want to be dependent on someone else's time and whims, she had to know how to do for herself. She could, if necessary, have chosen the right paints and pots to turn her into Mary, or Suzanna, or any other part she'd ever played. Tonight she was just Maddy.

Satisfied, she headed into the bedroom. There, spread on the bed, was what Chantel had left behind. Maddy picked up the note first and read the bold, looping writing.

Maddy,

After an exhaustive search and hard thinking, I decided this was for you. Happy birthday next month. Wear it tonight for your Reed. Better yet, wear it for yourself. Forget the first reaction that the color isn't right for you. Trust me. I'll be thinking of you. You know I love you, kid. Break a leg.

Chantel

Catching her bottom lip between her teeth, Maddy looked at Chantel's gift. The slinky silk slacks were a bold, flaming pink. Exactly the sort of color Maddy would avoid with her hair. She gave them a dubious look but reached down to touch. The skinny little camisole top was jade-colored. Together they were precisely the sort of outrageous combination she would have chosen herself. Maddy smiled as she picked the top up by the slender straps. But it was the jacket that she, who chose clothes with a careless eye for color and comfort, cooed over.

It was silk, as well, a bit oversize and as slinky as the slacks. Thousands of beads were sewed on it, creating a kaleidoscope of colors. Each way she turned it, a different pattern emerged. At first glance she would have said it was too sophisticated for her taste, too elegant for her style, but the ever-changing patterns caught both her imagination and her admiration.

"All right," she said aloud. "We're going to go for it."

Why was he nervous? Reed paced his too-quiet apartment for the tenth time. It was ridiculous to feel nervous just because he was going to entertain a woman for the evening. Even if the woman was Maddy. Especially because the woman was Maddy, he corrected.

They'd spent evenings together before. But tonight was different. He switched on the stereo, hoping the flow of music would distract him.

He'd purposely avoided contacting her all week to prove to himself he could live without her. Somewhere around Thursday, he had stopped counting the times he'd picked up the phone and dialed the first few digits of her number, only to hang up.

They were just going to talk, he reminded himself. It was becoming imperative that they outline what they wanted from each other, what the rules were, where the boundaries began. He wanted to make love with her. Needed to make love with her, he corrected, and a curl of desire began with just the thought.

They could be lovers and still keep things companionable. That's what they had to get straight before any more time passed. When she came, they would sit down and talk about their needs and their restrictions like reasonable adults. They would come to a logical understanding and go on from there. No one would be hurt.

He was going to hurt her. Reed ran a hand over the back of his neck and wondered why he was so certain of that. He could still remember the way her eyes had filled the last time he'd seen her. How she'd somehow looked both wounded and courageous.

How many times had he told himself he would use tonight to break it off, to sever it all before it went any farther? How many times had he ultimately admitted it wouldn't be possible?

She was getting under his skin, and he couldn't allow that. The best way, the only way, he knew to stop it was to set down the rules.

He paced again, to the windows and back before looking at his watch. She was late. She was driving him crazy.

What was it about her? he asked himself. She wasn't particularly beautiful. She wasn't smooth and sleek and alluringly cool. In short, she wasn't the sort of woman who caught his notice. She was the woman who'd caught him by the throat. He had to loosen her hold, gain control, go forward at his own pace.

Where the hell was she?

When the knock sounded, he was cursing her. Reed gave himself a moment to settle. It wouldn't do to open the door edgy and eager. If he started on solid ground, he'd stay on solid ground. Then he opened the door, and every logical thought deserted him.

Had he said she wasn't really beautiful? How could he have been so totally wrong? He's said she wasn't

alluring, yet she stood there, glittering, glowing, simmering with her own source of energy, and he'd never
been more captivated.

"Hi. How are you?" He couldn't tell her heart was
thudding uneasily as she smiled and kissed his cheek.

"I'm fine." That was the scent he'd carried with
him for days. It was absurd for a man to linger on
something that could be bought at a department-store
cosmetics counter.

Maddy hesitated a moment. "You did say you
wanted to see me Saturday night, didn't you?"

"Yes."

"Well, are you going to let me in?"

The humor in her eyes made him feel like a fool.
"Of course. Sorry." He closed the door behind her
and wondered if he'd just made the biggest mistake of
his life. And hers. "You look wonderful. Different."

"You think so?" Smiling again, she *pirouetted*.
"My sister breezed into town for a couple of days and
picked this out for me." She turned again, wanting to
share her pleasure. "Great, isn't it?"

"Yes. You're beautiful."

It was easy to pass it off with a laugh. "Well, the
outfit certainly is. You haven't been by rehearsals."

"No." Because he'd needed to give himself time
away from her. "Would you like a drink?"

"A little white wine, maybe." She crossed, as she
invariably did, to his view of the city. "It's really
coming together, Reed. Everything's starting to click."

"The accounting department will be glad to hear
it."

It was his dry tone that made her laugh. "How can
you lose? If we hit, you rake it in. If we flop, you write
it off as a tax break. But it's alive, Reed." She took the

glass from him, needing him to feel it with her. "Every time I walk out into a scene as Mary, it becomes more alive. I need that sort of vibrant, breathing center to my life."

A center to her life. He'd always scrupulously avoided having one in his own. "And a play does that for you?"

She looked down at her wine, then out at the city again. "If I were alone, with nothing more, without a chance for anything more, I could be happy. When I'm onstage . . . When I'm onstage," she began again, "and I look out and see a theater full of people, waiting for me . . . Reed, I don't know how to explain it."

"Try." He stood watching her, watching the city lights glow behind her. "I want to know."

She pulled a hand through the hair she'd so carefully styled. It fell back into place, just a little mussed. "I feel instant acceptance. I guess I feel loved. And I can give the love back, with a dance, with a song. It sounds hokey to say that's what I was born for. But it was. It just was."

"It would be enough if you could stand on stage and be loved by hundreds of strangers?"

She gave him a long, searching look, knowing he didn't understand. No one who didn't perform could. "It would be enough, would have to be enough, if that were all I could have."

"You don't need one single permanent person or thing in your life."

"I didn't say that." She kept her eyes on his as she shook her head slowly. "I meant that I've always been able to adjust. I've had to. Applause fills a lot of gaps, Reed. All of them, if you work hard at it. I imagine your work does the same for you."

"It does. I told you before I don't have the time or the inclination for a long-term relationship."

"Yes, you did."

"I meant it, Maddy." He drank again, because the words didn't come comfortably through his lips. Why, when he was trying so hard to be honest, did it feel as though he were lying? "We tried it your way. The friendship."

Her fingers were cold. She set her glass down and linked them together to warm them. "I think it worked."

"I want more." He ran his hand through her hair and brought her closer. "And if I take more, I'm going to hurt you."

That was the truth. She knew it, accepted it, then told herself to forget it. "I'm responsible for myself, Reed. That includes my emotions. I want more, too. Whatever happens, the choice was mine."

"What choice?" he demanded suddenly. "What choice, Maddy? Isn't it time to admit neither of us has had one all along? I wanted to push you aside. That was my choice. But I kept drawing you closer and closer." He had his hands on her shoulders now and slowly slid the jacket from them. It fell to the floor in a waterfall of color. "You don't know me," he murmured as he felt the quick tremble that moved through her body. "You don't know what's inside me. There's a lot there you wouldn't like, more you wouldn't even understand. If you were smart, you'd be out that door now."

"Guess I'm not smart."

"It wouldn't matter." His fingers tensed on her shoulders. "Because I'm past the point of letting you go." Her skin was warm, so warm and soft in his hands. "You'll hate me before it's finished." And he already regretted it.

"I don't hate easily. Reed . . ." Wanting to soothe, she lifted a hand to his cheek. "Trust me a little."

"Trust has nothing to do with this." Something flared in his eyes, quickly, vibrantly, then was gone. "Not a damn thing. I want you, and that hunger's been clawing inside me for weeks. That's all I have for you."

The hurt came, as promised, but she pushed it aside. "If that were true, I don't think you would have been fighting it so hard."

"I've finished fighting it." His lips descended upon hers. "You'll stay with me tonight."

"Yes, I'll stay." She put both hands to his face, wanting to ease the tension in him. "Because it's what I want."

He took her wrists, then slowly slid her hand through his until he could press his lips to her palm. It was a promise, the only one he could give her. "Come with me."

Leading with her heart, Maddy went.

Chapter Eight

There was a lamp in the hall that sent a shaft of light into the bedroom. Otherwise all was shadows and secrets. He'd left the stereo on, but it was hardly more than an echo of a sound now as they stopped to touch each other.

She'd wanted to see his eyes like this, intensely focused only on her and what he wanted from her. It made her smile as she yielded her lips to his again.

"You're making a mistake," he began.

"Shhh." She moved her lips over his. "Let's be logical later. I've wanted to know what it would be like with you from the moment I met you." Watching his face, she began to unbutton his shirt. "I've wanted to know what you looked like. What you felt like." She drew his shirt off, then ran her hands up his chest. It was hard, smooth and, at the moment, stiff. "I'd lie awake at night wondering when we'd be together like this." Seeking, curious, her hands stroked his shoulders, then moved slowly down his arms. "Reed, I'm not afraid of you, or of how I feel."

"You should be."

Her head tilted back. Her eyes challenged. "Then show me why."

With an oath he gave in to her, to himself, to everything. Dragging her against him, he crushed her mouth beneath his and plundered. He ran his hands all over the thin silk that covered her, until her body began to shiver. Was it fear or anticipation? He couldn't tell. But her fingers dug into his flesh, holding him close, and her mouth was open and eager.

He'd once wondered if she were a witch. The thought returned now, as what rose between them was all hellsmoke and temptation. There was nothing easy about her now, nothing light and simple. The passion that swirled around him seemed as complex and dangerous as Eve or the serpent who had dared her.

Desire clawed at him, fierce and heartless. He wanted to take her quickly, instantly, where they stood, living only for the moment, no strings, no promises. It would be better for her, better for him, if he did.

Then she murmured his name with a sound as soft and sweet as an evening breeze.

His hands gentled. He couldn't resist it. His mouth softened. He couldn't prevent it. There would come a time when he would hurt her. But tonight was special. He thought of nothing but her, not the past, not the future. Tonight he would give as much as he could, take as much as he dared. And perhaps he could give to himself, as well.

Gently he brushed the straps from her shoulders, and the brilliant silk slithered down to cling tentatively to her breasts. As if she sensed his change of mood, she went very still. Was she so willing to absorb his moods? He hoped for her sake she had some defenses left.

With a tenderness that surprised him more than it did her, he skimmed his lips over her bare shoulders, taking in the texture, as smooth as the silk, and her scent, just as tantalizing. She suddenly seemed so small, so fragile, so young. After a moment's hesitation, he brought his lips back to merge with hers.

She felt the change in him. The tug-of-war that always seemed to rage inside him seemed to cease. Her own open heart was ready to take him in.

She stroked carefully, pleased with the long, hard lines of his body. Though her breathing was no longer steady, she allowed her lips to nibble and tease only, to give him time to accept what was happening between them. He would fight it. She was nearly certain he would deny it, but his feelings were guiding him. Willing, pliant, they both moved to the bed.

She knew her body too well to feel awkward. Her hips were narrow, her legs long, her torso just a shade too thin. She was built like a dancer and didn't question it, just as she didn't question his cautious, careful exploration.

The camisole slipped off and was tossed aside. When his hands touched her skin, she merely sighed and let sensation rule. With her eyes half closed, she could see the dark, bronzed sweep of his hair as it brushed over her. She could feel her heart racing, pounding. Then his tongue traced over her nipple and her body contracted with a new, dizzying surge of pleasure.

She moved with him, as though the choreography between them had been long since plotted. Action and reaction, move and countermove. For Maddy it was as effortless and natural as breathing.

Wherever his desire took him, wherever his needs led, she was waiting, willing. He'd never experienced anything, anyone, like her. Her body sizzled with heat. He could feel the pulses throb wherever he touched, whenever he tasted. He'd never known anyone so open to loving, so free and uninhibited. When she unhooked his slacks and drew them down, her touch on his flesh was honest, generous, as though they'd known, touched and taken from each other since time began.

His own pulse was raging. She found it in the crook of his elbow and murmured as she pressed her lips against it. When he was naked, she looked at him with frank appreciation. With an easy smile, a gentle laugh, she gathered him close, embracing him with both passion and affection. A shudder rippled through him, leaving him dazed, confused and aching for her.

"Kiss me again," she murmured. When he looked, he saw her eyes half closed, with that tawny, feline look that shaded them so unexpectedly. "I love what happens to me when I'm kissing you."

She brought his face close and let herself be swept away.

"I've wanted you to touch me," she said against his lips. "Sometimes I'd imagine what it would be like to have your hands on me. Here." Nearly purring, she guided his hand. "And here. I can't get enough." She arched under him like a bow. "I don't think I'll ever get enough."

Something was slipping away from him—the control he kept tightly locked on his emotions. He couldn't afford to give her his heart, couldn't trust her with the power that went with the gift. Instead, he could give her the passion she sought and accepted so beautifully.

He pulled the silk pants off her, watching as they glided erotically over her flesh. The wisp that she wore beneath slid down and was discarded. Suddenly, so suddenly he couldn't mark the change, he was beyond being sensible, beyond being reasonable. Desire for her, for everything she was, everything she offered, clawed through his system. Perhaps this wasn't the kind of passion he'd been prepared for, but it raged through him, too strong and real to be harnessed. With her honesty and her zest for life, she'd begun this journey. He wouldn't be merely a passenger; here they would meet one to one. He would finally set free the needs she'd aroused in him from the first.

He forgot gentleness, so that when his mouth crushed hers it was with rough desperation. His hands, always so careful, raced over her until she was writhing and murmuring mindlessly beneath him. With each movement, each sigh, his heart thudded faster, pounding in his brain in a beat that somehow sounded like her name. Without hesitation she wrapped around him, and he took her. He heard a moan low in her throat before his own breath caught.

She was so warm, so unbelievably soft and welcoming. He struggled to regain that edge of control as her body began to move, graceful as a waltz, erotic as any primitive rite. He moved above her, wanting to see what the feel of him did to her. Pleasure shuddered over her face, but her eyes stayed open and on his.

She trembled, and the bedspread slithered through her fingers as she gripped it. Such power, such strength. Nothing she'd ever experienced could match it. If she'd left the world she'd known, she felt no need to return to it. Here, she could remain here, while centuries flew by.

Then they were tangled tightly as the storm plucked them both up and threw them together. Her body tensed, shivering on the edge before the release came in floods of unspeakable pleasure.

She would take the moon and the stars he offered. Maddy wrapped her arms around him and knew she would wait until he offered himself, as well.

She was gone when he woke up. Reed felt the loss swiftly, sharply, when he turned toward where she'd slept and found the bed beside him empty. From the living room, the stereo that had never been switched off droned out the Sunday-morning news as he lay back and explored the feeling of emptiness.

Why should he feel empty? He'd spent an exciting night with an exciting woman, and now she'd gone on her way. That was what he'd wanted. That was the way the game was played. Throughout the night they had given each other comfort, warmth and passion. Now the sun was up and it was over. He should be grateful she took it all so casually that she could slip out the door without even a goodbye.

Why should he feel empty? He couldn't afford to regret that she wasn't there to give him a sleepy smile and snuggle against him. He was the one who knew how transient and shallow relationships really were. He should admire her for being honest enough to acknowledge that what had passed between them during the night had been nothing more than mutual physical release. There had been no pledges given, no pledges asked for, just a few hours of mindless pleasure that required no excuses or explanations.

Why should he feel so empty?

Because she was gone, and he wanted to hold her.

Swearing, Reed pushed himself up in bed. As he raked a hand through his hair, he spotted a pool of pink silk on the floor beside the bed.

But she was gone. Reed tossed aside the sheet and got out of bed to pick up the slacks he'd drawn slowly down Maddy's legs the night before. Even Maddy couldn't get far without them. He was still holding them when he heard his front door open. Reed tossed the slacks over the back of the chair beside the bed, then reached for a robe.

He found her in the kitchen, setting a brown grocery bag on the counter.

"Maddy?"

She let out a muffled squeal and jumped back. "Reed!" With a hand to her heart, she closed her eyes a moment. "You scared me to death. I thought you were sleeping."

And he'd thought she was gone. Cautious, he held himself back. "What are you doing?"

"I went out to get breakfast."

He didn't feel empty any longer. But even as the pleasure came, so did the wariness. "I thought you'd left."

"Don't be silly. I wouldn't just leave." She combed her fingers through hair that hadn't yet seen a brush that morning. "Why don't you get back in bed? I'll have this put together in a minute."

"Maddy..." He took a step forward. Then his gaze slid slowly down her body. "What are you wearing?"

"Like it?" Laughing, she caught the hem of his shirt in her fingers and twirled around. "You have excellent taste, Reed. I was very fashionable."

His shirt hung loose over her shoulders, skimmed her thighs and made her look ridiculously attractive. "Is that one of my ties?"

She pressed her lips together to hold back a chuckle as she toyed with the thin black silk she'd used to secure the shirt at the waist. "It was all I could find. Don't worry, I can have it pressed."

Her legs were long and smooth and bare. He looked at them again and shook his head. "You went out like that?"

"Nobody looked twice," she assured him, so easily he thought she probably believed it. "Look, I'm starving." She wrapped her arms around his neck and kissed him with an easy affection that had his pulse thudding. "Get back in bed and I'll bring this in in a minute."

Because he needed a minute to adjust, he obliged her. She wasn't gone, Reed thought as he sat back against the pillows. She was here, in his kitchen, fixing breakfast as though it were the most natural thing in the world. It pleased him. It worried him. He wondered what he was going to do about her.

"I've got extra whipped cream if we need it," Maddy said as she walked in with a tray.

Reed stared at the breakfast she'd fixed as she scooted onto the bed and set the tray between them. "What is that?"

"Sundaes," she told him, dipping a forefinger into a mound of whipped cream. As she laid it on her tongue, she let out a luxurious sigh of pleasure. "Strawberry sundaes."

"Strawberry sundaes," he repeated. "For breakfast? Is this the same Maddy O'Hurley who worries constantly about nutrition and calories?"

"Ice cream's a dairy product," she reminded him as she offered a spoon. "The berries are fresh. What more do you need?"

"Bacon and eggs?"

"Much too much fat and cholesterol—especially since it doesn't taste this good. Anyway, I'm celebrating." She dipped into her bowl.

"Celebrating what?"

Their eyes met quickly and held. Then she seemed to sigh. How could he not know? And because he didn't, how could she explain? "You look wonderful. I feel wonderful. It's Sunday and the sun's shining. That should be enough." Maddy plucked a strawberry out of his bowl and offered it to him. "Go ahead. Live dangerously."

He closed his lips over the berry, drawing the tips of her fingers into his mouth briefly. "And I thought you subsisted on alfalfa sprouts and wheat germ."

"I do most of the time. That's why this is so great." She let the ice cream rest cool on her tongue and closed her eyes. "Usually I jog on Sunday mornings."

Reed sampled the ice cream himself. "Jog?"

"Only three or four miles," she said with a shrug.

"Only."

She licked the back of her spoon clean. "But today I'm being decadent."

He skimmed a hand along her knee. "Are you?"

"Absolutely. I'll pay for it tomorrow, so it has to be good."

"Did you plan to stay here and be decadent?"

"Unless you'd rather I go."

He linked his fingers with hers in an uncomplicated gesture that would have surprised him if he'd realized he'd done it. "No, I don't want you to go."

The smile lighted her face. "I can be very decadent."

"I'm counting on it."

Maddy swirled her finger through the whipped cream, then slowly, very slowly, licked it off. "You might be shocked." When she dipped again, Reed took her wrist, then brought the cream and her finger to his own mouth.

"You think so?" He felt her pulse jump as he sucked lightly on her fingertips. "Why don't we see?" Picking up the tray, he set it beside the bed. Her eyes were huge, her body aching, when he looked at her again. "I wondered how you'd look in the morning."

Tilting her head, she lifted a brow. "How do I look?"

"Fresh." With the lightest of touches he stroked her cheek. "Just a bit mussed. Appetizing."

She caught her tongue between her teeth. "I think I like the appetizing best."

"You know, Maddy, you never asked if you could borrow my shirt."

Humor danced in her eyes again, but she answered very seriously. "No, I didn't, did I? That was rude."

"I want it back." He hooked his fingers in the neck of the shirt and drew her closer. "Now."

"Now?" Fast and hot, anticipation rippled through her. "I suppose you want the tie, as well."

"I certainly do."

"I guess you're entitled," she murmured. Kneeling, she loosened the knot, slipped the silk off and handed it to him. She reached for the buttons, hesitated, then began to unfasten them. Her gaze stayed steady on his as the shirt fell open to reveal a thin panel of flesh. Then she smiled as she let the material slide from her shoulders. Without any self-consciousness she stayed as she was while he looked his fill, then took the shirt by the collar and held it out, kneeling in the center of the bed with sunlight streaming over her skin.

"This is yours, I believe."

He brushed the shirt aside, rising on his knees to cup her shoulders in his hands. "I'm becoming fonder of what's inside." He nipped at her chin as his hands slid down over her. "You have the most incredible body. Hard, soft, compact, limber." Compelled, he drew away just to look at her. "I wonder if— Maddy, what's that you're wearing?"

"What?" A little dazed, she followed his gaze downward. "Oh, that's a G-string, of course. Haven't you ever seen one?"

His eyes came back to hers, amused and intrigued. "As a matter of fact, yes. One wonders if you aren't taking your role of the Merry Widow a bit too seriously."

"You didn't say that while I was stripping for you," she pointed out, then linked her hands behind his neck. "I discovered G-strings when I was researching for the part."

"Researching?" He started to kiss her, then drew back again. "Exactly what does that mean?"

"Just what it sounds like. I couldn't go into a role like this without doing some research."

"You went to strip joints." Caught between fury and frustration, he took her chin firmly. "Are you crazy? Do you know what can happen in places like that?"

"Have you had a lot of experience?"

"Yes— No. Damn it, Maddy, don't change the subject."

"I didn't think I was." She smiled at him again. "Reed, I had to get inside Mary a bit. I figured the best way to do it was to talk to some strippers. I met some fascinating people. There was one called Lotta Oomph."

"Lotta—"

"Oomph," Maddy finished. "Her gimmick was poodles. See, she had five poodles, and—"

"I don't think I want to hear it." Though he wanted badly to laugh, he held her firmly. "Maddy, you've no business going into that kind of place."

"Don't be silly. I worked in places not much different than that when I was twelve. It's all fantasy, Reed. For the most part, all you have are people trying to make a living. And talking with some of the women really helped me understand Mary better."

"Mary is a fantasy," he corrected. "What goes on in those places, what can go on in those places, is hard reality."

"I understand reality very well, Reed." She lifted a hand to his cheek, touched that he would be concerned. "I'm not saying stripping's an admirable profession, or that every stripper's another Gypsy Rose Lee, but most of the people I talked with took a great deal of pride in their act."

"I don't intend to argue the morals or the social significance of exotic dancing, Maddy. I just don't like

the idea of you going into one of those joints downtown.''

"Well, I don't intend to make a habit of it." She
lowered her lashes, trailing a finger down his chest. "I
wouldn't mind seeing the poodles again."

"Maddy."

The lashes came up, revealing laughter. "They were
pretty amazing."

"So are you." He ran a hand over her hip where the
thin string rested. "And what's the story on this?"

"Comfort." She began to nibble quietly on his earlobe. "Every woman in America should wear a
G-string."

"You always wear one?" He spread his hand over
her, feeling soft skin, firm muscle.

"Mmm. Under street clothes."

"That day we went to see the exhibition of
Victorian architecture. You had on those baggy khaki
slacks that looked like army surplus."

"They are army surplus."

"You had one of these on underneath?"

"Mm-hmmm."

"Do you know what might have happened if I'd
known?"

Content, she rubbed her cheek against his.
"What?"

"Right there in front of the model of Queen
Victoria's summer home?"

The giggle bubbled out as he scooped her up.
"What?"

"With the family of four from New Jersey right
behind us?"

"Oh, God." She wrapped her arms around him.
"Maybe we can go back this afternoon."

"Not a chance." He buried his face in her throat.

He wasn't supposed to feel like laughing when he had a naked woman beneath him. Lovemaking was a serious business, to be respected and treated with caution and care. He wasn't supposed to feel like a teenager romping in a back seat on a darkened road. He was a grown man, experienced, aware.

But when he rolled over on the bed with her, the laughter was there. It was there when he held her hard against him, when she snuggled into him, when he touched, when she offered. His delight in her was so great, so immense, that laughter seemed the only answer. She accepted it so beautifully, answering with laughter of her own. Even later, not so very much later, when laughter turned to sighs, the joy wasn't dimmed.

There was so much love in her. Maddy wondered that it didn't burst out and light up the room. Every moment she was with him, he grew just a little brighter. Every time he looked at her, his eyes seemed to shimmer.

He was so kind, so gentle, so thorough. So desperate with need for her. If she hadn't already given him her heart, she would have done so then just as freely.

How could she have known there was so much to discover? So much pleasure, so many sensations. She'd never shown that much generosity to another, but with Reed, it was easy.

She knew her body intimately, its strengths, its weaknesses. How strange it was to discover she had known so little about its needs. When his mouth closed over her breast, she felt incredible sensations tighten inside her: pleasure, pain, desperation. A stroke of his hand down her thigh made her shudder. A brush of his lips at her throat made her moan. The body she disciplined so religiously became a morass of needs, of confusion, of anticipation, when he pressed against her.

Touching him made her weak. He was only flesh, blood, bone, but stroking her hands over him made her spirit soar. He was hers. She told herself it didn't matter that it was only for the moment. It didn't matter that it was only pretend. He was hers as long as they were flesh to flesh, mouth to mouth.

He needed her. She could feel the rush of excitement move through him. If, even for one brief moment, he untied the bonds on his emotions, he could love her. She was sure of it. There was more than passion when he held her, more than heat and lust. There was caring and compassion. When his lips brushed over hers, when he allowed the kiss to deepen slowly until they were both swimming in it, she knew that he was on the edge of giving her what she wanted so badly to give him.

Love. It healed, it soothed, it protected. She wanted to tell him how wonderful it was to feel so irrevocably bound to another. She wanted to offer him a glimpse of what it was to know there was someone there for him, someone who would always be there.

His skin was hot and damp. His hands lost their gentleness degree by degree as her excitement grew. She was wild, hungry, avid. Her energy seemed boundless and pushed him farther and farther, to the borders of his control.

The stereo blared on. Outside, the heat rose in waves. It didn't matter. Nothing mattered but them and what they could give each other.

She rolled over him, arms and legs snaking out to hold him close. Agile and desperate, she arched to take him into her. When their sanity shattered, then re-formed, they were still together.

Limp, drained, glowing, Maddy lowered herself to him. Her skin was damp and seemed to fuse naturally with his. She could hear his heartbeat through the dull buzzing in her head. When his hand came to stroke her back, she closed her eyes and surrendered everything.

"Oh, Reed, I love you."

At first she was too caught up in her own dream to feel the stiffening of his body beneath hers. She was too giddy to notice the quick tensing of his fingers on her back. But gradually her mind cleared. Maddy kept her eyes closed a moment longer, knowing that now the words had been said they couldn't be taken back.

"I'm sorry." She took a last long breath and looked up. His expression was shuttered. Though they were still tangled together, he'd distanced himself. "I'm not sorry I said it, or that I feel it, I'm sorry you don't want it."

He told himself that the rush of feeling was regret, not hope. "Maddy, I don't believe in catchphrases, or the need for them."

"Catchphrases." She shook her head as if to clear it. "You consider 'I love you' a catchphrase?"

"What else?" Taking her by the shoulders, he shifted them both until they were sitting. "Maddy, we have something good between us. Let's not cover it with comfortable lies."

What she swallowed wasn't bitterness but hurt. "I don't lie, Reed."

Something moved inside him, something warm. He didn't quite recognize it as another surge of hope before he forced it back. "Fantasize, then."

Her voice was quiet, not quite steady, when she spoke again. "You don't believe I could love you?"

"Love's just a word." He rolled out of bed, grabbing his robe again. "It exists, certainly. Father to son, mother to daughter, brother to sister. When it comes to a man and woman, there are things like attraction, infatuation, even obsession. They come and go, Maddy."

She could only stay where she was and stare at him. "You don't really believe that."

"I know it." He cut her off so sharply she flinched. He regretted his harshness instantly, but he swallowed the regret. "People come together because they want something from each other. They stay together until they want something from someone else. While they're together they make promises they don't intend to keep and say things they don't mean. Because it's expected. I have no expectations."

Suddenly cold, she drew the sheet up. To Reed, she looked terribly young and small and vulnerable. "I've never told another man that I loved him. I don't suppose that matters."

He couldn't let it. There was no way to explain it to her. "I don't want the words, Maddy." He walked to the window, his back to her. Why should he hurt? he wondered. He was only speaking the truth. "I can't give them back to you."

"Why, I wonder." Determined not to cry, she pressed the heels of her hands against her eyes for a moment. "What was it that happened to lock off your emotions, Reed? What's made you so hell-bent to stay untouched? I said I loved you." Her voice rose as she allowed the fury to overwhelm the pain. "I'm not ashamed of it. I didn't say it to pull some sort of declaration from you. It's simply the truth. You're looking for lies where there aren't any."

She wouldn't lose her temper, she told herself as she drew breath in and out slowly. But she wasn't finished. They weren't finished. "Are you going to try to tell me you didn't *feel* anything just now? Do you really believe we had sex and nothing more?"

When he turned, his struggle was all internal. Nothing showed on his face. "I don't have anything more to give you. Take it or leave it, Maddy."

Her fingers tightened on the sheet, but she nodded. "I see."

"I need some coffee." He turned on his heel and left her alone. His hands were shaking. Why did he feel as though everything he'd said had been someone else's thoughts, someone else's words?

What was wrong with him? Reed slammed the kettle on the burner, then leaned both palms on the counter. When she'd said she loved him, part of him had wanted and needed it. Part of him had believed it.

He was becoming a fool over her. That had to stop. He had a prime example of what happens to a man who trusts a woman, who devotes his life to her. Reed had promised himself he wouldn't allow himself the same vulnerability. Maddy couldn't change that. He couldn't let her.

She might actually believe she loved him. It wouldn't take long for her to realize differently. In the meantime, they simply had to go on carefully and play by the rules.

He heard the front door open, then close again. For a long time, Reed simply stood there. Even when the water began to steam and boil, he only stood there. He knew she was gone this time. And he felt hideously empty.

Chapter Nine

"I don't care if you've scheduled open-heart surgery, you are going to that party tonight."

Maddy pulled on a high-top sneaker. "Wanda, what's the big deal?"

"No big deal." Wanda pulled Maddy's eye-covered sweatshirt over her head, then studied the results. "You're going to go home and put on your fancy dress and party."

"I just said I was a little tired and not in the mood for a party."

"And I say you're sulking."

"Sulking?" Eyes narrowed, Maddy pulled on her second shoe. She was ready for a fight, primed for it. "I don't sulk."

Wanda plopped down beside her on the bench. "You're an expert at sulking."

"Don't push it, Wanda. I'm in a very mean mood."

Wanda seriously doubted that Maddy could be mean if she took a course in it. "Look, if you don't want to talk about what a jerk your guy is, fine."

"He's not my guy."

"Who's not your guy?"

Frustration came out in a low whistle under her breath. "*He*. He is not my guy. I do not have a guy, I do not want a guy. Therefore, whoever *he* is, he can't be mine."

"Uh-huh." Wanda examined her nails and decided that particular shade of red was very becoming. "But he is a jerk."

"I didn't say—" Her humor got the better of her, and she grinned. "Yeah, he's a jerk."

"Honey, they all are. The point is, Mr. Valentine senior's throwing us this bash, and the star of the show can't go home and pout in her bathtub."

"I wasn't going to." Maddy tied an elaborate bow with her laces. "I was going to pout in bed."

Wanda watched Maddy tie her other shoe. "If you don't go, I'm going to tell everyone in the company that you think you're too classy to party with us."

Maddy snorted. "Who'd believe you?"

"Everybody. 'Cause you won't be there."

Maddy lunged off the bench and began to drag a brush through her hair. "Look, why don't you lay off?"

"Because I like your face."

Wanda only grinned when Maddy scowled at her. "I'm just too tired to go, that's all."

"Bull. I've been rehearsing with you for weeks now. You don't get tired."

Maddy let the brush clatter into the sink. In the reflection, her eyes met Wanda's. "I'm tired tonight."

"You're sulking tonight."

"I'm not—" Yes, she was, she admitted silently. "He'll be there," she blurted out. "I don't— I just don't think I can handle it."

The saucy look was replaced by concern. Wanda rose to drape an arm around Maddy's shoulder. "Hit hard?"

"Yeah." Maddy pressed her fingers between her eyes. "Real hard."

"Had a good cry yet?"

"No." She shook her head, fighting for composure. "I didn't want to be any more of a fool than I already was."

"You're a fool if you don't cry it out." Wanda tugged her back to the bench. "Sit down here and put your head on Wanda's shoulder."

"I didn't think it would hurt so bad," Maddy managed as the tears started to fall.

"Who does?" Keeping her voice quiet, Wanda patted her arm. "If we knew how bad it can be, we wouldn't come within ten feet of a man. But we keep going back, because sometimes it's the best there is."

"It stinks."

"To high heaven."

"He's not worth crying over." She wiped the back of her hand over her cheek.

"Not one of them is. Except, of course, the right one."

"I love him, Wanda."

Wanda carefully drew back far enough to study Maddy's face. "The real thing?"

"Yeah." She didn't bother to wipe the tears away again. "Only he doesn't love me back. He doesn't even want me to love him. Somehow I always thought

when I got hit the other person would get hit, too, and
we'd go on to happy-ever-after. Reed doesn't even
think love exists.''

''That's his problem.''

''No, it's mine, too, because I've been trying for
days and days to get over him and I can't.'' She drew
in a deep breath. There would be no more tears. ''So
you see why I can't go tonight.''

''Hell, no. I see why you have to go.''

''Wanda—''

''Look, honey, go home and bury your head in the
sand and you're going to feel the same way tomorrow.'' When she spoke again, there was a toughness in
her voice that made Maddy's spine straighten. ''What
do you do when an audience freezes up on you and sits
there like a bunch of mummies?''

''I want to go stomp off to my dressing room.''

''But what do you do?''

Maddy sighed and brushed her hands over her
damp face. ''I stand onstage and sweat it out.''

''And that's what you have to do tonight. And if
I'm any judge of men, he's going to be doing some
sweating of his own. I saw the way he watched you
when he and his old man came to rehearsal. Come on,
let's get started. We've got to get dressed.''

Maddy revved herself up to see Reed again the same
way she revved herself up to face an audience. She told
herself she knew her lines, she knew her moves, and if
she made a mistake she'd cover it before anyone noticed. She chose a strapless dress that hugged her hips
and draped sensuously down her body and was slit up
the side to the middle of her thigh. If she was going to
flop, she was going to look great doing it.

Still, as she stood in front of Edwin Valentine's imposing front door, she had to talk herself out of turning around and running for cover.

Setting her chin, she knocked. She was prepared to face him again. She was prepared to act casual and cool. The one thing she wasn't prepared for was the possibility that Reed would open the door himself. She stared at him, astonished at how much emotion could churn inside the human body.

He wondered why his fingers hadn't simply crushed the faceted glass knob he gripped as he looked at her.

"Hello, Maddy."

"Reed." She wouldn't smile. It simply wasn't possible just yet. But she wouldn't collapse at his feet, either. "I hope I'm not early."

"No. As a matter of fact, my father's been waiting for you."

"Then I'll go say hello right away." The blare of a trumpet pealed out from down the hall. "I take it the party's down there." She skirted around him, ignoring the knot in her stomach.

"Maddy."

Bracing herself, she looked carelessly over her shoulder. "Yes?"

"Are you... how have you been?"

"Busy." The bell rang behind him, and she lifted a brow. "It looks like you've got your hands full, too. See you later." She walked blindly down the hall, blinking furiously to clear her vision.

The party was in full swing. Maddy stepped into it and allowed herself to be caught up in the good feelings, the excitement and the camaraderie. She exchanged a few quick, careless embraces and fended of a more intimate one from a member of the brass section.

"I was beginning to think you'd backed out." Wanda, who'd been talking to one of the musicians, came up beside her, a jerk of her head sending the horn player on his way.

"Nope. Nobody can call an O'Hurley a coward."

"Might help you to know that the younger Valentine has been watching the door for the last half hour."

"He has?" She started to turn around, to look for him, then stopped herself. "No, it doesn't matter. Let's have a drink. Champagne?"

"Yeah, Mr. Valentine's a real sport. You know, he's a nice man." Wanda took a glass of champagne and downed it in one shot. "Not stuffy. He acts as though we're real people."

"We are real people."

"Don't spread that around." A slow gleam came into Wanda's eyes as she looked over Maddy's shoulder. "There's Phil. I've decided to let him convince me he has serious intentions. Not necessarily *honorable*," she added as her smile widened. "Just serious."

"Phil?" Interested, Maddy eyed the dancer who played Wanda's partner. "Well, does he?"

"Maybe, maybe not." Wanda grabbed another glass of champagne. "The fun's in finding out."

Wishing she could agree, Maddy turned to the buffet table where groups of hungry dancers crowded together. Eat, drink and be merry, she told herself. For tomorrow we go to Philadelphia.

"Maddy."

Before she could choose between the pâté and the quiche, Edwin came up behind her.

"Oh, Mr. Valentine. What a great party."

"Edwin," he corrected, as he took her hand and kissed it in a courtly gesture that made her smile. "It has to be Edwin if you're going to give me the dance you promised."

"Then it's Edwin, and it will be my pleasure." With a hand on his shoulder, she moved into step with him. "I got in touch with my parents," she began. "They're in New Orleans, but they're going to make it for opening night in Philly. I was hoping you'd be there."

"Wouldn't miss it. You know, Maddy, this play is the best thing I've done for myself in years. I thought it was time I let myself grow old, you know."

"That's the most ridiculous thing I've ever heard."

"You're so young." He patted the back of her waist where his hand guided her. "When you come up on sixty, you look around and say to yourself, okay, it's time to slow down now. You've earned it. You should relax and enjoy your waning years."

"Waning years." She tossed her hair back and grinned at him. "Phooey."

"Well, that's about it." He chuckled down at her, and she wondered why Reed hadn't inherited those kind, dark eyes. "After I'd retired, I realized I wanted a bit more than eighteen holes every Wednesday. I needed youth around me, their vitality. Reed's always kept me young, you know. As much my best friend as my son. A man couldn't do any better."

"He loves you very much."

Something in her tone had him glancing down. "Yes, he does. I wanted to give him a chance with the business without me hanging around, poking into things. He's done well. More than well," he said with a sigh. "Reed's put his whole life into the business. Maybe that's a mistake."

"He doesn't think so."

"No? I wonder. Well, in any case, until this play came along I didn't know what the hell I was going to do with myself. Now I think I found out."

"Broadway fever?"

"Exactly." Somehow he'd known she would understand him. He could only hope she would understand his son, as well. "Once this play's established, I'm going to hunt myself up another. I figure I've got myself an expert whose opinion I can ask for and trust."

She saw the question in his eyes and nodded slowly. "If you want to play angel, Edwin, I'll be glad to play devil's advocate."

"I knew I could count on you. I've been around entertainers all my life, Maddy. Made my living off them. That kind of punch just can't be replaced with a golf ball." He gave her a quick, companionable pat. "Let's get you something to eat."

A glance at the buffet table had her sighing. "My hero."

The music changed from mellow to manic as three members of the cast jumped together to belt out a medley of Broadway hits. It didn't take long for Phil to pull Wanda stage center for an impassioned *pas de deux*. The chorus of cheers turned quickly into a challenge of champions as another couple swirled out.

"Come on, Maddy," Terry said, taking her by the hand. "We can't let them show us up."

"Sure we can," Maddy told him, and reached for the pâté again.

"No. We've got a reputation to uphold. Remember the number from *Within Reach*?"

"That was the biggest bomb I ever rode into the ground."

"So the play stunk," he said easily. "But the dances we had together were terrific. We got the only good reviews. Come on, Maddy, for old time's sake."

He tugged on her arm and grinned. Unable to resist, Maddy went into a series of pirouettes that ended with them caught close. The few dancers who recognized the moves went into a round of applause.

It was a slow, seductive number with long moves and extended holds that took perfect timing and muscle control. The routine came back to her, as though she'd rehearsed it that afternoon, rather than four years before. The file simply clicked open, and her body remembered.

She felt Terry brace for the lift and *plié* to help him. With the trust of dancer for dancer, she arched back until her hair nearly swept the rug.

Then she was laughing and bouncing back into his arms from the sheer fun of it. "Maybe it wasn't such a bomb," she said breathlessly.

"Baby, it was atomic." Then he gave her a friendly pat on the rump as the music changed tempo and other dancers merged together.

Reed was watching her. When her gaze was drawn to his, Maddy felt the heat rise to her skin along with wishes and regrets. Thinking only of escape, she turned and went through the doors onto the terrace.

The air was hot and sultry there, as if it bounced off the pavement and rose up. Maddy leaned on the banister and gave in to it. She absorbed the noise, the movement and the life of the city beneath her. She could need, she could wish, but she wouldn't regret. Steadying herself, Maddy drew on the strength she'd been born with. She wouldn't regret.

She knew Reed had stepped onto the terrace behind her before he spoke. It had been wrong of her to think of running, to think of hiding in her apartment. He was still what she wanted, like it or not.

"Tell me if you'd rather I go."

It was so like him, she thought, to lay the choices out front. She turned and let herself look at him. "No, of course not."

He curled his hands into his pockets. "Are you generous with everyone, Maddy, or most particularly with me?"

"I don't know. I've never thought about it."

He walked over to the railing, wanting to be just a bit closer. "I've missed seeing you."

"I'd hoped you would." The stars were out and the moon was full. She had that to hold on to, at least. "I was going to come here tonight and be very cool, very breezy. I don't seem to be able to carry it off."

"I watched you dance with my father, and you know what occurred to me?" When she shook her head, he reached out, compelled to touch her, even just a wisp of her hair. "You've never danced with me."

She turned just enough to study his profile. "You've never asked me."

"I'm asking now." He held out his hand, again leaving the choice up to her. She set hers in it without a second thought. They moved together until they were one shadow on the terrace floor. "When you left last week, I thought it was for the best."

"So did I."

He brushed his cheek over her hair. "There hasn't been a day that I haven't thought of you. There hasn't been a day that I haven't wanted you." Slowly, when he felt no resistance, he lowered his mouth to hers. Her lips were as warm and welcoming as always. Her body fit to his as though fate had fashioned her for him, or him for her. The longings that raced through him brought on a panic he rigidly fought down. "Maddy, I want you to come back."

"I want that, too." She lifted her hands to his cheeks. "But I can't."

He gripped her wrists as panic grew. "Why?"

"Because I can't keep to your terms, Reed. I can't stop myself from loving you, and you won't let yourself love me."

"Damn it, Maddy, you're asking for more than I can give."

"No." She stepped a little closer, and her eyes were bright and direct. "No, I'd never ask for more than you were capable of giving, any more than I can give you any less. I love you, Reed. If I came back, I couldn't stop telling you. You couldn't stop backing away from it."

"I want you in my life." Desperation made his hands tense on her. "Isn't that enough?"

"I wish I knew. I want to be part of your life. I want you to be part of mine."

"Marriage? Is that what you want?" He spun away to lean on the rail. "What the hell is marriage, Maddy?"

"An emotional commitment between two people who promise to do their best."

"For better or for worse." He turned back then, but his face was in shadow and she could only read his voice. "How many of them last?"

"Only the ones that people work hard enough at, I suppose. Only for the ones that care enough."

"Many don't last. The institution doesn't mean anything. It's a legal contract broken by another legal contract, the first of which is usually broken morally dozens of times in between."

Part of her heart broke for him just hearing what he said. "Reed, you can't generalize that way."

"How many happy marriages can you name? How many lasting ones?" he corrected. "Forget the happiness."

"Reed, that's ridiculous. I—"

"Can't even think of one?" he said.

Her temper snapped into place. "Of course I can. The—the Gianellis's on the first floor of my building."

"The ones who shout at each other constantly."

"They like to shout. It makes them deliriously happy to shout." Because she'd begun to shout herself, she spun on her heel and racked her brain. "Damn it, if you weren't quizzing me, I wouldn't have such a hard time at it. Ozzie and Harriet."

"Give it a break, Maddy."

"No." Setting her hands on her hips, she glared at him. "Jimmy Stewart's been married for a hundred and fifty years. Umm . . . Queen Elizabeth and Prince Philip are doing pretty good. My parents, for God's sake," she continued, warming up. "They've been together forever. My great-aunt Jo was married for fifty-five years."

"Had to work at it, didn't you?" He came out of the shadows then, and what she saw in his eyes was cynicism. "You'd have an easier time coming up with marriages that crumbled."

"All right, I would. It doesn't mean you give up on the system because the people involved in it make mistakes. Besides, I didn't ask you to marry me, I just asked you to feel."

He caught her before she could storm inside again. "Are you going to tell me marriage isn't what you want?"

She stood toe-to-toe with him. "No, I'm not going to tell you that."

"I can't promise marriage. I admire you, as a woman and as a performer. I'm attracted to you . . . I need you."

"All those things are important, Reed, but they're only enough for a little while. If I hadn't fallen in love with you, we could both be happy with that. I don't think I can handle too much more." She turned and gripped the railing as if it were a lifeline. "Please, just go."

It wasn't easy to fight her when he seemed to be fighting himself, as well. The moves weren't clear, the next step wasn't as well defined as it should have been. Seeing no other way, Reed backed off. "It's not finished. No matter how much both of us would like it otherwise."

"Maybe not." She drew in a breath. "But I've made a fool of myself in front of you for the last time. Leave me alone now."

The moment he left, she shut her eyes tight. She would *not* cry. As soon as she could pull herself together, she was going back inside to make her excuses and go home. She wasn't running away, she was simply facing reality.

"Maddy."

She turned and faced Edwin. One look told her she didn't need to paste on a bright smile.

"I'm sorry. I listened to a great deal of that, and you've a right to be angry with me. But Reed's my son and I love him."

"I'm not angry." Indeed, she found she couldn't dredge up any emotions at all. "I just have to go."

"I'll take you home."

"No, you have guests." She gestured inside. "I'll catch a cab."

"They'll never miss me." He stepped forward to take her arm. "I want to take you home, Maddy. There's a story you should hear."

They spoke very little on the way home. Edwin seemed to be lost in thoughts of his own. Maddy had lost her knack for bright, witty conversation. His only comment as they started up the stairs to her apartment was on the lack of security.

"You're becoming more well-known every time you step out onstage, Maddy. There's a price to be paid for that."

She glanced around the dimly lighted hallway as she reached for her keys. She'd never been afraid here, yet somehow she'd known that her time in the free-moving, transient world of the gypsies was almost up.

"I'll fix tea." She left Edwin to wander the cramped living room.

"This suits you, Maddy," he said a few moments later. "It's friendly, bright, honest." The glow of neon made him smile as he settled into a chair. "I'm going to embarrass you and tell you how much I admire what you've done with your life."

"You don't embarrass me. I appreciate it."

"Talent isn't always enough. I know. I've watched many, many talented people slip away into oblivion because they didn't have the strength or the confidence to make it to the top. You're there, and you haven't even noticed yet."

"I don't know about my reaching the top." She skirted the breakfront carrying a tray. "But I'm happy where I am."

"That's the beauty of it, Maddy. You like where you are. You like yourself." He accepted the cup of tea but put a hand lightly on hers. "Reed needs you."

"Maybe on some levels." She retreated a little, because it hurt too much. "I found out that I need more than that."

"So does he, Maddy. So does he, but he's too stubborn, and maybe too afraid, to admit it."

"I don't understand why. I don't understand how he can be so—" She cut herself off, swearing. "I'm sorry."

"Don't be. I think I understand. Maddy, has Reed ever told you about his mother?"

"No. That's one of the hands-off subjects between us."

"I think you have a right to know." He sighed and sipped his tea, knowing he was about to stir unwanted and painful memories of his own. "If I weren't sure you really cared for him, and that you were really right for him, I could never tell you this."

"Edwin, I don't want you to tell me something Reed would resent me knowing."

"Your concern for him is why I'm going to tell you." He set down his cup and leaned forward. Something told Maddy there would be no going back. "Reed's mother was a stunning woman. Is a stunning woman still, I'm sure, though I haven't seen her in many years."

"Has Reed?"

"No, he refuses to."

"Refuses to see his mother? How could he?"

"Once I explain, maybe you'll understand." There was a weariness in his voice that made her heart go out to him without question.

"I married Elaine when we were both very young. I had some family money, and she was a struggling singer, working the clubs... You understand."

"Yes, of course."

"She had talent, nothing show-stopping, but with the right management she could have made a solid living. I decided to give her that right management. Then I decided to marry her. It was almost as calculated as that, I'm sorry to say, because I was used to getting what I wanted. For a year or two, it worked. She was grateful for what I was doing for her career. I was grateful to have a beautiful wife. I loved her, and I worked very hard to make her a success because that's what she wanted most. Somewhere along the line, things began to change. Elaine was impatient."

Edwin sat back again, sipping tea as he looked around Maddy's apartment. He'd given his wife all he could, yet she'd never been satisfied.

"She was young," he said, knowing it was no real excuse. "She wanted better bookings and began to resent the fact that I was advising her on her clothes, her hair. She began to think that I was holding her back, using her to further my own career.''

''She couldn't have understood you very well.''

He smiled at that. Not everyone was willing to give such unconditional support. ''Perhaps not. But then, I didn't understand her, either. Our marriage was in trouble. I'd almost accepted the fact that it was ending when she told me she was going to have a child. You're a modern woman, Maddy. And a compassionate one. You should be able to understand that while I very much wanted children, had always wanted them, Elaine didn't.''

Maddy looked down at her tea, sympathizing with Edwin. ''I can only feel sorry for someone who didn't, or for whatever reason couldn't, want the child she carried.''

It was the right answer. He closed his eyes on it. ''Elaine was desperate for success. She had Reed, I think, because she was afraid to do otherwise. I had gotten her a small recording contract. Her decision to stay with me and have Reed was more a career move than anything else.''

''You still loved her.''

''I still had feelings for her. And there was Reed. When he was born, I felt as though I'd been given the greatest gift. A son. Someone who would love me, accept the love I wanted to give back. He was beautiful, a wonderful baby who grew into a wonderful child. My life changed the moment he was born. I wanted to give him everything. I had a kind of focus that hadn't been there before. I could lose a client, I could lose a contract, but my son was always there.''

''Families keep our feet on the ground.''

"Yes, they do. Before I go on, I want you to know that Reed has never given me anything but pleasure. I never considered him a duty or a burden."

"You don't have to tell me that. I can see it."

He rubbed his hand over his temple, then continued. "When he was five, I was in an accident. They did a lot of tests on me in the hospital." His voice was changing. Maddy tensed without knowing why. "One of the by-products of the testing was a report that I was sterile."

Her hand grew damp on the cup, and she set it down. "I don't understand."

"I couldn't have children." His eyes were direct, intense. "I'd never been able to have them."

The cold gripped her, squeezing her stomach into a frigid knot. "Reed." With the one word she asked all the questions and gave nothing but love.

"I didn't father him. It was a blow I can't describe to you."

"Oh, Edwin." She rose immediately to kneel in front of him.

"I confronted Elaine. She didn't even try to lie. I think she'd grown tired of the lies by then. The marriage had been over, and she knew she'd never hit it big as an entertainer. There'd been another man, one who'd left her as soon as he'd learned she was pregnant." His breath came out in a slow, painful stream. "It must have been a terrible blow to her. She'd known I wouldn't question but simply accept the child as mine. Moreover, she'd known, inside she'd known, that she'd never have gotten out of those dreary little clubs without me. So she'd stuck."

"She must have been a very unhappy woman."

"Not everyone finds contentment easily. Elaine was too restless to do anything but look for it. If she wasn't satisfied, she'd move on. When I got out of the hospital, she was gone. Reed was staying with a neighbor." He drew a deep breath because, after all the years that had passed, it still hurt. "Maddy, she'd told him."

"Oh, my God." She dropped her head on his knee and wept for all of them. "Poor little boy."

"I didn't do much better by him." Edwin laid a hand on her hair. He hadn't realized how cleansing it would be to speak of it aloud after all those years. "I needed to get away, so I paid the neighbor and left him there. I was gone nearly a month, pulling money together to finance Valentine Records. Until I met your family, I'm not sure I had any intention of going back. It's hard to forgive myself for that."

"You were hurt. You—"

"Reed was devastated," he said. "I hadn't considered the effect it would have on him. I'd thrown myself into the hustling game and tried to block out what I'd left behind. Then I met your parents. For just one night, I saw what family meant."

Rubbing a hand over her wet cheek, she looked up. "And you slept on a cot in their room."

"I slept on a cot and watched the love your parents had for each other and for their children. It was as though someone had drawn a curtain aside to let me see what life really meant, what was really important. I broke down. Your father took me out to a bar and I told him everything. God knows why."

"Pop's easy to talk to."

"He listened to all of it, sympathized some, but not as much as I thought I deserved." After all the years that had passed, Edwin could remember and even laugh a little. "He had a shot of whiskey in his hand. He downed it, slapped me on the shoulder and told me I had a son to think of and that I should go home to him. He saw clean through it, and he was right. I've never forgotten what he did for me just by speaking the truth."

She took his hands now, holding tight. "And Reed?"

"He was my son, always had been, always would be my son. I was a fool to have forgotten that."

"You hadn't forgotten," she murmured. "I don't think you'd forgotten."

"No." He felt the smoothness and strength of her hands in his. "In my heart I hadn't. I drove back. He was playing in the yard alone. This boy, not quite six, turned and looked at me with adult eyes." A shudder moved through him, quick and violent. "I've never been able to wipe out that one moment when I saw what his mother and I had done to him."

"You've no cause to blame yourself. No," she added before Edwin could speak again. "I've seen you and Reed together. You've no cause to blame yourself."

"I did everything I could to make it up to him, to make things normal. In fact, it didn't take me very long to forget what his mother had done. Reed never forgot. He still carries that bitterness, Maddy, that I saw in his eyes when he was five years old."

"What you've told me helps me to understand a great deal." Taking a deep breath, she sat back on her heels. "But, Edwin, I don't know what I can do."

"You love him, don't you?"

"Yes, I love him."

"You've given him something. He's beginning to trust in someone. Don't take it away now."

"He doesn't want what I have to give him."

"He does, and he'll come around. Just don't give up on him."

She rose and wrapped her arms around herself, then turned away. "Are you so sure I'm what he needs?"

"He's my son." As she turned back slowly, Edwin rose. "Yes, I'm sure."

He wasn't asleep. He couldn't sleep. Reed had nearly given in to the urge to lose himself in a bottle of Scotch, but he decided misery was better company.

He'd lost her. Because they hadn't been able to accept each other for what they were, he'd lost her. Oh, she was better off without him. That he was certain of. Yet, she'd been the best thing that had ever happened to him.

He'd hurt her, just as he'd known he would, but wasn't it strange how much he hurt, too?

She'd be gone tomorrow, he told himself. The best thing to do was to forget, and to put the handling of the play and the cast album in his father's hands. He'd divorce himself from it, and therefore purge himself of memories of Maddy O'Hurley.

He started to cross to the windows but remembered how Maddy had been drawn to them. Swearing, he paced away again.

The knock on the door surprised him. He didn't often have visitors at one in the morning. He didn't want visitors, he thought, and ignored the knock. It continued to sound stubbornly. Annoyed, Reed yanked the door open with the intention of blasting anyone who had the misfortune to be there.

"Hi." Maddy stood with a dance bag slung over her shoulders and her hands dipped into the pockets of a wide denim skirt.

"Maddy—"

"I was in the neighborhood," she began, and walked past him into the apartment. "I decided to drop in. I didn't wake you, did I?"

"No, I—"

"Good. I'm always cranky when someone wakes me up. So . . ." She tossed her bag down. "How about a drink?"

"What are you doing here?"

"I told you I was in the neighborhood."

Crossing to her, he held her by the shoulders and kept her still. "What are you doing here?"

She tilted her head. "I couldn't keep away from you."

Before he could prevent it, his hand had reached for her cheek. He dropped it again. "Maddy, a few hours ago—"

"I said a lot of things," she finished for him. "They were all true. I love you, Reed. I want to marry you. I want to spend my life with you. And I think we could do a pretty good job of it. But until you think so, we'll just have to coast."

"You're making a mistake."

She rolled her eyes. "Reed, you're putting those scratchy clothes on me again. If we were married, maybe—just maybe—you could suggest what was best for me. As things stand, I make my own decisions. I really would like a drink. Got any diet soda?"

"No."

"All right, whiskey then. Reed, it's very rude to refuse to serve a guest a drink."

He continued to hold her a moment longer, then
gave in and lowered his forehead to hers. "I do need
you, Maddy."

"I know." She lifted her hands to his face. "I know
you do. I'm glad you know it."

"If I could give you what you wanted—"

"We've talked about it enough for now. I'm leaving for Philadelphia tomorrow."

"Dancing to the piper," he murmured.

"That's right, and I'm going to work my tail off, so
I don't want to talk. I don't want to argue, not tonight."

"All right. I'll get us a drink."

He moved over to the bar and chose a decanter.
"You know, Reed, it's still a very odd feeling for me
to take my clothes off onstage."

He had to laugh. Somehow she always made him
laugh. "I imagine it is."

"I mean, I wear a bodysuit and spangles and don't
expose more than I would on a public beach, but it's
the act itself that's odd. I have to pull this off in front
of several hundred people in a few days. That means
practice, practice, practice."

When he turned back, she was smiling at him and
slowly unbuttoning her blouse. "I thought you might
give me an unbiased opinion on my. . . stage presence.
Stripping's an art, you know." She ran a hand down
the center of her body as her blouse parted. "Titillat-
ing. . ." She turned her back and looked at him over
her shoulder. "Fanciful." She let the blouse slip gently away. "What do you think?"

"I think you're doing great. So far."

"I just want to be sure I make Mary realistic." She
loosened the tie on her skirt and let it fall as she turned

back. The brief black merry widow she wore had him setting down his glass before he dropped it.

"I've never seen you wear anything like that."

"This?" She passed a hand down her body again. "Not really my style. Not comfortable enough. But for Mary..." She bent from the waist and unhooked a garter from the sheer black stocking. "It's sort of a trademark." She straightened again and ran both hands through her hair in an upward motion. "Do you think it'll sell?"

"I'm thinking that if you wear that onstage I'll strangle you."

With a laugh, she unhooked the second garter, then slowly rolled the stocking down her leg. "You have to remember I'm Mary once the curtain's up. And I'm going to help make your play a hit." She tossed the stocking at him, then began the same routine on the other. "It's too bad I don't have a more voluptuous figure."

"Yours does very well."

"Do you think?" Still smiling, she began to unhook the lace covering her breasts. "Reed, I hate to be a pest, but you haven't given me that drink."

"Sorry." He picked up her glass and carried it to her.

Maddy took it, and for a moment the humor in her eyes turned into something deeper. "This one's for my Pop," she said, and touched her glass to his.

"What?"

"You don't have to understand." She smiled again and tossed back the shot of whiskey. It poured through her like lava. "What do you think of the show so far? Worth the price of a ticket?"

He'd meant to be gentle. He'd wanted to be tender to show her how much her coming back to him meant. But the hands that dived into her hair were tense and urgent. "I've never wanted you more."

She tilted her head back and let her empty glass fall carelessly to the carpet. "Show me."

He dragged her against him, desperate. The sting of whiskey clung to her lips, intoxicating. Her arms went around him, welcoming the rage of desire. It was the first time, the only time, she had felt him come to her without control. Her blood began to pound with anticipation of facing unleashed passion. When he pulled her to the floor, she went willingly.

His hands were everywhere, touching, stroking, pressing. He lifted her up to a blinding peak where she could only gasp his name and ask for more.

There was more, much more.

Impatient, he tugged at the remaining hooks, freeing her body to his. Just as urgent, her fingers tore at the belt of his robe until she found warm, naked flesh and muscle.

The carpet was smooth at her back. His body was hard against hers. She heard her name whispered through his lips, harshly. Then he was filling her.

It had never been so fast before, so furious, so unrestrained. Heedlessly she threw herself into the whirl of pleasure. Her body shook, and so did his. Love and passion mixed so intimately that she couldn't tell one from the other and no longer tried.

She was there for him. As long as he accepted her arms around him, he was there for her.

Chapter Ten

"We'd be better off walking."

Maddy slowed and steered through yet another pothole before she tossed a grin at Wanda. "Where's your sense of adventure?"

"I lost it a mile back in that ditch we went through."

"It wasn't a ditch," Maddy corrected as she maneuvered her way through downtown Philadelphia traffic. "Why don't you look out the window and tell me when we pass something of great historical significance?"

"I can't look out the window." Wanda folded her long legs into a more comfortable position. It wasn't easy, as Maddy had chosen to rent a nifty little compact with bucket seats that all but sat on the dash. "It makes me seasick when the buildings bounce up and down."

"It's not the buildings, it's the car."

"That, too." Wanda grabbed the doorhandle for support. "Why did you rent this heap, anyway?"

"Because I never get to drive in New York. Is that Independence Hall?" When Maddy craned her neck around, Wanda gave her a none-too-gentle shove on the shoulder.

"Honey, you watch the road if you want to get back to New York."

Maddy bumped to a stop at a light. "I like driving," she said breezily.

"Some people like jumping out of planes," Wanda muttered.

"I'd have a car in New York if I thought I would ever have a chance to use it. How much time do we have?"

"Fifteen fun-filled minutes." Wanda braced herself as Maddy shot forward again. "I know I should have asked this before I got in the car, but when's the last time you drove?"

"Oh, I don't know. A year. Maybe two. I think we should try some of those little shops on South Street after rehearsal."

"If we live to see it," Wanda mumbled, then pressed the invisible brake on her side as Maddy whipped around a sedan. "You know, Maddy, the man on the street probably would think you're about the happiest human being alive. Somebody who knows you a bit better might tell you that your smile's going to crack around the edges if you don't ease up."

Maddy downshifted as the car jittered over yet another pothole. "That obvious?"

"Obvious enough. What's going on with you and Mr. Wonderful?"

Maddy let out a long, sighing breath. "One day at a time."

"And you're the type who needs to have a good grip on next week."

It was true, too true, but she shook her head. "He has a good reason for feeling the way he does."

"But that doesn't change the way you feel."

"I guess not. You know, Wanda, I never really used to believe it when people said life was complicated. Stop me if I get too personal," she began, and Wanda merely shrugged. "When you were married before, did you think it was forever?"

Wanda pursed her lips. "I guess you could say I did and he didn't."

"Well, would you . . . I mean, if you met someone you really cared about, would you get married?"

"Again?" Instinctively Wanda started to laugh, then thought better of it. "If there was someone who made everything click, I might do it. But I'd think about it for longer. No, hell, I wouldn't, either. I'd dive in with both feet."

"Why?"

"Because there aren't any guarantees. If I thought I had a chance, I'd take it. Like the lottery. Weren't you suppose to turn there?"

"Turn? Oh, damn." Muttering to herself, Maddy bumped her way around the block. "Now we'll be late."

"Better that you get what's on your mind out of your system first, anyway."

"I was just hoping he'd be here." Maddy turned again and got back on track. "I know he couldn't very well spend the whole week down here while we're in rehearsal, but we'd kind of planned that he would come today."

"No-show?"

"Something came up. He was vague about it, something about some problem with playlists and promoters or something."

"We've all got a job to do, kid."

"Yeah." With maneuvering even Wanda had to admire, Maddy squeezed into a minuscule parking space right across from the theater. "I guess I better think about my own. Two more full rehearsals and we're on."

"Don't remind me." Wanda set a hand on her stomach. "Every time I think about it a 747 lands in my gut."

"You're going to be great." Maddy stepped out of the car and slammed the door. At the end of the block, someone was selling cut flowers. She made a mental note to treat herself after rehearsal. "*We're* going to be great."

"I'm going to hold you to that. The last play I was in closed after two performances. I gave serious thought to sticking my head in the oven. But it was electric."

"Tell you what." Maddy paused by the stage door and grinned. "If we flop, you can use mine. I've got gas."

"Thanks a lot."

"That's what friends are for." Maddy pushed open the door, took one step inside, then let out a whoop. With some curiosity, Wanda watched her launch down the corridor and fling herself at a group of people.

"You're here. You're all here."

"And where else would we be?" Frank O'Hurley picked up his baby girl and swung her in a circle.

"But all of you!" The minute her feet touched the floor, Maddy grabbed her mother and squeezed her ribs until they threatened to crack. "You look great, absolutely great."

"So do you." Molly returned the hug. "And late for rehearsal, as usual."

"Missed my turn driving here. Oh, Abby." She reached for her sister, hugged and held on. "I'm so glad you could come. I was afraid you wouldn't be able to get away from the farm."

"It'll be there when we get back. How often does my sister have an opening night?" But concern clouded Abby's eyes. She knew her sister as well as she knew herself, and she didn't think the tension she felt from Maddy had anything to do with professional nerves.

Still hugging Abby, Maddy grabbed for her brother-in-law's hand. "Dylan, thanks for bringing her."

"I think it was the other way around." With a laugh, he kissed Maddy's cheek. "But you're welcome."

"It's too bad," she began with a wink to Abby, "that you couldn't bring the boys."

"We're right here."

Deliberately Maddy looked in the opposite direction. "Did I hear something?"

"We came, too."

"We're going to New York."

"I could have sworn I..." Maddy let her words trail off as she focused on her nephews. Carefully she kept her face blank for a moment, then widened her eyes. "You can't be Ben and Chris—can you? They're just little boys. You're both much too tall to be Ben and Chris."

"We are too," Chris piped up. "We grew."

Taking her time, Maddy studied both of them. "No fooling?"

"Come on, Maddy." Though he tried not to look too pleased, Ben grinned and shuffled his feet. "You know it's us."

"You're going to have to prove it to me. Give me a hug."

She bent down to hold them both tight. "We rode on a plane," Chris began. "I got to sit by the window."

"Miss O'Hurley, they want you in Wardrobe."

"Shoot." Maddy released her nephews and straightened. "Look, where are you all staying? There's a whole list of hotels on the call board. I can—"

"We're booked in your hotel," Molly told her. "Now go on, we'll have plenty of time."

"Okay. Are you going to stay for rehearsal?"

"Think they could stop us?" Frank asked.

When she heard her name again, she started down the hall, walking backward to keep them in view just a moment longer. "As soon as I'm done, we're going to celebrate. I'm buying."

Frank chuckled and draped an arm over his wife's shoulders. "Does she think we'd argue with that? Let's go get a front-row seat."

"Mr. Selby to see you, sir." Hannah kept a cool, professional smile on her face as she ushered Selby into Reed's office.

"Thank you, Hannah. Hold my calls." There would be no tray of coffee and sweet rolls today. Reed caught Hannah's look of disapproval before she shut the door. "Sit down, Selby."

"I guess your old man's proud of you." Selby cast a look around the office before he settled himself comfortably. "You've kept the label right up top. Heard you signed that little group from D.C. A risky move."

Reed merely lifted a brow and held his gaze steady. He knew Galloway had offered the group a contract. Valentine had simply offered them a better one. "We don't mind a few risks."

"Always a headache to get the stations to put new talent on their playlist. A record from an unknown's going to die without solid promotion." Selby took out a small, thin cigar, then fiddled with his lighter. "That's why I'm here. I thought it would be wise if we talked before the RIAA meeting this afternoon."

Reed continued to sit back, waiting for Selby to light his cigar. He'd known as soon as Selby had requested an appointment that the other man was running scared. The Recording Industry Association of America didn't have closed meetings every day. Those involved were aware that the label heads would vote on whether the organization should investigate independent promoters. Some major record companies, Galloway included, still used the independents, though the shadow of scandal, payola and kickbacks lurked around the edges of their profession.

"Look, Valentine," Selby began when Reed remained silent. "Neither of us started in this business yesterday. We know what the bottom line is. Airplay.

Without airplay on the important stations, a record dies.''

He was sweating, Reed observed calmly. Beneath the trendy pastel suit and the sunlamp tan, nerves ran hot. Just what would a full investigation mean to Galloway? Reed speculated.

"When you pay for airplay, Selby, you're riding a sick horse. Sooner or later it's going to fall down under you."

Letting out a quick stream of smoke, Selby leaned forward. "We both know how the system works. If it means slipping a few hundred to a program director, who does it hurt?"

"And if it means threatening that same program director if he doesn't play ball?"

"That's nonsense." But there was a tiny bead of sweat on his temple.

"If it is, an investigation will clear it up. In the meantime, Valentine Records will get its new releases played without independents."

"Throwing the baby out with the bathwater," Selby snapped, then rose. "Top 40 stations report their playlist to the trades. If a new release doesn't hit the trades, it might as well not exist. That's the system."

"Maybe the system needs a little reworking."

"Just as narrow-minded and straight as your old man."

A ghost of a smile touched Reed's lips. "Thank you."

"It's easy for you, isn't it?" Bitter, Selby turned on Reed. "You sit here in your cozy little office, never getting your hands dirty. Your daddy did that for you."

Reed checked his temper. "If you look," he said quietly, "you'll see my father's hands are clean. Valentine doesn't, and never has, run its business on payola, kickbacks or heavy-handed threats."

"You're not so lily-white, Valentine."

"Let's just say that in an hour Valentine Records will vote for a full investigation."

"It'll never fly." Selby smirked as he crushed out his cigar, but his hands weren't steady. He'd come to Reed because Valentine had the reputation and power to sway the vote. Now he was choking. Selby loosened the careful knot of his tie. "Too many labels know where the bread's buttered. Even if you probe, I won't lose. Oh, a few heads will roll down the line, but mine won't. Ten years ago, Galloway was a hole-in-the-wall. Today it's one of the top names in the business. I made it because I played the game, I watched the angles. When the dust settles, Valentine, I'm still going to be on top."

"I'm sure you will," Reed murmured as Selby stormed out of his office. Men like that never paid for their actions. They had plenty of fall guys and scape-goats littering their path. If Reed had wanted a per-sonal vendetta, he could have initiated an investigation of his own. Already he had information on a disc jockey who'd been beaten, allegedly for not playing certain releases. There was the program director in New Jersey whose wife had been threatened. There was another who made frequent trips to Vegas, trav-eling first-class and gambling heavily. More heavily than his annual salary would permit. Part of the game. Not a game Reed cared to play.

But it was unlikely Selby would pay for his actions. Did anyone?

Rising, he checked the contents of his briefcase. It was true that he had come into a business that had already been well established. He hadn't had to hustle his way to a label. If he had, would he have scrambled for a shortcut? Because he didn't know, couldn't be sure, Reed decided to leave the investigation up to the RIAA. He'd let the dust settle. It would be a long, probably ugly meeting, Reed thought as he stepped out of his office.

"I won't be back today, Hannah."

"Good luck, Mr. Valentine. You had a few calls while you were talking to that man."

His mouth twitched a little at her tone. "Anything important?"

"No, nothing that can't wait. You did get a call from Miss O'Hurley." Hannah sent him an entirely-too-innocent smile and hoped for a reaction. The fact that he hesitated told Hannah everything she needed to know.

"If she calls back, tell her . . ."

"Yes, Mr. Valentine?"

"Tell her I'll get back to her."

Disappointment ruled for a moment. "Ah, Mr. Valentine?"

"Yes?"

She could see the impatience, but pressed just a little further. "I wondered if you were going to Philadelphia for the opening, or if perhaps you'd like me to send flowers."

He thought of the meeting he had to deal with, of the work that couldn't be ignored. He thought of Maddy's face and the confusion that had been dogging him for days. Her feelings, his, his needs, hers.

Were they really the same, or were they so totally opposed that they could never come together?

"My father's going. If I don't, we'll be represented."

"I see," Hannah said primly, and stacked papers on her desk.

"I'll take care of the flowers myself."

"See that you do," she muttered as he went out the glass doors.

It had gone well. Maddy dropped crosswise on her bed and let the rehearsal play back in her head. She wouldn't jinx it by saying it was perfect, but she could think it. As long as she thought it very quietly.

Tomorrow night. Tomorrow night at this time, she thought with a little skip of the pulse, she'd be in her dressing room. Twenty-four hours. She rolled onto her back and stared at the ceiling. How in the hell was she going to get through the next twenty-four hours?

He hadn't called back. Maddy shifted her head so that she could look at the phone again. They had only spoken to each other a handful of times since she'd left for Philadelphia, and every time they had she'd sensed he was trying to distance himself from her. Maybe he'd succeeded.

A dancer was no stranger to pain. You felt it, acknowledged it, then went on and worked around it. Heartache might be a little more difficult to deal with than a pulled muscle, but she would go on. Survive. She'd always prided herself on being a survivor.

Her family was here. Rousing herself from the bed, Maddy went to the closet. She would change, put on her happiest face and take her family out on the town. Not everyone was as lucky as she, Maddy reminded herself as she stripped out of her sweats. She had a family who loved her, who stood behind her, who thought she was just fine the way she was.

She had a career that was on the rise. Even if she lost her grip on the brass ring, no one could take her dancing away from her. If she had to go back and play the clubs again, do regional theater, summer stock, she'd still be happy.

Maddy O'Hurley didn't need a man to complete her life, because her life was complete. She didn't want a knight on a white charger to scoop her up and take her away from all this. She liked where she was, who she was.

If Reed backed out of her life, she could— She leaned back against the closet door with a sigh. She could very possibly be the most miserable person alive. No, she didn't need him to save or protect her. She needed him to love her, and though she didn't think he could understand, she needed him to let her love him.

When she heard the knock on her door, Maddy shook herself out of what was dangerously close to depression. "Who is it?"

"It's Abby."

Leaving her robe untied, Maddy dashed to the door. Abby stood there, looking fresh and quietly lovely in a slim white dress. "Oh, you're all ready. I haven't even started."

"I dressed early so I could come down and talk."

"Before you say anything, I have to tell you how wonderful you look. Maybe it's Dylan, maybe it's the country air, but you've never looked better."

"Maybe it's pregnancy."

"What?"

"I found out right before we left home." She took Maddy by the shoulders, looking as though she could take on the world. "I'm going to have another baby."

"Oh, God. Oh, Abby, that's great. I'm going to cry."

"Okay. Let's sit down while you do."

Maddy searched fruitlessly in her robe pocket for tissue. "How does Dylan feel about it?"

"Stunned." Abby laughed as they sat together on the bed. Her eyes were soft. The hint of rose under her skin enhanced the curve of her cheeks. She pushed her wavy blond hair behind her back before she took Maddy's hands. "We're going to make the announcement at dinner tonight."

"And you're going to start taking better care of yourself. No more mucking out the stalls. I mean it, Abby," she continued before her sister could speak. "If I have to lecture Dylan, I will."

"You don't have to. He'd like to wrap me up in tissue for the next seven months or so. We weren't made for that, Maddy, you know we weren't."

"Maybe not, but you can ease off." She threw her arms around her sister and squeezed. "I'm so happy for you."

"I know. Now I want you to talk to me." Firm, Abby straightened her back. "Chantel called me and said you were making yourself crazy over some man."

"She would," Maddy muttered. "I'm not making myself crazy over anything. It's not my style."

Abby slipped off her shoes. "Who is he?"

"His name's Reed Valentine."

"Valentine Records?"

"That's right. How do you know?"

"I still keep up with the industry a little. And Dylan worked with him on a book some time ago."

"Yes, Reed mentioned it."

"And?"

"And nothing. I met him, I fell in love with him, I made a fool of myself." She tried to keep her voice careless and light, and nearly succeeded. "Now I'm sitting here staring at the phone waiting for him to call. Like a teenager."

"You never had much of a chance to be a teenager when you were sixteen."

"I don't care much for it. He's a good man, Abby. Kind and gentle, though he'd never see that in himself. Can I tell you about him?"

"You know you can."

She started at the beginning and left nothing out. It never occurred to her that she was betraying Reed's privacy. In truth, she wasn't. Whatever she said to Abby or to Chantel was like telling her thoughts to herself.

Abby listened in her calm, serene way while Maddy told her everything; the love, the compromises, the trauma that had marred Reed's childhood and affected his life. Because they were so in tune with each other, Abby hurt when her sister did.

"So you see, no matter how much I love him, I can't change what happened to him or how he feels."

"I'm sorry." They shifted together, with Abby's arm around Maddy's shoulder. "I know how painful it is. I can only tell you that I know absolutely that if you love hard enough you can work miracles. Dylan didn't want to love me. The truth is, I didn't want to love him, either." It was easy to look back and remember. "We'd both made a decision never to risk that kind of involvement again. It was a very logical decision made by two intelligent people.'' She smiled a little, leaning her head against Maddy's. ''Love has a way of wiping out everything but what really matters.''

''I've tried to tell myself that. But Abby, he wasn't dishonest with me. Right from the start he made it clear that he didn't want to get involved. It was to be a very casual relationship, which of course isn't a relationship at all. I'm the one who stepped over the line, so I'm the one who had to make the adjustments.''

''That's also very logical. What happened to your optimism, Maddy?''

''I left it in a drawer at home.''

''Then it's time you pulled it out again. This isn't like you, mooning around, looking at the dark side. You were the one who always planted her feet and refused to budge until things worked out your way.''

''This is different.''

''No, it's not. Don't you know how much I've always wanted to be as confident of myself as you are? I always envied that quality in you Maddy, when day after day I went on, afraid of failing.''

''Oh, Abby.''

''It's true, and you can't let me down now. If you love him, really love him, then you've got to plant your feet until he can admit he loves you, too.''

''He has to feel it first, Abby.''

''I think he does.'' She gave her sister a quick shake. ''Go back over everything you've just told me, but this time listen. The man's crazy about you, Maddy, he just hasn't been able to admit it to you or to himself.''

Hope, never far beneath the surface, began to stir again. "I've tried to believe that."

"Don't try, do. I've had the worst a relationship can offer, Maddy. Now I'm having a taste of the best." Instinctively she rested a hand on her stomach, where a new life slept. "Don't give up. But I'll be damned if I'm going to sit here and watch you wait for him to toss you a few crumbs. Get dressed," Abby ordered. "We're going to celebrate."

"Bossy." Maddy grinned as she walked to her closet. "You always were bossy."

Reed let the phone ring a dozen times before he hung up. It was nearly midnight. Where the hell was she? Why wasn't she in bed, resting up for the next day? The one thing he knew about her, was absolutely certain of, was that Maddy trained for a part as rigorously as an athlete. Training meant diet, exercise, attitude and rest. So where the hell was she?

In Philadelphia, he thought, disgusted as he walked to the windows and back again. She was miles away in Philadelphia, in her own world, with her own people. She could be doing anything, with anyone. And he had no right to question her.

The hell with rights, he told himself as he picked up the phone again. She was the one who spoke of love, of commitments, of trust. And she was the one not answering her phone.

He could still remember how disappointed she'd looked when he'd told her he couldn't be sure he'd be there for opening night. He'd had the damn RIAA meeting hanging over his head, and he still couldn't judge the backlash from it. There was bound to be a scandal now that the investigation had been approved. A scandal would affect everyone, every label, every record company executive, even the ones who'd kept their noses clean.

In the morning he was likely to have dozens of calls, from reporters, radio stations, consulting firms, his own employees. He couldn't very well drop everything and go off to watch the opening of a play.

Not just any play, he thought as the phone rang on and on. Maddy's play. No, his play, Reed reminded himself as he slammed the phone down again. Valentine Records was backing it and therefore had a duty to protect its interests. His father would be there, that would be enough. But *he* was president of Valentine, Reed reminded himself.

Was he excusing himself from going or from remaining behind?

It really didn't matter. None if it really mattered at all. What mattered was why Maddy wasn't answering the phone at midnight.

She had a right to her own life.

The hell she did.

Reed ran a hand through his hair. He was acting like a fool. Trying to calm himself, he walked over to pour himself a drink, and the plant caught his eye. There were new green shoots spreading out, young and healthy. The old, yellowed leaves had fallen off and been swept away. Compelled, he reached out to stroke one of the smooth, heart-shaped leaves.

A minor miracle? Perhaps, but it was only a plant, after all. A very stubborn plant, he conceded. One that had refused to die when it should have, one that had responded wholeheartedly to the proper care and attention.

So he had luck with plants. Deliberately, he turned away and stared at his empty apartment. It wouldn't be wise to make too much of its having been Maddy's. Just as it wasn't wise to make too much out of the fact that she wasn't in her room. He had other things to think about, other things to do. But he left the drink untouched.

The room was pitch-dark when knocking disturbed her sleep. Maddy rolled over, snuggled into the pillow and prepared to ignore it. When it continued, she shook herself awake, half believing it was a cue.

It was the middle of the night, she reminded herself with a huge yawn. She had hours yet before she had to step out onstage. But the knocking was definitely at her door and getting louder every minute.

"All right!" she called out irritably, and rubbed her eyes open. If one of the dancers had the jitters, she was going to send her back to her own room to sleep it off. She couldn't afford to be a pillar of strength at three a.m.

"Just hang on, will you?" Muttering, she found the light switch, then hunted up a robe. She unlocked her door, then pulled it open until the chain snapped into place. "Now look...Reed!" Instantly awake, Maddy slammed the door in his face and fumbled with the chain. When she pulled it open again, she jumped into his arms. "You're here! I didn't think you'd be here. I'd nearly gotten used to the idea that you weren't coming. No, I hadn't," she corrected immediately, and found his lips with hers. She felt it—the need, the tension. "Reed, what are you doing here at three in the morning?"

"Do you mind if I come in?"

"Of course not." She stepped back and waited while
he tossed a small overnight bag on a chair. "Is something wrong?" she began, then tugged at his shirt.
"Oh, God, is something wrong with your father?
Reed—"

"No, my father's fine. He should be here tomorrow."

Her fingers relaxed but stayed where they were.
"You're upset."

"I'm fine." He moved back from her and walked
around the room. She'd already made it her own, he
noticed, with tights, socks, shoes strewn here and
there. The dresser was a rubble of bottles and pots and
scraps of paper. She'd spilled a bit of powder and
hadn't bothered to dust it off. He ran a finger through
it, and her scent clung to his skin. "I couldn't reach
you tonight."

"Oh? I was out having dinner with—"

"You don't owe me an explanation." Furious,
though only with himself, he whirled around.

She pushed the hair away from her face and wished
she understood him. It was three in the morning, she
reminded herself. He was obviously edgy. She was
tired. It would be best to take it slow.

"All right. Reed, you're not going to tell me you
drove all the way to Philadelphia because I didn't answer the phone." Even as he stared at her, he saw
puzzlement turn to humor and humor to pleasure.
"You did?" Going to him, she slipped her arms
around him, pressing her cheek to his chest. "That's
about the nicest thing anyone's ever done for me. I
don't know what to say. I—" But when she looked up,
she saw it in his eyes. All the pleasure drained from
hers as she backed away.

"You thought I was with someone else." Her voice was very quiet, the words very distinct. "You thought I was sleeping with someone else, so you came to see for yourself." A bitter taste rose in her throat. It was a taste she'd rarely sampled. She gestured toward the empty bed. "Sorry to disappoint you."

"Don't." He grabbed her wrist before she could turn away, because he'd already seen the tears welling in her eyes. "That wasn't it. Or—damn it, maybe it was part of it, part of what went through my mind. You'd have a perfect right."

"Thank you." She pulled her wrist away and sat on the edge of the bed, but she couldn't stop the tears. "Now that you've satisfied yourself, why don't you go? I need my sleep."

"I know." He ran both hands though his hair before he sat beside her. "I know that, and when it was late and I couldn't reach you, I wondered." When her eyes lifted to his, he cursed himself. "All right, I did wonder if you were with someone else. I don't have any hold on you, Maddy."

"You're an idiot."

"I know that, too. Just give me a minute." Anticipating her, Reed took both her hands before she could refuse. "Please. I did wonder, and I hated the idea. Then I worried. The whole time I was driving here I worried that something had happened to you."

"Don't be ridiculous. What could happen?"

"Nothing. Anything." His hands tightened on hers in frustration. "I just had to be here. To see you."

The anger was draining, but she didn't know what would rise up to replace it. "Well, you've seen me. Now what?"

"That's up to you."

"No." She pulled away again and rose. "I want you to tell me. I want you to look at me right now and tell me what it is you want."

"I want you." He rose slowly. "I want you to let me stay. Not to make love with you, Maddy. Just to be here."

She could easily allow the hurt to overwhelm her. She could just as easily toss her hurt feelings aside and reach out to him. With a smile, she stepped closer. "You *don't* want to make love with me?"

"I want to make love with you until we both collapse." Shaken because it was true, he reached out to touch her cheek. "But you need your sleep."

"Worried about your investment?" She ran her fingers down his shirt, unfastening buttons as she went.

"Yes." He took her face in his hands. "Yes, I am."

"You don't have to be." Watching him, she slid his shirt off his shoulders. "Trust me. At least for tonight, trust me."

Chapter Eleven

He wanted to. Somewhere during the long, frustrating night, he'd realized that if he trusted her, what she was, what she said, what she felt, his life would turn around. He just couldn't be certain the answers would be waiting for him if it did.

But her touch was so easy, and her eyes were so warm. For tonight, for just one more night, nothing else really mattered.

He brought her hands, both of them, to his lips, as if he could show her what he didn't feel safe in saying, or feel safe in even thinking. She smiled at him, as always touched by the tenderness he was capable of.

Bright and steady, the light by the bed continued to burn as they lowered themselves onto already rumpled sheets.

Her eyes stayed open, darkening slowly, as he brushed kisses over her face. He stroked his fingers gently across her shoulder where her robe hung loose, up the long line of her throat and to her lips, where they traced the shape. With the tip of her tongue she moistened his skin, inviting, tempting, promising. Then she nipped, catching his fingertip between her teeth and holding it snug while her eyes dared him.

Watching her, he slid his hand up her leg, loitering on the tight, muscular calf, then lingering on the smooth, cool skin of her thigh. He felt her breath catch, then continued moving up, making her shudder once, twice, before he parted her robe and freed her body to his.

"I thought about touching you like this," Reed murmured as he caressed one small, firm breast, "since the last time I touched you this way."

"I wanted you to be here." She let her hands make their own explorations. Slowly, wanting to see the fire leap into his eyes, she drew his slacks over his hips. "Every night when I closed my eyes, I pretended that you'd be here in the morning. Now you will be."

She pressed a kiss to his shoulder, but her hands were never still. Nor were his.

They moved slowly, though not quite lazily, because the passion was too close to the surface. They savored, in silent agreement that they had all the time they needed. No rush, no hurry, no frantic, desperate merging that left the body and mind dazed. Tonight was a night for the soul first.

Desire me ... but quietly. Long for me ... but gently. Ache for me ... but patiently.

The sheets were tangled beneath her, disturbed by the restless night she had barely begun, warmed now by the passionate night she hoped wouldn't end. Their fingers linked, palm against palm, strength against strength, as their lips met for one more long, luxurious kiss.

Of all the food she had recklessly sampled that evening, there had been nothing to compare with the flavor of his kisses. The wine had lacked sparkle, the spices had been bland when compared with the taste of his lips on hers. He could indeed feed her soul. Somehow, in some way, she wanted to feed his. Her arms came around him as she sought to give back a portion of what she was given.

There seemed to be no limit to her generosity. He could feel it flow over him every time he held her. Now, even with the languorous, passionate movements of her body, he felt it pour out of her, quenching his soul's thirst like something cool in the midday heat.

Her body responded with every move, with every request he made. She was there with him, as desirable and urgent a partner as a man could want. But she was also, he knew, there *for* him, something soft and giving a man could sink into and be soothed by. He didn't know how to repay, to give back what she so selflessly offered. He knew only to love her with infinite care.

If it had been possible, she would have told him that was enough, at least for now. There could be no more words when her mind and body were floating so freely. When he touched her skin, she felt ablaze. He murmured her name and her heart rejoiced. When they came together with all the fire and intensity of lovers reunited, love for him consumed her.

By midmorning, Maddy was up and restless, filled with nervous energy. In a matter of hours, it would be make-or-break time, win-or-lose, all-or-nothing. It simply wasn't possible to stay away from the theater.

"I thought you didn't have to be there until late this afternoon," Reed commented as Maddy directed him down the shortcut she'd discovered from hotel to theater.

"There's no rehearsal, but everything's happening today."

"I was under the impression that everything happens tonight."

"Nothing happens tonight without today. The lights, the sets, the drops. Turn right, then right again."

Through a thick stream of traffic, he eased over and followed her directions. "I didn't think performers worried much about the technical points of a show."

"A musical would lose a lot of its punch if it wasn't trimmed properly. Try to picture *The King and I* without the throne room or *La Cage* without the nightclub. There's a space." Leaning out the window, she pointed it out to him. "Will this thing squeeze into that?"

Reed gave her a mild look, then, with a few turns of the wheel, maneuvered his BMW between two other cars parked at the curb. "Will that do?"

"That's great." She leaned over to kiss him. "You're great. I'm glad you're here, Reed. Have I mentioned that?"

"A few times." He cupped a hand around the back of her neck to keep her close. Keeping her close was becoming a priority. "I should have worked harder to talk you into staying in bed. To rest," he added when she lifted her brow. "You're ready to jump out of your skin."

"This is normal opening-night behavior. If I were relaxed, you could worry. Besides, I think you should see what you're paying for. You're not the kind of man who's only interested in the end product. Come on." She was out of the car and waiting on the sidewalk. "You should get a look at backstage."

They went through the stage door together. Maddy waved to the guard, then followed the noise. The electric sound of a saw came briefly, then was gone. For the most part there were voices, some loud, some lowered, some complaining. Men and women, dressed for work, milled around. Some gave orders, others followed them, in what looked to Reed like quiet confusion.

If he had to take bets that they would be ready for curtain in a matter of hours, he'd have called it a long shot. There was no greasepaint here, no glitter. There was dust, a little grime and a lot of sweat.

A man in a headphone stood downstage with his arms spread over his head. He spoke into the mike as he brought his hands a little closer together. A square of light on the backdrop adjusted with the movement.

"You met the lighting director, didn't you?"

"Briefly," Reed said, and watched him move a few feet to stage right.

"All the lights have to be focused, one at a time. He's doing the downstage lights, his assistant will take care of upstage."

"How many lights are there?"

"Dozens."

"The show starts at eight. Shouldn't this have been done already?"

"We made some changes in rehearsal yesterday. Don't worry." She linked an arm through his. "Whether it's done or not, the show will go on at eight."

Reed cast another look around. There were big wooden crates on wheels, some opened, some closed. Coils of cable littered the floor, ladders were set up here and there. On a Genie lift, a man fiddled with lights while another stood back, motioning down with his hands. A dark backdrop lowered slowly, then stopped on his signal.

"They've got to set the highs and lows on the drops," she told him. "They're all weighted, and the crew has to know how far to take them down, how far to bring them up. Come on, I'll show you the fly floor. That's where they make a lot of magic happen."

Maddy weaved her way backstage, around crates and boxes, carefully skirting ladders rather than walking under them. There was more rope dangling, more cable coiled. Reed saw a rubber chicken hanging by a noose next to where two men taped what looked like an electrical box to a wood panel.

"Miss O'Hurley." One of them turned to grin at her. "Looking good."

"Just make sure you make me look good tonight."

There were tall chests lined up along the back wall, most of them plastered with stickers from other shows. Maddy squeezed between the last drop and the chests.

"We have to cross underneath the stage in this theater," she explained. "Not enough room back here. It's better than having to run outside and around to make your next cue."

"Would it be more organized if—"

"This is theater." Maddy took his hand and led him through a narrow doorway. "This is as organized as it gets. Up here." She climbed up a skinny, steep stairway and through another opening.

It looked to Reed like the deck of a ship—one that had weathered a heavy storm. Ropes were everywhere, some as thick as Maddy's wrist, some thin and wiry. They hung from above and spilled out on the floor, without, it seemed to him, any rhyme or reason. A great many were grouped together, slanting up, then down over a long metal pole.

There was a small table wedged into a corner with papers tacked up around it and spread over it, with an overflowing ashtray on top of everything. A few men were tying ropes with the careless skill of veteran sailors. The place smelled of rope, cigarettes and sweat; the familiar scents that lingered in a theater.

"This is a hemp house," she began. "There aren't too many of them left in the States. It's too bad, really. You have more flexibility with rope and sandbags than you do with counterweights. All the moving pieces are handled from up here. The beaded curtain." She put a hand over a group of ropes that was bound together and labeled with a tag. "It weighs over five hundred pounds. When it's time to let it down in the third act, the stage manager cues the flyman verbally through the intercom. The lighting director backs it up with a light cue."

"Sounds simple enough."

"Sure. Unless you've got two or three cues on top of each other or a drop that's so heavy it takes three men on the ropes. This is a big show. The guys up here won't be taking many coffee breaks."

"I don't understand why you know so much."

"I've been in theater all my life." A man came through the doorway, muscled his way around them and began talking to two men who were tying off rope. "Come out on the paint bridge. It's quite a view."

She made her way around the various ropes, hunched under a steel bar and stepped out on a narrow iron platform. Below, stagehands were spread out. Though it looked no more organized from this angle, Reed began to sense a spirit of teamwork.

"If anything up here has to be painted, this is where they do it." She glanced down and shook her head. "Not my kind of job."

A stream of four-letter words rose up from below. A drop descended silently. Then a spotlight began to play on it, widening, then narrowing, then holding steady. Maddy ran her hands back and forth over the rail.

"That's my spot in act one, scene three."

"If I didn't know better, I'd say you were nervous."

"No, I'm not nervous. I'm terrified."

"Why?" He put a hand over hers. "You know what you can do."

"I know what I have done," she corrected. "I haven't done this yet. Tonight, when the curtain goes up, it's the first time. There's your father." Looking down, Maddy let out a long breath. "It looks like he's talking to the general manager of the theater. You should be down there with them."

"No, I should be here with you." He was just beginning to realize how true that was. He hadn't driven to Philadelphia in the middle of the night because he mistrusted her. He hadn't come with her that morning because he didn't have anything better to do. He'd done both because wherever she was, he belonged. She danced to the piper. And, perhaps, so did he. It scared the hell out of him.

Thirty feet above the stage, on a narrow iron platform, he experienced the fear of falling—but not fear of falling physically onto the floor below. "Let's go down." He wanted people around, strangers, noise, anything to distract him from what was blooming inside.

"All right. Oh. It's my family. Look." Nerves were gone, and the pleasure was so deep that she slipped an arm around Reed's waist without being aware that he stiffened. "There's Pop. See the skinny little man who's kibitzing with one of the carpenters? He could run any part of this show—lights, drops, props. He could direct it or choreograph it, but that's never been for him." She beamed down, all admiration and love. "Spotlight, that's for Pop."

"And for you?"

"I'm told I take after him the most. My mother's there. See the pretty woman with the little boy? That's my youngest nephew, Chris. He decided yesterday he wanted to be a lighting man because they get to ride up in the lift. And my sister Abby. Isn't she lovely?"

Reed looked down, focusing on a slender woman with wavy blond hair. There was an air of contentment around her, though she stood in the midst of chaos. She put her hand on the shoulder of another boy and pointed to the house.

"She's showing Ben where they'll be sitting tonight, I imagine. He's really more excited about going to New York tomorrow. Dylan has meetings with his publisher."

Reed watched Dylan reach down, then heft Chris on his shoulders. The little boy's squeals of delight bounced up to them.

"They're great kids." Because she heard the wistfulness in her own voice, she shook it away. She had enough, Maddy reminded herself. "Let's go say hello."

Back down onstage, she skirted around a row of colored lights bolted to the floor. Later that night they would shine for her. Hearing the signal, she took Reed's hand and drew him aside as the beaded curtain made its glittery descent.

"Pretty terrific, isn't it?"

Reed studied the thousands of beads. "It certainly makes a statement."

"We use this during my dream sequence, when I imagine I'm a ballet dancer instead of a stripper, and of course I *pirouette* right into Jonathan's arms. The nice thing about theater—and about dreams—is you can make anything you want happen."

As they walked around another drop, she heard her father's voice ring out.

"Valentine, I'll be damned." Frank O'Hurley, wiry and small, grabbed the huge, husky man in a rough embrace. "My girl told me you'd sprouted wings to back this play." Delighted, Frank drew back and grinned at him. "How many years has it been?"

"Too many." Edwin pumped Frank's hand enthusiastically. "Too damn many. You don't look any older."

"That's because your eyes are."

"And Molly." Edwin bent down to kiss her cheek. "Pretty as ever."

"There's not a thing wrong with your eyes, Edwin," she assured him, and kissed him again. "It's always good to see an old friend."

"I never forgot you. And I never stopped envying you your wife, Frank."

"In that case, I can't let you kiss her again. You might have a harder time remembering my Abby."

"One of the triplets." He took Abby's hand between his meaty ones. "Incredible. Which one—"

"The middle one," she answered easily.

"Maybe it was your diaper I changed."

With a laugh, Abby turned to Dylan. "My husband, Dylan Crosby. Mr. Valentine is obviously an old, intimate friend of the family."

"Crosby. I've read some of your work. Didn't you work with my son on one of your books?"

"Yes, I did." Dylan felt Ben's hand slip into his and linked fingers with him. "You were out of town at the time, so we never met."

"And grandchildren." Edwin sent another look at Frank and Molly before he hunkered down to the boys' level. "A fine pair. How do you do?" He offered his hand formally to each boy. "Here's something else I covet, Frank."

"I've got a soft spot for the little devils," Frank admitted, winking at them. "Abby's going to give us another one next winter."

"Congratulations." It was envy; he couldn't prevent it. But he felt pleasure, as well. "If you don't have plans, I'd like for you all to join me for dinner before the show."

"We're the O'Hurleys," Frank reminded him. "We never have plans that can't be changed. How's your boy, Edwin?"

"He's fine. As a matter of fact, he . . . Well, here he is now. With your daughter."

When Frank turned, a light went on in his head. He saw Maddy with her hand caught in that of a tall, lean man with sculpted features. And he saw the look in her eyes, warm, glowing and a little uncertain. His baby was in love. The quick twist in his heart was part pleasure, part pain. Both feelings softened when Molly's fingers linked with his.

Introductions were made again, and Frank kept his eyes sharply on Reed. If this was the man his baby had chosen, it was up to him to make sure she'd chosen well.

"So you're in charge of Valentine Records," Frank began. He didn't believe in subtle probing. "Doing a good job of it, are you?"

"I like to think so." The man before Reed was like a bantam rooster—small but scrappy. Frank's hairline was receding and his eyes were a stunning blue, and Reed wondered why, when he looked at Frank O'Hurley, he saw Maddy. There was little or no resemblance on the surface. If it was there—and somehow it was—it came from inside. Perhaps that was why he felt himself so drawn to the man and why he worked so hard to keep his distance.

"A lot of responsibility, a record company," Frank went on. "Takes a clever hand at a wheel. A dependable one. Not married, are you, boy?"

Despite himself, Reed felt a smile tugging. "No, I'm not."

"Never have been?"

"Pop, did I show you how we changed the timing for the finale?" Taking his hand, Maddy dragged him into the wings at stage left. "What do you think you're doing?"

"About what?" He grinned and kissed both her cheeks. "God, what a face you've got. Still look like my little turnip."

"Flattery will get you a punch in the nose." She drew him back behind the stage manager's desk as a group of stagehands wheeled out a crate. "You stop pumping Reed that way, Pop. It's so...so obvious."

"What's obvious is that you're my baby girl and I have a right to look after you—when I'm around to do it."

With her arms folded, she tilted her head. "Pop, did you do a good job of raising me?"

"I did the best job."

"Would you say I'm a sensible, responsible woman?"

"Damn right you are." Frank puffed out his chest. "I'd punch the first man who said different."

"Good." She kissed him hard. "Then butt out, O'Hurley." She gave his cheek two sharp pats, then walked out onstage again. "I know everyone has things to do this afternoon." She answered her mother's wink. "I'm going up to the rehearsal room to iron out a few kinks."

She warmed up slowly, carefully, stretching her muscles one by one to insure against injury. There was only her. Only her and the wall of mirrors. She could hear the washing machine humming in the wardrobe room across the hall. In the little kitchen down the hall, someone opened and slammed the refrigerator door. Two people from Maintenance were taking a break just outside the door. Their conversation ebbed and flowed as Maddy bent to touch her chin to her knee. There was only her and the wall of mirrors.

It had been Macke's idea to put in the dream sequence, with its balletic overtones. When she'd mentioned that she hadn't been *en pointe* in six months, he'd simply suggested that she dig out her toe shoes and practice. She had. The extra *pointe* classes every week had added hours to her schedule. She could only hope they paid off.

She'd worked, she'd rehearsed, and the moves and music were lodged in her head. Still, if there was one number that gave her the jitters, it was this one.

She'd be alone onstage for the first four minutes. Alone, the lights a filmy blue, the curtain behind her glittering and shimmering. The music would come up... Maddy pushed the button on her tape recorder and set herself in front of the mirrors. Her arms would cross her body, her hands would rest lightly on her own shoulders. Slowly, very slowly, she would rise *en pointe*. And begin.

The bustle outside the door was blanked out. A series of dreamy *pirouettes*. She wasn't Mary now, but Mary's most private dream. *Jeté*, arms extended. It had to look effortless, as if she floated. The bunching muscles, the strain, weren't allowed to show here. She was an illusion, a music-box dancer in tutu and tiara. Fluidity. She imagined her limbs were water, even as the strength rippled through them for a series of *fouet* turns. Her arms came over her head as she went to an *arabesque*. She would hold this for only a few seconds, until Jonathan came onstage to make the dream a *pas de deux*.

Maddy let her arms come down, then shook them to keep the muscles limber. That was as far as she could go without her partner. Moving to the recorder, she pressed the rewind button. She would do it again.

"I've never seen you dance like that."

Her concentration snapped as she glanced over and saw Reed in the doorway. "Not my usual style." She stopped the squawking tape. "I didn't know you were still around."

"You're a constant amazement," he murmured as he came into the room. "If I didn't know you, I would have looked in here and thought I'd walked in on a prima ballerina."

Though it pleased her, she laughed it away. "A few classic moves isn't Swan Lake."

"But you could do it if you wanted, couldn't you?" He took the towel she held and dabbed at her temples himself.

"I don't know. I'd probably be in the middle of *Sleeping Beauty* and feel an irresistible urge to do a tap routine."

"Ballet's loss is Broadway's gain."

"Keep talking," she said with a laugh. "I need it."

"Maddy, you've been in here nearly two hours. You're going to wear yourself out before curtain."

"Today I have enough energy to do the show three times."

"What about food?"

"Rumor has it the stagehands are fixing goulash. If I pick at some about four or five, I should be able to keep it down during the first act."

"I wanted to take you out."

"Oh, Reed, I couldn't, not before opening night. After." She reached out her hands for his. "We could have a late supper after."

"All right." He felt how cool her hands were even after her dancing. Too cool, too tense. He didn't know how to begin to soothe her. "Maddy, are you always like this before an opening?"

"Always."

"Even though you're confident that it's going to be a hit?"

"Just because I'm confident doesn't mean I don't have to work to make it a hit. And that makes me nervous. Nothing worthwhile happens easily."

"No." His eyes grew more intense on hers. "No, it doesn't."

But they weren't talking about opening nights or about the theater now. His fingers were tense when he spoke again. "You really believe that if you work at something hard enough, believe strongly enough, you can't miss?"

"Yes, I do."

"Us?"

She swallowed. "Yes, us."

"Even though the odds are against it?"

"It isn't a matter of odds, Reed. It's a matter of people."

He dropped her hands and moved away. Just as he had on the paint bridge, he'd felt that quick fear of falling. "I wish I could feel as optimistic as you. I wish I could believe in miracles."

She felt the hope that had ballooned inside her deflate. "So do I."

"Marriage is important to you." He could see her in the glass, small and standing very straight.

"Yes. The commitment. I was raised to respect that commitment, to understand that marriage wasn't an end but a beginning. Yes, it's important."

"It's a contract," he corrected, speaking almost to himself. "A legal one, and not particularly binding. We both know about contracts, Maddy. We can sign one."

She opened her mouth, then very slowly shut it again before she attempted to speak. "I beg your pardon?"

"I said we'll sign one. It's important to you, more important than I had realized. And it doesn't really matter to me. We can get blood tests, a license, and it's done."

"Blood tests." She let out a staggered breath and braced herself on the little table behind her. "A license. Well, that's certainly cutting out the romantic nonsense, isn't it?"

"It's only a formality." Something was moving uneasily in his stomach as he turned back to her. What he was doing was clear. He was closing his own cage door. Why he was doing it was another matter. "I'm not sure of the law, but if we have to we can drive into New York on Monday and take care of it. You can be back for the evening show Tuesday."

"We wouldn't want it to interfere with our schedules," she said quietly. She'd known he would hurt her, but she hadn't known he would quite simply break her heart. "I appreciate the offer, Reed, but I'll pass." She slammed down the button again and let the music come.

"What do you mean?" He took her arm before she could set into position.

"Just what I said. Excuse me, I have to rehearse."

Her voice had never been cold before. Never cold, never flat, as it was now. "You wanted marriage, and I agreed to it. What more do you want, Maddy?"

She jerked away to face him. "More, *much* more than you're willing to give. God, I'm afraid more than you're capable of giving. I don't want a piece of paper, damn you. I don't want you to do me any favors. Okay, Maddy wants to get married, and since I don't really care one way or the other, we'll sign on the dotted line and keep her happy. Well, you can go to hell."

"That's not what I meant." He would have taken her by the shoulders, but she backed away.

"I know what you meant. I know it too well. Marriage is just a contract, and contracts can be broken. Maybe you'd like to put an escape clause in this one so it can be neat and tidy when you're tired of it. No, thank you."

Had it sounded that cold, that...despicable? He was out of his mind. "Maddy, I didn't come up here knowing we'd get into all of this. It just happened."

"Too spontaneous for you?" This time there was sarcasm, another first. "Why don't you go punch up your lines, Reed?"

"What do you want, candlelight and me down on one knee? Aren't we beyond that?"

"I'm tired of telling you what I want." The fire went out of her eyes. They were cool again and, for the first time, aloof. "I have to be onstage in a few hours, and you've done enough for now to make that difficult for me." She pushed the recorder to take the tape back to the beginning again. "Leave me alone, Reed."

She picked up the count and began. She continued to dance when she was alone and the tears started to fall.

Chapter Twelve

As Reed came down into the corridor, he met his father.

"Maddy still upstairs?" Edwin clapped his arms around his son's shoulders. "Just finished talking with the general manager. Seems we're sold out for tonight's performance. In fact, we're sold out through the week. I wanted to tell her."

"Give her a little while." Reed dug his fists into his pockets and struggled against a feeling of utter frustration. "She's working on a routine."

"I see." He thought he did. "Come in here for a minute." He gestured toward the stage manager's office. When they were inside, he shut the door behind them. "You used to tell me when you had problems."

"You get to a point where you'd better know how to solve them yourself."

"You've always been good at that, Reed. It doesn't mean you can't run them by me." He took out a cigar, lighted it and waited.

"I asked Maddy to marry me. No," he went on quickly before the pleasure could dawn in Edwin's eyes. "That's not quite true. I laid out the arrangements for a marriage to Maddy. She tossed them right back at me."

"Arrangements?"

"Yes, arrangements." Reed was defensive, and his voice was sharp and impatient. "We need blood tests, a license; we have to fit it into our schedules."

"It?" Edwin repeated with a slight inclination of his head. "You make it sound very cut-and dried, Reed. No orange blossoms?"

"She can have a truckload of orange blossoms if she wants them." The room was too small to allow him to storm around it. Instead, he stood where he was and strained against the enforced stillness.

"If she wants them." Understanding too well, Edwin nodded and lowered himself into the one chair. "Reed, if you put marriage on that sort of level with a woman like Maddy, you deserved to have it tossed back at you."

"Maybe I did. Maybe it's for the best. I don't know why I started the whole business."

"It might be because you love her."

"Love's a word that sells greeting cards."

"If I thought you believed that, I'd consider myself a complete failure."

"No." Outraged, Reed turned to him. "You've never failed at anything."

"That's not true. I failed at my marriage."

"Not you." The bitterness rose up, too huge to swallow.

"Yes, I did. You listen to me now. We never talked about this properly. You never wanted to, and I let it go because I felt you'd been hurt enough. I shouldn't have." Edwin looked at his cigar, then slowly crushed it out. "I married your mother knowing she didn't love me. I thought I could keep her bound to me because I could pull the strings to give her what she wanted. The more strings I pulled, the more she felt hemmed in. When she finally broke free, it was as much my fault as hers."

"No."

"Yes," Edwin corrected. "Marriage is two people, Reed. It's not a business, it's not an arrangement. It's not one person wanting to keep the other indebted."

"I don't know what you're talking about," Reed said. "I don't see any reason to get into this now."

"You know there's a reason. She's upstairs right now."

Reed stopped even as he gripped the handle of the door. Slowly he let it go again and turned back. "You're right."

Edwin settled back. "Your mother didn't love me, and she didn't love you. I'm sorry for that, but you should know that love isn't something that comes just from giving birth or just from duty. It comes from the heart."

"She betrayed you."

"Yes. But she also gave you to me. I can't hate her, Reed, and it's time you stopped letting what she did run your life."

"I could be like her."

"Is that what this is about?" Edwin heaved himself up and took Reed by the lapels in the first gesture of violence he'd ever shown his son. "How long have you been carrying this around?"

"I could be like her," Reed repeated. "Or I could be like the man she slept with, and I don't even know who he was."

Edwin loosened his hold and stepped back. "Do you want to know?"

Reed combed both hands through his hair. "No, they're nothing to me. But how can I know what's inside of me? How can I know that what they were wasn't passed on?"

"You can't. But you can look in the mirror and think about who you are and have been, rather than who you might be. And you can believe, as I do, that the last thirty-five years that we've had together is more important."

"I know it is, but—"

"There are no buts."

"I'm in love with Maddy." With the words came a slow shattering of defenses he'd lived with since childhood. "How do I know that won't change next month, next year? How can I know I'm capable of giving her what it is she needs for the rest of our lives?"

"That's something else you can't ever know." Why couldn't the answers be simple ones? It seemed to Edwin that there had never been simple answers for Reed. "That's something you have to risk, something you have to want and something you have to work at. If you love her, you will."

"I'm more afraid of hurting her than I am of anything else. She's the best thing that ever happened to me."

"I don't suppose you mentioned all this when you were outlining the arrangements?"

"No." He rubbed his hands over his face. "I made a mess of it."

"I'd be more concerned if you'd been too smooth."

"You don't have to worry about that. I pushed her away because I was afraid to reach out for her."

Smiling, Edwin rocked back on his heels. "I'll tell you this. No son of mine would let a woman like Maddy O'Hurley slip through his fingers because he thinks he might not be perfect."

After running a hand over his face, Reed nearly laughed. "That sounds like a challenge."

"Damn right it is." Edwin put his hands on Reed's shoulders. "And my money's on you. Remember that game in your senior year? Ninth inning, two outs, the score was tied. You worked the batter to a full count."

"Yeah, I remember." This time he did laugh. "I threw a knuckleball and he knocked it over the fence."

"That's right." Edwin grinned at him. "But it was a hell of a pitch. Why don't you buy your old man a drink?"

With her hair pulled back by a thick band and the rattiest robe she owned tied loosely at the waist, Maddy sat at makeup mirror and carefully attached false lashes to her own. Her makeup was nearly done, and even with one eye lashed and the other naked, she'd already captured the exotic look that was Mary's. Just a little too much color on the cheeks. Just a little too much sparkle on the eyelids, and a rich ripe red for the lips. As she fastened the other lash, she waited for the knot in her stomach to untie itself.

Opening-night nerves, just opening-night nerves, she told herself as she carefully adjusted the liner on her left eye. But there was more than that rushing around inside her, and she couldn't get away from it.

Marriage. Reed had spoken of marriage—but on his terms. The part of her that was always open to hope had waited for the moment when he would accept the fact that they should be together. The part of her that was always willing to see the best of things had been certain that moment would come. Now that it had, she couldn't take it. What he offered wasn't years of joy but a piece of paper that would bind them together legally, leaving nothing to the emotions.

She had too much of it, Maddy told herself. Too much emotion, not enough logic. A logical woman would have accepted Reed's terms and made the best of it. Instead, she was ending things. Maddy stared at her reflection in the lighted mirror. Tonight was a night for beginnings—and a night for endings.

She rose and walked away from the mirror. She'd seen enough of herself.

Outside in the corridor, people were rushing by. She could hear the noise, the nerves, the energy that was opening night. Her dressing room was packed with flowers, dozens of arrangements that doubled themselves in the mirror and crowded the room with scent.

There were roses from Chantel. White ones. Her parents had sent her a clutch of daisies that looked wild and lovely. There was a bowl of gardenias that she had known had come from Trace before she'd looked at the card. It had merely said Break A Leg. She'd wondered briefly how he'd known where and

when to send them. Then she'd stopped wondering
and had appreciated.

Other arrangements sat here and there, but there
were none from Reed. She hated herself for overlooking the beauty of what she had in the quest for what
wasn't there.

"Thirty minutes, Miss O'Hurley."

Maddy pressed a hand to her stomach at the call.
Thirty minutes left. Why did she have to have Reed
dragging at her mind now? She didn't want to go on.
She didn't want to go out there tonight to sing and
dance and make a theater full of strangers laugh. She
wanted to go home and pull down the shades.

There was a quick knock at her door, but before she
could answer, her parents poked their heads through.
"Can you use a couple of friendly faces?" Molly
asked her.

"Oh, yeah." Maddy stretched out her hands to her
mother. "I need all I can get."

"The house is filling up." Frank beamed as he
looked around the dressing room. There was a star on
the door. He couldn't have asked for more for his
daughter. "You got standing room only, kiddo."

"Are you sure?"

"Sure I'm sure." Frank patted her hand. "I talked
to the general manager myself. He's wearing out the
leather on his shoes dancing around."

"He should wait until the curtain calls to do his
dancing." Maddy put a hand to her stomach again and
wondered if she had any Alka-Seltzer.

"You won't need it when the curtain goes up,"
Molly commented, reading her daughter easily.
"Opening-night jitters, Maddy, or is there something
else you want to tell us about?"

She hesitated, but there had never been any secrets between Maddy and her family. "Just that I'm in love with an absolute fool."

"Oh, well." Molly lifted a brow toward Frank. "I know how that is."

"Just a minute now," he began, but was summarily shooed from the room by his wife.

"Out, Frank. Maddy has to get into costume."

"I've powdered her bottom," he muttered, but allowed himself to be pushed out the door. "Knock them dead," he told his daughter. Then he winked and was gone.

"He's terrific, isn't he?" Maddy smiled as she heard him call out to one of the the dancers.

"He has his moments." Molly glanced at the costume of sequins and feathers hanging on the back of the door. "That for opening?"

"Yes."

"I'll give you a hand." Molly took it off the hanger as Maddy tossed her robe aside. "The fool wouldn't happen to be Reed Valentine, would it?"

"That's him." Maddy wiggled herself into the snug bikini.

"We had dinner with him and his father tonight." She helped Maddy hook the brief spangled bra that would go under the outer costume. "Seems like a nice young man."

"He is. I never want to see him again."

"Mm-hmmm."

"Fifteen minutes, Miss O'Hurley."

"I think I'm going to be sick," Maddy whispered.

"No, you're not." With competent hands, Molly pressed the Velcro together at her daughter's hip. "It seemed to me that your Reed was a bit distracted at dinner.''

"He's got a lot on his mind." Maddy turned this way and that to be certain the costume was secure. "Contracts, mostly," she added in a mutter. "Anyway, I'm not interested."

"Yes, I can see that. They don't make our lives easier, you know."

"What?"

"Men." Molly turned her daughter around. "They weren't put here to make our lives easier. They were just put here."

For the first time in hours, Maddy felt a laugh bubbling up. "Did you ever think the Amazons had it right?"

"The ones who killed off the men after they'd made love with them?" Molly seemed to consider the question seriously before shaking her head. "No, I don't think so. There's something comforting about having one man for a lifetime. You get used to him. Where are your shoes?"

"Right here." Studying her mother, Molly stepped into them. "You still love Pop, don't you? I mean really, really love him, just the way you always did?"

"No." When Maddy's mouth dropped open, Molly laughed. "Nothing stays the same. The way I love Frank now is different from the way I loved him thirty years ago. We've four children now, and a lifetime of fights and laughter and tears. I couldn't have loved him this much when I was twenty. I doubt I love him as much now as I will when I'm eighty."

"I wish . . ." Maddy let her words trail off, shaking her head.

"No, tell me what you wish." Molly's voice was gentle, as it rarely was. "A daughter can tell her mother anything, especially wishes."

"I wish Reed could understand that. I wish he could see that sometimes it can work, sometimes it can last. Mom, I love him so much."

"Then I'll give you one piece of advice." She took Maddy's wig off the stand. "Don't give up on him."

"I think I'm giving up on me."

"Well, that'll be a first for an O'Hurley. Sit down, girl. Maybe this wig will help keep the brains in your head."

"Thanks."

The five-minute call sounded. Molly walked to the door, then turned to give her daughter one last look. "Don't miss your cue."

"Mom." Maddy rose, keeping her shoulders straight. "I'm going to bring down the house."

"I'm counting on it."

Maddy stepped out of her dressing room with four minutes to spare. A member of the chorus came clattering down the stairs with an outrageous plume of ostrich feathers on her head. The overture was already playing. She walked toward the music, losing a little bit of Maddy O'Hurley with every step. Wanda was already in the wings taking long, cleansing breaths.

"This is it."

Maddy smiled at her before she looked over the stage manager's shoulder to the monitor on his desk. He could watch the play from there, seeing it as the audience did. "What's the top in curtain calls for you, Wanda?"

"We got seventeen in Rochester once."

Maddy put her hands on her hips. "We're going to beat the hell out of that tonight." She walked on-stage, faced the curtain and took her mark. As the other dancers filled the stage, she could feel the fear-laced excitement. The nightclub set was in darkness behind her. Hidden by the wings was Macke at stage right. Maddy glanced over at him and tossed her head. She was ready.

"House lights half...go."

She drew in oxygen.

"Cue one...go."

Above her head, lights flashed on, bathing her in a rainbow.

"House lights off...go."

The audience hushed.

"Curtain."

It rose, and so did the music.

By the time Maddy walked off stage right for the first scene change, the electricity was high. Immediately wardrobe began stripping off one cos-tume and bundling her into the next. She breathed a sigh as her wig was removed and her own hair fluffed out.

"You keep that energy up until the final curtain and I'll buy you the best meal in Philadelphia."

Maddy caught her breath as she stared at Macke. Her dress was zipped, her shoes changed and her makeup toned down, all in a matter of two minutes. "You're on." Then she made the dash that would take her under the stage and across for her cue.

She passed beneath the floor of the stage and crossed behind the orchestra pit, where the musicians now were silent. Her Jonathan and the actor who played his best friend were exchanging lines. She heard

the audience give a roll of laughter as she moved
through a makeshift lounge where enterprising members of the crew had gathered a couple of chairs and a
sagging sofa. Near the steps that would lead her back
up stage left, a group of stagehands loitered around a
small portable television. The sound was down to a
low buzz so that the business on stage could be heard
clearly. Maddy paused, knowing she had time before
the next cue. Obviously they did, too.

"Who's winning?" she asked as she caught a
glimpse of the ball game.

"No score. Pirates against the Mets. They're in the
third inning."

"My money's on the Mets."

One of the men laughed. "Hope you don't mind
losing it."

"Five bucks," she said as she heard Jonathan finishing up his song.

"You're on," he told her.

"I certainly am." She went up the steps and out
onstage for her first encounter with Jonathan C.
Wiggings III.

The chemistry was right. Mary and Jonathan met
on the library steps. They clicked. The audience's interest was caught up in the romance between the
stripper and the rich man's son with innocence shining out of his eyes.

The last number before intermission was Maddy's
striptease. She came rushing in, as she had in rehearsal, struggling out of her prim dress and into her
flamboyant costume and wig. Her dialogue with
Wanda was edgy and acerbic, her argument with Terry
tough. Then the lights came up in hot pinks and reds.

She began with her energy at peak and never let it slide.

She whipped the boa off and let it fly. The audience sent up a howl as it landed in her father's lap.

For you, Pop, she thought as she sent him a broad wink. Because you taught me everything.

Maddy kept her word and brought the house down.

Intermission wasn't a time for relaxing. There were costume changes, makeup to be freshened, energy to be recharged. Word was sent to Maddy that the Mets were down in the sixth, 2-zip. She took it philosophically. She'd lost more important things that day.

From her place in the wings, Maddy sipped a cup of water and peered out at the audience. The house lights were up, and she could see people swarming around the theater. The buzz of excitement was there. She had helped put it there.

Then she saw Reed with the lights from the chandeliers spilling over his hair. Her father stood beside him, inches shorter, years older but just as vital. As she watched, Frank laughed and tossed an arm around Reed's shoulder. It warmed her. She told herself it didn't matter, could no longer matter, but it warmed her to see her father laughing with the man she loved.

Maddy stepped back until the audience was blocked from her view.

"You look like that, you're going to scare them away before the finale."

Turning, Maddy looked at Wanda. They were both dressed in nightclothes for the scene in the apartment they shared. The beaded curtain would come down soon, and Maddy would do her dream sequence. "I can't do that. We still have to beat those seventeen curtain calls."

"He out there?" Wanda didn't bother to look, but motioned with her head.

"Yes, he's there."

The house lights flashed off and on, off and on. Wanda quietly began her deep breathing. "I guess you've got something to prove."

That I can survive, Maddy thought. That I can complete my own life if I have to. "To myself," she murmured before they moved out to their marks. "Not to him, to myself."

In plays, the writer can twist events, shift them, manipulate them to create a happy ending. In the end, Mary and Jonathan had each other. They had overcome differences and deceptions, backgrounds and lies, distrust and disillusionment. For them, happy-ever-after was there for the taking.

Then the applause began. It rolled, it thundered and echoed over the chorus as they took their bows. It continued, only stronger, over the principals. With her hands gripped together, Maddy waited. She would go out last.

With her head up and the smile already in place, Maddy strode out onstage. Applause rose like lava, warm and fluid. The cheers began in the balcony and rolled down, growing louder, still louder, until the theater was filled with them. She took her first bow with them ringing in her head.

Then they were standing, first one, then two, then a dozen. Hundreds of people rose up to their feet and shouted for her. Stunned, she could only stand there and look.

"Take another bow," Wanda said to her in an undertone. "You earned it."

Maddy broke out of her trance and bowed again before linking hands with Wanda and her partner. The cast as a unit bowed again, and the curtain came down. The applause kept coming, wave after wave, as Maddy threw her arms around Wanda and squeezed.

The unity was there, a line of dancers, a group of actors, all of whom had worked and studied and rehearsed endless hours for this one moment. So they held on to it as the curtain, for a moment, cut them off from the audience and ranged them together.

"Here we go again," Maddy said, and locked her hands tight.

The curtain rose and fell twenty-six times.

It took Maddy some time to work her way back to her dressing room. There were people to hug and a few tears to be shed. Macke scooped her up in his arms and kissed her full on the mouth.

"You better be just as damn good tomorrow," he told her.

It was a riot backstage, with dancers whooping around and planning a big celebration. They were a hit. Whatever adjustments, polishing or tightening that would have to be done before Broadway couldn't take away from the fact that they were a hit. No one could take it away from them. The hours and hours of work, sweat and repetition had paid off.

Feet clattered on stairs as members of the chorus scrambled up to their dressing rooms. Someone had a trumpet and was blaring out reveille. Maddy squeezed through the crowd in the hall and into her own room. There she collapsed on a chair and stared at her own reflection.

There were pots and tubes jumbled over the surface of the table. Greasepaint, powder, every color of the rainbow. Above it, she studied her own face, then broke into a grin.

She'd done it.

Her dressing room door opened, and part of the riot slipped in. She saw her father first, the boa slung around his shoulders like a mantle of victory. Energy poured back into her as she jumped out of her chair to fling herself into his arms.

"Pop. It was great. Tell me it was great."

"Great? Twenty-six curtain calls is better than great."

"You counted."

"Of course I counted." He squeezed her hard until her feet left the floor. "That was my girl out there. My baby girl knocking them dead. I'm so proud of you, Maddy."

"Oh, Pop, don't cry." Sniffling herself, she reached into his pocket for a handkerchief. "You'd have been proud of me if I'd flopped." She dried his eyes. "That's why I love you."

"How about a hug for your mother?" Molly held out her arms and gathered Maddy close. "All I could think of was the first time we put you in dance shoes. I could hardly believe it was you, so strong, so vital. Strong." Molly drew her back by the shoulders. "That's what you are, Madeline O'Hurley."

"My heart's still racing." Laughing, Abby embraced her sister. "Every time you came out, I'd grab Dylan's hand. I don't know how many fingers I broke. Ben kept telling the woman beside him you were his aunt. I just wish—"

"I know, I wish Chantel could have been here, too." She leaned down to hug Ben, then glanced up at Chris, who was nestled droopy eyed in Dylan's arms.

"I didn't fall asleep," Chris told her with a huge yawn. "I watched the whole thing. It was pretty."

"Thanks. Well, Dylan, do you think we're ready for Broadway?"

"I think you're going to rock Broadway back on its heels. Congratulations, Maddy." Then he grinned and let his gaze slide down her. "I also liked your costumes."

"Flashy, but brief," she said with a chuckle as she glanced down at the red merry widow she wore.

"We have to get the kids back." Abby looked at Ben. His hand was already caught in Dylan's. "We'll see you tomorrow, before we go. Call me." Abby touched Maddy's arm in a gesture that said everything. "I'll be thinking of you."

"We'll be going, too." Frank sent Molly a sidelong look. "You'll be running out of here to celebrate with the rest of the cast."

"You know you're welcome to come—" Maddy began.

"No, no, we need our rest. We've got a gig in Buffalo in a couple of days. Come on, let's leave the girl to change." Frank nudged his family along, then paused at the door. "You were the best, turnip."

"No." She remembered everything just then—his patience, the joy he'd given to her, the magic he'd passed on when he'd taught her to dance. "You were, Pop."

Maddy sighed and sat again. She drew a rose out of its vase to hold it to her cheek. The best, she thought, shutting her eyes. Why wasn't it enough?

When the door opened again, she straightened in her chair and had her smile ready. Reed stood in the doorway, with noise and confusion reigning behind him. Very carefully Maddy set the rose back in place. The bright smile didn't seem so necessary now.

"Do you mind if I come in?"

"No." But she didn't look at him. Deliberately she turned to the mirror and peeled off her lashes.

"I don't have to tell you how terrific you were." He shut the door on the stream of noise outside.

"Oh, I don't get tired of hearing it." She dipped her hand into a pot of cold cream, then smeared it on. "So you stayed for the show."

"Of course I stayed." She was making him feel like an idiot. He'd never pursued a woman before, not this way. And he knew if he made another mistake he'd lose her for good. When he came up behind her, he saw her hand hesitate, then tremble before she continued to rub in the cream. It eased the tension at the back of his neck. He hadn't lost her yet.

"I guess you know you got your money's worth." Maddy pulled out a tissue and began to wipe off the cream and layers of makeup.

"Yes, I do." He set a large blue box on the table at her elbow. She forced herself to ignore it. "But my father's taking over the show-business side. He wanted me to tell you how much he enjoyed tonight, how incredible he thought you were."

"I though he'd come back."

"He knew I needed to see you alone."

She tossed tissues in the wastebasket. Mary was gone, and there was only Maddy now. Rising, she reached for a robe. "I need to get out of costume. Do you mind?"

"No." He kept his eyes on hers. "I don't mind."

Because she decided he wouldn't make it easy, Maddy simply nodded and moved behind a Chinese screen. "So, you must be going back to New York tomorrow."

"No."

The hooks slipped out from between her fingers. Setting her teeth, Maddy attacked them again. "If your father's taking over, there's no need for you to stay."

"I'm not going anywhere, Maddy. If you want to make me crawl, I guess you're entitled."

She slammed the costume over the screen. "I don't want to make you crawl. That's ridiculous."

"Why? I've been a complete fool. I'm ready to admit it, but if you're not ready to accept it, I can wait."

She yanked the tie on her robe before she came around the screen. "You don't play fair. You've never played fair."

"No, I haven't. And it's cost me." He took a step toward her but saw from the look in her eyes that he could go no farther. "If it means I have to start over, from this point, I'll start over. I want you, Maddy, more than I've ever wanted anything or anyone."

"Why are you doing this?" She pulled a hand through her hair and looked for a way out. There wasn't one. "Every time I convince myself it's done and over with, every time I say okay, Maddy, give it up, you pull the rug out from under me. I'm tired of falling on my rear end with you, Reed. I just want to find my balance again."

This time he went to her, because nothing could stop him. His eyes were very dark, but she didn't see the panic in them. "I know you can live without me. I know you can shoot right to the top without me. And maybe, just maybe, I can walk away from you and survive. I don't want to risk it. I'll do whatever I can not to."

"Don't you understand, if the foundation isn't there, if we don't understand each other, don't trust each other, it won't ever work? I love you, Reed, but—"

"Don't say anything else." Though she held herself stiff, he drew her close. "Let me hang on to that for a minute. I've done a lot of thinking, a lot of changing, since I met you. Things were pretty black-and-white before you came along. You've added the color, and I don't want to lose that. No, don't say anything," he repeated. "Open the box first."

"Reed—"

"Please, just open the box first." If he knew her as well as he thought, as well as he hoped, that would say more to her than he could.

Strong. Her mother had told her she was strong. She had to believe it now. Maddy turned away and lifted the top on the box. For a moment, she could only stare.

"I didn't send you flowers," Reed began. "I figured you'd have plenty of them. I thought—I hoped—this would mean more. Hannah had a hell of a time getting it up here."

Speechless, Maddy lifted the plant out. When she'd given it to him, it had been soggy and yellowed and already rotting away. Now it was green and vivid, with strong young shoots. Because her hands were unsteady, she set it down on the table.

"A minor miracle," Reed murmured. "It didn't die when it should have. It just kept fighting, just kept thriving. You can make miracles happen if you want them badly enough. You told me that once, and I didn't believe it. I do now." He touched her hair and waited until she looked back at him. "I love you. All I want is for you to give me a lifetime to prove it."

She stepped into his arms. "Start now."

With laughter and relief he brought his lips to hers and felt the welcome. She drew him closer with a sigh, holding on with all the love, all the strength, she would promise him.

"I never had a chance," he murmured. "Not from the first minute I saw you. Nothing, thank God, has been the same for me since." But he drew her away, needing to pass the last hurdle. "Those things I said this afternoon—"

Placing a finger over his lips, she shook her head. "You're not going to try to back out of marrying me now."

"No." He held her close again, then let her go. "No, but I can't ask you until you know everything about me." It was hard, harder than he'd thought it could be. He let his hands drop away from her. "Maddy, my father..."

"Is an exceptional man," she finished for him, taking his hand. "Reed, he told me everything weeks ago."

"He told you?"

"Yes." She reached up to soothe the tension before it could form. "Did you think it would make a difference?"

"I couldn't be sure."

She shook her head. Rising on her toes, she kissed him again, letting the love pour out. "Be sure. There's no candlelight," she pointed out. "And I don't want you to get down on one knee. But I do want you to ask me."

He took both of her hands, and as he brought them to his lips, his eyes never left her. "I love you, Maddy. I want to spend my life with you, have children with you, take chances with you. I want to sit in the front row and watch you explode on the stage and know when it's over you'll come home to me. Will you marry me?"

The smile came slowly, until it lighted her whole face. She opened her mouth, then let out a groan as a sharp knock sounded at her door.

"Get rid of them," Reed demanded.

Maddy gave his hands a quick squeeze. "Just don't move. Don't even breathe." She yanked the door open, prepared to shut it again just as quickly.

"Your five, Miss O'Hurley." One of the stage-hands grinned at her and offered her a bill. "Mets took it 4–3. Looks like you just can't lose tonight."

She took the bill and ran it through her hands. Looking over her shoulder, she smiled at Reed. "You're so right."

* * * * *

SKIN DEEP

Prologue

"I don't know what we're going to do with that girl."

"Now, Molly." With his eye on the mirror, Frank O'Hurley added a touch of pancake makeup to his chin to make certain his face didn't shine onstage. "You worry too much."

"Worry?" As she twisted to pull the zipper up the back of her dress, Molly remained at the dressing room door so that she could watch the corridor backstage. "Frank, we have four children and I love every one of them. But Chantel's middle name is trouble."

"You're too hard on the girl."

"Because you're not hard enough."

Frank chuckled, then turned around to scoop his wife into his arms. More than twenty years of marriage hadn't dulled his feelings for her a whit. She was still his Molly, pretty and bright, even though she was the mother of his twenty-year-old son and his three teenage daughters. "Molly, my love, Chantel's a beautiful young girl."

"And she knows it." Molly peeked over Frank's shoulder at the backstage door, willing it to open. Where was that girl? They had fifteen minutes before they were due onstage, and Chantel had yet to make an appearance.

When she had given birth to her three daughters, each within minutes of the next, she hadn't known that the first one would give her more to worry about than the other two combined.

"It's her looks that are going to get her in trouble," Molly muttered. "When a girl looks like Chantel, boys are bound to come sniffing around."

"She can handle the boys."

"Maybe that worries me, too. She handles them too well." How could she expect a man as simple and kindhearted as her Frank to understand the complexities of women? Instead, she fell back on an old standard. "She's only sixteen, Frank."

"And how old were you when you and I—?"

"That was different," Molly said, but she was forced to laugh at the grin Frank sent her. "Well, it was." She straightened his tie, then brushed powder from his lapels as she spoke. "She might not have the good fortune to meet a man like you."

Cupping his hands under her elbows, he held her still. "What kind of man is that?"

With her hands on his shoulders, she looked at his face. It was thin, and already lined, but the eyes were the eyes of the smooth-talking boy she'd lost her head over. Though he'd never quite come up with that moon on a silver platter that he'd once promised her, they were partners in every sense of the word. For better or worse—through thick and thin. There had been a lot of thin. She'd spent more than half of her life with the man, Molly thought, and he could still charm her.

"A dear one," she told him, and brought her lips to his. At the sound of the back door closing, Molly pulled away.

"Now don't jump on her, Molly," Frank began as he caught his wife's arm. "You know it'll just put her back up, and she's here now."

Grumbling, Molly drew away as Chantel danced down the corridor. She was wearing a vivid red sweater and snug black slacks that showed off her blooming young shape. The brisk fall air had whipped color into her cheeks, highlighting already-elegant bones. Her eyes were a deep, deep blue and held a breezy, self-satisfied expression.

"Chantel."

With her natural flair for drama and timing, Chantel paused outside the door of the dressing room she shared with her sisters. "Mom." Her lips turned up at the corners, and the smile spread farther when she saw her father wink at her over Molly's shoulder. She knew she could always count on Pop. "I know I'm a little late, but I'll be ready. I had the most wonderful time." Excitement added spark to beauty. "Michael let me drive his car."

"That fancy little red number—?" Frank began. Then he coughed into his hand as Molly leveled him with a look.

"Chantel, you've only had your license a few weeks." How she hated to lecture, Molly thought as she wound herself up for it. She knew what it was to be sixteen, and because of that she knew there was no way around what she had to do. "Your father and I don't think you're ready to drive unless one of us is with you. And in any case," she continued before Chantel could get out her first protest, "it isn't smart to get behind the wheel of someone else's car."

"We were on the back roads." Chantel came over and kissed her mother on both cheeks. "Don't worry so much. I have to have some fun or I'll just shrivel up."

Molly recognized the ploy too well, and she stood firm. "Chantel, you're too young to go off in some boy's car."

"Michael's not a boy. He's twenty-one."

"That only makes my point."

"He's a creep," Trace announced calmly as he came into the corridor. He only lifted a brow when Chantel turned on him, eyes flashing. "And if I find out he's touched you I'll rip his face off."

"It's none of your business," Chantel told him. It was one thing to be lectured by her mother, quite another to hear it from her brother. "I'm sixteen, not six, and I'm sick and tired of being hovered over."

"Too bad." He took her chin in his hand, holding it steady when she tried to jerk away. He had a rougher, masculine version of Chantel's beauty. Looking at them, Frank felt pride swell in him until he thought he was going to burst. They were the fire-eaters of the family, more like their mother than him. He loved them with all his heart.

"All right now, all right." Playing peacemaker, he stepped up. "We'll get into all this business later. Right now, Chantel has to change. Ten minutes, princess," he murmured. "Don't dawdle. Come on, Molly, let's go warm up the crowd."

Molly sent Chantel a quiet look that warned her the business wasn't over, then softened and touched her daughter's cheek. "We've a right to worry about you, you know."

"Maybe." Chantel's chin was still high. "But you don't need to. I can take care of myself."

"I'm afraid you can." With a little sigh, she walked with her husband down toward the small stage where they would earn their living for the rest of the week.

Far from mollified, Chantel put her hand on the knob of the door behind her before she faced her brother. "I decide who touches me, Trace. Remember that."

"Just make sure your friend with the fancy car behaves himself. Unless you'd like both his arms broken."

"Oh, go to hell."

"Probably will," he said easily. Then he tugged her hair. "I'll be clearing a path for you, little sister."

Because she wanted to laugh, Chantel yanked open the door, then shut it in his face.

Maddy glanced over as she buttoned the back of Abby's costume. "So, you decided to show up."

"Don't you start." Moving quickly, Chantel pulled a dress that matched her sisters' off an iron bar that spanned the width of the room.

"Wouldn't dream of it. Sounded interesting out in the hall, though."

"I wish they'd stop fussing over me." Chantel tossed the dress down, then peeled off her sweater. The skin below was pale and smooth, the curves already soft and feminine.

"Look at it this way," Maddy said as she finished Abby's buttons. "They're so busy fussing at you, they hardly ever pick on Abby and me."

"You owe me." Chantel slipped out of her slacks with brisk movements and stood in bra and panties.

"Mom really was worried," Abby interjected. Since her own makeup and hair were finished, she arranged the tubes and pots that would set Chantel's face for the stage.

Feeling a little pang of guilt, Chantel plopped down in front of the mirror the three of them shared. "She didn't have to be. I was fine. I had fun."

"Did he really let you drive his car?" Interested, Maddy picked up a brush to fix Chantel's hair.

"Yeah. It felt . . . I don't know, it felt important." She glanced around the cramped, windowless room with its concrete floor and dingy walls. "I'm not always going to be in a dump like this, you know."

"Now you sound like Pop." With a smile, Abby handed her a makeup sponge.

"Well, I'm not." With years of experience already behind her, Chantel added the color to her face in quick strokes. "One day I'm going to have a dressing room three times this big. All white, with carpet so thick you'll sink up to your ankles."

"I'd rather have color," Maddy said, dreaming herself for a moment. "Lots and lots of color."

"White," Chantel repeated firmly. Then she stood to put on her dress. "And it's going to have a star on

the door. I'm going to ride in a limo and have a sports
car that makes Michael's look like a toy." Her eyes
darkened as she pulled on the dress, which had been
mended too many times to count. "And a house with
acres of garden and a big stone pool."

Because dreams were part of their heritage, Abby
elaborated as she did up Chantel's buttons. "When
you walk into a restaurant, the maître d' will recognize you and give you the best table and a bottle of
champagne on the house."

"You'll be gracious to photographers," Maddy
went on, handing Chantel her earrings. "And never
refuse an autograph."

"Naturally." Enjoying herself, Chantel clipped the
glass stones at her ears, thinking of diamonds.
"There'll be two enormous suites in the house for each
of my sisters. We'll sit up at night and eat caviar."

"Make it pizza," Maddy instructed, resting an elbow on her shoulder.

"Pizza *and* caviar," Abby put in, then stood on the
other side.

With a laugh, Chantel slipped her arms around her
sisters' waists. They were a unit now, just as they had
been in the womb. "We're going to go places. We're
going to be somebody."

"We already are." Abby tilted her head to look at
Chantel. "The O'Hurley Triplets."

Chantel looked at the reflection the mirror tossed
back. "And nobody's ever going to forget it."

Chapter One

The house was big and cool and white. In the early-morning hours, a breeze came through the terrace doors Chantel had left unlatched, bringing in the scents of the garden. Across the lawn, hidden from the main house by trees, was a gazebo, painted white, with wisteria climbing up the trellises. Sometimes, when the wind was right, Chantel could catch the perfume from her bedroom window.

On the east side of the lawn was an elaborate marble fountain. It was quiet now. She rarely had it turned on when she was alone. Near it was the pool, an octagonal stone affair skirted by a wide patio and flanked by another, smaller, white house. There was a tennis court beyond a grove of trees, but it had been weeks since she'd had the time or the inclination to pick up a racket.

Surrounding the estate was a stone fence, twice as tall as a man, that alternately gave her a sense of security or the feeling of being hemmed in. Still, inside the house, with its lofty ceilings and cool white walls, she often forgot about the fence and the security system and the electronic gate; it was the price she paid for the fame she had always wanted.

The servants' quarters were in the west wing, on the first floor. No one stirred there now. It was barely dawn, and she was alone. There were times Chantel preferred it that way.

As she bundled her hair under a hat, she didn't bother to check the results in the three-foot mirror in her dressing room. The long shirt and flat-heeled shoes she wore were chosen for comfort, not for elegance. The face that had broken men's hearts and stirred women's envy was left untouched by cosmetics. Chantel protected it by pulling down the brim of her hat and slipping on enormous sunglasses. As she picked up the bag that held everything she thought she would need for the day, the intercom beside the door buzzed.

She checked her watch. Five forty-five. Then she pushed the button. "Right on time."

"Good morning, Miss O'Hurley."

"Good morning, Robert. I'll be right down." After flipping the switch that released the front gate, Chantel started down the wide double staircase that led to the main floor. The mahogany rail felt like satin under her fingers as she trailed them down. Overhead, a chandelier hung, its prisms quiet in the dim light. The marble floor shone like glass. The house was a suitable showcase for the star she had worked to become. Chantel had yet to take any of it for granted. It was a dream that had rolled from, then into, other dreams, and it took time and effort and skill to maintain. But then she'd been working all her life and felt entitled to the benefits she had begun to reap.

As she walked to the front door, the phone began to ring.

Damn it, had they changed the call on her? Because she was up and the servants weren't, Chantel crossed the hall to the library and lifted the receiver. "Hello." Automatically she picked up a pen and prepared to make a note.

"I wish I could see you right now." The familiar whisper had her palms going damp, and the pen slipped out of her hand and fell soundlessly on the fresh blotter. "Why did you change your number? You're not afraid of me, are you? You mustn't be afraid of me, Chantel. I won't hurt you. I just want to touch you. Just touch you. Are you getting dressed? Are you—"

With a cry of despair, Chantel slammed down the receiver. The sound of her breathing in the big, empty house seemed to echo back to her. It was starting again.

Minutes later, her driver noticed only that she didn't give him the easy, flirtatious smile she usually greeted him with before she climbed into the back of the limo. Once inside, Chantel tipped her head back, closed her eyes and willed herself to calm. She had to face the camera in a few hours and give it her best. That was her job. That was her life. Nothing could be allowed to interfere with that, not even the fear of a whisper over the phone or an anonymous letter.

By the time the limo passed through the studio gates, Chantel had herself under control again. She should be safe here, shouldn't she? Here she could pour herself into the work that still fascinated her. Inside the dozens of big domed buildings, magic happened, and she was part of it. Even the ugliness was just pretend. Murder, mayhem and passion could all be simulated. Fantasyland, her sister Maddy called it, and that was true enough. But, Chantel thought with a smile, you had to work your tail off to make the fantasy real.

She was sitting in makeup at six-thirty and having her hair fussed over and styled by seven. They were in the first week of shooting, and everything seemed fresh and new. Chantel read over her lines while the stylist arranged her hair into the flowing silver-blond mane her character would wear that day.

"Such incredible bulk," the stylist murmured as she aimed the hand-held dryer. "I know women who would sell their blue-chip stocks for hair as thick as this. And the color!" She bent down to eye level to look in the mirror at the results of her work. "Even I have a hard time believing it's natural."

"My grandmother on my father's side." Chantel turned her head a bit to check her left profile. "I'm supposed to be twenty in this scene, Margo. Am I going to pull it off?"

With a laugh, the stringy redhead stood back. "That's the least of your worries. It's a shame they're going to dump rain all over this." She gave Chantel's hair a final fluff.

"You're telling me." Chantel stood when the bib was removed. "Thanks, Margo." Before she'd taken two steps, her assistant was at her elbow. Chantel had hired him because he was young and eager and had no ambitions to be an actor. "Are you going to crack the whip, Larry?"

Larry Washington flushed and stuttered, as he always did during his first five minutes around Chantel. He was short and well built, fresh out of college, and had a mind that soaked up details. His biggest ambition at the moment was to own a Mercedes. "Oh, you know I'd never do that, Miss O'Hurley."

Chantel patted his shoulder, making his blood pressure soar. "Somebody has to. Larry, I'd appreciate it if you'd scout up the assistant director and tell him I'm in my dressing room. I'm going to hide out there until they're ready to rehearse." Her co-star came into view carrying a cigarette and what Chantel accurately gauged to be a filthy hangover.

"Would you like me to bring you some coffee, Miss O'Hurley?" As he asked, Larry shifted to distance himself. Everyone with brains had quickly figured out that it was best to avoid Sean Carter when he was dealing with the morning after.

"Yes, thanks." Chantel nodded to a few members of the crew as they tightened up the works on the first set, a train station, complete with tracks, passenger cars and a depot. She'd say her desperate goodbyes to her lover there. She could only hope he'd gotten his headache under control by then.

Larry kept pace with her as she crossed the set, walking under lights and around cables. "I wanted to remind you about your interview this afternoon. The reporter from *Star Gaze* is due here at twelve-thirty.

Dean from publicity said he'd sit in with you if you wanted."

"No, that's all right. I can handle a reporter. See if you can get some fresh fruit, sandwiches, coffee. No, make that iced tea. I'll do the interview in my dressing room."

"All right, Miss O'Hurley." Earnestly he began to note it down in his book. "Is there anything else?"

She paused at the door of her dressing room. "How long have you been working for me now, Larry?"

"Ah, just over three months, Miss O'Hurley."

"I think you could start to call me Chantel." She smiled, then closed the door on his astonished pleasure.

The dressing room had been recently redecorated for her taste and comfort. With the script still in her hand, Chantel walked through the sitting room and into the small dressing area beyond. Knowing her time was limited, she didn't waste it. After stripping out of her own clothes, she changed into the jeans and sweater she would wear for the first scene.

She was to be twenty, a struggling art student on the down slide of her first affair. Chantel glanced at the script again. It was good, solid. The part she'd gotten would give her an opportunity to express a range of feeling that would stretch her creative talents. It was a challenge, and all she had to do was take advantage of it. And she would. Chantel promised herself she would.

When she had read *Strangers* she'd cast herself in the part of Hailey, the young artist betrayed by one man, haunted by another; a woman who ultimately finds success and loses love. Chantel understood

Hailey. She understood betrayal. And, she thought as she glanced around the elegant little room again, she understood success and the price that had to be paid for it.

Though she knew her lines cold, she kept the script with her as she went back to the sitting room. With luck she would have time for one quick cup of coffee before they ran through the scene. When she was working on a film, Chantel found it easy to live off coffee, a quick, light lunch and more coffee. The part fed her. There was rarely time for shopping, a dip in the pool or a massage at the club until a film was wrapped. Those were rewards for a job well done.

She started to sit, but a vase of vivid red roses caught her eye. From one of the studio heads, she thought as she walked over to pick up the card. When she opened it, the script slid out of her hand and onto the floor. "I'm watching you always. Always."

At the knock on her door, she jerked back, stumbling against the counter. The scent of the roses at her back spread, heady and sweet. With a hand to her throat, she stared at the door with the first real fear she'd ever experienced.

"Miss O'Hurley... Chantel, it's Larry. I have your coffee."

With a breathless sob, she ran across the room and jerked open the door. "Larry—"

"It's black the way you— What's wrong?"

"I—I just—" She cut herself off. Control, she thought desperately. You lose everything if you lose control. "Larry, do you know anything about these flowers?" She gestured back, but couldn't look at them.

"The roses. Oh, one of the caterers found them while she was setting up breakfast. Since they had your name on them, I went ahead and put them in here. I know how much you like roses."

"Get rid of them."

"But—"

"Please." She stepped out of the dressing room. People. She wanted lots of people around her. "Just get rid of them, Larry."

"Sure." He stared at her back as she walked toward the set. "Right away."

Four aspirin and three cups of coffee had brought Sean Carter back to life. It was time to work, and nothing could be allowed to interfere with that—not a hangover, not a few frightening words printed on a card. Chantel had worked hard to project an image of glamour and style. She'd worked just as hard not to develop a reputation as a temperamental actress. She was ready when called and always knew her lines. If a scene took ten hours to shoot, then it took ten hours. She reminded herself of all of this as she approached Sean and their director.

"How come you always look as though you stepped out of the pages of a fashion magazine?" Sean grumbled, but Chantel observed that makeup had dealt with the shadows under his eyes. His skin was tanned and shaved smooth. His thick, mahogany-colored hair was styled casually, falling across his brow. He looked young, healthy and handsome, the dream lover for an idealistic girl.

Chantel lifted a hand and let it rest on his cheek. "Because, darling, I did."

"What a woman." Because the aspirin had made him feel human again, Sean grabbed Chantel and leaned her back in a dramatic dip. "Let me ask you this, Rothschild," he said, calling to the director while his lips hovered inches from Chantel's. "How could a man in his right mind leave a woman like this?"

"It hasn't been established that you—or Brad," Mary Rothschild corrected, referring to the role, "is in his right mind."

"And you're such a cad," Chantel reminded Sean.

Pleased to remember it, Sean brought her up again. "I haven't played a real cad in about five years. I don't think I've properly thanked the writer yet."

"You can do it later today," Rothschild told him. "He's over there."

Chantel glanced over to the tall, rangy man who stood, chain-smoking nervously, on the edge of the set. She'd met him a handful of times in meetings and during preproduction. As she recalled, he had said little that hadn't dealt directly with his book or his characters. She sent him a vaguely friendly smile before turning back to the director.

As Rothschild outlined the scene, she pushed everything else out of her mind. All that would be left was the heartbreak and hope her character felt as her lover slipped away. Mechanically, their minds on angles and continuity, she and Sean went over their brief but poignant love scene.

"I think I should touch your face like this." Chantel reached up to rest her palm on his cheek and looked pleadingly into his eyes.

"Then I'll take your wrist." Sean wrapped his fingers around it, then turned her palm to his lips.

"I'll wait for you and so forth." Chantel skipped over the lines as one of the crew dropped a barn door into place with a clatter. She gave a small, broken sigh and pressed her cheek to his. "Then I'll start to bring my arms up."

"Let's try this." Sean took her shoulders, held her for a moment while they stared at each other, then placed two nibbling kisses on either side of her mouth.

"Oh, Brad, please don't go... Then I kiss you until your teeth rattle."

Sean grinned. "I'm looking forward to it."

"Let's run through it." Rothschild held up a hand. Women directors were still the exception to the rule. She couldn't afford to give herself, or anyone else, an inch. "I want a lot of steam when you get to the kiss," she told both of them. "Keep the tears coming, Chantel. Remember, deep in your heart you know he's not coming back."

"I really am a cad," Sean said pleasantly.

"Places." Extras scrambled to their marks. A few members of the camera crew broke off making plans for a poker game. "Quiet on the set." Rothschild moved over, too, until she had the best angle for Chantel's entrance. "Action."

Chantel dashed out on the platform, looking around frantically while groups of people milled around her. It all showed on her face, the desperation, the last flames of hope, the dream that wasn't ready to die. There would be a thunderstorm brewing, thanks to special effects. Lightning flashing, thunder rolling. Then she spotted Brad. She called out his name, pushing her way through the crowd until she was with him.

They rehearsed the scene three times before Rothschild was satisfied enough to roll film. Chantel's makeup and hair were freshened. When the clapper came down, she was ready.

Throughout the morning they perfected the first part of the scene, her search, the impatience and rush of the crowd, her meeting with Brad. Take after take she repeated the same moves, the same words, at times with the camera no more than a foot away.

On the sixth take, Rothschild finally gave the signal for the rain. The sprinklers sent down a drizzle that misted over her as she stood facing Brad. Her eyes filled and her voice trembled as she begged him not to leave. Wet and cold, they continued to go over what would be five minutes on the screen until lunch break.

In her dressing room, Chantel stripped out of Hailey's clothes and handed them to the wardrobe mistress so that they could be dried. Her hair would be styled again, then soaked again, before she could call it a day.

The roses were gone, but she thought she could still smell them. When Larry came to the door to tell her that the reporter had arrived, she asked him to give her five minutes, then send him along.

She'd put it off too long, she told herself as she picked up the phone. It wasn't going to stop, and she'd reached the point where she could no longer ignore it.

"The Burns Agency."

"I need to speak to Matt."

"I'm sorry, Mr. Burns is in a meeting. May I—"

"This is Chantel O'Hurley. I have to speak to Matt now."

"Of course, Miss O'Hurley."

Chantel couldn't resist a slight smirk at how quickly
the receptionist had changed her tune. Searching a
drawer for the pack of cigarettes she kept for emerg-
encies, she waited for Matt to come on the line.

"Chantel, what's up?"

"I need to see you. Tonight."

"Well, sweetheart, I'm kind of tied up. Why don't
we make it tomorrow?"

"Tonight." Some of the panic fought its way
through. Chantel lighted the cigarette and drew deeply.
"It's important. I need help." She let the smoke out in
a slow stream. "I really need your help, Matt."

Because he'd never heard fear in her voice before,
he didn't question her. "I'll come by, what...eight?"

"Yes, yes, that's fine. I appreciate it."

"Can you tell me what it's about?"

"I can't. Not over the phone, not now." She was
calming again, just knowing she was about to take a
step seemed to help.

"Whatever you say. I'll be there tonight."

"Thanks." She hung up the phone just as the knock
came at her door. Chantel carefully stubbed out her
cigarette, tossed her still-damp hair back and ushered
the reporter in with a gracious smile.

"Why in the hell didn't you tell me about this before?" Matt Burns paced around Chantel's spacious
living room with an unfamiliar feeling of helplessness. In twelve years he'd scrambled his way up from
mail clerk to assistant to top theatrical agent. He
hadn't gotten there by not knowing what to do in any
given situation. Now he had a hornet's nest on his

hands, and he wasn't sure which way to toss it. "Damn it, Chantel, how long has this been going on?"

"The first phone call came about six weeks ago." Chantel sat on a low oyster-colored sofa and nursed a glass of mineral water. Like Matt, she didn't like the feeling of helplessness. She disliked having to ask someone else to do something about a problem of hers even more. "Look, Matt, the first couple of calls, the first couple of letters, seemed harmless." Ice clinked in her glass as she set it down, then picked it up again. "With my face plastered all over magazines and all over the screen, obviously I'll attract attention. Not all of it's healthy. I figured if I ignored it it would stop."

"But it didn't."

"No." She looked down at her glass, remembering the words printed on the card. *I'm watching you always. Always.* "No, it got worse." She shrugged, trying to pretend to herself, and to him, that it wasn't as bad as it sounded. "I had my number changed, and for a while it worked."

"You should have told me."

"You're my agent, not my mother."

"I'm your friend," he reminded her.

"I know." She held out a hand. Real friendships were few and far between in the world she'd chosen. "That's why I called you before I went off the deep end. I'm not a hysterical woman."

He laughed, then released her hand to pour himself another drink. "Anything but."

"When those roses— Well, I knew I had to do something, but I didn't know what."

"The *what* is to call the police."

"Absolutely not." She lifted a finger when he started to object. "Matt, I imagine you can write the scenario as easily as I can. We call the police, then the press gets hold of it. Headline: Chantel O'Hurley Haunted by Twisted Admirer. Whispered Phone Calls. Desperate Love Letters." She pulled a hand through her hair. "We might be able to laugh that off, even use it to a point, but it wouldn't be long before a few more unbalanced personalities decided to write me some fan letters. Or camp out at the front gate. I don't think I can handle more than one at a time."

"What if he's violent?"

"Don't you think I've thought of that?" She plucked one of his French cigarettes from his pocket and waited for him to light it.

"You need protection."

"Maybe I do." She took a quick, hurried drag. "Maybe I'm just about ready to admit that, but I'm in the middle of a film. You bring cops on the set and people wouldn't stop talking."

"Since when has gossip worried you?"

"Never." She managed an easy smile. "Except when it's about something really personal. My, ah . . . extraordinary love affairs and hedonistic lifestyle are one thing. My life, as it really is, is quite another. No police, Matt, at least not yet. I need another alternative."

He took the cigarette from her and inhaled thoughtfully. Chantel's first job on the screen had been negotiated by him. He'd seen her through everything from shampoo commercials to feature films, and it was rare, very rare, for her to ask for help with something personal. In all the years he had known her, even Matt had seldom gotten beneath the image of the woman they had both manufactured.

"I think I have one. Trust me?"

"Haven't I always?"

"Sit tight. I'm going to make a call."

Chantel settled back and closed her eyes when Matt left the room. Maybe she was overreacting. Maybe she was being foolishly jumpy about a fan who'd taken admiration just a few steps too far.

I'm watching you . . . watching you. . . .

No. Unable to sit, Chantel sprang up to pace around the room. She enjoyed being watched—on the screen. She could accept being photographed whenever she swept in or out of a club, whenever she attended a party or a premiere. But this was . . . frightening, she admitted. As if someone were just outside the windows, looking in. The thought made her glance nervously over her shoulder. Of course there was no one there. She had the electronic gate, the walls, the security. But she couldn't stay locked in her house twenty-four hours a day.

She stopped by the antique mirror above the white marble fireplace. There was the face she was familiar with, the face critics had called devastating, incomparable, even heartlessly beautiful. A lucky accident, she sometimes thought, the combination of pearly skin, Nordic blue eyes and ice-sharp cheekbones. She'd done nothing to earn the face, the classic oval shape of it, the full, lush mouth or the thick mane of angel-blond hair. She'd been born with that, but she'd worked for the rest. And worked hard.

She'd been performing since she could walk, traveling endlessly around the country with her family in clubs and regional theater. She'd paid her dues long before she had come to Hollywood at nineteen, not starry-eyed but determined. In the years that had passed, she had won roles and lost them, had hawked shampoo and sold gallons of perfume in unapologetically sexy, often silly commercials. When her first break had come she'd been ready, more than ready, to play the soulless man-eater who stayed on screen less than twenty minutes. She'd stolen that movie from a pair of veterans and had gone on to star in one of her own. There'd been no looking back.

That first break had brought her the stardom she had always craved. And had, indirectly, nearly destroyed her life.

Yet, she'd survived, Chantel reminded herself as she faced her own reflection. She hadn't allowed what had happened all those years ago to ruin her. She refused to allow what was happening now to ruin her, either.

"He's coming right over."

She turned away from the mirror as Matt strode into the room again. "What?"

"I said he's coming right over. Let me fix you a real drink."

"No, I have to be on the set at six-thirty. Who's coming right over?"

"Quinn Doran. He might just be the answer, and since we go back a ways, I was able to...persuade him to think about it."

Chantel stuck her hands in the pockets of her white satin loungers. "Who is Quinn Doran?"

"He's sort of a private investigator."

"Sort of?"

"He runs a security business . . . corporate, small business, whatever. At one time he worked in some sort of covert operation. Might have been for our government, but I couldn't swear to it."

"Sounds fascinating, but I don't think I want a spy, Matt. A three-hundred-pound wrestler might be more appealing."

"And obvious," he reminded her. "You could hire yourelf a couple of bruisers for bodyguards, sweetheart, but what you want here is brains—and discretion. That's Quinn." He finished off his drink and contemplated having another. "He doesn't do much of the legwork himself now. He has plenty of operatives or whatever they're called to handle that. Keeps himself available as a troubleshooter. But in this case I want you to have the best."

"And that's Quinn," Chantel mimicked, dropping onto the arm of the sofa. "What's he supposed to do?"

"I don't have any idea. That's why I called him. He's a moody bastard," he said reminiscently. "Not too, well . . . polished, but I'd trust him with my life."

"Or, in this case, mine."

Matt's expression changed immediately. "Chantel, if you're really that worried—"

"No, no." With a wave of her hand, she brushed off his concern. "I have the feeling that this Quinn Doran of yours is likely to listen to what I have to say, roll his eyes and give me a lecture on how to handle the obscene phone caller. I don't like him already."

"You're just nervous." Matt patted her knee as he crossed to the bar. "You're allowed to be nervous, Chantel."

"No, I'm not." She smiled, determined to lighten her own mood. "Nerves don't fit the image. It's an image you helped me mold."

"You didn't need any help with that." With a smile for her, he turned back and studied the flow of white satin that suited her so well. "You were born with the talent. I just helped you expand it."

She tilted her head and gave him a long, luxurious smile. "How'd we do?"

"I'll say this, no one looking at you today would think that you'd once mended your panty hose."

She laughed and slid down on the sofa. "You're so good for me, Matt."

"I've been telling you that for years. There's the bell. I'll get it."

Chantel picked up her warming mineral water and swirled it. If Matt thought Quinn Doran was an answer, she'd have to take his word for it. But it galled her, it galled her right down to the ground, to tell her personal problems to a stranger.

Then the stranger walked in.

If she had had to cast someone in the roll of a spy, a private investigator or an alley fighter, her choice would have been Quinn Doran. He filled the archway to her living room, inches taller than Matt, inches broader in the shoulders, yet with a wiry leanness that made her think he could move fast and move well. The quick flutter of feminine approval she accepted as natural even before she looked at his face. Then she thought it unnatural.

He wasn't leading-man handsome, but he had tough go-to-hell looks that would make any woman's pulse uneven. Dark, thick hair curled over his ears and trailed over the collar of a denim work shirt. His skin was tanned and taut over strong facial bones, and the pale shade of his eyes seemed almost startlingly cool. His lashes were too long, too thick for a man, but they were anything but feminine. There was nothing about him that wasn't totally masculine. When he walked, he walked with the soft, measured stride of a man who knew how to stalk. His mouth turned up slightly as he crossed to her, but Chantel didn't see humor or appreciation in his eyes. She saw, recognized and stiffened against derision.

"So this is the ice palace," he said in a surprisingly beautiful voice. "And the queen."

Chapter Two

He'd seen her before, of course. On the screen she looked larger than life, indomitable, untouchable. The face, almost mystically perfect, could rule a man's fantasies. A facade. Quinn understood facades, how they could be formed, altered or hacked away as circumstances demanded. He wondered, as with a casual glance he took in everything about her, how much substance there was beneath that silk-and-satin exterior.

Matt had known Quinn too long to be disturbed by his cavalier attitude. "Chantel, Quinn Doran."

Satin slid over satin as she crossed her legs. With a lazy kind of grace, she offered her hand. "Charming," she murmured, stiffening as his fingers curled firmly over hers. He didn't shake her hand, nor did he bring it to his lips in the casual European gesture she

suddenly felt he was capable of. He just held it while
his pale green eyes held hers. Her skin was like the
satin she wore, smooth, fragrant and coolly feminine. His was hard, unyielding and darkened by the
sun. They froze for a moment, her on the sofa, him on
his feet, with their hands still locked. Chantel had been
in combat with men before, and only once had she
lost. She understood that the glove had been tossed
down, and she accepted the challenge.

"Is it still vodka rocks?" Matt asked Quinn as he
turned to the bar.

"Yeah." With a slight inclination of his head,
Quinn indicated that he knew the game was on. He
relaxed his fingers slowly to let her hand slide from his.
"Matt tells me you have a problem."

"Apparently I do." Chantel plucked a cigarette
from a porcelain holder on the table, then lifted a
brow. When Quinn drew a lighter out of his pocket
and flicked it on, she smiled and leaned a bit closer.
"I'm afraid I don't know if you're the man to deal
with it—" her gaze lifted and held his before she
leaned back again "—Mr. Doran."

"I'm inclined to agree with you…Miss O'Hurley."
For the second time their gazes locked, and some-
thing not entirely pleasant hummed between them.
"But since I'm here, why don't you tell me about it?"
Quinn accepted the glass from Matt, then shot him a
look before he could speak. "Why don't we let Miss
O'Hurley fill me in, since it's her problem?"

As an agent, Matt knew when to negotiate and when
to back off. "Fine, I'll just fill my mouth with a few
of these canapés." He sat, leaving them to each other.

"I've been getting some annoying phone calls." She said it casually, but the tension showed briefly in the way her fingers curled and uncurled. Quinn was used to picking up on small details. At the moment he noticed that her hands were quite small and narrow, with long fingers, the rounded tips painted with clear lacquer. The fingers themselves were never quite still.

"Phone calls?"

"And letters." She moved her shoulders and the satin whispered quietly. "It started about six weeks ago."

"Obscene phone calls?"

Chantel lifted her chin, unable to resist the urge to look down her small, straight nose. "I suppose that would depend on your definition of obscene. Yours might be quite different than mine."

Humor touched his eyes and made them strangely appealing. She wondered fleetingly how many woman had stepped into his lion's den and been devoured. "I'm sure it is. Go on."

"At first—at first you could say I was almost amused. It seemed harmless enough, though annoying. Then..." She moistened her lips and brought the cigarette to them. "Then he became a bit bolder, more explicit. It made me uneasy."

"You should change your number."

"I've done that. The phone calls stopped for about a week. They started again today."

As he leaned back, Quinn sampled the vodka. Like her, it was a quality brand. "You recognize the voice?"

"No, he whispers."

"You could change your number again." The ice clinked in his glass as he shrugged. "Or have the police put a tap on it."

"I'm tired of changing my number." With quick impatience, she stubbed out the cigarette. "And I don't want the police. I prefer to keep this discreet. Matt seems to think you're the answer to that."

Quinn drank again. The room was done in different shades of white, but it wasn't virginal. The very absence of color, with her at the center, was outrageously alluring. He was sure she knew it. In every one of her films she had acted the role of a woman who deliberately played on a man's needs, his weaknesses, his most private dreams. Quinn could drum up little sympathy for a woman who deliberately projected an image designed to arouse men, then complained about a few harmless phone calls.

"Miss O'Hurley, you're probably aware that men who make these kind of calls don't do anything but talk. I'd suggest you change your number again, then have one of your servants answer the phone for a while, until he gets tired of it."

"Quinn." Matt swirled his own drink. He had a habit of keeping in motion when under pressure, his hands, his feet. Now, he cleared his throat and tried to settle. "That's not much help."

"She can hire a bodyguard if it makes her feel better. Her security here could certainly be tightened."

"Maybe I need barbed wire, vicious guard dogs," Chantel interjected, and rose.

"That's the price you pay," Quinn told her coolly, "for being what you are."

"What I am?" Her eyes, already a vivid, searing blue, sharpened. "Oh, I see. I parade myself on the screen, I don't dress in burlap and wear a veil over my face, therefore I asked for what I got. And I deserve it."

Her cool beauty was compelling, but her passionate outburst was like seeing fire in ice. Quinn ignored the tightening in his gut and shrugged. "That's close enough."

"Thank you for your time," she said, and turned away. Before she could stop herself, she was whirling back. "Why don't you take a walk into the twentieth century? Just because a woman is attractive and doesn't disguise the fact doesn't mean she deserves to be abused—verbally, physically or emotionally."

"I don't believe I said an attractive woman, or any woman, deserves abuse," Quinn commented.

His careless tone only stoked the fires. "Just because I'm an actress and sexuality is part of my craft doesn't mean I'm fair game for any man who wants a piece of me. If I play the part of a murderer, it doesn't mean I should go on trial."

"You appeal to a man's most primitive fantasies, Miss O'Hurley, and you do it in Technicolor. There's bound to be a little backwash."

"So I should just take my medicine," she murmured. "You're an idiot. You're the kind of man who wears his brain below his belt. The kind who thinks if a woman agrees to have dinner with him she should pay for it with a romp between the sheets. Well, I can pay for my own dinner, Mr. Doran, and I can handle my own problems. I'm sure you can find the door."

"Chantel," Matt began, but she turned on him like a cat. "I'll just have a few more canapés," he muttered.

"Miss O'Hurley."

"What?" Chantel spun around to face her tall, aging majordomo, then drew in a long, cleansing breath. "Yes, Marsh, what is it?"

It was the tone that had Quinn narrowing his eyes. There was an underlying straightforward quality to it that ignored any domestic caste system and spoke human to human. Though nerves had her body strung tight, she smiled at the old man.

"These were just delivered for you."

"Thank you." Chantel crossed the room to him and took the vase of daylilies. "I won't need you any more tonight, Marsh."

"Very good, Miss."

Stepping behind Quinn, she went to a table by the windows. "Why don't you show your friend out, Matt? I don't think—"

She had the card in her hands and was staring at it. Her fingers trembled momentarily before she crushed the paper. Before she could drop it on the floor, Quinn had her wrist and was slowly drawing the mangled note from her. What he read made his stomach tighten, this time in disgust.

"No more than I deserve?" Chantel's voice was cold, almost detached, but her eyes, when Quinn looked into them, were terrified. He slipped the paper into his pocket as he took her arm.

"Why don't you sit down?"

"Was it another one?" Matt started toward them, but Quinn motioned to the bar.

"Get her a brandy."

"I don't want a drink. I don't want to sit down. I want you to go." When she started to pull her arm away, Quinn merely tightened his hold and led her to the sofa. "How often do you get one of these?"

"Nearly every day." She picked up a cigarette, then put it back.

"All of them as . . . direct?"

"No." She took the brandy and sipped at it, hating to admit she needed it. "That started a couple of weeks ago."

"What did you do with the notes?"

"I tossed out the first few. Then, when the tone started to change, I was going to burn them." The brandy warmed her but did nothing to settle her. "I kept them. I'm not sure why. I suppose I thought I should have them if things got out of hand."

"Call your servant back in. I want to ask him some questions. And go get the other letters."

His orders did what the brandy hadn't. Chantel felt her spine straighten. "It's none of your concern, Mr. Doran. We've already settled that."

"This just unsettled it." He drew the paper out of his pocket and watched her slight but definite recoil.

"I don't want your help."

"I didn't say I'd give it yet." He let that hang as they continued to stare at each other. "The letters? Unless you've got a better idea what to do about all this."

At that moment, at that one shimmering moment, she despised him. She could have hidden it. She was skilled enough. She didn't bother. Before she could speak, Matt laid a hand on her shoulder. His fingers moved as restlessly as hers.

"Please, Chantel. Think before you say anything."

She kept her eyes on Quinn's. "I wouldn't want to say what I'm thinking." When his lips curved again, she gritted her teeth. "Or perhaps I would."

"Chantel." Matt gave her shoulder a light squeeze. "I don't like ultimatums, but if we can't deal with Quinn, I'm going to call the police. No," he continued when her head shot back, "I mean it. You're a smart woman. Be practical."

She hated being backed into a corner. Quinn could see it. She was a woman who insisted on having the choice and the control in her own hands. It was something he could admire, even respect. Maybe, just maybe, there was more to Chantel O'Hurley than met the eye.

"All right, we'll do it your way. For now." She rose, at once regal and strong. "Don't badger Marsh." She met Quinn's eyes levelly. "He's old and getting frail. I don't want him upset."

"I haven't kicked a dog all day," Quinn told her.

"Only small children and kittens," she murmured, then swept from the room.

"Quite a woman, your client."

"She's all of that," Matt agreed. "And she's scared right down to her toes. She doesn't scare easily."

"I bet she doesn't." Quinn took out a cigarette and tapped it idly against the pack. He was forced to admit that he had thought she was simply dramatizing. The few sentences printed on the card had changed his mind. They were just short of vile. For Quinn, the line of demarcation between right and wrong was flexible, but the card fell well on the wrong side. Still, before he decided just how much he wanted to be involved, there were a few things he had to know.

He glanced back at Matt, watching him pace. "Just how close are the two of you?"

"We have a solid, mutually advantageous arrangement." Matt gave Quinn a sober smile. "And she doesn't sleep with me."

"You're slipping."

"She knows what she wants, and what she doesn't want. She wanted an agent. But I do care about her." He cast a worried look at the doorway. "She's already gone through enough."

"Enough of what?"

With a shake of his head, Matt sat again. "Another story, and nothing to do with this. Are you going to be able to help her?"

Quinn drew slowly on his cigarette. "I don't know."

"Excuse me." Marsh stood in the doorway, still dressed in his black suit and starched collar. "Miss O'Hurley said you wanted to speak with me."

"I wondered if you could tell me about the person who delivered the flowers." Quinn gestured toward them and watched the old man squint. Nearsighted, he thought.

"They were delivered by a young man, eighteen, perhaps twenty. He rang from the gate and explained that he had a delivery for Miss O'Hurley."

"Was he wearing a uniform?"

Marsh's brows knit as he concentrated. "I don't believe so. I can't say for certain."

"Did you happen to see his car?"

"No, sir. I took the flowers at the back door."

"Would you recognize him if you saw him again?"

"Perhaps. I think I might."

"Thank you, Marsh."

Marsh hesitated. Then, remembering his position, he bowed stiffly. "Very good, sir."

As he walked back into the hallway, Quinn heard Chantel stop him for a brief, murmured conversation. Her voice, he noticed, was soothing from a distance, quiet and easy. Up close, its smoky quality could twine around a man's nerve endings and make him want. She came back in, carrying a small pack of letters.

"I'm sure you'll find it fascinating reading," she said as she tossed them into Quinn's lap. "My guess is it's close to the technique you use to court women."

She'd regained her spirit, Quinn decided as he ignored her and opened the first envelope. The address on it, like the text inside, was printed in small block letters. The paper was dime-store quality. He could work for weeks and never trace it.

The first few notes he read were fawning in their admiration and subtly suggestive. And well written, Quinn added silently. The work of an educated person. As he went on, the prose and syntax remained good but the content deteriorated. Even a man who had seen and done what he had felt instant distaste. The writer went into graphic and pitiless detail, outlining his fantasies, his needs and his intentions. The last few letters added veiled hints that the writer was close by. Watching. Waiting.

When he'd finished, Quinn stacked the letters in a neat pile. "You sure you don't want the cops in on this?"

Chantel had seated herself across from him, and now she folded her hands in her lap. She didn't like him, she told herself. She didn't like the way he looked, the way he moved. She didn't like the fact that his voice was almost poetic, so very different from his lived-in face. So why, if all this was true, did she feel as though she wanted, even needed, his help. She kept her eyes on his. Sometimes you made bargains with the devil.

"No, I don't want the police. I don't want publicity on this. What I want is for this man to be found and stopped."

Quinn rose and poured himself another drink. Both the glasses and ice bucket were Rosenthal. He appreciated elegant things, just as he appreciated the cruder things in life. Beer from a bottle or wine from a crystal glass, it hardly mattered, as long as your thirst was quenched. He appreciated beauty, but he wasn't duped by it. An outer shell meant nothing. He'd shed plenty of his own when the occasion had called for it.

Chantel O'Hurley had beauty, had elegance. If he took the job, by the very nature of it he was bound to discover how much was shell, how much was substance. That was what had him hesitating. He understood just how dangerous knowledge of another person could be—to all involved.

He could control the attraction he felt for her looks, as long as he chose to. His mood on that could change from day to day. What he wouldn't control, had never been able to control, was his curiosity as to what lay beneath the skin.

Swallowing his vodka, he turned back around. She was sitting back in her chair, and one would have thought from looking at her that she was relaxed, even aloof. The fingers on her left hand moved, just a little, curling together, spreading apart, as if she had managed to center her nerves only there. He shrugged and matched his mood to hers.

"Five hundred a day, plus expenses."

She lifted a brow. It was the only movement she made. With it, she conveyed a range of feeling— amusement, consideration and dislike. What it didn't show was the surge of relief that passed through her.

"That's a princely sum, Mr. Doran."

"You'll get your money's worth."

"That's something I insist on." Leaning back, she steepled her fingers under her chin. Her wrists were slender, and her hands were as delicate as her face. A diamond flashed on her right hand, then became as white and cool as the rest of her. "Just what do I get for five hundred a day plus expenses?"

His lips curved just before he brought the glass to them. "You get me, Miss O'Hurley."

She smiled a little. Sparring helped. She was back in control again, and the fear was ebbing. "Interesting." The look she sent him was designed to pin a man to the wall and make him beg. Quinn felt the punch and acknowledged the power. "What do I do with you?"

"You've got it backward." He walked to her then, stopping by her chair to lean close. She caught a hint of scent, not cologne, not soap or powder, but raw and completely comfortable masculinity. Though she didn't retreat from it, she braced herself, recognizing her own attraction.

"Just what do I have backward, Mr. Doran?"

She looked like a painting, one he thought he'd seen in the Louvre a lifetime ago. "It's what I do with you. Five hundred a day, angel, and your trust. That's my price. You pay it and you get twenty-four-hour protection, starting with one of my men posted as a guard at that gate of yours."

"If I already have the gate, why do I need a guard?"

"Did it ever occur to you that a gate doesn't do a hell of a lot of good if you're going to open it up to anyone who asks?"

"What didn't occur to me was that I'd have to lock myself in."

"Get used to it, because whoever's sending you flowers doesn't have a clean bill of health."

Panic came and went in her eyes. He gave her points for how quickly she mastered it. "I'm aware of that."

"I need your schedule. Starting tomorrow, one of my men goes with you every time you stick your pretty nose out the door."

"No." The O'Hurley stubbornness came through as she rose to face him. "For five hundred a day I want you, Doran. You're the one Matt trusts, and you're the one I'm paying for."

They stood close, very close. He could smell the scent that seemed to seep through her pores, neither quiet nor subtle. The perfection of her face could take a man's breath away. Her hair swept back from it in a glorious cascade, like an angel's. If a man touched it, would he find heaven or be cast from the clouds?

546 SKIN DEEP

When it came to that, Quinn wouldn't worry about the consequences.

"You might regret it," he murmured, then smiled slowly.

So she might. Chantel already knew that, but pride wouldn't let her back down. "I pay for you, Mr. Doran. That's the deal."

"You're the boss." He lifted his drink to her. "Two of my men will come by in the morning to wire the phone."

"I don't want—"

"I don't take the job if you tie my hands." His easy smile was gone as quickly as it had formed. "We tap the phone, maybe he says something to give himself away, maybe we get lucky and trace it. Just think of us as doctors." He smiled at her again, enjoying himself. "If you want to say something intimate to one of your... friends, don't worry. We've heard it all and more."

Temper had always been the most difficult of her emotions to master. It surged up and was fought back down before she spoke again. "I'm quite sure you have. What else?"

"I'll take the letters with me. It's doubtful we'll be able to trace the paper, but we'll give it a shot. Now is there anyone you know who you think could be doing this?"

"No." The answer came immediately and with complete confidence. He decided to run a check on everyone close to her.

"Dump anyone in the last few months that may be carrying a torch for you?"

"Thousands."

"Cute." He drew a pad and the stub of a pencil out of his pocket. "I need the names of who you've slept with. We'll go back three months."

"Go to hell," she said sweetly, then started to sit. He caught her by the wrist.

"Look, I'm not going to play games with you. I'm not personally interested in how many men you've had in your bed. This is business."

"That's right." She tossed her head back. "My business."

Her skin was warmer than it looked. That was something he filed away to think about later. "One of them might just have gone off the deep end. Maybe you slept with him a couple times and it gave him delusions of grandeur. Think about it. This all started six weeks ago, so who were you with before that?"

"No one."

Annoyance covered his face as he tightened his hold. "Give me a break, angel. I haven't got all night."

"I said no one." She yanked her arm away. For a moment she wished she could rattle off a dozen names, two dozen names, just to see him sweat. "Believe whatever you like."

"I tell you what I don't believe, and that's that you spend your evenings alone, darning socks."

"I don't jump into bed with every man who passes within five feet of me." In a calculated move, she dropped her gaze down as if measuring the distance between them.

"It looks like about ten inches to me," he murmured.

"Sorry to disappoint you, but I have to be interested first, and I haven't been. Besides, I've been working, and it tends to take up a great deal of my time." Unconsciously she rubbed at her wrist, where his fingers had pressed. "Satisfied?"

"Come on, Quinn, ease off." Feeling trapped in the middle, Matt moved over and put an arm around Chantel's shoulders. "She's had it rough enough."

"It's not my job to hold her hand." Quinn scooped up the letters, annoyed by the twinge of self-disgust he felt. "I'll be back tomorrow. What time do you get up?"

"Five-fifteen." She couldn't resist a smirk when he only stared at her. "I leave for the studio at five forty-five. That's a.m., Mr. Doran. Can you handle it?"

"You just write the check. Fifteen hundred in advance."

"You'll have it. Good night, Mr. Doran. It's been unusual."

"Do yourself a favor and don't answer your phone any more tonight." With that, he nodded to Matt and strode out. Chantel waited for the sound of the door closing behind him. She went to the coffee table and drew out another cigarette.

"Your friend's a bastard, Matt."

"Always has been," he agreed. "But he's the best."

Chapter Three

Chantel had thought she wouldn't sleep. The house had seemed so enormous around her, and so enormously quiet. But she had climbed into bed with a vision of Quinn Doran hovering in her mind. Just the thought of him made her furious, insulted her intelligence, nipped at her ego. And made her feel safe.

She slept only six hours, but she slept deeply.

Music woke her, pouring from the wall unit beside the bed. She rolled over, surrounded by pillows, covered with ivory linen sheets and nothing else.

The bed had been one of the first luxuries she had indulged herself with, almost before she could afford it. It was huge and old, with a carved cherrywood headboard that had made her think of princesses waking up from a hundred years of sleep. Growing up, she had invariably slept in hotel beds, and she'd decided that a sinfully beautiful bed was something she deserved to indulge herself in when she signed her first film contract. A small part in a full-length feature had been enough to pin her hopes on. Years later, when she awoke in the antique four-poster it still gave her the same satisfaction.

She thought back to the time when she had still lived in the small apartment in L.A. The bed had taken up the entire room, and she had had to crawl over it to reach the doorway. Her two sisters had visited once, and the three of them had stretched across it and talked and giggled for hours.

She wished they could be with her now. The feeling of safety would be more tangible.

She'd nearly told Maddy about the letters and calls when she'd gone to New York a few weeks before. Part of her had wanted to, needed to, but Maddy had been so preoccupied. She'd been entitled, Chantel reminded herself as she sat up and stretched. Her play had been nearly ready to open, and her heart had been wrapped up in the man who was backing it. All for a good cause, Chantel thought with a smile. The play was a smash, and Maddy was planning her wedding.

He'd better be good to her, Chantel thought as the old protective instinct rose up in her. She had had to watch one sister go through a miserable marriage. She couldn't bear it if Maddy was hurt, as well.

Maddy would be fine, she reassured herself. Just as Abby was fine. They had both found the right man at the right time. So she had one sister planning a wedding and the other preparing for the birth of her third child. She couldn't spoil all that by dumping her problems on them now. Besides, she was the eldest triplet, if only by a matter of minutes. To Chantel, that meant that she had the responsibility to be the strongest. They would be there for her, of course, just as she would be there for them. But she was the oldest.

They'd come so far. Chantel sat in the middle of the lush bed and looked around a room that was larger than the whole of her first apartment in California. Why was it she felt as though she still had so far to go?

Now wasn't the time for philosophizing. After turning up the volume on the radio, she climbed out of bed and prepared to face another day on the set.

Quinn wasn't accustomed to rising before dawn. It was much more his style to see the night through and find his bed at sunrise rather than climbing out of it at that hour. Not that he didn't appreciate an L.A. sunrise. It was simply more to his taste to watch the sky take on color after a night of celebration—in bed or out.

He drove across town under a pink-and-mauve sky, casting an occasional look of mild contempt at a jogger. Designer sweat suits weren't his style. If he wanted to tone up, he went to the gym. And not one of those pastel-walled spas where they piped in classical music, a real gym. You didn't see cute leotards there, and the sweat ran as free and healthy as the four-letter words. A man's world—and no one drank carrot juice frappé. A woman like Chantel O'Hurley wouldn't poke her million-dollar nose through the front door.

Quinn shifted in his seat and scowled at nothing in particular. He couldn't remember the last time a woman had made him uncomfortable. Chantel's looks were designed to make a man squirm—and ache. The hell of it was she knew it and, Quinn was certain, enjoyed it.

He couldn't let that be a problem. She was paying him to do a job. The only thing he could be concerned about from this point on was her security. The check she would give him entitled her to the best, and he *was* the best. Besides, he didn't care for the content of the letters she'd shown him.

Not that Quinn was a supporter of the women's movement. To his way of thinking, men and women were different. End of story. If a woman walking by a construction site was insulted because she got a few whistles or invitations, he figured she should walk someplace else. After all, that was just good clean fun. There'd been nothing clean, or fun, in the letters, though. And Chantel hadn't looked insulted, either. If he knew anything, Quinn knew what genuine fear looked like.

Sooner or later he would find out who had written them. That would take patience. In the meantime, he'd give Chantel the round-the-clock protection she was paying for. Remembering her face, Quinn acknowledged that that would take willpower. He had it, he thought with a shrug as he pulled up to the iron gates. Besides, chances were that she'd look like a hag at this hour of the morning.

He reached out the window and leaned on the buzzer.

"Yes?"

The frown moved into his eyes. Even in one word, Chantel's voice was easily recognizable. He hadn't expected her to answer the intercom herself. "Doran," he said curtly.

"You're prompt."

"You get what you pay for."

There was no answer, but the gates slowly swung open. Quinn cruised through them, then stopped to make certain they shut behind him.

In the daylight, he got a better look at the lay of the land. Anyone determined enough could find his way over the wall. He and a partner had once scaled a sheer cliff in Afghanistan with nothing more than rope and nerve.

The trees that flowered over the lawn sent up a sweet scent. And would provide more-than-adequate cover for an intruder. He was going to have to get a good look at the alarm system in the house, though he knew anything that could be put in could be deactivated.

Quinn pulled up just beyond the steps, then got out to lean on the hood of his car. You couldn't hear any traffic from here. Just the sound of birds. He took out a cigarette. A glance around showed him a few floodlights, maybe a dozen ground lights, obviously placed more for aesthetic purposes than for added security. After a look at his watch, Quinn decided to walk around the house and check a few things out for himself.

Perhaps out of spite, Chantel decided to let Quinn cool his heels outside while she dallied in her dressing room. Under other circumstances she might have invited him in for a quick cup of coffee before the limo arrived. She wasn't feeling gracious. Instead, she took her time, bundling her hair back from her face, checking the contents of her bag, then writing a few instructions for her maid. When the buzzer from the gate rang again, she spoke to her driver, then gathered up her script. She turned toward the bedroom and walked into Quinn. He watched initial shock turn to anger.

"What the hell are you doing in here?"

"Just checked out your security system." He leaned against the doorway and noted, with a quick twinge, that regardless of the hour she looked fantastic. "It's pitiful. A Boy Scout with two merit badges could get past it."

Chantel settled the strap of her bag on her shoulder and promised herself she would pay Matt back if it was the last thing she ever did. "When it was installed I was assured it was the best on the market."

"Supermarket, maybe. I'll have my men beef it up."

She'd been born practical, and the years had done nothing to change that. "How much?"

"Don't know for sure until they're into it. Three to five, I'd say."

"Thousand?"

"Sure. Like I said, you—"

"Get what you pay for," she murmured, walking around him. "All right, Mr. Doran, you go right ahead." As she spoke, she moved to her nightstand. "But the next time you decide to check out the system, I wouldn't advise you sneaking into my bedroom." When she turned, she had a pearl-handled .22 in her hand. "I tend to be nervous."

Quinn regarded the gun with a raised brow. He'd been on the wrong end of one plenty of times before. "Know how to use one of those, angel?"

"You just pull this little trigger here." She smiled. "Of course, my aim's terrible. I'd point at your leg and end up shooting you right through the brain."

"There's only one rule about guns," he began, then scowled over her shoulder. When Chantel turned to look, he was on her. With a move too quick to judge, he had the gun in his hand and her beneath him on the bed. "The rule is, don't point one unless you intend to use it."

She didn't squirm beneath him, but lay still, letting the heat of fury and dislike pour out. With a casual gesture he flipped open the pistol's chamber.

"It's not loaded."

"Of course it's not. I wouldn't keep a loaded gun in the house."

"A gun's not a souvenir." He closed it again before he looked down at her. Her face was untouched by makeup, and it was as beautiful as it was furious. Despite himself, Quinn found the combination very much to his liking. Her body was small and strong beneath his, not as cushioned and feminine as he'd expected. But her scent was there, as it had been the night before, outrageously feminine.

"Nice bed," he murmured, unable to resist the urge to sweep his gaze down to her mouth. He thought, but couldn't be sure, that her heartbeat increased.

"Your approval means everything to me, Mr. Doran. Now, if you don't mind, I have to get to work."

How many other men had pinned her between their bodies and this wide, firm mattress? How many other men had felt this wild, edgy flare of desire? Both thoughts ran through his head before he could stop them. Because they did, he rolled aside and yanked her to her feet. But she was still close.

"Maybe we'll keep this business," he told her quietly. "And maybe we won't."

Though her pulse was racing, Chantel wasn't dishonest enough to blame it on temper. Desire was something she understood, even if she had rarely felt it for a man. It was also something that could be controlled. Instinct warned her that it was vital to do that now, and to continue to do so, when it applied to Quinn.

"You tempt me to put bullets in that gun, Mr. Doran."

"It wouldn't hurt." Quinn dropped it back in her bedside drawer. "And make it Quinn, angel. After all, we've been to bed together." Taking her arm, he escorted her downstairs and outside.

"Good morning, Robert." Chantel smiled at her driver as he opened the back door of the limo. "Mr. Doran will be accompanying me to the studio for a few days."

"Very good, Miss O'Hurley."

Quinn didn't miss the wistful look the driver sent him before they were closed in behind smoked glass. "How does it feel to infatuate the male of the species?"

Chantel settled back. "He's just a boy."

"Does that make a difference?"

Behind her dark glasses, Chantel shut her eyes. "Oh, I forgot. I'm one of those heartless women who tease and flaunt, then toss men aside after I've drained them, like empty pop bottles."

Amused, Quinn stretched out long legs. "That pretty much covers it."

"You have a remarkable disdain for women, Mr. Doran."

"No, you're wrong. Women happen to be one of my favorite pastimes."

"Past—" Chantel caught herself before she sputtered. She drew her glasses completely off, wishing she could see if he was baiting her or speaking the simple truth. Wanting to believe the worst of him, she went with the latter. "You're a classic chauvinist, Mr. Doran. I'd thought your species nearly extinct."

"We're a hardy breed, angel." He pushed a button and watched the compact bar rotate toward him. Quinn considered mixing a Bloody Mary but settled for straight orange juice.

Replacing her glasses, Chantel decided against beating her head against a brick wall. "I prefer not to introduce you as my bodyguard. I can do without that sort of speculation."

"Fine. How do you want to handle it?"

"They'll just assume you're my lover." Coolly she took the glass of juice from him and sipped. "I'm accustomed to that sort of speculation."

"I bet. It's your game. Play it any way you want."

She handed him back the glass. "I intend to. And what will you do?"

"My job." As they passed through the studio gates, he drained the glass. "You just smile pretty at the cameras, angel, and don't worry about it."

She found that her jaw was tensed so tightly it hurt. Acting on impulse, Chantel turned to him, and curled her fingers into his shirt. "Oh, Quinn, it's just that I'm so frightened. I'm so very frightened. Not knowing from one minute to the next if I'm safe." Her voice broke as she leaned closer. "I can't tell you what it means to me just to know you'll be there. Protecting me. I'm defenseless, vulnerable. And you're so...strong."

She was close, so close he could see her eyes flutter shut behind the tinted glasses. Her body trembled lightly as she leaned into him. Desire flared, along with a need to comfort and protect. She was soft, pliant and helpless. As he drew her nearer, her scent tangled around his senses until his head throbbed with it. "You don't have to worry," he murmured. "I'm going to take care of you."

"Quinn." Her head tilted up until her lips were only a whisper away from his. When she felt him tense, she jerked back and pressed something into his hand. "Your check," she said carelessly, then stepped out of the limo.

Quinn sat for a full ten seconds and wondered why he'd never entertained thoughts of strangling a woman before. When he stepped out beside her, he curled his fingers around her arm. "You're good. Very, very good."

"Yes, I am." She gave him a slow, easy smile. "And I get much better."

As Chantel went through her morning routine of makeup and hairstyling, Quinn simply observed. There were a dozen people Chantel came in contact with during the first hour alone. There were other actors, technicians and a parade of assistants. He'd want a list, and he was beginning to realize just how extensive it would be. Whoever was hounding her obviously knew her routine. That made the people she worked with his priority.

"Miss—ah, Chantel." Larry stopped by her side with a cup of fresh coffee.

"Oh, thanks. You read my mind."

He preened a bit, pleased. "I knew the hair was going to take longer this morning." He watched as the stylist patiently threaded pearls through the already-complicated arrangement. "You're going to be just beautiful for the ballroom scene."

"A far cry from yesterday." She sipped the coffee. "If they'd watered me one more time, I'd have melted."

"Miss Rothschild said the dailies were great. I checked."

"Thanks." She caught sight of Quinn's reflection in the mirror and decided that moment was as good a time as any. "Larry, this is Quinn Doran, a friend of mine." Only years of training kept her from choking on the word as she held a hand over her shoulder for Quinn's. "Larry's my right hand. And often my left, as well. Quinn's going to watch the filming for a few days."

"Oh, well . . ." Larry cleared his throat. "That's nice."

Quinn saw that the young man thought it was anything but. Another conquest, he thought. But he couldn't afford to feel sympathy, only suspicion.

"I'll keep out of the way," Quinn promised, making the most of it by rubbing his thumb over Chantel's knuckles. "I just want to see Chantel at work."

"Isn't that sweet?" Chantel said with a brilliant smile. "Quinn's between jobs at the moment and has time on his hands. Now don't be sensitive, darling." She gave his hand a pat before drawing hers away.

"We all understand how difficult the job market is, especially for botanists." Satisfied, Chantel rose. "I have to get into costume."

"They've scheduled publicity shots this morning," Larry told her after an uncertain glance at Quinn. "As soon as you're ready, you're supposed to go to the ballroom set."

"Fine."

"I'll go with you, darling." Quinn slipped an arm around her shoulders and squeezed, just a few degrees too hard. "You might need some help with buttons and snaps."

"Ease up, Doran," she muttered as they walked away. "I'm wearing a strapless dress for this scene, and I can't afford the bruises."

"You tempt me to put them where they won't show. A botanist?"

"I've always been attracted to the sensitive, introspective type."

"Like Larry?"

"He's my assistant. Leave him alone."

"Don't tell me how to do my job."

"He's a nice boy, he came with excellent references and—"

"How long ago?"

Annoyed, Chantel yanked open the door of her dressing room. "About three months."

When the door shut at his back, Quinn drew out a notebook. "Let's have his full name."

"Larry Washington. But I don't see—"

"You don't have to. What about the makeup guy?"

"George? Don't be absurd, he's old enough to be my grandfather."

Quinn merely shifted his gaze until it met hers. "The name, angel. There's no age limit on a disturbed mind."

She muttered it, then swept back into the private dressing alcove. "I don't like the way you work, Doran."

"I'll notify the complaint department." Lowering to the arm of a chair, he took a quick, interested look around her dressing room. Like her home, it was meticulously decorated in white on white. "While we're at it, give me the names of the rest of the men you deal with on the set."

There was a brief, pregnant pause. "All of them?"

"That's right."

"That's impossible," she told him. "I couldn't possibly remember everyone. Oh, most by sight and by first name, but not everything about everyone."

"Then find out."

"I have a job to do. I can't—"

"So do I. Get me the names."

Chantel yanked up the zipper at her back and scowled at the wall that separated them. "I'll see if Larry can get me a list."

"No, you won't. I don't want to rouse anyone's suspicions."

"All right, all right." For a moment she was convinced the cure was more trouble than the problem. Then she remembered the contents of the last note. Like it or not, she needed Quinn. "The assistant director's name is Amos Leery. The cinematographer's Chuck Powers. And damn it, they didn't walk into town yesterday. They've been in the business for years. They have families."

"What difference does that make? An obsession's an obsession." When she walked back into the room, Quinn was still sitting, scribbling in his notebook.

"What about the director?"

"The director's a woman." Chantel slipped off her watch and laid it aside. "I think we can rule her out."

"What about the—" He made the mistake of looking up as he spoke. The words stopped because his thought processes simply disintegrated. She was wearing red, a hot, vibrant red that seemed to lick at her skin. The dress scooped low and snug at her breasts, then followed the lines of her body. The skirt hung straight, hitched up on one side nearly to the hip, where it was secured by a circlet of glittering stones. His mouth went suddenly and completely dry.

Chantel saw the look, recognized it. Normally it would have made her smile, either with pleasure or in automatic response. Now she found she couldn't, because her heart was thudding too hard. He rose slowly and she stepped back. It wouldn't occur to her until much later that it was the first time in her life she had retreated from a man.

"I'll have to give you the rest later," she said quickly. "They'll be waiting for me on set."

"What are you supposed to be in that?" He didn't take another step toward her. Self-preservation held him back.

Chantel moistened her lips. "A woman out for revenge."

He looked at her again, gradually, up, then down, then up again until their eyes met. "I'd say you get it."

Making a conscious effort, she drew in a breath, then let it out again. Play the role, she told herself. It

was always possible to play the role. "Like it?"
Deliberately she turned a slow circle, revealing the
daring plunge at the back.

"It's a bit much for seven-thirty in the morning."

"Think so?" She smiled, more comfortable now.
"Wait until you see the hardware that goes with it.
Cartier's lending us a necklace and earrings. Two
hundred and fifty thousand dollars worth of all that
glitters. We'll have two armed guards and a very
nervous jeweler here shortly."

"Why not use paste? It shines, too."

"Because the real thing makes for better publicity.
Coming?"

He stopped her at the door with just a fingertip on
her bare shoulder. Each of them felt the jolt. "One
question. You wear anything under that?"

She managed another smile only because her hand
was already on the knob. "This is Hollywood, Mr.
Doran. We leave little details like that up to your
imagination." She stepped out, hoping the constric-
tion in her chest would ease before the first take.

By noon, Quinn had been forced to revise his
opinion of Chantel at least in one area. She wasn't the
pampered, temperamental prima donna he had expected. She worked like a horse—a thoroughbred,
perhaps, but she went through her paces time and time
again without complaint.

She'd been gracious to the photographers even when
the session had run on for ninety minutes. She hadn't
snapped at the makeup artist, as one of her co-stars
had, when it had been time for yet another retouch.
The temperature on the set was sizzling, thanks to the

lights, but she didn't wilt. Between takes she sipped from an ever-present glass of mineral water, unable to sit, because wardrobe had fussed about creases in her costume.

Two armed guards kept their eyes trained on her, and on the quarter million in jewels she wore. They suited her, he was forced to admit—the thick gold band crusted with diamonds and rubies that circled her neck, the symphony of diamonds and hot red stones that dripped from her ears. She wore them with the ease of a woman who knew she deserved them.

Quinn stayed well off the set and wondered how the actors could take the sheer monotony of repetition.

"Incredible, isn't it?"

Quinn turned his head and glanced at the tall, graying man beside him. "What's that?"

"How it takes them hours and hours to film a two-minute scene." He pulled out a thin black cigarette and lighted it from the butt of another. "I don't know why I come. It makes me nervous, but I can't stay away while they dissect my brainchild."

Quinn lifted a brow. "No, I suppose not."

He drew in smoke deeply before he smiled. "I'm not mad—or perhaps I am. I wrote the screenplay. Rather, I wrote what it appears this will loosely resemble." He offered a well-kept, rather thin hand. "James Brewster."

"Quinn Doran."

"Yes, I know. You're Miss O'Hurley's friend." He smiled again with a negligent shrug. "Word travels fast in small towns. She's quite brilliant, isn't she?"

"I don't know much about it."

"Oh, I assure you, she is. There was really no one else who could be Hailey. Cold, vindictive, clawing, and at the same time vulnerable and desperate for love. One of the few things I don't worry about as far as this little extravaganza goes is Chantel's interpretation of Hailey."

"She seems to know what she's doing."

"More, she feels what she's doing." Brewster took another quick puff as the crew set up for the next take. "It gives me enormous pleasure just to watch her."

Quinn slipped his hands into his pockets and mentally added Brewster to his growing list of men to check out. "She's an extraordinarily beautiful woman."

"That goes without saying. But then, to use a cliché, that's only skin deep. It's what's inside Chantel O'Hurley that fascinates."

Quinn's eyes narrowed fractionally. "And what's that?"

"I would say, Mr. Doran, that every man would have to discover that for himself."

The director called for quiet, and Brewster lapsed into a nervous silence. Quinn contemplated his own considerations.

She did seem to feel the part. The key scene called for her to confront her lover three years after he had left her, alone and abandoned. Even after a half a dozen takes, her eyes would frost over on cue, her voice would take on just the necessary hint of venom. On a dance floor crowded with people, she set out to seduce and humiliate. Chantel did both with such apparent ease that Quinn felt she must enjoy it.

Even to him, a man who'd learned how to look beyond illusions, it seemed that she was only aware of the man in whose arms she danced. There might not have been any cameras, any technicians, any dollies or lifts.

It went on for hours, but Quinn was patient. It interested him to see that whenever a break lasted longer than five minutes her assistant appeared at her elbow with a fresh glass of mineral water. More than once the assistant director came over to take her hand and murmur to her. The makeup artist retouched her face time and again, as though it were a rare canvas.

It was after seven before they wrapped. They had taken an hour for lunch, and apart from that, Quinn calculated, she had been on her feet for fourteen hours. All in all, he decided, he'd rather spend eight hours digging ditches.

"Ever think of another line of work?" Quinn asked her as they closed themselves in her dressing room again.

"Oh, no." Chantel eased out of her shoes and felt her arches cramp instantly. "I love the glamour."

"Where was it?"

The smile came automatically. "You catch on fast. If she'd called for one more take, just one more, I was going to ask you to shoot her in the knee. Get the zipper for me, will you? My arms are like rubber."

"That's because you had them wrapped around Carter for most of the day."

"Just one of the perks of the job." She arched her back as Quinn brought the zipper down below her hips.

"He's okay, if you like the smooth poster-boy type."

She looked over her shoulder with a half smile. "I adore them."

"Ever think it might be Carter who's sending you flowers?"

She stiffened a bit, then walked into the dressing area. "He's too busy trying to untangle himself from his third wife. Besides, I've known him for years."

"People change, or do the unexpected. And you spend several hours a day in a clinch with him."

"That's work."

"Nice work if you can get it. In any case, you shouldn't trust anyone."

"Except you."

"That's right. Brewster seemed pretty taken with you, too."

"Brewster? The writer?" Really amused, Chantel walked back in, still buttoning her blouse. "James is much more interested in his characters than the people who play them. And he's been happily married for twenty-odd years. Don't you ever read the gossip columns?"

"Never miss them." He stopped in the act of reaching for a cigarette when she sat abruptly and grabbed her foot. "Problem?"

"It's always after you take those damn things off that you're in agony." She winced, swore and kneaded. "I can tell you, it was a man who invented the high heel—the same one who invented the bra."

"It's you women who wear the things," he pointed out, but knelt down and took her foot in his hand. "Got you in the arch?"

"Yes, but—" Her protest died on her lips as he began to press. With a long, sincere sigh, she leaned back. "Yes, that's wonderful. You've missed your calling. You could make a fortune as a masseur."

"You should see what I could do for the rest of you."

She opened one eye. "We'll just stick with the feet, thanks. If I were a few inches taller, or Sean a few inches shorter, I could have gotten away with flats for most of the shots."

"I'll tell you this, his love scenes with you seemed pretty sincere."

"They're supposed to." Bone-tired, she opened both eyes. "Look, we're professionals. It looked that way because we played it that way, not because either one of us has any physical interest in the other."

"It looked like interest from my angle. Especially when he put his hand on your—"

"Try another tune, Doran."

"I think you're about to tell me how to do my job again."

"I'd like you to do your job," she shot back, "instead of harping on a man just because he's good at his work."

"Just checking him out, angel."

"I don't want my friends and associates spied on."

"If you want someone who's afraid to step on toes, you hired the wrong man."

"I've come to that conclusion several times myself." She couldn't have said why her temper was building so quickly, but his hands moving slowly up and down the arch of her foot were doing things they shouldn't to her system. She wanted him out and gone.

"Why don't you take a walk, Doran?" She jerked her foot away. "You're just not my style." Rising, she stepped around him. "You can keep the change."

"Fine." He was as angry as she, and just as baffled as to the cause. He only knew that for one quick moment he'd felt something for her, something soft and easy. It was gone now, erased as if it had never been. In its place was the anger, and a need, just as strong, that demanded physical release. "I might as well take a bonus while I'm at it."

He grabbed her. She'd known he wouldn't be gentle. His hand tangled in her hair as his mouth came down on hers. She'd known he would show little finesse. What she hadn't known, or hadn't admitted, was that she could respond so completely.

No man held her when she didn't choose to be held. No man took from her what she didn't willingly offer. Yet he *was* holding her, and she found nothing within herself to make him stop. His face was rough against her, and his fingers dug into her skin as he held her close. Defending herself should have been simple, even automatic, yet she didn't struggle in his arms. Her knees trembled, but she didn't even feel it. Everything was bound up in the sensation of his mouth on hers and the explosion of the taste of him. Delectable. Her lips parted and invited him in.

He rarely worried about consequences, and even less frequently questioned his instincts. When he had felt the need to touch her, to take her this way, he had done so. He was already paying for it. She was more than he had imagined she could be. Softer, smoother, warmer. It wasn't an image he held in his arms but a passionate, hot-blooded woman. Even as he discovered and explored the flavor and texture of her lips, he understood that he needed more. That was the trap, and he'd fallen right into it.

He drew her away because he wanted to see her face after she had tasted him. Her eyes opened slowly, so dark, so very blue that for an instant he was more vulnerable to her than either of them could have guessed. He felt the need shift to an ache, and the ache to uncertainty, before he pulled himself back.

"It's been an interesting day, angel." And one he was afraid he wouldn't easily forget. "Why don't you tell Matt to find you somebody else?"

It had been a long time since she had felt rejection. It hurt more than she remembered. Training and pride had her straightening and kept her voice icy cool. "If you've finished your show of male dominance, you can go." The image was back, even before her pulse had started to level. "If I hear of someone who needs a bodyguard for their poodle, I'll give them your card."

Chantel turned away when the phone rang. She picked up the receiver, then looked over her shoulder until she saw Quinn open the door. With a toss of her head, she brought it back to her ear. "Yes, hello."

The voice was too familiar now, and a degree more frightening. "I've waited all day to talk to you. You're so beautiful, so exciting. All day I've been imagining how we would—"

"Why don't you stop?" Control snapped as she shouted into the phone. "Why don't you just leave me alone?" Before she could slam the receiver down, Quinn snatched it out of her hand.

"Don't be angry." The edgy desperation in the voice had him tensing. "I love you. I can make you happy, happier than you've ever been."

"Miss O'Hurley's happier without you," Quinn said calmly. "You really should stop bothering her."

There was a long silence, and Quinn heard the breathing on the other end of the phone grow heavier. "She doesn't need you. She needs me. She needs me," the voice repeated before the connection was broken. Quietly Quinn replaced the receiver. Chantel's back was to him, but after a moment she turned around.

He could see that she'd worked hard, even in those few moments, to regain her composure. But her skin was as white as the room around them. "I thought you'd gone."

"So did I." He made it a policy never to apologize for his actions. It was not that he didn't believe he could be wrong, just that apologies tended to weaken his position. In this case, he decided to come as close as possible without crossing the line. "Look, we don't have to like each other much to get this job done, and I don't like to leave things before they're finished. Why don't we just forget about what happened before."

She didn't care for compromises any more than Quinn did for apologies. But she cared less for the thought of going on alone. To satisfy both her needs and her pride, she gave him a bland smile. "Did something happen before?"

He acknowledged the gibe with a slight nod. "Not a thing. Let's get out of here."

Chapter Four

Chantel had long ago acknowledged that one couldn't have both privacy and fame. In order to achieve and maintain the second, the first almost invariably had to be sacrificed. If she went out for a quiet dinner with a friend, she would read about it the next day. If she danced with another celebrity, there would be pictures and speculation before the music stopped. According to the press, her life was full of men, full of wild, sizzling romance and blistering affairs. She accepted that. She was also shrewd enough to know that if she were rude or belligerent to the paparazzi both her reputation and her photographs would be unflattering. So she was willing, within reason, to court them and present a glamorous and unflappable image to the public.

But the tap on her phone and the guard at her gate were entirely different. They weren't part of the creamy silk-and-diamonds mystique she'd chosen to develop. If she had the choice... Every time that thought ran through her head, Chantel gritted her teeth and reminded herself that she didn't.

She should be grateful. It was difficult to acknowledge that fact, but she knew she should be. Since the phone call in her dressing room there had been nothing—no letters, no flowers, no whispering voice. She told herself she should be relieved. Instead, she felt as though she were waiting for the other shoe to drop.

During the week her work kept her too busy to think. She could, for a few hours a day, plunge herself into Hailey's character and her problems. As long as the film was rolling and the pressure was on, it was difficult to think of her own personal crises. Work had gotten her through other rough periods. She counted on its doing the same for her now.

But it was Saturday and the film was going smoothly, so she had no call. Normally she treasured mornings when she could lounge in bed for a few extra hours, indulging in the things that were reported to be part of her everyday life.

By seven she was awake. Disgusted, she ordered herself back to sleep. At seven-fifteen she was staring at the ceiling and thinking a great deal too much for her own peace of mind. Beautiful, glamorous women were supposed to sleep until noon, then pamper themselves with massages and facials. She'd have believed that herself if she hadn't been in the game so long.

Tossing the covers aside, she went into the office that adjoined her dressing room. Of all the rooms in her home, this one, and only this one, showed the other side of her. The furnishings, though sophisticated, were simple and functional; the material for the curtains might have been imported from Paris, but the space as a whole was imbued with a sense of organization and practicality. Her desk had been purchased for its usefulness as well as its appearance. And she did use it. She also used the computer that rested on it.

It was true that she had an agent and personal manager, a team of publicists and an assistant, but Chantel believed in keeping a handle on her own life, her own business. She knew what stocks she owned and the gross she received from the pictures she'd made. Copies of her contracts were meticulously filed. Chantel didn't simply sign them, she read them.

She went directly to her desk and, ignoring her thick appointment book and the pile of phone messages left by her maid, picked up a fat stack of papers. There were three scripts she hadn't so much as glanced at. The filming on *Strangers* wouldn't last forever. The sooner she started thinking about her next project, the less idle time she'd have.

Chantel got back into bed, propped the first script on her knees and told herself she would wait until eight o'clock for coffee. It only took half that time for her to discover that the first script was hopeless. The story itself had a few things going for it, but most of them were scenes with her naked, wrapped in one passionate embrace after another. She wasn't a prude, but neither was she willing to use her body as a selling point for a mediocre script. In any case, she was tired of playing the vamp or the victim. She tossed the script aside and picked up another. It caught her from the first page.

A comedy. At last someone had sent her an intelligent story that didn't rely exclusively on her sexuality to sell it. Not only was the dialogue sharp, the plot had twist after twist and made her chuckle out loud. The jokes were as much physical as verbal and would, she knew, exhaust her. Her character would make a fool of herself on-screen time after time. She'd end up with her face in the mud. And Chantel would love it.

Bless you, Matt. Halfway through the script, Chantel hugged it to her breast. He knew she wanted to do something at odds with the image they had both carefully created over the last six years. It would be a risk. Would people pay to see her face with mud on it? Chantel was willing to bet they would.

Happier than she'd been in weeks, Chantel pushed the intercom button and ordered breakfast brought up. She wasn't budging until she finished the last page. And when she did, she was going to call Matt. If she had to go to a casting call for this one, she would. If she had to read for the part, she'd read for it. She'd take a cut in salary if need be, but this was going to be hers.

Chantel snuggled back against the pillows, brought up her knees and turned the next page.

When the knock came at her door, she was totally absorbed. She answered absently, then began to chuckle as the character, *her* character, punched her way out of another crisis.

"Must be pretty funny stuff," Quinn commented.

Chantel's head whipped around. The amusement in her eyes turned instantly to annoyance. It was too bad, she thought, that he had to look so damn good. "A pity I didn't load that gun."

"You wouldn't shoot a man who's bringing you breakfast in bed." He moved across the room, set the tray on her lap, then made himself comfortable on the bed beside her. He wore a T-shirt and faded jeans and didn't seem to mind that his sneakers were on her handsewn spread. "What are you reading?" he asked, then stretched out his legs and crossed his arms behind his head.

"The stock market reports."

"Yeah, I always get a kick out of them, too." The pillows carried her scent, sexy, exotic and alluring. She was a bit rumpled from sleep, her hair tumbling around her shoulders and down her back. Even in the strong morning light he couldn't find a single flaw on her face. There were two skinny straps over her shoulders and a very little bit of lace low at her breasts. He remembered what he shouldn't have—what it felt like to hold her against him and kiss her until his mind went dim. He plucked a piece of toast off the tray and reached for the jelly.

"Help yourself," she muttered, fighting the urge to inch away.

"Thanks." He leaned over the tray as he spread on a healthy portion of jelly. When his breath whispered warm over her bare shoulder, she stiffened and reminded herself how much she disliked him. "Like I said before, this is a great bed."

"When I get the bill for laundering the spread, I'll deduct it from your fee." Determined not to show any reaction, Chantel reached for the pot of coffee and poured a cup. "What can I do for you, Doran?"

He nibbled on the toast and just looked at her. The smile bloomed slowly, very slowly.

"Don't embarrass yourself," she told him, and sipped the coffee while it was too hot. When it scalded her tongue, she decided she didn't simply dislike him. She detested him.

"Ask a silly question," he began, then proceeded to pour himself a cup of coffee.

"Look, I'm busy, so if—"

"Yeah, I can see that."

"I happen to be reading some scripts."

"Any good?"

Chantel drew a deep breath. Some men were more thickheaded than others, she reminded herself. Perhaps if she humored him a little... "As a matter of fact, yes. I want to finish this one this morning, so if we've business to discuss—"

"You going to chew up another man in this one?"

Patience, Chantel told herself. It was compassionate to show patience to an idiot. "No. As it happens, this is a comedy."

"A comedy?" He let out one quick laugh before he drank. "You?"

Her eyes narrowed. "Don't push your luck, Doran."

"Come on, angel. Yours isn't the kind of face that a man pushes a pie into."

"It's mud."

"What?"

"In this case, my face gets pushed in mud."

He chose a piece of melon from her bowl. "That I'd have to see."

"I'm counting on several million people having your attitude." With a natural flair, she whipped the napkin from its ring and passed it to him. "You are, after all, the common man, aren't you?"

"As common as they come," he said easily.

"Now, why don't you tell me why you're here this morning with your feet on my bed and your hands in my breakfast."

"Just part of the service. Great coffee."

"I'll give your compliments to the chef. Now, why don't you get to the point?"

"Aren't you going to eat?"

"Doran."

"Okay." He took a small folder out of the side basket of the tray and opened it. "I have a couple of preliminary reports. Thought you'd be interested."

"Reports on what?"

"Larry Washington, Amos Leery, James Brewster. Also have a bit on the makeup guy and your driver."

"My driver? You're investigating Robert?" Her appetite gone, Chantel pushed herself farther up in bed. Quinn saw dark rose silk beneath the lace and wondered how far down it went. "That's the most ridiculous thing I've ever heard."

"Angel, don't you ever read mysteries? The one you least suspect is always the one who done it."

"I'm not paying you to play Sam Spade, and I'm damned if I can see paying you to run investigations on people like Robert and George."

After brief consideration, Quinn decided on a strawberry. "Have you ever noticed how your Robert looks at you?"

The lace rose up, then settled again with her breathing. Deliberately Chantel tilted her head. "Darling, *all* men look at me like that."

He gave her a long stare before he sipped his coffee again. Even he had problems separating her act from reality. "Since I have to start somewhere, I'm starting with the men closest to you."

"The next thing you'll tell me is you're investigating Matt." When he said nothing, she looked at him again. "You must be joking. Matt's—"

"A man," Quinn finished for her. "You just said that was all it takes."

Furious, Chantel picked up the tray, then dumped it in his lap. Coffee sloshed over the rims of the cups. "Look, let's just stop this right now. I'm not going to have people I care about spied on and embarrassed. Matt's the closest friend I have, and I was under the impression he was your friend, too."

"This is business."

"Let's say our business is concluded. The calls have stopped, and so have the letters."

"For a whole forty-eight hours."

"That's enough for me. I'll pay your fee through today and we'll—" She broke off, the words sticking in her throat as the phone beside the bed began to ring. Without realizing it, Chantel found her hand in Quinn's, her fingers locked tight.

"They'll pick it up downstairs," he murmured. "Don't panic. If it's him, just keep calm. Try to get him to talk, to stay on the line as long as possible. We need time to run a trace." When the intercom buzzed, she jumped. "Pull yourself together, Chantel. You can handle it."

Working at keeping her breathing steady, Chantel spoke into the intercom. "Yes?"

"There's a man on the line, Miss O'Hurley. He won't give his name, but he says it's important. Shall I tell him you're unavailable?"

"Yes, I—" Quinn's hand curled around her wrist. "No, no, I'll take it. Thank you."

"Take it slow," Quinn told her. "Just let him talk."

Her fingers were stiff and cold as she picked up the receiver. "Hello." Quinn only had to look at her face to know she was hearing the familiar whisper.

"Don't lose it," he said quietly, keeping her free hand in his. "Just keep him on the line. Stay calm and answer him."

"Thank you," she managed, despite the block in her throat. "Yes, yes, I've gotten all your letters. No, I'm not angry." She closed her eyes and tried to pretend that the things he was saying didn't make her skin crawl. "I wish you'd tell me who you are. If you'd—" Caught between frustration and relief, she brought the receiver away from her ear. "He hung up."

"Damn." After setting the tray on the floor beside the bed, Quinn leaned over her and punched a few buttons on the phone. "It's Quinn." He swore again. "Yeah, just keep on it. Right. Not enough time," he told Chantel as he hung up the phone again. "Did he say anything that rang a bell, anything that makes you think of someone you know?"

"No." She trembled once before she regained control. "No one I know has a mind like that."

"Drink some coffee." He poured more into her cup, then handed it to her. She drank to ease the tightness in her throat.

"Quinn." She had to swallow again. "He said—he said he had a surprise for me, a big surprise." When she turned her head to look at him, her eyes were huge and dark. "He said it wouldn't be much longer."

"Let me worry about him." He'd always had a soft spot for the defenseless. It had gotten him into trouble before—in South America, in Afghanistan, and in countless other places. Even though he knew it might be dangerous in a more personal way, he slipped an arm around her shoulders and brought her close. "That's what you're paying me for, angel."

"He's going to get to me." She said it with such flat finality that he tightened his hold. "I can feel it."

"He'll have a hard time doing that with me in the way. Listen, I've got two men patrolling the grounds, two others monitoring the phones."

"It doesn't seem to help." She closed her eyes and for a moment let herself lean on him. "Maybe it's because I can't see them."

"You can see me, can't you?"

"Yeah." And she could feel him, could feel the hard, working muscles of his arm and shoulder, the not-so-smooth skin of his face.

"Want to see more of me?"

Cautious, Chantel lifted her face to look into his. There was humor there, but—she was sure she was mistaken—it looked as though there were genuine concern, as well. "I beg your pardon?"

"I like the way you do that. Angel, you could cut a man off at the knees without lifting a finger."

"It's a talent of mine. Explain, Doran."

"Why don't I move in for a while? Now don't let your ego get the best of you," he warned as she started to stiffen. "You've got plenty of rooms in this place, and though I am developing a real fondness for your bed, I can make do with another. What do you say, angel? Want a housemate?"

She frowned at him, hating to admit how much safer she would feel with him around all the time. The house was certainly big enough to keep them out of each other's way, though privacy would go out of the window. The real problem would be remembering just how he'd made her feel during that one sizzling kiss. If he were around twenty-four hours a day, remembering might not be enough.

"Maybe I should buy that vicious dog," Chantel muttered.

"Your choice."

That was true. It was. And she knew exactly how to handle it—and him. "Go ahead and get your duffel bag, Doran. We'll find a corner for you to sleep in." Sitting up, she flipped through the script again. She felt better, she couldn't deny it. The icy fist in her stomach had loosened. "How much extra is this going to cost me?"

"Meals—and I want more than a bowl of fruit in the morning—use of the facilities and, since this is going to play hell with my social life, another two hundred a day."

"Two hundred?" Chantel gave a quick, unladylike snort. "I can't imagine your social life's worth more than fifty. Isn't that the going rate in the massage parlors?"

"What do you know about massage parlors?"

She slanted him a look. "Just what I see in the movies, darling."

"How about a hands-on demonstration?" He lifted a finger and slid a strap from her shoulder. Instead of replacing it, Chantel simply studied the script.

"No, thanks. I doubt if there's anything you could teach me."

"I was thinking more the other way around." When he nudged the other strap aside, Chantel lifted her gaze to his. He was baiting her, and she wasn't ready to nibble.

"Try me when I've got a few weeks to spare, Doran. With you, I'm afraid we'd have to start from scratch."

"I'm a fast learner." He slid his hand up her shoulder until his thumb brushed her jaw.

She grabbed his wrist before she could stop herself, but her voice remained steady. "Watch your step."

"If you watch your step, you miss too much."

He'd wanted to touch her again, to feel her skin smooth and warm under his hands. He'd wanted to see her eyes darken, partly from anger, partly from temptation, when he did. She looked ready to rake his face, but the bite of her nails wouldn't stop him from sampling the fire she held so well banked inside her. The fire she let flame so explosively on screen.

When her free hand came up, he grabbed it. She held one of his, he held one of hers. As far as Quinn was concerned, they were even. He thought it was pride that kept her from struggling, pride and the confidence that she could bring him to his knees whenever she chose. He wasn't as certain as he wanted to be that she couldn't.

He was just about to let her go when her chin lifted and her eyes dared him. He'd always been a sucker for a dare.

With his eyes open and on hers, he lowered his mouth. But he didn't kiss her. Chantel felt the impact, both surprised and aroused, when he caught her bottom lip between his teeth. The chilly nonresponse she'd been determined to give him began to heat.

She could have stopped him. Her brother Trace had taught her and her sisters how to defend themselves from overamorous members of the male sex. Chantel was aware that she could take Quinn by surprise and have him bent over double and gasping for air with one quick jerk of her knee. She lay still, hypnotized by the green eyes that watched her.

She wasn't supposed to have these kind of feelings, this kind of hunger. She had blocked them out years before, when her emotions had made a fool of her. She wasn't supposed to have this slow, curling sensation in her stomach. Her bones weren't supposed to liquify at a touch. She'd done love scene after love scene—choreographed, blocked out, shot and reshot for the camera—and had felt nothing that hadn't been programmed into her character. She knew just how little the most passionate embrace could mean to the two people involved.

This light, nibbling sensation on her lip should have done nothing but annoy her. But she lay still, trapped by an urgent desire to absorb the rushing range of feeling it brought to her.

Impossible. It had to be impossible, but he felt innocence shimmering around her. If it was an act, she was more skilled than she had a right to be. If it wasn't— But he couldn't think. She did something to his mind that she shouldn't be permitted to do. She pushed her way into it and filled it until he was ready to forget everything but her.

Desire. Desire was something easily quenched and easily forgotten. It would pay to remember that. Any man was bound to want her. But he wasn't sure any man would be able to forget her. There was too much power in her, the power to make a man hunger, to make him ache, to make him weak. Quinn couldn't afford to lose his hold. With her lips warm and soft under his, he reminded himself that he had two priorities. One was to keep her safe. The other was to look out for himself.

When he felt himself sinking, he pulled back. The ground was too unsteady here. For once he would indeed watch his step. "You pack a punch, angel."

Steady, she told herself, struggling to find a foothold. It meant nothing to him, nothing more than the eternal war of wills men and women fought. He hadn't gone soft inside or felt the need to be loved, the need to believe that maybe, just maybe, this was right. She wouldn't give him the satisfaction of knowing she had.

"Next time it'll flatten you."

"You might be right," he muttered, and shifted away. "Your skin's a little pale." He skimmed his gaze over her bare shoulders and cursed himself for the twist of need he felt. "Get dressed and meet me out by the pool. I'll bring you up to date on what we have so far." He rolled from the bed and, taking the file with him, left her alone.

He needed some air, fast.

* * *

Quinn cut through the water of the pool like an eel, smooth, fast and quiet. When Chantel came onto the patio, she stood in the sunlight and watched him. She hadn't been wrong about the feel of his muscles. She could see them now, rippling with each stroke of his arm, bunching with each kick of his leg. He'd chosen brief black trunks from the stack she kept in the pool-house for guests. They fit low and snug over his hips.

Still, she imagined he'd picked them for comfort rather than impact. As far as she could tell, Quinn Doran considered himself too irresistible to think about such things. She chose a chair by an umbrellaed table and waited for him to surface.

The physical exertion helped. Quinn realized he'd pushed himself closer to the limit with her than he'd intended. He still wasn't sure why he'd made a move toward her when he knew she was the kind of woman a smart man kept his distance from. He'd always been smart. That was the way you survived. But he'd also always had a habit of giving in to temptation. That was the way you lived. Though his life had never been dull, Chantel O'Hurley was his biggest temptation so far.

By the time he'd crossed the length of the pool and back thirty times, most of the tension had drained. Under other circumstances he would have used a punching bag to relieve it, but he was willing to make use of whatever was available.

Tossing wet hair from his face, he stood in the shallow end, water lapping at his thighs. And he saw her.

Tipped back in the chair, her face shaded by a big, white umbrella, she was the epitome of cool, gut-wrenching beauty. She'd pulled her hair up and back so that her face was unframed. It needed no framing. The sleek, severe style only accented that fact. The snug top she wore was cut deep at the shoulders and cinched into the waistband of cropped shorts that showed off long, long legs. His gaze lingered on those legs as he hauled himself out of the pool.

"You've got a hell of a foundation, angel."

"So I'm told." Reaching beside her, she picked up a towel. "I see you're finding your way around all right." She tossed the towel to him, but he did no more than sling it around his neck. The sunlight shimmered on the drops of water on his bronzed skin.

"Nice pool."

"I like it."

"Then you should use it more. Swimming's a great way to keep in shape."

"I'll worry about my shape, Doran." Temper was licking its way to the surface. Chantel coated it with sarcasm. "Is this going to take long? I want to get my nails done this afternoon."

"We'll fit it in."

"We?" She couldn't prevent a smile as he sat across from her. "Somehow I can't picture you in a chi-chi little place like Nail It Down."

"I've been in worse." He shifted the chair slightly, placing himself in full sunlight. "Anything else on your agenda today?"

"Oh, maybe a little window-shopping on Rodeo Drive," she said on the spur of the moment, just to make things tougher. "Lunch at Ma Maison, I think, or perhaps the Bistro." She rested her chin on the back of her hand. "It's been *days* since I've seen anyone.

You do have something appropriate to wear, don't you?''

"I'll get by. Then there's that charity dinner tonight."

Her smile faded. "How did you know about that?"

"It's my job to know." Though he didn't need them Quinn flipped through his notes. "My secretary contacted Sean Carter and explained you had another escort."

"Then she can contact him again. Sean and I arranged to go together to help promote the film."

"Are you willing to get into a dark limo with a man who might be—"

"It's not Sean." After cutting him off, Chantel reached for the pack of cigarettes Quinn had tossed on the table.

"We'll just play this my way." Quinn picked up his lighter and flicked it on. "I'll take you to your little party, and if you like you can cuddle with Sean for the cameras. What about tomorrow?"

Chantel gave him a poisonous look. "You tell me."

Quinn patiently flipped open his file. "You've got a reporter and photographer from *Life-styles* coming at one to do a story on you and the house. That's all I've got."

She dropped the cigarette in an ashtray and let it smolder. "Because that's all there is. I have some personal things to attend to here at home, then I go to bed early because Monday's a working day."

"Matt said you were practical." Quinn flipped the page over. "Larry Washington."

"Get on with it," she told him. "You won't be happy until you do."

"The kid looks clean enough on the surface. Graduated UCLA last year with a degree in business management. Seems he always had a thing for the theater, but preferred the setups and backstage stuff to the acting."

"Which is exactly why I hired him."

"Apparently he had a pretty heavy thing going with a co-ed until about six months ago. A very attractive blue-eyed blonde. She dumped him."

He didn't have to spell out the implications. "A lot of women have blue eyes, and a lot of college romances break up."

"Amos Leery," he continued, ignoring her. "Did you know his first wife divorced him because he couldn't keep his hands off other women?"

"Yes, I know. And it was fifteen years ago, so—"

"Old habits die hard. George McLintoch."

"That's pitiful, Doran. Even for you."

"He's been a makeup artist for thirty-three years. Has five grandchildren and another due in the fall. Since his wife died a couple of years ago, he's had a few problems with the bottle."

"That's enough." She rose and paced to the edge of the pool. The water was calm and crystal clear. So had her life been only a few weeks before. "That's really enough. I'm not going to sit here and listen to you dissect the personal problems of people I work with." She looked back over her shoulder. "You're in a filthy business."

"That's right." Not by a flicker did he reveal his feelings on the subject. "James Brewster. Seems like a pretty stable family life. Married twenty-one years, one son studying law in the east. Interesting that he's been in analysis for over ten years."

"Everyone in this town's in analysis."

"You're not."

"I will be if I keep you around."

He smiled briefly, then turned the page. "Your driver, Robert, is an interesting character. Young Robert DeFranco has himself a string of ladies."

"Just your kind of man."

"Can't help but admire his stamina. Matt Burns."

She turned all the way around then. This time he saw not anger but revulsion. It ripped at something inside him. "How could you?" She said it quietly and painfully. "He's your friend."

"This is my job."

"It's your job to spy into the personal lives of people you're supposed to care about?"

He kept his eyes on hers. "I can't afford to care about anyone but my clients when they're paying me. That's the service."

"Then keep this part of it to yourself. Whatever you dug up about Matt, I don't want to know."

He wouldn't allow her to make him regret what he'd done. He'd done worse, much worse. He wondered how she'd look at him if she knew. "Chantel, you're going to have to consider all the possibilities."

"No, *you* are. And at this point you're getting seven hundred a day to do it. It's your job to find who-ever's hounding me and to keep me safe while you're doing it."

"This is the way I do it."

"Fine. Since it is, all I want to see from you is the bill."

She started to storm back into the house, but he blocked her path. "Grow up." Taking her by the shoulders, he held her still. She was hurting, he realized, really hurting for the people she cared for. He had to convince her that she couldn't afford to. "Anyone at all could be making those calls. Maybe it's someone you've never even met, but my instincts tell me different. He knows you, lady." He gave her a quick shake to accentuate his point. "And he wants you real bad. Until we find him, you're going to do just like I say."

That morning's call was still too fresh in her mind. If a compromise had to be made, she'd make it. But she wouldn't like it. "I'll do what you say, Doran, to a point. I'll have my phone tapped, I'll have the damn guards at the gate and you in my house, but I won't listen to this garbage."

"In other words, you'll make a good showing, but you don't want the details."

"You got it."

He dropped his hands. "I thought you had more guts than that."

She opened her mouth to yell, then shut it again because he was right. She just didn't have the stomach for it. "Dry off, Doran."

She turned on her heel and walked away. As he stood watching her, Quinn decided his instincts were as reliable as ever. When push came to shove, she wouldn't crumble.

Chapter Five

When they got through the weekend without chewing any pieces off each other, Chantel decided they might make it. It hadn't pleased her to go to dinner with him and pretend, in front of three hundred other people, that she enjoyed being with him. Chantel had told herself to look at it as a job—a particularly difficult and unappealing job. Then Quinn had thrown her a curve. He'd been charming.

Surprisingly, black tie suited him. Though it didn't quite disguise his rough edges, it made them all the more appealing. He would never be suave or smooth or glossy. For some reason, Chantel found she was pleased to know that. He might wear a silk tie and the trappings of sophistication, but you knew—at least if you were a woman you knew—that a barbarian lay underneath.

Before the evening was over, he had drunk champagne with this year's top box-office draw and had danced with a three-time Oscar-winning actress. The seventy-year-old veteran had patted Chantel on the knee and told her that her taste in men was improving. Though that had been difficult to swallow, not once during the evening had Quinn given Chantel the opportunity to smirk at him.

On Sunday he left her to herself. When the reporters came and she gave them an interview and a tour of her home, it was as if he weren't even there. She knew he was around, somewhere, but he didn't infringe on her privacy. She was free to get back to her reading, to indulge in a long, soothing whirlpool bath and to catch up on correspondence and a few niggling business matters. By the time they left the house on Monday morning, Chantel was almost ready to revise her opinion of him.

She felt rested and eager for work. The night before, she had finished the script she'd begun on Saturday morning and was more enthusiastic than ever. She'd woken Matt out of a sound sleep to tell him to go after the part. It might have been shy of 6:00 a.m., but Chantel felt wonderful.

She glanced over at Quinn beside her, legs stretched out, eyes closed behind tinted glasses. From the look of him, he hadn't shaved since Saturday. It seemed unfair that the slightly dissipated aura suited him so.

"Rough night?"

He opened one eye. Then, finding it too much effort, he closed it again. "Poker game."

"You played poker last night? I didn't know you'd gone out."

"In the kitchen," he muttered, wondering how soon he could get his hands on another cup of coffee.

"My kitchen?" Chantel frowned, a little annoyed that she hadn't been asked to play. "With whom?"

"Gardener."

"Rafael? He hardly speaks English."

"Don't have to to know a full house beats a straight."

"I see." A smile tugged at her lips. "So you and Rafael played poker in the kitchen, got drunk and told lies."

"And Marsh."

"And Marsh what?" She stopped in the act of reaching for a glass. "Marsh played cards? *My* Marsh?"

"Tall guy, not much hair."

"Really, Quinn, he's nearly eighty and quite creaky. I'm surprised even you would take advantage of him."

"Took me for eighty-three dollars. Canny old son of a—"

"Serves you right," she said with satisfaction. "Sitting down in my kitchen, swilling beer and smoking cigars and bragging about women when I'm paying for your time."

"You were asleep."

"I hardly think that matters. You're being paid to watch out for me, not play five-card stud."

"Five-card draw, jacks or better. And I was watching out for you."

"Really?" She brought a glass of juice to her lips. "That's odd. I didn't see hide nor hair of you yesterday."

"I was around. You enjoy your whirlpool?"

"I beg your pardon?"

"You spent damn near an hour in that tub." He took the glass from her and drained it. Maybe it would wash the cotton out of his mouth. "Funny, I figured a woman like you would have two dozen bathing suits. Guess you couldn't find one."

"You were watching me."

He handed the glass back to her, then settled back again. "That's what you're paying me for."

Indignation rippled through her as she slammed the glass back in its holder. "I'm not paying you to be a Peeping Tom. Get your prurient kicks on your own time."

"My time is your time, angel. I saw nearly that much of you when I plunked down four-fifty to see *Thin Ice*. Besides, if I'd been out for kicks, I'd have joined you."

"I'd have drowned you," she tossed back, but he only smiled and shut his eyes again.

His head was pounding like a jackhammer. He'd gotten less sleep before, but that had usually been of his own choosing. The poker game had been his way of distracting himself from the knowledge that she was sleeping upstairs, his way of trying to forget the way she'd looked stretched out in the foaming water of the spa that afternoon.

He hadn't, as he wanted her to believe, watched her. He'd seen her go into the poolhouse. Then, when she hadn't come out, he'd gone to check on her. She'd been lounging in the big tub, Rachmaninoff wafting from the overhead speakers. Her hair had been left down and floated in the frothing water. And her body...her body had been long and slender and pale.

He could still feel the impact, like a sledgehammer straight to the solar plexus.

He hadn't stayed to tease and taunt, but had left as quietly as he'd come. There had been a fear, a definite fear that if she'd opened her eyes and looked at him he'd have crawled.

Thoughts of her haunted him day and night. He knew he should be able to prevent it. Nothing and no one was permitted to have power over him. But he was beginning to understand how a woman could become an obsession by simply existing. He was beginning to understand how a man could become overwhelmed by his own fantasies.

It made him worry about himself, but it made him worry more about her. If another man had become obsessed with her, and that other man had crossed certain lines, to what lengths might he go to have her? The letters and calls were gradually becoming more urgent. When would he stop them and try something more desperate?

As frightened as she was, Quinn didn't believe Chantel had any conception of just how far that kind of madness could push a man. The longer he was around her, the more he realized just how far that was.

They would shoot on the back lot that day. Another camera crew was already in New York filming exteriors. Chantel was looking forward to the time when she and other members of the crew would fly east for the handful of scenes to be shot on location. It would give her a chance to see her sister Maddy and, with any luck, catch her play on Broadway.

The thought of it brought back her earlier cheerful mood. It lasted even through an hour's delay while technicians worked out a few bugs.

"Looks like New England," Quinn commented as he glanced around the open-air set.

"Massachusetts, to be exact," Chantel told him, nibbling on a sticky bun. "Ever been there?"

"I was born in Vermont."

"I was born on a train." Chantel broke off another piece of her bun and laughed. "Well, nearly. My parents were on their way to a gig when my mother went into labor. They stopped off long enough to have my sisters and me."

"Your sisters *and* you?"

"That's right. I'm the oldest of triplets."

"There are three of you. Good God."

"There's only one of me, Doran." She popped a piece of the bun in his mouth, enjoying the fresh air and sunshine. "We're triplets, but each of us manages to be her own person. Abby's raising horses and kids in Virginia, and Maddy's currently wowing them on Broadway."

"You don't look like the family type."

"Really." She felt too good to be offended. "I also have a brother. I can't tell you what he does, because no one's quite sure. I lean toward professional gigolo or international jewel thief. You'd get along beautifully with him." She watched one of the prop men pick up a boulder and move it a few feet. "Amazing, isn't it?"

Quinn studied the trees. They looked real, just like the ones back home, until you saw the wood base they sat on. "Anything real around here?"

"Not a great deal. Give them a few hours and they could make this a jungle in Kenya." Stretching her back, she toyed with the ice in her cup. She was used to waiting. "We were going to shoot this on location, but there were some problems."

"There's a lot of wait-around in this business."

"It's not for the restless. I've gone back to my dressing room and sat for hours to be called back for a five-minute scene. Other days you put in fourteen hours nonstop."

"Why?"

"Why what?"

"Why do you do it?"

"Because it's what I've always wanted to do." It was a stock answer. Why she felt obliged to elaborate on it, she didn't know. "When I was little and I sat in a theater and saw what could happen, I knew I had to be a part of it."

"So you always wanted to be an actress."

She tossed her hair back and smiled. "I've always been an actress. I wanted to be a star."

"Looks like you got what you wanted."

"Looks like," she murmured, shaking off a hint of depression. "What about you? Did you always want to be a—whatever it is you are?"

"I wanted to be a juvenile delinquent, and was doing a pretty good job of it."

"Sounds fascinating." She wanted to know more. To be honest, she wanted to know everything about him, but she'd take care how she asked. "Why aren't you serving ten-to-twenty in San Quentin?"

"I got drafted." He grinned, but she sensed the joke was very much his own.

"The army builds men."

"Something like that. Anyway, I learned to do what I was good at, make a profit and stay out of jail."

"And what are you good at?" He turned his head, just enough that she could see the amusement and the challenge in his eyes. "Forget I asked. Let's try something else. How long were you in the army?"

"I didn't say I was in the army." He offered her a cigarette, then lighted it himself when she shook her head.

"You said you were drafted."

"I was. Drafted and government-trained. Want some more coffee?"

"No. How long were you in?"

"Too long."

"Is that where you learned not to give a direct answer?"

"Yeah." He smiled at her again. Then, before either of them realized his intention, he reached out to touch her hair. "You look like a kid."

Her heart shouldn't have been hammering, but it was. It was only a touch, after all, only a few words and a long look in a pretend world teeming with people. "That's the idea," she managed after a moment. "I'm twenty in this scene, innocent, eager, naive . . . and about to be deflowered."

"Here?"

"No, actually, just over there." She pointed to a small clearing in the forest the crew had created. "Brad the cad seduces me, promising me his everlasting devotion. He taps the passion that so far I've only given to my painting, then exploits it."

Quinn clucked his tongue. "With all these people watching."

"I love an audience."

"And you got mad because I watched you in the tub."

"You—"

"They're ready for you, Chantel."

After giving her assistant a nod, Chantel stood up, then carefully brushed off the seat of her pants. "Get yourself a good seat, Doran," she suggested. "You might learn something."

Taking her advice, Quinn watched her run through the scene several times on low power. From his angle, it seemed a lukewarm stock scene—a gullible woman, a clever man in a pretty springtime setting. Plastic, he thought, pure plastic, down to the leaves on the trees. Quinn kept his eyes on George as the makeup artist retouched Chantel's face to keep that dewy, never-been-touched look intact. One of the prop men handed her back her sketchpad and pencil.

"Places. Quiet on the set." The hubbub died away, to be replaced by silence. "Speed. Roll film." The clapper came down for take 1. "Action."

It began the same way, with Chantel sitting on a rock sketching. Sean made his entrance and stood watching her for a moment. When Chantel glanced up and saw him, Quinn felt his mouth go dry. Everything a man could want was in that look. Love, trust, desire. If a man had a woman look at him that way, he could win wars and scale mountains.

He'd never wanted to be loved. Love tied you down, made you responsible to someone other than yourself. It took as much as or more than it gave. That was what he'd thought, that was what he'd been certain of, until he'd seen the look come into Chantel's eyes.

A movie, he reminded himself when he realized he'd missed five minutes of shooting. They were already doing a second take. The look in her eyes was as much an illusion as the forest they were in. And it hadn't been aimed at him, in any case. It was a movie, she was an actress, and it was all part of the script.

The first time Sean Carter touched her, Quinn felt his jaw lock tight. Fortunately for him, the director cut the scene.

When they continued, Quinn told himself he was under control. He told himself that he was only there because he was paid to be. She meant nothing to him personally. She was a case. It didn't matter to him how many men she made love with, on- or off-camera.

Then he watched her touch her lips softly, hesitantly, to Sean's, and he thought of murder.

It was only a scene in a movie, with fake rocks, fake trees and fake emotions. But it seemed so real, so honest. There were dozens of people around him with machines to run the lights, the mikes. Even as Sean gathered Chantel closer, a camera edged in on them.

But she trembled. Damn it, he saw her quiver as Sean pulled the band from her hair and let it tumble free. Her voice shook when she told him she loved him, she wanted him, she wasn't afraid. Quinn found his hands were balled into fists in his pockets.

Her eyes shut as Sean rained kisses all over her face. She looked so young, so vulnerable, so ready to be loved. Quinn didn't notice the camera come in close. He only saw Sean unbuttoning her blouse, and her eyes, wide and blue, locked on her lover's. Hesitantly she unbuttoned his shirt. Color washed her cheeks as she drew the shirt aside and pressed her cheek to his chest. They lowered to the grass.

"Cut."

Quinn came back to reality with a thud. He watched Chantel sit up, then say something to Sean that made him laugh. She was wearing a brief strapless bra that would stay below camera range and a pair of baggy jeans. Larry draped her discarded blouse over her shoulder, and she gave him an absent smile.

"Let's take it again. Chantel, after you take off his shirt, I want you to lift your head." Mary Rothschild hunkered down as Chantel rebuttoned her blouse. "I want a kiss there, a good long one, before you two go down on the grass."

Sometime during the fifth take, Quinn found his objectivity. He searched the faces of those looking on. If there was an uncomfortable stirring in his stomach, he could ignore it now. His job was to find out who might be watching Chantel, not clinically, not approvingly as she completed the scene, but someone who might be eaten alive with jealousy. Or fantasizing. It wasn't going to do either one of them any good if it was him.

Quinn took out another cigarette and watched the faces around him. He had reports coming in on everyone from the cinematographer to the prop man. Gut instinct told him that whoever was sending her letters was someone she knew, someone she might speak to casually every day.

Quinn wanted to find him, and he wanted to find him quickly. Before he developed an obsession of his own.

The assistant director put his arm around Chantel's shoulders and, with his head bent close to her ear, led her off the set. Before they reached the trailer that was Chantel's dressing room, Quinn was in front of them.

"Going somewhere?"

Chantel shot him a narrowed look but hung on to her temper. "As a matter of fact, I was going to get out of the sun for awhile. Amos was giving me the rest of today's schedule. You'll have to forgive Quinn, Amos. He's a bit . . . possessive."

"Hard to blame him." Good-natured and a bit tubby around the middle, Amos patted her shoulder. "You were terrific, Chantel, just terrific. We'll call when we need you for the close-ups and reaction shots. You should have about a half hour."

"Thanks, Amos." She waited until he was out of earshot before she turned on Quinn. "Don't do that."

"Do what?"

"All you needed was a knife between your teeth," she muttered, jerking open the door of the trailer. "I told you Amos was harmless. He—"

"Has a habit of touching women. One of those women is my client."

Chantel chose a diet drink from the small refrigerator and collapsed with it onto the sofa. "If I didn't want him to touch me, I assure you, he wouldn't. This isn't the first time I've worked with Amos, and unless you insist on acting like an idiot, it won't be the last."

Quinn opened the refrigerator and, to his satisfaction, found a beer. "Look, angel, I can't narrow down the list of suspects to suit your requirements. It's time you stopped pretending that the person you're so afraid of isn't someone you know."

"I'm not pretending," she began.

"You are." He chugged back some of the beer before he sat beside her. "And you're not pretending with half as much style as you were out there rolling on the grass a few minutes ago."

"That's work. This is my life."

"Exactly." He took her chin in a way that made her eyes flash. "I'm supposed to take care of it. If it makes you feel better, I've just about eliminated Carter."

"Sean?" She felt a quick surge of relief, then one of caution. "Why?"

"Simple enough reasoning." He took another sip of beer and kept her hanging. "Seems to me that if a man was obsessed with a woman— We'll agree that we're dealing with an obsession?"

"Yes, damn it." She snatched the bottle out of his hand. "What are you getting at?"

"Just that if I were going over the edge about a woman I wouldn't be able to stand up, dust myself off and turn aside after I'd spent a good part of the day tangled half-naked with her."

"Is that so?" Chantel handed him back his beer. "I'll be sure to keep that in mind." Relaxed again, Chantel leaned back against the pillows and stretched out her legs. "So, what did you think of the scene?"

"It ought to fog up a few bifocals."

"Oh, come on, Quinn." She held up her drink and watched moisture bead the sides of the bottle. "It wasn't just a matter of sex, you know. It was a betrayal of innocence and trust. What happened to Hailey in that New England wood will affect the rest of her life. A quick tumble on the pine cones doesn't do that."

"But a quick tumble on the pine cones sells tickets."

"This is television. We're after ratings. Damn it, Quinn, I put a lot into that scene. It's the turning point of Hailey's life. If it doesn't mean more than—"

"You were good," he cut in, and had her staring at him.

"Well." She set her drink down. "Mind repeating that?"

"I said you were good. I don't hand out the awards, angel."

She brought her knees up and dropped her chin onto them. With the thin slash of sunlight coming through the curtains, she still looked young and innocent. "How good?"

"How do you manage to feed that ego when you're alone?"

"I've never denied the size of my ego. How good?"

"Good enough to make me want to give Carter a black eye."

"Really?" Delighted, she caught her bottom lip between her teeth. She'd play it light. It wouldn't do to let him know just how much it meant to her to hear him praise her work. "Before or after the cameras were rolling?"

"Before, during and after." Unexpectedly he reached over and took the front of her shirt in his hand. "And don't push your luck, angel. I've got a habit of taking what looks good to me."

"You've such class, Doran." She uncurled his fingers from her blouse. "Such low class."

"Just keep that in mind. You know, angel, you gave me a twinge or two when I watched you and Carter paw each other."

"We weren't—"

"Give it any name you want. But good as you are, I didn't spend all my time watching you. I looked around and saw a few interesting things."

"Such as?"

"Brewster smoked a half a pack of cigarettes while you and Carter were . . . working."

"He's a nervous man. I've seen writers do worse when their script's being filmed."

"Leery practically fell in your lap trying to get a closer look."

"It's his job to look."

"And your assistant nearly swallowed his tongue when Carter took your shirt off."

"Just stop it." Springing up, she paced to one of the windows. They would call her soon. She wouldn't be any good if she let what Quinn was saying get her all churned up. "As far as I'm concerned, you're giving your own gutter-height views to everyone on set."

"That brings up another thought." He settled back and waited for her to look around at him. "Matt's yet to show up on the set. Strange. Aren't you his top client?"

She stared at him for a long moment. "You're determined to leave me without anyone, anyone at all."

"That's right." He ignored the quick, bitter taste in his throat. "For the moment, you trust me and only me."

"They'll be calling me soon. I'm going to go lie down." Without looking at him again, she walked to the back of the trailer and through a doorway.

Quinn had a sudden fierce urge to throw the bottle against the wall. Just to hear it shatter. She had no business making him feel guilty. He was looking out for her. That was what he was paid for. And it was easier all around if she was suspicious. If that meant she shed a few tears, it couldn't be helped. He wasn't worried about it. He didn't give a damn.

Swearing, he slammed the bottle down on the table beside him. Lecturing himself all the way, he strode through the trailer to the bedroom. "Look, Chantel—"

She was sitting at the foot of the bed, staring down at an envelope in her hands. He smelled the dark, sweet scent of wild roses before he saw them on the dresser.

"I can't open it," she murmured. When she looked up at him, something twisted in his stomach. It wasn't just her pallor. It wasn't just the fear he could see in the way her fingers shook. It was the complete and utter despair in her eyes. "I just can't take any more."

"You don't have to." With a compassion he thought had been erased in him years before, he sat beside her and gathered her close. "That's what I'm here for." He slipped the envelope out of her numb fingers. "I don't want you to open any more of the letters. If they come, you give them to me."

"I don't want to know what it says." She shut her eyes and hated herself for it. "Just rip it up."

"Don't worry about it." He stuffed the letter into his back pocket as he pressed a kiss to the top of her head. He had questions to ask, a lot of questions as to who might have gone into her dressing room that day. "Part of the deal is that you trust me. Just let me take care of things."

The head resting against his shoulder shook once in quick denial. "You can't take care of the way this makes me feel. I always wanted to be someone. I always wanted to feel important. Is that why this is happening?" With a dry sob, she pulled away from him. "Maybe you were right. Maybe I asked for this."

"Stop it." He took her hard by the shoulders and prayed she'd control the tears he could see were threatening. "I was out of line. You're beautiful, you're talented, and you've made use of it. That doesn't mean you're to blame for someone's sickness."

"But it's me that he wants," she said quietly. "And I'm afraid."

"I'm not going to let anything happen to you."

She let out a deep breath as her hand wrapped around his. "Sign that in blood?"

He smiled and ran a fingertip down her cheek. "Whose?"

Needing the contact, she rested her cheek against his for a moment. The gesture left him shaken. "Thanks."

"Sure."

"Look, I know I haven't been making this easy for you." She drew back again. As he'd hoped, the tears hadn't fallen. "I haven't wanted to."

"Trouble is my business. Besides, I like your style."

"While we're being nice to each other, I guess I'll say I like yours, too."

"A red-letter day," he murmured, and brought her hand to his lips.

It was a mistake. They both realized it the instant the contact was made. Over their joined fingers, their gazes met and held. She thought she could feel the tension jump from his palm to hers. This wasn't a matter of temptation, or of anger, or of passion flaring quickly, but of need. She needed to feel his arms around her again, holding her tight. She needed to feel his lips on hers, warm, hard, demanding. Everything else would fade, she knew, if only they came together now.

Their hands were still joined, but she didn't protest as his fingers tightened painfully on hers. What was he thinking? It suddenly seemed imperative that she understand, that she see, what he felt in his mind, in his heart. Did he want her, could he possibly want her as badly this moment as she wanted him . . . ?

No other woman had ever made him ache like this. Not just from wanting. No other woman had ever made his blood swim. Not just from looking. He thought it would be possible to sit there through eternity and just look at that face. Was it only her beauty? Could it possibly be that he was twisted around inside because of a flawless facade?

Or was it something else, something that seemed to glow from within? There was something elusive, almost secretive, that showed in her eyes only if you looked quickly and carefully enough. He thought he saw it now. Then all he could think of was how much he wanted her.

With his free hand he reached up to trail his fingers through her hair. Spun gold, like an angel's. That's what it made him think of. But she was flesh and blood. Not a fantasy, a woman. He leaned closer, then watched her lashes flutter down.

The knock on the trailer door had her shooting up like an arrow out of a bow. She put both hands to her face but shook her head when Quinn reached for her.

"No, it's all right. That's just my call to go on the set."

"Sit down. I'll tell them you're not feeling well."

"No." She dropped her hands to her sides. "No, this isn't going to interfere with my work." The fingers of her left hand balled into a fist, but he could see she was working to regain control. "I can't let that happen." Turning her head, she stared at the roses on the table. "I won't let it."

He wanted to overrule her but knew this was the one thing he'd admired about her from the first. She was strong, strong enough to fight back. "Okay. You want a few more minutes?"

"Yeah, maybe." She walked to the window and drew the curtains aside to let in more sun. It was frightening, much too frightening to think about darkness. At night she was alone with her thoughts and her imagination. The sun was out, she reminded herself, sighing deeply. She had work to do.

"Would you mind letting them know I'll be out in a minute?"

"I'll take care of it." He hesitated, wanting to go to her, knowing it would be a mistake for both of them. "I'll be right outside, Chantel. Don't come out until you're ready."

"I'll be fine."

She waited until she heard him walk away before she dropped her forehead onto the glass. Weeping would be such a relief. Weeping, screaming, just letting go, would ease the hammerlock her nerves had on her system. But she couldn't let go, any more than she could allow herself to get churned up like this. There were hours more to put in that day. She needed her wits, and her stamina.

She'd make it, Chantel promised herself. Drawing a deep breath, she turned from the window. The flowers were gone. She stared at the table with a foolish sense of relief. He'd taken them away. She hadn't even had to ask.

What kind of a man was he? Rude and rough one moment, tender the next. Why couldn't he be easy to understand and easy to dismiss? With a shake of her head, she started down to the front of the trailer. He was impossible to understand. And he stirred things in her. He was anything but the kind of man a woman could be comfortable with. And she felt so safe knowing he was close by.

If she hadn't known herself so well, been so certain of her own control, she would almost have believed she was falling in love with him.

Chapter Six

It was anything but a quiet, restful week, though Chantel spent a good chunk of it in bed. The bed was big and plush and ornate—and it was on the set, on soundstage D. The major scene to be shot was her wedding night—Hailey's wedding night—not to the man she loved but to the man she wanted to love.

The props included an ice bucket with champagne, a full-length sable draped over a chair and a table laden with roses that had to be spritzed constantly to keep them fresh under the lights. Don Sterling, a relative unknown, had been chosen to play the man she would marry. He'd been selected mainly because of looks and chemistry. Though his final reading with Chantel had been excellent, his nerves had him blowing the scene a half-dozen times during the morning.

Locked in his arms, Chantel felt him tighten up. Before he could do so himself, she flubbed the scene, hoping to take some of the pressure off him.

"Sorry." She gave a delicate shrug. "Can we take five, Mary? I'm getting stale."

"Make it ten," Rothschild ordered, then turned to consult with her assistant.

"How about a cup of coffee?" Chantel accepted the robe she was handed and slipped into it as she smiled at Don.

"Only if I can drown myself in it."

"Let's try drinking it first." She signaled to Larry, then found two seats in a relatively quiet corner. When she saw Quinn start to approach, she shook her head and leaned closer to Don. "It's a tough scene."

"It shouldn't be." He ran a hand through a mass of thick, dark hair.

"Look, the order they're shooting this miniseries in, we've only had a couple of scenes together so far. The first thing you know, we're married and on our honeymoon." She took the coffee from Larry. "I don't know about you, but I think it's easier to jump into bed with someone if you have more than a passing acquaintance."

He held the coffee in both hands and managed a chuckle. "I'm supposed to be an actor."

"Me too."

"You could run through this scene with your eyes closed." He sipped the coffee, then, with a sound of disgust, set it aside. "I'll be honest. You intimidate the hell out of me." When she only lifted a brow, he let out a long breath and looked away. "When my agent called and told me I had this part and that I'd be playing opposite you, I almost went into a coma."

"That makes it tough to work up any passion." She put a hand on his. "Look, your reading with me was great. No one else even came close."

"The bit in Hailey's art studio." He picked up his coffee with a rueful look. "Not a bed in sight."

"The first love scene I ever played was opposite Scott Baron. Hollywood legend—the world's sexiest man. I had to kiss him, and my teeth were chattering, I was so scared. He took me aside, bought me a tuna-fish sandwich and told me stories, half of which were certainly lies. Then he told me something true. He said all actors are children and all children like to play games. If we didn't play the game well, we'd have to grow up and get real jobs."

The tension she'd spotted around his mouth had already relaxed. "Did it work?"

"It was either that or the tuna fish, but we went back on the set and played the game."

"You stole that movie from him."

She smiled. "I've heard it said." She continued to smile as she sipped coffee. "Don't think I'm going to let you steal this one from me."

"You blew that last line on purpose."

She could become a prima donna with little more than a tilt of her head. "I don't know what you're talking about."

"You have a reputation for being cold and driven," he mused. "I never expected you to be, well, nice."

"Don't let it get around." Rising, she offered him a hand. "Let's get this honeymoon off the ground."

The scene went like clockwork. Quinn didn't know what Chantel had said during her brief huddle with her co-star, but it had turned the trick. For himself, he was learning not to tense up when Chantel was in someone else's arms. It was difficult to work up any resentment when so much technology went into setting the scene. The lights had to be adjusted to simulate candlelight. Chantel and Don lay in the bed, he stripped to the waist, she in a thigh-length chemise. The camera was nearly on top of them. The director knelt on the bed and went over the moves. On cue, Chantel and Don turned to each other as if they were the only two people on earth.

It was so easy for her, Quinn reflected, to fabricate passion. When he watched her like this, he wondered if she had any real feelings at all. Her emotions were turned off and on as direction indicated. Like an exquisitely crafted puppet, he thought, beautifully formed on the outside, hollow within.

Yet he'd held her himself. He'd felt passion shimmer in her. The feelings, needs, uncertainties had been there for him to touch. Had that been just part of her act, as well? It shouldn't matter to him, he reminded himself as he lighted a cigarette. He couldn't let it matter. She was an assignment and nothing more. If she stirred feelings in him, as she did with uncanny regularity, he would just have to take a step back. Involvement with a woman like Chantel O'Hurley was suicide for a man who didn't have himself under complete control.

But when he looked at her, his mouth went dry.

Just desire, he told himself. Or, more accurately, lust. There was no denying that wanting her was as

easy, as natural, as drawing breath. But it hadn't been
desire or lust he had felt when he'd held her in his arms
moments ago.

So he had some compassion left in him. Quinn
found a chair, then discovered he was too wired to sit.
He'd have been pretty low if he hadn't felt sympathy
or been able to offer comfort to a frightened and vulnerable woman.

But it hadn't been sympathy, it had been rage. He
recognized it even now, that hot, bubbling fury at the
thought of his woman being threatened. His woman.
That was the problem. The longer he was with her, the
easier it became to think of her as his.

Take a step back from that, Doran, he ordered
himself. And make it fast. If he didn't pull himself
together soon, he was going to be in over his head. A
man could only hold his breath for so long.

He crushed out his cigarette and wished the
interminable day would end.

There had been two more letters that week, letters
he hadn't shown her. The tone had shifted from
pleading to near-whimpering. It worried Quinn more
than the subtle menace the earlier letters had con-
tained. The author was about to break. When he did,
Quinn was certain it would be like a geyser, fast and
violent. Because his own patience was thin, he hoped
it would be soon. It would give him some outlet for the
fury building inside him.

"That's a wrap, people. Don't have too much fun
over the weekend. We want you alive and coherent on
Monday."

Still in her chemise, Chantel sat on the edge of the
bed and held an earnest conversation with Don.

Jealousy. Where it had come from and why, Quinn couldn't begin to answer. Quinn had always been a live-and-let-live sort of person. If a woman, even a woman he was involved with, decided to look to another man, that was her prerogative. No strings, no pain, no complications. He'd managed very well that way for years. He'd never experienced this sharp twist in the gut over a woman before. He felt it now, and he didn't like it, or himself. Unable to stop himself, he walked over and drew Chantel to her feet.

"Playtime's over," he said, and pulled her with him.

"Let go of me," she told him under her breath as he walked toward her dressing room. Larry started forward with her robe, saw the look on Quinn's face and backed away.

"Just shut up."

"Doran, this is my place of business, but if you keep it up I'm going to create the biggest, juiciest scene even your twisted brain can imagine. You'll read about it in the paper for weeks."

"Go ahead."

She set her teeth. "Just what is your problem?"

"You're my problem, lady. For a woman who should be watching her step, you were awfully chummy with that kid."

"Kid? Don? For God's sake, he's an associate, and he's not a kid. He's two years older than I am."

"You were steaming up his contact lenses."

"Don't you get tired of playing the same tune?" She jerked her arm free and pulled open her dressing room door herself. "If you've been doing your job, you already have a report on Don Sterling and you know

he's practically engaged to a woman he's been involved with for two years.''

''And the woman in question is three thousand
miles away in New York.''

''I know that.'' As she pushed her hair out of her
face the chemise shifted, whispering silkily over her
skin. ''He was just telling me that he's going to catch
the red-eye to the east coast so that he can spend the
weekend with her. He's in love, Doran, though I realize you might not understand the term.''

''A man could be in love with another woman and
still want you.''

She slammed the dressing room door and leaned
back against it. ''What would you know about love?
What would you know about any genuine emotion?''

''You want emotion?'' He slapped his palms on the
door at either side of her head. Though her eyes
widened in shock, she stood firm. ''You want a taste
of the kind of emotion you push out of a man? The
real thing, angel, not something out of the pages of a
script. Think you can take it?''

Her heart was beating in her throat. It was crazy to
actually *want* to be dragged against him, to be plundered, drained and weakened. She could see nothing
but raw fury in his eyes, but somehow she relished it.
If it was all he could feel for her, it was almost enough.
She'd be willing to settle, and that scared the hell out
of her.

''Just leave me alone,'' she whispered.

''You're smart to be scared of me.''

''I'm not scared of you.''

He leaned a little closer. ''You're trembling.''

"I'm furious." She pressed her damp palms against the door.

"Maybe you are. And maybe that's because you're not quite sure of what happens next. It's not written out for you, is it, Chantel? Not so easy to turn the switch off and on."

"Get out of my way."

"Not just yet. I want to know what you feel." His body pressed lightly against hers. "I want to know *if* you feel."

She was losing ground, and what she had left was shaky. If he touched her now, really touched her, she was afraid she would lose everything. How could she tell him what she felt, when what she felt was against all the rules? She wanted to be held, protected, cherished, loved. If she told him that, he'd only smile and take what he wanted. She'd been left empty before, and it would never, never happen to her again.

Chantel lifted her chin and waited until his lips hovered an inch from hers. "You're no better than the man I hired you to protect me from."

He stepped back as if she'd slapped him. The stunned look on his face made her want to reach out to him. Instead, she pressed back against the door and waited for his next move.

"Get some clothes on," he told her, and turned aside. As she walked away, he reached into the refrigerator for a beer. She was right. Quinn twisted off the top and took two long swallows. He'd wanted to frighten, to weaken, then take her there, on his terms. If he could have proven to himself that what happened between them was cold and calculated, he might have believed she meant nothing to him.

He'd wanted to hurt her. She was threatening his peace of mind, and he'd needed to strike back. He would have used sex to purge himself and to repay her for the restless nights. The wave of self-disgust was as unfamiliar and as unpalatable as the surge of jealousy he'd felt earlier.

He'd told himself to take a step back, yet he'd taken a leap forward and had landed in the mire. He'd done things and seen things in his life that would have left others pale and speechless. Yet, for the first time in his life, he felt truly soiled.

When he heard her coming back, he tossed the bottle into the trash. She wore rose-colored linen slacks and a jacket with a muted floral design. She looked cool, composed and nothing like the restless, questing character she'd played all day.

Without a word she walked by him and put her hand on the knob. Before she could open the door, Quinn placed his hand over hers. He cursed himself when she stiffened and sent him a cool, disinterested look.

"You're entitled to take a few shots," he said mildly. "I won't even duck."

For a moment she said nothing. Then, as the anger dissipated she sighed. She was tired, drained from the constant play and replay of emotion. "I'll take a rain check."

As she twisted the knob, he tightened his hand on hers. "Chantel..."

"What?"

He wanted to apologize. It wasn't his style, but he wanted badly to tell her he was sorry. The need was there, but the words wouldn't come. "Nothing. Let's go."

They rode home in silence while guilt ate at him. It would fade, he assured himself. It was just one more of the odd emotions she drew out of him. She looked exhausted now, though he remembered she'd looked fine—in fact, she'd looked wonderful—before he'd...

Damn it, he couldn't waste his time worrying about things like that. He had a job to do, and if he'd stepped out of line, it wouldn't happen again. Case closed. He'd see her into the house, make certain the doors were locked and the alarm on. Then he'd relax. He needed to go over the report from his field man, though he was already aware they'd turned up nothing on the stationery. They needed a mistake. So far, no matter how mentally unstable Chantel's admirer was, he'd been smart.

Quinn sat back as the limo cruised through the gates, wishing he could say the same thing about himself.

He preferred to act on impulse. As he stepped out of the car, he didn't hesitate or think twice. Taking Chantel by the hand, he began to lead her around the side of the house.

"What are you doing?"

"It's Friday night and I'm sick of being cooped up in that house. We're going out to eat." He stopped by his car and nodded to one of the men who patrolled the grounds.

"Did it ever occur to you that I might not feel like going out?"

"Where I go, you go." He opened the door and started to nudge her inside.

"Doran, I've put in sixty hours this week and I'm tired. I don't want to go to a restaurant and be stared at."

"Who said anything about a restaurant? Just get in, angel, you don't want to embarrass yourself in front of my man over there."

"I'm not hungry."

"I am." He gave her a quick shove, then shut the door behind her.

"Has anyone ever mentioned that you're totally lacking in manners or any of the other social graces?"

"Constantly."

He gunned the motor and sent the car barreling down the drive. Chantel reached for her seat belt. "If you wreck this heap with me in it, the producers are going to have your head on a platter." For a moment she wondered if it wouldn't be worth it.

"Nervous?"

"You don't make me nervous, Doran, you simply annoy me."

"Everyone's got to be good at something." He turned the radio dial, and loud, throbbing rock poured out. Chantel closed her eyes and pretended to ignore him.

When the car came to a halt, she didn't move. Determined to show nothing but indifference, she sat still as the silence grew. Outside the car she heard the bump and grind of weekend traffic heating up. She had no idea where they were and told herself she didn't care. Quinn's door opened and closed, and she still didn't move. But she did open her eyes.

She saw him stride up to the little fast-food joint and fought back a chuckle. She would not be amused. At home she could have had a nice glass of wine and a crisp salad with her cook's special herb dressing. God knew what Quinn was carrying back to the car in the white bag. She simply wouldn't eat, she told herself. She'd let him get whatever he had in his system out, but she wouldn't eat.

Closing her eyes again, she tried not to react as aromas, really wonderful aromas, filled the car. He glanced over, smiled, then started the car again.

Again she didn't know where he was heading, but the road began to wind and the sounds of traffic faded. She very nearly dozed off as her system absorbed the quiet sunset drive. She hadn't realized how much she'd needed to get away, from work, from her house, maybe from herself. It was going to be hard not to be grateful to him. But Chantel told herself she would manage.

When the car stopped again, she refused to move. Curiosity gnawed at her, but she kept her eyes firmly shut. Saying nothing, Quinn reached for the bag, rattling it so that the scent seeped through the car. Then he stepped out and closed the door behind him.

Chantel's stomach contracted, reminding her that the plate of fruit and cheese she'd had for lunch wasn't enough. The least he could do was force her to eat something, the way he'd forced her to do other things she hadn't wanted to. But no, she thought as her temper began to rise, he would just go off and gobble up whatever was in that bag and let her starve.

Opening her eyes, Chantel pushed open her door. As she let it slam behind her, the noise seemed to echo forever. Astonished, she looked around her.

They were farther up in the hills than she had ever gone before. Below, miles below, L.A. stretched forever, glistening just a bit as lights winked on. She could see the separate levels of color in the sky as the sun went down. Deep blue led to paler blue, and paler blue to mauve and rose and pink, all glistening with gold. The first star blinked to life overhead and waited patiently for others to join it. The breeze whistled through the brush, but the city she knew so well seemed encased in glass, it was so quiet.

"Pretty impressive, isn't it?"

She turned and saw Quinn leaning against a giant *H*. The Hollywood sign, she realized, and nearly laughed. She'd seen it so often it no longer registered. From the hills it looked white, invulnerable and perhaps immortal. Up close, like the town it heralded, it was mostly illusion. It was big and bold, certainly, but a little grimy, a little shaky. Graffiti was etched in clumps near the base.

"It could use a fresh coat of paint," she murmured.

"No, it's more honest this way." He kicked aside a beer can. "Teenagers come up here to hang out—and make out."

She tilted her head. "And you?"

"Oh, I just like the view." He climbed over a few rocks effortlessly and planted himself on the base of an *L*. "And the quiet. If you're lucky, you can come up here and not hear a thing, except for a coyote now and again."

"Coyote?" She glanced over her shoulder.

"That's right." Not bothering to hide a grin, he dug in the bag. "Want a taco?"

"A taco? You dragged me all the way up here to eat tacos?"

"Got some beer."

"Lovely."

"It's getting warm. You'd better drink up."

"I don't want anything."

"Suit yourself." He unwrapped a taco and bit into it. "Got some fries, too," he said with a full mouth. "A little greasy, maybe, but they're not cold yet."

"I don't know how I can resist." She turned away from him to look down at the city again. As fate would have it, the breeze carried the spicy scents to her. Her mouth watered. Chantel scowled down at the lights and wished Quinn Doran to hell.

"I guess a woman like you turns her nose up if it isn't champagne and caviar."

Spinning around, Chantel stood with the city and the sunset at her back. Quinn felt his heart turn over in his chest. She'd never looked more beautiful. "You know nothing about me, nothing at all." Her voice had an edge to it now, a dull, gritty edge that had his eyes narrowing. "I spent nearly the first twenty years of my life shuffling from town to town, eating in greasy spoons or over a hot plate in a motel room. Sometimes, if we were lucky and the gig was good, we got to wolf down a meal in the hotel kitchen. If we weren't so lucky, there were always hard-boiled eggs and coffee. Don't you sit there in your smug little world and toss stones at me, Doran. You don't know what I am, or who I am. All you know is what I've made myself."

Slowly he set the beer on the rock behind him. "Well, well," he said quietly. "I wouldn't read any of that in your official bio, would I?"

She could only stare. What was it about him that made her lose control? Why had she been compelled to yank herself out and expose her roots to him?

"I want to go back."

"No, you don't." His voice wasn't curt now, but gentle. It was that gentleness that chipped away her defenses. "There's no one here but me, Chantel. Why don't we just sit up here and look down at the rest of the world for a while?"

Before she'd thought it through, she'd taken a step toward him. When he rose and held out a hand to help her up, she reached for it without hesitation. Hesitation came the moment his palm met hers. She remembered the feel of it, the strength of it, and her gaze lifted and locked with his. They stood there a moment with the sky darkening around them. Then he hauled her up.

"I'm sorry." The apology surprised him as much as it did her.

"For what?" She started to draw her hand from his, but he reached up to brush back her hair.

"For what happened before. I don't know why, but something about you makes me edgy."

She kept her eyes level with his. "Then we're even."

The wind tossed the hair back from his face. In every situation, he knew, there came a time for honesty. Perhaps this was such a time. "Chantel, I want you. I'm having a hell of a time dealing with that."

Other men had wanted her, other men had told her so in more beautiful ways. But the words had never made it difficult for her to breathe. "I could fire you."

"It wouldn't matter."

"No, I don't suppose it would." She looked away, surprised at how strong a longing could be. "Quinn, I can't go to bed with you."

"I figured you'd feel that way."

"Quinn." She took his hand again as he started to step away. "I don't know what you think my reasons are, but I guarantee you, you're wrong."

"Not your style," he said, picking up his beer again. "Not your league."

Chantel snatched the bottle from him and heaved it. Spray spewed against the rocks before the glass shattered. "Don't tell me what I think. *Don't* tell me what I feel."

"Then you tell me." He grabbed her and pulled her against him.

"I don't have to tell you *anything*. I don't have to explain myself to you. Damn you, I just want some peace. I just want a few hours where the pressure's off. I don't know if I can take being squeezed at all sides for much longer."

"Okay, okay." His hold gentled immediately. As he murmured, his hand stroked up and down her back. "You're right. I didn't bring you up here to fight with you, but you make me edgy."

"Let's just go back."

"No, sit down. Please," he added, brushing his lips over her hair. "Let's see if we can stay here for an hour together and not pick on each other. Have a taco."

He smiled at her as he pulled her down to sit. Chantel took one look at the bag and gave up.

"I'm starving."

"Yeah, I figured as much." He handed her a wad of paper napkins. For the next few minutes they ate in companionable silence. "Was your childhood rough?"

Chantel stopped in the act of opening a little packet of salt for the fries. "Oh, no, I didn't mean that. It was just different. My parents are entertainers. They've been a song-and-dance team for over thirty years. The six of us trouped around the country, and some of the places we played were dives. But my family..." She smiled, absently accepting a beer. "They're wonderful. Trace did some routines, but he was best on the piano. It always used to frustrate me that no matter how hard I tried I couldn't play better than he did."

"Sibling rivalry."

"Sure. Life would be pretty dull without it. Trace and I were always so much alike that we couldn't stay off each other's backs for very long. There was never much of that between my sisters and me. We were just too much a part of each other." She sipped the beer straight from the bottle and looked down at the city below. "We still are. God, sometimes it's so hard to be away from them. When we were little we made all these plans for keeping the act together forever." She remembered them with a little pang of regret. "Then we grew up."

"What kind of an act?"

Laughing, she licked salt from her fingers. "You never heard of the O'Hurley Triplets?"

"Sorry."

"You'd probably be sorrier if you had heard of us. Three-part harmony, show tunes and popular music, a few old standards thrown in."

"You sing?"

"Doran, I don't just *sing*, I'm terrific."

"You never sing in your movies."

She shrugged a shoulder. "It hasn't come up. Matt keeps saying we should give the public a surprise one of these days and get a guest spot where I can do a few numbers, and dance, maybe too. Yes," she added when he slanted a look at her, "I can dance—my father would have died of shame otherwise."

"Why don't you do it?"

"The time just hasn't been right. Besides, I've been concentrating on what I'm best at."

He balled up the empty bag and set it beside his feet. "What's that?"

She gave him a quick, mocking look. "Playing roles."

Instead of smiling back, he tucked her hair behind her ear. "My guess is you're not playing one now."

She turned her head quickly and looked out. The sky was nearly dark, but there was only a smattering of stars. "You can't be sure. I'm not sure myself half the time."

"I think you're sure."

When she turned her head back, his mouth was close. Close and tempting. "Don't. I told you I can't—" But his lips brushed over hers, light as a whisper, and stopped her cold.

"Do you know how I felt when you were lying on that bed with Sterling today?"

"No. I don't want to know. I've told you, it's my job."

She was already half seduced; he could hear it in her voice. There was a thrill of anticipation along his skin as he thought of taking her beyond the next step. "I wasn't sure if I wanted to put my hands around his throat or yours, but I did know I wanted you to look at me the way you were looking at him."

"It's just a part. I'm supposed to—"

"There aren't any cameras here, Chantel. Just you and me. And that's what I think you're afraid of. No one's here to tell you what you're supposed to be feeling. No one's going to yell 'Cut' before things go just a little too far."

"I don't need anyone to tell me what to feel. I don't need anyone," she repeated, and tugged his mouth back to hers.

She wanted it. She wanted to experience the wild flood of sensation he could bring her. No one else. She could tell him there'd been no one else who had touched her just this way, but he'd never believe her. The image, her image, was all but carved in stone, and she'd polished it herself. What she was inside belonged to her. She was determined that no one would ever share that part of her again.

But she could have this, the heat, the need, the desperation. She could take this, and she could give it back to him as long as she promised herself she wouldn't give him too much. As long as she didn't give him everything.

The sky darkened above them, and the wind whistled through the brush.

She was pulling something from him, drawing something out of him. He couldn't seem to stop her. His hands weren't steady as they reached up to tangle in her hair. His mind was swimming in a mist of his needs, but the needs weren't as simple as he'd told himself they had to be. Desire could make you ache, but it shouldn't be allowed to slice you open.

He wanted to take her there, there in the rocks and dirt. He wanted to treat her like porcelain, delicately and with intense care.

His body was coiled tight, ready to explode. God, he had to touch her, even if it was only once. In one smooth stroke he brought his hand along her leg, over her hip, until he found and cupped her breast. She was small, incredibly fragile, and as soft as water. Compelled, he flicked open the two buttons on her jacket to feast on the warm flesh inside.

It had been so long, so long since she had allowed herself to be touched, since she'd felt the need for intimacy. She wanted his hands on her, his lips on her, his body hard and demanding against hers. The hell with where they were, who they were. The hell with the price she would surely pay for allowing herself to love him.

In an act of surrender that left him shaken, she brought her arms around him and buried her face against his throat.

"Chantel . . ." He started to tilt her face up, longing, for reasons he couldn't be sure of, to see what was in her eyes. Then he heard it, a rustling in the brush that came once, then twice, and had him tensing.

"What? What is it?" She had heard it, too, and she dug her fingers into his arm. "An animal?"

"Yeah, probably." But he didn't think so. His nerves were humming as he drew her aside.

"Where are you going?"

"To take a look. Just stay here."

"Quinn—" She was already standing.

"Just sit tight. It's probably just a rabbit."

It was no rabbit. She heard it in his voice. He wasn't nearly the actor she was. Fear made her want to cringe away. Pride had her matching him step for step. "I'm going with you."

"Chantel, sit down."

"No." She held his arm and scrambled over the rocks.

Resigned, Quinn helped her regain her balance. "All right, then, be careful. You get any scratches on that skin and I'll get blamed for it."

"Damn right."

Because the light had faded, he went to his car and found a flashlight. "Why don't you just sit—"

"No."

Swearing under his breath, he took her by the arm again. He walked slowly toward the brush, casually angling his body to shield hers. "Lot of game up here," he began, but his muscles were coiled and ready. He moved softly, quietly pushing brush aside as Chantel hung on to his hand.

"I remember, coyote."

"Yeah." He crouched down when he spotted prints in the soft dirt. The beam of his light swept over them, then held.

Chantel pressed her lips together. "I guess coyote don't wear shoes."

"None that I've seen." He hated hearing that hint of fear in her voice. "Look, it was probably just a kid."

"No. You don't believe that and neither do I." She stared down at the scuffed prints. The brush where they were wasn't more than five yards from where they'd been sitting a moment before. "Someone was watching us, and I think we both know why. God." She pressed her fingers to her eyes. "He was here. He was right here, just watching. Why doesn't he stop? Why doesn't he—"

"Get a hold of yourself." Quinn took her by the shoulders and shook. She took a deep breath, then nearly screamed when the sound of an engine starting echoed back to them.

"He followed me." She stopped trembling. Her body felt too numb even for that. "How many other times has he been there, watching me?"

"I don't know." Frustrated, Quinn stared out at the darkening road. Even if he dared leave her there alone, he'd never catch up with the other car now. "Just remember, he's watching us now. I'm not going to let him get to you."

"For how long?" she said quietly, then turned away. "I want to go back."

Chapter Seven

"It just doesn't seem like we're getting anywhere." Chantel poured herself a brandy, then freshened Matt's glass.

"I'm sorry, Chantel. I'd have sworn if anyone could dig up an answer it would be Quinn."

"I'm not blaming him." Cupping her brandy in both hands, she walked to the window. The sun was setting. It reminded her of another dusk. With the snifter at her lips, she watched night fall.

"You've changed your tune from the first time we talked about him."

More than you know, she thought, but shrugged her shoulders. "I can't claim he's not doing everything he can, that's all."

"Then maybe I have to," Matt returned, hating to hear the tired resignation in her voice. "He hasn't come up with anything solid. What about the letters?''

"The stationery the letters were written on could have come from any of dozens of dime or drugstores in the L.A. area. There's no way for him to trace it.''

"But the flowers." Restless, Matt walked to the white baby grand, then back to the fireplace, his cigarette trailing expensive smoke behind him. "There has to be a way to trace where they were bought.''

"Apparently not. Most of the time they just appear in my dressing room or somewhere on the set. So far no one's seen who delivers them.''

"Florists keep records.''

"If you pay cash and pick up the flowers yourself, there wouldn't be any reason to ask for ID.'' She pressed her fingers to the back of her neck, pressed and released, fruitlessly working at a knot of tension.

"Someone might remember who—''

"Quinn tells me his men have done a sweep of the florists in the area. There's nothing.''

"The phone calls.''

"They haven't been able to get a trace.''

"Damn it.'' If something—or someone—existed, Matt felt there must be a way to find him. "Chantel, maybe you should reconsider the police.''

She turned back. With him, she could allow the weariness to show. "Matt, do you really think they could do more than Quinn's done?''

"I don't know." The quiet desperation in her eyes was difficult to face. He scowled down at his brandy. "I just don't know." Setting down his drink, he crossed to her. "I was sure this thing would be tied up in a matter of days.''

"It's not as simple as that. It seems he's clever, or cautious, at any rate."

"Are you sure you've told Quinn everything you know?"

"What I don't tell him, he finds out." Nerves had her swirling the brandy around and around in her glass but not drinking. "He's running investigations on everyone I know."

"Well, that—"

"Including you."

He stopped to stare at her. With a grimace, he stuck his hands in his pockets and nervously pulled out his lighter. "He's thorough, anyway."

"I don't like it, Matt." For the first time, real emotion came into her voice, into her eyes. "I feel...I don't know, sleazy when I think of him poking into the keyholes of people's lives, and on my account."

Not quite comfortable, Matt slipped an arm around her shoulder. "Look, baby, if rattling a few skeletons in my closet helps get to the bottom of this thing, then it's worth it." He was silent a moment, then cleared his throat. "So, what did he find out?"

"About you?"

"That's a good place to start."

"I don't know." Letting out a long breath, she leaned her head on his shoulder. The sun had disappeared completely, leaving only a hint of color streaking the clouds. "I told him I didn't want to know, Matt. He started to give me reports on people like Larry and James Brewster, and I hated it." She could still remember his cool disapproval of her cowardice. Chantel gritted her teeth against the memory. "We agreed that I'd take the precautions he'd outlined, and that he'd keep what information he had to himself.''

With one hand he flicked on the silver monogrammed lighter he'd been toying with. "That's burying your head in the sand, Chantel."

"I don't care."

"Listen, there's no one, certainly no one who's made it past twenty, who hasn't done something they're ashamed of, something they'd prefer to keep covered." He shifted but made himself speak matter-of-factly. "Quinn's got a right to investigate, and because of who he is, nothing he finds out would go any farther."

"Thanks for the vote of confidence." Quinn paused in the doorway and studied them. Matt still had his arm around her. Chantel's head rested on his shoulder as the dim light through the window behind them settled over her hair. She looked comfortable with him, Quinn realized with a twinge of resentment. She looked as though she'd be content to snuggle up against him and sit for hours.

"I'm the one who recommended you," Matt said easily. "I'd hate to say I'd made a mistake."

"You didn't." Quinn crossed to the bar to pour himself a double shot of brandy. "How've you been, Matt? I thought we'd be seeing more of you."

"I've been tied up."

Sensing the restraint between them, Chantel took a step forward. "Just stop it," she told Quinn. "Don't start on him."

"You're telling me how to do my job again, angel."

"I'm not going to allow you to use your third degree on my friends."

Quinn tossed back his brandy. "Too bad I left my rubber hose upstairs."

"Why don't we sit down?" Matt put a hand on Chantel's shoulder. "I appreciate it, babe, but it isn't necessary." His gaze locked with Quinn's. "I guess when I told Chantel to hire you I should have figured you'd dig it up."

Quinn met the look, but there was nothing to show his feelings. "Yeah, you should have."

"Dig what up?" she demanded.

Quinn lifted his glass in a half salute. "Maybe you'd like to tell her yourself."

"Yes, I would. Sit down, Chantel." When she only looked at him, Matt squeezed her shoulder. "Please, sit down."

She felt the now-familiar churning in her stomach as she chose a chair. "All right, I'm sitting."

"A few years back, almost ten now, I ran into some financial problems." He retrieved his brandy and took a deep swallow.

"Matt, you don't have to tell me about this."

"Yes, I do." He looked back at Quinn. "I want you to hear it from me." He held up a hand before she could protest again. "Just hear me out. When I'm finished maybe I won't feel as though the blade's about to fall on my neck."

"All right," she said evenly, but her left hand moved restlessly on the arm of her chair.

"Gambling," he said with a hint of fear in his voice.

"Matt, that's absurd." She nearly laughed. "You won't even play gin for matchsticks."

"That's now. This was then. I couldn't keep away from the horses." With a self-mocking smile, he looked back at her. "It's a fever, and mine ran pretty hot until I'd dropped more than I could afford. I was desperate. I'd borrowed money from a certain group of people—the kind who break small bones in your body if they don't get their weekly payment."

"Oh, Matt."

"I needed ten thousand I didn't have. I forged a check. A client's check." He closed his eyes before he took another swallow. Chantel sat in silence. "Of course, it didn't take long for it to come to light. My client didn't want the publicity, so he didn't press charges. I mortgaged my soul, then hocked the rest to pay him back. You could call it a turning point in my life." This time he laughed, but there was no humor in it. "My career was on the line, so I took a good hard look at myself. Because what I saw left me pretty shaken, I checked into an organization for obsessive gamblers. It's been nearly eight years since I've been to the track. Even though gambling nearly ruined my life, I have to fight the urge every day to place just one bet." He set down his glass and looked at her. "If you want another agent, I'll understand."

She rose slowly and walked to him. Without a word, she put her arms around him and gathered him close. Over his shoulder she sent Quinn a long, neutral look. "I don't want another agent. You know I insist on the best."

With a muffled laugh, he pressed a kiss to her brow. "You're a special lady."

"Someone's always telling me that."

He gripped her fingers hard, and she felt how damp his palms were. "I wouldn't let you down, Chantel."

"I know."

He kissed her again before he drew away. "I've got to get going. You'll call if there's anything I can do?"

"Of course."

He turned to Quinn. For a moment the men studied each other across the room. If there was regret on either side, they didn't show it. "Take care of her."

"I intend to."

With a brief nod, Matt let himself out.

Chantel turned on Quinn immediately. "How could you? How could you humiliate him that way?"

"It was necessary." But necessary or not, it left a foul taste in his mouth. Quinn poured another brandy, knowing that taste wouldn't be so easily washed away.

"Necessary? Why? What does a gambling debt nearly ten years ago have to do with what's happening to me now?"

"If a man can develop one obsession, he can develop another."

"That's ridiculous."

"No, that's a fact."

A quiver ran through her, not of fear but of anger. "Matt Burns has never attempted to be anything to me other than my agent and my friend. And he's had abundant opportunity."

"Would you have let him?"

Chantel took a cigarette, then flicked the table lighter three times before she managed to get it to flame. "What does that have to do with it?"

He came closer, curling his hand firmly around her arm. "Would you?"

"No." Tossing her head, she blew out smoke. "No."

"And he knows it." When she jerked her arm away, he watched her pace the room. "You're good with scenarios. Try this one. The man works with you for years, he watches you soar straight to the top. He's helped you, layer by layer, to build that illusion of cool, ice-hard sexuality. Maybe he wants what he helped to create."

A shiver ran down her spine, but her eyes were calm and level when she turned to him. "It doesn't play, Doran."

"It plays as well as anything else."

"No, it doesn't." The fear was back. She fought hard to keep it from showing. "Why wouldn't a man I know, a man I'm close to, just approach me openly?"

"Because he's a man you know, a man you're close to," Quinn countered. "He knows he doesn't have a chance with you on that level."

Impatient, she stubbed the cigarette out. "How would he know if he's never asked?"

Quinn put a hand to her cheek to stop her nervous pacing. "Don't you think a man knows when a woman's interested?" Running a thumb down her jaw, he brought her an inch closer. It was there, as it had been from the first, humming between them. She felt it, damn it, he knew she felt it, even though she refused to show that she did. "Don't you think he can look at a woman, see the way she looks at him, and know if they're going to be lovers?"

She put a hand to his wrist and carefully drew his away. Her skin felt as though it would stay warm for hours. "I'm tired," she told him. "I'm going to bed."

When he was alone, the brandy tempted him. Because it seemed too easy a way out, he turned his back on it. He went outside to walk the grounds.

Chantel was finding sleep harder and harder to come by. In the late hours she would toss and turn, then fall into a light doze, only to awake again, nervous and groggy, to toss and turn some more. Several times she had been tempted to give in and get a prescription for sleeping pills. Each time she remembered her promise never to tranquilize herself against pressure, personal or professional.

She thought of Matt, of the self-disgust and apology in his voice as he'd told her something she had no business knowing.

She thought of Quinn, firm and unyielding but offering Matt the chance to explain for himself.

Oddly enough, she thought of her brother and an argument they'd had when she'd been a teenager. Trace had threatened to knock some boy's block off if he got too familiar with her. Chantel remembered being furious at him for interfering, and telling everyone she could handle things.

Why wasn't she in control now?

She always had been. Even Trace had known then she hadn't needed him to stand up for her. Perhaps because she'd been one of three in the womb, she'd been born ready to handle her own problems. She'd faced tragedy, personal loss and disillusionment but had always managed to fight her way back. She wasn't fighting now, and she should be. It had never been necessary for her to look to a man for protection, and yet . . .

Then she thought of Quinn again and his promise to protect her. She wanted to believe him. When he was there, right beside her, she did.

But it was the middle of the night, and her brain was hazy. She only wanted to sleep. The sheets twisted around her as she turned again and finally drifted off.

When the phone rang, she groped for it. Half dreaming, she thought it was her mother calling to scold her for being late for rehearsal. "Yes," she mumbled into the receiver. "Yes, I'm coming."

"I can't sleep. I can't sleep for thinking of you."

The whisper had a low, desperate edge to it that shocked Chantel fully awake.

"You have to stop this."

"But I can't. I've tried, but I can't. Don't you know what you do to me? Every time I see you, every time I'm near you, I—"

"No!" she shouted into the phone. Then, to her disgust, she began to weep. "Please leave me alone. Please. I don't want to hear any more."

But she could hear him as she turned her face into the pillow. She could hear him still as she fumbled to hang up the phone. Even when she had the receiver cradled, she could hear his voice echoing in her head. Chantel curled into a ball and let the tears come.

Quinn was staring out his window when the phone rang. Cursing, he dashed across the room, hoping to get to it before it awakened Chantel. But the whispering had already started. For a moment he thought he recognized something—a speech pattern, accent, or turn of phrase. He tried to focus on it, block out the words themselves and Chantel's terror. Then his mouth tightened to a grim line as he heard Chantel plead, then begin to cry. He heard her hang up, then heard a man sobbing before the connection was broken.

After slamming down the receiver, Quinn plunged his hands into his pockets, his fingers balling into fists. He'd lost something, maybe something vital because his concentration and his objectivity had been broken when she'd begun to cry.

The woman was making him soft. He couldn't allow it. Wouldn't allow it. He had to leave her alone. She'd *want* to be alone, he told himself. She wouldn't like to have him see her now that she'd lost control. A woman like Chantel would shed her tears in private. Even if she looked for consolation, the last person she'd want it from was him. Struggling against an overpowering sense of rage and helplessness, he stalked back to the window.

She'd sounded so frightened.

He couldn't leave her alone now. Not now, he thought as he pounded his clenched hand lightly against the windowsill. She might want to be alone, but she needed to be with him. He only hoped he could figure out what to do once he was with her.

There were a few slashes of moonlight coming through her windows. They turned everything to silver. He came in quietly, hoping she'd fallen asleep again and that he could just check on her, maybe sit with her awhile without her being aware of it. If she knew how badly he wanted to be with her, protect her—damn it, cherish her—wouldn't that give her all the more reason to push him aside?

He'd never had to use caution with a woman before. Because, he was forced to admit, no woman had really mattered until her. And she mattered too much.

She wasn't asleep. Quinn could hear her muffled weeping as he crossed to the bed. He stopped where he was, terrified by the small, helpless sound. He knew how a grenade sounded when it exploded in the dirt and sent shrapnel hurtling through the air. He'd heard the horrific noise of gunfire and the unspeakable sound of a bullet striking flesh. Those were things he'd faced with more confidence than he faced Chantel's quiet sobbing with now.

If she had been angry, he could have played on it. If she had merely been frightened, he could have insulted her out of it. But she was weeping.

Soundlessly he went to the side of the bed and crouched down. Wishing he knew the right words but knowing he didn't, he laid a hand on her hair. At his touch she sprang up, screaming.

"It's me. It's only me." He took both her hands and squeezed. "Relax. No one's going to hurt you."

"Quinn." Her hand went limp in his, then tensed again as she fought for control. "You startled me."

"Sorry." The moonlight was strong enough that he could see her face, and the tears damp on her cheeks. "You okay?"

"Yes." Her chest was hurtfully tight, her throat raw from unshed tears. "Yes, I'm fine. I guess you heard the phone."

"I heard it." He dropped her hands because he was afraid he'd break her fingers. "Why don't I get you something? Water." He stuck his hands in his pockets again. "Something."

"No. I don't need anything." She brought the heels of her hands over her face to dry her tears. "I couldn't keep him talking. I just couldn't do it."

"It's all right."

"No, it's not." Bringing her knees up, she dropped her head on them. "It's my problem, and as long as I keep running from it it's not going away. Everything you've said so far has been true, everything you've done has been right, and I haven't been holding up my end."

"Nobody's blaming you, Chantel." He started to reach out for her again, to touch her creamy shoulders, which were slumped in despair. Catching himself, Quinn clenched his hand. "You should try to get some sleep."

"Yeah."

He strained against his own helplessness. Where had he gotten the stupid idea that she needed him? He didn't know the way to comfort and soothe. He didn't have the pretty words that would relax her and help her sleep again. He had nothing but a rage boiling inside him and a fierce desire to keep her safe. Neither of those would help her now.

"Look, I can get you something. Go downstairs and make, I don't know, some tea."

With her face still pressed against her knees, she squeezed her eyes tight. "No, thanks. I'll be fine."

"Damn it, I want to do something." The explosion ripped out of him before he could stop it. "I can't stand seeing you like this. Let me get you some aspirin, or sit in the chair until you can get to sleep. Something. You can't ask me to just leave you alone."

"Hold me." The words came out in a sob as she lifted her head. "Could you just hold me a minute?"

He sat beside her and, gathering her close, pressed her head to his shoulder. "Sure. As long as you want. Go ahead and let go, angel."

She didn't have the strength to stop it, and she no longer wanted to. With his arms strong around her, she let the full force of the tears come. Quinn cradled her close and murmured things he hoped would help, things he wasn't even certain she heard. When she began to quiet, he stroked the hair back from her face and said nothing at all.

"Quinn?"

"Hmmm?"

"Thanks."

"Any time."

"I don't make a habit of it." She sniffled. "Got a handkerchief?"

"No."

Reluctant to shift away even slightly, she reached for a tissue on her bedside table. "I guess I figured a man like you would head for the hills when a woman started—" she sniffled again "—blubbering."

"This is different."

She tilted her head back. Her eyes were swollen, her cheeks tear-streaked. "Why?"

"It's just different." He brushed a tear from her lashes. Then, though he felt foolish, he let the moisture linger on his thumb. "Feel better?"

"Yes." She did, unaccountably, for she'd never believed tears solved anything. Now that they were shed she felt drained and embarrassed. "I'd, ah...appreciate it if we both forgot about this lapse in the morning."

"Never give yourself an inch, do you?"

"I hate to cry."

She said it with such bitter finality that he knew she'd shed hot tears over something before. Or someone. "Me too."

That made her smile. "You're a nice guy when you put a little effort into it."

"I try not to let it happen often." He stroked her hair again before he shifted her closer. It hadn't been so hard to comfort, he discovered. It wasn't so hard to be needed. "Think you can sleep now?"

"I guess." She closed her eyes, discovering it felt enormously good to let her cheek rest against his.

He ran a comforting hand over her back, then tensed when he felt silk give way to flesh. "Tomorrow's Sunday. You can stay in bed all day."

"I have a photo session at one." With her eyes still closed, she explored the muscles of his shoulders with her fingertips.

"You can cancel it."

"I'll be okay. The photographer's accommodating me because of the shooting schedule."

"Then you'd better get some rest or you'll look like hell."

"Thanks a lot."

"You're welcome."

When he drew her back, she tilted her head up and smiled at him. His fingers tensed on her shoulders, and hers on his, and her smile faded. The need vibrated between them so urgently that it set the air humming.

"I'd better go."

"No." The decision had already been made, she knew, perhaps before they'd even met. Her heart had just accepted it. She loved. There was no changing it. Until now, until him, she hadn't known how much she needed to have the chance to love again. "I want you to stay." She slid her hands over his shoulders. "I want you to make love with me."

The ache that had begun to throb just from looking at her turned sharp and stabbing—a painfully sweet sensation. Her hands felt so cool on his skin. Her eyes looked so warm and dark. The moonlight dappled over her like a dream, but he couldn't afford to forget reality.

"Chantel, I want you so much right now I can hardly breathe. But..." He slid his hands up to her wrists. "I don't know if I could live with the fact that this happened between us because you were scared and shaky."

A smile curved her lips as she brought them closer to his. "Haven't you figured out yet that I know what I want?" She turned her head slightly so that her kiss brushed his chin. "Didn't you say that a man could tell just by the way a woman looked at him? Can't you see the way I'm looking at you?"

"Maybe I only see the way I want you to look." But his fingers had tangled in her hair.

"I want you to stay," she repeated, "not because I'm scared. I want you to stay because of the way you make me feel when you kiss me. When you hold me. When you touch me." She rubbed her cheek against his. "I want you to stay because you can make me forget there's anything outside of this room."

Something snapped inside him. Some would call it control. With an oath, he dragged his hands through her hair and plundered her mouth.

She was everything dark and desperate and desirable. She was pure aphrodisiac. As they knelt on the bed he let his dreams spring to life and rained kisses over her face, her hair, her throat. The scent that was so much a part of her misted through his brain like a fog. And she trembled. Not on cue but from pleasure, from the pleasure he gave her. Half-mad, he crushed his lips to hers again and tasted her passion.

Never before and, she was certain, never again, would a man bring her to life this way. Never before and never again would she want like this. Her body was like a furnace, pumping heat and energy while her mind was flooded with a brilliant kaleidoscope of sensation. No, never again would a man bring her this, because there was only one man. She'd known it, somehow, from the first.

Everything was so clear. She felt the scrape of his chin over her shoulder, felt the mattress sink under their combined weights as they knelt torso-to-torso. She could see the moonlight against his skin as she ran her hands over his shoulders and down. His muscles contracted at her touch, and she heard the soft hiss of his indrawn breath. Desperation flavored his kisses and fueled her own need. A kaleidoscope, a whirlwind, a race. The scents from her garden crept into the room. With a gurgle of delight, she lowered her lips to his shoulder and nipped.

A man could lose his mind and his soul to her. Quinn felt his chest constrict as he ran his hands freely over her. Pain and power... they were both twined together in his need for her. She made him hurt and made him soar just by being in his arms.

It wasn't just the perfection of form, of face, but the wild, wanton sexuality she had encased in glittering ice. Released, it was a Pandora's box of emotions, some dark, some dangerous, some desperately exciting.

He wouldn't resist her. He couldn't. He could feel her tremble, hear her moan as he touched and tasted and tempted. Her skin was hot, already damp. Her breath caught on his name. Tonight, even if it was just for tonight, he would make her as frenzied as he.

He gathered her hair in his hand, drawing her head back to expose the long white line of her throat. Her pulse beat frantically as he traced his tongue over it. Her hands moved over his chest, then lower, and his stomach muscles quivered at her touch. As she tugged at the snap on his jeans, he found her breast through the thin silk she wore. When he drew both silk and flesh into his mouth, she strained against him, shuddering. Her throat filled with indistinct murmurs of pleasure, she tugged the denim over his hips.

The feel of her hands on him drove every rational thought from his mind. In one crazed movement he ripped the silk from her, rending it down the middle. Her gasp was muffled against his mouth as he dragged her down beneath him.

He couldn't think. He could only feel. When he plunged into her she was so warm, so moist. He wondered if a man could die from being given his ultimate wish. Then she was wrapped around him, driving him even as he sought to drive her. He could see her, her hair spread out on tumbled white sheets, her eyes half closed, her lips slightly parted as the breath trembled out.

"Quinn." His name whispered from her as she was tossed by titanic waves of sensation. Heat, light, wind. Nothing had prepared her for this. She tried to tell him, but his lips were on hers again. She was a part of him. Release came in a torrent that left her too stunned for speech.

She didn't know what to say. Would he expect some clever phrase, some easy words? It wasn't possible to explain that she had given herself to only one other man and never, truly never, like this. If it hadn't mattered so much—if he hadn't mattered so much—she was sure she could have come up with something to break the long silence and the tension she felt building again.

He didn't know what to say. He'd taken her like a madman. She deserved better, more care, certainly more finesse. If only he hadn't lost control. But he had, Quinn reminded himself ruthlessly. He couldn't change that any more than he could change the fact that he'd damaged whatever might have been growing between them. He could only hope it wasn't too late to repair it.

Both of them tensed, then turned, then spoke each other's names at the same time. The awkwardness lasted only a moment before they grinned.

"I was thinking you were right," she began, "about me needing a script. I can't think of what I want to say."

"I've been having some trouble with that myself." He took her hand and brought it to his lips. "I guess I was a little rough."

"Were you?" Amused and relieved, Chantel groped for the remains of her silk teddy. Lifting a brow, she dropped it on his chest.

Quinn rubbed the material between his thumb and forefinger. "You could deduct it from my check."

"I intend to. Three hundred and fifty."

"Three hundred and fifty?" He rose on one elbow and examined the ripped silk more carefully. "You've got to be crazy to spend three-fifty on something you sleep in."

"I enjoy indulging myself." To prove her point, she leaned over and nibbled on his lips. "And under the circumstances, I think it only fair that I deduct half the price."

"Half?"

"It was a joint effort." She smiled and ran a fingertip over his chest. "Besides, it was worth it."

"Was it?" His hand came up her leg to rest on her hip. "You sure?"

"Well, I'm a cautious woman, and you know what they say in the business."

"No." Her hair teased his shoulders as she leaned over him. "What do they say in the business?"

"Take 2," Chantel sighed, lowering herself to him.

Chapter Eight

"Quinn, I promise you, this is going to take a good three hours, maybe four." Chantel got out of the car, then leaned over to take her garment bag from the hook by the passenger door.

He noticed how nicely the slim skirt fit over her bottom. "I can be patient."

"A photo session is often very tedious for the people involved, much less for someone who just has to sit there."

"Let me worry about that," he advised, and took the bag from her.

"I have to worry about it. Knowing you're hanging around, grumbling under your breath, is going to make me tense." Chantel pressed a buzzer on the outside door, then tipped down her sunglasses to peer over them. "And tension will show in the pictures. This layout for *The Scene* is very important."

He pushed the glasses back up on her nose. "So are you."

It warmed her. She no longer knew how to pretend it didn't. Chantel rose on her toes to brush a kiss over his lips. "I appreciate that. But I'll be perfectly safe. Margot will be there to do my hair, and the makeup artist is a free-lancer I've worked with before. Mrs. Alice Cooke. They have to stay for the whole session. I'll be surrounded by well-meaning women."

"And the photographer," he reminded her. "I'm not letting you alone with this Bryan Mitchell or any other man."

Chantel started to correct him, then thought better of it. A woman was entitled to take every advantage offered. She ran a finger over the collar of his shirt. "Jealous?"

"Cautious."

"Bryan Mitchell." The voice coming through the intercom was low, smooth and feminine.

"It's Chantel O'Hurley for the one o'clock session."

"Right on time."

There was a mechanical buzz from inside the door, and then it unlatched.

"Bryan Mitchell is a tall, gorgeous blonde," Chantel began as they climbed the inside stairs. "We've been friends for years."

Quinn wrapped his fingers around hers. "All the more reason I'm not leaving you alone with him. Until this thing is settled, the only man you're having solitary dealings with is me."

"Well." Chantel paused at the studio door and wrapped her arms around him. "I like that," she murmured, and met his lips with hers.

"I bet you do." Bryan stood in the open doorway, grinning.

"Quinn Doran." Chantel laid a hand lightly on his arm. "Bryan Mitchell."

The photographer was indeed tall, blond and gorgeous. She was also a woman. Quinn shot Chantel a look as she smiled. "Nice meeting you."

Bryan offered him a hand, already wondering if she could convince him to sit for her. "Welcome to chaos," she told them as she gestured them inside. "I'm still setting up. Chantel, you know where the cold drinks are. Hairdressing and makeup are in the back room having an argument about fashion. Personally, I can't get emotionally involved over whether henna is back to stay." As she spoke, she walked over to a set of white umbrellas and adjusted them.

Chantel walked to a cramped little room off the side of the studio and poked in the refrigerator. "Quinn, it's going to be like this for hours. There must be something else you want to do."

He could hear the other two women chattering in the back room. Something about facial packs and eye tucks. "I can think of a couple dozen."

"Then go do them." Chantel set down the bottle of soda to take both of his hands. "Bryan had the security system installed a few months ago when there was a rash of robberies in the neighborhood. No one gets through the outside door unless she releases the lock. I'm surrounded by women who'll be fussing over me for hours, and you'll distract all of us. Go play some handball or something.''

She was right. She'd be safe here, and he'd be in the way—as well as unmercifully bored. Then, too, it would help him to have a couple of hours away from her, a couple of hours of pure physical exertion. Would he work her out of his system?

"Gym's a couple of blocks down," he muttered.

"Jim who?"

"*The* gym," he corrected, putting his hands on her hips.

"You mean one of those places with weights and nasty machines that make you grunt and sweat?"

"More or less." Taking out his notebook, he wrote down a name and number. "Call me when you're finished and I'll come back and pick you up."

"Rizzo's." She kept her face bland as she looked up at him. "Sounds serious."

"Just call." He leaned down to bite her lightly on the bottom lip. "Why don't you go make yourself beautiful?"

She kept her arms around him as she lifted a brow. "Aren't I already?"

He knew she hadn't so much as picked up a tube of mascara that morning. Her eyes were blue and brilliant, her skin luminous and pale. Fresh and dewy, as it was now, her beauty was heartbreaking. He lifted a hand to skim it over her cheek. "Such a hag."

Before she could retaliate he had her close, cutting off her breath in a kiss that seemed to last for hours. He needed to lift weights, Quinn thought. He had to sweat some of the need for her out of his system.

"Try to do something about that face, will you?"

"Take a walk, Doran."

He grinned at her, then slipped back into the studio. Chantel let out a shaky breath and leaned her palms against the cluttered counter beside the refrigerator. There was nothing she could do, and she was nearly ready to admit there was nothing she wanted to do, about the fact that she was in love with him. It was probably a mistake, a desperate one, but it had already been made.

Somehow, if she could somehow draw back a part of herself, she wouldn't be so devastated when he went his own way. And he would, wouldn't he? A man like Quinn lived alone, worked alone, walked alone. When his job was over he'd kiss her goodbye and go. She caught her bottom lip between her teeth and straightened. No, he wouldn't. Not if she had anything to do with it.

You're going to lose this match, Doran, she promised herself. No way was he going to walk away and leave her.

"Chantel, they're ready for you."

She was ready, too. Chantel left the drink on the counter. She was more than ready.

For two hours she worked nonstop. Her hair was frizzed, smoothed, sprayed and gelled. Her face was painted and powdered. Every time she changed her outfit her hair and face were subtly altered to enhance the look. Bryan worked with a slow, steady enthusiasm, as she always did.

"I haven't asked you how Shade is."

"Put your right hand on your left shoulder," Bryan instructed. "Spread your fingers. Good. Shade's terrific. He's home changing diapers." She caught Chantel's quick, mischievous grin on film.

"That I'd like to see."

"He's great at it. Organized, you know."

"Well, I can tell you, you don't look as though you had a baby two months ago."

"Who has time to eat? Tilt your chin up and try for aloof. That's it." She crouched, shifting angles. "Andrew Colby is a ten-pound slave driver."

"And you're crazy about him."

Bryan lowered her camera and beamed. "He's the most fantastic baby. Between Shade and me, we've taken at least five hundred rolls of film. Every day there's some little change." She tossed her long blond braid behind her back. "You can see how bright he is just by the way he looks at things. Just yesterday he—" She cut herself off with a laugh. "Stop me. It's an obsession."

"No." Chantel smiled, though the quick pang of envy she felt surprised her. "It's lovely."

"It is, you know. I never saw myself as a mother." She lifted the camera back into place. "Now I can't imagine life without Andrew. Or Shade."

"The right man can change your outlook, I guess."

Bryan decided the wistful expression that flitted across Chantel's face would be the best shot yet. "You sure make my work easier."

Bringing herself back, Chantel looked at the camera. "How's that?"

"Turn to the side and look over your shoulder. A bit more. Smolder a little." She pressed the shutter four times in rapid succession. "A face like yours is always a pleasure to shoot, especially when you bring so much to it. But I didn't expect the bonus."

"What bonus?" Chantel asked as she shifted to look over her other shoulder.

"There's nothing more terrific than photographing a woman in love. Close your mouth," she ordered, then lowered her camera to stretch her shoulders.

Slowly Chantel turned to face Bryan again. "It's that obvious?"

"Don't you want it to be?"

"No... yes. I don't know." She pushed a hand through her carefully groomed hair. "I don't want to make a fool of myself."

"That kind of goes hand in hand with falling in love, but I think you'll survive it. He's got a great face. I don't suppose you could talk him into sitting for me."

"Maybe if you bound him hand and foot. Bryan, how did you handle Shade?"

Bryan took a chocolate bar out of her back pocket. "*You're* asking *me* for advice on men?"

Chantel accepted a sliver of the chocolate. "Don't let it get around."

"Have you felt like murdering him yet?"

"Several times."

"You're making progress. The best thing I can tell you is to let things happen. We're wrapped here." She bit into the candy. "If I were you, I wouldn't waste what's left of the weekend."

The gym smelt like men. Damp, athletic men. The air was filled with sweat and swearing. Most of the patrons had stripped down to shorts, and a few had added T-shirts. On a mat, a man with weights on his legs grunted his way through a series of sit-ups. On a bench press, another man swore repetitively every time he extended the bar over his head. The equipment was top-notch, but it had long since lost its shine.

Chantel strolled in and absorbed, both brows lifted. The first one who saw her was a young man pulling weights up the walls with two ropes. He was working steadily, the veins in his neck bulging out as he rotated his arms. His mouth dropped open and the ropes snapped back against the wall. Chantel smiled at him.

Careful to keep her skirts clear, she circled around the bench press. The man stopped swearing as his eyes bugged out. It took less than ten seconds for the noisy, steamy gym to drop into silence. Then she saw Quinn.

He hadn't noticed the sudden quiet. With his back to the room, he was systematically jabbing at a punching bag. Its buffeting noise was the only sound in the room. He looked magnificent, legs spread, eyes intense, his powerful back tensed as he concentrated on his timing. The small brown bag was a blur as his fists never let it rest. Chantel walked over to him, waited a moment, then ran a fingertip down his back.

"Hello, darling."

He swore and spun, his hand still fisted and lifted. Chantel raised a brow, then her chin, as if inviting him to take his best shot.

"What the hell are you doing here?"

"Watching you." She took a finger and pushed at the bag. "Tell me, what's the purpose of beating at this little thing?"

"I told you to call me." He swiped sweat out of his eyes in order to glare at her better.

"I felt like a walk. Besides, I wanted to see where a man like you...played." Deliberately she looked over her shoulder and scanned the room. "Fascinating."

Every man in the room sucked in his stomach.

With an oath, Quinn took her by the arm. "You must be crazy. You don't belong in a place like this."

"Why ever not?" As they passed the man on the bench press, Chantel sent him a brilliant smile. The weights clattered against the safety bar.

"Cut that out," he muttered. "Rizzo, I'm using your office."

"Oh, where is he?" As he dragged her out, Chantel glanced back. "I'm dying to meet him."

"Shut up. Do you have to walk in here with legs like that?"

"They're all I have to walk on."

"Sit." He shoved her into a torn plastic chair. "What the hell am I supposed to do with you?"

"Would you like a multiple choice?"

"This isn't a joke, damn it." He pushed at the clutter on Rizzo's desk until he found a crumpled pack of Camels. "Look, Chantel, we made an arrangement. You were supposed to call. There are reasons." He shook out a cigarette and lit it.

"Quinn, it's a beautiful afternoon and it wasn't far. There isn't much opportunity to stroll in L.A., and I couldn't resist. If you're going to tell me I can't walk two blocks on a public street in broad daylight, I'll scream." She glanced toward the door. "I can't imagine what your, ah, associates would make of that."

He exhaled a long stream of smoke, then crushed the cigarette into a mess of brown tobacco and white paper. "You go nowhere without me. You had instructions, Chantel, and I trusted you to follow them."

"Oh, lighten up." She rose and put her palms on his bare chest.

"I'm sweating like a pig," he muttered, taking her wrists.

"I noticed. I don't know what it is that attracts men to a place that smells like old athletic socks, but if this is how you keep in shape—" she glanced down approvingly "—I might just have to install a gym at home."

"Don't change the subject."

"What subject was that?"

"I don't want anything to happen to you."

She touched her tongue to her upper lip and edged closer. "Why? You've already been paid for this week."

"I don't care about the damn money," he said with violence.

"What do you care about, Quinn?"

"You." He said it between his teeth before he spun away. He'd thought he needed space, just some space and time to get his equilibrium back. There wasn't that much space in the whole world. "Don't pull anything like this again."

"All right. I'm sorry."

"I've got to shower. Stay in here."

When the door slammed at his back, Chantel sat again. He cared. She closed her eyes and hugged the knowledge to her. He cared about her. If she'd gotten him to say it, the next step was getting him to like it.

* * *

"How long are you going to be angry?"

They were driving home with the top down. Chantel had let the first fifteen minutes pass in silence.

"I'm not angry."

"You're clenching your teeth."

"Consider yourself lucky that's all I'm doing."

"Quinn, I've already said I was sorry. I'm not going to apologize again."

"No one's asking you to." He downshifted around a curve. "What I am asking is that you take the situation you're in seriously."

"You don't think I am?"

"Not after that little stunt of yours this afternoon."

She shifted in her seat. The wind picked up her hair and tossed it as her temper snapped. "Stop treating me like a child. I understand the situation I'm in perfectly. I live with it twenty-four hours a day, every day, every night. Every time the phone rings, every time I go through my mail. When I go to sleep at night, that's what I'm thinking of. When I wake up in the morning, that's what I'm thinking of. If I can't have an hour now and then when I can push it aside, I'll go crazy. I'm trying to survive, Doran. Don't talk to me as though I'm irresponsible."

She shifted away again, and again silence reigned. He was right, Quinn told himself as he slacked his speed. But so was she. There were times, because she put up such a good front, when he believed she'd forgotten she was in any danger. She never forgot, he realized. She just refused to buckle—except in her private moments. He didn't know how to tell her he loved her for that above everything else.

Loved her. That was a tough one to swallow, but then the truth often was. The more his feelings for her grew, the more he worried about her well-being. He knew she worked hard, and for long hours. With the kind of strain she was under, she could only keep up that pace for a limited time. Even a woman as strong willed as Chantel would lose eventually.

Damn it, he wished he had something, anything, to go on. They were moving into their third week, and he was no closer to putting things right than he had been on the first day. He needed to see her safe, secure, content. Even though he was afraid that once she was she'd write him a check and kiss him off.

Quinn's hands tightened on the wheel, then gradually relaxed. She was going to have a fight on her hands when it came to that.

Relax, he told himself. She wasn't going to get away. Moving only his eyes, he took in the stiff, angry way she sat. Angel, he told her silently, I'm just the man to clip your wings.

Quinn tossed his arm casually over the back of the seat. "You're pouting."

"Go to hell."

"You're going to get lines all over your face if you keep that up. Then where will you be?"

"Kiss my—"

"Love to." He pulled over to the side of the road. She didn't even have the chance to snarl at him before he gathered her close. "Why don't I start with that homely face of yours and work my way down?"

"No."

"Okay, if you'd rather I take it from the bottom up."

When he started to shift her, she began to struggle in earnest. "Stop it. I don't want you to kiss me anywhere."

"Are you sure?" He brought her wrist to his lips and brushed them over the inside. "How about there?"

"No."

"Here, then." He pressed his mouth to the side of her throat. She stopped struggling.

"No."

"Well, other options are a little risky on the side of the road, but if you insist—"

"Stop." The laughter bubbled up as she shoved him away. Chantel leaned against the door and crossed her arms. "You creep."

"I love it when you insult me."

"Then you're going to love this," she began, but he was too quick. Whatever she'd had in mind was muffled against his mouth. Response came instantly, from the heart. Her arms went around him and her lips parted. For a moment there was nothing but the warm late-afternoon sun and sheer, unbridled pleasure.

Her eyes stayed closed, seconds after he'd drawn his lips from hers. When they opened, slowly, the irises were dark and clouded. "Are you trying to make up?" she murmured.

"For what?"

Her lips curved as she framed his face with her hands. "Never mind. Let's go home, Quinn."

He touched his lips to hers again, lingering, before he sat back and started the engine. "By the way, Rizzo wanted to know if he could have an autographed picture for his office."

Chantel laughed, then sat back to enjoy the rest of the drive. As they rode by the high wall surrounding her grounds, she began to toy with the idea of a long dip in the pool. Bryan was right. It would be a pity to waste what was left of the weekend. Even as she turned to ask Quinn to join her, he was bringing the car to a fast stop.

"Quinn, we really should wait until we're *inside*."

"There's a car in front of the gates." His tone had her tensing as she looked around. "A man's there, see? Looks like he's causing quite a bit of commotion."

"You don't think that—" She moistened her lips. "He wouldn't come right to the front gate."

"Why don't we find out?" He took the keys from the ignition and unlocked the glove compartment. Chantel watched as he drew out a revolver. It was nothing like her dainty little .22. And she was just as certain it wasn't unloaded.

"Quinn."

"Stay here."

"No, I—"

"Don't argue."

"But I don't want you to..." As the argument at the gate heated up, the voices drifted to her. Listening intently, Chantel tightened her grip on Quinn. "I don't believe it," she murmured. She squinted, trying to make out the figure in the distance. "I just don't be-

lieve it," she repeated, and sprang out of the car before Quinn could stop her.

"Chantel!"

"It's Pop." Laughing, she spun back to Quinn.
"It's Pop. My father." Her long legs flashed as she
sped up the rest of the road. "Pop!" Still laughing,
she threw her arms wide.

Frank O'Hurley turned from his spirited argument
with the guard. His thin face erupted into a grin.
"There's my girl." Spry and wiry, he pumped down
the remaining distance and caught Chantel close. With
a whoop, he spun her in three dizzying circles. "How's
my little princess?"

"Surprised." She kissed his baby-smooth face, then
hugged him again. He smelled, as he always did, of
powder and peppermint. "I didn't know you were
coming."

"Don't need an invitation, do I?"

"Don't be silly."

"Well, tell that to the joker on the other side of the
gate. The idiot wouldn't let me in even when I told him
I was your own flesh and blood."

"I'm sorry, Miss O'Hurley." The stiff-faced man
behind the gate speared Frank with a look. The crazy
old man had threatened to pull out his tongue and
wrap it around his neck. "There was no one here to
verify."

"That's all right."

"All right?" Frank piped up. He was primed and
ready for a donnybrook. "All right when your own
father's treated like a trespasser?"

"Don't be cranky." Chantel brushed at his lapels.
"I've added to the security, that's all."

"Why?" Immediately alert, he cupped Chantel's chin. "What's wrong?"

"It's nothing. We'll get into all that later. Now I'm just glad to see you." She glanced back at the dusty rental car. "Where's Mom?"

"Said she wasn't fit to see anyone until she'd been to the beauty parlor. I wasn't going to sit around cooling my heels while she's getting primped up. She'll be taking a cab out later."

"But tell me what you're doing here, how long you can stay. What—"

"God be praised, girl, can't it wait until a man's washed the dust out of his throat? Drove clear from Vegas today."

"Vegas? I didn't know you had a gig in Vegas."

"You don't know everything." He tweaked her nose, then looked over her shoulder as Quinn pulled up. "Now who might this be?"

"That's Quinn." She shot him a quick look. "Quinn Doran. You're right, Pop, we can talk better inside—especially after you've had a glass of the Irish."

"Now you're talking." Frank hopped back in his car, then sailed through the now-open gates. Chantel saw him look down his nose at the guard.

"Your father?" Quinn asked when she climbed back in the car.

"Yes, I wasn't expecting him, but that's nothing new." Her fingers twisted together. "You put the gun away?"

He lifted a hand to the guard as he drove through. "Don't worry."

"But I am. I didn't want to bring my family into all this." Chantel pressed the bridge of her nose between her thumb and forefinger. "I'm going to have to tell them something. He's seen the guard at the gates. He's bound to notice the men patrolling the grounds."

"Why don't you try the truth?"

"I don't want to worry my parents. Damn, I only get to see them three or four times a year, and now this." She looked at Quinn as he slowed at the end of the drive. "And I have to explain you."

"The truth," he repeated.

"All right. I can't think of anything else." She put a hand on his arm before he could climb out. "But I'll do it my way. I want to play it down as much as possible."

"Well now." Beaming and affable, Frank strolled over to the car. "Looks like you've got yourself a fine strong fellow here, Chantel."

"Quinn Doran, my father, Frank O'Hurley."

"Pleased to meet you." Frank offered a hand and pumped Quinn's exuberantly. "Wouldn't mind helping me in with the bags, would you, son?"

Chantel had to smile when Frank popped open his trunk and took out a small shoulder bag, leaving two large cases for Quinn. "You never change," she murmured hooking an arm through his to lead him into the house.

"Just leave them there," she told Quinn, gesturing to the base of the staircase. "You can take them up later."

"Thanks."

She met his sarcasm with an easy smile. "Why don't you two go into the living room and have a drink? I want to tell the cook there'll be two more for dinner.'' Leaving Quinn with a brief warning look, she started down the hall.

"Well, son, I don't know about you," Frank said, giving Quinn a solid slap on the back. "But I could use a drink." He trotted off into the living room and headed directly to the bar. "What's your pleasure?"

"Scotch."

Frank shrugged his narrow shoulders, then poured. "To each his own." Locating the bottle of whiskey, he gave a satisfied grunt and poured a generous three fingers. "Well, now... Quinn, is it? Why don't we drink to my girl?" He tapped his glass solidly against Quinn's without regard for the pricey Rosenthal crystal, then swallowed deeply. "Now that's a drink a man can wrap his heart around. Have a seat, son, have a seat." Still playing the congenial host, he gestured to a chair before finding one for himself. "Now..." He settled back and sighed. Then, abruptly, his eyes were shrewd and sharp. "Just what are you doing with my daughter?"

"Pop." Grateful for her timing, Chantel strolled into the room, then sat on the arm of her father's chair. "You'll have to excuse him, Quinn. He's never been subtle."

Quinn regarded his Scotch for a moment. "Seems like a reasonable question to me."

"There." Satisfied with what he saw, Frank nodded. "We're going to get along just fine."

"I wouldn't be surprised," she murmured ruffling her father's hair. "So tell me how it went in Vegas."

"Be glad to." He sipped his whiskey again, appreciating its smooth heat. "Just as soon as you explain why you have a trained gorilla at your front gate.''

"I told you, I added some security." But when she started to rise, Frank put a firm hand on her knee.

"You wouldn't try to con an old hand like me, would you, princess?"

It would be useless, she admitted, and settled back. "I've been getting some annoying phone calls, that's all. It seemed wise to take a few precautions."

"What kind of phone calls?"

"Just nuisance calls."

"Chantel." He knew his daughter too well. A few nuisance calls would have been brushed off, laughed off and forgotten. "Is someone threatening you?"

"No. No, it's nothing like that." Realizing she was being backed into a corner, she shot a pleading look at Quinn.

"I still opt for the truth," he said simply.

"Thanks for the help."

"Just be quiet," Frank told her, and there was such uncharacteristic authority in his tone that she closed her mouth instantly. "You tell me what's going on," he ordered Quinn. "And what you have to do with it."

"Quinn—"

"Chantel Margaret Louise O'Hurley, shut your mouth and keep it shut."

When she did, Quinn could only smile. "Nice trick," he said to Frank.

"I use it selectively to keep it fresh." Frank swallowed the rest of his whiskey. "Let's hear it."

Briefly, concisely, Quinn outlined what Chantel was dealing with. As he spoke, Frank's brows lowered, his thin face reddened and the hand still resting on Chantel's knee clenched.

"Slimy bastard." Frank rose out of the chair like a terrier ready to charge. "If you're a detective, Quinn Doran, why in hell haven't you found him?"

"Because he hasn't made a mistake." Quinn set down his glass and met Frank's outraged glare levelly. "But he will, and I'll find him."

"If he hurts my girl—"

"He's not going to get near her," Quinn interrupted flatly. "Because he has to go through me first."

Frank swallowed his fury—it was something he didn't often bother to do—and measured the man in front of him. He'd always prided himself on being a good judge of character. You needed to know whether to raise your fists or laugh and back off. The man in front of him was hard as a rock and mean as they came. If he had to trust his daughter to someone, this was the one.

"So. You're staying here, in the house, with Chantel."

"That's right. I'm going to take care of her, Mr. O'Hurley. You have my word on that."

Frank hesitated only a moment before his teeth showed in a smile. "If you don't, I'll skin you alive. And make it Frank."

Cool and regal, Chantel rose. "Perhaps I could say a word now."

"Don't put that face on with me, girl." Frank crossed to her, then gently framed her face in his hands. "You should have come to your family with this."

"There was no point in worrying you."

"Point?" Frank shook his head from side to side. "We're family. We're the O'Hurleys. We stick together."

"Pop, Maddy's getting married at the end of the week. Abby's pregnant. Trace is—"

"You'll kindly leave him out of it," Frank said stiffly. "Family business has nothing to do with your brother. That's his choice."

"Really, Pop, after all this time you should—"

"And don't change the subject. Your mother and me, and your sisters, are entitled to worry about you."

It wasn't the time to go to her brother's defense. And Chantel wasn't entirely sure he'd care one way or the other. Now she wanted to smooth those lines of worry from her father's face.

"All right, then." She kissed him soundly. "Worry all you want, but everything that can be done is being done."

He kept his hand on her shoulder but turned to Quinn. "We're off to New York on Friday to see my daughter married off. You'll be going with us?"

"I didn't think it was necessary to drag Quinn to—"

"I'm going," he interrupted. His eyes met Chantel's in something like a challenge. "I've already made the arrangements."

"You never mentioned it to me."

"Why should I?" he countered for the simple pleasure of watching fury rise in her eyes.

"It hardly seems I'm necessary, does it?" Feeling squeezed from all sides, she bristled. "If you'll both excuse me, I'm going to go soak my head."

"Nasty little number, isn't she?" Frank asked with obvious pride as she stalked out.

"All that and more."

"It's the Irish, you know. We're either poets or fighters. O'Hurleys are a bit of both."

"I'm looking forward to meeting the rest of your family."

And they'll want to get a look at you, Frank said to himself. "Tell me, Quinn," he began in an amiable tone. "Do you intend to, ah, keep your eye on Chantel, so to speak, after this business is settled?"

Quinn studied the man across from him. It seemed it was still time for truths. "Yes. Whether she likes it or not."

Frank gave a quick laugh. "Let's have another drink."

Chapter Nine

"Mom, there's no reason for you to do that."

Molly O'Hurley carefully folded a white silk jacket in tissue. "Why should you call a maid up here?" Years of experience had Molly packing Chantel's clothes with a minimum of fuss.

"It's her job."

Molly brushed her objections away with the back of her hand. "I never feel I can speak my mind in front of maids and butlers."

Chantel looked at the suitcase and at her stacks of clothes. She'd spent the first twenty years of her life packing and unpacking. As a matter of principle, she hadn't done so in years. But she'd never been able to win a fight with her mother. Resigned, Chantel began a careful selection of her toiletries.

"I'm sorry we haven't had much time together the past few days."

"Don't be silly." Brisk and practical, Molly rattled more tissue paper. "You're in the middle of that film. Your father and I didn't expect to be entertained."

"Pop seemed to be entertained the day you came to the set."

Chuckling, Molly glanced up. She was a pretty, trim woman who managed to look a decade younger than her years with a minimum of effort. Looking at her, Chantel acknowledged that the rush and craziness of her parents' life-style suited Molly just as much as it did Frank. "He did, didn't he? Still, I don't think he should have argued with the director about how to set the scene."

"Mary has a—a sense of humor."

"Good thing." For the next few moments, they packed in silence. "Chantel, we're worried about you."

"Mom, that's exactly what I don't want you to do."

"We love you. You can't expect us to love you and not be concerned."

"I know." She slipped a bottle of perfume into a padded travel box. "That's why I didn't want to tell you about what was going on. You had to worry enough about me when I was growing up."

"You don't expect a parent to turn off the juice just because a child's past the age of twenty-one?"

"No, I suppose not." She smiled and slipped her set of makeup brushes into their cases. "But it seems like you should have less to worry about after a certain age."

"I can only tell you that one day you'll find out differently yourself."

There was that pang again. Chantel's brows drew together as she tried to ignore it. "I don't know about that," she murmured. "I *do* know I don't want this business to affect the family."

"What affects one of us affects all of us. That's that." Molly said it so matter-of-factly, Chantel was forced to smile.

"Your Irish is showing."

"And why shouldn't it?" Molly wanted to know. "Your father and I think we should come back with you after the wedding."

"Back here?" Chantel stopped to stare. "You can't. You have a gig in New Hampshire."

Molly folded a pair of linen slacks by the pleats and said with a little smile, "Chantel, your father and I have been performing for over thirty-five years. I don't think canceling one engagement is going to make much of a ripple."

"No." Chantel set down the bottles and pots in her hands to reach for her mother. "I can't tell you how much it means to me to know that you would. But what could you do?"

"We could be with you."

"You could hardly even do that. Mom, I'll be filming for weeks more. You've seen in the last few days how little I'm home. I'd be a wreck thinking about you sitting around here twiddling your thumbs when you'd want to be working."

"Sitting around here, as in lounging by the pool?"

Chantel's lips curved, but she shook her head. "If I could believe you'd be content for more than forty-eight hours, it would be different. Be logical, Mom. If you stayed I'd be worried because you were worried. Pop would drive the staff crazy, and I wouldn't even be around to enjoy it."

"I told Frank you'd feel this way." With a sigh, Molly touched Chantel's hair. "I always worried about you the most, you know."

"I guess I gave you the most cause."

"You did what you had to. And Trace also was going to go his own way, no matter what. Your father refused to see it, but it was there from the time he could walk. Somehow I always knew Abby and Maddy would be all right, even when Abby was going through the mess of her first marriage and Maddy was struggling to keep herself in dancing shoes. But you..." Molly caressed her daughter's cheek. "I was always afraid you'd miss what was beside you because you were always looking so far ahead. I want you to be happy, Chantel."

"I am. No, I am, really. These past few weeks, even with this other business hanging over my head, I've found something."

"Quinn."

Chantel made a restless movement before walking to the windows. "It's obvious to everyone but him the way I feel."

Molly had formed her own opinion of Quinn Doran. He wasn't an easy man, nor would he often be a gentle one, but her daughter didn't need an easy, gentle man. She needed one who'd give her a run for her money.

"Men are more thickheaded," Molly commented. She was a woman who knew well just how thickheaded men could be. "Why don't you tell him?"

"No." She turned back, then rested the heels of her hands on the windowsill. "At least not yet. This is going to sound foolish, but I want...I need him to respect me. Me," she repeated. "For what I am. I need to be certain he's not just passing the time."

"Chantel, you can't use Dustin Price as a yardstick."

"I'm not." Anger crept into her voice. She managed to control it only because her mother's eyes remained so steady. "No, I'm not. But it isn't something that's easy to forget."

"No, it's impossible. But you can't live your life with that as the foundation. Have you told Quinn about him?"

"No, I can't. Mom, there are so many complications now, why bring up another? It's been nearly seven years."

"Do you trust Quinn?"

"Yes."

"Don't you think he'd understand?"

She pressed her fingers to her eyes for a moment. "If I was sure he loved me, really sure that what's between us is real, I could tell him anything. Even that."

"I wish I could tell you there were guarantees, but I can't." Molly crossed to her and gathered Chantel close. "I can tell you that I wouldn't consider leaving you, not for a minute until everything was resolved, if I wasn't sure Quinn was going to protect you."

"He makes me feel safe. Until I met him, I didn't know anyone could." She squeezed her eyes shut. "I didn't know I needed anyone who could."

"We all need to feel safe, Chantel. And loved." Molly stroked her hair, the light silver-blond locks she'd brushed and braided so often in the past. "There's something I haven't told you. Something I should have told you a long time ago." She embraced Chantel. "I'm very proud of you."

"Oh, Mom." As the tears welled up, Molly shook her head.

"Now, none of that," she murmured. "If we go downstairs with puffy eyes, your father will be pinching at me to find out why we've been sitting up here crying." She kissed Chantel's cheek and held on for another moment. "Let's finish packing."

"Mom."

"Yes, dear."

"I've always been proud of you, too."

"Well." Molly cleared her throat, but her voice was still husky when she spoke. "That's quite a thing to hear from a grown daughter. You're going to be all right?"

"I'm going to be fine. I'm going to be terrific."

"That's my girl. Now let's be about our business." Turning away, Molly made herself busy. "Look at this." Clucking her tongue, she held up a brief night-gown fashioned of black silk and lace. "It looks like sin."

Chantel rubbed a knuckle under her eyes to dry them and giggled. "I can't give it an evaluation yet. I just bought it."

Molly held it up to the sunlight. "I think it speaks for itself."

"You like it." Pleased, Chantel came over, folded it carefully and handed it back to her mother. "A souvenir from Beverly Hills."

"Don't be silly." But Molly couldn't resist rubbing a thumb over the silk. "I couldn't wear a thing like this."

"Why not?"

"I'm the mother of four grown children."

"You didn't pick us from under cabbage leaves."

"Well, your father would..." She trailed off, speculating. Chantel watched a wicked gleam come into her eyes. "Thank you, dear." Molly set the nightgown apart from the rest of Chantel's lingerie. "And I'll thank you for your father in advance."

By the time they went downstairs again, Frank could be heard picking his banjo.

"He's practicing," Molly said, "so he can play at the reception. They'll have to knock him unconscious to keep him from performing."

"You know Maddy wouldn't have it any other way."

"It's about time, woman." Frank looked up as his family walked in, but his fingers never stilled. "A man needs some backup, you know. This one here—" he jerked his head toward Quinn "—won't sing a note."

"Just doing you a favor," Quinn said easily as he lounged back on the sofa.

"Never heard of a body that wouldn't sing," Frank commented. "Heard plenty that couldn't, but never one who wouldn't. Sit here, Molly, my love. Let's show the man what the O'Hurleys are made of."

Obligingly Molly sat beside him, picked up the count and launched into the song with a strong, practiced voice. Chantel sat on the arm of the sofa beside Quinn and listened to the familiar sound of her parents working together. It was good, it was solid. The tension of the past weeks drained away.

"Come on, princess, you remember the chorus."

Chantel joined in, the words and rhythm of the bright novelty number coming easily. She rarely sang on her own. To Chantel, singing was a family affair. Even now, as she added her voice to her parents', she thought of Trace and her sisters and the countless times they'd all sung that same old song.

She'd surprised him. Quinn sat back, enjoying himself, as Frank merged one tune into another. Chantel wasn't the cool movie star now, nor was she the restless, passionate woman he'd discovered beneath that facade. She was at home with the nonsense songs her father played. She was a daughter, a loving one. The innocence he'd once sensed in her was apparent as she laughed and accused her father of missing a note.

Her scent was there, dark and sultry, in contrast to her relaxed, playful behavior. He'd never seen her like this. Never known she could be like this. He wondered if she realized how much her family meant to her, if she knew how her Hollywood image faded when she was with them.

It had been a good week. Chantel didn't know of the letters that had come, because he'd intercepted them. Nor did she know that they had traced one of the calls to a phone booth downtown. Quinn saw no reason to tell her or to hit her with the fact that two of the letters had begged for a meeting in New York.

He knew her plans.

Quinn lifted a hand and ran it down her arm. Chantel's fingers linked naturally with his. There was no point in telling her. She wouldn't be alone in New York, not for a moment. He'd already arranged for three of his best men to fly to Manhattan. Every step Chantel took would be monitored.

Frank interrupted Quinn's train of thought as he shot a challenging look at his daughter. "Do you still play that thing? Or do you use it as a doorstop?"

Chantel glanced at the white baby grand, then examined her nails. "I manage to hit a few keys."

"With a big, beautiful instrument like that you should be able to do a lot more."

"I don't want to show you up, Pop."

"That'll be the day."

With a shrug, she stood and moved to the piano. Deliberately she fluttered her lashes, sat, then went into a long, complicated arpeggio.

"You've been practicing," Frank accused, then cackled with delight.

Chantel shot a look at Quinn. "I don't spend my evenings darning socks."

Quinn acknowledged the hit with a slight inclination of his head. "Your daughter's full of surprises, Frank."

"No need to tell me that. The stories I could tell you. Why, there was the time—"

"Requests?" Chantel interrupted sweetly. "Unless Pop wants me to tie his tongue in a nice, neat bow."

Always cautious, Frank cleared his throat. "Why don't you do that little number your mother wouldn't let you sing until you turned eighteen?"

"Abby always did that one best."

"True enough." Frank's grin was crooked and amiable. "But you weren't half-bad." Molly managed to hide a smile as Chantel's eyes narrowed.

"Half-bad?" She wrinkled her nose at him as she gave herself a flowing introduction.

The low, torchy ballad prickled along Quinn's skin. Her voice was as smooth as the Scotch in his hand, and just as potent. The words were plaintive, vulnerable, but with her voice they became seductive. She wore white as she sat behind the glossy white piano. But he no longer thought of angels. The room grew warmer just from the sound of her voice. It seemed to weigh on him, pressing down until he was no longer sure he was even breathing.

Then she brought her gaze up from the keys to meet his.

It wasn't a song of love, but of love lost. The thought came to him then that if he lost her there were no words written that could describe his desperation. She'd made him ache before. And she'd made him burn. Now, for the first time, she made him weak.

She played the last chords with her eyes still locked on his.

"Not half-bad," Frank repeated, pleased with her delivery. "Now if you'd—"

"It's late, Frank." Molly patted his hand, loving him for the knucklehead he was. "We should go up to bed. Tomorrow's going to be a long day."

"Late? Nonsense, it's barely—"

"Late," Molly repeated. "And getting later by the minute. I have a surprise for you upstairs."

"But I was just getting— A surprise?"

"That's right. Come along, Frank. Good night, Quinn."

"Molly." But he couldn't take his eyes off Chantel.

"All right, all right, I'm coming. Good night, you two. Chantel, see if that cook of yours can make waffles in the morning, will you?"

"Night, Pop." She tilted her cheek for his kiss, but her eyes stayed locked on Quinn's.

As he climbed the stairs with his wife, Frank could be heard demanding what his surprise was.

"You were right," Quinn murmured when the room was silent again.

"About what?"

"You are terrific." He rose and came to her. Taking both her hands, he turned them palm up and pressed his lips to the center of each one. "The more I'm with you," he murmured, "the more I know you, the more I want."

With her hands still in his, she stood. Light glowed in her eyes. "I've never in my life felt about anyone the way I feel about you. I need you to believe that."

"And I need to believe it." They were close, very close, to taking that final step. Commitments, promises, dependence. He felt himself teeter on the edge, ready, but was afraid she would pull back and away if he pressed too soon. "Tell me what you want, Chantel."

"You." She could give that answer truthfully enough without demanding more than she thought he was ready to give. "I only want to be with you."

For how long? he wanted to ask, but fear stopped him. He would take today, tonight, and fight for tomorrow. "Come to bed."

Hands linked, hearts lost, they climbed the stairs.

They left a low light burning beside the bed. Odd, she thought, that her pulse should be hammering so hard, that her nerves should be fluttering so wildly when she already knew what they could bring to each other. Why should it feel so different this time? So special. So much, she realized dimly, like the first time. The only time.

She offered her mouth, anticipating the hard demand of his.

He was gentle. He was . . . tender. As he brushed his lips lightly over hers she felt her muscles go lax and her bones melt. He cupped her face with his hands so that his thumbs traced like whispers, like promises, over her throat. She sighed his name as she felt herself float.

What kind of passion was this that crept in so quietly? Desire was there, already thrumming, but with each caress he soothed it—and stoked it. His mouth was patient, gliding over her face as if he wanted to memorize the essence of her through touch and taste. He strung small, feathery kisses down her cheekbones, then sought her mouth. His tongue traced the outline, then lingered to stroke lazily over her bottom lip. The room began to whirl inside her head.

She was priceless. This time, he promised himself, he would show her. She had a beauty he knew now reached beneath the skin. He would cherish it. He combed his fingers through her hair, delighting in the silken feel of it. He murmured, and she sighed and pressed herself against him.

As his mouth continued to explore, he began to undo the row of buttons at her back. When the material parted, he ran his hands along her spine, gently, as a man touches fragile glass. As the silk slithered to the floor, she trembled. She was warm and naked beneath it. His heart hammered in his throat. It was as though she had waited all evening for this moment with him.

Quinn drew her away to look at her, all of her, in the lamplight. She was so small, so delicate, with skin like porcelain and a form that might have been carved from alabaster. Her hair tumbled over her shoulders, ending just before the curve of her breasts. Her rib cage was narrow. He ran his hands down it, amazed that the strength he knew she possessed came from such delicacy. Her waist tapered so that he could almost span it with his hands before flaring out gently to slender hips and long, slim thighs.

"You're so beautiful." His voice was strained as he brought his gaze back to hers. "You take my breath away."

She stepped forward into his arms.

The material of his shirt was rough against her bare skin. With her eyes half closed, Chantel moved against him, urging his mouth to take its fill. Her tongue found his and began a silent, exotic seduction. All the while, his fingertips played over her as exquisitely as hers had played over the piano keys.

Through the window the breeze stirred, threatening rain. Chantel inhaled the fragrances of the night as they tangled with the musky scent of passion. Slowly, and with as much care as he had shown her, she undressed Quinn.

She rubbed her palms over the hard, coiled muscles of his shoulders, delighting in the feel. Temptingly she pressed her lips to his chest. There was a power and discipline in his body that urged her to touch, to tease. The ridges of muscles in his torso fascinated her. With a murmur of approval, she bought her lips back to his.

They lowered themselves onto the bed.

No hurry. No rush. The moment was drawn out, dreamlike, as they pleasured each other. Chantel shifted to look down at him. How could she tell him what he'd come to mean to her? How could she explain how much she needed him to be with her—now, tomorrow, forever? Did a man like Quinn believe in forever? She shook her head quickly, thrusting the questions aside. She couldn't tell him, she couldn't ask him. But she could show him.

Softly Chantel brought her mouth to his, then ran her fingertip over it as if to test the warmth she'd elicited. Approving, she brought her lips to his again, to savor.

He hadn't known it could be like this. Even in the wildest rages of passion they'd incited in each other, he hadn't known there could be such wonder. He'd told himself before that she belonged to him, but now, with her pliant and soft in his arms, he could finally believe it. And what was more, he was hers. Completely, utterly. Love fueled by tenderness was more consuming than any madness.

He slipped into her easily, naturally. With a sigh, she accepted him. They rose together in a harmony of movement that was its own kind of beauty.

When there was nothing left to give, they gathered each other close and slept.

"Don't rush me, don't rush me." With a spring in his step, Frank waltzed in front of the skycap desk. "I'm going to make sure they don't send my banjo to Duluth."

"La Guardia." With a grin, the skycap showed Frank the stubs. "Don't worry about a thing."

"Easy for you to say. I've had that banjo longer than I've had my wife." Then, with a chuckle, he squeezed Molly's shoulder. "Not that you mean less to me, my love."

"But we run neck and neck. Did you take your Dramamine, Frank?"

"Yes, yes, don't fuss."

"Frank's a hideous air traveler," Molly put in as she pocketed the tickets and boarding passes. "That's where Chantel got it from."

Surprised, Quinn stopped in the act of hefting his small carry-on bag. "You don't like to fly?"

"I'm fine." She'd already downed half a roll of antacids and two air sickness pills.

Molly glanced at the watch on her wrist. "We'd better get moving."

"Women. Always rushing." Frank gave Quinn a slap on the back. "Why do we put up with it, boy?"

"Only game in town."

"Right you are." Delighted with the world in general, Frank cackled as he strolled through the automatic doors.

"You're feeling chipper this morning," Chantel commented dryly, refusing to acknowledge the leaden feeling in her own stomach.

"And why not?" Frank beamed as they rode up the escalator toward their gate. "A good night's sleep's just the ticket." He quirked his brow at Molly and wondered if she'd wear that little black number again anytime soon.

As they passed through gate security, Chantel began the slow and even breathing technique that helped her get on board.

"Angel." Quinn drew her off to the side. "Don't you have a tranquilizer or something?"

"I don't take them." She twisted the strap of her bag in her fingers. "Besides, I'm fine."

He unclenched her fingers and soothed them with his. "Your hands are like ice."

"It's chilly in here."

Quinn noted a man mopping his brow as the room filled with body heat. "I didn't realize you were nervous about flying."

"Don't be silly, I fly all the time."

"I know. It must be rough."

Disgusted with herself, she stared over his shoulder. "Everyone's entitled to a phobia."

"That's right." He brought her hand to his lips. "Let me help."

She started to draw her hand away but found it held firmly. "Quinn, I feel like an idiot. I'd rather you just let it go."

"Fine. But you wouldn't mind holding my hand during the flight, would you?"

"It's six hours," she muttered. "Six incredibly long hours."

He tilted her face to his. "We ought to be able to think of something to pass the time." As he lowered his mouth to hers, neither of them noticed a man wearing dark glasses slip into a seat in the corner of the departure lounge. Neither of them noticed the way his hands clenched into fists as he watched them.

"If we do what you're thinking of, we'll be arrested," Chantel murmured, but the tension in her shoulders eased.

Quinn nipped at her lip. "I'm surprised at you. I was thinking of gin rummy."

"Like hell." When their flight was called, she drew a deep breath and kept her hand in his. "A dollar a point?"

"You're on."

Laughing, she walked with Quinn and her parents through the gate.

The man in dark glasses rose and pulled a low-brimmed hat over his head, then took out his boarding pass. He merged with the crowd that surged onto the plane.

Chapter Ten

"Are you sure you don't mind being drafted into the family?" Chantel carefully zipped a dress into her garment bag. She'd hired one of Hollywood's leading designers to create it, but it wasn't for the stage or the screen. It wasn't every day she was maid of honor at her sister's wedding.

"Is that what you call it?" Amused, Quinn sat on the unmade bed, dressed only in a towel. There was a freshly pressed suit in the closet that he didn't even want to think about.

"I don't know what else." Preoccupied, Chantel checked her makeup bag. If she'd forgotten anything, Maddy was sure to have it—probably still in the box. "Pop said you had to be at Reed's suite an hour before the ceremony." She paused and glanced back at him. "Just what is it men do before a wedding?"

"State secret, and no, I don't mind."

She stopped again, tapping a brush against her palm. "What did you think of Reed, Quinn? I know we only had a few hours together last night, but you must have formed an impression."

"Worried about your sister?"

"It goes with the territory."

He settled back against the pillows and looked at her. Trim slacks, a silk blouse, silver-blond hair pulled back from an extraordinary face with hammered gold combs. Chantel O'Hurley didn't look anything like a mother hen, but he'd learned to see farther than skin deep. When it came to her family, she was a marshmallow.

"Dependable, certainly successful. Meticulous, I'd guess. Conservative."

"And Maddy?"

"Scattered, theatrical and a shade wide-eyed."

"That's Maddy," Chantel murmured. "It doesn't seem as though they'd have enough in common for more than a ten-minute conversation. But—"

"But?"

"It feels right." With a sigh, she dropped the brush into her bag. "It just feels right."

"Then what are you worried about?"

"She's my baby sister."

"By how many minutes?" he asked dryly.

"Time has nothing to do with it." She said it with such offhand certainty that he was sure the question had been put to her before. "She *is* my baby sister, and she's always been the most trusting one, the most loving one. Abby's so... solid," she said. "And I've got enough meanness in me to keep my head above water.

But Maddy... Maddy's the kind of woman who believes the check *is* in the mail, the alarm didn't go off or the gas gauge was broken.''

"I think your sister knows exactly what she wants and how to make it work."

"So do I, really. I guess I'm just being sentimental."

Quinn arched a brow. "Why don't you come over here and be sentimental?"

She sent him a slow smile. "I thought you were waiting for room service."

"Hate to wait alone."

"Quinn, if I get back in that bed ..."

"Yeah?"

"I'm going to make incredible love to you."

"Threats, huh?" He lay back and crossed his arms behind his head. "Why don't you come over here and say that?"

She tossed her cosmetic bag aside and walked to him. "You haven't got a chance."

"Big talk."

"I can do more than talk," she murmured, and ran her fingertips up his leg to where the towel skimmed the top of his thigh. "Much more."

Before she could prove it, Quinn grabbed her wrist and yanked so that she tumbled across his chest. Her laughter came first, then was muffled to a sigh against his lips.

It didn't seem possible that she could want him as much as she had the night before, when they'd first slipped between the linen hotel sheets, but the excitement was just as new now, just as vital.

The scent of his shower was on him, fresh and tangy. His hair was slightly damp as it brushed across her face. His body was there for her, strong, virile, unclothed. With another laugh, she pressed her lips to his throat.

"Something funny?"

"I feel safe." She tossed back her head to smile at him. "So wonderfully safe."

He brushed the hair away from her face, holding it a moment, then letting it stream through his hands. How had she come to mean so much to him in so short a time?

"Safe's not the only thing I want you to feel."

"No?" She lowered her lips to his shoulder and let her tongue glide across his skin. "What else?"

Love, loyalty, devotion. It was frightening that those were his first thoughts. To protect himself, and maybe to protect her, he didn't tell her that. The physical loving wouldn't hurt either of them—not the way emotions could.

"Why don't I show you?" In one quick move he had Chantel on her back beneath him. The towel around his waist was held in place only by the press of their bodies. When his lips found hers, she began to tug the towel aside. Aroused, he laughed and made quick work of the buttons on her blouse. A knock on the door of the adjoining parlor had them both groaning. Chantel rose on her elbow and tossed her mussed hair back.

"You had to have breakfast, didn't you?"

"Let him bring it back later." Quinn slipped a hand under her skirt to explore her thigh. The knock came again, more insistently this time.

"I'll get it." Shifting away from Quinn, she adjusted her blouse. Then, with a grin, she picked up the towel and tossed it across the room. "You stay here." She kissed him again, quickly. "Right here."

"You're the boss."

"Keep that in mind." Chantel was smiling as she hurried into the parlor. Quinn would have his breakfast, but he was going to eat it cold.

In bed, Quinn reached over and idly turned on the radio. A little music, he thought. With the drapes still drawn, the room was dim. They might be anywhere. For a moment he let himself imagine they were in their bedroom—not in her house, not in his, not in some plush hotel, but in a home they'd made between them. When you loved, he realized, you didn't just think of now, but of always.

Maybe it was time to tell her, time to admit to her, not just to himself, that he loved her and wanted to share his life with her. His life—that meant past, present, future, not just the fleeting urge to satisfy passion, to quench desire. There was passion, but it would never be satisfied. Desire would never be quenched. And more, much more, there was emotion that swelled and expanded every moment he was with her.

He wanted her for his wife. That should have terrified him, but it almost amused him. He wanted her in all the traditional ways, the ways he'd always shrugged aside as restrictive and unimportant. A home, a family, his ring on her finger and hers on his. Quinn Doran, family man. It suddenly seemed to fit.

She might balk. She probably would. He'd just have to apply the right kind of pressure. Thinking of it made him smile a little. Persuading Chantel O'Hurley to marry him might just be the toughest nut he'd ever cracked.

"Quinn."

"Yeah?"

"Would you come out here a minute?"

He heard it in her voice, just a hint of tension. Quinn pushed aside his fantasies and reached for his robe. He saw the flowers as soon as he stepped into the parlor. A dozen blood-red roses with their petals just opened sat on the table by the door. Chantel stood beside them, her face as white as the card she held in her hand.

"He knows I'm here." She managed to keep her voice even, almost calm. "He says he'd follow me anywhere." Her fingers were steady as she handed the card to Quinn, but when his brushed over them, he found them cold. "He says he's waiting for the perfect time."

Quinn took the note and glanced briefly at the message. In the corner of the envelope was the printed name of the florist's shop. "He's made his first mistake," he murmured. "Who brought these up?"

"A bellboy." She stared at the far wall, at a Monet print, and wondered why she felt nothing, nothing at all. "I didn't even tip him."

"Stop it."

His voice snapped her back. After one long shudder, Chantel looked at him. She wouldn't get sympathy from Quinn, or soothing words or empty promises. She didn't want them. She wanted the truth. "He's here, isn't he? He might even be in this hotel."

"Sit down." He started to take her arm, but she backed away.

"I don't need to sit down. I need some answers."

"Chantel—"

At the next knock, she pressed a hand to her mouth to muffle a scream. Swearing, Quinn pushed her into a chair, then went to the door. Through the peephole he saw a room-service waiter with a breakfast tray. "It's all right," he tossed over his shoulder. "Just room service."

Quinn opened the door to let the waiter roll the cart to the table by the window. After scrawling his name on the tab, he followed the waiter to the door to take a quick scan of the hall.

"You could use some coffee," Quinn said, moving past Chantel to the breakfast tray.

"No, answers." Though her knees were wobbly, she rose. "I'm not sure why, but I think you have them. You knew he'd be here."

Despite her refusal, Quinn poured two cups. "Yeah."

"Yeah." A dry laugh came from nowhere as she pressed her fingers to her temple. "You're not a man to elaborate, are you, Quinn? How did you know he'd be here? Sixth sense, gut hunch, instinct?"

"Any of those would do." He felt a sick curling in his stomach as he turned to face her again. "I expect him to go where you go, but in addition to that he said he'd be here in the last few notes he sent."

She crossed her arms over her chest. The chill had sprung to her skin quickly. She was beginning to feel now, and feel sharply. "You didn't think I should know?"

"If I'd thought you should know I'd have told you. Why don't you eat something?"

Yes, there were feelings now. They were boiling inside her, threatening to bubble out with the first word she spoke. Chantel walked to the table and, keeping her eyes on Quinn's, picked up a plate and very deliberately dropped it on the floor.

"Just who the hell do you think you are?" Her voice carried more venom when it was low and steady. "How dare you treat me as though I'm some brainless, gutless female who needs to be led around by the nose? I had a right to know he intended to follow me, that things would be the same here as they were on the Coast."

He could let his temper go or he could control it. Quinn sat down and picked up his coffee. Anger had taken the dazed look out of her eyes. He'd let her take it as far as she could. "I handled it my way. You pay me to handle things my way."

Caught off guard, she stepped back. She paid him. How could she have forgotten he was only doing a job? An arrow of pain passed through her. Even that, somehow, was better than the numbness. "I expect to be kept informed of your progress, Doran."

"Fine." He picked up a piece of toast and began to heap on jelly.

"I'll just leave you to enjoy your breakfast."

"Chantel." His voice was soft, but it had enough punch to stop her before she crossed the room. "You might as well sit down. You're not going anywhere by yourself."

"I'm going down to Maddy's room."

"You can try to leave." He set his knife very deliberately on the side of his plate. "You won't make it. I'll take you down myself as soon as I'm dressed." He sent her a cool, challenging look. "And you'll stay there, inside the room, until I come back for you."

"I don't—"

"I've got a man stationed in the room across the hall, and another in the room across from your sister's. You're perfectly safe inside, but I want to take you down myself."

She was almost angry enough to take her chances. Chantel measured the distance to the door, and the look in Quinn's eyes. Without a word, she dropped down onto a chair and ignored him while he finished his breakfast.

Quinn found the cramped little flower shop in the West Sixties. In spite of the air-conditioning, the air was sultry inside and heavy with a barrage of floral scents. Three customers were crowded in, two of them in front of a long, chipped counter covered with scraps of papers and a shrilling phone the harried little man behind the counter ignored. Another customer stood in front of a display window and studied arrangements.

"Can't have them there before four. Can't." The owner scrawled on a form and kept shaking his head. He took a credit card and ran it through a machine for authorization. "Yes, it'll be pretty," he answered to the customer's murmured question. "Big pink carnations, some sprays of baby's breath. Tasteful, very tasteful. Sign here."

Quinn wandered to a grouping of lilies while the man dealt with the other customers.

"Okay, okay, you want to buy flowers or just look at them?"

Quinn glanced over to see the man piling the papers on the counter. "Pretty busy today."

"You're telling me nothing." The little man pulled out a handkerchief to wipe the back of his neck. "Got problems with the air conditioner, my clerk gets appendicitis, and too many people are dying." When Quinn lifted a brow, the man settled down a bit. "Funerals. Got a run on gladiolas this week."

"Tough." Quinn skirted a spray of daisies in a watering can. "This one of yours?"

He glanced at the card in Quinn's hand. "Says so right there." The man's squat finger punched at the name. "Flowers by Bernstein. I'm Bernstein. You have a problem with a delivery?"

"A question. Red roses, a dozen, delivered to the Plaza this morning. Who bought them?"

"You ask me who bought them?" Bernstein gave a long, nasal laugh. "Young man, I sell twenty dozen roses this week if I sell one. How am I supposed to know who buys?"

"You keep records?" Quinn gestured toward the register. "Receipts. You should have a receipt for a dozen red roses delivered to the Plaza at, let's say, ten-thirty, eleven this morning."

"You want me to go through my receipts?"

Quinn reached in his pocket and drew out a twenty. "That's right."

The little man stood straight. His drooping jowls quivered with indignation. "I don't take bribes. You got twenty dollars, you buy twenty dollars' worth of flowers."

"Fine. How about the receipts?"

"You a cop?"

"Private."

Bernstein hesitated. Then, grumbling, he went into the drawer that held the day's receipts. He mumbled to himself as he flipped through them. "Nobody bought red roses today."

"Yesterday."

That earned Quinn a disgusted look, but Bernstein went into another drawer. "Red roses to Maine, two dozen to Pennsylvania, a dozen to Twenty-seventh Street…" He mumbled out a few more addresses. "A dozen to the Plaza Hotel, suite 1203, for delivery this morning."

"Can I take a look at that?" Without waiting for an answer, Quinn plucked it out of his hand. "Paid cash."

"I got no problem taking cash."

But cash meant no signature. Quinn passed the receipt back. "What did he look like?"

"What did he look like?" The man let out another snort of laughter. "How am I going to remember what you look like tomorrow? People come in here and buy their flowers. I don't care if they got an eye in the middle of their forehead so long as their credit's good or their cash is green."

"Just think about it a minute." Quinn pulled out another twenty. "You got some great flowers here."

The florist gave him a shrewd look. "The carnations on display here are getting wilted."

"I happen to be very fond of carnations."

With a nod, the man pocketed the two twenties, then took the slightly drooping carnations from behind the glass. "I remember he said to send the roses to Chantel O'Hurley. Things were pretty busy here yesterday. They hauled my clerk out in an ambulance. My other clerk's on vacation, and we've got two weddings." Because the florist had a genuine love for flowers, he took out a plastic bottle and spritzed the carnations. "Anyhow, he says to send them to her, so I say, hey, is that the actress? You know, the wife and I go to the movies a lot. Oh, yeah, I ask him if he's from California. He was wearing a hat, one of those panama types, and dark glasses."

"What did he say?"

"I don't think he did. And don't ask me what he looked like again, 'cause I don't know. I had Mrs. Donahue in here fussing about her daughter's wedding. Rose petals—bags of 'em. Pink." He shook his head. "He was a guy, and I never saw much of his face."

"How old?"

"Could've been younger than you, could've been older. But he wasn't built so big. Nervous hands," he remembered suddenly, and in a moment of conscience added some fresh greenery to the carnations.

"Why do you say that?"

"Came in here smoking some foreign cigarette. I don't allow smoking, no matter how classy the tobacco. Not good for the flowers."

"How do you know it was foreign?"

"How do I know? How do I know? I know an American cigarette when I see one," the florist said testily. "And this wasn't one of them. Made him put it out too. Don't care how much money you spend in here, you ain't gonna pollute my flowers.''

"Okay, so he had nervous hands.''

"Couldn't keep them still once he put the thing out. Look, I had enough trouble in here yesterday without this character. Mrs. Donahue was driving me to grief and my clerk was getting her appendix out. Next thing you know, she'll want to claim it on workman's compensation.''

"Anything else?'' Quinn steered him patiently away from his clerk's appendectomy. "Anything he did or said that sticks in your mind?''

"Money clip,'' he said abruptly. "Yeah, he took the cash out of a clip instead of a wallet. A nice one, nothing you'd pick up on the street. Silver. Monogrammed.''

"What initials?''

"Initials?'' The florist began to file away his stack of receipts. "What do I know from initials? It had squiggly lines on it.''

"Any rings? A watch?''

"I don't know. I notice the clip because the guy's got a nice fat wad tucked into it. Maybe he's got jewelry, maybe he doesn't. I'm taking his cash, not giving him an appraisal.''

"Thanks.'' Quinn took out a card and wrote his number at the hotel on the back. "I'd appreciate it if you'd call if you remember anything else. Or if he comes back.''

"He in trouble?''

"Let's just say I'd like the chance to talk to him.''

"Don't forget your carnations.''

Quinn tucked the arrangement under his arm and headed for the door.

"Guess you get some weirdos out in California," Bernstein commented.

"Our share."

"Movie stars." He gave another quick snort. "Guy said he worked close with Miss O'Hurley. Real close."

Quinn's fingers tightened around the knob. "Thanks." As he stepped onto the sidewalk, he thrust the flowers into the arms of a woman dragging a shopping cart. He didn't look back to see her staring at him. There was a sick feeling starting in his stomach. He knew someone who occasionally carried a silver money clip. A clip that had been a present from Chantel. Matt Burns.

He didn't want to believe it. Matt was a friend, and no one knew better than Quinn how hard it was to make and keep friends in his business. Yet how well did he really know Matt Burns?

He hadn't known about the gambling until he'd dug it up. Matt had betrayed a client then because of a weakness. Didn't that make him first in line to betray Chantel because of another kind of weakness?

A lot of men carried money clips, Quinn reminded himself as he headed away from the hotel rather than toward it. He needed to think things through before going back to Chantel. A lot of men carried silver money clips, Quinn continued, just the way a lot of men smoked foreign cigarettes. But he wondered how many men who knew Chantel, who worked closely with Chantel, did both.

He was being stupid, Quinn decided as he stopped at a phone booth. The word was soft, he corrected.

That's what the woman had done to him. It wasn't his job to find reasons why it couldn't be Matt, but find reasons why it could.

Flipping open his notepad, he scanned for Matt's number and dialed.

"Answering for Matt Burns."

"I need to speak with him."

"I'm sorry, Mr. Burns is unavailable until Monday."

"Make him available, sweetheart. It's important."

The voice became very prim. "I'm sorry, Mr. Burns is out of town."

Nerves skimmed down Quinn's spine. "Where?"

"I'm not permitted to give out that information."

"This is Quinn Doran. I'm calling for Chantel O'Hurley."

"Oh, I'm sorry, Mr. Doran. You should have told me who you were. Mr. Burns is out of town, I'm afraid. Should I have him get in touch with you if he checks in?"

"I'll get in touch with him on Monday. Where is he?"

"He flew to New York, Mr. Doran. On some personal business."

"Yeah." He bit off an oath as he hung up the phone. It was very personal. This was going to hurt her, Quinn thought. And it was going to hurt deep.

"Three more hours." Maddy O'Hurley jumped up from her chair, paced across the room and plopped onto the sofa. "We should have gotten married in the morning."

"It'll be afternoon soon enough." Chantel sipped at her third cup of coffee and wondered when she would hear from Quinn again. "Shouldn't you be enjoying your last hours as a single woman?"

"I'm too wired to enjoy anything." Maddy was up again, her mop of red hair bouncing with the movement. "I'm so glad you're here." She stopped long enough to give Chantel a quick squeeze. "I'd be going crazy now if you weren't. I wish Abby would come down."

"She will, as soon as she dumps Dylan and the boys on Pop. Think about something else."

"Something else." Maddy's slim dancer's body spun in a circle. "How can I think of something else? Walking down that aisle is the biggest entrance I'll ever make."

"Speaking of entrances, tell me about the play."

"It's terrific." Her amber eyes lighted with love of the theater. "Maybe I'm prejudiced because it was the play that brought Reed and me together, but it's the best thing I've done. I was hoping you'd be able to see it."

"I'll be back in New York shooting on location soon. You'll be back from your honeymoon and onstage." Chantel reached restlessly for a cigarette. "And if the reviews are any indication, the thing's going to be running for years."

Maddy watched her sister toy with, then light, the cigarette. It was something she did rarely, and only when she was tense. "How's the filming going?"

"No complaints."

"And this Quinn? Is it serious?"

Chantel moved her shoulders. "He's just a man."

"Come on, Chantel, this is Maddy. I've seen you with just a man before. Did you have an argument?" She managed to keep herself still long enough to sit on the arm of Chantel's chair. "Last night you seemed so happy. You practically glowed every time you looked at him."

"Of course I'm happy." She gave Maddy's arm a quick pat. "My baby sister's getting married to a man I've decided is nearly worthy of her."

"Don't hedge, Chantel." Abruptly serious, Maddy took Chantel's restless hands in hers. Nerves seemed to leap from one sister to the other. "Hey, something's really wrong, isn't it?"

"Don't be silly, I—" She broke off at the knock on the door. Maddy felt her sister's fingers tense.

"Chantel, what is it?"

"Nothing." Disgusted with herself, Chantel made her muscles relax. "Just make sure who it is, darling. We don't want an overexuberant bridegroom walking in."

Far from satisfied, Maddy rose and walked to the door. "It's Abby," she said as she looked through the peephole. And with Abby's help, she thought, she'd get to the bottom of what was worrying their sister. "How come you're not fat yet?" she accused as she opened the door.

With a laugh, Abby put one hand on her stomach and the other on Maddy's cheek. "Because I have over five months to go. How come you're not getting ready yet?"

"Because the wedding's not for three hours."

"Just enough time." Abby draped a garment bag over the back of a chair and went to Chantel. "Think we can whip her into shape?"

"Maybe. At least if we start on her she can't pace around the suite. Thank God Reed talked you into giving up that apartment. We'd have been sitting on top of each other."

"I still miss it." With a grin, Maddy moved over to wrap an arm around each of her sisters. "I have such a hard time picturing me in a penthouse uptown. Are Dylan and the boys with Pop?"

"I left them at his door. Mom's getting her hair done, and Pop was about to talk Dylan into a prewedding toast. I can't wait to see Ben in his tux again. He looks like such a little man. And Chris is annoyed that we're renting them instead of buying them. He thinks it's just the thing to show off to his friends at home. And by the way—" she gave Chantel a squeeze before she released her "—I liked your Quinn."

"The possessive pronoun's a bit premature." Chantel managed a smile. Then, on impulse, she went to the phone. "I know what's missing here," she told them, punching up Room Service. "I'd like a bottle of champagne, three glasses. Dom Pérignon '71. Yes, Madeline O'Hurley's suite. Thank you."

Abby arched a brow and leaned her arm on Maddy's shoulder. "It's barely eleven."

"Who's counting?" Chantel wanted to know. "The O'Hurley Triplets are going to celebrate." Without warning, her eyes filled. "Oh, God, sometimes I miss the two of you so much I can hardly stand it."

In an instant they were together, holding close in the bond that had cemented them even before birth. Maddy sniffled, Abby soothed, and then, to her sisters' amazement, Chantel broke down completely.

"Oh, baby." Abby lowered her to the sofa, casting a quick, concerned look at Maddy. "What's wrong, Chantel?"

"It's nothing, nothing." She brushed her tears aside. "Just being sentimental. I guess I'm a little edgy, working too hard. Just seeing the two of you, you with your beautiful family, Abby, and Maddy about to start one of her own. I wonder if things had been different..." She let her words trail off with a shake of her head. "No, I made my choices, now I have to deal with them."

Abby brushed the hair from Chantel's face. Her voice was always calm, her hands always gentle. "Chantel, is this about Quinn?"

"Yes— No." She lifted both hands, then dropped them. "I don't know. I'm having a little trouble with an overenthusiastic fan," she said, downplaying her problem. "I hired Quinn to more or less keep him at a distance, and then I fell in love with him and..." She trailed off again, letting out a deep breath. "I just said it out loud."

Maddy bent down to kiss the top of her head. "Did it help?"

Some of the tension uncurled. "Maybe. I'm being an idiot." She fumbled for a tissue. "And I'll be damned if I'm going to walk down the aisle as maid of honor with puffy eyes."

"That sounds more like Chantel," Maddy murmured. "And besides, if you're in love with Quinn, everything's going to work out."

"Always the optimist."

"Absolutely. Abby found Dylan, I found Reed, so it's your turn. Now if we could just pin down Trace..."

"You're really reaching," Chantel said with a laugh. "If there's a woman out there who can put a hobble on big brother, I'd love to meet her." She started at the knock on the door, but brought herself back quickly. "Must be the champagne." Stuffing the tissue in her pocket, Chantel went to the door but checked the peephole first. "Uh-oh." A smile hovered on her lips as she glanced over her shoulder. "We've got the champagne, all right, but there's more. Abby, drag Maddy into the bedroom. There's a lovesick maniac at the door."

"Reed? Is it Reed?" Maddy was halfway to the door before her sisters headed her off.

"No way." She might be nearly four months pregnant, but Abby was still agile. She had an arm hooked around Maddy's waist. "Bad luck, honey. You get into the bedroom. Chantel and I can transmit any messages."

"This is silly."

"I'm not opening the door until you're out of the room," Chantel said simply, and leaned back on it. "All the way out."

After wrinkling her nose, Maddy slammed the door behind her. As a precaution, Abby posted herself in front of it. With a nod of satisfaction, Chantel pulled open the door to the hall. "Just over there," she told

the waiter. "And you—" she put a slender, manicured finger to Reed's chest "—not a step farther."

"I just want to see her for a minute."

Chantel managed to force back a smile and shook
her head. She could almost feel the love coming from
him, the nerves, the longing. He hadn't changed into
his tux yet, and he was wearing a pair of casual slacks
and a shirt that reflected his conservative style. He
looked like an executive. He *was* an executive, she
thought with another shake of her head. And the
farthest thing from the type one would have imagined
with her free-spirited, bohemian sister. Yet they fit.
Chantel imagined Maddy had fallen for those calm
gray eyes first. The rest would have been a smooth
drop.

"Look, I have something for her." Used to getting
his own way, Reed took a step forward, only to be
blocked easily by Chantel. "I'll be in and out before
you know it."

"You won't be in at all," Chantel corrected. "We're
Irish, Reed, and we're theater people. You're not go-
ing to find a group more superstitious. You'll see
Maddy at the church."

"That's right." Hearing a stirring behind her, Abby
hooked her hand firmly around the knob of the bedroom door. "I'm sure you're too much of a gentleman to try to get through both of us." Using the
ultimate weapon, she smiled and put a hand to her
stomach. "Or should I say all three of us?"

Reed wasn't so sure. He wanted to see Maddy, touch
her, if only for a minute, to assure himself it was all
real. Abby smiled at him with warm, sympathetic eyes,

but she didn't budge. Chantel signed the receipt for the wine without moving from the doorway.

"Go down to the eighth floor and have a drink with Pop," she advised.

"I just want to—"

"Forget it." Then she softened and kissed his cheek. "Just a couple of hours, Reed. Believe me, it'll be worth the wait."

Only minutes before, Reed had managed to talk his way around Dylan and override Frank's objections. But he knew when he was out of his depth. "Would you give her this?" He took a small box from his pocket. "It was my grandmother's. I was going to give it to her later, but, well, I'd like her to wear it today."

"She'll wear it." She started to hustle him out again, then stopped. "Reed."

"Yeah?"

"Welcome to the family." Then she shut the door in his face. "Lord, another minute of that and I'd have been in tears again. Let her out."

"What did he give you?" Maddy was already nudging past her sister. She took the box from Chantel and opened it. Inside was a tiny heart of diamonds on a thin silver chain. "Oh, isn't it lovely?"

"It's going to look even lovelier against your dress." Abby ran a fingertip over the stones. "Here, I'll clasp it for you."

"Now *I'm* going to cry." Maddy closed her hand over the heart. He was going to be hers, truly hers, in a matter of hours. And her new life would begin.

"No more tears." Chantel released the cork from the wine with a swoosh. It landed on the carpet, to be ignored as she poured wine to overflowing into three glasses. "We're going to get just a little drunk— Well, two of us are going to get a little drunk, and Abby's going to have half a glass. Then, between the three of us, we're going to create the most beautiful bride to ever walk down the aisle at St. Pat's. Here's to you, little sister."

"No." Maddy touched her glass to Chantel's, then to Abby's. "Here's to us. As long as we have each other, we're never alone."

Chapter Eleven

At Chantel's insistence, she and Quinn caught the
red-eye to L.A. Saturday night. New York hadn't been
the haven she'd hoped for. With the wedding over and
her sister off on a Caribbean honeymoon, Chantel
could only think of getting home.

The reception had been a strain. She'd caught herself watching strangers, studying familiar faces and
wondering. Even when she willed herself to sleep on
the plane, she promised herself that the next time she
came back to New York, it would be without fear.

And what could she say to Quinn? She felt betrayed by his silence, yet had she, by the extent of her
dependence on him, asked for it? Was she so weak, so
cowardly, that he felt it necessary to shield her from
everything? She wanted his protection, but she also
wanted his respect. Had she forfeited that by refusing

to listen to his reports, by allowing him to intercept the notes and keep the contents from her? It was time that stopped. All her life, except for one brief period, she had had her hand on the controls. Now, through fear, she'd relinquished them. Starting now, she was taking back the helm.

Quinn wondered how long it would take her to unfreeze. She'd certainly been cool enough throughout the afternoon and evening. Cool, aloof, distant. It was something he had no choice but to accept. Yet when he'd seen her walking down the aisle in front of her sister, wearing that pale blue dress, all filmy and romantic, he'd wanted to step out of his seat, scoop her up and carry her off. Somewhere. Anywhere.

He wondered what it would feel like to stand where Reed Valentine had stood, to watch Chantel, as Reed had watched Maddy, walk toward him wearing white lace. What would it be like to hear her make the promises her sister had made? He shook himself out of the mood.

They were almost ready to land, and Chantel was dozing restlessly beside him. Couldn't she understand that he'd done what he'd done for her sake, because he'd needed so badly to see her relax, even if only for a couple of days? She didn't understand, or wouldn't, and he hadn't tried to explain. He didn't know how.

He didn't have the flair of one of her leading men. He didn't have the words all neatly typed in a script he could memorize. He had only what was inside him, and there didn't seem to be a way to explain that. Words weren't feelings. Phrases weren't emotions. And emotions were all he had.

When they landed, Chantel looked fresh and rested, as though she'd spent eight hours sleeping on a soft bed rather than snatching naps on a plane. They got their luggage without incident and within twenty minutes were riding in the back of a limo toward Beverly Hills.

Chantel lighted a cigarette, then glanced casually at her watch. Right now she felt wired, restless. Jet lag would hit tomorrow, but she would function.

"I'd like to see your reports, all of your reports, by noon tomorrow."

Streetlights flashed intermittently against the windows. His face was in shadow, but Chantel doubted she would have been able to read his expression in any case. "Fine. I have the file at your place."

"I'd also like an update on anything you came up with in New York."

"You're the boss."

"I'm glad you remember that."

He could have strangled her. He thought about ways that were quick and quiet, but instead he simply sat back and bided his time. He stepped out of the limo at the gate. Though Chantel had been gone, he'd thought it best to leave the twenty-four-hour guard in place. A few brief words and he was back in the limo, gliding through the open gates.

At the entrance, Chantel sailed past him. She had reached the head of the main staircase before he caught her.

"Something eating you, angel?"

"I don't know what you're talking about. You will excuse me now, Quinn?" Delicately she peeled his fingers from her arm. "I want to take a long, hot bath."

No one did it better. He had to give her that as he watched her walk down the hall to her room. She could, with a look, with an inflection, slice a man in half without leaving a drop of blood.

He thought he was calm. He thought he was controlled—until the moment he heard the lock click on her door. Then the rage he'd held in throughout the day clawed free. He didn't hesitate. Maybe he wasn't even thinking. Quinn walked to her bedroom door and kicked it in.

She wasn't often speechless. Chantel just stood there. The jacket of her suit had already been discarded, leaving her in a pale pink teddy and a rose-colored skirt. One hand remained frozen on top of her head where she had begun to pin up her hair.

She'd seen fury before, real and simulated, but she'd never seen anything like what was boiling in Quinn's eyes.

"Don't you ever lock a door on me." His voice was so quiet after the crash of splintering wood that she shivered. "Don't you ever walk away from me."

Slowly she lowered her hand so that her hair tumbled to her shoulders. "I want you to leave."

"Maybe it's time you learned even you can't have everything you want. I'm here to stay. You're going to have to do a hell of a lot more than turn a key to keep me out."

When he came toward her, she stiffened but refused to retreat. She was through backing away from anything, even him. He took her hair and wrapped it around his hand.

"You wanted to slap me down, and that's fine. But I'll be damned if I'll take it from you for doing my job."

"I won't be treated like a fool, or a weakling." The lace of the teddy trembled over her breasts as she took an unsteady breath. "You knew he was going to follow me to New York. You knew I'd be no safer there than I was here."

"That's right. I knew, you didn't. And you had one night when you didn't toss in your sleep."

"You had no right—"

"I had every right." The hand in her hair tightened. She wanted to wince, but she didn't seem to be able to move at all. "I have the right to do anything, everything, to keep you safe, to give you some peace of mind. And I'm going to keep on doing it, because there's nothing that matters to me more than you."

Chantel let out a breath she hadn't been aware of holding. She'd seen it in his eyes, beneath the anger, beneath the frustration, but she hadn't been certain she could believe it. "Is that your—" She stopped, pressing her lips together. It wouldn't do for her voice to tremble now. She wanted to be strong, for him, as well as herself. "Is that your way of telling me you love me?"

He stared down at her, a good deal more stunned by his announcement than she. He hadn't meant to throw it at her like a threat. He'd wanted to give them both time, to give them both room, so that he could coax her along until she realized she needed him. But he'd never been good at coaxing.

"Take it or leave it."

"Take it or leave it," she repeated in a murmur. How like him. "Would you mind letting go of my hair? I need it for a couple of scenes on Monday. Besides, that way you'd have both arms to put around me."

Before he could, she was pressed against him, holding tight and hard and praying it wasn't a dream.

"I guess this means you're taking it." He buried his face in her hair and wondered how he'd ever survived without her scent, without her touch.

"Yeah. I've been trying to figure out a way to make you fall in love with me so you wouldn't be able to walk away." She tossed her head back to look at him. "Tell me you're not going to walk away."

"I'm not going anywhere." Then he found her mouth and made it a promise. "Let me hear you say it." He took her hair again but drew it back gently until their eyes met. "Look at me and say it. No lights, no camera, no script."

"I love you, Quinn, more than I thought it was possible to love. It scares the hell out of me."

"Good." He kissed her again, harder. "It scares the hell out of me, too."

"We've got so many things to talk about."

"Later." He was already drawing down the zipper of her skirt.

"Later," she agreed, tugging his shirt out of the waistband of his slacks. "Want to take a bath?" As she asked, she yanked his shirt over his shoulders.

"Yeah."

"Before?" With a laugh, she nipped at his chin. "Or after?"

"After." And he pulled her with him onto the bed.

It had been wild before, fierce, violent, passionate, and it had also shimmered with gentleness. But now there was love, felt, spoken, answered. She'd stopped believing that her life would lead her to this—love, acceptance, understanding. In the end she'd only had to open her hand and take it. In a burst of emotion they were caught close, mouths open and hungry, bodies heated and aware. She heard his long indrawn breath as he buried his face in her hair, as if he, too, had just realized what a gift they'd been given.

She thought he trembled. Her hands, pressed against his back, felt the quick tensing of muscle. She didn't want to soothe it. She wanted him to be as she was, stunned, a little afraid, and deliriously happy. When she pressed her lips to his throat she felt the throb of excitement, tasted the heat. In one long, possessive stroke she ran her hands down his back, then up again. He was hers. From this moment, he was hers.

She was there for him, soft, yielding, yet strong enough to hold him. He'd never looked for her. Quinn understood himself well enough to know he'd never looked for anyone to share his life. Still, he'd found her, and in her he'd found everything. A mate. There was something primitive yet soothing in the word. It meant someone to tumble between the sheets with on hot, sultry nights. It meant someone to wake with in the cool, lazy mornings. It was someone to confide in, someone to protect, someone to reach out to.

Just the thought of it made him close his eyes, as if to keep the fantasy trapped forever. With his fingertips he traced her face so that her image hovered there, in his mind.

"So beautiful," he murmured. "Here..." His finger lingered on her cheek. "And here." Slowly he slid his hand down her body. Then he opened his eyes to look into hers. "And inside."

"No, I—"

"Don't contradict the man who loves you." He brought her palm to his lips, watching her. He turned her hand over, kissing each finger. The diamond glittered on one, a symbol of what she was to the world. Cool sex, glamour with a hard polish. Her hand trembled like a young girl's.

He brushed kisses along her jawline, and her breath came in slow, quiet gasps. She could almost hear her skin hum as his fingers whispered over it. With each touch she drifted deeper into a dark, liquid world where sensations were her only guide.

Only he could make her forget the boundaries she'd once set for herself. Only he could make her forget that when you loved, you risked. With him she could give without fear, without reservations or restrictions. There would be a tomorrow with Quinn. There would be a lifetime of tomorrows.

He wasn't sure he knew how to show her how he felt. He wasn't used to pampering. Romance was for books, for movies, for the young and foolish. Yet he had a need, a growing one, to show her that his feelings went so far beyond desire that he couldn't measure them.

Rising to his elbow, he brushed the hair carefully away from her face, combing his fingers through it as it fell, silvery-blond, over the spread. Gently, as though she might crumble at the slightest touch, he cupped her face in his hand. Could she be more beautiful now? Somehow it seemed so to him as he watched the first beams of daylight steal through the windows and over her skin.

He ran his thumb over her lips, fascinated by the shape, by the softness, by the flavor he imagined would linger on his own flesh. As if it were the first time—and perhaps it was—he touched his lips to hers.

Her body went weak. As his lips lingered, the hand she had pressed to his back slipped down, limp. She'd thought she understood possession, but she'd been wrong. She'd thought she could imagine what it was like to be loved, loved fully. But she'd had no idea. Something fluttered through her, so softly that it might have been a dream. But it expanded within her, and a promise was made.

The heat centered, focused and grew. Strength flooded back into her, and with it a passion so rich that she moaned from the pleasure. Together they rolled until she lay over him. Together they let themselves go.

His hands were quick, but no more urgent than hers. His lips were hungry, but his desperation had met its match. Sanity was discarded as easily as silk and lace. They came together like thunder, in a storm that lingered into the morning. As dawn rose, they took each other into the dark.

"I'm so glad it's Sunday." Chantel eased her shoulders down into the hot, frothy water. She picked up a wineglass from the side of the tub and laughed at Quinn over the rim. "You're not supposed to scowl at the bubbles. You're supposed to enjoy them."

Quinn shifted to reach for his own glass. Chantel's tub was easily big enough for two, and the skylight overhead showed a perfect blue sky. The water that lapped nearly to the edge was layered with white, fragrant bubbles.

"I'm going to smell like a woman."

"Darling." She touched her tongue to the rim of her glass. "No one's going to smell you but me."

"With all the stuff you dumped in here, I'll be lucky if it wears off in a week." He shifted again, and his leg slid over hers. "But it has its compensations."

"Mmmm." With her eyes half closed, she leaned back. "For both of us. I need this. The shooting schedule next week is murder. There are three scenes in particular that I know will leave me limp. The one where Brad and Hailey nearly die in the fire is the worst."

"What fire?"

"Read the script," she said lazily, smiling when he tossed bubbles at her. "I trust Special Effects, but it doesn't make it any easier to crawl around in a shack on the back lot or on the set on the soundstage while they're shooting flames and pumping smoke in. That's why it's especially nice that it's Sunday and I can lie in the tub and think about making love with you." She looked at him through eyes that were hardly more than slits. "Again."

"You can lie in the tub *and* make love with me." He twisted his body, bringing it forward until his face was close to hers. "At the same time."

Chantel laughed and linked her hands behind his head as water lapped over the tub and onto the floor. "Too much water."

"You filled it up."

"My mistake. I usually bathe alone."

"Not anymore." Bubbles burst between them as he kissed her. "Why don't you pull the plug?"

"Can't get to it." She tilted her head to change the angle of the next kiss. "It's, ah, behind me. Now I bet a big strong man like you could manage it all by himself."

"Back here?" His hand trailed over her breast, then slipped to her rib cage.

"Close. Very close." She felt his fingers slide over her hip. "Getting closer. Why don't we—" The words were cut off as she found herself submerged, his mouth hard on hers. Up again, she drew in air, swiped at her face and squinted at him. " Quinn!"

"Slipped." He found the lever easily and flipped it down.

"I bet. Now I've got soap in my eyes." He started to grin, but his mouth went dry when she rose up, magnificent, and let water drain from her skin as she reached for a towel. "Remind me to bring a snorkel next time we take a bath."

"Chantel."

She was holding the towel to her face, but she lowered it with a half smile that faded when he stood beside her. Without a word, he gathered her to him. They stood where they were while the bubbles drained beneath them and dried on their skin.

"I never knew it could be like this," she murmured. "Not like this."

"That makes two of us." He'd found her. It seemed so incredible that he'd found her, found everything, without looking. "You're getting cold." Feeling the chill on her skin, he took a towel and wrapped it around her. "I guess I'd have a lot to answer to if you went to work tomorrow with a red nose."

"I never get a red nose." She took a towel in turn and wrapped it around him. "It's in my contract."

"Think you could take a break when you finish filming?"

"That depends." She smiled again. "On where and with whom."

"With me. We can talk about the where."

"I should be wrapped in three weeks. You pick the where." She started to step from the tub, then braced herself against the wall. "Careful. We've flooded the place."

"Just toss down a couple towels." Quinn plucked another from the shelf and let it fall to the floor to soak up the water.

"My housekeeper's going to love you." Out of habit, Chantel picked up a jar of moisturizer and began to rub a light cover over her skin.

"After we're married, there's going to have to be a change in the rules of the tub." He was hooking the towel at his waist and didn't notice the way her fingers froze in place on her cheek. "Bubbles are okay, but they've got to be unscented. It's one thing for the staff to sniff, but we can't have the kids wondering if their father wears perfume."

Somehow she managed to get the lid back on the jar and set it down without dropping it. "We're getting married?"

He didn't have to look at her to know she'd taken three paces back. He heard it in her voice. "Absolutely."

Her heart was hammering in her throat, but she'd trained herself to speak clearly over nerves. "You want children?"

"Yeah." One by one, the muscles of his stomach knotted. "Is that a problem?"

"I... Things are moving pretty fast," she managed.

"We're not teenagers, Chantel. I think we both know what we want."

"I have to sit down." She didn't trust her legs, so she moved quickly back to the bedroom and took a chair. She held the towel together in front of her with hands that had gone white at the knuckles.

Quinn waited a moment. The steam had fogged the wall-length mirror opposite the tub, but he could imagine her sitting there, her beauty reflected, slim, young, perfect. She was a dream and, more, she was a star, someone who lighted up the screen and created fantasies. His jaw was tight when he walked into the bedroom.

"Looks like I pushed the wrong buttons." Digging up his shirt, he found his cigarettes. "I thought that's what you wanted, too." Lighting one, he drew smoke in deeply. "I guess a husband and kids don't go with the image."

She looked up slowly. Her eyes were dry, but he recognized pain, something deep and dull and lasting.

"Chantel—"

"No." She stopped him with a gesture of her hand. "Maybe I deserved that." Rising, she went to the closet and chose a robe. With deliberate motions she dropped the towel, then slipped the robe on and belted it. She linked her fingers a moment, then let them fall to her sides. "My career is important to me, but I've never let it interfere with my personal life—or vice versa. My work is demanding. You've seen for yourself that the hours can be brutal."

"So there's no room for me and a family?"

Something came into her face again. Pain again, but with a touch of anger this time. "My parents raised four children on the road. There was always room, always time for family."

"Then what is it?"

She dipped her hands into her pockets, then took them out again, unable to keep them still. "First, I want to tell you that there's nothing I want more than to marry you and start a family. Please, don't," she said quickly when he started to come to her. "Sit down, Quinn. It would be easier for me if you would sit."

"All right."

When he had, she drew a deep breath. "There are things you have to know before we go any farther. It's difficult, at least for me, to admit past mistakes, but you have a right to know. If I'd listened to my mother, I would have told you before. It might have been easier then."

"Look, if you want to tell me you've been with other men—"

Her low laugh cut him off. It was strained. "Not exactly. This doesn't fit the image, either, but I only slept with one other man before you. Surprise," she said quietly when he simply stared. She went to stand at the window. "I was barely twenty when I met him. I was doing commercials, going to acting classes. I even had a part-time job selling magazines on the phone. I kept telling myself it was just a matter of time, and I believed it, but it was tough. Oh, God, it was so tough to be alone. Then Matt called and said he'd gotten me a test for a small part on a feature. *Lawless*, my first real break. The producer was—"

"Dustin Price."

Chantel turned back from the window. Her hand was curled in a fist. "Yes. How do you know that?"

"A lot of movie buffs might, but the fact is, I already know about Price. He turned up when I did a background check on you."

"You did a check on me?" She found herself braced against the windowsill. "On me?"

"It's standard, Chantel. I do a run on you, maybe somebody turns up you've forgotten, or forgotten to mention. Like Dustin Price. He's clean, by the way. Been in England eighteen months."

"Standard," she repeated, letting the rest sift away like sand. "I guess I should have expected it."

"What difference does it make now? So you slept with him. You needed a break, he could give you a break. It was years ago, and I don't give a damn."

Every muscle in her body went rigid. "Is that what you think? You think I slept with him to get a part?"

"I'm telling you I don't care."

"Don't touch me." She whipped away from him as he reached for her. "I don't have to sleep with anyone to get a part, and I never have. I may have made compromises, I may have given up more than I should, but I never prostituted myself."

"I'm sorry." This time he took her arms, ignoring her resistance. "I'm trying to tell you that whatever happened between you and Price doesn't matter."

"Oh, it matters." She pulled away and poured wine into a fresh glass. "It matters. When Matt called me to tell me I had the part, I was so happy. I knew it was the beginning. I was going places, I was going to be somebody." She pressed her fingers to her lips until she was sure she could speak calmly. "Dustin sent me a dozen roses, a bottle of champagne and a lovely letter of congratulations. He said he knew I was going to be a star and suggested we have dinner to discuss the film and my career."

She drank because her throat was dry, then set down the glass, refusing to rely on wine to get her through the story. "Of course, I agreed. He was one of the top producers, riding on a wave of three box-office smashes. Of course, he was married, but I didn't think of that." The derision was in her voice again, self-derision, self-disgust.

"Chantel. It was years ago."

"There are some things you never stop paying for. I was going to be sophisticated. We were just having dinner, colleagues. God, he was charming." The memory still hurt, but the pain was dull now, covered with scar tissue. "The flowers kept coming, the dinners. He knew so much about the business, the people. Who to talk to, who to be seen with. All of that was so important to me then. I thought I could handle it. The truth was I was just a naive young girl on her own for the first time.

"I fell in love with him. I believed everything he said about him and his wife living together for appearances only, about the quiet divorce that was already in the works. About the two of us making the best and brightest team Hollywood had seen since the golden age. The whole thing might have run its natural course as I got a little smarter, and he a bit bored, but before all that happened, I made a mistake." She ran her damp palms down her robe, then linked them. "I got pregnant." She managed to swallow. "You didn't find that in your background check, did you?"

Rage hit, and he smothered it. "No."

"He had enough money, enough influence, to keep it quiet. And it wasn't an issue for very long."

He was struggling, fighting desperately to understand. "You had an abortion?"

"That's what he wanted. He was furious. I suppose a lot of men would be when their mistress—and that's what I was, really—turns up pregnant and threatens his very comfortable marriage. Of course, he'd never planned on getting a divorce or marrying me. All of that came out when I told him I was going to have his baby.''

"He used you," Quinn spit out. "You were twenty years old and he used you."

"No." Strange that she could say it so calmly now. "I was twenty years old and I pretended I knew all the rules. I pretended very well. I made one mistake, then I made another mistake. I told him he could go to hell, but I was keeping the baby. Things got ugly then. He threatened to destroy my career if I didn't play his way. Well, there's no use going into what was said, except that the affair was over and my eyes were wide open."

"You're still hurting," Quinn said quietly.

"Yes, but not for the reasons you might think. I thought I loved him, but as soon as the glitter washed off I knew I never had. I called my parents. I was ready to run home and leave everything behind. I bought plane tickets. Quinn, I don't know what I would have ultimately done once I was thinking clearly. That's the worst of it, not knowing. There was an accident on the way to the airport." She took a deep breath, struggling to finish. "Nothing major, the taxi driver had a couple of broken bones, and I—I lost the baby."

With a broken sob, she pressed her fingers to her eyes. "I lost the baby, and I tried to tell myself it was for the best. But all I ever could think was that it had never had a chance. I was only six weeks pregnant. Six weeks. Here, then gone. Matt pulled me out of it, got me back to work almost as soon as I was out of the hospital. Everything clicked for me then, the parts, the people, the fame I'd always wanted. All I had to do was lose a baby."

"Chantel." He came to her, running his hands over her face, her hair, her shoulders. "There's nothing I can say. Nothing I know how to do."

"There's more."

"No more." He started to gather her close, but she backed away.

"When I lost the baby, there were complications. The doctors told me, well, they said it was possible I could have other children, but it wasn't something they could guarantee. Possible, just possible, not even probable. There might never be another baby, another chance. Do you understand?"

He took her hands. "Are you going to marry me?"

"Quinn, aren't you listening? I just told you—"

"I heard you." His fingers linked with hers and held firm. "You might not be able to have children. I want them, Chantel—yours, mine. If we can have them, that's great. But first, always..." He bent to touch his lips to hers. "I want you. I need you, angel. The rest is up to chance."

"Quinn, I love you."

"Then let's get married tomorrow."

"No." She put her hands to his chest to hold him off. "I want you to think about this, really think about it. You need some time."

"I need you," he corrected. "I don't need time."

"I feel I owe it to you. Let's leave things as they are. A few days."

He could have pushed. He could have won. But the hurt seemed too close to the surface just then. "A very few days. Come here." This time she went willingly into his arms. "I'm not going to let anyone hurt you again," he murmured.

She closed her eyes, hoping she could promise him the same thing, even if she were speaking of herself.

Chapter Twelve

The day started at six and never let up. Filming began at a shack on the back lot. The interior was no more than that, a small frame building that had been used in a handful of films. For *Strangers* it had been given a face-lift, a false front that had turned it into a rustic cabin in the woods of New England. In a climactic scene, Special Effects would burn it down, the fire starting under mysterious circumstances with Hailey and Brad inside.

The interior scenes would be shot later, on a two-story set on the soundstage, but the morning was spent on exteriors. Chantel drove Hailey's Ferrari to the deserted cabin. She was older now, but still caught between the man she had married and the man who had betrayed her. The scene called for her, on the verge of a breakdown, to seek solace in the remote cabin, searching for the roots of her art, which she'd lost in the tangle of success.

All the scenes were shot out of sequence and then would be edited together. For several hours of this shoot there was no dialogue. She was filmed unloading her art equipment, setting an easel on the narrow porch, walking through the door and out again with costume changes. There was a long, lingering close-up of her leaning on the porch rail with a cup of coffee in her hand. Without words, Chantel could use only her face to show the turmoil her character was feeling.

She painted on the porch, sketched on the porch steps, planted flowers. Through posture and gestures and by relaxing the set of her face, Chantel showed her character's gradual healing.

From the sidelines, Quinn watched her and felt his pride in her grow. He didn't know the story, but he understood the woman she became for the cameras. And he began to root for Hailey.

There was a poignant scene in which Hailey sat on the porch and poured out her heart to a stray dog. It was the examination of a life, with all its flaws, its wrong turns, its regrets. Even when it was reshot to change the angle, the emotion generated remained intense. Quinn saw more than one member of the crew wipe their eyes.

Before lunch they had wrapped a number of scenes, including a short, vicious argument between Hailey and Brad on the porch. During an hour's break Chantel took a quick, necessary nap, then shored up her energy with fruit, cheese and a protein drink before going to the soundstage for the interiors.

The set was as rustic as the outside of the cabin had promised, but there were a few of Hailey's paintings on the wall. The props included a large carved music box that had been a wedding present from her husband. The earlier tension was back in her character as Chantel opened the box and let the strains of the *Moonlight Sonata* out.

Dissatisfied with the way the scene was going, Chantel and the director went into a discussion on mood and motion.

"What do you think of our little story?"

James Brewster appeared beside Quinn. The two of them watched Larry Washington bring Chantel a glass of juice.

"Hard to say when you see it chopped up this way." Quinn kept his eye on Larry as the young man hovered around Chantel, ready to jump at the tiniest gesture. "But I expect it'll sell. It has it all—sex, violence, melodrama."

"You don't write a best-seller by leaving them out," Brewster said easily. "Of course, Hailey is the key, the hinge. What she does, what she feels, affects every character. When I started the book, I thought I was telling a tale of betrayal and birth. But it became a story of how one woman—and what happens to her—determines the destiny of everyone she touches." He broke off with a laugh. "It sounds pretentious, and perhaps it would be without Chantel. She is Hailey."

"She does make you believe," Quinn murmured.

"Exactly." Pleased, Brewster gave a quick nod. "As a writer, there's no greater reward than watching one of your characters come to life, particularly one you feel strongly about. I nearly killed her in the fire, you know."

Quinn stiffened. "What do you mean?"

Brewster laughed again and drew out a cigarette. "You're a very literal man, Mr. Doran. I meant I nearly ended the book here, in this cabin, with Hailey losing everything, including her life, in a fire set by the only man who really loved her. I found it impossible. She had to go on, you see, and survive."

They both watched as the stage was set for the next take. "An extraordinary woman," Brewster murmured. "Every man here is just a little bit in love with her."

"And you?"

A wry smile in his eyes, Brewster turned. "I'm a writer, Mr. Doran. I deal in fantasies. Chantel is very much flesh and blood."

At the assistant director's signal, the set fell silent and filming began again.

Quinn watched Brewster carefully. The writer seemed less nervous than he had in the early days of shooting. Perhaps he was pleased with the progress. It was Larry Washington who seemed on edge now. Chantel's assistant was never still for long, was always moving from one spot to the next. Did the tension Quinn felt on the set come from him? It was there. Quinn sensed it sparking the air, something nervy and desperate. Yet, everywhere he looked, people were going about their jobs with the drum-tight efficiency the director insisted on.

Perhaps the tension was just within himself. There was plenty of cause. Chantel was still just out of reach, not yet ready, or not yet able, to commit herself. When a man who had lived his life avoiding commitments finally found one he wanted, he was bound to be impatient. So Quinn told himself as he watched Chantel listen to the music box with pain and indecision in her eyes.

Were her thoughts on him, he wondered, or was she in character? Her talent made it nearly impossible to separate the actress from the role.

Every eye was on her, but she was alone, in a cabin in the woods, at a turning point in her life.

"Cut. Print. Wonderful." Mary Rothschild straightened from her position behind the camera operator. "Really wonderful, Chantel."

"Thanks." She drew a deep breath and tried to shake off the emotion that had carried her through the scene. "I'm glad I don't have to do that again."

"We're going to go to the confrontation with Brad." As she spoke, Mary began to knead Chantel's shoulders. "You know what you're feeling. You still want him. After everything he's done, everything you know, you can't quite remove yourself from the young woman who fell in love with him. You want to love your husband, you've tried, but the only thing you've managed to do is hurt him. You're on the edge of your life here. You know if you go with Brad you'll never survive. Yet you're drawn."

"I'm fighting myself more than him."

"Exactly. Let's run through it."

They worked until six. Before it was over, Special Effects had pumped smoke onto the set. Hailey, dazed by the smoke, terrified of the fire that had begun to

roar through the cabin, crawled along the wooden
floor in a desperate search for the door. All she carried
was the music box.

"Hell of a day," Quinn commented later when they
were in Chantel's dressing room.

"Tell me about it." Weary, she creamed off the
streaks of soot Makeup had smeared her face with. "I
don't even want to eat, just sleep."

"I'll tuck you in."

She smiled and, after drying her face, swung her bag
over her shoulder. "Tuck me in? I prefer having
someone to snuggle against."

"You'll have that, too, in a few hours." They
walked out of the dressing room, past the soundstage, where the director and cinematographer were
having an impromptu meeting.

"Going somewhere?"

"I've got some business." He thought of Matt, his
friend, and of Chantel, the woman he loved. "I'll tell
you about it when I get back."

"I'd rather you told me now." When they were
outside, Chantel headed straight for the waiting limo.
"Quinn, I don't want to be protected this way. Not
anymore."

She was right, and he'd known that sooner or later
he'd have to tell her. When she settled into the limo, he
slid his arm behind, ready to comfort her.

"I didn't want to get into it in New York. You had
your sister's wedding, and we had our own problems
to deal with. Yesterday…" He hesitated, still not sure
how to describe what that one twenty-four-hour period

had meant to him. "I wanted yesterday for both of us."

"I understand." She lifted a hand to his. "So, what is it, Quinn?"

"I got a lead on the man who ordered the flowers." He felt her tense, but didn't try to soothe her. She wouldn't want soothing now. "He paid cash, so there's no record. The florist couldn't give me much of a description. The guy wore dark glasses and a hat. There were a couple things the florist noticed, though." He hesitated, hating to be the one to destroy a trust and a friendship. She was more important than both. Than anything. "He smoked a foreign brand of cigarette and carried a monogrammed silver money clip."

For a moment her mind was blank. Slowly, the meaning came through. Rather than disillusionment, he saw a quick flash of determination. "A lot of men prefer foreign tobacco and clips."

"A lot of men don't work closely with you. This one said he did."

"He could have been lying."

"Could have been. We both know he wasn't. All along the one thing we could bank on was that this man knows you, and you know him. Chantel, you gave a silver money clip to someone who works with you."

"It's not Matt."

"Angel, it's time to separate what you want from what is, or at least what might be."

"It doesn't matter what you say, I won't believe it."

"I called Matt while we were in New York." He lifted a hand to cup her face. His grip was firm. "He was out of town, Chantel."

"So he was out of town." There was a quick flutter just beneath her heart, but she ignored it. "A lot of people go out of town on weekends."

"He was in New York on personal business."

She paled, but just as quickly shook her head. "Quinn—"

"I have to go talk to him."

"I don't want you to accuse—" A look from him cut her off. "All right," she murmured, turning her head to stare out the window. "I'm not supposed to tell you how to do your job."

"That's right, angel. Look." He took her shoulder and turned her toward him. "Look at me." When she did, he swore under his breath and brushed the hair back from her face. "I don't want this to hurt you."

"You're telling me that my closest friend is your top suspect. I can't help but be hurt."

"Go home." He leaned closer and touched his lips to hers. "Go to bed. Stop thinking about it tonight. For me," he said before she could speak. "I love you, Chantel."

"Stay home and show me."

"No." He caught her face in his hands. "I won't be long. And this is going to be over. I promise you that."

They went through the gate and up the long, quiet drive. "I trust you," she told him, and forced herself to relax. "I'm going to wait for you."

"Wait for me in bed," he murmured, hoping for her sake that she'd fall asleep quickly.

They stepped out of the limo. "You'll be careful?"

"I'm always careful."

She started up the steps, then stopped and turned back. "I hate this, but I can't regret it anymore, because it brought you. Come back soon." She walked into the house without looking back.

She wouldn't think. The day's work had drained her body, and she would concentrate on that. She'd have a late supper brought upstairs when Quinn came back. For now, she would wind down with a swim and a whirlpool.

If it was Matt, it could all be over tonight. Over. For a moment, her hope centered there. Abruptly she felt the sickness hit the pit of her stomach. No, she wouldn't wish for that. Running away from her own thoughts, she hurried upstairs to change.

"I'm glad I caught you in."

"Even superagents don't party every night." Matt was dressed in a casual sweater and slacks and comfortable boat shoes and was wound tight as a spring. "Actually, I'm having a quiet dinner at home tonight. I didn't expect to see you. Want a drink?"

"No. Thanks."

Matt set the decanter down. "How's Chantel?"

"She's fine." Rather, he was going to see that she was fine, no matter what he had to do. "Funny, I thought you'd be checking a bit more closely on that yourself."

"I figured she'd be in good hands with you." Matt rocked back and forth on his heels, not sitting, not offering Quinn a chair. "And I've been a little tied up on some personal business."

"The business take you into New York over the weekend?"

"New York?" Matt's brows drew together. "What makes you think that?"

"The florist got a pretty good look." Quinn drew out a cigarette, watching Matt as he lighted it.

"Yeah?" With a half laugh, Matt finally sat. "What the hell are you talking about, Quinn?"

"The roses you sent to Chantel. You made a mistake this time. The envelope for the card had the florist's name on it."

"Roses I sent?" Matt dragged a hand through his hair as he shook his head. "I don't know what you're getting at. I—" He stopped then, as understanding came into his eyes. "Good God, you think I've been doing this to her? You think it's me? Damn it, Quinn." He sprang out of the chair. "I thought we knew each other."

"So did I. Where'd you spend the weekend, Matt?"

"None of your damn business."

Blowing out smoke, Quinn remained in his chair. "You can tell me, or I can find out. Either way, I'm going to see to it that you're out of her life."

Fury showed in clenched fists. Quinn glanced at them, almost hoping Matt would put them to use. A physical outlet would be more to his taste than this psychologic sparring, hoping to wear down his opponent's resistance. "I'm her agent, I'm her friend. When she hit rock bottom, I was there for her. If I'd had those kind of feelings, I could have acted on them then."

"Where were you over the weekend?" Quinn demanded, determined to play this through to the bitter end.

"I was out of town," Matt snapped. "Personal business."

"You've had a lot of personal business going lately. You haven't shown up at all during the filming. You're such a good friend of Chantel's, but you've only seen her twice since you found out what was going on."

Guilt flashed briefly in his eyes, but then temper obscured it. "If Chantel had wanted me, she would have called me."

"I wonder if it's you who's been calling her."

"You're crazy." But Matt's hands shook a bit as he went to pour a drink.

"You use a money clip, Matt. A silver one," Quinn continued. "One Chantel gave you. The florist picked up on a couple little details like that."

"You want to see my money clip?" Furious, Matt reached into his pocket and yanked out a wad of bills held together by a small metal clip. It hit the table with a quiet thud.

Frowning, Quinn picked it up. It was gold, not silver, with Matt's initials engraved on it.

"I've been using that for two months, since you're so interested. Ever since Marion gave it to me." He picked up his drink and tossed it back. "If it wasn't for Chantel, I'd take a shot at tossing you out."

"You're entitled to try." Quinn dropped the clip again. "Maybe you'd be smarter to level with me. Where were you over the weekend, Matt?"

"New York." Swearing, he walked to the window and back. "Brooklyn. From Friday night until Sunday afternoon—I was meeting Marion's parents. Marion Lawrence, a twenty-four-year-old schoolteacher. Twenty-four," he repeated under his breath, rubbing a hand over his face. "I met her about three months ago. She's twelve years younger than me, bright, innocent, trusting. I should have walked away. Instead, I fell in love with her." After sending Quinn a furious look, he fumbled for a cigarette of his own.

"I've spent the last three months thinking about how I relate to houses with picket fences. This young, beautiful woman is going to marry me, and I spent the weekend trying to convince her conservative and very concerned parents that I wasn't some Hollywood playboy out to take their daughter for a ride. I'd rather have faced a firing squad." He puffed on his cigarette without inhaling.

"Listen, Quinn, if I haven't been around as much as Chantel needed, it was because I've lost my head over an elementary schoolteacher. Look at her." Matt flipped a photograph out of his billfold. "She looks like she could still *be* in school. I've been living on nerves for weeks."

Quinn believed him. With a mixture of relief and frustration, Quinn shut the billfold. It could have been a lie, but one man in love easily recognizes another. "What the hell does she see in you?"

Matt gave a shaky laugh. "She thinks I'm terrific. She knows about the gambling, about everything, and she thinks I'm terrific. I want to marry her before she finds out any different."

"Good luck."

"Yeah." Matt put the billfold away. His temper was gone, as were his embarrassment and his nerves. But guilt remained. "If we've got that straightened out, I'd like you to fill me in about Chantel. This character sent her flowers in New York?"

"That's right."

"He looked like me?"

"I don't know what he looked like."

"But you said—"

"I lied."

"You always were a bastard," Matt said without heat. "How's she holding up?"

"She's struggling. She's going to be better knowing you're clear."

"Let me ride out with you." He rubbed the back of his neck. "I would've told her about Marion before, but I felt—I guess I felt like an idiot. Here lies Matt Burns, agent of the stars, knocked unconscious by a woman who helps kids tie their shoelaces all day."

With her hair wet and loose, Chantel came into the poolhouse after a quick swim. The water and exercise had helped clear her head. Now all she wanted was to soothe her body. Hitting the switch for the whirlpool, she sent the bubbles gushing. A sigh of gratitude purred out as she lowered her body into the hot, churning water.

Quinn would be back soon, and one way or the other they would work things out. She had to concentrate on that, and not on the circumstances that had brought them together. Not on the circumstances that had taken him away tonight.

Beams from the setting sun came through the ribbon of high windows. The skylights above were deep blue with early evening. Chantel let the jets of water beat the fatigue out of her muscles and soothe the lingering tension from her limbs.

She was on the verge of having everything she wanted. She had only to say yes to Quinn. He loved her. Chantel closed her eyes on that thought. He loved her for what she was, not what she appeared to be on the surface. No one but her family had ever accepted her totally, with her flaws, her insecurities, her mistakes. Quinn did. A woman could live a lifetime and not find a man who loved what she was on the inside.

What held her back from taking what she needed was the fear that she might not be able to give him everything—not a family of his own.

She wanted children. His children. What if she ultimately disappointed him that way? What if he, too, had to pay for her past mistakes? If she didn't love him so much, it would be so easy to say yes.

She wanted him to come back, to be with her now. If he could just hold her now, she'd know, somehow, the right answer to give him. Chantel closed her eyes and let herself sink a little deeper. When he came back to her she would know, and whatever she did would be right for both of them.

She heard a sound, a soft one, at the back of the poolhouse. Straightening, Chantel pushed the wet hair away from her face. "Quinn? Don't say anything now." She closed her eyes again. "Just come here."

Then she heard the music, and her heart shot to her throat.

It was quiet, lovely, with the bell-like quality only the best music boxes achieve. The sky was nearly dark as the strains of the *Moonlight Sonata* flowed over the sound of churning water.

"Quinn." But she said his name knowing he wasn't there. Her hand shook as she reached over and turned off the jets. In the silence, the music box continued to play. Putting the heels of her hands behind her, Chantel pushed herself out of the tub.

"I've waited so long for this."

At the whisper, the air clogged in her throat. She had to breathe, she told herself. If she was to get to the door she had to breathe, and the door was so far away. The lights dimmed, and the fear raced along her skin.

"You're so beautiful. So incredibly beautiful. Nothing I could imagine or create could be as perfect. Tonight, we'll finally be together."

He was in the shadows near the rear door. Chantel forced herself to look, but even then she couldn't see who it was. "There are guards outside." She balled her hand into a fist, refusing to allow her voice to quiver. "I could scream."

"There's only the guard at the gate, and he's too far away. I had to hurt the others. Sometimes you have to hurt when you love."

She gauged the distance to the front door. "How did you get in?"

"Over the wall by the tennis courts. You haven't been using the tennis courts. I've been watching for you."

"The alarm—"

"I took care of the alarm. I have some knowledge. My reputation for careful research is well deserved." Brewster stepped out of the shadows with the music box in his hands.

"James." The air in the poolhouse was sultry, but Chantel began to shiver. "Why are you doing this?"

"I love you." His eyes were glazed, and she could see no emotion in them as he walked closer. "When you first formed in my mind, I knew I had to have you. Then you were there, flesh, blood. Real. I had this made for you."

He held out the music box, and Chantel stepped back.

"Don't be afraid of me, Hailey."

"James, I'm Chantel. Chantel."

"Yes, yes, of course." He smiled at her, then set the box down on a little table beside the tub. It continued to play, romantic and sweet. "Chantel O'Hurley, with the perfect face. I've dreamed of you for months. I can't write. My wife thinks I'm agonizing over my new book. But there is no book. There'll never be another book. Chantel, you wouldn't keep my flowers."

"I'm sorry." Quinn would be back, she told herself. The nightmare would be over. She felt exposed in her brief suit, so she reached for her wrap. Training kept her gestures casual, even as her heart roared in her head. "It was the way you sent them, James. You frightened me."

"I never meant to. Hailey—"

"Chantel," she corrected, a flutter of panic in her voice. "I'm Chantel. James, I think we should go into the house and talk about this."

"Chantel?" He looked momentarily puzzled. "No, no, I want to be alone with you. I've waited too long for tonight. The perfect night, when the moon is full. The song." He looked at the music box. "It was meant for you."

"Why didn't you just talk to me?"

"You would have rejected me. Rejected me," he repeated in a rising voice. "Do you think I'm a fool? I've seen you with those young men, all muscles and smooth faces. But none of them love you like I do. You've driven me mad with waiting. You were obsessed with Brad. It was always Brad."

"There is no Brad!" she shouted. "He's a character. There is no Hailey. You made them up. They're not real."

"You're real. I've seen you with him. I've watched the way you look at him, let him touch you, when it should be me. But I've been patient. Tonight." He started toward her. "I've waited for tonight."

Chantel raced for the front door, knowing that if she could beat him she'd have a chance. Grabbing the knob, she pulled, but it held firm.

"I locked it from the outside," Brewster told her quietly. "I knew you'd try to run away. I knew you'd throw my love back in my face."

Chantel spun around, pressing her back to the door. "You don't love me. You're confused. I'm an actress, I'm not your Hailey."

He winced as if in pain and pressed his fingers to his eyes. "Such headaches," he murmured. "No, don't," he warned when she edged toward the back door. He blocked her way, then stepped back into the shadows to pick something up. "I know what I have to do, and there's no running for either of us now, Hailey."

"I'm not—"

"It's too late," he said viciously. "Too late. I guess I've always known. I hate what you've done to me." He pressed his fingers to his temple as tears welled up in his eyes. "But as God is my witness, I can't let another man have you. You're mine. From the first moment, you were mine. If you could only understand that."

"James." She was afraid to touch him, but she took a small step closer. "Please, come into the house with me. I'm—I'm cold," she said quickly. "I'm wet, I need to change. Then we can sit down and talk."

He looked at her, but saw only what he wanted to see. "You can't lie to me. I created you. You're going to try to leave. You want to see them put me away. My doctor wants to put me away, but I know what I have to do. For both of us. It ends here, Hailey."

He held up the can, and she smelled the gasoline. "Oh, God, no."

"You were meant to die in the fire before, but I couldn't do it then. Now I have to."

He turned the can over as she lunged at him. It hit the floor with a clatter, then skidded, gas soaking into

the wood. She fought to get past him. Chantel heard
him sob as he shoved her down and her head hit the
table. Suddenly there were shooting stars in front of
her eyes.

"Chantel's going to want to open a bottle of champagne."

"I think we could all use it," Matt commented as
they walked into the house. "Quinn, I'd appreciate it
if you'd let me tell her."

"You're entitled." He looked around the cool, quiet
hall. "You were entitled to take a swing at me back
there."

"You're bigger than I am," Matt said easily.

"I overreacted, Matt. I'm not used to that." He
thought about Chantel waiting for him upstairs, and
what he would have done, would continue to do to
keep her safe. "The thing is I jumped on you with
both feet because it was the first solid lead I've had in
this whole mess."

"From what you told me, it looks like everything
the florist told you fit me."

"What fits you fits someone else. I'm missing it,"
Quinn murmured. "I'm missing it because I'm too
close. You know what the first rule of law enforce-
ment, private or public service, is? Don't get involved."

"A little late for that I take it."

"Way too late. She believed in you," he added. "I
think you should know that. Even after I spelled it all
out for her she stood behind you."

Touched, Matt fiddled with the lapel of his jacket. "She's a very special woman."

"She's the most beautiful woman I've ever met, inside and out. Integrity. You don't see the integrity when you look at her, or the guts, or the loyalty. It's taken me awhile to get under the surface and see all there is to her." He moved his shoulders, restless, dissatisfied. "Maybe if I'd had a little more of her faith in the people she cares for, I wouldn't have chased down a blind alley."

Matt followed Quinn's gaze up the stairs. If Quinn had overreacted, he thought, then he himself had underreacted. The past few weeks he'd been too involved with his own world to give one of his closest friends the kind of time and attention she needed. He turned the bottle in his hand. He was going to start making up for it now.

"Look, I was pretty steamed before, but I think you're as crazy about Chantel as I am about Marion. I probably would have done the same thing myself."

"Maybe." Quinn glanced at the stairs again. He didn't want champagne. He only wanted to be alone with Chantel, but she needed to see Matt, needed to talk to him. She'd be relieved, and yet he wondered if she would feel the same frustration he was experiencing. They'd come so far, yet they'd gone nowhere. "I hate what she's going through."

"So do I." Matt laid a hand on his shoulder. "The past couple months have taught me that love can drive anybody crazy. I guess it's like Brewster said in that interview."

"What interview?"

"It was in the paper tonight. They did an article on *Strangers*, focusing on Hailey. The way he described her, hell, you'd have thought she was real. But he said something that rang true—about how when a man really loves a woman, he sees her as no one else does, that no matter what he accomplishes, what he fails at, she stays at the center of his life, rules it just by being. I guess I was feeling sentimental when I read it," Matt said with a trace of embarrassment. "But I thought I knew what he meant. He even got Chantel and Hailey's names mixed up once."

"What?"

"You could tell the reporter got a charge out of that. He played up how Chantel must be turning in an Emmy-winning performance to have the writer confuse the actress with the character."

"Damn." Quinn slammed his fist against the newel post and started up the stairs. "He practically confessed this afternoon. He all but spit it in my lap."

"What are you—" But Quinn was gone. Matt just shrugged and wondered if he had time to telephone Marion.

"Call the fire department." Quinn shouted, taking the steps three at a time. "The poolhouse is going up."

"It's on fire?"

"She's in there." Quinn was at the door before Matt picked up the phone. "He's got her in there."

Chantel shook her head to try to clear it. The room swam, and she struggled to her hands and knees. She smelled the smoke first, thick and pungent, as it had been that afternoon during the filming. But this wasn't special effects, she remembered. She heard the crackle of flames and looked over to see the floor turn to fire.

He was still blocking the back door, standing there as if hypnotized by the fire, which was spreading fast. He wasn't trying to leave. He would die here, he wanted to die here. And he would take her with him.

Chantel stood, choking on smoke as she looked around frantically. Her head throbbed and spun, but she couldn't allow herself the luxury of passing out. The windows were too high. She'd never get out that way. The front door was barred. There was only one exit. She had to get past him before the fire closed it off.

Her breath came in a fit of coughing, but he didn't hear. The flames held his attention as they ate greedily at the far wall. The heat was growing, visible in waves that shimmered between her and the door. Moving fast, Chantel grabbed a towel and dumped it in the tub. Then, draping it over her face, she looked for a weapon.

The music box sat on the table, playing though the tune was muffled by the sound of flames. She took it and, on legs that threatened to buckle, walked behind Brewster.

He was crying. She heard it now as she raised the heavy wooden box over her head. Tears were streaking her own face, blurring her vision. It was so much like the scene she had studied, rehearsed, tried to understand.

Hailey, she thought as smoke clouded her brain. It was the cabin, her New England retreat. She was Hailey and she'd brought tragedy on herself, on those who had loved her. Past mistakes, past loves, past lives. If only she hadn't given her love and her innocence to Brad.... To Dustin?

Her vision went gray, and she fought to clear it. There was no Brad. Only Quinn. Quinn was real and she was Chantel. An O'Hurley. O'Hurleys were survivors.

Weeping, she smashed the box down on Brewster's head.

When he crumpled at her feet, she could only crouch, panting, struggling to find air in a room consumed by smoke and flame.

Had she killed him? She looked at the doorway, framed now by flames. Her only way out. Survival. She took a step forward, stopped, then bent over Brewster.

He'd loved her. Mad or sane, whatever he'd done had been tied to her. Somehow, later, she would sort it out, but she couldn't save herself without trying to save him.

She snatched off the towel and covered his face with it. The ceiling gave an ominous crack, but she didn't dare look. She didn't think. Everything was centered on living. Hooking her hands under his armpits, Chantel began to drag him toward the door and closer to the flames.

She was losing. There was no air to fill her lungs as she dragged the deadweight of Brewster's unconscious body. The fire was winning, edging closer. She felt the furnace blast of heat on her skin and wished desperately that she'd taken the time to wet some towels.

Inches from the door, she stumbled and fell, light-headed from lack of oxygen. A little farther, she demanded, dragging herself and Brewster across the floor. Oh, God, just a little farther.

She watched, too dazed to be frightened, as a beam fell, flaming, into the hot tub.

"Chantel!"

She heard the shout dimly as her consciousness started to waver. Somehow she managed to gain another two inches.

Quinn kicked in the front door and saw nothing but a wall of flame. He screamed for her again and heard nothing but fire. The roof was going. He ran for the doorway, but the heat drove him back. It was then he saw her, or thought he did, slumped by the far wall, with the flames separating them.

Coughing on the smoke he'd swallowed, he raced around the building, praying for the first time in his adult life.

She'd almost made it. That was his first thought as he saw her, collapsed against Brewster near the door. Burning wood showered from the ceiling as he hurled his body over hers. He felt it hit and sear his hand before he dragged her out onto the grass.

"In the name of God—" Matt began as he raced to them.

"Brewster's in there," Quinn managed. "Take care of her."

Quinn fought the heat again, nearly giving way at what had been the back doorway. Crawling on his belly, he inched closer, until he managed to grip Brewster's wrist. If there was a pulse, he couldn't feel it, but he dragged him back. As the roof collapsed inward, he left Brewster lying on the grass and rolled onto his back to draw in air.

"Chantel." Still coughing, he crawled to her. Her face was smeared with soot. He heard the sirens as she opened her eyes to look at him.

"Quinn. He—"

"I got him out. Don't try to talk now." She began to shiver, though the heat was still intense. Quinn stripped off his shirt and covered her. "She's in shock," he said tersely. "Smoke inhalation. She needs the hospital."

"I told them to send an ambulance." Matt peeled off his sweater and added it to Quinn's shirt. "She's going to be all right. She's tough."

"Yeah." Quinn cradled her head in his lap. "Yeah."

"He thought I was Hailey." She groped for his hand as she wavered in and out of consciousness.

"I know. Shhh." He took her hand and squeezed. The pain from his burns was real. She was real. And they were alive.

"I . . . for a little while in there, so did I. Quinn, tell me who I am."

"Chantel O'Hurley. The only woman I've ever loved."

"Thanks," she whispered, and drifted off.

By the time he was allowed to see her, Quinn had gone twenty-four hours without sleep. He'd refused to leave the hospital to change, and his clothes were streaked and reeking of smoke. Throughout the night he'd paced the halls and driven the nurses crazy.

She'd been treated for shock and smoke inhalation. The doctors had assured him that all she needed was rest. He intended to see and speak to her himself before he went anywhere. And when he went, she was going with him.

At dawn the day after the fire, Chantel awoke from a drugged sleep. When the doctor came out of her room, he was shaking his head. He looked at Quinn, noting his bandaged hand and singed clothing. "You can see her now. I'm going to process her discharge papers, though if you have any influence you should talk her into staying one more day for observation."

"I can take care of her at home."

The doctor sent a dubious look in the direction of the door. "Maybe you can. Mr. Doran?"

Quinn stopped with his hand on the knob. "Yes?"

"She's a very strong-willed woman."

"I know." For the first time in hours, Quinn smiled. He opened the door to see Chantel sitting up in bed, frowning into a mirror.

"I look horrible."

"Beauty's only skin deep," he said as she lowered the mirror to look at him.

"It's a good thing, because you look worse than I do. Oh, Quinn..." She spread her arms wide. "You're really here," she whispered as she used all her strength to squeeze. "It's all right now, isn't it? Everything's going to be all right."

"It's over. I should have taken better care of you."

"I'll dock your pay."

"Damn it, Chantel, it's not a joke."

"You saved my life," she told him as she drew away.

"When I think of what might have happened—"

"No." She put her fingertips to his mouth. "I don't want to think of 'what ifs' anymore, Quinn. I'm safe and so are you. That's all that matters now. And...and James..."

"He'll live," Quinn said, answering her unspoken question. He stood and began to prowl the room. "He's going to be put away, Chantel. I'm going to help see to that."

"Quinn, he was so pathetic, so confused. He created something that overwhelmed him."

"He would have killed you."

"He would have killed Hailey," she corrected. "I can only pity him."

"Forget him," Quinn told her, knowing he would have to if he didn't want to be eaten alive by bitterness. "Your family's coming."

"Here? All of them?"

"Your sisters, your parents. Nobody knows how to reach Trace."

"Quinn, I don't want to disrupt Maddy's honeymoon. And everyone else—"

"Wants to make sure you're all right. That's what families are for, right?"

"Yes." She folded her hands. "It is. Quinn, you deserve a family, your own family."

He turned to her, ready to fight for what he needed. "I know what I want, Chantel."

"Yes, I think you do." She'd made her decision when she'd opened her eyes on the grass and seen his face. "Quinn, before all of this happened last night, I was waiting for you. I knew when you came back and held me I'd make the right choice, for both of us." She glanced around the room, then into the mirror. With a grimace she set it facedown on the table beside her. "This isn't exactly how I expected things to be, but it would help a lot if you'd come here and put your arms around me."

He sat on the bed beside her and gathered her close. "Listen, I have to tell you this. When I got there last night and the poolhouse was burning, I knew you were inside because my heart had stopped. If I had lost you, it would never have started again."

"Quinn." She lifted her head, searching for his lips. Finding them, she found all the answers she needed. "I'd like a short engagement," she said, smiling. "Very, very short."

* * * * *

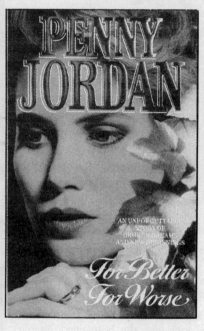